John Pilger

HIDDEN AGENDAS

VINTAGE

Published by Vintage 1999

10

Copyright © John Pilger 1998

The right of John Pilger to be identified as the author
of this work has been asserted by him in accordance
with the Copyright, Designs and Patents Act, 1988

Grateful acknowledgement is made to Mainstream Press for
permission to reproduce an extract from *Flash! Splash! Crash!
All at Sea with Cap'n Bob* by Mike Maloney

First published in Great Britain by
Vintage 1998

Vintage
The Random House Group Limited
20 Vauxhall Bridge Road, London SW1V 2SA

Random House Australia (Pty) Limited
20 Alfred Street, Milsons Point, Sydney, New South Wales 2061, Australia

Random House New Zealand Limited
18 Poland Road, Glenfield, Auckland 10, New Zealand

Random House (Pty) Limited
Endulini, 5a Jubilee Road, Parktown 2193, South Africa

The Random House Group Limited Reg. No. 954009
www.randomhouse.co.uk

A CIP catalogue record for this book
is available from the British Library

ISBN 0 09 974151 2

Papers used by Random House are natural, recyclable products made
from wood grown in sustainable forests. The manufacturing processes
conform to the environmental regulations of the country of origin.

Typeset in 10½/12 Sabon by
MATS, Southend-on-Sea, Essex
Printed and bound in Denmark by
Nørhaven A/S, Viborg

HIDDEN AGENDAS

John Pilger grew up in Sydney, Australia. He has been a war correspondent, author and film-maker. He has twice won British journalism's highest award, that of Journalist of the Year, for his work all over the world, notably in Vietnam and Cambodia. Among a number of other awards, he has been International Reporter of the Year and winner of the United Nations Association Media Peace Prize. For his broadcasting, he has won France's Reporter sans Frontières, an American television Academy Award, an 'Emmy', and the Richard Dimbleby Award, given by the British Academy of Film and Television Arts. He lives in London.

BY THE SAME AUTHOR

The Last Day
Aftermath: The Struggle of Cambodia
and Vietnam (with Anthony Barnett)
The Outsiders
(with Michael Coren)
Heroes
A Secret Country
Distant Voices

TO THE MEMORY OF MARTHA GELLHORN,
AND FOR JANE, JOSÉ, SAM AND ZOË

CONTENTS

Acknowledgements   ix
Introduction   1

I   THE NEW COLD WAR
     The Terrorists   19
     Unpeople 1   44
     The Crusaders   59
     Unpeople 2   99

II   FLYING THE FLAG
     Arming the World   115

III   INSIDE BURMA
     The Golden Land   155
     We Shall Have Our Time   190

IV   AUSTRALIA
     Secret Waters   223
     Anzac Day   249

V   WE RESIST TO WIN
     Xanana   283
     José Ramos-Horta   296
     Bishop Belo   305
     Jo, Andrea, Lotta and Angie   313
     The Invisible Revolution   323
     The Dockers   334

VI   ON THE FAMINE ROAD
     The Roots of War   361

VII   THE RISE AND FALL OF POPULAR
JOURNALISM
Forward with the People   371
Breaking the Mirror   410

VIII   THE MEDIA AGE
A Cultural Chernobyl   445
Guardians of the Faith   485
The Last Voice   526

IX   RETURN TO VIETNAM
Still a Noble Cause   549
The Final Battle   564
China Beach   589

X   EPILOGUE
The View from Dimbaza   597

Notes   611

Index   653

ACKNOWLEDGEMENTS

I WOULD LIKE to thank the following people who, in one way or another, have given me help and encouragement: Jim Aubrey, David Boardman, John Booth, David Bowman, Roger Bratchell, Carmel Budiardjo, Scott Burchill, Mike Carden, Robert Clough, John Cody, Ian Craig, Hazel Croft, Hugh Cudlipp, Roger Diski, Faith Doherty, Paul Donovan, Margaret Duerden, Elizabeth Duggan, Nic Dunlop, John Garrett, Allen Myers and the writers of *Green Left Weekly*, Rachel Hagan, Jörg Hensgen, Tom Hyland, Roger James, Myra Jones, Shona Kirkwood, Nicholas Lom, Helen Long, Greg McLaughlin, Helen Martin, Razi Mireskandari, Bobby Morton, Don Mullan, David Munro, Joe Murray, Andrea Needham, Lorraine Nelson, friends on *The New Internationalist*, Helen Oldfield, Deborah Orr, Alex Palmer, Greg Philo, Graham Pilger, Jaine Roberts, Vicki Robinson, Peter Schumpeter, Gil Scrine, Michael Seva, Julie Stoner, the Third World Network in Penang, Allan Ticehurst, Jill Tomkinson and Jo Wilson. I would especially like to thank Liz Cowen, my excellent editor, Will Sulkin of Vintage, Jacqueline Korn, my agent and friend, and Jane Hill, whose skilled and comradely hand is evident throughout this book.

Who controls the past controls the future. Who controls the present controls the past.

George Orwell, Nineteen Eighty-four

INTRODUCTION

THERE IS SOMETHING in journalism called a slow news day. This usually falls on a Sunday or during the holiday period when the authorised sources of information are at rest. Nothing happens then, apart from acts of God and disorder in far-away places. It is generally agreed that the media show cannot go on while the cast is away.

This book is devoted to slow news. In each chapter, the setting changes, from Iraq to the East End of London, from Burma to the docks of Liverpool and the West of Ireland, from Vietnam to Australia and the 'new' South Africa. In all these places, events have occurred that qualify as slow news. Some have been reported, even glimpsed on the evening news, where they are unremembered as part of a moving belt of images 'shot and edited to the rhythms of a Coca-Cola advertisement', wrote one media onlooker, pointing out that the average length of the TV news 'soundbite' in the United States had gone from 42·3 seconds in 1968 to 9·9 seconds.[1]

That is the trend. In American television, a one percentage point fall in the ratings can represent a loss of $100 million a year in advertising. The result is not just 'infotainment', but 'infoadvertising': programmes that 'flow seamlessly into commercials'.[2] This is how commercial television works in Australia, Japan, Italy and many other countries. Britain is not far behind; the ever-diminishing circle of multinational companies that control the media, especially television, take their cue from the brand leader, Rupert Murdoch, who says his role in the 'communications revolution' is that of a 'battering ram'.

1

In Britain, on what is still lauded as 'the best television service in the world', only 3 per cent of peak-time programmes feature *anything* about the majority of humanity, and almost all of that is confined to the 'minority' channels, if you exclude Clive James laughing at the Japanese. In the media's 'global village', other nations do not exist unless they are useful to 'us'.[3]

Regardless of the BBC's enduring façade of 'impartiality' and 'standards', news is now openly ideological and uniform, as the demands of the 'market' supercult are met. When slow news is included, it is more than likely dressed in a political and social vocabulary that ensures the truth is lost. Thus, in Britain, as in the United States (and Australia), the systematic impoverishment of a quarter of the population is routinely filed under 'underclass', an American term describing a corrupting, anti-social group outside society. The solution to poverty, which is the return of vast wealth taken from the poor by the rich, is seldom given a public airing. The 'new' system of capitalism for the powerless and socialism for the powerful, under which the former are persecuted and the latter are given billions in public subsidies, is rarely identified as such. Terms like 'modernisation' are preferred.

Wars can be notoriously slow news. Not the fireworks, of course. Indeed, like fast food, the whizz-bang of war has been made 'convenient' for the 'consumer' at home in front of the TV set. The Gulf War in 1991 was reported as a technological wonder, an event of bloodless science in which, rejoiced one editorial writer, there were 'miraculously few casualties'.[4] It was one of the most covered wars in history, yet few journalists reported the truth, still widely unknown, that a quarter of a million Iraqis were wantonly slaughtered or died unnecessary deaths.[5]

Since that bloodfest, the fate of the children of Iraq has been the slowest of news. Who knows that at least half a million children have died as a direct result of the economic sanctions imposed by the Western powers? Who understands that the sanctions are aimed not at bringing down Saddam Hussein, or deterring him from building some mythical nuclear bomb, but at preventing the 'market' competition of Iraqi oil from forcing down the price of oil produced by Saudi Arabia, the West's most important Middle Eastern proxy, next to Israel, and biggest arms customer?[6]

The children of Iraq are Unpeople. So, too, are the half a million children who, according to UNICEF, die beneath the burden of unrepayable debt owed by their governments to the West.[7] One Filipino child is said to die every hour, in a country where more than half the national budget is given over to paying just the interest on World Bank and IMF loans. These facts are not allowed to interrupt the cosy British ritual of Red Nose Day, when the money raised for 'the poor of the world' is but a fraction of that paid by the governments of the poor to Western banks on the same day.[8] Britain, which has an 'ethical' foreign policy, demands levels of debt repayment that far outweigh new loans or aid; only the United States has a longer record of taking more money from the developing world than it gives out.[9] It was not until the government of Mexico threatened to repudiate its debt, an action that might have brought down the Western banking system, that the wider issue was retrieved from media oblivion.

Unpeople are the heroes of this book. Their eloquent defiance and courage are as important as the secret histories of their neglect. In Part V, 'We Resist to Win', I chart the journey of 500 Liverpool dockers who were summarily sacked in 1996, most of them after a lifetime of service. Replaced by casual and part-time workers, their remarkable struggle is that of millions of people against what Prime Minister Blair, echoing President Clinton, euphemistically calls 'flexible working'.

Hidden Agendas is about power, propaganda and censorship. It picks up where my previous books, *Heroes, A Secret Country* and *Distant Voices*, left off. In order to tell the story so far, I have included brief sections from these books. Several chapters began life as essays in the *Guardian* and the *New Statesman* and have been substantially expanded and brought up to date. Otherwise, the material is new; and all of it is close to my heart.

Having spent much of my life as a reporter in places of

upheaval, including many of the wars of the second half of the century, I have become convinced that it is not enough for journalists to see themselves as mere messengers, without understanding the hidden agendas of the message and the myths that surround it. High on the list is the myth that we now live in an 'information age' – when, in fact, we live in a media age, in which the available information is repetitive, 'safe' and limited by invisible boundaries.

In the day-to-day media, much of this is the propaganda of Western power, whose narcissism, dissembling language and omissions often prevent us from understanding the meaning of contemporary events. 'Globalisation' is a prime example. This smokescreen extends to journalists themselves who, wrote Michael Parenti in *Inventing Reality: The Politics of the Mass Media*, 'rarely doubt their own objectivity even as they faithfully echo the established political vocabularies and the prevailing politico-economic orthodoxy. Since they do not cross any forbidden lines, they are not reined in. So they are likely to have no awareness they are on an ideological leash.'[10] Thus, the true nature of power is not revealed, its changing contours are seldom explored, its goals and targets seldom identified. This is counterfeit journalism because the surface of events is not disturbed. It is ironic that, while corruption among the system's managers and subalterns is at times brilliantly exposed by a small group of exceptional journalists, the wider corruption is unseen and unreported.

In *The Serpent*, Marc Karlin's film about Rupert Murdoch (originally entitled *The Cancer* as a tribute to the playwright Dennis Potter, who named his lethal tumour 'Rupert'), the director ruminates on how easily Murdoch came to dominate the British media and coerce the liberal elite. He illustrates this with clips from a keynote speech which Murdoch gave at the Edinburgh Television Festival. The camera pans across the audience of television executives, who listen in respectful silence as Murdoch accuses them of waging the same kind of thought control as the Established Church before the invention of the printing press. 'This is the silence of the democrats,' says a disembodied voice-over, 'and the Dark

Prince could bathe in that silence.'[11]

The silence of the democrats has been gathering for almost a generation, since the defection of those who once prided themselves on their resistance to the rapacity of power and who understand how fragile is the vital link between the people's right to know and be heard and liberty itself. One of the characters in Arthur Miller's *The Price* put it succinctly: 'We invent ourselves to wipe out what we know.' This is examined in the centrepiece chapters of 'The Media Age', particularly in 'Guardians of the Faith', which questions the false assumption of many liberal communicators that their position at the 'centre' is representative of the 'broad band' of society and its 'best interests'; some, like Tony Blair, even claim that it is non-ideological. Indeed, the ideology he shares with many in the media is one of the most powerful of the modern era and more pervasive for its concealed and unconscious attachment to a status quo of inequity based on class and wealth. The late Steve Biko described this political illusion in the context of South Africa when he remarked that the civilised collaborators' view of apartheid was of 'an eyesore spoiling an otherwise beautiful view'.[12]

These are surreal times, as if 'mainstream' politics has come to the end of the road. In Britain, the United States, much of Europe and Australia, the policies of the principal parties have converged into single-ideology states with rival factions, which are little more than brotherhoods of power and privilege. Their rhetoric is tendentious. Democratic accountability and vision are replaced by a specious gloss, the work of fixers known as 'spin-doctors', and assorted marketing and public relations experts and their fellow travellers, notably journalists. A false 'consensus' is their invention, such as that invested in the events following Princess Diana's death. Did it occur to those who gorged themselves on her death that the public's reaction might largely be that of a people despairing at the whole political class, politicians and media alike? In one of the rare pieces about Diana that did not surrender social analysis to psychobabble, Mike Marqusee wrote that 'in her life and death the pre-modern met the post-modern, the world of feudal right and blood status entered the media-refracted "society of the spectacle". The result should alarm ... all those who want to live in a community shaped by informal, critical, genuinely pluralistic debate.'[13]

In one sense, the media have never held such sway. We have government by the media, for the media. In Britain, New Labour constructed itself, its policies, its campaign, then its government with a media-supplied kit. The campaign never ends; one stunt begets another. The new government's solution to the problem of the 'underclass' was dreamt up by Peter Mandelson, the propaganda minister in all but name. He says there is to be a Social Exclusion Unit, a fine Orwellian moniker. In his announcement he praised the politician responsible for the greatest transfer of public wealth from the poor to the rich: Margaret Thatcher. None of it is to be given back. His is the speech of a political March Hare, juxtaposed on the front page of the *Guardian* with news that the Ministry of Defence's £10 billion-a-year budget to buy arms and equipment has been overspent by £1·4 billion. There is no link, no suggestion that Britain's defence budget might be reduced to the European average, thereby releasing £7 billion, or that obsolete fighter aircraft and Trident submarines might be scrapped, releasing many more billions. These are taboo subjects, matters for self-censorship.

Having announced an 'ethical' foreign policy, the Foreign Secretary, Robin Cook, embarked on a series of media stunts in south-east Asia. In Malaysia he declared a 'war on drugs', a hand-me-down from former President Bush, who was previously director of the CIA, an organisation as deeply involved in the drugs trade as the British were in the nineteenth century. Did this mean war with the United States? No. Burma was singled out for opprobrium, while Thailand, the most important Western-backed corridor for the drugs trade, was not mentioned. Neither was the almost total absence of a drugs' treatment programme in Britain.

On arrival in Indonesia, Cook introduced high farce by presenting one of the world's most vicious dictatorships with a 'deal on human rights' that included 'a series of lectures on

6

non-violent crowd control given by senior British police officers'. The unfunny and unreported side to this was that while Cook was in Indonesia his hosts were conducting 'Operation Finish Them Off' in East Timor, using the same type of British arms whose delivery he refused to stop. This 'ethical' policy is designed for the media and to co-opt the voluntary agencies; for the public it is a hoax. While 'defending' human rights, Cook used the Official Secrets Act to conceal the re-supply of the Indonesian regime with everything from bombs and ammunition, to nuclear equipment and rapid-firing machine-guns, with which Indonesia's gestapo has caused, in East Timor, the equivalent of the horror of Dunblane many times over.[14]

Those who doubt the true consequences of Western power might reflect on the secret machinations described in Part II, 'Flying the Flag'. Since the Second World War, the arms trade, dominated by the Western powers and conducted principally with murderous tyrannies, has caused the death of an estimated twenty million people.[15] This is slow news indeed.

At the time of writing, President Clinton is re-arming much of Latin America, and a £22 billion bonanza beckons for American and British arms companies as NATO expands into Eastern Europe. These developments have passed virtually unnoticed. 'Whoever gets in first will have a lock for the next quarter-century,' said Joel Johnson of Aerospace Industries Association. 'The market for fighter jets alone is worth $10 billion. Then there's transport aircraft, utility helicopters, attack helicopters, communications and avionics. Add them together and we're talking real money.'[16]

Even slower news – in this case, almost extinct news – is the nuclear re-arming of the world. People rightly regard the 'peace dividend' as a bad joke, but what they do not know is that all the nuclear powers are upgrading their nuclear arsenals at such a furious pace that the old Cold War might never have ended. The 'first strike' nuclear arms programmes set in train by Ronald Reagan and George Bush have not missed a beat under Bill Clinton; only one relatively minor air-to-ground missile has been cancelled. Otherwise, billions of dollars are being spent on Reagan's favourite Star Wars anti-missiles system, called Theatre High Altitude Area Defence, or THAAD. In response, the Russians are developing their own anti-ballistic-missile system, while both powers collude in the deception that their irresponsibility does not breach the ABM Treaty, signed in 1972. For the Americans, whether or not there is a Comprehensive Test Ban Treaty is irrelevant; they have now developed a computer modelling believed to be every bit as reliable as an actual test.

In the Media Age, 'history without memory confines Americans to a sort of eternal present', says *Time* magazine.[17] As the rest of us are drawn into this eternal present, the memory struggles to rescue the truth that our rights come not from something called consumerism or from commercial invention, known as technology, but from a long and painful history of struggle. 'Rights belong solely to people,' wrote David Korten. 'They do not extend to corporations or other artificial entities.'[18] Nor do they belong to unelected committees, known in Britain as quangos and 'review' bodies, or the international bureaucrats who are redefining our very concept of rights in 'agreements' with which most of us would disagree. In *The Solution*, Bertolt Brecht defined the problem:

> The Secretary of the Writers' Union
> Had leaflets distributed in the Stalinallee
> Stating that the people
> Had forfeited the confidence of the government
> And could win it back only
> By redoubled efforts. Would it not be easier
> In that case for the government
> To dissolve the people
> And elect another?

In the absence of vigilant journalism, the meaning of political language has been reversed. 'Reform' has lost its dictionary meaning; it is now destruction. 'Wealth creation' actually refers to the *extraction* of wealth by the relentless stripping and merging of companies. That noble concept, 'democracy', has become, along with universal suffrage, just another rhetorical device. As the Chartists' revolt of the 1830s and 1840s showed, the vote was only valuable if people's lives improved.

In the eternal present, media technology is promoted as an extension of human consciousness, not as the most powerful tool of a new order controlled by the few at the expense of the many. 'The threat to independence in the late twentieth century from the new electronics', wrote Edward Said in *Culture and Imperialism*, 'could be greater than was colonialism itself. We are beginning to learn that de-colonisation was not the termination of imperial relationships but merely the extending of a geo-political web which has been spinning since the Renaissance. The new media have the power to penetrate more deeply into a "receiving" culture than any previous manifestation of Western technology . . .' Compared with a century ago, he says, when 'European culture was associated with a white man's presence, we now have in addition an international media presence that insinuates itself over a fantastically wide range'.[19]

There is only one way now, say the Big Brother media and other mythographers of 'the market', which is the equivalent of 'Our Ford', the divinity that ruled the totalitarian Utopia in Aldous Huxley's *Brave New World*. Opposition is apostasy; fatalism is ideal. 'The core conviction of the centre-left', wrote John Gray, the academic and media political commentator, 'is the belief that social cohesion and enduring economic success go together. There is no way of escaping global market competition. There can be no way of going back to regulated labour markets . . .' Earlier in his observations, Gray had described how 'necessities' of global markets had 'wiped out the life savings of 80 per cent of the Russian population' and 'excluded a fifth of British households from work'. That has to be accepted: the 'core' divinity says so.[20]

There is no news from Africa. In the Media Age, the continent hardly exists. Rwanda was merely a vale of tears, while the memory struggles with the French, British and American manipulation of that tragedy, as it struggles with the imperial carnage in southern Africa in the 1980s, and in Nicaragua, El Salvador, Somalia, Panama and in all of Indo-China. The devastation of Vietnam 'was *America's* version of the Holocaust', says a Hollywood movie writer.[21] The italics are mine; the astonishment is not. This recasting of our history is the subject of the chapter 'Return to Vietnam'. The American attack on that country was a pivotal event of the twentieth century for a number of reasons, not least because it dramatically raised people's consciousness across the world and gave millions another way of seeing. It was this that earned the true spirits of the remarkable decade of the 1960s their retrospective trashing by those dedicated to bringing back the 'values' of a time when everybody knew their place.

I have described the attempt to re-impose these 'values' on the Vietnamese, whose resistance to them may well be their final, most decisive battle. That the gunfire is unheard makes it no less important than the great military siege of Dien Bien Phu. They have been told the price of their entry into the 'global economy': cities of sweatshops, a countryside of landlords: everything they fought against. The new foreign banks and private enterprises, wrote the journalist, Nhu T. Le, 'are meant to create a Hobbesian world of scarce resources inhabited by desperate people willing to do almost anything to feed their families. The marketeers are making an argument about human nature – that fear and greed are the fundamental human motivations. But in Vietnam, three million people in the grave serve as its greatest refutation.'[22]

The regression is already failing in one sense. There is, to paraphrase Graham Greene, a subterranean world of the mind where most people think what they want to think, and their thoughts are invariably at odds with and more civilised than those of their self-appointed betters. What they offer is not Utopia, simply a hidden reality.

In the United States, national surveys show that overwhelming majorities believe government is 'run for the benefit of the few and the special interests, not the people'; that the economic system is 'inherently unfair'; that 'business has gained too much power'; that 'the federal government must protect the most vulnerable in society, especially the poor and the elderly, by guaranteeing minimum living standards and providing social benefits', including support for the disabled,

unemployment insurance, medical and child care. By twenty
to one, Americans want corporations to 'sacrifice some profit'
for the benefit of 'workers and communities'.[23] There is no
doubt that some propaganda campaigns have had a profound
effect, such as that described in Robert Parry's *Fooling
America*, which built a false 'conservative consensus'
(extreme right wing) in the 1970s and 1980s; but, as Noam
Chomsky has pointed out, the sheer resilience of social
democratic attitudes is particularly striking in the light of such
relentless brainwashing projects, on which billions of dollars
are spent year upon year marketing 'the capitalist story'.[24]

In Britain, in the wake of New Labour's victory, the *laissez-
faire* guru Samuel Brittan wrote in the *Financial Times* that
his followers should count themselves lucky to have Blair, as
Labour would have certainly won on a socialist platform. The
British public, he lamented, remains 'hopelessly collectivist'.[25]

Whether or not they are 'collectivist', there is a critical
intelligence and common sense in the way most people arrive
at their values. The crusaders in power must despair that in
attacking single mothers and 'naming and shaming' deprived
schools, they do not gain in popularity. Along with other
surveys, the venerable *British Social Attitudes Survey* shows
that the British people are not innately conservative, as
journalists and politicians caricature them. On the contrary,
they are increasingly tolerant and often supportive of the
variety of ways people try to construct their personal lives.
They reject overwhelmingly the growing divide between rich
and poor – by a remarkable majority of 87 per cent, the
highest in the survey's history – and support the redistribution
of wealth and income and tax-funded support for public
services. Three-quarters believe that profit should be invested
and go to the benefit of working people; barely 3 per cent
believe that shareholders and managers should benefit.

The marketed wisdom is that the influence of class is less
than it used to be: that there is even a classless 'new Britain'.
The reverse is true; sons and daughters of unskilled workers
are no more likely to go to university than they were in the
1970s, especially now that New Labour has ended free higher

education. Three-quarters of the people surveyed believe that a class war is still being fought – here again, they represent the highest proportion since surveying began.[26]

In my experience, these attitudes reflect qualities that endure throughout the world, regardless of whether people are tagged 'developed' or 'undeveloped'. In Papua New Guinea, a society the economists would describe as primitive but which, in reality, is sophisticated and civilised, there is a village socialism known as *wantok*. This ensures that no one ever has to face a serious problem alone. Whether it is finding money for an electricity bill or nursing for an elderly relative, there is a system of reciprocal care that keeps hardship and discontent at bay and evens out the distribution of wealth.

In Australia, Aboriginality means similar qualities of generosity and reciprocity among an ancient people who could not imagine extremes of wealth and poverty until these were forced upon them by European predators. Ironically, their undoing was partly due to their belief that all land was common and none of it was owned. In inviting the colonists to share it, and assuming they would not steal it, they set their own trap.

The same invasion continues by other means. The privileges of 'discovery and conquest' granted to Christopher Columbus in 1492, in a world the Pope 'considered his property to be disposed according to his will', have been replaced by other acts of piracy transformed into divine will. The World Bank, the International Monetary Fund and other 'international' institutions are invested with the privileges of conquest on behalf of the new papacy in Washington.[27] The objective is what Clinton calls the 'integration of countries into the global free market community', the terms of which, says the *New York Times*, 'require the United States to be involved in the plumbing and wiring of nations' internal affairs more deeply than ever before'. In other words: a *de facto* world government.

This world government was assiduously at work following the collapse of 'model capitalism' in Asia. Reported in the West as a 'bail out' by the International Monetary Fund, the IMF's 'rescue packages' represent an audacious takeover of Asian economies, notably that of South Korea, where local companies are being forced to surrender to foreign control and workers' rights are diminished under plans designed in Washington.

The success of the new Western mission is, however, far from certain. The present order, built on money, electronic technology and illusions, is chronically insecure. People everywhere feel this. The globalised stock market is threatening to follow the disintegration of the 'tiger' economics. More than 700 million are unemployed, thirty-five million in the wealthy countries. Most are young people and many are disaffected and angry. In the United States, where genuine trade union activity was pronounced dead twenty years ago, the victory of the United Parcels Service (UPS) workers in 1997, backed by the public, has shifted the mood of American workers. The Liverpool dockers, denied their union's backing at home and ignored or dismissed by the British media, have seen unprecedented demonstrations of solidarity around the world. While Europe's politicians, central bankers and establishment journalists debate with each other how best to impose a 'single currency' and so further destroy proper employment and social services, French workers have stopped their country and German, Spanish and Greek workers have demonstrated a similar resistance.

As for the 'underdeveloped' world, where the majority live, there are far too many politicised people for the finality of the imperial mission to be accepted. In the revolution that consumed South Africa in the 1980s, 'the anonymous individuals of a humiliated community', wrote Allister Sparks, 'seemed to draw strength from the crowd, gaining from it ... an affirmation of their human worth. Their daily lives might seem meaningless, but here on these occasions the world turned out, with its reporters and its television cameras, to tell them it was not so, that their lives mattered, that humanity cared, that their cause was just; and when they clenched their fists and chanted their defiant slogans, they could feel they were proclaiming their equality and that their strength of spirit could overwhelm the guns and armoured vehicles waiting outside.'[28] And so it did: even if the euphoria may yet have to overcome an enduring system of economic apartheid administered by a black government.

'The hope for peace and justice in the world comes only from the tireless crusade of the common citizen,' wrote José Ramos-Horta, the East Timorese leader in exile. 'The mighty Soviet military arsenal did not prevent the break-up of the Soviet Union, the freedom of the captive Baltic and Eastern European nations, and the dismantling of the Berlin Wall. The tanks of Ferdinand Marcos and Nicolae Ceausescu could not hold back the demands of Filipinos and Romanians for freedom. The Eritreans fought a dogged battle of resistance against Ethiopia for thirty years while all around them said it was a hopeless struggle, yet Eritrea has now won its freedom. In East Timor we have survived Indonesia's brutal occupation, American, French and British complicity, the hypocrisy of countries like Australia and New Zealand that have put mercantile goods above morality and justice – none of this has crushed the Timorese will to be free.'[29]

There are many such examples. In almost every country today – even in blighted Haiti – people's solidarity with each other in the form of vibrant grass-roots organisations enables a form of democracy to function in spite of and in parallel with oppressive power often dressed up as democracy. The anarchist Colin Ward called this 'the seed beneath the snow'.

Eduardo Galeano, master poet of black irony, wrote, 'It seems there is no place for revolutions any more, other than in archaeological museum display cases, nor room for the left, except the repentant left willing to sit at the right of the bankers. We are all invited to the world burial of socialism. All of humanity is in the funeral procession, they claim. I must confess, I don't believe it. This funeral has mistaken the corpse.'[30]

This book is a tribute to people who, in refusing to attend the funeral, have brought light into the hidden agendas of governments, corporations and their bureaucracies. They are those of the calibre of Mordechai Vanunu, who has endured twelve years of solitary confinement in Israel for heroically warning the world about Israel's nuclear threat, and Aung San Suu Kyi, who told me, with exquisite certainty while steel-helmeted troops waited outside her door, that Burma would be free 'within ten years'.

If this book is something of a 'J'accuse' directed at a journalism claiming to be free, it is also a tribute to those journalists who, by not consorting with power, begin the process of demystifying and disarming it. 'Truth is always subversive,' an Indonesian journalist friend told me, 'otherwise why should governments spend so much energy trying to suppress it?'

The other day I met Rotimi Sankore from Nigeria (it's not a recognisable name) in a pub in London. A shy and sardonic man in his early thirties, he is part of the resistance to a vicious regime of generals and colonels shored up by Western oil companies. The Lagos magazine he writes for, *Tempo*, survives in amazing circumstances. His editor-in-chief has spent nine months in prison and the assistant editor, George Mbah, is being held at Biu prison in northern Nigeria, and has suffered head injuries. Three other editors, Chris Anyawu, Ben Charles Obi and Kunle Ajibade are in prison, and very sick. They were convicted by a secret military tribunal of being 'accessories after the fact of treason'. Known as the Innocent Four, they are immensely popular with the public for the physical and moral courage they have shown. Each was given a life sentence which, after public outrage, was commuted to fifteen years.

'That's a lifetime in a Nigerian prison,' said Rotimi Sankore. He described how *Tempo* still publishes and circulates from a network of safe houses and with printers and vendors willing to risk their freedom, even their lives. 'It is guerrilla journalism,' he said. 'We depend on the people for intelligence. When they tell us the soldiers are coming, we are on our way to the next location where the presses are waiting. When a military lorry parks near the vendors, they signal, and other vendors, out of sight, pick up the papers. We are all fugitives; it is a strange life, but a necessary one.' He was flying home that week. 'I will keep going until they catch me,' he said. 'That is my job: that is what people expect of me.'

JOHN PILGER

I
THE NEW COLD WAR

THE TERRORISTS

I use very big money. I use guns, too. The bums who insist on double-crossing me know what they are up against. City Hall understands what I'm saying. At least I hope they do.

Al Capone, American Mafia gangster

You just give me the word and I'll turn that fucking little island into a parking lot.

Al Haig, American Secretary of State

DIEGO GARCIA IS a British colony in the Indian Ocean, from which American bombers patrol the Middle East. There are few places as important to American military planners as this refuelling base between two continents. Who lives there? During President Clinton's attack on Iraq in 1996 a BBC commentator referred to the island as 'uninhabited' and gave no hint of its past. This was understandable, as the true story of Diego Garcia is instructive of times past and of the times we now live in.

Diego Garcia is part of the Chagos Archipelago, which ought to have been granted independence from Britain in 1965 along with Mauritius. However, at the insistence of the United States, the Government of Harold Wilson told the Mauritians they could have their freedom only if they gave up the island. Ignoring a United Nations resolution that called on the British 'to take no action which would dismember the territory of Mauritius and violate its territorial integrity', the British Government did just that, and in the process formed a new colony, the British Indian Overseas Territories. The reason and its hidden agenda soon became clear.[1]

In high secrecy, the Foreign Office leased the island to Washington for fifty years, with the option of a twenty-year extension.[2] The British prefer to deny this now, referring to a 'joint defence arrangement'.[3] This is sophistry; today Diego Garcia serves as an American refuelling base and an American nuclear weapons dump. In 1991, President Bush used the island as a base from which to carpet-bomb Iraq. In the same year the Foreign Office told an aggrieved Mauritian government that the island's sovereignty was 'no longer negotiable'.[4]

Until 1965, the Ilois people were indigenous to Diego Garcia. With the militarisation of their island they were given a status rather like that of Australia's Aborigines in the nineteenth century: they were deemed not to exist. Between 1965 and 1973 they were 'removed' from their homes, loaded on to ships and planes and dumped in Mauritius. In 1972, the American Defense Department assured Congress that 'the islands are virtually uninhabited and the erection of the base will cause no indigenous political problems'. When asked about the whereabouts of the native population, a British Ministry of Defence official lied, 'There is nothing in our files about inhabitants or about an evacuation.'[5]

A Minority Rights Group study, which received almost no publicity when it was published in 1985, concluded that Britain expelled the native population 'without any workable re-settlement scheme; left them in poverty; gave them a tiny amount of compensation and later offered more on condition that the islanders renounced their rights ever to return home'. The Ilois were allowed to take with them 'minimum personal possessions, packed into a small crate'. Most ended up in the slums of the Mauritian capital, leading wretched, disaffected lives; the number who have since died from starvation and disease is unknown.[6]

This terror violated Articles 9 and 13 of the United Nations

Declaration of Human Rights, which states that 'no one should be subjected to arbitrary exile' and 'everybody has the right to return to his country'.[7] The Labour Foreign Secretary, Michael Stewart, told the US Secretary of State, Dean Rusk, 'The question of detaching bits of territory from colonies that were advancing towards self-government requires careful handling.' He later boasted to a Cabinet colleague, 'I think we have much to gain by proceeding with this project in association with the Americans.'[8]

No one caused a fuss. The islanders had no voice in London. 'Britain's treatment of the Ilois people', wrote John Madeley, author of the Minority Rights Group report, 'stands in eloquent and stark contrast with the way the people of the Falkland Islands were treated in 1982. The invasion of the Falklands was furiously resisted by British forces travelling 8,000 miles at a cost of more than a thousand million pounds and many British and Argentinian lives. Diego Garcia was handed over without its inhabitants – far from being defended – even being consulted before being removed.'[9]

While there was silence in the media on the British atrocity in Diego Garcia, there was resounding condemnation of the Argentinian invasion of the Falklands. Both were British territories; the difference was between a brown-skinned indigenous nation and white settlers. The *Financial Times* called the Falklands invasion an 'illegal and immoral means to make good territorial claims', as well as an 'outrage' that should not be allowed to 'pass over the wishes of the Falkland Islanders'.[10] Echoing Prime Minister Thatcher, the *Daily Telegraph* said 'the wishes of the [Falkland] islanders were paramount', that 'these islanders' must not be 'betrayed' and that 'principle dictates' that the British and American governments could not possibly 'be indifferent to the imposition of foreign rule on people who have no desire for it'.[11]

Diego Garcia is a microcosm of empire and of the Cold War, old and new. The unchanging nature of the 500-year Western imperial crusade is exemplified in the suffering of the forgotten Ilois people, whose story has been consigned to oblivion, routinely, by the reporters and historians of power. To my knowledge, the shocking detail has been recorded by no one, with the honourable exception of Mark Curtis.[12] This is hardly surprising, as much of mainstream Western scholarship has taken humanity out of the study of nations, congealing it with jargon and reducing it to an esotericism called 'international relations', the chess game of Western power. Such orthodoxy, observed Richard Falk, Professor of International Relations at Princeton and a distinguished dissenter, 'which is so widely accepted among political scientists as to be virtually unchallengeable in academic journals, regards law and morality as irrelevant to the identification of rational policy'. Thus, Western foreign policy is formulated almost exclusively 'through a self-righteous, one-way moral/legal screen [with] positive images of Western values and innocence portrayed as threatened, validating a campaign of unrestricted political violence . . .'[13] In contemporary historiography, a similar discipline applies. In serious journalism, the 'self-righteous, one-way moral screen' is such a time-honoured tradition that the most important terrorists are rarely seen.

At times, orthodox opinion finds respectability and violence a difficult union to celebrate. 'We must recognise', wrote Michael Stohl, in *Current Perspectives on International Terrorism*, 'that by convention – and it must be emphasised *only* by convention – great power use and the threat of the use of force is normally described as coercive diplomacy and not as a form of terrorism', though it involves 'the threat and often the use of violence for what would be described as terroristic purposes were it not great powers who were pursuing the very same tactic'. (By 'great power', he meant exclusively *Western* power.)[14] 'From Machiavelli to Niebuhr, Moorgenthau and Kissinger', wrote Falk, 'there has been inculcated in public consciousness an ethos of violence that is regulated, if at all, only by perceptions of effectiveness. A weapon or tactic is acceptable, and generally beyond scrutiny, if it works in the sense of bringing the goals of the state more closely toward realisation . . . Considerations of innocence, of human suffering, of limits on the pursuit of state policy are treated as irrelevant, [and to be] scorned.'[15]

In other words, the Henry Kissingers rule. The 'statecraft' that Kissinger personified in the 1970s is widely appreciated in circles of 'post-modern' expertise. Presidents and governments consult him. Douglas Hurd, when Foreign Secretary, arranged an honorary knighthood for him. The BBC pays him $3,000 for less than a minute's wisdom. That he secretly and illegally bombed a neutral country, Cambodia, causing tens of thousands of deaths, is immaterial. That he worked to overthrow the elected government in Chile is irrelevant. That he defied Congress and clandestinely supplied the Indonesian dictators with weapons with which they pursued the genocide in East Timor is of no consequence. That he encouraged the Kurds to fight for nationhood, then betrayed them, is by the way.[16]

Illusion is all-important. Leaving aside its declared 'mistakes', Western colonialism is benevolent, the Cold War was rational. Countries are 'protected' from or 'defended' against 'insurgents' whom the former US Secretary of State George Shultz described as 'the depraved opponents of civilisation itself'.[17] The West itself is never terrorist. That it has invaded, stolen land and resources, subverted local culture and abused and enslaved indigenous populations is beyond comparison with terrorism: that was divine work. The distrust and fear of colonialism felt by societies all over the world is easily explained. According to the Foreign Office, it is 'often strictly psychopathic' as colonised peoples 'have practically no social consciousness'.[18]

Critical to our understanding of current world events is the way we view imperial machinations of the recent past. Malaya is a case in point. To the celebrated historian Lord Hailey, Malaya was 'ceded by local Sultans' and 'voluntarily applied for British protection'.[19] There was no invasion; the people were not subjugated. When British military forces attacked Malaya between 1948 and 1960, this benign view prevailed. There was no attack; the British establishment was 'defending' Malaya against a 'counter-insurgency campaign'. British companies then controlled most of the Malayan 'prize', as Lord Milverton described the country's natural resources, notably its wealth of rubber and tin.[20]

There was never an external threat to Malaya; the 'emergency' was purely an internal affair. Yet the accredited propaganda was that the 'free world' was defending Malaya from Soviet/Chinese-backed aggression: a theme embraced by academics and journalists alike. Malaya was a 'good war'. Only in its secret documents did the British Foreign Office admit that the war 'is very much in defence of [the] rubber industry'.[21]

British behaviour in Malaya in essence was no different from the American record in Vietnam, for which it proved inspirational. Collective punishment was official policy; food was withheld from villages judged guilty of sheltering 'insurgents'; other villages were turned into concentration camps and more than half a million people were forcibly dispossessed. This 'resettlement' was described by the Colonial Office in London as 'a great piece of social development'. Predating the American chemical assault on the Vietnamese countryside, which destroyed half the forests and caused widespread genetic damage, the British secretly dropped defoliants and crop destroyers on Malaya from the early 1950s. The chemicals, according to the Colonial Office, provided 'a lucrative field for experiment'.[22]

The pattern was the same in Kenya, where another 'good war' was waged against amoral 'insurgents'. The approved version is still cherished by the media, having been popularised in numerous novels and feature films. In fact, it was a skilfully promoted lie. 'The task to which we have set our minds', declared the Governor of Kenya in 1955, 'is to civilise a great mass of human beings who are in a very primitive moral and social state.' The reality was a kind of colonial fascism. The slaughter of thousands of nationalists was British Government policy – the British policy in Ireland of 'shoot to kill' practised on a massive scale.

The murder of one 'insurgent' was worth £5 to the killer. A British Army 'counter-insurgency' expert later commented, 'Three Africans appeared walking down the track towards us: a perfect target. Unfortunately, they were policemen.' In fact, the myth of the Kenyan uprising was that the Mau Mau

24

brought 'demonic terror' to the heroic white settlers. The Mau Mau killed thirty-two Europeans, compared with an estimated 10,000 Africans who were killed by the British colonial authority.[23]

The British ran concentration camps in Kenya in which the conditions were so harsh that 402 inmates died in just one month, June 1954. Torture, flogging, forced labour, the denial of rations and the abuse of women and children were commonplace. 'The special prisons', wrote the imperial historian V. G. Kieman, 'were probably as bad as any similar Nazi or Japanese establishments.' A former rehabilitation officer noted that 'Japanese methods of torture' were practised by one British camp commandant. This terror was enshrined in colonial law, which was maintained and rigidly enforced by the post-colonial regimes of Jomo Kenyatta and Daniel arap Moi in their dual roles as opponents of popular democracy and 'friends of the West'. The Registration of Natives Ordinance, similar to apartheid South Africa's infamous pass laws, was strengthened. The Masters and Servants Ordinance became the Masters and Servants Act; the draconian Emergency Powers Order became the Preservation of Public Security Act. Today, Kenya is in a turmoil because its democracy movement is still, in effect, fighting colonialism.

When post-colonial regimes took the wrong political turn they generally did not last long. Official records from 1953 show that in British Guiana, the elected socialist government was overthrown by British and CIA terrorism in order to secure the flow of cheap sugar and bauxite. That was a busy year. The elected nationalist government in Iran met the same fate; claiming ownership of the nation's own oil resources was beyond the pale.[24] British governments supported repression and killing in Uganda, Chile and South Africa. In Vietnam in the 1960s, unknown to Parliament and the public, British SAS troops fought alongside American 'special forces'.

The American invasion of Vietnam was supported by Labour Prime Minister Harold Wilson, just as his government and its successors supported the American-fuelled genocide in Indonesia when General Suharto took over in the mid-1960s.

British approval of the Indonesian killings, which in 1965 passed half a million, is expressed in a secret Foreign Office file, declaring that 'while the present confusion continues, we can hardly go wrong by tacitly backing the Generals'.[25]

The transition from a British to an American world led to internal complaints in the Foreign Office, apparently bereft of irony, about 'American imperialism . . . seeking to determine the future of Asia'. [26] But generally the handover was smooth, as demonstrated by the gift of Diego Garcia. Thereafter, British support for the new order was universal and steadfast. In the 1980s, Foreign Secretary Geoffrey Howe declared that Britain 'absolutely endorsed' American 'objectives' in Central America.

Reporting from that region in the early 1980s, I saw the evidence of these objectives. Between 1981 and 1985, an American terrorist army, the Contra, trained, armed and funded by the CIA, murdered 3,346 Nicaraguan children and teenagers and killed one or both parents of 6,236 children.[27] On the day I arrived at El Regadio, a town near the border with Honduras, Celestina Ugarto had been kidnapped and had her throat slit by an American-directed death squad. Hers was a typical case; recently qualified as a midwife, she had been given new skills in her fifties, such as reading and writing, and she was loved and respected in her community. She was the fifth midwife in the valley to be murdered by the Contra.

The American objectives for which Geoffrey Howe pledged British support were outlined by former CIA analyst David MacMichael in evidence he gave to the International Court of Justice. The American terror, he said, was designed to 'provoke cross-border attacks by Nicaraguan forces and thus serve to demonstrate Nicaragua's aggressive nature', to pressure the Nicaraguan Government to 'clamp down on civil liberties within Nicaragua itself, arresting its opposition, demonstrating its allegedly inherent totalitarian nature and thus increasing domestic dissent within the country'. The aim was to destroy the Nicaraguan economy.[28] In 1986, the World Court condemned the United States for its 'unlawful use of force' and illegal economic warfare against Nicaragua. Undeterred, American representatives on the United Nations Security Council vetoed a resolution calling on all governments to observe international law.[29]

The 'coercive diplomacy' and 'terroristic purposes', described by Michael Stohl, were Western specialities in Latin America. In 1996, an activist group obtained secret Pentagon files which confirmed that the US Army's academy for Latin American military and police officers in Georgia 'recommended' the torture of dissidents, threats, bribery and blackmail. Manuals written in Spanish advocated 'motivation by fear, payment of bounties for enemy dead, false imprisonment, executions and the use of truth serum'.[30]

In El Salvador in the 1980s, I befriended two of six Jesuit priests who, with their cook and her teenage daughter, were murdered by army officers in 1989; nineteen of the twenty-seven assassins were trained at the 'School of the Americas'. Other graduates included General Galtieri, former head of the Argentinian junta, under whose regime 30,000 people 'disappeared'; former President Suarez of Bolivia, whose paramilitary forces brutally suppressed the country's tin miners; more than 100 of the 246 Colombian officers cited for war crimes by a 1993 international human rights tribunal; Manuel Callejas, chief of Guatemalan intelligence in the 1970s and 1980s, an organisation of notoriety even by local standards; and Roberto d'Aubuisson, the Salvadorean death squad leader who planned the assassination of Archbishop Oscar Romero in 1980 – shortly after Romero had pleaded with Washington not to support the killers of his people.[31]

According to the United Nations Commission on Human Rights, in a fifteen-month period, more than 20,000 civilians in El Salvador were murdered by death squads related to or part of the 'security forces' trained by the United States and funded with $523 million in American 'aid'.[32] When I reported from El Salvador following Archbishop Romero's murder, I interviewed many among the 600 frightened people who had taken refuge in the garden of the Archbishop's palace. They were unarmed and all that separated them from the black helmets and black boots of the American-trained National Guard were two rickety gates of corrugated iron. Not knowing when the Guard would strike was a familiar symptom of the terror.

A twelve-year-old boy, Domingo Garcia, whose job was to open and shut the gates quickly, told me how guardsmen had killed his father for belonging to an agricultural workers' union. 'They killed my three brothers and they thought I was dead, too,' he said. He had scars on his scalp, neck and arms, caused by a machete. Archbishop Romero's successor, Archbishop Rivera y Damas, described the American-run terror as 'a war of extermination and genocide against a defenceless civilian population'.[33]

When Gore Vidal described the Cold War with the Soviet Union as 'an American fiction', he exaggerated, though not by much. Western orthodoxy says it was a war of attrition between the two superpowers, between the Stalinist Soviet Union and the democratic West when, in fact, there was broad agreement between them on strategic boundaries and 'spheres of influence'. The United States had no intention of rescuing the Hungarians when Soviet tanks rolled into Budapest in 1956 or the Czechoslovaks when they were invaded in 1968. For its parts, the Soviet Union showed no desire to join the Vietnamese in expelling the American invader, or to fight alongside nationalist guerrillas in Latin America. Periods of tension came and went between the two superpowers, but mostly their 'war' was rhetorical theatre.

This is made quite clear in secret British planning documents, which dismiss the 'Soviet threat' as non-existent in most of the Third World, even in the Middle East, a Cold War 'flashpoint'. And yet it was in the arena of the Third World that the real Cold War was fought by the Western powers – not against Russians, but against expendable brown- and black-skinned people, often in places of great poverty. It was not so much a war between East and West as between North and South, rich and poor, big and small. Indeed, the smaller the adversary, the greater the threat, because triumph by the weak might produce such a successful example as to be contagious – 'the threat of a good example', Oxfam once called it.[34] Thus the weak are the true enemy, and they still are.

The end of the old Cold War and the collapse of the Soviet Union have removed the most important restraint on Western terrorism. 'Never before in history has one nation had more power over more people in more spheres of life than does the United States,' wrote the Nicaraguan scholar Alejandro Bendana. 'For us in Central America, the new looks pretty much like the old, as the United States has been the dominant power in our region for the past century and a half. Maybe we can now speak of the Central Americanisation of the world [for] what we are witnessing today is far more serious as it consists of a fully fledged attempt by the United States to rebuild the international political and economic system . . . to ensure an open door for its goods, services and capital.'[35]

Shortly after he invaded Panama in the valedictory year of 1989, George Bush declared a 'new world order' that would provide a post-Cold War 'peace dividend'. Fellow travellers became almost lyrical. 'Like King Lear', wrote Adrian Hamilton in the *Observer*, 'the US seems intent on dividing up the world in a rush of magnanimous gestures . . . No one should complain of the effort or question the sincerity of the gestures. In Angola and Ethiopia as much as the Middle East and the Gulf and even Vietnam and Cambodia, Washington seems intent on clearing the stage of past disputes and ushering in a new order in which it can retire to a carefree life.' Moreover, implored Hamilton, sceptics should leave the retired old gent alone and 'welcome the signs that the US no longer wishes to be the policeman of the world, *at least with its own troops*' (my italics).[36]

Such a noble concept ran into promotional difficulties beyond the usual propaganda network, for it was obvious to all that the new 'order' was more violent than the old. 'The global number of conflicts', reported *World Military and Social Expenditures*, 'rose rapidly in 1991 and 1992 . . . War deaths were the highest in 17 years.'[37] Most of these deaths occurred when the United States, Britain and their allies attacked Iraq in January 1991. The most reliable estimate is that a quarter of a million people died.[38]

Another 6,000 died when American troops invaded Somalia the following year.[39] During the same period, American arms sales rose by 64 per cent, the greatest increase ever; and the Pentagon's war budget increased accordingly. In Britain, by 1994 a revitalised arms industry employed one worker in ten and accounted for 20 per cent of the world market.[40]

Bereft of the 'Soviet threat', the West's challenge was to find a suitable public rationale for the new state of war. An intense period of market testing followed; and the 'War on Drugs' was invented.

Colombia was deluged with more American military 'assistance' than any other country in the world, and a new enemy was identified: the 'narcoguerrilla'. Lumping together drug traffickers and nationalist guerrillas, Washington dispatched Special Forces on the pretext of fighting the one and imprisoning the other. (Britain helped out by secretly sending the Strategic Air Services.) Drugs, wrote Gabriel García Márquez, were 'a most convenient Satan for US national security policies', which allowed yet another invasion of Latin America.[41]

With the Americans came the familiar – money, 'market opportunities', corruption and eventually a full-scale war. Meanwhile the United States remained the largest consumer of illegal drugs in the world, with some twenty million addicts, and no equivalent domestic campaign against corrupt American authorities and leading traffickers.[42]

The War on Drugs took bleak irony beyond Orwell. While Nancy Reagan, wife of the President, promoted a 'Just Say No to Drugs' campaign, the secret agencies of her husband's government were saying yes. As the landmark work of Alfred McCoy has shown, a longstanding hidden agenda of American intelligence has been drug trafficking, which those who work with addicts and the AIDS epidemic regard as an insidious and especially effective form of terrorism.[43] 'Under the cover of anti-communism,' wrote Clarence Lusane, of the US Center for Drug Abuse Research, 'every US administration from Truman to Bush justified global covert operations that led directly to the opening and expansion of trafficking routes for illegal narcotics. Operatives associated with US intelligence ... supported the flow of drugs that predictably followed.'[44]

In the Indo-China wars, the CIA was deeply involved in drugs: its 'secret army' in Laos was run by General Vang Pao, the famous drug lord, entirely with money from drug trafficking. In Central America in the 1980s, after Congress had denied it funding, the CIA's 'secret war' against the Sandinistas was substantially funded by drugs. The congressional hearings conducted by Senator John Kerry's Subcommittee on Terrorism, Narcotics and International Relations found that 'on the basis of the evidence, it is clear that [the Contras] knowingly received financial and material assistance from drug traffickers ... In each case, one or another agency of the US government had information about the involvement ... Indeed, US policy-makers were not immune to the idea that drug money was a perfect solution to the Contras' funding problems.'[45]

In 1997, *Le Monde diplomatique* disclosed that after the military coup in Bolivia in 1980, 'the CIA had its hands free to finance its Central American operations thanks to cocaine produced in a secret workshop in Huanchaca [Bolivia] ... The US Drug Enforcement Agency knew about the drugs factory and said nothing about it. When a Bolivian Congressman was about to demand the expulsion of the DEA's agents from Bolivia, he was assassinated shortly after making his charges.'[46]

After years of reviewing classified files, the chief investigator to the Kerry Committee, Jack Blum, concluded: 'If you ask: in the process of fighting a war against the Sandinistas, did people connected with the US Government open channels which allowed drug traffickers to move drugs to the United States, did they know the drug traffickers were doing it and did they protect them from law enforcement? The answer to all those questions is yes.'[47]

The War on Drugs was followed by the War on Demons. Demons are those who stand in the way of what was known in the nineteenth century as 'America's manifest destiny'. Demons can be entire religions like Islam, entire nations like Iran, or individuals like Fidel Castro, Saddam Hussein and Colonel Muammar al Gaddafi.

The kidnapping of a lesser demon, General Noriega, an old pal of George Bush when Bush was director of the CIA, required the killing of some 2,000 Panamanians as part of a full-scale invasion of their country. Noriega was duly satanised as a drug-pusher and child pornography collector. His graduation from the 'School of the Americas' and his long relationship with the CIA, and Bush, were deemed immaterial. The subsequent restoration of Panama and its canal to unfettered American sovereignty, managed by more reliable Noriegas, which was the reason for the invasion, created little interest.

One of the most successful demons of all, Saddam Hussein, was another former pal of George Bush and also of the American and British arms industries, which supplied him during the 1980s in his war against those early model Ultra Demons, the Iranian mullahs. About a million people died in that decade-long Western-sponsored slaughter. When Saddam got uppity in 1990 and invaded Kuwait over the disputed ownership of oil fields, his former pal described him as 'another Adolf Hitler'. Within a few months another quarter of a million people had lost their lives, in the American-led slaughter in Iraq.

A demon who never lost his usefulness is the Cambodian genocidist Pol Pot. In recent years Pol Pot has once again been promoted as a unique monster who single-handedly brought untold suffering to his people. There is no mention of the monster's Faustian partners in the West, without whom he would never have seized power and who later restored and sustained him in exile, in the service of their own imperial imperatives.

The Western version is that Cambodia's nightmare began in 1975, 'Year Zero', when the Khmer Rouge took power. In fact, 'Year Zero' was 1969, when President Nixon and his Secretary of State, Henry Kissinger, launched their secret and illegal bombing of neutral Cambodia, with American pilots' logs being falsified to conceal the crime. Between 1969 and 1973, American bombers killed three-quarters of a million Cambodian peasants in an attempt to destroy North Vietnamese supply bases, many of which did not exist. During one six-month period in 1973, B-52 aircraft dropped more bombs on Cambodians, living mostly in straw huts, than were dropped on Japan during all of the Second World War: the equivalent of five Hiroshimas.

Evidence from US official documents, declassified in 1987, leaves little doubt that this American terror provided the catalyst for a revolution which, until then, had had no popular base among the Cambodian people. 'They are using [the bombing] as the main theme of their propaganda,' reported the CIA Director of Operations on May 2, 1973. 'This approach has resulted in the successful recruitment of a number of young men [and] the propaganda has been most effective among refugees subjected to B-52 strikes.'[48]

What Nixon and Kissinger began, Pol Pot completed. And when the Khmer Rouge were finally driven into Thailand by the Vietnamese on Christmas Day, 1978, they were received and welcomed into border camps by American covert operations officials, including the same Defence Intelligence Agency colonel who had planned the secret bombing that had helped bring them to power. Headquartered in the American Embassy in Bangkok, the Kampuchea Emergency Group set about restoring the Khmer Rouge as the 'resistance' to the Vietnamese-backed regime in Phnom Penh.[49] Two American relief aid workers, Linda Mason and Roger Brown, later wrote, 'The US Government insisted that the Khmer Rouge be fed ... the US preferred that the Khmer Rouge operation benefit from the credibility of an internationally known relief operation.'[50] Under American pressure, the World Food Programme handed over $12 millions' worth of food to the Thai Army to pass on to the Khmer Rouge. '20,000 to 40,000 Pol Pot guerrillas benefited,' according to former Assistant Secretary of State Richard Holbrooke.[51]

In 1980, I travelled in a UN convoy of forty trucks,

seventeen of them loaded with food, seventeen with seed and the rest with what the UN people called 'goodies'. We headed for Phnom Chat, a Khmer Rouge operations base set in forest just inside Cambodia and bunkered with land-mines. The UN official leading the convoy, an American, Phyllis Gestrin, said, 'I don't know what this aid is doing [but] I don't trust these blackshirts.' After her trucks had dropped off their 'goodies', she solicited the signature of a man who had watched in bemused silence from a thatched shelter. 'Well, I guess what I got here is a receipt,' she said. 'Not bad, from a butcher like him.' The 'butcher's' military alias was Nam Phann, also known as 'Pol Pot's Himmler', a man wanted for the murder of thousands of people in Siem Reap province.

Five months later, Dr Ray Cline, a former deputy director of the CIA and a foreign-policy adviser to President-elect Ronald Reagan, made a secret visit to a near-by Khmer Rouge operations base, where he conferred with senior Khmer Rouge officials. American satellite intelligence and money followed. By 1983, Pol Pot's American allies were joined by a contingent from Britain's SAS, who taught the Khmer Rouge-led 'resistance' the technology of land-mines and how to lay them. When the British returned to Cambodia eight years later as members of a UN 'peace-keeping' force, they were greeted as old comrades by Pol Pot's senior commanders.[52]

How is it that Western establishments can invert the public truth of their own power and terrorism? The answer is that it is apostasy in Britain and the United States to describe the democracies as terrorist states. That distinction is reserved for the likes of Libya and Iran, which of course are pipsqueak terrorists. Stereotypes are much preferred, such as the 'Muslim fanatic'. In fact, not only have Muslims been responsible for a tiny proportion of deaths caused by terrorism, but in recent years it is they who have been the greatest sufferers from state terrorism: in Palestine, Iraq, Bosnia, Chechenya and Somalia. The omission from public debate of these truths is given respectability by a legion of Western academics, think tanks, 'defence' correspondents and popular Western culture. Arnold Schwarzenegger, in his successful film *True Lies*, kills eighty terrorists, all of them Arab Muslims.

'Terrorists', wrote the historian Frank Furedi, 'become any foreign people you don't like. Moreover, terrorism is redefined to serve as an all-purpose metaphor for the Third World, demanding concerted action from the West.'[53] He cited a report by the Trilateral Commission, warning that international migration, with its connections to such issues as environmental degradation, drugs and terrorism, is a 'new fact of national and international life that requires co-operation of all kinds among all nations'.[54] The emphasis on demographic themes, he noted, 'creates a situation in which the West, rather than being the aggressive invader in the Third World, becomes the target of alien invasion.'[55] A prominent British terrorism 'expert', Professor Paul Wilkinson, wrote, presumably with a straight face, that terrorism presented a 'threat to the US' and other 'powerless Western governments'.[56]

The Malthusian spectre is once again popular. A leading American defence journal has identified the new enemy as 'that swirling pot of poison made up of zealots, crazies, drug-runners and terrorists'.[57] Not only was the United States threatened, warned a writer in *International Affairs*, but 'Europe is increasingly confronted with ... AIDS, drugs, pollution and the proliferation of chemical and biological weapons in the Third World'.[58]

Serious blueprints are at hand to deal with this nightmare. The most famous is the work of Professor Samuel Huntington, Director of Harvard's Institute of Strategic Studies. Called *The Clash of Civilisations*, it has been hailed as a 1990s equivalent to George F. Kennan's historic essay on 'containment', which rationalised American imperial supremacy following the Second World War. Huntington's argument is that Western culture must be preserved in splendid isolation from the rest of humanity in order to 'generate a third Euro-American phase of Western affluence'. 'The leaders of Western countries', he wrote, 'have instituted patterns of trust and co-operation among themselves that, with rare exceptions, they do not have with the leaders of other societies.' He described NATO as 'the security organisation of Western civilisation [whose] primary purpose is to defend and preserve that civilisation'. NATO member-ship should be closed to 'countries that have historically been primarily Muslim or Orthodox' or in any way non-Western 'in their religion and culture'.

Huntington's language relies upon racial stereotypes and a veiled social Darwinism that is the staple of fascism. It is a vision of global apartheid. Of course, the responsibility to police this Western laager 'falls overwhelmingly on the most powerful Western country, the United States'. Huntington's call for a new Mandate from Heaven has been endorsed by Henry Kissinger as 'the most important since the Cold War'.[59]

Everybody will know their place in the global apartheid system. The European Union has shown the way. Anti-refugee and asylum-seeker laws now ensure that people are sent back to regimes that want to imprison or kill them. In 1997, refugees escaping from Albania drowned after an Italian naval ship deliberately rammed their boat. One of the first acts of the Blair Government was to speed up the deportation of 'failed' asylum seekers, removing a 'backlog' of reportedly 50,000 people.[60]

However, as the drawbridges are pulled up and the refugees are sent packing, the Third World Nuclear Threat is revealed. There are the 'Atomic Ayatollahs' in Iran; and Saddam Hussein has been long suspected of 'going nuclear'. That the International Atomic Energy Agency has dismissed the former as nonsense, and the Stockholm Research Institute for Studies of Conflict and Terrorism, a respected body, found the latter unsupported by any evidence, is beside the point. Like 'drug barons' in Latin America, 'nuclear terrorists' require a response from the civilised West.

Among a number of proposals is a Nuclear Expeditionary Force, 'primarily for use against Third World targets'.[61] In 1997, six new radar-evading Stealth bombers were com-missioned into the US nuclear strike force. They will carry a new type of bomb, the B61-11, or 'penetrator nuclear weapon'.

Designed to drill deep into the earth before exploding in a blast whose shockwaves can destroy 'command bunkers' thousands of feet below, these low-yield 'mini-nukes' can also be delivered by F-16 fighter planes.[62]

No fuss is made about the Middle East's only genuine nuclear-armed power, whose murderous invasions of a neighbouring country, all of them in violation of at least six UN resolutions and overwhelmingly condemned by the UN General Assembly, have been carried out with impunity. This is Israel, whose terrorism, known as 'self-defence', is under-written by the United States. In 1982, the Israelis invaded Lebanon and killed some 20,000 people. Israeli fighter aircraft bombed refugee camps; death squads of Shin Beth, the Israeli secret police, kidnapped and murdered at will. The unstated reason for this barbarism was, wrote Noam Chomsky, 'to overcome the threat of PLO diplomacy'.[63]

In 1996, the Israelis massacred 102 refugees, including women and children, in the United Nations' base at Qana in southern Lebanon. The shelling had been aimed at a Hizbollah base near by, they insisted: a claim quickly discredited by UN observers. The press coverage in Britain and the United States was instructive. The headline in *The Times* was 'CLINTON LEADS CALL FOR PEACE AFTER 97 DIE', followed by 'Attack on Lebanon will go on unless Hizbollah calls cease-fire'. The *Daily Telegraph* juxtaposed a banner headline, 'ISRAELI SHELLS KILL 94 REFUGEES' with a quote in bold type from Shimon Peres, the Israeli Prime Minister: 'We had no choice but to defend our people and soldiers.' *Newsweek* said the victims had died 'in the crossfire'.[64]

In Palestine, as elsewhere, the victims, not the oppressors, are the terrorists: a perception widely held, according to Richard Falk, because of 'the domination of *fact* by *image* in shaping and shading the dissemination of images that control the public perception of reality . . . even left critics generally start from the prefabricated association of terrorism with the politics of the dispossessed, and try from that vantage point to explain and argue why such patterns of violence have emerged . . .'[65] That all but a few members of the UN General

Assembly vote year upon year for a resolution calling on Israel to withdraw from the occupied territories is, like so much else, irrelevant. What matters is that Israel represents Western, mostly American, power.

Today, an American-sponsored 'peace process' means the opposite. It is a war process that has corralled the Palestinians between Israeli military forces and foreign invaders, known as 'settlers', who are sponsored and armed by the Israeli government and subsidised by the United States. It is entirely appropriate, if heartbreaking, that the beleaguered cantons that comprise 3 per cent of the West Bank, which the 'peace process' has allotted the Palestinians in their own country, resemble the impoverished Bantustans or 'homelands' of apartheid South Africa. In the meantime, the Palestinians must put up with clichés about Islamic terrorism when almost nothing is said about the dehumanising terror of Jewish and Western fundamentalism. Although failing to achieve the ideal of pacifying the indigenous population, the 'peace process' has petrified them, muting their hopes and dreams, while the Western powers go about their task of exploiting a region long recognised by the United States as 'a stupendous source of strategic power, and one of the greatest material prizes in world history'.[66]

One of the striking features of the new Cold War is the rehabilitation of the concept of imperialism. Like Prime Minister Harold Macmillan in the 1950s, the Samuel Huntingtons in the 1990s grieve the 'loss of white prestige' that was imperialism.[67] 'It is easy to forget', wrote Frank Furedi in The New Ideology of Imperialism, 'that until the 1930s the moral claims of imperialism were seldom questioned in the West. Imperialism and the global expansion of the Western powers were represented in unambiguously positive terms as a major contributor to human civilisation ... To be an imperialist was considered a respectable, political badge.'[68] Future Labour Prime Minister Harold Wilson, who described himself as a socialist, argued in 1949 that 'no party can or should claim for itself the exclusive use of the title Imperialist, in the best sense of the word'.[69]

As the United States emerged from the Second World War and shed what 'Atlanticists' like to call its 'age of innocence' (forgetting the slaughter of the American Indians, slavery, the theft of Texas from Mexico, the subjugation of Central America, Cuba and the Philippines, the Monroe Doctrine and other innocent pursuits), 'imperialism' was dropped from American textbooks and declared a European affair. One of the difficulties for proud imperialists in the post-war period was that Hitler and fascism, and all their ideas of racial and cultural superiority, had left a legacy of guilt by association.

'The discovery that imperialism was immoral', wrote Furedi, 'took some time to sink in [and] strongly disoriented the British ruling class.'[70] A serious, if farcical, campaign to expunge the word from the language followed, 'on the grounds that it falsely attributed immoral motives to Western foreign policy'. The term was deemed no longer to have 'relevance'. Those who persisted in using it as a pejorative term were 'disreputable' and 'sinister'. They were, wrote one American historian, 'inspired by Communist doctrine' or they were 'Negro intellectuals who had grievances of their own against white capitalism'.[71]

In the best Stalinist tradition, imperialism no longer existed. There followed a historical sleight of hand. 'The Cold War intelligentsia', wrote Furedi, 'by denying the centrality of the imperial identity to Western society, were denying their own past. They did not deny that imperialism was something to be ashamed of, they merely denied all association with it.'[72]

With the end of the old Cold War, a new opportunity arose. The economic and political crises in the Third World could now serve as retrospective justification for imperialism. Although the word remained unspeakable, imperialism's return journey to respectability had begun. For the first time in half a century the past was openly celebrated. The *Wall Street Journal* described American opposition to the Franco-British invasion of Suez in 1956 as 'perhaps the biggest strategic mistake in the post-war era'.[73] Shortly before the American attack on Iraq in 1991, the right-wing Cambridge academic John Casey announced that the Western powers 'can now do what they like [in the Third World]'.[74]

And he was right. Today, with the expansion of NATO, the American legitimisation of ethnic cleansing in the Balkans, the 'containment' of the Middle East, and the restoration of American influence throughout Africa and in the Central American 'backyard', the retired Douglas Hurd can understandably sigh with relief when he says that 'we are slowly putting behind us a period of history when the West was unable to express a legitimate interest in the developing world without being accused of "neo-colonialism".'[75]

New brand names come and go: 'preventative diplomacy' and 'humanitarian intervention', the latter a veteran of the Gulf slaughter. Although satisfying the criterion of doing what you like where you like, as long as you're strong enough, they have yet to capture the popular imagination; 'United Nations peacekeeping' and 'peace operations' are current favourites.

'Like its role in the Gulf War', wrote Phyllis Bennis in her 1996 study of the United Nations, 'the UN's function in the years since has increasingly become one of authorising and facilitating the unilateral interventionist policies of its most powerful member states – especially those of the US', while its own power remains 'contingent on the scraps and dregs of resources bestowed on or denied it by Washington . . .'[76] The UN Security Council was still meeting on January 16, 1991, debating whether to authorise the attack on Iraq, when a reporter came into the chamber and said, 'They're bombing Baghdad. It's on CNN.'[77]

Since 1996, 'peace operations' have passed quietly from the United Nations to the North Atlantic Treaty Organisation (NATO), originally set up in Washington to fight the Russians. The policing of Bosnia, which effectively legitimised 'ethnic cleansing' in the Balkans, was handed over to NATO forces and is seen as a model for policing the world. In preparation for this new role, NATO has reorganised and re-equipped itself with 'crisis reaction forces', which are capable of intervening anywhere. A new command, known as the 'combined joint task forces', will allow the use of NATO weapons and intelligence without consultation with members who have 'insufficient interest in a particular region'. Of course, Washington retains a veto.

Those who predicted that NATO's function in Europe would pass into history with the fall of the Berlin Wall were mistaken. NATO has expanded rapidly into Eastern Europe, right up to the borders of Russia. The Russian response is hardly known in the West, being the slowest of news. 'The Defence Ministry in Moscow', wrote Andreas Zumach, a German journalist specialising in the UN, 'has already announced plans to deploy new tactical nuclear weapons near Russia's western border. Russia's National Security Council also intends to drop Moscow's longstanding doctrine of "no first use" nuclear weapons. The claustrophobic encroachment on Russia's borders has strengthened the influence of nationalistic forces in the Russian parliament [which] will not ratify the second Strategic Arms Reduction Treaty with the US . . . Rather than provide "more stability and security for Europe", as its proponents promise, NATO's expansion east will be a cause of possible open crises on the Eurasian continent for years to come.'[78]

Since the re-invasion of Russia by the forces of globalisation, Russia's economy has halved and its Gross Domestic product has been reduced to that of the Netherlands. The availability of food has again become desperate and unemployment is at its highest for sixty years. With male life expectancy down to fifty-eight, Russia is the first country in history to experience such a sharp fall in life expectancy. (It was sixty-nine in the late 1950s.)[79] 'Under the masque of liberal democracy,' wrote Michel Chossudovsky, 'the totalitarian state remained unscathed: a careful blend of Stalinism and the "free" market with the IMF and the other instruments of the triumphant imperialism [intent] on neutralising a former enemy and forestalling the development of Russia as a major capitalist power.'[80]

This is not the way Russia is reported in Britain and the United States. There is no public debate about unfolding dangers, no sense of what has been done to former Soviet society. Imperialism may be rehabilitated, but its conse-quences remain unspeakable. Throughout the world people are still paraded on television as the victims of their own misfortune. No matter that their predicament has causes rooted in the imperial past, in shifting imperial alliances and 'spheres of influence', as in Rwanda. When the cameras move on, as sure as the seasons, the people no longer exist.

Cambodia is a vivid example. In 1992, when the Western powers returned to Cambodia, they came under the United Nations' flag. This time, they imposed a 'peace plan' devised by US Congressman Stephen Solarz, a leading Cold War warrior. Under the Solarz Plan, Cambodia would be opened to the 'global market', indebted, and expunged of the influence of its liberators, the Vietnamese.

In order to undermine the Vietnamese-supported Hun Sen Government, the United Nations welcomed back to Phnom Penh the exiled politicians and generals of the 'Coalition Government of Democratic Kampuchea', which was an invention of the United States and dominated by the Khmer Rouge. Pol Pot's guerrillas were handed a quarter of the Cambodian countryside, where, contrary to propaganda that they are 'finished', they continue to operate with impunity and in their 'thousands', according to US State Department spokesman Nicholas Burns.[81] This is not surprising; in 1992, Eric Falt, the UN spokesman in Phnom Penh, told me, 'The peace process was aimed at allowing [the Khmer Rouge] to gain respectability.'[82]

Thanks to the United Nations' 'peace operation', with its by-products of corruption and an AIDS epidemic, Cambodia was left with a government impossibly divided between Hun Sen, an opponent of the Khmer Rouge, and Prince Norodom Ranariddh, a Khmer Rouge ally. It was Ranariddh's eagerness to bring the Khmer Rouge into the government as a means of boosting his own power that led to Hun Sen's so-called 'coup' in 1997 and the subsequent sideshow of Pol Pot's public 'trial', staged by the Khmer Rouge for the Western media. This allowed them once again to step back into the shadows. Ranariddh's royalists are once again their allies. 'The most successful UN peace operation in history' merely reinforced the status quo, denying Cambodia opportunities for an authentic peace.

A runner-up for the mantle of the UN's 'greatest success' is George Bush's 'humanitarian intervention' in Somalia in 1992, in the midst of his re-election campaign. Here it was generally agreed that the US Marines were finally doing what Bush called 'God's work . . . saving thousands of innocents'. This was 'Operation Restore Hope', which, like the assault on Iraq the previous year, had UN 'legality'. The American TV crews were waiting as the Marines landed in a beautiful African pre-dawn: 'prime time' at home. From the Somalian side there was perpetual darkness: 'chaos' and 'tribalism' and 'warlords'. When the American warlords had completed their adventure in Somalia and taken the media home with them, the story died, as they say. The Marines had left 7,000–10,000 people dead. This was not news.[83]

'The objective in Somalia was noble,' wrote Henry Kissinger in the *Guardian*. 'In fact, moral purpose has motivated every American war this century . . . The new approach [in Somalia] claims an extension in the reach of morality . . . "Humanitarian intervention" asserts that moral and humane concerns are so much part of American life that not only treasure but lives must be risked to vindicate them; in their absence, American life would have lost some meaning. No other nation has ever put forward such a set of propositions.'[84]

UNPEOPLE 1

Few of us can easily surrender our belief that society must
somehow make sense. The thought that the State has lost
its mind and is punishing so many innocent people is
intolerable. And so the evidence has to be internally
denied.

Arthur Miller

THE GULF WAR was the first real major action of the new
Cold War. Like a videogame all the family could play, it was
fun. There was a demon to fight, hi-tech weapons to fight him
with, it was all over quickly and 'we' won. The bonus was the
'miraculously small number of casualties'.

'GO GET HIM BOYS', said the *Daily Star* on the day war
broke out. The *Daily Mirror* juxtaposed pictures of a soldier
and an airman beneath the banner headline, 'THE HEROES',
with a scowling Saddam Hussein, headlined 'THE VILLAIN'.
'The time has come', opined the *Sun*, to 'punish the guilty
party . . . Iraq and Saddam Hussein must be destroyed once
and for all.'[1] After all, President Bush had declared Saddam
'another Adolf Hitler'; and the Foreign Secretary, Douglas
Hurd, had agreed '100 per cent'.[2]

So it followed that anything short of resolute military
action was, like the Munich Agreement in 1938, the work of
the 'spineless appeasers' (said the *Sun*) and 'the give-
sanctions-a-chance-brigade' (*Daily Express*).[3] A Central
Intelligence Agency report disclosing that sanctions had
already stopped 97 per cent of Iraqi exports was ignored by

all but the *Guardian*. The fact that most of the population of Iraq were Kurds and Shi'a, ethnic peoples oppressed by and opposed to Saddam Hussein, was not news. The war was 'inevitable'. 'Iraq', like 'Russia' during the Cold War, had ceased to be a human community and become a 'guilty party' and a target for extraordinary weapons.[4]

'The world watched in awe', reported the *Daily Mirror*, 'as Stormin' Norman played his "home video" – revealing how allied planes are using *Star Wars* technology to destroy vital Iraqi targets. Just like Luke Skywalker manoeuvring his fighter into the heart of Darth Vader's space complex, the US pilots zeroed into the very heart of Saddam Hussein's Baghdad.'[5]

The similarity between the 'coverage' in the tabloids and on television was striking. Only the style was different. The BBC's David Dimbleby spoke urgently about the 'surgical' effect of the new bombs, which were known by the name 'smart', as if to endow them with human intelligence. As Greg Philo and Greg McLaughlin wrote in their review of the reporting of the war, the assumption that the 'surgical' weapons ensured low civilian casualties freed journalists from their humanitarian 'dilemma'.[6]

'Like two sports commentators, David Dimbleby and the BBC defence correspondent, David Shukman, were almost rapt with enthusiasm,' they wrote. 'They called for freeze-frames and replays and they highlighted "the action" on screen with computer "light-pens". "This is the promised hi-tech war," said Shukman. "Defence contractors for some time have been trying to convince everybody that hi-tech weapons can work . . . Now, by isolating [the target], they are able to destroy [it] . . . without causing casualties among the civilian population around." '[7]

Interviewing the American Ambassador to Britain, David Dimbleby was especially excited. 'Isn't it in fact true,' he said to him, 'that America, by dint of the very accuracy of the weapons we've seen, is the only potential world policeman? You may have to operate under the United Nations, but it's beginning to look as though you're going to have to be in the Middle East just as, in the previous part of this century, we and the French were in the Middle East.'[8]

Quite so.

The first graphic result of the 'surgical precision' was the American bombing of the Al-Amiriya bunker in Baghdad, in which between 300 and 400 women and children died; most of them burned to death. The *Sun* reported this as a fabrication of Iraqi propaganda. 'Saddam Hussein tried to trick the world yesterday', it said, 'by saying hundreds of women and children died in a bomb attack on an "air-raid shelter". He cunningly arranged TV scenes designed to shock and appal . . . The hidden "civilian" casualties may have been Iraqi military casualties.'[9]

Like most of the *Sun*'s reporting of the war, this was false. What was instructive was the speed with which the respectable media promoted the same falsehoods, if less crudely, while at the same time minimising evidence of the carnage inside the bunker and American culpability. ITN, in announcing that it was censoring its report because the material was 'too distressing', set the tone.[10]

Six months later, the unedited CNN and WTN 'feeds' of footage of the bunker were obtained by the *Columbia Journalism Review*. They had been censored for transmission in Britain, the United States, Australia and for other Western clients. 'They showed scenes of incredible carnage,' wrote the reporter who viewed the videotape. 'Nearly all the bodies were charred into blackness; in some cases the heat had been so great that entire limbs were burned off. Among the corpses were those of at least six babies and ten children, most of them so severely burned that their gender could not be determined. Rescue workers collapsed in grief, dropping corpses; some rescuers vomited from the stench of the still-smoldering bodies.'[11]

The US military briefers insisted that the bunker was a 'military facility'. People living in the vicinity told researchers it was 'unbelievable' that the Americans did not know the shelter was used mostly by women and children, who came and went twice a day.[12] Abu Kulud, who lost his wife and two daughters, said, 'It was impossible for them not to know there were only civilians in the shelter. Their air [communications] were everywhere.' A woman who lost her mother and two sisters, said, 'How could they not know? They had to know. They had the satellite over our heads twenty-four hours a day, as well as photographs the planes took before they bombed.'[13]

On the day of the attack, the BBC's *Nine O'Clock News* presenter, Peter Sissons, prefaced a report from Baghdad with the American statement that the bunker was a military installation. This exchange followed:

Sissons: A few moments ago, I spoke with [the BBC's] Jeremy Bowen in Baghdad and asked him whether he could be *absolutely sure* that there was no military communications equipment in the shelter, which the allies believe was there.

Bowen: Well, Peter, we looked very hard for it . . . I'm pretty confident, as confident as I can be, that I've seen all the main rooms . . .

Sissons: Is it conceivable that it could have been in military use and was converted recently to civilian use?

Bowen: Well, it would seem a strange sort of thing to . . .

Sissons: Let me put it another way, Jeremy. Is it possible to say with *certainty* that it was never a military facility?

Sissons concluded the interview by saying that Bowen was 'subject, of course, to Iraq's reporting restrictions'.[14]

Long after the war was over, a senior American official admitted privately that the bunker bombing had been 'a military mistake'. As this was never broadcast, the 'mistake' was never challenged.[15]

The bunker atrocity was passed over quickly, and the 'coverage' returned to its main theme of a sanitised, scientific war which the Allied military command in Saudi Arabia promoted, thanks to the 'pool' system. The 'pool' is a British invention, used to considerable effect in the Second World War, Korea and the Falklands. The Americans used the Falklands model for their invasions of Grenada (1983) and Panama (1989).

Under the rules, only selected journalists can visit 'the front', and then under military escort. Their reports are then shared with colleagues remaining behind. Thus the 'news' is the same. Those who attempt to strike out on their own are often blackballed and denied military co-operation, such as transport, which means they see no more of the 'action'. The obedient see what the military want them to see. The control of journalists and the management of news are almost total. That was how it worked in the Gulf.

Press 'conferences' became the arena for dispensing propaganda, such as the entertaining videotapes showing pinpoint bombing. Here claims could be made without journalists being able to authenticate them. The Allies' claim that they were progressively 'knocking out' Scud missile sites in Iraq with 'smart' weapons was dutifully reported. In fact, no Scud sites were destroyed. So enthralled were some journalists with the wondrous performance of the hi-tech weapons – as seen on the military videotape – that few questioned their 'surgical precision' or asked to see the unedited videotape. Unknown to reporters in Saudi Arabia, less than 7 per cent of the weapons used in the Gulf War were 'smart', as the Pentagon admitted long after the war.[16]

Most were old-fashioned 'dump' bombs, like those dropped by B-52 aircraft, and famously inaccurate. Seventy per cent of the 88,500 tons of bombs dropped on Iraq and Kuwait – the equivalent of more than seven Hiroshimas – missed their targets completely and many fell in populated areas, causing widespread 'collateral damage': the jargon for civilian casualties.[17] This was not reported. 'War is never pleasant,' declared the *Independent on Sunday*. 'There are certain actions that a civilised society can never contemplate. This carpet-bombing is undeniably terrible. But that does not make it wrong.'[18]

Editorial writers are seldom witnesses. In another war, in paddy fields not far from Saigon, I watched three ladders curve in the sky, and as each rung reached the ground there was a plume of fire and a sound which welled and rippled rather than exploded. These were the bombs of three B-52s flying in formation, unseen above the clouds; between them they dropped about seventy tons of explosives in a 'long box' pattern. Everything inside the 'box' was destroyed.

When I reached the nearest village, the street had been replaced by a crater; people a hundred yards from the point of contact left not even their scorched shadows, which the dead had left at Hiroshima. There were pieces of heads and limbs, and the intact bodies of young children who had been thrown into the air by the blast.

And so it was in Iraq. The Clark Commission – chaired by former US Attorney-General Ramsey Clark – heard evidence from Paul Roberts, a freelance journalist who had travelled with Bedouins during the bombing, that he had watched three waves of bombing every night. 'I experienced bombing in Cambodia,' he said, 'but this was nothing like that . . . After twenty minutes of this carpet-bombing there would be a silence and you would hear a screaming of children and people, and then the wounded would be dragged out. I found myself with everyone else trying to treat injuries, but the state of people generally was one of pure shock. They were walking around like zombies . . .'[19] His evidence, like that of many others before the Clark Commission, was never published in the mainstream media.

Perhaps, like the Vietnamese, Iraqi civilians were obliterated in order to save them. Certainly, George Bush, in his victory speech, said the Gulf War had 'freed America from the memory of Vietnam' – though not before the truth began to trickle out. As the ceasefire was signed, a column of Iraqis retreating from Kuwait City along the Basra road towards Iraq were attacked by American carrier-based aircraft. They used a variety of rockets, cluster bombs and Napalm B, the type that sticks to the skin while continuing to burn. Returning pilots bragged to 'pool' reporters on the carriers, describing the event as a 'duck shoot' and a 'turkey shoot'. Others likened it to 'shooting fish in a barrel'. Defenceless people had been incinerated in their vehicles or strafed as they ran for cover.[20]

Television crews travelling with the Allied forces in Kuwait came upon the aftermath by chance. As the first pictures appeared on American television, the White House justified the attack by referring to the dead as 'torturers, looters and rapists'.[21] However, it was obvious that the convoy included not only military lorries, but civilian vehicles: battered Toyota vans, Volkwagens, motorbikes. Their occupants were foreign workers who had been trapped in Kuwait: Palestinians, Bangladeshis, Sudanese, Egyptians and others.

In the British press, the *Observer* published a shocking photograph of a charred corpse still at the wheel of a truck. With the lips burned away, it appeared to be grinning. Most newspapers preferred a front-page photograph of a US Army medic attending a wounded Iraqi soldier. Here was the supreme image of magnanimity and tenderness, a 'lifeline' the *Daily Mirror* called it, and the exact opposite of what had happened.[22]

In a memorable report for BBC radio, Stephen Sackur who, like Jeremy Bowen, distinguished himself against the odds in the Gulf, described the carnage in such a way that he separated, for his listeners, ordinary Iraqis from Saddam Hussein. He converted the ducks, turkeys and fish to human beings. The incinerated figures, he said, were simply people trying to get home; he sounded angry.[23]

Kate Adie was there for the BBC. Her television report showed corpses in the desert and consumer goods scattered among the blackened vehicles. If this was 'loot', it was pathetic: toys, dolls, hair-dryers. She referred to 'the evidence of the horrible confusion'. She interviewed a US Marine Lieutenant, who appeared distressed. He said the convoy had had 'no air cover, nothing', and he added ambiguously, 'It was not very professional at all.' Adie did not ask him what he meant, nor did she attempt to explain *why* the massacre had taken place. But she did say that 'those who fought and died for Iraq here turned out to be from the north of the country, from minority communities, persecuted by Saddam Hussein – the Kurds and the Turks'.[24]

This was probably the most revealing news of the war; but without context or the barest explanation, it was almost meaningless. The massacre on the Basra road was mainly of troops conscripted from people oppressed by Saddam Hussein and who were his bitter opponents – the very people whom George Bush, John Major and General Schwarzkopf had called on to 'take heart' and 'rise up in revolt'. While Saddam's Republican Guard escaped, Iraq's coerced and demoralised army of mostly Kurds and Shi'a was slaughtered.

Basra road was only one of many massacres. The others were not reported. Throughout the short 'war', the slaughter was carried out beyond the scrutiny of the 'pool'. Unknown to journalists, in the last two days before the ceasefire American armoured bulldozers were ruthlessly deployed, mostly at night, burying Iraqis alive in their trenches, including the wounded. Six months later, *New York Newsday* disclosed that three brigades of the 1st Mechanised Infantry Division – 'the Big Red One' – 'used snow plows mounted on tanks and combat earth movers to bury thousands of Iraqi soldiers – some still alive – in more than 70 miles of trenches'. A brigade commander, Colonel Anthony Moreno, said, 'For all I know, we could have killed thousands.'[25] The only images of this to be shown on television were used as a backdrop to a discussion about the reporting of the war on a late-night BBC arts programme.[26]

'Not a single armoured vehicle of the US [or its allies] was hit by enemy fire. Not one,' wrote Ramsey Clark.[27] American pilots became so bored with the task of killing defenceless Iraqis that they began joking about 'tank plinking', as if the armoured vehicles were tin cans. The operations officer for 'Desert Storm', General Richard Neal, admitted that most Iraqi vehicles were destroyed from the rear.[28]

General Schwarzkopf's policy was that Iraqi dead were not to be counted.[29] One of his senior officers boasted, 'This is the first war in modern times where every screwdriver, every nail is accounted for.' As for human beings, he added, 'I don't think anybody is going to be able to come up with an accurate count for the Iraqi dead.'[30] In fact, Schwarzkopf did provide figures to Congress, indicating that at least 100,000 Iraqi soldiers had been killed. He offered no estimate of civilian deaths.[31]

The war was not a war at all. It was a one-sided blood-letting. Kate Adie, like most of her colleagues, had reported the news, but not the story. Long after it was all over, the BBC's foreign editor, John Simpson, commented in a documentary, 'As for the human casualties, tens of thousands of them, or the brutal effect the war had on millions of others . . . we didn't see much of that.'[32]

In the post-war period some journalists and their editors gave the impression that they knew they had been misled. There was something of an air of atonement. Editorial writers and studio presenters became exercised about 'safe havens' for the Kurds in the north of Iraq, policed by the same military force that had slaughtered thousands of Kurds on the Basra road and elsewhere. Star Wars over, the story was suddenly humanitarian. And close to home. Speaking as one, the British media accused the government of 'covering up the truth' about the deaths of nine British servicemen in the Gulf, all of them killed by American 'friendly fire'. Having been led by the nose in the cover-up of the slaughter of 'tens of thousands' of Iraqis, their indignation gave no hint of irony.

In the United States, there was some attempt to root out the truth. However, this was confined to a few newspapers, such as New York Newsday and its outstanding reporter Knute Royce, and samizdat publications like Z magazine and Covert Action Quarterly. In Australia, ABC television and radio sustained the most virulent establishment abuse for daring to give time to dissenters.

The famous American TV anchorman, Dan Rather, told Americans, 'There's one thing we can all agree on. It's the heroism of the 148 Americans who gave their lives so that freedom could live.' In fact, a quarter of them had been killed, like their British comrades, by other Americans. Moreover, official citations describing how Americans had died heroically in hand-to-hand combat with Iraqis were fake.[33] American forces had bombed five Iraqi military hospitals; and American newscasters seldom referred to the Iraqi dead, let alone how they had died. These were a shocking omissions, as the cost of the human tragedy in Iraq was now available.[34]

Shortly before Christmas 1991, the Medical Educational

Trust in London published a comprehensive study of casualties. Up to a quarter of a million men, women and children were killed or died as a direct result of the American-led attack on Iraq.[35] This confirmed American and French intelligence estimates of 'in excess of 200,000 civilian deaths'.[36]

In evidence submitted to the Parliamentary Foreign Affairs Select Committee, the major international relief agencies reported that 1·8 million people had been made homeless, and Iraq's electricity, water, sewage, communications, health, agriculture and industrial infrastructure had been 'substantially destroyed', producing 'conditions for famine and epidemics'.[37]

The Clark Commission concluded that the nature of the American-led attacks violated the Geneva Convention of 1949, which expressly prohibits attacks on 'objects indispensable to the survival of the civilian population, such as foodstuffs, agricultural areas ... crops, livestock, drinking water installations and supplies and irrigation works', as well as 'dams, dykes and electrical generating stations', without which there will be 'consequent severe losses among the civilian population'.[38]

In 1995, the United Nations Food and Agriculture Organisation (FAO) reported that the military devastation of Iraq, combined with the effect of sanctions imposed by the Security Council – in reality, by the American and British governments – had been responsible for the deaths of more than 560,000 children in Iraq.[39] The World Health Organisation confirmed this figure.[40] Jean Lennock, a field worker, reported this as the equivalent of the unnecessary death of a child every six minutes. 'At Ibn-al-Baladi hospital in Baghdad', she wrote, 'I witnessed the death of eight-month-old Ali Hassan from diarrhoea. His life could have been saved with simple antibiotics. I also witnessed the grief of his mother. Like many of us, she could not understand why her child had been punished for the actions of the Iraqi government.'[41]

In a letter to the Security Council, Ramsey Clark, who has

carried out investigations in Iraq since 1991, wrote that most of the deaths 'are from the effects of malnutrition including marasmus and kwashiorkor, wasting or emaciation which has reached twelve per cent of all children, stunted growth which affects twenty-eight per cent, diarrhoea, dehydration from bad water or food, which is ordinarily easily controlled and cured, common communicable diseases preventable by vaccinations, and epidemics from deteriorating sanitary conditions. There are no deaths crueller than these. They are suffering slowly, helplessly, without simple remedial medication, without simple sedation to relieve pain, without mercy.'[42]

In October 1996, UNICEF, the children's relief organisation, launched an appeal for help from governments, saying that 'over 50 per cent of women and children are receiving less than half their calorific needs'. In other words, they were close to starvation. Only the Government of the Netherlands made a contribution.[43]

In the meantime, the UN has sought to negotiate an 'oil-for-food' arrangement, by which Iraq would be allowed to sell $1 billion's worth of oil every three months on the world market. Half of this would go in war reparations to Kuwait and be allocated to the Kurds in the 'safe havens'; the other half would buy food and medicines and basic spare parts for water and sewage treatment facilities.

The American representatives on the UN Sanctions Committee have used every opportunity to obstruct the plan, which now appears frozen, in spite of having the approval of the Secretary-General.[44] When the US Ambassador to the United Nations, Madeleine Albright, later to be appointed Secretary of State, was asked whether the lives of half a million Iraqi children were too high a price to pay, she replied, 'I think this is a very hard choice, but the price, we think, is worth it.'[45]

Ramsey Clark replied, 'The United States has forced this decision on the Security Council. Three of the five permanent members – China, France and the Russian Federation – have sought to modify the sanctions. [The US] blames Saddam Hussein and Iraq for the effects [on the Iraqi people], most recently arguing that if Saddam stopped spending billions on his military machine and palaces for the elite, he could afford to feed his people. But only a fool would offer or believe such propaganda. If Iraq is spending billions on the military, then the sanctions are obviously not working. Malnutrition didn't exist in Iraq before the sanctions. If Saddam Hussein is building palaces, he intends to stay. Meanwhile, an entire nation is suffering. Hundreds are dying daily and millions are threatened in Iraq, because of US-compelled impoverishment.'[46]

To report the real reasons why children are dying in Iraq, even to recognise the extent of their suffering, is to bracket Western governments with dictatorships and totalitarian regimes. Thus the victims become unmentionable. They become, wrote Mark Curtis, 'unpeople: human beings who impede the pursuit of high policy and whose rights, often lives, therefore become irrelevant'.[47] As Unpeople, they are not news, and their plight, as Kate Adie said of the slaughter on the Basra road, is merely 'evidence of the horrific confusion'.

There were a number of reasons for the American-led attack on Iraq, and none of them had much to do with concern for the freedom-loving tyranny in Kuwait. Saddam Hussein said he invaded Kuwait because the Kuwaiti regime was moving in on disputed oil fields on the Iraq–Kuwait border. This was probably correct, as the US Chairman of the Joint Chiefs of Staff, Colin Powell, indicated when he argued against military intervention, predicting that Saddam would withdraw and put 'his puppet in [and] everyone in the Arab world will be happy'.[48] The documented fact that Saddam Hussein tried to extricate himself from Kuwait on a number of occasions was ignored by most of the American and British media, which preferred the countdown to war.[49]

As in the American invasion of Panama in 1989, Bush wanted to demonstrate the United States' new single-superpower status, and Iraq was the perfect venue. Here was an opportunity to show off American military power, and thereby conceal the decline of its economic power, as well as to test a range of new weapons. For example, munitions made from Depleted Uranium (DU) were used for the first time in Iraq. DU has a radioactive half-life of 125,000 years, and like the effects of 'Agent Orange' in Vietnam, its effect on the population and on future generations will be insidious and devastating.

There was no burning desire to get rid of Saddam Hussein. He had been the West's man, whom Reagan and Thatcher had armed and backed against the mullahs in Iran; and the last thing the West wanted was an Iraq run by socialists and democrats. For this reason, as the 1991 slaughter got under way, the British Government imprisoned as many Iraqi opposition leaders as it could round up. In 1996, the *New York Times* reported that the administration longed for the good old days when Saddam's 'iron fist held Iraq together, much to the satisfaction of the American allies, Turkey and Saudi Arabia'.[50]

The Americans also wanted to protect Saudi oil and the faltering Saudi economy from the competition of cheaper Iraqi oil. That remains Washington's real reason for opposing the lifting of sanctions. 'If Iraq were allowed to resume oil exports,' wrote Phyllis Bennis, one of the most astute American commentators, 'analysts expect it would soon be producing three million barrels a day and within a decade, perhaps as many as six million. Oil prices would soon drop ... And Washington is determined to defend the kingdom's economy, largely to safeguard the West's unfettered access to the Saudis' 25 per cent of known oil reserves.'[51]

An important factor in this is the arms trade. In 1993, almost two-thirds of all American arms export agreements with developing countries were with Saudi Arabia, whose dictatorship is every bit as odious as the one in Baghdad.[52] Since 1990 the Saudis have contracted more than thirty billion dollars' worth of American tanks, missiles and fighter aircraft. According to the authors, Leslie and Andrew Cockburn, 'Every day, the Pentagon ... disburses an average of 10 million dollars – some days as much as 50 million – to contractors at work on the Saudi shopping list.' As an insight into the

US-sponsored 'peace process' in the Middle East, they wrote that a Pentagon officer had told them, 'If the Saudis had cancelled their F-15 [fighter aircraft] program [as a result of the fall in oil prices], Israel probably would not have bought any. Basically, that's the only thing keeping the F-15 line open.'[53]

In 1996, President Clinton attacked Iraq with Tomahawk missiles – ostensibly to 'defend' Kurds in the north of the country, but the presidential election campaign was well under way. Once again military technology dominated the news, celebrated with Dan Dare maps and missiles looking sleek against the dawn light. Both the BBC news and ITN used Pentagon footage. The Tomahawks and B-52s were said to have struck only 'radar sites' and 'strategic control centres'. ITN's Trevor McDonald spoke inexplicably about 'the balance of power' and 'urgent Western diplomacy'.[54] Addressing the American people, Clinton invoked the paramount rule of the Old West: 'When you abuse your own people . . . you must pay a price.'[55]

It was Unpeople who paid the price, and we saw virtually nothing of them. A shot of a demolished building in a crowded part of Baghdad was, explained McDonald, 'allegedly hit' by a Tomahawk. 'And finally,' said McDonald, 'Lottery winners say their millions have given them security for life. Good night.'[56] There was clearly no time for Iraq's dying children.

As I write this, Clinton is again threatening to attack Iraq, with an unquestioning Tony Blair as his principal ally. In contrast to the voluminous coverage of Clinton's sex life, there has been minimal genuine debate about this looming war and its danger – such as the real possibility that the United States will use the B61-11 'nuclear penetration bomb' against Saddam Hussein's bunkers. The reason given for this attack is the unproven charge that Saddam is manufacturing 'weapons of mass destruction'. With more than 1·4 million Iraqis dead as a result of Western sanctions, the source of the real weapon of mass destruction is proven, if unreported.

'Have we grown more wary of instant response to disaster,

more indifferent to the stream of seemingly baffling conflicts which flit past on the screen?' asked Kate Adie in a reflective article. 'Do the pictures of the displaced, the homeless and injured mean less when they are so regularly available? Have we, in short, begun to care less . . .?'

She did not explain the 'we'. 'What has not changed', she wrote, 'is the need to choose news priorities, to judge the importance and relevance of a story against all else that is happening in the world. And the need endlessly to debate whether some stories should be covered for a moral or humanitarian reason, *even though the majority of the audience expresses little desire to view them*' (my italics).[57]

She offered no evidence to support this last assertion. On the contrary, the generosity of those who can least afford to give is demonstrable, vivid and unending, as I know from personal experience. It is compassion, as well as anger, that gives millions of people the energy and tenacity to lobby governments for an end to state crimes committed in their name in East Timor, Burma, Turkey, Tibet, Iraq, to name but a few. Far from not wanting to know, the 'majority of the audience' consistently make clear, as the relevant surveys show, that they want *more* current affairs and documentaries which attempt to make sense of the news and which explain the 'why' of human events.[58]

During the Thatcher years, broadcasters and journalists invented the public affliction called 'compassion fatigue', which represented, not the public's sentiments, but conformism long served by journalists. Following the Gulf War, researchers scrutinised more than 8,000 images of the British television coverage and found that only one per cent dealt with human suffering.

There is a self-fulfilling element in this age of saturation media. In a related survey, a sample group of children were asked, 'What sticks in your mind about the television coverage of the war?' Most referred to the hi-tech weapons and equipment; some mentioned specifically the Pentagon war 'videogames'. None mentioned people.[59]

THE CRUSADERS

Everyone has the right to work, to just and favourable
conditions of work and to protection for himself and his
family [and] an existence worthy of human dignity ...
everyone has the right to a standard of living adequate for
the health and well being of himself and his family,
including food, clothing, housing and medical care.
                    Universal Declaration of Human Rights, 1948

We have 50 per cent of the world's wealth, but only 6·3
per cent of its population. In this situation, our real job in
the coming period is to devise a pattern of relationships
which permit us to maintain this position of disparity. To
do so, we have to dispense with all sentimentality ... we
should cease thinking about human rights, the raising of
living standards and democratisation.
                    George Kennan, US Cold War planner, 1948

THE FOOTBALL IN Sonia's hands bears the picture and
signature of Eric Cantona, together with the legend 'Eric the
King'. Sonia is stitching the ball, which is her job in a village
in India's Punjab. She is eleven years old and blind. She
remembers the moment she lost her sight. 'It went completely
dark in front of my eyes and I was scared,' she said.

She has since learned to stitch footballs by touch alone: her
Aunt Satya matches up the panels and passes them to her
niece. The two of them support an extended family since
Sonia's mother fell seriously ill. When asked about the fun of

being a child, Sonia said there was no fun in what she did. 'I have no choice,' she said. It takes her a day to stitch two balls, for which she earns the equivalent of fifteen pence, or about a quarter of one dollar – not enough to buy a litre of milk.

Before he retired from Manchester United in 1997, Eric Cantona earned around £19,000 a week, not including fees from advertising and commercial sponsorship, such as the use of his face and signature on footballs. In 1995–6, Britain imported £8 million's worth of sporting goods from India, made with cheap labour. Other European countries and the United States, Australia and Japan also 'out-sourced', as they say in the global economy, much of their sports manufacturing to untold numbers of Sonias in the poorest countries.[1]

For several months before Christmas, toy shops in Britain's high streets are packed with parents anxious to please their expectant children. In China and Thailand, there are parents for whom toys and children have another association. In 1993, two of the world's worst industrial fires razed toy factories in Thailand and China, killing 275 workers, most of them in their early teens. Hundreds were terribly burned. Most were girls from very poor families.

Accidents in toy factories are endemic, as production is speeded up to meet an apparently insatiable demand from Europe, North America, Japan and Australia, which import 80 per cent of their toys from Asia. The girls in the Kadar factory in Bangkok were making Bart Simpson and Cabbage Patch dolls. In China, the popular Barbie and Sindy dolls, Power Rangers and Fisher-Price toddlers' toys are made by mostly rural girls working twelve to sixteen hours a day for the legal minimum wage of £27 a month, if they are lucky. Many will suffer from chronic industrial diseases, caused by the effects of plastics, paints and glues used without protection or ventilation.[2]

Using subcontractors, the Western and Japanese brand-owners often insist they have no direct responsibility for the conditions under which their products are made. For the consumers, 'signed' footballs, toys, Nike shoes, caps that Western youths like to wear back to front, all types of clothing made in sizes into which two of its seamstresses would fit, leather bags, electronic circuits, computers and TV sets are manufactured in places of impoverishment and exploitation that exist only as labels. This is 'globalisation'.

Globalisation is a jargon term which journalists and politicians have made fashionable and which is often used in a positive sense to denote a 'global village' of 'free trade', hi-tech marvels and all kinds of possibilities that transcend class, historical experience and ideology. According to one of its chief proponents, Prime Minister Tony Blair, the very notion means that 'the grand ideological battles of the twentieth century are over'. What matters now, he says, are 'recovery' and 'growth', 'competitiveness' and 'flexible working'; all else is obsolete.[3]

These terms could easily replace their equivalents in George Orwell's 1984, for their true meaning is the dictionary opposite. Devoid of social and moral content, rather like the rows of Barbie dolls on the shelves of Hamley's toy supermarket in London, they point to the nightmare of ordinary people like Sonia and the toy workers, and to a class war waged at a distance by technocrats of the new Cold War.

It is the confluence of globalisation and state terror that defines the new Cold War. 'New' is deceptive, for the nature of the modern assault derives from the liberal economic theory of the eighteenth and nineteenth centuries, which gave birth to 'capitalism writ large', or modern imperialism. Backed by the power of the state, British and other European trading companies fell upon the world's riches and peoples like pirates on buried treasure. Their 'competitiveness' created the conditions for the slaughter of 1914–18; Henry Ford's ensuing 'new era of endless prosperity' became the Great Depression of the 1930s, and imperial retributions contributed to the rise to Nazism and the slaughter of 1939–45.[4]

What followed was the simultaneous defeat and recolonisation of the European empires by American capital. This was made possible by a government-subsidised production boom in the United States during the Second World

61

War, which left half the world's wealth in American hands, and by a conference of the Western Allies at Bretton Woods in New Hampshire in July 1944. Like Versailles in 1919, it was described as 'negotiations'; in reality it marked the American conquest of most of the world.

'What the US imperial master demanded, and still does', wrote Frederic F. Clairmont in *The Rise and Fall of Economic Liberalism*, 'was not allies but unctuous client states. What Bretton Woods bequeathed to the world was a lethal totalitarian blueprint for the carve up of world markets.'[5] Having secured Europe and its markets and ensured that Marshall Plan 'aid' was repaid at exorbitant interest rates, the United States at Bretton Woods established the World Bank and the International Monetary Fund, based in Washington, as instruments of a *Pax Americana* that knew no boundaries in the non-communist world. The Asian Development Bank, the Inter-American Bank and the African Development Bank followed: 'international' institutions, in which capital subscription, not membership, determined influence. That is to say, Washington ran them.

The new masters initially called their imperialism 'liberal containment'. For example, in the first years of the American invasion of Vietnam, the early 1960s, huge 'loans' funded a limited redistribution of wealth in 'American protected' South Vietnam in order to bring 'stability' to a nation consumed by a liberation struggle. ('Stability' is probably the most important word in the new imperial vocabulary.) The 'loans' went into civil projects and to favoured farmers and businessmen, but mostly the money bribed local elites – while American-led death squads conducted terror campaigns against those suspected of supporting the 'internal aggression' of the 'insurgents'. In this way, as many as 100,000 Vietnamese civilians were murdered in the CIA's infamous Operation Phoenix.[6]

'I don't see why', said Henry Kissinger, 'we need to stand by and watch a country go communist because of the irresponsibility of its own people.' Kissinger was referring to another 'Vietnam': the American conquest of Chile, for which he was partly responsible and which provided a lesson to Third World nations seeking alternative economic routes by democratic means. In 1971, Chileans elected Salvador Allende, a socialist whose attempts at wealth redistribution were destroyed by an unrelenting CIA campaign of subversion. Economic chaos was achieved, Allende was assassinated and Washington's man, General Augusto Pinochet, began a military reign that saw 130,000 Chileans murdered, tortured and 'disappeared'.[7]

Although plenty of other countries, such as Guatemala, Iran, Brazil and the Congo, had been similarly dispossessed of popular governments and nationalist leaders who sought a non-American way for their people, Chile was the first to be 'structurally adjusted'. Structural Adjustment Programmes, or SAPs, were dreamt up in the late 1970s when American, European and Japanese banks pressured poor countries to borrow petro-dollars accumulated following the boom in oil prices. There followed a rapid rise in interest rates, which coincided with the fall in the world price of commodities like coffee. As a consequence Third World governments found themselves in grave difficulties.

Under a plan devised by President Reagan's Secretary to the Treasury, James Baker, indebted countries were offered World Bank and IMF 'servicing' loans in return for the 'structural adjustment' of their economies. This meant that the economic direction of each country would be planned, monitored and controlled in Washington. 'Liberal containment' was replaced by *laissez-faire* capitalism, known as the 'free market'. Industry would be deregulated and sold off; public services, such as health care and education, would be diminished. Subsistence agriculture, which has kept human beings alive for thousands of years, would be converted to the production of foreign exchange-earning cash crops. 'Tax holidays' and other 'incentives', such as sweated labour, would be offered to foreign 'investors'. It was the surrender of sovereignty, and without a gunboat in sight.

Chile was to be the 'laboratory' for this new imperial order. Frank Field, now Social Security Minister in the Blair

Government, went there in 1996 with a group of other MPs. Assigned by Blair to 'think the unthinkable' on welfare policy, Field has studied the way the regime has dealt with welfare, specifically pensions. Employed Chileans pay at least 10 per cent of their wages into a private scheme; unemployed Chileans pay and receive nothing. Field is likely to introduce a similar system in Britain.

He is one of many to find 'free market' inspiration in Chile, especially since a tenuous respectability was restored with the election of a civilian government in 1990. Presided over by the World Bank, the IMF and General Pinochet's military machine, which remains the real power, Chile is the very model of what is known in Washington as a New Democracy.

What impressed Field had long impressed Margaret Thatcher, a still frequent pilgrim to Santiago and dinner guest of the 'retired' Pinochet. In Chile, the 'unthinkable' was realised in the late 1970s by a group of economists trained at the University of Chicago under the *laissez-faire* cult leader Milton Friedman. A decade later, almost all state enterprises had been sold off to multinational corporations.

The World Bank and IMF were proud of the results, producing numerous celebratory papers. This was puzzling. Chile's debt was higher than when the 'Chicago boys' took over. By 1991, it had officially risen to almost half the Gross National Product and was certainly higher, as most of Chile's debt was concealed in foreign equity holdings: the notorious 'debt-equity swaps'. A country which, prior to Pinochet, had maintained a reasonable standard of living for most of its people, even managing in Salvador Allende's brief time to double the growth rate, was ravaged. Industry was dismantled, the currency was devalued and the majority of Chileans were plunged into poverty.[8]

When General Pinochet stepped into the shadows but not out of power, and a civilian government took over, 40 per cent of his people were so poor and their calorie consumption so low that hunger and malnutrition blighted most of them.[9] Today, far from serving a long prison sentence for crimes against humanity, he is touring Europe and the United States, shopping for guns and missiles with which to defend his New Democracy.

Haiti is another type of New Democracy. When I reported from Haiti in the 1960s and early 1970s, it seemed a pioneer of the 'free market' of the future, if not the distant past. The Americans had difficulties with the unpredictable 'Papa' Doc Duvalier, the murderous dictator, but this did not interrupt business. I saw another side to all those misty-eyed Hollywood movies about baseball's 'greats'. Almost all the baseballs used in the United States come from Haiti. Whereas Eric Cantona's fame and wealth owe something to children in India, America's Major League heroes have a debt to Haiti. At the Port-au-Prince Superior Baseball Plant, girls stooped in front of whirring, hissing, binding machines. Many had swollen eyes and lacerated arms. There was no protection, and a large man barked orders at them. When I produced a camera, I was thrown out.

'Haiti has a monopoly [on making baseballs] not because of any special skill or resources,' reported the *Los Angeles Times* in 1974. 'The monopoly is there because of cheap labour . . . Tomar Industries, one of several American companies that put baseballs together in Haiti, pays its workers 38 cents for every dozen baseballs sewn. The average girl can sew three and a half to four dozen baseballs a day. That's $1.33 to $1.52 a day. Baseballs are sewn in Haiti because of desperation.'[10]

Haiti is the poorest country in the western hemisphere. Settled in the nineteenth century by freed slaves, there has not been a time when Haiti has not been dominated by the United States. Along with the manufacture of baseballs, textiles, toys and cheap electronics, Haiti's sugar, bauxite and sisal are all controlled by American multinational companies. The exception is coffee, which relies upon the American market.

As a direct result of the imposition of this 'free market', half the children die before they reach the age of five. A child of two is called in Creole *youn to chape* – a little escapee from death. Life expectancy is about fifty-three years.[11] Most American companies pay as little as they can get away with. More than 20,000 people work on assembly lines, a third of which produce goods for that symbol of all-American wholesomeness, the Walt Disney Company. Contractors making Mickey Mouse and Pocahontas pyjamas for Disney in 1996 paid eight pence an hour. The workers are all in debt, knowing that if they lose their jobs they will join those struggling against starvation.[12]

In 1990, following the fall of the Duvalier dynasty, Father Jean-Bertrand Aristide won a national election with a modest programme of reform, giving hope to Haiti's suffering people. Within two years he was overthrown by generals trained in the United States and in the pay of the CIA. As a product of Haitian popular democracy, Father Aristide attracted international support and was given exile in the United States.

It was 1992. Bill Clinton was running for president, promoting himself as another Kennedy, a man 'of all the people, the little people, the middle class people, the caring, hard-working people'.[13] The problem for Clinton was that on the nation's television screens were pictures of the little, hard-working people of Haiti trying to escape to jobs in the United States. This was not helpful in an election campaign. In the meantime, nothing had been heard of the exiled Father Aristide who, rather like Alexander Dubček in Moscow in 1968, was being given the terms of his return to Haiti, or what is known in Washington as a 'geo-political lobotomy'.

He would drop all nonsense about redistributing wealth and accept a World Bank Structural Adjustment Programme that would ensure that the baseballs, Mickey Mouse ears and Pocahontas pyjamas kept coming. Like a similar offer from Al Capone, a refusal would have been unwise; and he complied. He was given assurances that the United States would not intervene in Haitian 'domestic affairs'. He was not told that American covert agencies would continue to arm the Haitian death squads, including the most notorious, known as 'Fraph', which was a creation of the CIA.[14]

In 1994, Clinton invaded Haiti under the flag of the United Nations. (The 'international contingent' arrived a week later.) The United States, said the President, intended to make Haiti 'safe and secure' and to end a period of 'unacceptable human rights violations that shame our hemisphere'. A BBC report referred to 'Mr Nice Guy ... bringing democracy back to a sad and troubled land'.[15] Soon afterwards, the World Bank announced its plan for Haiti, which would bring 'new life' to American manufacturing on the island. Naturally, one of the world's poorest peoples would repay the debt with interest.[16]

True democracy needs no Jeffersonian *imprimatur*; Thomas Jefferson's notion of liberty was not extended to his slaves. George Washington, father of the American nation, set the tone for every president save Franklin Roosevelt. 'Indians', he said, 'have nothing human except the shape ... the gradual extension of our settlements will as certainly cause the savage, as the wolf, to retire; both being beasts of prey though they differ in shape.'[17] James Madison was less crude, though no less honest, when, in addressing the Constitutional Convention in 1787, he said the aim of the new republic was 'to protect the minority of the opulent against the majority'.[18]

True democracy is expressed not on Georgian tablets but in Articles 23 and 25 of the 1948 Universal Declaration of Human Rights. These say that everybody has the right to life and to a decent life: a right not only to employment, but to decent pay, decent working conditions, 'the right to form and join trade unions', the right to a proper home and the right to feel secure, 'in sickness, disability, widowhood, old age': the right to dignity. Nowadays, this is a subversive document, to be perverted and circumvented.[19]

New Democracy is now the way. 'First and foremost,' wrote Peter Gowan, 'a New Democracy is run by strong capitalist proprietors funding the political process and offering electors a choice of leaders who share opinions on most things but have different styles of leadership ... This guarantees that public policy stays politically correct. At the same time New Democracy makes it easier for multinationals to advance their influence and for the "global" [i.e. Western] media to shape public opinion. [In this way] we get leaders in the target country who "want what we want". Hence there is no need to use the big stick ...'[20]

The Americanising of political, economic and cultural life is essential. Since the Berlin Wall came down, a revision of John F. Kennedy's famous utterance at the Wall in 1961 might be: 'We are all Americans now.' In the industrial countries American ideology has been so successfully reconstituted that cultural refuges are now hard to find. 'America sets the tone for the world,' says the voice over the opening titles of the movie *Jerry Maguire*. That is a concise way of saying that the world is ruled by the institutions of money, which are the cathedrals of the American Dream. No relationship is now more important than that between a human being and his or her cash. You must be a consumer/customer. Railway passengers and hospital patients are consumer/customers. People who drink water are consumer/customers. Time, music, cultural heritage and the forests are there to be consumed. Moreover consumers have *rights* which non-consumers do not share.

'Our enormously productive economy', wrote Victor Lebow, a leading retailing analyst, '. . . demands that we make consumption our way of life, that we convert the buying and use of goods into rituals, that we seek spiritual satisfaction, our ego satisfaction, in consumption. We need things, consumed, burned up, worn out, replaced and discarded at an ever increasing rate.'[21]

Children are not exempt. In 1992, Saatchi and Saatchi, the advertising multinational corporation that helped bring the 'spiritual satisfaction' of consumption to Britain and much of the world, formed a 'Kids Division'. Its 'targets' are children between two and fourteen years of age. In 1995, the company was paid $100 million for this service.[22] As Sharon Beder points out in *Global Spin*, Saatchi and Saatchi has realised the 'unprecedented' opportunities offered by the Internet, which is watched by about a million children around the world. This is how the firm explains its Kid Connection service:

> 'We at KID CONNECTION are committed to understanding kids: their motivations, their feelings and their influences. In keeping with our mission to connect our clients to the kid market with programs that match our clients' business

68

objectives with the needs, drives and desires of kids ...
Interactive technology is at the forefront of kid culture,
allowing us to enter into contemporary kid life and com-
municate with them in an environment they call their own.[23]

Consumerism is 'packaged' American culture, which dominates as never before. The majority of films shown worldwide
are American. Like Coke and Pepsi, they drown the local
competition. Made as 'targeted products', many of them
promote self-aggrandisement and violence, inviting the
viewer to join in the shooting and knifing and raping. In a
celebrated Hollywood box-office triumph called *One False
Move*, a psychopath holds a knife to a woman's throat and
she coos at him. Those arbiters of reactionary chic, the critics,
loved it, just as they love and promote Quentin Tarantino and
the other cinematographic salesmen of gratuitous, cash-
flowing violence. General Norman Schwarzkopf, whose
forces in the Gulf killed around a quarter of a million people,
tours the world giving 'motivational speeches' for the World
Masters of Business, for 'around $100,000 an hour', says his
promoter.[24]

'Integrated marketing' ensures that this 'culture' now
permeates much of what we see and read and listen to. Disney
has a 'tie-in' with McDonald's, Warner Bros with Burger
King. The Olympic Games are virtually owned by Coca-Cola,
Nike, Reebok, the oil companies and the other conglomerates
which pay for multi-million-dollar 'endorsements'. Multi-
media Murdoch controls much of the rest.

'In Barbados', lamented Harold Hoyt, President of the
Caribbean Publishing and Broadcasting Association, 'we have
a saying which goes "we is we". It means that we understand
who we are and that we have a sense of belonging to one
another. There is no doubt in my mind that we are being
bombarded by American television, American news,
American everything, which is saying loud and clear that
there are only winners and losers. The way it's going we'll no
longer have a political identity of our own; we'll no longer be
we.'[25]

The condition of Americans themselves best explains this.

The United States, says a Congressional study, has become 'the most unequal of modern nations', in which the most prominent feature of everyday life is class divisiveness. At the end of the Reagan years, the top 20 per cent of the population held the largest share of total income, while the bottom 60 per cent had the lowest ever recorded. Wages have fallen below 1973 levels; the majority of workers are no longer in full-time employment. Ordinary Americans have been so thoroughly 'downsized' that up to 50 million live below the poverty line, most of them without health care of any kind, and with more than half of them dependent on charity so that they can eat.[26]

Outflanking the Republicans from the right in the 1996 election campaign, Clinton signed into law a bill that wiped out the last of Roosevelt's 'New Deal' reforms of the 1930s. By cutting $13 billion from welfare, he excluded millions of the poorest from any form of public assistance. 'The war on poverty is over,' commented the National Urban League. 'A Democratic President and the Congress have decided to wage war against the poor themselves.' The poor, says Clinton (he means blacks and Hispanics), have been 'demotivated' by welfare and forced into a 'welfare' culture.

With the homeless now crowding the streets of cities that once hardly knew them (like Portland, Oregon), Clinton has effectively criminalised the poor, approving laws that have increased the American prison population to more than 1·5 million people. Many are serving long sentences for offences related to the stark deprivation of their lives. Under new state and federal laws, petty and serious offenders are treated the same; and once inside, if you break the rules, such as speaking to a guard the wrong way, your sentence can start all over again.

Of course, there is a 'market' incentive to this. Prisons have become the fastest-growing business in the United States; more people are now employed in what are known as 'prison industries' than in any of the country's top 500 corporations, with the exception of General Motors. Cold War defence contracts have been replaced by Crime War prison contracts.[27] Several states now require prisoners to work six days a week for less than the minimum wage, making consumer goods in 'enterprise zones', which are run on exploitative lines similar to those in Haiti.

In the state of Georgia, always ahead in regression, a company called the United States Corrections Corporation runs prisons which produce a variety of manufactured goods on which it will ultimately realise huge profits. Under Georgia's law, prisoners cannot be paid for their labour; and so that they will not be distracted by rehabilitation and education programmes, the Georgia Department of Corrections has sacked more than 200 teachers, counsellors and librarians. Prisoners who were being taught to read and write have had their courses cancelled. Seventy per cent of them are black and Hispanic. As one of Georgia's biggest contributors to political campaigns, the prisons company is dictating state policy: a trend that will see other captive factories inaugurated throughout the United States.[28]

By contrast, the prosecution of serious corporate crime, which is rife, is unusual. While small-time dealers are pursued in Clinton's 'war on drugs', money laundering, much of it related to the international 'narco-trade', flows unimpeded through the Caribbean tax havens cherished by US multinationals, banks and pension-fund managers.[29] In Clinton's New Democracy, one per cent of the population now controls 40 per cent of the national wealth; profits are at an all-time high, having risen by 19 per cent in the last five years while wages and welfare benefits, put together, have grown by a mere one per cent. This is what economists mean when they say that the American economy is 'booming'.[30]

This is not to suggest that socialism is unknown in the United States. I recall the shock when I was living there in the 1960s when it was disclosed that forty cents in every dollar of tax went towards subsidising what President Eisenhower called the 'military industrial complex'. This is unchanged. In his rhetoric about 'welfare dependency', Clinton omits to mention the most important welfare dependants, such as the 'defence' and aircraft industries and the farming industry, known as 'agribusiness', the recipients of billions of tax dollars since the 1940s. Today, the Federal Government pays out $15 billion a year in farming subsidy, most of it to the giants of 'agribusiness'.[31]

This has led to a massive overproduction of food, with surpluses flooding the world market and destroying the agricultural base in many countries. In Korea, American surpluses, known as 'Food for Peace', have so distorted the local market that up to 90 per cent of Korea's food is now imported from the United States.[32] As a consequence, six American companies control 70 per cent of the world trade in grain. The income of the Cargill Corporation, the world's largest grain trader, is equivalent to that of the nine largest sub-Saharan African countries.[33] Under this system of 'free trade', 40,000 children under the age of five die from malnutrition every day.[34]

Indeed, almost half the world's 'free trade' is not conducted between nations at all, but as transactions *within* 180 multinational corporations. Most are American and Japanese, the rest French, German, British and Swiss. Annual sales of the top eight companies exceed the Gross Domestic Product of the fifty countries which have over half the world's population. These companies control the range of economic life, from food to communications, banking to advertising, retailing to financial services.

They are totalitarian by nature: 'private tyrannies', as Noam Chomsky calls them. It seemed to mystify commentators at the time of Hong Kong's handover to China why the richest capitalists in the former colony warmly welcomed the communist dictatorship on the mainland. In fact, their union is a perfect match. Both sides share a virulent opposition to and fear of true democracy. While the capitalists build the factories and sell and distribute the goods, the dictators supply, control and discipline the workforce. When elections can be arranged, with people voting for one or other identical faction, China will qualify as a 'New Democracy'.

The nature of multinational corporations is exemplified by Coca-Cola, one of the most powerful. During the Second World War, the company claimed that 'next to wives and sweethearts and letters from home, among the things our fighting men overseas mention most is Coca-Cola'. 'Coke' was said to represent the spirit of the United States in its struggle against the forces of fascism. Allied Supreme Commander General (later President) Dwight Eisenhower ordered eight Coca-Cola plants to be set up immediately after his armies landed on the beaches of North Africa.

However, beloved Coke also served the enemy. Max Keith, the company's man in Berlin, so ingratiated himself with the Nazis' Office of Enemy Propaganda that he was appointed administrator of soft drinks' production in occupied Europe. Unable to import the Coca-Cola syrup, Keith concocted another formula from available ingredients and called it Fanta – a brand that is today one of the company's most profitable.[35]

'It does not matter whether the product does good or evil,' wrote a disaffected executive of the giant IBM, 'what counts is that it is consumed – in ever increasing quantities. Since everything the corporation does has as its ultimate goal the creation of profit, it offers its workers no deep personal satisfaction, no feeling of contributing anything worthwhile to society, no true meaning to their activities. Go to work for a corporation and you are, through good salaries and various fringe benefits, installed as a faceless link in the lengthening chain – completing the circle by becoming one more consumer of all that junk.'[36]

Multinational corporations are not the equivalent of independent, sovereign states, as some of their opponents believe. They are the shock troops of the imperial powers, the United States, Japan and Europe, and their web of clubs, notably the Organisation for Economic Co-operation and Development (OECD) and the World Trade Organisation (WTO). These exist to 'open up' countries to 'competitiveness', a current euphemism for plunder. To add to the bewildering array of imperial acronyms (TRIMS, TRIPS, NAFTA, SAPs and so on), there is now MAI, the Multilateral Agreement on Investment.

At a conference on MAI staged by the World Trade

Organisation in 1996, the hum of global power was interrupted by one angry voice. It belonged to Basoga Nsadhu, Finance Minister of Uganda, who said, 'We were told that if we had democracy, we would get funds. We had democracy, but no funds came. We were told if we had structural adjustments, foreign direct investment would come. We had Structural Adjustment Programmes, but no funds came. We were told if we had trade liberalisation and privatisation, investment would come, but none came. Now we are told we will get funds if there is a Multilateral Investment Agreement. You are trying to cheat Africa.'[37]

The MAI 'negotiations' represent the most important imperial advance for half a century, yet they do not qualify as headline news. Once formalised, they will remove the last restrictions on the free movement of foreign capital anywhere in the world, while effectively transferring development policy from national governments to multinational corporations. At the same time, multinationals will be freed from the obligation to observe minimum standards in public welfare, the environment and business practices.

Under the new rules, corporations will be able to challenge local laws before an international tribunal – but governments or their citizens will have no corresponding right to take action against offending corporations. For instance, they will have no right to conserve their environment or protect people against the harmful effects of foreign investment. Colombia will have to repeal laws against the disposal of toxic and radioactive waste; Brunei, Pakistan and Brazil will no longer be able to stop foreign ownership of agricultural land and areas around national reserves and borders; Venezuela will have to surrender its national film, television and publishing industries to foreign interests.

As 70 per cent of foreign investment is not really investment at all, but the buying and stripping of local companies, infant industries in Third World countries will face new obstacles in entering the 'world economy'. Under MAI, protection of local employment and local content in manufactured goods will be banned, and political parties will no longer promote the goal of full employment. This is calculated to stop the rise of more 'tiger states', like South Korea, which at first subsidised and protected local industry. The result will be a world even more divided between the owners of capital and those supplying cheap commodities and cheap labour. So why should poor countries sign up? The simple answer is that, having obeyed their Western creditors and 'restructured' their economies in order to accommodate foreign investment, most countries have no choice.

In 1995, more than 80 per cent of investment ended up in just twelve countries. The forty-eight least developed countries attracted only 0·5 per cent. The MAI, says the World Development Movement, 'is being held out as a stamp of approval for investors, and the poorer countries are being told they will not get foreign investment until they sign up. Faced with this choice and intense pressure from [rich] countries, few will be able to resist.'[38]

This is not to suggest that traditional forms of piracy have been abandoned. The world's banana trade is a case in point. Most bananas sold in Western supermarkets are grown in Latin America, especially the Central American 'banana republics', such as Honduras, a fiefdom of American capital for sixty years. However, 7 per cent of bananas imported by the European Union come from the Caribbean, notably Grenada, a British colony, and the other Windward Islands. Although under the protection of Britain, minuscule Grenada was invaded by President Reagan in 1983 when 'Marxists' were said to be taking over the island and Cubans were building an airstrip that 'threatened' the United States. It was fantasy; the airstrip was for tourists.

Fourteen years later, one of the world's powerless countries is again under attack from the most powerful. In 1996, the American representative in the World Trade Organisation, Mickey Kantor, complained that Chiquita Brands, the American banana multinational, was the victim of discrimination by European tariffs, which allowed a trickle of slightly more expensive, organically grown Caribbean bananas. The day after Kantor spoke up for the principles of 'free trade', the billionaire who controls Chiquita, Carl Lindner, gave half a million dollars to the Clinton presidential campaign via the 'discreet route' of Democratic Party funds in Wyoming. Thereafter, the tycoon was invited by the President to stay overnight at the White House.

As a result, not a single banana has left Grenada since January 1997. They rot in the warehouses and on the wharves, and those who farm them grow poorer and poorer. The young on Grenada now have little hope of work and some have turned to trafficking in cocaine. In his war on drugs, perhaps President Clinton will send the US Marines against them.[39]

The true scale of this worldwide social engineering, of which little countries and poor people are the victims, is seldom reported in the West. That is left to mostly Third World journalists who maintain an allegiance to the freedoms in the Declaration of Human Rights. They are, for example, the writers and publishers of the Third World Network in Malaysia and the defiantly incorrigible journalists of the Philippines and Thailand, who are sometimes murdered for doing their job.

A shaming contrast is Australia, a developed country where Rupert Murdoch owns almost 70 per cent of the press most people read and where hardly a media voice is raised against the growth of the great cartels. On the contrary, the new rules are enthusiastically supported; in 1994, a media chorus celebrated Australia's 'pioneering role' in helping to establish a regional cartel, the Asia Pacific Economic Conference (APEC).

At the APEC conference in Jakarta, Australian newspapers described Prime Minister Keating's 'absolute triumph' in attending 'the birth of his dream'. Keating's claim that APEC would lead to 70,000 new jobs in Australia went unchallenged. Instead, it was described as 'the prize of free trade'. However, the *Australian* newspaper gave a hint. 'There will, in all likelihood, be big job losses,' it said, 'and some local dislocation as unemployment forces some families to relocate and workers [are forced] to retrain.' Three years later, part-time and casual working practices engulfed Australia, where the notion of full employment was pioneered, giving rise to what the *Sydney Morning Herald* called the 'American phenomenon' of the working poor – workers who 'relocate' and 'retrain' and whose wages are little more than the minimal welfare payments.[40]

On his return from the United States in 1997, Keating's successor, John Howard, said how impressed he was with America's 'low unemployment rate' based on 'lower wages' and minimal unemployment benefits. He said what Australia needed was a lower minimum wage and reduced dole payments. He made no mention of the fact that with a third of the Australian population living on welfare benefits as the main item of family income, with almost half of males aged between twenty-four and forty-four receiving close to poverty wages, Australia was already embracing the American Way. 'We've got to meet the exciting challenge', he said, 'of the new world being shaped around us.'[41]

It is said that Tony Blair began his election campaign in January 1996 on a tour of Asia, during which he declared that the 'success' of the Singapore autocrat Lee Kuan Yew 'very much reflects my own philosophy'.[42] Considering New Labour's convergence with conservative forces in Britain and abroad, this was a revealing statement.

The parallels that Blair draws between his 'vision' or 'third way' and that of the rulers of the tiger states makes perfect sense. The Asian 'success' he referred to has been the restoration of rapacious capitalism's modern essentials – centralised state power and a rigged 'market'. For all Margaret Thatcher's rhetoric about the rights of the individual and the 'withering of the state', this fundamentalism is her true legacy, to which Lee Kuan Yew has paid due homage. His high regard for Blair is as Thatcher's creature and successor. None of them, understandably has since revised their comments following the collapse of the tiger economies.

The promotion of the tiger states was a brilliant public

relations ruse by the 'philosopher king' of Singapore and his neighbour, Mahathir bia Mohamed of Malaysia, who cast their repressive orders as exemplars of the 'best' of the late twentieth century. Their gleaming towers were much more than symbols of mere money, not to mention precarious stock markets. They were beacons in a morally polluted world built by crusaders devoted to 'the family' and 'Asian values'. It was this social authoritarianism, in a place designed on clean, straight lines, which Blair made clear had so impressed him.

Like many Westerners who *shiko* at the courts of Asia, he offered no political context to his admiring remarks; no glimpse of what the writer on Singapore, Ann Tellman, has described as 'happy face fascism'; no suggestion that in most of the tiger states democratic institutions are considered deeply harmful to the 'wider macro-economic purposes'. There was not a hint of what Waldon Bello of the Centre for the South has documented as 'restrictions on individual rights, the banning of labour organisations, tight controls on the press and subordination of citizens' rights to internal security'.[43] Singapore's real achievement is social control and its attendant fear, making democratic debate impossible and conversations with educated, intelligent people routinely circumspect. Singaporeans are turning to born-again Christianity for relief from the oppressive uniformity, a trend the regime has responded to with characteristic alacrity. A Racial Harmony Act now prohibits sermons on social and political issues that are deemed 'non-relevant'.

Like Lee Kuan Yew, Blair has attacked single mothers and homeless young people. His Home Secretary, Jack Straw, would appreciate Malaysia's answer to the 'problem' of such people, and the 'squeegie merchants' and other itinerant youth. In Malaysia it is illegal for young people to congregate, no matter how innocently, in a way that offends the authorities. Public shaming and detention without trial keep matters orderly.

Soon after he was elected Britain's first Labour Prime Minister in eighteen years, Blair made a number of symbolic gestures. One of them was to visit what the *Independent* described as a 'dark estate' in London, where the 'underclass' live. The stairs of the Aylesbury Estate in south London were perfumed for him and people looked out of their doors in mostly bemused silence as he tried to greet them. He was photographed standing alone in the rough-cast concrete landscape, looking pensive, if decidedly uncomfortable, and next to a senior police officer. These were the required images.

Purpose-built with tiers of tiny flats, damp on the inside and peeling on the outside, an exercise yard and no community facilities, the Aylesbury Estate is like an open prison. Fifty-nine per cent of the households are so poor they are on housing benefit, 17 per cent are registered unemployed and 78 per cent of the seventeen-year-olds are not in full-time education.[44]

Blair's visit was reminiscent of the visit of Edward, Prince of Wales, to the Welsh slums in the 1930s, when the future king said immortally, 'Something must be done.' The social gulf between the leader of the People's Party and the people on the estate was striking. However, Blair did not say that something must be done about the poverty, rather that it ought to be tidied up and policed and the people put to some use, out of the way: single mothers in McDonald's, young lads weeding the grass in the cracks in the concrete. (The words of Lady Bracknell came to mind: 'Really, if the lower orders don't set a good example, what on earth is the use of them?')

There was no suggestion that the underlying causes, such as eighteen years of spectacular wealth redistribution, the eradication of real jobs and genuine training and the running-down of schools for the majority, would be addressed. The problem was cultural and the response punitive.

Like Los Angeles, parts of London and other British cities now belong to the Third World. The violence and menace are not the same, but the roots of them are. 'Poverty', wrote Peter Townsend, Emeritus Professor of Social Policy at Bristol University, a man who has devoted most of his life to making people aware of its causes, 'is not something people impose on themselves for want of effort and community organisation. It is *constructed* by divisive and discriminatory laws, inflexible organisations, acquisitive ideologies of wealth, a deeply-rooted class system and policies which serve privilege in the short term and destroy society in the long term.'[45]

The rising number of poor people is the mark of a New Democracy; and Britain is the laboratory to the First World that Chile was to the Third. No modern ideological figure created more poor and more rich so rapidly than Margaret Thatcher. The UN Human Development Report for 1997 says that in no other country has poverty 'increased as substantially' since the early 1980s, and that the number of Britons in 'income poverty' leapt by nearly 60 per cent under her Government.[46] Should there be doubt about the class nature of British poverty, a House of Commons investigation into infant mortality dispels it. Infant mortality for the rich is 4·3 per 1,000 and for the poor 18·5 per 1,000. The author of the report, Dr Richard Harding, says that 2,000 children die in Britain every year because they are poor.[47]

It is only when these statistics take a human shape that the complete, unnecessary horror presents itself: such as a warning by Dr Ian Banks, the British Medical Association spokesman on men and health, that suicide is 'the big new killer of men and is shockingly popular – it has doubled in the last ten years. The one clear cause is uncertainty at work. Short-term contracts are a constant strain that makes men ill.'[48]

Thatcher and her successors made Britain into a two-thirds society, with the top third privileged, the middle third insecure and the bottom third poor: a rigid class stratum copied by other former social democracies. So it made sense that she was among the first invited by Blair to Downing Street for 'consultations'. The gravity of Blair's 'project' is not universally recognised as yet, but I believe it will be, as the managed adulation recedes and the government's extremism reaches beyond Thatcherism. Theirs is a ruthlessness known only to the ideologically born again – as their attacks on even disabled people make clear. The Blairites have become the political wing of the City of London and the British multinational corporations and, in natural order, the trusted servitors of European 'central bankism' and American economic and military hegemony. They are indeed more trustworthy and more 'modern' than the Tories, many of whom are still smitten by English nationalism, some even by paternalism.

'The key move [for Blair]', observed Robin Ramsay, 'was to see the City ... and the asset-stripping of the domestic economy in the 1980s, not as the problem but as the solution.' Ramsay compares two critical Labour Party policy documents. In the draft report of the committee headed by Bryan Gould, the major cause of Britain's economic problems was identified as 'the concentration of power and wealth in the City of London' and the domination of 'City values' and 'the interests of those who hold assets rather than produce'. This was re-written by the emerging 'new right' of the party under Neil Kinnock.

By 1996, with Blair, Gordon Brown and Peter Mandelson in control of the party, the Gould view of Britain had been reversed. In *The Blair Revolution: Can Labour Deliver?*, Mandelson and his co-author Roger Liddle highlighted Britain's 'economic strengths' as its multinational corporations, the 'aerospace' industry (arms) and *'the pre-eminence of the City of London'* (my italics).[49] No doubt in recognition of their new-found pre-eminence under a Labour government, the City of London celebrated Christmas 1997 by awarding its dealers a record £1 billion in bonuses, a rise of 30 per cent in one year – while New Labour's Paymaster-General, Geoffrey Robinson, dismissed criticism of his £12·5 million trust fund, salted away in tax-free Guernsey.

Overlaying this is a particular social authoritarianism – Blair used 'moral' and 'morality' eighteen times in a speech he gave at a conference in Australia as a guest of Rupert Murdoch – in which the new party brings another dimension to British politics. Mandelson expressed this forthrightly in *The Blair Revolution*. New Labour, he and Liddle wrote, demanded 'a tough discipline' and a 'hardworking majority' and the 'proper bringing-up [sic] of children'.[50]

(Mandelson has since abolished 'poverty', replacing it with 'social exclusion'. In announcing that he was setting up a Social Exclusion Unit in Downing Street, Mandelson said that the Prime Minister shared Margaret Thatcher's 'rock-hard determination to deal with poverty': a statement as perplexing as it was bizarre.)[51]

For Blair, even more than his mentor Thatcher, the issue is class. Whereas she set about remaking the establishment with infusions of new blood and new money, he is the embodiment of the *bourgeoisie*, arguably the most class-conscious of the English social tribes, especially when under threat.

When times were more secure, the liberal wing of the middle class would allot a rung or two of their ladder to the working class, as ordinary people were known in the days when there was work. The ladder was hauled up as the Thatcher revolution spread beyond miners and steelworkers and into the suburbs and gentrified terraces, where middle managers suddenly found themselves 'shed' and 'redundant'. It was to people like these that Labour under Neil Kinnock, then John Smith, then Tony Blair, looked in order to win power. *Middle-classness* became the political code, as the middle classes sought, above all else, to restore their status and privileges.

For a time, following the death of John Smith, the liberal wing of the middle class indulged in a sort of ideological Scrabble in order to justify the Blair project's class aims. The 'stakeholder' theory was briefly promoted. This reminded me of something tried by the World Bank in its 'liberal containment' phase under Robert McNamara, who was keen on creating 'stakeholders' and 'smallholders' in Third World societies not as the means of real change, but as barriers to it.

There was also chatter about 'civil' and 'civic' society, which was code for new elites; liberal columnists used the archaic word 'governance' a great deal and there was enthusiasm for the ideas of the American 'communitarian' Amitai Etzioni, who wrote psychobabble books that were briefly fashionable in the United States. This is Etzioni's thought: 'The sociological challenge is to develop societal formations that leave considerable room for the enriching particulars of autonomous subcultures while sustaining the core of shared values'.[52] For this great thinker, the root of society's problems lay not in political and economic problems, but in the collapse of the family, in 'rampant moral confusion and social anarchy'. The trouble with the world was that people had 'too many freedoms' and not enough 'responsibility'. He read like a Blair speech, taken from a Clinton speech.

Indeed, the guru so impressed Clinton that the President made him a special adviser. 'Thank you very much, Dr Etzioni,' Clinton effused. 'Thank you for the inspiration that your work has given to me and to so many others [and] for your wonderful book. There are no institutions really for bringing us all together, across the lines that divide us, in our common cause of building what is good about America and building up what is good within the character of our people.'[53]

On a visit to Britain, Etzioni was asked by the writer Joan Smith if his theories were merely reinforcing traditional gender roles. He erupted. 'How would you feel if I called you a fascist?' he demanded. 'You're stupid and ignorant and I'm not going to talk to you.'[54]

A 'think tank' called Demos filled up the *Guardian* on slow days with a range of dinner-party topics of little relevance to a society where one in four live in poverty. Said to be 'centre left', one of its board members is Sir Douglas Hague, who was Margaret Thatcher's economic adviser. A founder of Demos, Geoff Mulgan, himself rewarded with a job in one of Tony Blair's 'policy units', wrote a book called *Connexity* which had a message similar to Amitai Etzioni's. 'In much of the world today,' Mulgan wrote, 'the most pressing problems on the public agenda are not poverty or material shortage . . . but rather the disorders of freedom: the troubles that result from having too many freedoms that are abused rather than constructively used.' As if celebrating life on another planet, he wrote, 'For the first time ever, most of the world's most powerful nations do not want to conquer territory.'[55]

New Labour's public relations managers, assisted by the

stereotyping media, created something called 'middle England', a middle-class idyll similar to that described by John Major when he famously yearned for cycling spinsters, cricket and warm beer. The real middle England, if such a place exists at all, is more like the Larches Estate in Preston, Lancashire. Unlike the Aylesbury Estate, it was never a dumping ground, but a once fairly prosperous habitat for skilled workers from Thatcher's favourite industry, 'defence'. Now, with even those jobs lost, almost a quarter of the men are unemployed and half the eligible young people have never had jobs, because there are none. When I was there a group of the youngest played on strips of asbestos outside a bricked-up youth club, which the 'capped' council could not afford to support any more. In the Larches Labour Club, two dozen pensioners sat in the warmth, able to afford only a few glasses of beer between them.

Like so much else, Blair's campaign against people like these draws its inspiration from the United States. Clinton's spleen against 'welfare mothers' became Blair's against single mothers. Shortly after taking over as Labour leader, he was invited by the Thatcherite TV interviewer Brian Walden to 'pass a crucial test' by attacking single mothers. Blair rose to the occasion and was rewarded with headlines in the *Daily Mail* and the other Tory newspapers.

Unlike the old Tories, who were careful not to attack publicly those beneath them, Blair has displayed no such reticence. With his own family cocooned in wealth and privilege, he now aimed at deprived and troubled children who truant. There was no question of a Labour commitment of resources to children with special needs. Instead, he threatened a 'crackdown' as he lectured the most vulnerable on their 'responsibilities' to their 'community'. He made no mention of the responsibilities of the rich and powerful, nor did he threaten to crack down on corporations like Murdoch's News International which, in the decade to 1996, deprived the community of tax on profits of almost a billion pounds.[56]

Of course, Blair did not want to *appear* like Thatcher, who, like some Victorians, regarded whole classes of society as effectively outlaws. He demonstrated this concern for image by pleading with the *Independent on Sunday* to drop a story on Cherie Booth, his barrister wife. The paper had learned that Booth had asked a court to send a bailed poll-tax defaulter to prison regardless of the fact, which she acknowledged, that he had no means to pay his poll-tax arrears. The man was not even a protester: just dirt poor. Her defenders claimed she had to take the case on the 'first-cab-off-the-rank' principle. In practice, barristers and their clerks can often choose cases.

When the paper published the story, it was inundated with protests from New Labour women that Booth was being picked on because she was Blair's wife. This was disingenuous. She was a former Labour candidate who had shared every major platform with her husband, and was part of his triumphal march to Downing Street. This included numerous staged 'photo-opportunities' and accompanying him to strategic, secret dinners with Rupert and Anna Murdoch, and to Murdoch's Newscorp conference on Hayman Island in Australia. Moreover, Blair had spoken about the 'moral challenge': whether or not to send a penniless man to prison had provided such a challenge for his political partner.[57]

In the 1997 election, the truth of Blair's 'landslide' victory was that it represented fewer votes than John Major won in 1992. In inner-city seats, the vote was less than 60 per cent, extremely low for a British general election. In Liverpool Riverside it was less than 52 per cent; in the constituency of the future Social Security Secretary Harriet Harman, who had declined to send her son to school in the area, the vote was 56 per cent. The two million votes Labour gained on its vote in 1992 were mainly in middle-class marginals, which delivered more than 100 seats. Roy Hattersley, the party's resident chameleon, announced that the new government had succeeded because it was 'untainted by dogma' and that Blair 'is taking the politics out of politics'.[58]

Among Blair's first appointments was Lord Simon, who

was made Minister for Competitiveness. Lord Simon was chairman of British Petroleum and a director of Rio Tinto Zinc, two of the most voracious multinational corporations in the world. In Colombia, according to the Union Syndical Obrera, the national workers' union, 'BP is the most aggressive oil company in Colombia. Workers have no rights to organise ... There are disgraceful human rights violations.'[59] An investigation by ITV's *World in Action* found that BP had contracted former British SAS soldiers to train paramilitary squads; and a report by the Labour Euro MP Richard Howitt says that the company supplied the murderous Colombian Army with photographs and videotapes of workers, peasants and environmental campaigners. Six activists were subsequently kidnapped and found dead.[60] The company denies all allegations of human rights abuse.

Rio Tinto Zinc (RTZ) is notorious for exploiting mineral deposits in countries run by dictatorships, notably apartheid South Africa and Indonesia. Lord Simon was also a director of Grand Metropolitan, another multinational, which owns Burger King, the chain that paid an employee in Glasgow £1 for five hours' work.[61] As Minister for Competitiveness, he will sit in the unelected House of Lords.

Blair also assigned Alan Sugar, the Thatcherite computer millionaire, to travel the country persuading young people to take up a life in business. Other advisers include Lord Donoghue, a former close associate of Robert Maxwell and Lord Hollick, who, having sacked hundreds of staff from his companies, Anglia TV and Express Newspapers, has been appointed a senior adviser at the Department of Trade and Industry.

The most revealing appointment is Martin Taylor, Chief Executive of Barclays Bank. An Old Etonian, Taylor is to work on 'welfare dependency' and the 'disincentives that keep people unemployed'. Soon after his appointment, Barclays' staff staged the most widespread strike ever known in the financial sector. They were protesting against what the unions call a 'policy of wage cutting and general hostility to personnel'. As the head of another multinational,

Courtauld's, Taylor liberated thousands of people from the tyranny of employment and earned the sobriquet 'Hatchet Man'. He will work closely with the Social Security Minister, Frank Field while Field is 'thinking the unthinkable'.[62]

Field is the man assigned to do something about the people on the Aylesbury Estate and the rest of the poor. As chairman of the House of Commons Social Security Select Committee, he wanted an investigation into 'single motherhood'. He has written widely on 'welfare dependency', a theory that originated with the extreme right in the United States, notably Charles Murray, a guru admired by Rupert Murdoch and promoted by the *Sunday Times*. It was Murray's writings which helped to launch Clinton on his campaign against the 'underclass' and led to the abolition of welfare payments for some of the poorest Americans.

As for Britain, Murray concluded, 'Illegitimacy in the lower classes will continue to rise and inevitably life in lower class communities will continue to degenerate.' Welfare simply leads to 'more crime, more widespread drug and alcohol addiction, fewer marriages, more drop-outs from work, more homelessness, more child neglect'. He uses words like 'disease', 'plague' and 'contamination' to describe poverty. He is the co-author of a book, *The Bell Curve*, which says that black people are naturally less intelligent than whites.[63]

Murray has praised Field's 'moral courage'. While Field says that he does not share Murray's brand of extremism, for both, 'moral factors' lie at the root of poverty. 'Mine is a Christian view that we are fallen creatures, but capable of redemption,' Field has said. In his precise scale of punishment for the unredeemed, the unemployed, the poor or the simply 'disorganised' who failed to conform should get no more than £30 a week benefit. In other words, they are to be starved into submission, or more likely into crime. The mentally ill should be subjected to 'sanctions', said Field. His proposals evoke those who, a century ago, sorted the poor, the inadequate and the mentally ill into first and second class, infirm and guilty, idle and profligate.

If his proposed rules are obeyed, says Field, West End

theatre-goers will not have to 'step over' such people. By using 'an SAS-type core of officers countering [benefit] fraud', he said, 'literally billions of pounds' can be saved.[64] Like Blair, he has not commented on the £23 billion owed by big business in uncollected corporate tax and Value Added Tax. 'The key is self-interest,' he said. 'It's not an unclean thought . . . it's a most fundamental one.'[65]

It is this fundamentalism and its vocabulary of class rejection that propels Britain now. New Labour and its ermine-rack of lords and bankers and downsizers will not allow unprofitable spending on the relief of poverty. After all, the poverty that exists is a condition of their wealth, as it is of the affluence of the middle class. When the government broke an election promise and 'froze' the implementation of the European Union's Social Chapter, there was no explanation. The Social Chapter would have raised issues of jobs and working hours and conditions. These are not now on the agenda.

Central to Blair's agenda is another American import: 'flexible working'. When Blair made his first trip to Europe as Prime Minister, he lectured the European social democratic parties on the virtues of the American economic 'miracle'. He failed to point out that most new jobs in the United States were part-time or casual and the real unemployment rate in the United States was considerably more than 10 per cent, or twice the figure claimed by the Clinton administration.[66]

Chancellor Gordon Brown's first budget was celebrated in the media as 'brilliant' and 'inspired'. The IMF praised his 'excellent start', although it warned that spending would have to be cut.[67] The contrast with the Keynesian policies of his Tory predecessor, Kenneth Clarke, was striking. Instead of increasing government deficits in response to the recession, Labour's 'Iron Chancellor' accepted *all* the economic premises and restrictions that Clarke had preached but not practised. Never before has a Labour Government done anything like this. Brown's first act was to hand over to the Bank of England the authority to fix interest rates: the most important economic power that any government faced with serious unemployment can exercise, because it determines whether the production of real goods will expand or retract, and whether men and women will work or not. As the Institute for Fiscal Studies pointed out, the austerity Labour planned for the majority of the British people would almost certainly be far harsher than any during the Tories' eighteen years.[68]

Having cut corporate tax, Brown made no attempt to create real employment. A welfare-to-work scheme, borrowed from Clinton's Workfare, will provide a scattering of temporary, menial, mostly demoralising jobs. For each new employee, an employer receives £60 a week and £750 training costs. The wage is 'negotiable' and the young workers can be sacked after six months with no redress for unfair dismissal. The discarded youngsters will show up in the statistics as short-term employed, so the scheme will appear to work even if not a single job is created. 'Workshy' single mothers are granted £2 a week with which to pay for the care of a child while they are cutting grass or painting the church wall for the moral exhilaration of it.

The Trades Union Congress has made no protest; its leaders' collaboration is an article of faith, having become established practice under the Tories. Unlike their French, German, Spanish, Belgian, Dutch and Greek comrades, they have accepted 'flexible working' as willingly as they accepted laws that prevent concerted action in defence of sacked and victimised men and women – like the Liverpool dockers and the Hillingdon hospital cleaners. The second biggest union, the Transport and General Workers (TGWU), has condoned the reintroduction of casual and 'flexible practices' on the docks. Bill Morris, the General-Secretary, says that trade unions are responding to 'the new national mood, and have extended the hand of partnership' to companies in 'the global marketplace'.[69] At the union's 1997 conference, Morris made not a single reference to the new welfare-to-work. He described Chancellor Brown's budget as 'a very welcome first step' and praised the Prime Minister's passion for 'education, education, education'.

Education is advertised as the Blair project's 'big idea'. One of the Labour Government's first 'dynamic' decisions was to abolish universal free tuition and replace student grants with loans. Thatcherism never went this far. It means that universities will be run on 'market' lines, with the price of tuition increased as the state of the economy worsens. This happened in Australia, a model for the 'reforms'. There tuition fees almost doubled in seven years, with subjects and courses carrying different price tags according to 'consumer appeal'. Only the well off will be able to afford, for example, an engineering degree at a specialist university. In Britain it is estimated that a working student will graduate with a £6,480 debt, more than double that of a student from a better-off background. That alone will drive many working-class children away from the colleges.[70]

The 'big idea' does not include the restoration of run-down school buildings (the 1997 budget commitment would scarcely mend the leaking roofs), the expansion of opportunity and the payment of proper salaries to teachers. It reflects middle-class fears of a truly equitable system and will ensure that selection in schools is even more rigorously enforced – Blair uses the business jargon, 'fast tracking'. Schools denied resources in those parts of Britain denied investment and employment are publicly 'shamed' by a Labour Secretary of State, while their teachers are demoralised and often victimised by an inspectorate established on strictly ideological terms by the Tories' former Thatcherites and retained by Labour.

A week seldom passes without the Education Secretary David Blunkett, who once had a reputation for being a humane politician, insulting teachers, perhaps the most valuable professional group in any society. His rage appears to be in reaction to the unwillingness of many teachers to accept the zeal of his political apostasy. The denigration of the less by the more powerful is, of course, always a way of obscuring truth. This same politician, like Blair himself, gave an undertaking before the election that he would not introduce fees. 'The end-users of education', wrote Michael Barber, one of New Labour's principal advisers, 'are the employers.'[71] Forget education as an enriching human re-source. As for Blunkett, he says that Britain has to keep up with 'our [business] competitors in North America and the Asian tigers'. His assumption of a link between higher standards in education and greater prosperity is false. As a study by the Centre for Economic Performance discovered, instead of academic performance affecting economic per-formance, the reverse is true. It is the economic and social dis-advantages suffered by so many working-class children which create the conditions for failure at school. Poverty alone overwhelms all the factors propagated by the government, such as teaching methods and homework policy. In Blair's 'end-user' society, 40 per cent of all jobs and 80 per cent of unskilled jobs require reading skills no better than those achieved by many infant school children.[72]

In his great work, *Equality*, R. H. Tawney pointed out that the English educational system 'will never be one worthy of a civilised society until the children of all classes in the nation attend the same schools ... The idea that differences of educational opportunities among children should depend upon differences of wealth represents a barbarity.'[73] In other words, 'freedom' in a society riven by class division is no freedom at all. The truths in *Equality* have been publicly recognised by every leader of the Labour Party – including Tony Blair. Knowing the truth and acting otherwise is, to paraphrase Benjamin Disraeli, not so much politics as organised hypocrisy, which also serves as an apt description of the modern Labour Party.

In Britain, as in other Western countries, the left is said to be in 'crisis'. It is a crisis, it seems to me, of those who once regarded themselves as principled thinkers and true demo-crats. Many have recanted after being critically silent for so long: a failure of nerve in both instances. Now they embrace identity politics and cultural relativism in order to fill the niches left by rapacious global capitalism. To Hugh Macpherson, a rare independent voice in British journalism, they have become Blair's 'poltroons'.

Ironically, the poltroons' most obedient recruits include

women who describe themselves as feminists: a word they have all but discredited. Certainly, it has been a measure of the success of the women's movement that women have found more authority in established institutions, such as the state bureaucracy, the universities, Parliament and the mainstream parties. While their new status appears to legitimise their 'feminism', it also serves to suppress the views of women outside the system, especially those who insist that feminism and socialism are indivisible – that it is not possible to have one without the other.

Among these newly elevated women are former activists who, like their male counterparts, fell silent long before the 1997 election for fear of 'jeopardising Labour's chances' or their own promising careers. I recall the same phenomenon in Australia helping to keep in power the Labour governments of Bob Hawke and Paul Keating, whose electoral success and Thatcherite policies provided inspiration for Blair. As the Australian feminist Pat Brewer has written, these women 'look instead to the appointment of high-profile women to positions of parliamentary or bureaucratic "power" as the realistic way to stop the backlash against feminism. However, the appointment of women to such positions actually serves to prevent or contain any resistance to the attacks being made on the gains [of women].'[74]

In both countries this has become known as 'prettifying'. It has become a whispered panacea, as Labour women choose to 'prettify' the 'reforms' demanded by the 'market' and the party leadership as somehow being in women's interests, as the positive 'feminisation' of politics, like the 'feminisation of work'. In reality, the latter has meant the impoverishment of work as women are exploited as cheaper and more malleable labour than men.

'Prettifying' is essentially middle-class: Barbara Follett's 'Emily's List' being the most telling example. In her promotion of mostly privileged women as a feminist advance, Follett lifted the idea of 'Emily's List' straight from the United States and launched it as a 'foundation' at a £120-a-plate media event. It was little more than a vehicle for stacking the Labour

Party's all-women selection lists with candidates the leadership considered 'safe'. These excluded socialists, notably Liz Davies, who was rejected as a candidate as a result of a vendetta against her socialist principles.[75]

New Labour's blueprint was partly the work of Patricia Hewitt, the director of a pre-election body set up by Blair which called itself the Commission on Social Justice. A former adviser to Neil Kinnock, Hewitt became one of the wealthy principals of a City of London consulting firm, whose clients include Barclays Bank and BP. She describes herself as a feminist and is now a Labour MP. In her book, *About Time: The Revolution of Work and Family Life*, she says that the 'model of full-time permanent employment was always based on the lives of men rather than women, and simply does not fit modern industrial countries'. Translation: to keep profits high, future employment should be part-time, insecure, poorly paid and done by women.

With its pretence of independent scholarship, the Commission on Social Justice was useful in obfuscating and speeding up Labour's move to the right. It had nothing worthwhile to recommend about eradicating the structural piracy of Thatcherism. The redistribution of wealth from the poor to the rich was not seriously discussed. Instead, it recommended a minimum wage of £3.50 an hour, far below the 'decency threshold' and below even the conservative Trades Union Congress figure of £4.15. The usual craven threat of loss of benefits was levelled at single parents unless they found work when their youngest child reached the age of five. The principle of free, universal nursery education was rejected, along with student grants. All of this has happened.

Following the 1997 election Hewitt praised the lone parents of Leicester as 'the heroes and heroines of my constituency [who] will be the heroes and heroines of the new Britain'. Five months later she attacked those Labour MPs who dared to vote against the Blair Government's legislation cutting benefits to lone parents.[76]

There are three other famous feminists in the Blair Cabinet: Clare Short, the Secretary of State for International

Development, who, according to the *Independent*, 'is perceived as A Decent and Outspoken Human Being . . . an asset that the party can ill afford to dispense with'. Contrary to her populist image, Short is a conservative politician, who supported the threat to bomb Iraq in 1998, has spoken admiringly of her Thatcherite predecessor, and abused people in Montserrat who believe Britain ought to fulfil its responsibilities towards its volcano-ravaged colony. She says she wants to halve the world's poverty by 2015, but has sought no extra resources from the Treasury to do so; 'aid', she says, is not the answer.[77]

Her colleague, Margaret Beckett, Secretary of State for Trade and Industry, remains silent on the export of British 'riot control' vehicles and water cannon to the genocidal dictatorship in Indonesia, together with Hawk ground-attack aircraft (which, as the Foreign Secretary, Robin Cook, confirmed in 1994, 'have been observed on bombing runs in East Timor in most years since 1984').[78]

Harriet Harman, now the Social Security Secretary, is currently running the government's project to get single mothers into low-paying jobs and to cut their benefits. From April 1998, single parents will lose benefits amounting to £300 million. For all the hype of a 'revolt' by Labour backbenchers against this attack on Britain's poorest, the decision to cut was endorsed by the Parliamentary Social Security Standing Committee, which included a clutch of New Labour's female MP's elected in 1997 'to end male-dominated, Conservative policies', and none spoke up for the million and a half women who would be further impoverished. When it came to a vote in the House of Commons, most Labour women voted for the cut.[79]

In foreign affairs, the Americanising of foreign policy has been consolidated. In his address to Rupert Murdoch's Newscorp conference, Blair said, '*The Americans have made it clear* [my emphasis] they want a special relationship with Europe, not with Britain alone. If we are to be listened to seriously in Washington or Tokyo, or the Pacific, we will often be acting with the rest of Europe . . . The real patriotic case, therefore, for those who want Britain to maintain its traditional global role, is for leadership in Europe . . . the Labour Government will be outward-looking, internationalist and committed to free and open trade . . .'.[80]

He could not have been more candid. The Americans 'have made it clear' that Britain's 'traditional role' is now best served watching over US interests in Europe. Being 'outward-looking' and 'internationalist' means protecting far-flung British capital, which under Thatcher amassed the largest overseas investments in the world after the United States. It also means fulfilling Britain's sub-imperial obligations as an American lieutenant in the United Nations and the other US-dominated international institutions, as well as in key areas of the world, like the Gulf: indeed in all theatres of the new Cold War where British support is required.

Blair is committed to the largest military budget in Europe and to NATO. NATO's expansion into Eastern Europe has generated an arms race that will profit the American and British weapons industries, which between them dominate the world market. The Anglo-American alliance, which has consistently and violently intervened in other people's affairs, fuelled countless wars and otherwise caused havoc throughout the world since the Second World War, is stronger than ever.

The new Labour elite is probably the most 'Atlanticist' of any British establishment since the Second World War. That is to say, it is devoted to *Pax Americana*. All those years of Kennedy scholarships, trade union 'fellowships' at Harvard and assorted secondments, study trips and fraternal seminars paid for by American government agencies, 'foundations' and 'endowments', have worked wonders. The Bilderberg Group, for example, 'forum' of the Anglo-American elite, has welcomed both Gordon Brown and John Monks, the 'modernising' General-Secretary of the Trades Union Congress. Edward Balls, Brown's economic adviser, was, like Brown himself, at Harvard. David Miliband, Blair's head of policy, was at the Massachusetts Institute of Technology. Like Balls, he was a Kennedy Scholar.

Five senior members of the Blair Government – Peter

Mandelson, George Robertson, Marjorie Mowlam, Chris Smith and Elizabeth Symons – along with Blair's chief of staff Jonathan Powell, have been members of the British-American Project for the Successor Generation, an ambitious, highly structured and little-known transatlantic network of 'chosen' politicians, journalists and academics. 'By virtue of their present accomplishments,' says BAP literature, '[the chosen few] have given indication that, in the succeeding generation, they would be leaders in their country and perhaps internationally.'

The Successor Generation is funded by the Pew Charitable Trusts of Philadelphia, established by the billionaire J. Howard Pew, chairman of the Sun Oil Company, a devoted supporter of the Republican Party and right-wing groups. These include the Heritage Foundation, a pillar of the Reagan 'project' and far-right causes, and the Manhattan Institute for Policy Research, set up by William Casey, former head of the CIA, and described by the *New York Times* as 'an aggressive foundation' and the sponsor of books 'widely regarded as influencing Reagan Administration economic and social thinking'. (One such book was *Losing Ground* by Charles Murray, the extreme-right inventor of the term 'underclass' and advocate of the abolition of welfare.)[81]

Although its roots go back to the Labour Party's Gaitskellite wing and David Owen's SDP, the idea for a 'successor generation' was put forward at a meeting in the White House in March 1983. Attended by Rupert Murdoch and Sir James Goldsmith, among others of similar political outlook, it was addressed by President Reagan himself. The subject was the mounting opposition in Europe to the stationing of Cruise and Pershing missiles in Britain and elsewhere. Opposition within the Labour and Liberal Parties was especially alarming and seen as the first major challenge to NATO for thirty-five years. Reagan told them:

> Last June I spoke to the British Parliament, proposing that we – the democracies of the world – work together to build the infrastructure of democracy. This will take time, money and efforts by both government and the private sector. We need

96

particularly to cement relations among the various sectors of our societies in the United States and Europe. *A special concern will be the successor generations, as these younger people are the ones who will have to work together in the future on defense and security issues.* (My emphasis.)[82]

At BAP conferences there are 'introducers', 'alumni' and 'rapporteurs' and other trappings of a casual freemasonry. Games are played, with participants taking different power roles. Subjects discussed include 'Sharing the Defense Burden', 'The Power of the Fellowship', 'Creatures of the Enlightenment' and 'The Welfare State on Trial'. The debate is varied and lively; the assumptions are shared and deeply orthodox. 'America's proper role as the largest player in the capitalist system', as one contributor put it, 'is that of an efficient agent of free trade, stable monetary order and leadership by example – in short, the system's ready, dependable hand . . .' There is always a scattering of defence and security specialists: Defence Ministry think-tank people, NATO advisers, a counter-insurgency expert, a man from the Heritage Foundation-funded Institute for European Defence and Strategic Studies and the usual Foreign Office people.

The Successor Generation's tenth anniversary get-together at Windsor in 1995 included the smiling presence of Jonathan Powell, then a Foreign Office diplomat in Washington. In its 1997 newsletter, the BAP warmly welcomes the elevation of Successor Generation members to the Blair Cabinet: 'Congratulations from all of us!' One of them, George Robertson, the Defence Secretary, as well as belonging to the Successor Generation, is a former member of the British Atlantic Committee and the Council of the Royal Institute for International Affairs (Chatham House).

All Blair's new political appointees at the Ministry of Defence are part of the wider 'Atlanticist' network, having been members of or associated with the Atlantic Council and its labour movement wing, the Trades Union Committee for European and Transatlantic Understanding. Like Robertson, all believe in an 'independent [nuclear] deterrent'. Blair himself has assured the nation he has what it takes to squeeze the nuclear trigger. President Clinton has been to Downing Street to express his delight. The empire is safe in their hands.

'What we've got now in the United States,' said the black leader Jesse Jackson, 'is one party, two names. We've got Republicans and Republicans Lite.'[83] In Britain, too, it is no longer possible to justify a vote every five years on the basis of lesser-of-two-evilism. Like the United States, Britain has become a single-ideology state with two principal, almost identical factions, so that the result of any election has a minimal effect on the economy and social policy. People have no choice but to vote for political choreographers, not politicians. Gossip about them and their petty intrigues, and an occasional scandal, are regarded as political news. When, in the 1950s, Aneurin Bevan described Parliament as 'a social shock absorber placed between privilege and the pressure of popular discontent', he could not have imagined how exact his truth would become.[84]

On the eve of Blair's ascendancy, with his party's internal democracy replaced by twelve-foot images of himself and talk of 'a new social order' and preparing for a 'thousand years', even that most devoted of parliamentarians and Labour loyalist Tony Benn was moved to write, 'It is not surprising that more and more people are coming to the conclusion that the ballot box is no longer an instrument that will secure political solutions ... They can see that the parliamentary democracy we boast of is becoming a sham.'[85]

UNPEOPLE 2

We are told that the poor are grateful for charity. Some of them are, no doubt, but the best among the poor are never grateful. They are ungrateful, disobedient and rebellious. They are quite right to be so. Disobedience, in the eyes of anyone who has read history, is man's original virtue.

Oscar Wilde

TRISHA AND AMY are nineteen and twenty years old and they shine with youth when they laugh. But their laughter also comes from a sense of irony beyond their years. 'My middle name is No Frills,' said Amy. 'I eat Kwik Save No Frills beans, and No Frills soup, and No Frills beans again. In the bathroom I've got No Frills shampoo and No Frills bubble bath; that means it hasn't got any bubbles. I'm a No Frills girl living a No Frills life.'

'My first bedsit', said Trisha, 'had the sort of bathroom you had to have a shower after you went into it. It was *that* dirty. It was £35 a week. After benefits, I was left with £36 a week to pay all the bills. That's when I found the Red Rose Freezer, which is a penny or two cheaper than Kwik Save. I'll walk an hour for a tin of beans that's only 10p. You can't beat that! When you get there, though, it's a peculiar feeling standing in a queue with a lot of elderly people, really poor pensioners, sort of hidden away, waiting for the cheap stuff and the almost-past-its-sell-by stuff to be handed out.'

'What else do you eat?' I asked.

'Mainly beans,' said Amy. 'Beans on toast: breakfast, lunch

and tea. A can of soup Sundays. The real food goes to Jemma [her infant], who gets burger and veg; now and then a chop . . . I get £75 a week and I have to pay out £87.90. That's for gas, electric, water, catalogues, phone, food, nappies, baby wipes, cream. I am twenty years old and and I am £3,000 in debt. When the baby came along, everything I had went on her. I could only use catalogues; that's all I could afford. Owing all that money really *worries* me. The Water Board are still taking me to court; they've done it once already. I owe them £144. One good thing about having an electric meter is it takes off what you owe. For every £5 I put in, my meter takes £2.50 off my debt. But it makes for short nights, I tell you.'

Trisha has Ben, who is two. The two children seem hyperactive within the confines of Amy's small sitting room. As you enter, the boards groan; they are bare, every other one rotting. There is a fake Oriental rug with the texture of tarpaper. The damp brown carpet on the stairs needs stapling and is dangerous, as the stairs are steep. The walls are scabrous with damp; there are two small pictures hanging, one of Brad Pitt, the movie star, in a gilt frame, another of a china John Bull, which Trisha found in the park.

The television is 1970s style, on legs with brass bands. One of the legs is held together with the scaffolding of a coat-hanger. The cooker, framed in the doorway, is of a corresponding vintage. Dust hangs in a shaft of light from a window in the kitchen, the only one downstairs. When the electricity meter says your time is up there is a sound like a steel trap closing. Such are the artefacts of modern poverty.

Amy says she has attempted suicide thirteen times. She repeats the figure. Her growing up 'in care', the euphemism for an institution, and her stepfather's abuse of her, offer ready explanation. But as shocking as that is, it is not untypical among the impoverished young. 'It was like a long dark night,' is all she will say. Amy is seriously overweight and covers herself in a large T-shirt and baggy tracksuit bottoms. She has no 'good' clothes, whereas two-year-old Jemma is dressed like an expensive doll. Amy chain-smokes, dispatching each cigarette with long drags, a habit she acquired as a ten-year-old 'in care'.

Trisha is strikingly different. She might have stepped out of the pages of a teenagers' magazine. She has a finely boned face, jet black hair and Betty Boop eyes, which, despite their size, seem quiet, almost opaque, as if they are living another life. Her skin is skeined grey. 'I left home because I had to,' she said. 'We were a big family, living on top of each other. I didn't get on with my parents. We fought cat and dog. One day I just filled a couple of plastic shopping bags and left.'

'When did it strike you,' I asked them both, 'that life was different for you?'

'You mean, how old was I when I worked out that I was born at the bottom of the pile?' said Amy. 'I know *exactly*. I was six . . . no, seven . . . yeah, seven. That's when I can remember back to. I remember the smooth cold green walls of the council home I was in and the high windows I could never reach to, and never see out of and people saying, "*Don't . . .*"'

Amy has had four nannying jobs. 'They all say Jemma is the problem,' she said. 'They never want me to bring her, as if she'll give the kids I'm looking after a disease, or something. The most I got was £3 an hour. It's hard for single mums working. Maybe the job will cover your rent and bills and food; but you've also got to find a child-minder. How much does that cost? There's no help with that for a young mother, or a young father – let's not be sexist – who wants to go out and earn a living.'

Trisha said, 'I spend half the morning looking for a job that'll cover Ben's minding, like Amy says. I've got a City and Guilds [certificate] so I can work with the elderly, the disabled or children. I've just applied for a job – £3 an hour, split shifts, starting at half-eight in the morning, until three in the afternoon, and the next day it's three to ten-thirty at night. But Ben would never see me. If there was support for a young mum like me, I'd be no problem to anyone. I'm also trying for a pub job. They say I've got the right personality: *perky*!'

'Do you go out?'

'Can't afford to,' they chorused.

'Pictures?'

'If you're like us,' said Trisha, 'even if you've got the money, you can't afford to dress up nicely, so what's the point? You can't enjoy yourself because you don't feel good about yourself. The pictures is the only place where you don't have to get dressed, whereas the clubs and that are out of the question . . . I'd love to go to an all-night party, wouldn't you, Amy? I went to an all-night party when I was sixteen . . . it was *lovely*.'

Amy said, 'I haven't been to the pictures since I was fourteen. It was my birthday. The telly, teabags and a bottle of milk do now. The thing is not to grumble. I say that every morning when I wake up; a friend at the Centre told me to say it [the 'Centre' is a support club for young people run by Save the Children Fund]. I try to get to the Centre at least once a day. They're lovely; they look after Jemma for me while I look for a job, or just walk around, looking at the shops. It's nice doing just that. You slip into a bit of a dream . . .'

Trisha said, 'You soon snap out of it, mind, if you wander into one of the big posh stores, like Marks and Spencer. Amy gave me a gift voucher for my birthday – a tenner – and I had the security following me around all the time I was there. People know you're on the dole. They can tell by the way you're dressed; and people on the dole are slower than people with jobs and families, I mean they walk slower, because they've got more time. The security can spot that sort of thing: ooh, they *are* bright. It's because I can't afford to go to the launderette sometimes and I have to wear the same clothes for weeks. I'll hand-wash the baby's clothes, but if you've got one pair of jeans it's difficult, isn't it?'

'But you two seem jolly. What do you laugh about?'

'Anything at all,' said Trisha. 'Just before you came, we were skipping and laughing till we fell over. I mean, here we are, grown women with children skippin' like bloody kids! We laugh when I perm Amy's hair. That's like going out. We do our best; we probably laugh because we've got a sad life and we don't want to admit it.'

'That's *very* wise of you, Trisha,' said Amy.

'But it's true, love . . .'

'Do you have boyfriends?'

'I've just had Ben's dad,' said Trisha. 'Actually, we were going to stay together, always and always, we said, but we were only seventeen. That's only two years ago; it seems like ages . . .'

'*Men!*' said Amy. 'They're good for one thing only, and they make a mess of *that*, don't they? Jack, my bloke, and I got married when I was nineteen. We borrowed £200 from a loan company and, with the interest, had to pay back £311. We were always worrying about money, and both being Leo, we were always going at each other . . . But he's all right . . .'

The television was on, as it usually is, unwatched. It was the Labour Party conference in Blackpool, twenty miles away. Gordon Brown, the Chancellor to be, was saying that his government would be 'prudent and disciplined' because responsible people 'these days are prudent'. He wagged a finger. I asked the girls if they knew the meaning of 'prudence'.

'It's a posh name,' said Trisha.

'It means being really careful with money,' said Amy.

'We're *that*, all right,' said Trisha.

'Do the politicians mean anything to you two?'

'Only when they attack us,' said Amy. 'Other than that, they might as well be from the moon.'

'Do you read newspapers or watch the news?'

'I don't see the point,' said Trisha. 'They don't have any good news about young people. Or if they do, they make out it's absolutely amazing that a young person has done something good. Young people are meant to go around mugging people, or on drugs, aren't they?'

'Or being scroungers,' said Amy. 'It's a hateful thing to call us and it's not true. They don't *know* how hard we try to get jobs; they don't know that you're turned down the moment they know you've been in care. They don't know how few jobs there are, and what a con a lot of them are . . .' Amy seems close to tears.

'Or maybe they do know,' said Trisha. 'When you turn on

the telly and hear them talk about scroungers, you wonder if we're all in the same world ... I don't want anything for myself, just for my baby. I want to be able to fix the ceiling and paint the walls and do her bedroom ... I think people like her and me deserve a bit of bloody credit, just for coping.'

'*Up 'em!*' said Amy, recomposed.

'A prolonged and ferocious class war is under way,' wrote the author of a United Nations Development Programme study, adding, 'You cannot hide the poorest behind national boundaries.'[1] In rich countries like Britain, the rumble of this war grows louder as social Darwinism is applied. A quarter of the adult British population now lives in poverty, more than double the figure in 1979.[2] One child in three is born into poverty.[3] Britain is now the most unequal society in the Western world, a distinction it shares with Australia. The gap between well-off and poor in Britain and Australia is the same as in Nigeria, much worse than in Jamaica, Ghana or the Ivory Coast and twice as bad as in Sri Lanka or Ethiopia.[4]

Although the British and Australian poor are much better off in absolute terms than the poor in the Third World, there are similarities. Up to 2 million British children suffer ill health and stunted growth because of malnutrition, which the School Milk Campaign says has been caused by the reduction of free and cheap school meals: a 'right' that took a century to establish.[5] Research in West Yorkshire has found that poor children entering school are four centimetres shorter and weigh less than their better-off peers.[6] In Bristol, Dr John James has found that a quarter of the children he sees as inner-city patients, children between the ages of fourteen months and two years, are anaemic from lack of iron – a common condition in the poorest countries on earth, affecting mental and physical development.[7]

The modern poor are not the visible homeless and alcoholics rummaging in litter bins. They are those like Amy and Trisha and their children, who appear 'normal', whose poverty is enclosed and internalised. Meeting her, you might never guess that Amy has repeatedly tried to end her life.

In the 1997 election, the politicians' singular interest was the 'floating voter' in marginal middle-class constituencies. The poor and near poor, a third of the population, were disenfranchised. They are Unpeople.

And, as they have no voice, it is easy to mythologise them as 'scroungers' and cast them aside as the 'undeserving poor'. 'Welfare fraud', which has long been a fashionable issue, is a case in point. In a study for the Child Poverty Action Group (CPAG) Roy Sainsbury pointed out that the true picture was 'subtly transformed' by the propagandists, who, by adding estimates of 'suspected fraud', double the final figure. 'Suspected fraud' includes misdemeanours and trivia, and the mistaken actions of those who fail to understand an increasingly complex system. In 1996, an average year, between £2·3 billion and £3·5 billion of benefits were not claimed because people were unaware they were eligible or because they were too proud.[8]

'The favourite stereotype', said Sally Witcher, the CPAG director, 'is the teenage mother who gets pregnant just to get on the council housing list. In fact, a very small proportion seeking council accommodation are single mothers and most of these are from a traditional, stable relationship that has ended. There is, of course, no equivalent stereotype of the very different people who regularly defraud the tax system; and no real public discussion of the *causes* of poverty. The two are not unrelated.'[9]

Unemployment, the abolition of the National Housing Programme, the running down of social services: these are all known causes. What is not discussed is the most important cause. Between 1979 and 1992–3, the poorest tenth of the British population experienced a fall in their real income of 18 per cent after housing costs, compared to an unprecedented rise of 61 per cent for the top tenth.[10] According to *Economic Trends*, the post-war improvement of life for the poorest 'has been put into reverse [since 1979]. Income has not trickled down but filtered up from the poorer sections of society to the richer ones.'[11] Put another way: since the year Margaret Thatcher came to power, more than £63 billion has been transferred, in subsidies, from the poor to the rich.[12]

Danny has much in common with Amy and Trisha and their children, even though he is eighty-two. Brought up in the East End of London, he went from childhood into the 'rag trade'. As a young man, he was a shop steward dedicated to introducing decent pay and safe conditions in the textile sweatshops that dotted London, from the East End to Tottenham, and are still there. He was wounded in the Second World War. His wife, whom he loved dearly, died in 1993. He has a habit of crossing the room and picking up a framed picture of her.

A life-long asthmatic, he lives in a damp council flat which is like stepping back in time, neat and clean, but gradually being reclaimed by the elements, as the wallpaper over long damp streaks indicates and the floorboards ripple and the carpet curls underfoot. Following an interview Danny gave on BBC television, the flat was fitted with central heating after years of requests; most of the other flats, which house old people, have no heating. A nugget of a man, his passionate fluency and dry, sometimes dark, sense of humour are born of the East End and a life's struggle. He has only the state pension and help from his son.

'At Christmas,' he said, 'I got a note from the pensions, saying I'd been granted a bonus.'

'How much?'

'A *tenner*. Now look, that gave me the Christmas of a lifetime. Well, the wrapping paper, if nothing to wrap. Still, the benevolence of the higher authorities is in my heart. They surpassed themselves when I turned eighty years of age . . .'

'*Two* tenners?'

'Twenty-five pence extra a week.'

He rolled out a chuckle that almost left him breathless. 'Here is my budget,' he said, producing a neat list. 'I get £70 a week plus £3 income support. My outgoings are £26 a week rent, £7.50 a week electricity, £7.50 gas, £14 phone and £3 council tax and £2 TV licence. That leaves me with £13 a week to live on: food, that sort of thing.'

'How do you live?'

'My son is my lifeline. Without him, I wouldn't live, would I?'

'What about your war pension?'

'Let me advise you. I was wounded in both arms and the shrapnel is still there. I have thirty-three and a third per cent disability. But I was like thousands . . . I was so glad to get out of the army, I didn't claim. I was an independent man. I *am* an independent man. I didn't want anything from anybody; and I don't want charity now. I didn't claim income support, or whatever they called it then, until I was forced to . . . I've been opposed to means testing all my life. It's no less degrading today than it was in the time of the Poor Laws. I *paid* for my pension in contributions all my working life; no one has a right to question that now and to interrogate me, no matter how poor I am . . .'

'Are you bitter at being poor?'

'Well, I'll tell you about my life. Before the war there was means testing and there were food tickets. Those were the "benefits" then. My old man would get a ticket that stipulated cocoa. And I hated cocoa! And another ticket got you condensed milk. We couldn't afford fresh milk and the tin of condensed milk used to last us a week. We never had any stocks in the house. [His kitchen cupboards today are almost bare.] My mum used to send me to the shop for a penn'orth of jam and a penn'orth of tea, and a penn'orth of crumb biscuits. The thing is, there was no reason for us to live like that; this was a rich country and it still is.

'When the war broke out, I was twenty years of age. Unlike the rosy myths, most of the lads had not the slightest wish to go. Yes, we wanted to fight fascism; but this country, the people who ran it, had given us nothing. I was stationed at Newbury; I got to know the cook, who gave me butter, and a sergeant taught me how to snare rabbits. I'd never even seen butter or a rabbit until then. These seemed to me hints of what life could be. When it was all over, an old colonel came out and addressed us, saying he wanted chaps to volunteer to stay on in the forces. We nearly fell over laughing. That old guard didn't have a clue about us, least of all that they were about to get a Labour Government.

'I was over the moon when I got home, but my mum was ill. We got her to the doctor, who wouldn't lift a hand until he got 3s 6d. We didn't have it, so she went to the mission, which had a big room of forms, you know, seats that the patients sat on like it was a church. They had to sit there and sing hymns before a doctor would see them. My mum never knew any bloody hymns, so she was going, "La, la, la, la . . .", the old sweetheart. If you wanted to see a doctor, you did the "la, la, la, la" routine. If you didn't, no doctor. And if you needed a tooth out, well that was half a crown. No one could afford it, so we'd go to two blokes, Moss and Roberts, who did it for a shilling. He'd say, "Right, which is it?" and without further ado, he'd pull it out, whether or not it needed pulling out.

'It was just before the Health Service was established that my wife had our baby. She went to the German Hospital and got a bill for a tenner. I couldn't pay it, and they wouldn't take the baby back. They gave me hell. When we got the NHS, we got the beginning, just the *beginning*, of a civilised society.'

'How do conditions compare now in the East End?'

'I watch people. They're dressed better, of course, and many are better fed. There are fridges and washing machines. But what about happiness? What about peace of mind? What about warmth and all the things that make life good? The old habits have come back. I watch people walking up and down, looking at the stalls, looking in the shop windows, counting their change over and over. We used to do that.

'The difference these days is you're expected to sacrifice the few things you've gained, things that are taken for granted, in order to qualify as being poor. Am I making sense? The poor mustn't drive a car, even if it's an old banger. They mustn't go to the pictures. They mustn't have a packet of fags. They mustn't have a pint. Not that they can afford these things, but if they somehow hang on to the little conveniences of life, that are really the basics now, that keep them sane, they are treated as if they're pulling off a bank robbery if they go to the Social Security.'

'How does the media reflect this?'

'They moralise, and they never look beneath the surface. I

worked in textile factories all over the East End. We got a few bob an hour, and the safety was lousy ... unprotected machines, long shifts that left people so exhausted they'd make mistakes. A luxury dress would cost a quid to make and it would sell for twenty.

'What's changed? I've been asking myself that since I've been making my own inquiries lately. Every now and then I wander in and out of the textile factories around here. The workers aren't Jews like in the thirties; they're what they call ethnic: Turks and Asians and people from eastern Europe ...'

'Do you just turn up?'

'Sure ... If I'm asked who I am, I say I'm looking for scraps of cloth, or an hour's work cleaning. How can they be suspicious of a harmless old pensioner like me? What they don't know is that I'm interviewing the people at the sewing machines, asking them what they get, how long they work, if they can go to the toilet without asking, what happens when they get sick, that sort of thing.

'And what I find out is that *nothing* has changed. Some of these people get a pound an hour. They're lucky getting £3. They work up to twelve, fifteen hours a day. They've got no security, no sick days, no holidays. They do it to get cash in hand and because there is nothing else. The dust gets in their mouth and down in their chest. I can't stay in there for long, I tell you.

'They never see an inspector, because there aren't enough of them. In one place, the workers were producing 600 jackets a day, working eighty hours a week, seven days a week. You never know who really owns these places. Sometimes people aren't paid at all when the company goes bankrupt, but then in steps another company and the people are cheated out of the little they get.These are places the media never sees.'

'What should be done?'

'They should be closed down and people given proper jobs as a *right*. It's the same with us, the pensioners. We should be talking about rights. In Hackney, the poorest borough in London, there are 35,000 pensioners, 10,000 one-parent families and a lot of disabled people. And Hackney is cutting

5 million quid off its budget. For instance, they're starting to close down the public libraries, which old people use. We're getting better organised, because there are more pensioners than ever before. At eighty-two, it makes me bloody angry, I can assure you of that. Anger is what's needed; unfortunately, I can't be angry for everybody.'

Since I saw Danny, his son, his 'lifeline', has become gravely ill. Danny has stopped touring the sweatshops in order to care for him. And his income has diminished further.

In Britain, a third of single pensioners have incomes of less than half the national average. In 1979, the Thatcher Government abolished 'index linking' between the state pension and earnings. As a result, the value of the single pension has dropped by £21 a week and a married couple's by £32. In his autobiography, the Chancellor responsible, Nigel Lawson, described this as his 'single greatest achievement'.[13] The Blair Labour Government says it will not restore the vital link with earnings.

'No one in his right mind thinks a third of us are poor,' wrote the liberal commentator Richard Thomas in the *Guardian* business pages. He was attacking a report by the Child Poverty Action Group, which had laid out the evidence, based on official statistics. Thomas urged his readers to 'forget about the poverty tourists' and concentrate on 'the chronic, persistent poor – probably accounting for 5–10 per cent of the population – who really matter'.

This is a familiar approach to the poor in the serious media. There is the glibness, the trivialising of struggling people as 'tourists', the use of an arbitrary figure to discredit credible research, which 'no one believes any more', and, of course to diminish the problem: to confine the poor to their ideologically correct status as an 'underclass' that is 'stubbornly still with us'.[14] With unwitting irony, Thomas complained that the poor had 'vanished from public debate'. He is right there.

In 1996, Liverpool's Department of Public Health issued its annual report, which disclosed that one in three children living in the inner cities was suffering 'moderate to severe mental health problems' as a direct result of poverty. This was not reported in the media.[15] In 1995 and 1996, the National Pensioners' Convention held 'pensioners' parliaments', attended by 2,400 delegates representing some three million activists and, indirectly, a quarter of the electorate. On the agenda was the kind of poverty Danny describes. The first conference was covered by regional BBC and ignored by the national press. The second was covered only by the *Independent*.

During the 1997 election campaign, the BBC's *Newsnight* had a poor person in the studio one night, facing three politicians. She invited them to see how she lived. They accepted, but there was no follow-up. The *Observer* published a large photograph of a pair of down-at-heel children's shoes, symbolising poverty.[16]

Generally speaking, there was the customary silence.

II

FLYING THE FLAG

ARMING THE WORLD

The Queen knelt and shops fell silent for the dead of
Dunblane . . . GEC in £5 billion Middle East arms deal.

Guardian, *front page*

The price of one British Aerospace Hawk is roughly the
amount needed to provide 1·5 million people in the Third
World with fresh water for life.

Campaign Against the Arms Trade

BENEATH THE UNION JACK a BL755 'multi-purpose'
British cluster bomb gleamed in the soft backlight, like the
latest showroom Jaguar or an exhibit at the Ideal Home
Exhibition. Spruced salesmen of the Hunting Engineering
company of Bedford hovered with colour brochures. A large
display photograph showed the bomb mounted on a Hawk
aircraft, beneath which the company promised prospective
buyers 'containers suitable for world-wide transport', an
'extended shelf life' and a 'truly competitive price'. I asked one
of the salesmen what it did.

'I beg your pardon?' he said.

'What does it do?' I repeated. 'You know, what's it for?'

'Just a minute please,' he said. 'Public relations will have to
handle this.'

A public relations man arrived and my question was
whispered to him. 'Is there a problem here?' he said.

'No,' I replied. 'I would like somebody to explain what

the multi-purpose cluster bomb does.'

'I shall need that request in writing,' he said, 'for MoD approval. All media inquiries must go to the MoD. An *ad hoc* reply from me here and now might be taken out of context. We've had this problem of context before. I'm not saying you would take it out of context, but context is all important, and policy is policy . . .'

At this point I realised I was speaking to an incarnation of Major Major from Joseph Heller's *Catch-22*.

'What does the BL755 do?' I tried again.

'That's classified,' said Major Major.

'Why?'

'That's classified, too.'

Refined absurdity is always close at hand in the arms business. It squeezes into bed with secrecy, corruption and stupendous greed. The public relations man's reticence was quite understandable. The BL755 is not really a bomb at all, but an 'area denial sub-munition', a land-mine in all but name. It is dropped from the air and explodes into forty-seven little mines, which are shaped like spiders. These are scattered over a wide area and 'deny' life to anything that moves or grows. They have been found in Bosnia and Croatia, where between two and four million mines threaten to maim and kill long after the end of that war against civilians.

My exchange with Major Major took place at the Farn-borough Air Show, which is really an arms market offering everything from aircraft, missiles and bombs (and 'bomblets') to razor wire. Seated beneath a 'Welcome!' sign, the representative of the Birmingham Barbed Tape company looked like Father Christmas in a department store. He was surrounded by coils of razor wire.

'What does it do?' I asked.

'It fills a niche market for a more aesthetically pleasing product.'

'Spikes are more aesthetically pleasing?'

'It depends whether they are traditional or de luxe.'

'Who are your customers?'

'We're at Heathrow airport, and we're in Angola and

the Far East, wherever there is the need.'

'How do you distinguish between customers who want to secure an airport and those building concentration camps?'

'Very difficult, very difficult . . . I keep an eye on the TV news for our products. This business is strictly commercial. You can't *imagine* the competition we're up against.'

'Cut-throat, is it?'

'I'll say. The French are always looking over our shoulder. Take our electro-foil concept . . .'

'What does it do?'

'Depends. We offer the option of a standard electrical current, or the de-luxe mesh concept that combines the traditional razor wire with electrification.'

'What is the effect on people?'

'I'm not with you . . .'

At the Paris arms fair, I asked a salesman to describe the working of a 'cluster grenade' the size of a grapefruit. Bending over a glass case, as one does when inspecting something precious, he said, 'This is *wonderful*. It is state of the art, unique. What it does is discharge copper dust, very very fine dust, so that the particles saturate the objective . . .'

'What objective?' I asked.

He looked incredulous. 'Whatever it may be,' he replied.

'People?'

'Well, er . . . if you like.'

The one pleasure to be had at these events is in helping the salesmen relieve their verbal constipation. They have the greatest difficulty saying words like 'people' and 'kill' and 'maim'. I have yet to meet one who has seen his products in use against human beings. The 'unique' grapefruit bomb took me back almost twenty years: to a hot, still day at the end of the war in Vietnam. Broken masonry and shattered cooking pots crackled underfoot like bracken as I walked through the ruins of Hongai, a northern provincial capital on the Gulf of Tonkin. American aircraft had flown fifty-two sorties against the town, round the clock, and had dropped a new type of bomb, the size and shape of a grapefruit.

At the town's school, which was destroyed, I found a letter

117

pinned to a classroom wall. It read, 'My name is Nguyen Thi An. I am fifteen years old. It was a sunny, glorious day when my mother had just told me to lay the table for lunch. The next thing I heard was the air-raid siren and I hurried to the shelter. But when I came out my mother and father were lying there covered in blood, and my sister, Binh, had pieces of metal in her, and so did her doll. My street had fallen down.'

The street had been hit by the new bombs, which sprayed small darts. These had entered Binh's body and continued to move about inside her for several days, causing internal injuries from which she died an agonising death. The darts looked like metal, but they were of a type of plastic difficult to detect under X-ray. They were first tested in Hongai, although, to my knowledge, this was not reported at the time; so much of what happened in this 'laboratory war' was a precursor to the way wars of the future would be fought, using 'anti-personnel' weapons such as the BL755 and the cluster grenade, against both military and civilian targets.

The modern arms trade was invented by the British in the 1860s when an ambitious lawyer from Newcastle upon Tyne, William Armstrong, set up in competition with the German arms manufacturer, Alfred Krupp. Armstrong was one of those Victorian industrialists of high moral tone, who believed his machines bore the sanctity of the British state. However, he was soon persuaded that selling arms to foreigners was patriotic because it made them dependent and that this was a new market ripe for British domination.

By the 1880s, Armstrong's factories were facing their first serious rival: the Vickers brothers based in Sheffield, who had taken over the Maxim-Nordenfelt company and were making the highly successful machine-gun invented by Sir Hiram Maxim. 'My gun', said Sir Hiram, 'is especially useful in stopping the mad rush of savages.'[1] Empire builders were delighted. In 1898, Hilaire Belloc wrote in *The Modern Traveller*:

> Whatever happens, we have got
> The Maxim gun and they have not.

The most famous arms dealer of all was Sir Basil Zaharoff, whose reputation popularised the term 'merchant of death'. In 1905, Vickers paid him £86,000 as their chief salesman, and quickly made him a millionaire. Zaharoff understood the connections between arms and power, diplomacy, spying and bribery, and flying the flag, regardless of whose flag it was. 'I made wars so that I could sell arms to both sides,' he declared. 'I must have sold more arms than anyone else in the world.'[2]

Essentially nothing has changed. The one difference today is that the arms business is run mainly for and by governments. In Britain this is called 'defence procurement' and justified less forthrightly than in Zaharoff's day. 'The British are really rather good at making certain kinds of weapons,' said Prince Charles at the Dubai arms fair, where he was promoting the British arms industry, as his family frequently does. He happened to be standing near an 'anti-personnel' weapon designed specifically to destroy, not objects, but as many people as possible. 'It's the hoary old chestnut,' he said. 'If we don't sell them, someone else will.'[3]

Douglas Hurd, when Tory Foreign Secretary, alluded to higher motives. 'Under the United Nations Charter,' he said, 'all Sovereign States have the right to their own self defence. So there is nothing wrong with selling arms to friendly countries to allow them to defend themselves.'

He was referring then to Indonesia, whose military dictatorship, one of the most bloodthirsty of the twentieth century, gets most of its arms from Britain – Hawk ground-attack aircraft, Sea Wolf and Rapier surface-to-air missiles, Tribal class frigates, Marconi and other battlefield communications equipment, sea-bed mine-disposal equipment, Saladin, Saracen and Fernet armoured vehicles, Tactica 'riot control' vehicles (with water cannon optional) and a fully equipped Institute of Technology for the Indonesian Army.

Indonesia's special forces, known as Kopassus, patrol East Timor in civilian dress in unmarked vehicles, armed with Heckler and Koch automatic weapons supplied by British Aerospace. Their marksmen train on simulators used by the SAS and their death squads train in British equipment officially known as 'close-quarter battle houses', also known as 'killing houses'. Indonesian military officers and pilots are trained in Britain. As for the Hurd maxim of its 'right to self defence', Indonesia is under no external threat nor likely to be. Moreover, its military establishment, reports Amnesty International, 'is organised to deal with domestic rather than international threats'.[4]

Britain is a major arms supplier to at least five countries where there is internal conflict and where the combined death toll runs to almost one million people. A British company, Mil-Tac, armed the genocidal Hutu militia in the former Zaire. In Turkey, armoured Land Rovers are used by the murderous 'anti-terrorist' police, while British missiles, guns and 'command and control' systems are secretly supplied to the Turkish military, whose war against Turkey's Kurdish population has claimed more than 20,000 victims. As Turkey is a NATO 'partner', it receives RAF photo-reconnaissance of Kurdish resistance bases.

Then there is Nigeria. Despite denials by government ministers, Britain continues to supply arms to the military regime, a famous human rights' abuser, which is waging a war against the Ogoni people. In Central America's wars of oppression, Britain has a long record. For example, training is currently provided to police and military officers from Guatemala, a country whose army has been terrorising the countryside for more than forty years. The list does not end there.[5]

True to Sir Basil Zaharoff's boast of selling arms to both sides in war, British manufacturers supplied both Iran and Iraq during their war in the 1980s, in which a million died. When the Pakistani dictator General Zia declared, 'We have to match India sword with sword, tank with tank and destroyer with destroyer,' British arms salesmen were quick off the mark. Having supplied India with Sea King helicopters, Hawk and Harrier aircraft and Sea Eagle anti-ship missiles, they offered Pakistan a strikingly similar arsenal.

What has certainly changed since Sir Basil's day is the importance of the arms industry in the political economy of

Britain. Not long ago, non-military manufacturing was a source of British pride. In the 1960s, the motor industry was the country's biggest single manufacturer. With the coming to power of Margaret Thatcher and her heirs, much of traditional manufacturing has been dismantled, disinvested and sold off, with the exception of arms, in which Britain is still a world leader.

Today, Britain is the world's second-largest arms exporter, after the United States, capturing a quarter of the world market in 1996, up from 16 per cent in 1994 and 19 per cent in 1995. In no other export sector is Britain so successful as in the arms business, which is cosseted like no other industry and in a manner otherwise heretical to Thatcherism, Majorism and now Blairism. Almost half of all research and development funds are allocated to 'defence'; and there is an ingenious scam known as the Aid for Trade Provisions (ATP), which accounts for more than half of all British 'aid' to the developing world.

In 1988, Alan Clark, Thatcher's Trade Minister, set up a little-known special fund of £1 billion, from which the Export Credit Guarantee Department (ECGD) of the Department of Trade and Industry financed indebted Third World regimes wishing to buy British arms. It was the first time the ECGD had extended credit to a whole industry, and by 1993 more than half of all credit guarantees underwrote arms sales, mostly to Indonesia and Malaysia.

The Malaysian deal was a mite too ingenious. More than £1.3 billion in arms sales (mostly Hawk jets) were barely concealed in an 'aid package' financing the Pergau hydro-electric dam, which was being built by British firms. Douglas Hurd, the Foreign Secretary, was strongly advised by his senior aid official, Sir Tim Lankester, that the dam was 'uneconomic' and 'a very bad buy' which would be detrimental to the real needs of Malaysia. Hurd overruled him because of 'wider considerations' and because Britain 'had given her word'.[6] In 1994, in an action brought by the World Development Movement, the High Court in London ruled the deal illegal and ordered all further payments stopped.

121

In 1996, the National Audit Office found similar corruption in the link between British 'aid' to Indonesia and future arms sales to the dictatorship. The Minister for Overseas Development, Linda Chalker, said in Parliament that this was 'helping the poor in Indonesia'.[7] If aid to police installations, airports and other strategic infrastructure is helping Indonesia's poor, the situation in other countries, beneficiaries of Baroness Chalker's largesse, is also puzzling.

However, there is a pattern. Malaysia, nowhere near the poorest of nations, is the fifth largest recipient of British aid. The tiny Sultanate of Oman gets double the aid per person received by other nations. Yet Oman is relatively well off, with an average income higher than Portugal's. Oman happens to be the third largest buyer of British arms in the world. British aid to Ecuador has inexplicably leapt 176 per cent and is now eight times more than to El Salvador, which is poorer. Ecuador is the fifth largest buyer of British arms in the world.[8]

In 1995, a study by the tenacious World Development Movement revealed that British taxpayers were paying at least a fifth of the total value of British arms exports in hidden subsidies and that the government spent more than ten times as much promoting arms as civil exports. 'Nearly £5 billion of taxpayers' money has been pawned against arms sales in the last five years,' said the report, *Gunrunners' Gold*.

What this means is that much of the British economy has been militarised. One in ten workers in manufacturing now works on military equipment. The Ministry of Defence is industry's biggest customer, spending in excess of £20 billion of taxpayers' money every year and a great deal more, in terms of Gross National Product, than most developed nations spend on defence. To help pay for this, British manufacturers are licensed to sell to almost anybody who will buy from them. When Sir Alan Thomas, the head of the government's Defence Sales Organisation, said, 'no other major manufacturing nation has a more responsible and restrictive policy', he provided a memorable example in the Orwellian tradition of a statement that represented the diametric opposite of the truth.[9]

Britain is on the United Nations Security Council, a body distinguished by the fact that its five permanent members – the others are the United States, Russia, China and France – are the world's biggest arms dealers. Their 'responsibility', to quote Sir Alan again, can be measured against the fact that they, and the other members, export every year some $36 billion's worth of arms. As for a 'restrictive' British arms policy, some 80 per cent of British exports go to poor and developing countries, while exports to Asia and the Middle East, the world's most dangerous flashpoints, have increased fourfold.[10]

When the US Congress voted in 1994 to ban small-arms sales to Indonesia, because of the genocide in East Timor, a spokesman for the dictatorship said, 'No problem. We can always turn to Britain.'[11] The truth of this assumption is illustrated by the facts of Britain's longstanding relationship with another dictatorial regime, in Chile. Although Chile today has a civilian government, its armed forces are still run by General Augusto Pinochet, whose documented atrocities fill shelves at the offices of Amnesty International. Jeremy Corbyn MP has estimated that Pinochet has been responsible for 50,000 civilian deaths since he overthrew the elected government of Salvador Allende in 1973.

I ran into one of Pinochet's arms buyers at the Paris arms fair. He was receiving an impressive across-the-counter pitch from a British Aerospace salesman. The eager young salesman, in colourful tie and fashionably baggy suit, had all the fluency of a Petticoat Lane huckster: a little smoother perhaps and more technical. Performing at the sand-bagged entrance to the British Aerospace exhibition, he clearly fascinated the Chilean with his promotion of the Merlin mortar bomb.

When a film crew with me began to film this, they were waved away by a public relations man. 'You are not being helpful,' he remonstrated. The notion that we should be 'helpful' in the selling of a weapon that showers shrapnel over a wide area, killing people and making the environment uninhabitable, was salutary. I half-expected him to quote Margaret Thatcher, heroine of the arms industry. 'An order means the best of Britain has won through', she had said, 'and I am batting for Britain.'[12]

Thatcher admired Pinochet, and still does. Even out of office, she has visited Chile and dined with the man whose systematic use of torture and extra-judicial killing has given his name a notoriety to compare with Hitler and Pol Pot. When Alan Clark visited Chile as Thatcher's devoted Trade Minister, he recorded in his diary an argument among Chileans about, as he put it, 'who denounced whose sister during the period of military rule. Frankly, I'd have put them all under arrest as they left the building. I might say that to Pinochet, if I get to see him [the next day].'[13]

While his arms buyer was shopping in Paris, Pinochet was in Britain, as the guest of British Aerospace. A lunch was held in his honour, during which the company's Rayo multiple-launch rocket system was discussed. Pinochet was said to 'have his heart set on the Rayo', which, reported a company spokesman, is 'potentially worth tens of millions of pounds'. He added, 'As you know, we operate within the rules of the government. [Pinochet] is a most valuable customer, and so long as we have the support of the government, it is good for us, very good business indeed.'[14]

Although British companies have long sold arms, legally and illegally, to the world's leading tyrannies – Saracen armoured cars took part in the Sharpeville massacre in South Africa in 1960 and British communications equipment helped the Ugandan mass murderer Idi Amin to track down his victims – it was Margaret Thatcher who brought a crusading zeal to the task of arming much of the world.

She became a super-saleswoman, making deals, talking up the finer points of fighter aircraft engines, hard-bargaining with Saudi princes, cajoling buyers and sellers alike. At the annual dinner at the Farnborough arms fair in 1980, she banged the table. 'Look here,' she said, '£1.2 billion . . . it's not enough!' Soon afterwards she was in Kuwait, announcing, 'There's a tremendous lot for Britain here . . . like military communications systems. We are all very good at that. After all, it's *we* who discovered radar!'[15]

When she ordered the nation to 'Rejoice!' during the Falklands War in 1982, she omitted to mention that the first Harrier aircraft lost was shot down by Argentinian fighters using British ammunition. From the day she took office, her ministers set out to court another future adversary, Saddam Hussein, then the Anglo-American favourite to vanquish Iran's hated Ayatollah. A ministerial procession wound its way from Whitehall to Baghdad – Lord Carrington, Cecil Parkinson, John Nott, John Biffen, Tony Newton, Paul Channon, William Waldegrave. The *Baghdad Observer* featured photographs of them, smiling, or perhaps wincing, on the dictator's famous visitors' couch.

In 1981, Douglas Hurd, then a Foreign Office minister, flew to Baghdad to 'celebrate' with Saddam the coming to power of the Iraqi Ba'athists in 1968, one of the bloodiest events in modern Middle Eastern history, and one which extinguished hope of a pluralistic Iraq. Hurd knew that the man to whom he offered his government's congratulations was renowned as the interrogator and torturer of Qasr-al-Nihayyah, the 'Palace of the End'. But Hurd had another mission; he was, reported the *Guardian* at the time, 'a top-level salesman' who had tried to sell Saddam an entire British Aerospace air defence system which 'would be the biggest sale of its kind ever achieved'.[16]

When, in 1985, Britain eventually banned the sale of arms to Iraq, the flow of British arms, money and 'top-level salesmen' did not stop. The following year, Trade Minister Alan Clark led the way back to Baghdad. On his return, he encouraged machine-tool manufacturers to trade with Iraq, and his ministry issued export licences to at least five British companies. In 1988, David Mellor, then a Foreign Office minister, joined Saddam Hussein on his couch, and the obligatory *Baghdad Observer* photograph shows them both smiling in an oddly similar way.

While Mellor was being entertained, his host ordered the gassing of 5,000 Kurds in the town of Halabja. 'There was the plump baby', reported Nicholas Beeston of *The Times* from Halabja, 'whose face, frozen in a scream, stuck out from under the protective arm of a man, away from the open door of a house that he never reached. Nearby, a family of five who had been sitting in their garden eating lunch were cut down – the killer gas not even sparing the family cat or the birds in the tree, which littered the well-kept lawn.' Halabja was the worst-ever act of genocide using poison gas to be documented.

The response of the British Government, which was now trading secretly and illegally with Saddam Hussein, was to assign a junior Foreign Office official to tell the Iraqi Ambassador that he was 'shocked'. However, it was unclear if this 'shock' was directed at Iraq's behaviour or at the decision by British newspaper editors to publish photographic evidence of the atrocity committed by Britain's friend. 'It would look very cynical,' said Lord (Geoffrey) Howe, 'if so soon after expressing outrage over the Kurds we adopted a more flexible approach to arms sales.'[17]

Within a month of the gassing of the Kurds, Alan Clark's successor at the Department of Trade, Tony Newton, flew to Baghdad and offered Saddam Hussein £340 million in export credits. He returned to Baghdad later that year to celebrate the deal and the fact that trade with Iraq had risen from £2.9 million the previous year to £31.5 million. Iraq was now Britain's third biggest market for machine tools, many of which were for 'dual use' – that is, they made weapons.

Mark Higson was the Iraq Desk Officer at the Foreign Office in 1989. In a setting that might have been conjured by Dennis Potter, Higson sat behind a little Iraqi flag and directly opposite the Iran Desk man, who sat behind the Ayatollah's flag. He told me how ministers and officials systematically lied to Parliament. 'The draft letters I wrote for various ministers', he said, 'were saying that nothing had changed, the embargo on the sale of arms to Iraq was the same.'

'Was that true?' I asked.

'No, it wasn't true. I'm not proud of my role in it . . . I was simply doing what I regarded as my job.'

'And your superiors knew it wasn't true?'

'Yes. If I was writing a draft reply to a letter from an MP for

Mr Mellor or Mr Waldegrave [then Foreign Office ministers]
I wrote the agreed line. But they knew things had changed. I
also wrote replies to go to members of the public who were
concerned about the gassing of the Kurds at Halabja and
wanted to know what the government was doing about it. A
lot of MPs and members of the public thought the £340 million credit guarantees we gave to Iraq were absolutely disgusting. The letters I wrote were awfully polite . . .'

I said, 'You and your colleagues at the Foreign Office had
seen the end-user certificates with Jordan on them, but you
knew the equipment was going to Iraq. Is that correct?'

'Oh yes, yes. We were quite well aware that Jordan was
being used . . . Iraq was regarded as the big prize.'

'So how much truth did the public get?'

'The public got just as much truth as we could squeeze out,
given that we told downright lies . . .'

'You had a conscience about this?'

'Yes . . . there were eleven of us in my joining group. There
are only five still there. The others left not necessarily because
of political conscience but because they couldn't stand the air
of sycophancy that pervades the Foreign Office.'

The company best known for its part in getting arms
secretly to Iraq was the machine-tools manufacturer, Matrix
Churchill. But the case of the former fireworks firm, Astra,
which rose to prominence as an arms manufacturer during the
1980s, is more instructive, especially as it remains unresolved.
According to the former chairman, Gerald James, Astra was
'taken over' by MI6 and used as a channel to Iraq. 'I found
out', he told me, 'that my company was heavily involved in a
massive arms deal with Jordan, which Mrs Thatcher had
personally negotiated. It was reported to me that we were
supplying £100 million worth of propellant.'

'And you weren't aware of this?'

'Absolutely not . . . that amount exceeded our group
turnover!'

'How could you not be aware of it?'

'Well, because our names were being used for contracts
which were being operated by people who belonged to IMS

... that's International Military Services. It's a company owned by the Ministry of Defence and is quite separate from Defence Sales and handles the more covert operations of the government. When I investigated I found out that the end-user certificates, which said "Jordan", were a fiction, a total fiction ... tank parts, certain other weapons, missile-launching equipment, all of it ended up in Iraq and was almost certainly used in the Gulf War.'

Although Gerald James submitted a statement to the arms-to-Iraq inquiry chaired by Lord Justice Scott, he was not called to give evidence. Neither was his chief executive, Christopher Gumbley, who is now widely believed to have been wrongly convicted on a minor bribery charge after he had discovered the secret life of his company.

Nor did Scott call any executive or director of Astra and its shadowy subsidiaries, such as PRB, makers of parts for the infamous Iraqi supergun – nor any of those deeper in the shadows, who had passed through the arms industry's legendary revolving door: men like Sir John Cuckney, the former MI5 officer who features in Peter Wright's book, *Spycatcher*, and who was chairman of the Ministry of Defence's secret arm, International Military Services.

Tim Laxton was the auditor brought in to examine the books of Astra and its subsidiary PRB. As a result of his own investigations, Laxton supports the main thrust of Gerald James's charge that Astra was used by the intelligence services to get arms to Iraq through their subsidiaries. Having attended most of the sittings of the Scott inquiry, he says it is a 'mystery' why Scott failed to question those who made the weapons, promoted them, bankrolled them and were privy to decision-making at the highest level.

'We heard nothing from any of the ministers' private secretaries,' he told me. 'They knew what their bosses knew. We heard nothing from Mrs Thatcher's private secretary, Sir Charles Powell, who was responsible for passing documents to her. The inquiry reserved the worst flak for the middle-ranking public servants, not the big guns. Lord Scott himself was unduly deferential to Lady Thatcher. He appeared afraid that she was going to walk out. He actually said to her, "Lady Thatcher, we'll try and trouble you with as few papers as possible." '

Laxton believes that if there was a full and open inquiry, 'hundreds' would face criminal investigation. 'They would include', he said, 'top political figures, very senior Civil Servants from right throughout Whitehall: the Foreign Office, the Ministry of Defence, the Department of Trade and Industry . . . the top echelon of government.'

Scott ensured this would not happen by passing out the ammunition of exoneration and acquittal to those found guilty on the evidence in his own report. At the end of a report so long and dense that few could be expected to read it, he concluded that Cabinet ministers had acted 'honestly and in good faith' in having culpably approved the supply of weapons to a murderous tyrant. He judged that the same ministers had deliberately misled Parliament, but had not intended to mislead Parliament!

In his draft (which was leaked and published), Scott accused William Waldegrave, the Foreign Office Minister, of writing letters in 'terms that were apt to mislead the readers as to the nature of the policy on export sales to Iraq . . . Mr. Waldegrave was unquestionably in a position to know that this was so.' In the final version, there is the following change: 'Mr. Waldegrave was in a position to know that was so although I accept that he did not intend his letters to be misleading and did not so regard them.'[18] Waldegrave and others had been allowed to read the judgements Scott had made on them and successfully to demand amendments.

There is evidence in the body of the report that John Major concealed the truth about the changes to the guidelines for arms sales to Iraq. A memo written by his private secretary John Wall (when Major was Foreign Secretary) strongly suggests that he knew about the changes. Major denied this unreservedly to Scott. And although Scott described a letter of denial written by Major as 'misleading', he largely accepted his plea of ignorance without explaining why.

Margaret Thatcher was similarly let off, as the transcript

of her evidence makes clear. She admitted to the inquiry that she had underlined the crucial words, 'more flexible interpretation' (of the guidelines for arms sales to Iraq), and had written 'doubtful' in the margin of an official paper suggesting that the government 'could argue that the sale [to Iraq] would be within the revised guidelines'. Yet she had told the House of Commons that 'the Government have not changed their policy on defence sales to Iraq . . .'[19]

No matter the weight and careful marshalling of his investigation, Scott's conclusions were absurdly contradictory or lost in obfuscation; and there was something for everybody. The former Tory Defence Minister, Tom King, quipped that everyone could quote sentences from the Scott Report to suit themselves. 'It's a game,' he said approvingly.[20]

Speaking from the saddle of his hunting horse a few days after the release of his report, Scott denied having watered down his conclusions under pressure and said the very suggestion deserved a 'ruder' reply, 'but I don't want to offend. Excuse me, I would like to continue with my day's hunting.' And off he galloped.[21]

In 1992, Robert Sheldon, the Labour MP who chaired the House of Commons Public Accounts Committee, a 'watchdog' body, was handed a report by the National Audit Office that both shocked and silenced him. The report was about the 'commissions' paid in arms deals, specifically the £20 billion in sales of Tornado fighter-bombers and naval vessels to Saudi Arabia, known as Al-Yamamah (The Dove). It is said to be the biggest arms deal in history.

The Saudis had made clear that if their rake-offs became public – they were understood to be demanding £15 million added to the price of a £20 million Tornado – the deal was off. Sheldon decided not to publish. I requested an interview for a television documentary I was making; he refused. The Tory minister then responsible for arms sales was Jonathan Aitken, the 'Minister for Defence Procurement'. Aitken, who doubled as an 'adviser' to the arms industry, had long been deeply involved with the Saudis.

At almost exactly the time that Sheldon was locking up the NAO report, Aitken was flying to his fateful weekend at the Ritz Hotel in Paris to meet his Saudi friends and 'save' the arms deal: in other words, to discuss the question of commissions. That was why he lied about the trip during his famously failed libel action against the *Guardian* and Granada Television. He had been found out; and ignominy followed swiftly.

The Al-Yamamah deal was signed by Prime Minister Margaret Thatcher. Of all the issues left unresolved from the 1980s, the most outstanding are questions arising from the Thatcher family's omnipresence in the arms trade. After years of speculation, specific allegations emerged in 1994. Mark Thatcher was said to have received a £12 million 'commission' on Al-Yamamah.

The allegations were based on transcripts of recorded telephone conversations between Saudi princes and their agents. They purported to show Mark Thatcher and others competing for commissions in 1984 and Thatcher trading on his name and access to his mother.[22] 'Commissions' are the way the system works in Saudi Arabia; in the kingdom that is the world's greatest oil well, billions are raked off on every conceivable deal. For Thatcher and his cronies this was not illegal.

In any case, he vehemently denied the allegations. In an interview with the *Financial Times*, he admitted that he was a friend of Wafic Said, the powerful millionaire businessman who acted as a go-between for the British in the Al-Yamamah negotiations in the mid-1980s. 'Merely because I know this man', he said, 'does not mean to say that he is going to pay me £12 million because I am a nice guy.' He claimed he was worth no more than £5 million. Had he enjoyed such 'tremendous success', he said, 'I would be sitting on my private island in the South Pacific.' As it turns out, most of his money is in such places, beyond the scrutiny of reporters and tax investigators.

The *Financial Times* reported that Thatcher had 'secured backing for one of his biggest US investment deals from some of his mother's closest business supporters – Hanson, the UK-quoted conglomerate, and Mr Li Ka-Shing, the Hong Kong billionaire, both of whom have been substantial donors to the Conservative Party . . .'[23]

When the allegations broke, I interviewed Howard Teicher, a top official in the Reagan administration in the 1980s. Teicher had held two senior posts on the National Security Council, the powerful body that advises the President; he was Director of Near East and South Asian Affairs and Senior Director of Political-Military Affairs. He told me he had first read about Mark Thatcher's 'involvement' in the Al-Yamamah deal in secret dispatches from the US Embassy in Saudi Arabia and from other intelligence and diplomatic reports from European capitals. He said he regarded the reports as 'totally reliable, totally accurate'.

'What was your reaction at seeing this?' I asked.

'I was quite surprised to read about the son of the Prime Minister of the United Kingdom making himself a player in an arms transaction for the obvious reason that it would create the appearance of a direct relationship between the [Thatcher] family . . . I became increasingly concerned, because it was clear that the volume of reporting stated that he was genuinely involved . . . There was no doubt in my mind that Mark Thatcher was a principal in the group of individuals promoting the UK arms transaction and that he undoubtedly would benefit economically from this transaction.'

I showed him a copy of a document from a current court case in the United States related to the Saudi deal, which referred to the lobbying of British Aerospace and Rolls-Royce to delay the decision by the Saudi Government to fit the Tornado aircraft with American General Electric engines. It says, '$4 billion was mentioned in connection with M. Thatcher's son.' Teicher said the document seemed genuine and 'very credible' and that the $4 billion would have been shared among 'Mark Thatcher's group'.[24]

'What kind of commission would that represent?'

'Well, do the math,' he said. 'Five per cent on four billion dollars; it's a pretty hefty commission.'

Margaret Thatcher's interest in arms deals was

'extraordinary', according to Robin Robison, a Cabinet Office official from 1985 to 1990. Robison told me that she was the only prime minister regularly to read the intelligence intercepts and to attend the top-secret Joint Intelligence Committee (JIC) meetings, at which arms deals were frequently discussed. 'The JIC had masses of stuff on the arms trade,' he said. 'It also had specific information on the gassing of the Kurds before the news broke . . .'

I asked him if human rights were ever a consideration, or ever discussed.

'Never,' he replied.

In maintaining that her interest in arms deals meant that she was 'batting for Britain', Thatcher was demonstrating her extreme form of nationalism; but there was another, less obvious element to the gathering of power this represented. The Thatcher years saw the rise of what has been called the 'national security state', whose pillars of power are 10 Downing Street, a Civil Service widely politicised by Thatcherite placemen and responsible to the executive, principal quangos directed from Downing Street, and the intelligence and security services, which have wide and publicly unaccountable powers. Central to this is an ostensibly 'free market', though one that is rigged, as privatisation has demonstrated, and dependent to a significant degree on a subsidised arms industry. Far from changing this since he came to power, promising 'clean government', Tony Blair has reinforced it.

None of it, of course, has to do with 'national security' but with the retention of power by those establishment crusaders who built more and bigger nuclear weapons and continue to rationalise it as ensuring 'peace and security'.

In justifying the retention of 'first strike' nuclear weapons, the Ministry of Defence claims to have given Trident a 're-ordered posture' and a 'sub-strategic capability'. A hint of what that might mean was contained in a brief announcement in 1994 that the Ministry would conduct a £5 million study into defending Britain 'against a ballistic missile attack, focusing on the potential threat from the Third World'.[25]

When I was last at the Ministry of Defence in Whitehall, I noticed on the wall of a reception room a framed centre-spread from the *Sun*, which carried a large photograph of the Trident submarine beneath the headline: 'WORTH EVERY PENNY'. Keeping Trident allows the British establishment to retain its 'nuclear club' membership of the United Nations Security Council, which remains an immensely powerful imperial tool.

In 1994, the British Government displayed its anxiety at losing this 'seat at the top table' when, together with the United States, China, Russia and France, its legal right to maintain and use nuclear weapons was challenged at the World Court and in the General Assembly of the United Nations.

In order to defeat the UN resolution, the nuclear powers needed the support of important Third World countries. Among the resolution's most vociferous backers was the Non-Aligned Movement, chaired by Indonesia. Without warning, Indonesia changed its vote and successfully lobbied on behalf of the pro-nuclear powers to delay the issue reaching the floor of the General Assembly.

The irony was exquisite.

Having lectured the West on the 'independence' of Indonesian foreign policy and its 'right' to act as it wished in East Timor, the Suharto regime clearly did exactly as it was told in the time-honoured way of a Western client. It was a model demonstration of the power of the West over an indebted dictatorship increasingly dependent on Western 'aid', capital and technology. There can be little doubt that similar pressure could begin to free East Timor from Indonesia's grip. Those who question the power of public opinion in the West to embarrass and move their governments ought not to forget this.

The 'national security state', armed to the teeth and arming the world, originated in the United States. In 1981, President Reagan embarked on the biggest peacetime military arms spending programme in American history. With finance borrowed on the international money markets, this led to a rapid rise in interest rates and the over-valuation of the dollar. As money then being borrowed from British and other Western banks by Third World countries was in dollars, the cost of 'debt-servicing' accelerated, causing a 'debt crisis' that has seen government after government lose its economic sovereignty to IMF-imposed 'structural adjustment pro- grammes', the notorious SAPs.

It is to these struggling, debt-burdened countries that British and other Western companies have sold most of their weapons. For ordinary people in the Third World, the effect has been catastrophic, as their national resources are squandered on ever-rising debt repayments and the likes of British Aerospace Hawk aircraft, one of which, it has been estimated, would buy fresh, running water for a million and a half people.

In Britain, meanwhile, extra-parliamentary groups opposed to such a world view and the secretive 'state within a state' have seen their rights diminished by autocratic legislation that has crowded the statute book since Thatcher was elected. Tony Blair, as Opposition leader, played an important part in this. By tabling amendments to the Criminal Justice Bill, the most repressive legislation ever put forward in modern Britain, he conceded the bill's principle of limiting freedom of movement, association and dissent.

Six weeks before the 1997 general election, when the Tories had already lost their majority, Labour helped the government to 'fast track' legislation of one of the most repressive and despised Home Secretaries in modern times: Michael Howard's Crime Bill and Police Bill, which legislates for American-style mandatory sentences and still more powers for the police. In his first Queen's Speech, Blair pointedly refused to honour an election pledge to enact a Freedom of Information Bill, the single piece of legislation that would erode the secret state and which he described in 1996 as a 'change that is absolutely fundamental to how we see politics developing in this country over the next few years'.[26]

From the day they took office Blair and Straw acted secretly on vital issues. Blair approved eleven arms deals with Indonesia under cover of the Official Secrets Act. Straw planned legislation which 'would give to courts jurisdiction over acts of conspiracy performed in this country in respect of criminal acts committed abroad'. What this meant was the end of the much-vaunted British tradition of giving refuge to exiled political dissidents plotting to overthrow repressive regimes. It would have excluded the African National Congress from having a base in London during the apartheid years, not to mention Karl Marx and many others. 'I cannot go into details,' said a Home Office official.[27]

My only visit to the Foreign Office was in 1989 when I went to interview Lord Brabazon of Tara. I had asked for the Foreign Secretary, Douglas Hurd, and was instead given His Lordship, one of the Bertie Wooster junior ministers who help the FO keep in touch with its past. The subject of the interview was Cambodia. I had questions about Britain's military support for the exiled Khmer Rouge-dominated coalition (the SAS were training them to lay land-mines) and Prime Minister Thatcher's statement that the 'more reasonable' Khmer Rouge should 'play some part in a future government'.[28]

I was met by a minder from the news department, Ian Whitehead, who took me aside, as he was no doubt used to doing with journalists, and told me to 'go easy' on His Lordship, whose knowledge of Indo-China was limited. With a film camera turning, I began by asking the minister who exactly these reasonable Khmer Rouge were. 'Um . . .' he replied. When I asked for their names, Whitehead threw himself in front of the camera, yelling, 'Stop this *now*! This is *not* the way we were led to believe the line of questioning would go!' No 'line' had been agreed. Nevertheless, he refused to allow the interview to proceed until he had approved the questions.

Over the years, I have been able to observe the contemptuous way the Foreign Office, perhaps the greatest citadel of the British establishment, treats the public. From time to time, documentary films I have made have caused people to write to the government and their MPs, seeking answers to serious questions about the effect of British policies on large numbers of human beings all over the world. The result, almost invariably, as Mark Higson pointed out, has been a form of low-intensity lying.

When people have written to the Foreign Office about East Timor, they have been told that 'Indonesia's human rights record remains imperfect, but progress is being made. The Indonesian government has declared its commitment to human rights.' This is as false as the specious claim that British officials are engaged in 'quiet diplomacy' to improve human rights in Indonesia.

The senior briefer dealing with East Timor and Indonesia is Carol Robson, deputy head of the south-east Asian department. The manner in which Robson has defended the Suharto regime has greatly impressed those attending her briefings. When Indonesian troops brutally attacked demonstrators, this was dismissed as 'squaddie indiscipline'. Robson has worked especially hard, though unsuccessfully, to discredit East Timorese eye-witness accounts of bombing by British-made Hawks. 'It takes twenty years' plane-spotting', she said, 'to identify a Hawk.' She has claimed that the Indonesians lack the technical skill to convert the Hawks from trainers to attack aircraft. (British Aerospace's own promotional material makes clear that 'Hawks can be modified on site to the five-pylon ground-attack standard' and that conversion is 'relatively simple'.)

In 1995, Ahmad Taufik, a correspondent of the banned Jakarta weekly *Tempo* and a founder of the Alliance of Independent Journalists, came to Britain to seek support for those like him campaigning for democracy and freedom of speech in Indonesia. The trip required extraordinary courage. He saw Carol Robson at the Foreign Office, who told him, 'The human rights situation is improving in your country.' He replied that this was untrue. She cited the 'lighter punishment' given out to journalists who had protested in the streets (they were beaten, some of them senseless, by police) as proof that 'conditions have improved'. On Taufik's return to Jakarta, he was arrested, found guilty of 'insulting the government', and sentenced to two years and eight months in prison.

On a sunny day in May 1997, Robin Cook, the new Labour Foreign Secretary, held a media event at the Foreign Office. An impressive video display showed Tony and Cherie Blair arriving at 10 Downing Street, Union Jack-waving crowds, Blair juxtaposed with Nelson Mandela and Britons doing good work in the Third World. Both the Foreign Secretary and the head of the Diplomatic Service looked decidedly uncomfortable; others, waiting for Cook to speak, inspected their shoes. The Americanisation of British mainstream politics has a way to go yet.

Still, by the time the heroic images had faded, there was the expectation of an Important Announcement. In fact, it was described as a 'mission statement'. 'We will not permit the sale of arms to regimes that might use them for internal repression or international aggression,' declared Cook. 'We shall work through international forums and bilateral relationships to spread the values of human rights, civil liberties and democracy which we demand for ourselves.' Human rights, he emphasised, would be at the 'heart' of British foreign policy. To further this end, there would be a 'review' of Britain's trading arrangements and the 'ethical implications'.

The announcement was at odds with the historical record, which shows that since 1945 Tory and Labour governments have had almost identical foreign policies, none of which have upheld human rights. On the contrary, in serving what are known as 'British interests', they have played a significant part in some of the century's worst abuses of human rights. What is more, it has been Labour, not Tory, governments which have been the most zealous in pursuing these 'interests'.

In the post-war Attlee Government, the Foreign Secretary, Ernest Bevin, was the architect of a policy of 'mutuality' and 'partnership' with some of the world's most vicious despots, especially in the Middle East, forging relationships that endure today, often sidelining and crushing the human rights of whole communities and societies. For all the iniquities of the Thatcher years, it was not the Tories but Labour who set up the Defence Sales Organisation at the Ministry of Defence specifically to boost the arms trade and make money from selling lethal weapons.

In announcing this in 1966, Defence Secretary Denis Healey told the House of Commons, 'While the government attach the highest importance to making progress in the field of arms control and disarmament, we must also take what practical steps we can to ensure that this country does not fail to secure its rightful share of this valuable market.'[29]

When I asked Denis Healey about this, he claimed that his decision had made no difference to the volume of military exports which, he said, was 20 per cent of the world market – about what it is now. In fact, it led to almost a doubling of Britain's share of the arms market.[30]

In the 1960s, the Wilson Government, far from promoting human rights around the world, supported the American invasion of Vietnam, sold arms to racist South Africa and armed and conspired with the Nigerian military regime to crush Biafra. Less well known is Labour's bloody record in Indonesia. Declassified Foreign Office files show that in 1965 Britain aided in the slaughter of more than half a million Indonesians, many of them opponents of the present dictator, General Suharto. 'I have never concealed from you my belief', cabled the British Ambassador in Jakarta, Sir Andrew Gilchrist, in 1965, 'that a little shooting in Indonesia would be an essential preliminary to effective change.' A series of covert British operations, directed from Singapore, supported the 'little shooting', which turned out to be the murder of hundreds of thousands of members of the PKI, the Indonesian Communist Party and others, mostly poor farmers of no party allegiance.[31]

Within a year of this extermination campaign, Wilson's Foreign Secretary, the mild-mannered Michael Stewart, visited Jakarta and reported that the 'economic chaos of Indonesia' promised 'great potential opportunities for British exporters . . . I think we ought to take an active part and try to secure a slice of the cake ourselves.'[32] Stewart wrote that he had 'reached a good understanding' with the Indonesian Foreign Minister, Adam Malik, a 'remarkable man' who was 'resolved to keep his country at peace'.[33] This remarkable man was later to play a key role as apologist for the Indonesian atrocities in East Timor. In 1977, he was reported as saying: '50,000 or 80,000 people might have been killed during the war in East Timor . . . It was war . . . then what is the big fuss?'[34]

Again, it was not a Tory minister who sold the first Hawk fighter-bombers to Suharto, but David Owen, Foreign Secretary in the Callaghan Government. The year was 1978. When asked about the implications for East Timor, Owen said the estimates of the killings had been 'exaggerated' and that the 'most reliable' figure was 10,000 and, anyway, 'the scale of fighting had been reduced'. The opposite was true. Owen's 'reliable estimates' were Indonesian Government propaganda passed through the Foreign Office; and the genocide was then actually reaching its height.[35]

In the same year, Robin Cook, the young Labour MP for Edinburgh Central, was making his name as a critic of the arms trade. In two long articles in the *New Statesman*, entitled 'Britain's Arms Bazaar' and 'The Tragic Cost of Britain's Arms Trade', Cook lamented that 'wherever weapons are sold there is a tacit conspiracy to conceal the reality of war' and 'it is a truism that every war for the past two decades has been fought by poor countries with weapons supplied by rich countries'. He attacked 'those governments who are so unpopular they only stay in power by terrorising their civilian population', singling out the dictatorship in Indonesia.

'The current sale of Hawk aircraft to Indonesia is particularly disturbing,' he wrote, 'as the purchasing regime is not only repressive but actually at war on two fronts: in East Timor, where perhaps a sixth of the population has been slaughtered . . . and in West Papua, where it confronts an indigenous liberation movement.' In deriding the Tory

Government's suggestion that the Hawk was only a training aircraft, Cook quoted a sales catalogue which described the Hawk as a powerful fighter-bomber that could easily be converted 'to carry a weapon load of 5,600 lbs'. 'No one need pretend', he wrote, 'that such a plane will not have a devastating potential against secessionist movements who have no air cover of their own.'

When Labour's Defence Minister, Roy Mason, flew to South Korea to sell arms to a regime that had just imprisoned twelve members of the opposition for appealing to the West for help, he was roundly denounced by Cook. 'It may be that the Foreign Office takes the view that democracy will never be restored in South Korea,' he wrote. 'But if they are wrong Britain will never be forgiven by the new regime for what we are doing now for the sake of a fast buck. Nor do we deserve to be forgiven.'[36]

Sixteen years later and now on Labour's front bench, Cook seemed to have lost none of his spark. Lambasting the Tory Trade Minister, Richard Needham, for selling more Hawks to Indonesia, he said, 'He will be aware that Hawk aircraft have been observed on bombing runs in East Timor in most years since 1984.'[37] Cook was right; of course the Minister was aware. As Mark Higson confirmed, the Foreign Office knew where and how the Hawks were being used in East Timor. Indeed, as Shadow Trade Minister, Cook was impressive in exposing the deceit of ministers involved in the Matrix Churchill affair, which was also about sending British arms to a tyrant: in this case Saddam Hussein. However, Cook limited his role to that of a champion of businessmen treated unjustly. He was never the front-bencher fearlessly explaining to a puzzled nation what the arms-to-Iraq affair *meant*: that it was a British scandal of Watergate proportions. Looking back, his passionate performances at the Dispatch Box and on television probably helped to contain it.

In June 1995, I sent Cook a fax asking him if a Labour government would continue to arm the dictatorship in Indonesia. He replied that Labour's policy was not to sell arms to any country that used them for 'internal repression' and that a Labour Government would look closely at every 'fresh application' for weapons. I faxed back, asking him what this meant exactly, and if Labour would let Suharto have the Hawks that were still on the assembly line.

I received a reply from his assistant with a copy of *Hansard* of May 11, 1994, when Cook had sought 'assurances' from the Trade Minister that the twenty-four Hawks approved for sale would not be used in East Timor, as they had been 'observed . . . in most years since 1984'. Needham had issued the standard denial, which Cook let pass.

The *Hansard* that Cook did not send me was for November 17, 1994, when, in a volte-face, he defended the decision of the Wilson Government to sell Hawks to Suharto. These were 'trainers', he said, sold 'on the clear understanding' that they would not be used for any other purpose. Moreover, there was no evidence 'whatever' that they had been used in East Timor. This was the very opposite of what he had said in Parliament six months earlier: that the Hawks had been bombing East Timor 'in most years since 1984'. And what of his earlier rebuttal of the 'trainers' myth: that the Hawks could be converted to 'carry a weapon load of 5,600 lbs'?

But now Cook was Foreign Secretary, promising a 'thorough review of arms sales' and a 'firm commitment not to permit the sale of arms to regimes that might use them for repression or aggression'. The test would be whether he stopped the export to Indonesia of a batch of sixteen Hawk aircraft which were almost ready to be shipped from the factory at Warton in Lancashire.

In a television investigation by Martyn Gregory, Nick Oliver, the managing director of the second largest British arms supplier to Indonesia, Procurement Services International, said that he had spoken personally to Tony Blair before the general election and had been assured that 'the type of equipment the Conservatives have given export licences to will present no difficulty for the Labour Government'.

Blair's office issued a statement in which the Prime Minister said he had 'no recollection' of meeting Oliver and that it was 'vacuous in the extreme' to suggest that he would have discussed export licences in opposition. The statement did not say why it was vacuous – with Labour on the verge of taking office.

Subsequently, Labour's Defence Minister, John Spellar, was asked by the Labour MP Ann Clwyd to 'publish the minutes of meetings and other documents' relating to any contact between the government and Procurement Services International. Spellar's reply could have been written by his Tory predecessor. He said, 'Details of meetings between [the government] and its customers cannot be released due to their commercial confidentiality. I am withholding the information requested . . .' Under 'ethical' New Labour, the company's record £700 million business with Indonesia has proceeded unimpeded.[38] Clwyd got a similar secretive rebuttal when she asked the Trade Minister which British banks were funding the sales to Indonesia with government credit. She was told that getting the information would incur 'disproportionate costs' – exactly what the Tories used to say.[39]

During the first two months of the Blair Government, Procurement Services International was able to export all but thirty of its Tactica 'riot control' vehicles. These had already been involved in demonstrations in which two students had died. '[The others] will soon be out there on the streets,' Nick Oliver boasted to Martyn Gregory. Oliver confirmed that the vehicles were headed for East Timor, where he said he, as a Territorial Army captain, had been on patrol 'regularly' with the notorious Kopassus forces. He dismissed the slaughter in East Timor, comparing it with Northern Ireland. 'The difference', he said, 'is that in East Timor they do it in blocks of 200, and in Northern Ireland they do one or two a day.'[40]

With his 'review' of arms sales under way, Cook had meetings at the Foreign Office with two 1997 Nobel Peace Prize winners, Bishop Carlos Felipe Ximines Belo and José Ramos-Horta, of East Timor. He assured them Britain would 'speak up' for East Timor in Europe and that his government would not license any weapons that might be used for internal repression. At a public meeting in London, Bishop Belo made a direct appeal. 'Please, I beg you,' he said, 'do not sustain any longer a conflict which without these sales could never have been pursued in the first place, nor for so very long.' Apart from the *Morning Star*, no one reported his words.

Journalists were, however, out in force at the Foreign Office the following week to hear Robin Cook speak on 'human rights in a new century'. This was his 'mission statement' mark two. However, this time, instead of a heroic video to introduce him, Zeinab Bedawi, the Channel 4 news presenter, and Martin Bell, the former BBC war correspondent, were there to give a warm welcome to the Foreign Secretary and his 'ethical' stand. In the invited audience were editors, foreign editors and representatives of 'non-governmental' organisations. While they were taking their seats, Foreign Office officials lied to diplomatic correspondents that there was 'no evidence' of Hawk aircraft deployed in East Timor.

Cook began his speech by saying that 'all nations belong to the same international community' and are 'neighbours in a global village [who] share a global economy'. This, as the aid workers in the audience knew, was manifestly false; there was one economy for the rich and one for the poor, causing the greatest wealth disparity since records were kept. They also knew that British policy and the British arms trade were pillars of this distortion. 'Countries with the strongest authoritarian rule', Cook went on, 'are more often than not countries which the global economy has passed by.'

The opposite is true; authoritarian regimes are often those that benefit most from the 'global economy': such as the Suharto regime, the recipient not only of British arms but of tens of millions of pounds in 'soft' loans to help pay for them. Cook announced that Britain would fund an 'NGOs' centre to enable the voluntary aid agencies to have 'a fuller opportunity to put forward their views'. This is a sinister development. The problem for non-governmental organisations is that they are already drawn too close to government through funding and their tax-exempt charitable status and they serve increasingly to neutralise and de-radicalise movements for real change, often remaining silent on the true complicity of their Western donors in the denial of human rights. What Cook, or rather the Foreign Office, wants is a more efficient way of co-opting and controlling them.

Cook pledged that Britain would help pay for a tribunal to try war crimes in the former Yugoslavia. How ironic. An international criminal tribunal on the causes and effects of the international arms trade would see the British Government not as a contributor, but as a defendant. More than two-thirds of British arms exports go to countries with appalling human rights records; and falsified end-user certificates, as exposed in the Scott Report, make this a conservative estimate.[41]

Cook's speech was a familiar exercise in Foreign Office cynicism, in which the new incumbent sought to justify his loyalty to the status quo by abusing noble words like 'solidarity', 'hope' and 'freedom' and exploiting the sentiments of the Universal Declaration of Human Rights. 'These are duties we claim for ourselves,' he said, 'and which we therefore have a duty to demand for those who do not yet enjoy them. As Tony Blair has often reminded us, rights bring with them responsibilities . . .'

The most indigestible Cookism was his call for a 'national effort to defend human rights wherever they are under threat'. Almost as an insult, it seemed, to those who work selflessly for human rights around the world, often in adverse conditions aggravated by the British Government's policies, Cook preached, 'If Britain as a nation wishes to promote our values and defend human rights then it cannot all be left to government. Every part of civic society has its role to play [in] bringing hope to those who look to us for help.'[42]

No questions were allowed. And no journalists, to their shame, spoke up. One would have been forgiven for thinking it was all an elaborate hoax. Less than a fortnight later, Cook announced the results of his 'thorough review'; again, no questions were allowed. Instead of addressing the House of Commons, he issued a press release. 'It was', he wrote, 'not realistic or practical to revoke licences which were valid and in force at the time of our election.' The problem, whispered the Foreign Office briefers, was that the government would be 'liable to pay out huge compensation'.

In fact, the Export of Goods (Control) Order 1994 clearly states that a licence granted by the Secretary of State 'may be revoked or varied by the Secretary of State at any time'. Legal advice commissioned by the World Development Movement confirmed 'a wide discretion in [the Act] to allow the Secretary of State to revoke any licence that has been granted'. There was nothing in private law that would allow action against ministers and 'a revocation of the licence therefore will not lead to the government having to pay damages or compensation to the licensee'. Moreover, with a change in government, 'it would be a proper use of the powers [of the Act] to consider the revocation of these licences [to Indonesia]'.[43]

This was never tested; and those vulnerable faraway people fighting for their freedom, 'who look to us for help', now face the arrival of more British aircraft 'designed . . . to shoot high velocity cannon and deliver ordnance at low levels against unprotected human beings'.[44] Riot control vehicles and water cannon, of the same type used to crush pro-democracy demonstrators, would be soon on their way. ('I was personally surprised that we export water cannons, which we don't use in Britain,' Cook told BBC Radio. 'I will be asking some searching questions about that.')[45]

Cook's 'review' amounted to a ban on electric-shock batons, leg-irons and other 'torture equipment' which, like his earlier ban on land-mines, merely enshrined in law a *de facto* ban that was already in force. The contrast between these mostly symbolic actions and the lucrative sale of military aircraft and other repressive equipment to Indonesia meant that Labour, like the Tories, was prepared only to limit arms sales when there was little financially at stake.

The Blair Government's ban on handguns is not dissimilar. Following the massacre at Dunblane, the Shadow Home Secretary, Jack Straw, declared, 'We cannot take risks with public safety in the interests of sport. Allowing .22 calibre weapons to remain legal would be fraught with difficulty . . .

Such guns have no place in a decent society. If there is any doubt, remember the children of Dunblane.'[46]

What he did not say was that, under Labour, it would be perfectly all right to continue sending British guns to 'decent societies' abroad. The British American Security Information Council has monitored an extraordinary rise in the number of export licences for handguns issued by the Department of Trade and Industry, now presided over by Margaret Beckett. This means that large numbers of guns prohibited in Britain are sold wholesale abroad. The Department of Trade refuses to say how many guns because, says an official, details of the trade are 'commercially confidential'. What is known is that the Blair Government has approved the sale of handguns to most of Europe, the United States, the Far East, Algeria, Sri Lanka and Colombia: countries beset either by war, state violence or a great deal of violent crime.[47]

Indonesia's gestapo, Kopassus, will continue to get British Aerospace Heckler and Koch machine-guns that can fire 400-metre-per-second bullets at the rate of 800 rounds per minute. Major-General Prabowo, the storm troopers' commander and Suharto's son-in-law, is so grateful for his hi-tech tools of repression from Britain that he has pronounced himself 'an admirer of the British'.

In the first year of the Labour administration, the government staged one of the biggest-ever arms jamborees, at Farnborough. Some 300 UK arms companies mounted exhibitions under Ministry of Defence auspices. The government invited buyers from more than ninety countries, including those on Amnesty International's 'Torture List', such as Turkey, Saudi Arabia and Indonesia.

General Feisal Tanjung is Commander-in-Chief of the Indonesian armed forces, and General Wiranto is Army Chief of Staff. In the build-up to the rigged elections in 1997, Tanjung oversaw a huge military show of force, including Scorpion tanks from Britain, and announced a policy of 'contained repression' in which troops would be ordered to 'shoot on sight' anyone who 'violates the law'. Wiranto, a particularly ruthless Suharto loyalist, was even more forthright:

'Those who want to disturb the elections will be wiped out.'[48]

When Douglas Hurd was Tory Foreign Secretary, he occasionally referred to the 'moral imperative' in foreign policy-making. 'We should penalise particularly bad cases of repression and abuse of human rights,' he once said. Of course he did the opposite, and only the naïve were surprised. The difference was that he did not bother with Mandelson-style media shows and 'reviews' that are deceptions.

In the week that Cook announced his 'ethical mission statement', the Indonesian Minister for Defence, Edi Sudradjat, was telling the Jakarta press that talks were already under way with Britain for the purchase of eighteen *more* Hawks. 'The political change in Britain will not effect our negotiations for an additional purchase of eighteen Hawks,' he said.[49] In fact, the eleven new military contracts recently approved by Blair were then under way, covering everything from bombs and ammunition to nuclear equipment.[50]

Perhaps the most sinister side to Cook's 'ethical' policy was revealed in a confidential letter sent by his private secretary to 10 Downing Street. The letter said the Foreign Secretary wanted a 'better grip' on the 'unfocused' and 'wayward' campaigns by Members of the European Parliament in support of human rights. In future, these should be directed along lines 'more supportive' of the British Government. He cited the MEPs' 'negative' opposition to Britain's murderous arms customer in Turkey as typical of their waywardness. In other words, as Britain takes over the European presidency, its new controllers want to gag those in the EU who object to its gun-running and death-dealing.[51]

The truth is that Labour's relationship with the crusaders in the Foreign Office and military establishment is no different from that of its Tory predecessors. If anything, it is more obedient. The new Defence Secretary, George Robertson, quickly exhibited the obligatory deference to the Ministry of Defence and its fiefdom. He seems to have gone further, even proposing a 'military experience' for new Labour MPs, who, he says, should spend at least twenty-one days 'getting to know' the Army, Navy or Air Force. 'I want them to be able to see from the inside', he said, 'what is done and why our troops have got such a world-wide reputation.' In an internal memorandum, the Armed Forces Minister, John Reid, effused, 'This is a marvellous scheme . . . interesting, challenging, exciting and out of the ordinary.'[52]

Also said to be 'driven' by a new 'ethical' policy, Robertson's own 'review' pointedly excludes two principal items. The first is the Eurofighter, designed specifically for combat with aircraft of the Soviet Union, which no longer exists. In 1997, the costs of this more than doubled to £42 billion, the equivalent of the GDP of the Republic of Ireland. The second is Trident, which, like the Eurofighter, was designed exclusively for a war against the defunct Soviet Union and whose long-term costs exceed the Eurofighter's. It requires little imagination to apply these figures to the National Health Service, schools, a literacy campaign, poverty, the transport system.

Asked about Trident when in opposition, Blair assured the nation he was prepared to 'pull the trigger'.[53] His defence spokesman at the time, David Clark, devoted himself to laying out New Labour's 'long-term defence policy'. He began by dismissing the campaign against nuclear disarmament as 'a zany idea of the past'.[54] In a long Commons statement of 'principles', Clark attacked the Major Government for not giving *enough* support to the arms industry.

'It is because we believe', he said, 'that it is in Britain's national and economic interest to have a defence industrial base and because the Tories have inflicted such damage on it that we have launched our own strategy for a secure future for the defence industry. [Labour] believe, unlike the government, that the British defence industry is a strategic part not only of our defence effort but of our manufacturing capability. We will work with the defence industry to identify technologies in which we lead the world and to ensure that they realise their potential.'[55]

When I interviewed Clark at the time, he gave me the up-to-date Washington/Ministry of Defence line about 'unstable' dictators rattling their missiles – missiles supplied, of course, by British Aerospace and its 'market' competitors. 'You must understand', he said, 'that the threat is now coming from dictators who can actually cause damage to your civilised West.'

I asked him which dictators justified Britain keeping a nuclear-armed Trident. He replied, 'Some unstable dictator might have the wherewithal to lob a missile at France or Spain or Portugal or Turkey or Greece . . . even if he can't hit Britain at the moment.'

'Which dictator?' I asked. 'Where?'

'Er, down there, in Africa . . .'

He boasted that, whereas the Tories spend on average 'only' 5·8 per cent of GNP on defence, Labour Governments have consistently spent 6·45 per cent. 'It's no wonder,' he said, 'that military men throughout the country have been telling us that they always do better under a Labour Government than under the Conservatives.'

Or as Prime Minister Blair put it, 'Britain must maintain its historic role as a global player.'

Occasionally, out of the bent morality and intellect required in the arms business, there is a glittering flash of honesty. In July 1994, I attended a ceremony at Sir Basil Zaharoff's old firm, Vickers plc, when 290 Challenger tanks were handed over to the British Army at a cost of £2.5 million each. The Vickers public relations officer, a sardonic man only weeks away from retirement, reminded me that the company also made baby incubators. 'You see,' he said, 'we blow them to bits at one end of the spectrum and stick them together at the other end.'

Sam Cummings, the biggest dealer in small arms in the world, is just as honest in his cynicism. His six-storey Manchester warehouse, standing next to a Gothic church, contains some 300,000 weapons which he exports to governments and various intermediaries – 'under HMG regulations, of course,' he says with a nodding grin.

Cummings dresses like an old-fashioned bank manager and neither smokes nor drinks. He and his accountant, Mr

Spence, have sandwiches for lunch. Yet he clearly relishes his fame, as his walls are covered with photographs of himself with celebrities. In his book, *The Arms Bazaar*, Anthony Sampson describes Cummings as 'genial and innocent, with a beatific smile, like a boy who has been a gun-freak, and has suddenly found all his wishes come true – which is, more or less, what he is'.[56]

When I went to see him, Cummings happily posed with a Kalashnikov automatic weapon in front of a Vietnamese flag. 'You see, my friend,' he said, shaking his world-weary head, 'if weapons did not exist, human folly would find something else.' He used the expression 'human folly' a great deal, as if it had nothing to do with Sam Cummings. He also said, 'I am just a simple businessman' and 'business is business', and 'if I didn't do it, somebody else would'.

The slave traders said as much.

Professor Michael Cooley was a leading aircraft design engineer who, during a distinguished career at Lucas Aerospace, helped pioneer strategies to convert the arms industry to peacetime production. 'In my twenty-two years in defence,' he said, 'I never met one worker, either a scientist or an engineer or a manual worker on the shop floor, who said they only wanted to work on weapons – not one.'

I asked him how he replied to those who insisted that defence contracts sustained jobs. 'In many ways,' he said, 'that's a downright lie. If they want to have a defence industry for military reasons, that's their political issue, but it must not be confused with jobs. In some areas of the defence industry, it costs £600,000 to create just one job. Now if the government put a fraction of that money into alternatives, almost anything would be possible.

'I can list 5,000 new products, beginning with systems for renewable energy to monitoring and control devices, used in aircraft design, that could combat our biggest killer, cardiovascular disease. At the end of the Second World War in Britain, 3·5 million people were demobbed and 3·25 million were taken out of the defence industry. How? There was a national plan and government support.

'I'm not saying conversion is easy, but it can be done; it needs only the political will. At the same time I think it's important that all of us understand that the future has yet to be built by people like you and me, and that the choices are becoming stark; and one of them is to use the skill and ability we now have concentrated in the defence industry. I don't think that's Utopian. When you consider the human and environmental problems facing us, it seems to me entirely practical.'

In Britain, almost half of all government research and development funds goes on the military and the arms industry. This could be redirected to a Conversion Agency in the Department of Trade and Industry, which would administer a low-interest fund to finance conversion and retraining. There are plenty of imaginative alternatives; and some companies have already shown what can be done. Babcock Thorn used to refit warships at the Rosyth naval dockyards; it now refits London Underground and mainline railway carriages, and its defence work has dropped to less than a quarter of total production.

It is generally agreed that if Britain's military spending was cut by half, it would still equal the average of other European nations. And if the billions released – £42 billion over six years, according to the World Development Movement – were invested in making possible Michael Cooley's vision, and in rebuilding vital industries and restoring the devastated public services, the modest premises upon which civilised life used to be based in Britain might even return. 'The values of human rights, civil liberties and democracy', to quote Robin Cook, might also return. 'If we betray these basic principles for the sake of a fast buck,' said Cook, 'we deserve not to be forgiven.'[57]

III

INSIDE BURMA

THE GOLDEN LAND

I call on governments to enact sanctions against the
oppressors of my people in the name of democracy and
decency.

Aung San Suu Kyi, the democratically elected
(and banned) leader of Burma

AT DAWN CROWS glide without a quiver among the great
silhouettes that rise like cathedrals in the desert. The only
sound is the chiming of a tree of bells, the only visible
humanity an urchin asleep on a parapet below a gilded pin-
nacle and its great diamond: the signpost to Nirvana. The
sunlight refracted through mist reveals a city whose secular
life has vanished, leaving buildings the equivalent of Chartres
and as grand as anything the Greeks raised to their gods. Built
in the eleventh and twelfth centuries by kings seeking
redemption, this is Pagan, the ancient capital of Burma and
described in its scriptures as its secret heart.

In the most celebrated temple, Ananda, with its mitre-like
pyramid, there are four colossal Buddhas, each standing more
than thirty feet above its throne. As the light catches one of
them, it is smiling. As you get closer, the smile becomes enig-
matic, then it fades. As you walk to one side and look back,
the expression is melancholy. Walk on and it becomes fear
veiled in pride. I have not seen anything like it. For the devout,
no doubt, it symbolises Buddha's timeless wisdom. For me, it
is the face of modern Burma.

In 1990 more than 4,000 people lived here. They were

given two weeks to leave: some a few days. The city was being opened to foreign tourism and only guides and the staff of a planned strip of hotels could stay. The people's homes were bulldozed and they were marched at gunpoint to a shadeless, waterless stubble that is a dustbowl in the dry season and runs with mud during the monsoon.

Their new houses are of straw and poor-quality bamboo and stand mostly out of sight of the tour buses that will come down a new and empty dual carriageway with its freshly-painted double yellow line. Those villagers who objected were sent out on to the barren plain or they were subdued with beatings, or they were taken away in the night. Two are believed to be still in prison.

The dispossession of the descendants of those who built one of the last wonders of the ancient world was mild by the standards of Ne Win and the military dictatorship which has ruled Burma since 1962. In February 1995, the International Confederation of Free Trade Unions reported that a million people had been forced from their homes in Rangoon alone, in preparation for tourism and foreign investment.[1]

In order to bring the city's golf course up to standard for rich foreigners, mostly Japanese businessmen, the army seized adjacent land, where a community had lived for forty years. When an armed blockade failed to make them move, one member of each family was arrested and taken to prison. The rest were driven in trucks to a satellite town fifteen miles away.[2]

This happens frequently. In 1996, a thousand people were expelled from the village they had occupied for generations near Lashio in Shan state, so that the army could extend the golf course for tourists. They were dumped on a dry mound where it is not possible even to sink a well and from where they can watch their water nourishing the greens of the golf course. Throughout Burma an estimated 5 million people have been forcibly exiled in 'satellite townships', where they are compelled silently to construct Burma's new façade of 'economic growth'.

'I pass in the spirit amid the courts of the great golden pagoda in Rangoon,' wrote an Edwardian traveller. '[There is] the light of a hundred tiny candles guttering on the ground. The smell of incense is wafted to my nostrils, and the fragrance of the frangipani perfumes the air like scent. I could go on with a hundred of such scenes, all different, and all indelibly impressed on my brain; for the charm of the most fascinating country in the world, the country of Burma, has laid hold upon me and will be with me to the end.'[3]

The subtle and ethereal are unchanged. In the capital, Rangoon, frangipani perfumes the air and incense fills the covered bridges, wrapped as if in tinfoil, surrounding the great golden pagoda of Shwe Dagon, built in the lifetime of Buddha 2,500 years ago. Here, astrologers announce the future, and families seek the blessings of a passing monk and his place of honour in a group photograph. There is a normality to this: eyes that have cultivated an opaqueness, allowing them to navigate through constant states of fear, come to life here; even a few words exchanged with a foreigner can seem safe with Lord Buddha close by.

The golden dusks change that. Like ruined Pagan, the streets of Rangoon, a city of 4 million, are suddenly quiet except for the wind in the confusion of overhead wires. Colonial colonnades frame people, motionless before they move on quickly. Traffic lights turn red, yet a lorryload of troops drives through. The only *cyclo* driver on this street dismounts and slips into the shadows. 'People are kidnapped at night,' said an informant, 'and never seen again. Once the *cyclo* drivers were taken away to become porters for the army, pack animals with ammunition and sometimes human mine-sweepers. You never know when it will happen.'

A Baptist pastor interviewed secretly said, 'We are not free to have meetings, not free to print books, not free to gather together in any way we want. In sermons we must leave out certain words, like "democracy". My wife tells me, "Be careful about your sermon. You are not the only one who will disappear." She is referring to herself and our children. This means for us fear – fear all around.' A United Nations Special Rapporteur has described 'an atmosphere of pervasive fear in Burma'.[4]

Isolated for thirty-four years, this 'land of golden hues', of spires and gem-encrusted woods and forests of teak and mahogany, has been relegated to among the poorest on earth, its people terrorised and subdued on such a scale that, for me, the parallels with Indonesia's military rule in East Timor are striking. Last year the United Nations Commission on Human Rights reported, as it has done year after year, that the following violations were 'commonplace' in Burma: 'Torture, summary and arbitrary executions, forced labour, abuse of women, politically motivated arrests and detention, forced displacement, important restrictions on the freedoms of expression and association and oppression of ethnic and religious minorities . . .'[5]

One can take at random any of the numerous studies by Amnesty International. There is this, from September 1995: 'Conditions in labour camps are so harsh that hundreds of prisoners have died as a result. In the largest detention facility at least 800 political prisoners are being held. Military Intelligence personnel regularly interrogate prisoners to the point of unconsciousness. Even the possession of almost any reading material is punishable. Political prisoners are liable to be sent to "police dog cells", where police dogs are normally kept. Elderly and sick people and even handicapped people are placed in leg-irons and forced to work.' Burma, concludes Amnesty, is 'a prison without bars'.[6]

During the genocide in Cambodia, Pol Pot's Minister of Information, a woman called Yun Yat, quipped, 'The problem is becoming extinguished. Hence there is no problem.'[7] Pick up a travel brochure from any of the famous names in British tourism – British Airways, Oriental Express, Kuoni – and there is no problem. To British Airways, Burma offers 'the ultimate in luxury' and a 'fabulous prize' for its Executive Club members. 'To find an unspoilt country today may seem impossible,' says the Orient Express brochure. 'But Burma is such a place. It has retained its charm, its fascinating traditions and the inexhaustible politeness of its people.'

Indeed, Rangoon 'means "end of strife". It is easy to see why. Its easy-going ways are a tonic to the Western traveller.'

What's more, this 'truly unique experience' includes a 'free lecture on Burma's history and culture'. The lecture makes no mention of the history made in 1988.[8]

In 1988, the year before the democracy movement in China was crushed in Tiananmen Square, the people of Burma rose up and as many as 10,000 were killed by the army. Unlike the Chinese leadership, the generals in Rangoon moved quickly to curtail foreign media coverage. There were no TV cameras and no satellite images to shock the world. This cryptic Telex message reached the Associated Press in Bangkok from its office in Rangoon: 'Daddy has been taken away. He won't be able to answer your queries.'[9] Aung San Suu Kyi, the Nobel Peace Prize winner, told me, 'Countries and events keep slipping from the headlines, and we slipped.'

On May 27, 1990, 82 per cent of the eligible population voted for the parliamentary candidates of the National League for Democracy, the party led by Aung San Suu Kyi, who was then under house arrest. Stunned by an election result they believed impossible, the generals threw into prison those MPs who tried to form a government, then waited as the world forgot about Burma.

Milan Kundera's aphorism that 'the struggle of people against power is the struggle of memory against forgetting' might well have been written for the Burmese.[10] In 1995, during the fiftieth anniversary celebrations of victory over the Japanese, a BBC reporter asked a British veteran of the Burma campaign, 'What about the Burmese?' He replied that they had 'vanished' during the fighting at Mandalay. To my knowledge, that was one of the few references to them in the television commemoration of Britain's 'forgotten army' in Burma and the prisoners of war who built the Burma–Siam railway. Yet alongside the 16,000 British and Allied soldiers who died as slaves on the 'death railway' were more than 100,000 Burmese and other Asian dead.

There is, as I found, scarce reference to them on a brass plaque erected not long ago by Australian veterans outside the gates of the Commonwealth war cemetery at Thanbyuzayat, near Moulmein, in the south of Burma. The death railway began here and the graves are in neat rows on the site of one of the field hospitals. 'Deep in my heart', says the inscription on the grave of Lance-Corporal A. H. Wilson of the Sherwood Foresters, 'a memory is kept of the son I lost but will never forget.' And on the grave of Private C. R. Bayly of the Australian Army Service Corps: 'Loving husband of Jane, daddy of Janice, Gwenda and Judith'. Like a suburban lawn laid in the jungle, with the list of names in a visitors' book lovingly kept by the Burmese caretaker in a woollen bag he hangs from a tree, it leaves the casual visitor deeply moved.

Outside the gates, the railway is still there: the same rusted lines, the same sleepers laid by the young men in the cemetery: a life for every sleeper, one of the survivors has calculated. A Japanese locomotive stands as if abandoned on the day the horror ended. It is jet black and on the track in front of it is a square of barbed wire enclosing three petrified figures in cement: a Japanese guard with a rifle and two emaciated, shaven-headed PoWs working with pickaxes. A few hundred yards further on, the line connects with a railway going south to the town of Ye. This is being extended to Tavoy on the Andaman Sea, where history is repeating itself.

This is Burma's great secret. In a bid for the dubious respectability and the hard currency that comes with tourism and foreign investment, the junta that goes by the Orwellian acronym of SLORC, which stands for State Law and Order Restoration Council, declared 1996 'Visit Myanmar Year'. (They renamed the country Myanmar, which, as the travel writer James Strachan pointed out, is the same as Germany insisting upon everyone calling it Deutschland.)

In a crash programme to restore the neglected infrastructure of the country – roads, bridges, airports, railways – the regime has turned Burma into a vast slave-labour camp. The moat around the imperial palace in Mandalay has been excavated and rebuilt almost entirely by forced labour, including chain gangs guarded by troops. The regime has claimed that 'contributing labour' is a noble Asian tradition and, anyway, many of the workers are convicted criminals who 'volunteered to work in the open air'.

In a state where the law is arbitrarily decreed, the term 'convicted criminal' can embrace a person guilty of having been elected to office, or of handing out leaflets calling for democracy (five years' hard labour), or of singing a song the generals don't like (seven years' hard labour), or of speaking to the BBC (fourteen years' hard labour), or of sending a report to the United Nations (fifteen years).[11]

The new death railway is the symbol of Burma's suffering. Although human rights studies have documented the testimonies of its slave workers, few outsiders have seen it or the slave camps along the route. This is because most of the southern part of the country, close to the Thai border, remains a restricted zone and foreigners are unwelcome. It is Burma's gulag.

Having entered Burma in 1996 posing as travel consultants ('specialists in adventure and exotic travel'), my film-making partner David Munro and I headed south, hoping to find the railway construction site by tracing it along the old Second World War death railway. We carried small cameras, including one with a lens the size of a pinhole concealed in a shoulder strap: an improvisation based on the camera bag David had designed for our secret filming in East Timor in 1993. We left Rangoon well before dawn, travelling over spine-gutting roads, often without headlights, and passing watchtowers near where prisoners in chains were already quarrying rock. The roadblocks were guarded by boys who were asleep or uninterested; money fluttered across to them.

As the sun rose, small silhouettes became young girls holding out silver urns for contributions to the welfare of their villages, a Buddhist tradition. Their face masks of *thanaka*, a yellow paste made from tree-bark that protects and nourishes the skin, gave them a surreal and ancient quality, like small ghosts emerging from the jungle or exotic faces in a Victorian album.

The towns, too, appeared as a step back in time, as if the British were merely away at their hill stations. Ancient sewing machines whirred on balconies; the roads were filled with bicycles not cars, save a few 1940s Austins and Morrises; piles of carbon paper were for sale, and sleeveless sweaters and 78 rpm vinyl records. In the street, a professional letter writer demonstrated his copperplate. Everyone, men and women, wore the *longhi*, the traditional sarong.

People studied us with due curiosity; in remote Burma a whole generation has grown up having never laid eyes on Europeans. They would catch themselves and look away. To take too great an interest in a foreigner is to alert the local snoop for 'MI', the hated Military Intelligence. To talk openly to a foreigner is to invite arrest, interrogation and worse. Surveillance is a way of life, though inefficient. Hotels must copy guest-registration forms as many as fourteen times. On the day we arrived in Tavoy, all 'independent travellers' were barred in this part of Mon state. Fortunately, all Myanmar Airways flights back to Rangoon had been commandeered by the army and there was no way back.

Tavoy is suspended somewhere between Queen Victoria's birth and the 1950s. It is one of those so-called backwaters that seem unaware of their beauty, with streets of decorous teak houses in the gingerbread style, the grandest with lace iron balconies. Other buildings are dungeon-like, with iron bars and damp trickling over last year's calendar and torn posters of coy females holding parasols. Drays carrying great jugs of water and jack-fruit plod up and down; our car was as unusual as its occupants. With the Tavoy River and the Andaman Sea near by, there is a lushness that is menacing: a sense that given half a chance the jungle would reclaim everything.

On a hill above the town is the Lyaung-daw-mu, one of the largest reclining Buddhas in the world. Built in 1931, it is 243 feet long and 69 feet high; the palm of one hand is 33 feet across and the big toe more than twice my height. Two awe-struck soldiers kneeling in its vast shadow without their boots were no longer oppressors. Yet at the end of the long flight of stone steps down to the road a truck with steel-helmeted troops ground its brakes and forged ruthlessly through the scattering bicycles.

In the centre of Tavoy is a government guest house built in

the late nineteenth century in the grand Scottish manner. It has teak floors and vast verandas, louvred doors and windows and arthritic ceiling fans. In the gardens are the lush mohur and pyinkado trees that George Orwell describes in *Burmese Days*. The power comes and goes. As everywhere else, the water is undrinkable and the mosquitoes malarial. At night, if there is a wind off the sea, it pitches and creaks like an oak-hulled barque riding below its Plimsoll line. Apart from a nearby warren of plywood, padlocked cages, it is the only hotel in Tavoy. David and I decided to take a risk. With our false papers as tour operators, we presented ourselves to the civilian District Governor and sought lodgings for the night.

The District Governor was U Pan Ko (the 'U' stands for 'uncle', a term of respect) and we found him a few weeks away from retirement after forty-two years in the Civil Service. The shape of Buddha himself, he seemed a memory of the last days of the Raj. Educated by Scottish priests at St Paul's School in Rangoon, he said he loved things Scottish. 'Is it true', he asked, 'that Glenfiddich, not Glenlivet, is the best malt? Good God, have I had it wrong all these years?' He spoke of Burma, not Myanmar, Rangoon, not Yangon (the SLORC word).

Wedged behind a teak desk heaped with yellowing, beribboned files that fluttered beneath the turning fan directly above, he sucked pills from a variety of bottles assembled on an inkstand dated 1920. A modern white phone looked out of place. Every now and then he would pick it up, listen and mumble, 'Engaged.'

It never rang.

'Did you know', he said, without lifting his gaze from his papers, 'that Caribbean is a Scottish word?' He reminded me of the scoundrel in *Burmese Days*, U Po Kyin, a venal magistrate 'whose earliest memory was watching the British troops march into Mandalay'.[12] Such a comparison did not seem unkind after we had glimpsed him the following night draining a bottle of Johnnie Walker with a SLORC general and two colonels, whose troops oversee the work on the death railway.

David and I calculated we had a day and a half to find the railway construction sites before we were caught. From Tavoy, we followed the line of embankments north into the jungle, got lost, despaired, then came upon a clearing that presented what might have been a tableau of Victorian industrial England. Scores of people were building a viaduct across a dry river bed. From out of jungle so dense that its bamboo formed great wickerwork screens, they were carving the railway. A twenty-foot-high embankment had been built with earth dug by hoe and hand from huge holes. The majority were slave labourers, of whom many were children.

Laboriously and clumsily they wrested clay from the excavations, sharing a hoe between three. One small girl in a long blue dress struggled to wield a hoe taller than herself, then fell back exhausted and winced, holding her aching shoulder. 'How old are you?' I asked. 'Eleven,' came the reply.

The children carried loads of mud mixed with straw in baskets and dishes on their heads and agonised under the weight of it. They poured it into a vat and grinder, turned by two tethered oxen. The sticky clay, almost as hard as rock, was gathered by the smallest, one of them ten years old and small enough to fit up to his shoulders in a hole directly beneath the grinder. Horrified, I watched a load of clay tip over him, almost burying him. Another child rushed to help, but did not have the strength to drag him free. I reached under his arms and pulled him out.

The others laughed, as if this was normal. How many children are trapped and injured or die like that? The bridge we saw under construction was one of forty, with children engaged on all of them.

The system works like this. Every village along the way must give its labour 'voluntarily', regardless of age or the state of people's health. Advanced pregnancy is no excuse. If people protest that, as peasant farmers, their labour is all they have to keep them and their families alive, they are fined and their possessions confiscated. If a whole village objects, the headman is made a public example of, beaten or killed, and all the houses razed. The army provides neither implements nor food. Cerebral malaria, the type that kills, is so virulent here that the only safe preventative is an antibiotic virtually unknown in Burma.

'I had malaria but still they made me work on the railway,' a former Civil Servant told me in a nearby safe area controlled by the Karen National Union. 'I was so sick I kept falling down as I worked. I saw one old man accidentally drop his load into the river. As he tried to retrieve it, the soldiers shot him in the head. I could see the water turn red with his blood, then the river carried him away.

'No one can escape them. SLORC officials or the army go from village to village. They take even a child, as long as he is strong enough, without asking permission of the parent. If the villagers give them Toddy juice [local palm-based alcohol], maybe they are happy. Otherwise, just walking past them can be dangerous. When a woman is asked to give "voluntary service" by the army, even if she is pregnant, she has no choice; some give birth while they work. On the railway, prisoners are used like cows and buffaloes, having to pull rollers. If the rollers don't move, the soldiers beat them with huge canes. I saw this. They were shackled and given no water.'

A man who escaped with his wife expressed a sense of the past converging with the present. He said, 'The SLORC are no different from the Japanese in forcing us to build the railway. I worked for months on it before I ran away. I saw people dying because of landslides or fever. Some of the bodies were never found. Oh dear, dear, in some cases only the head was found or a foot. They didn't bother to bury the bodies properly, with a funeral. They just dug a hole and left them there.'

His wife said, 'I feel for the children. They are too young to anticipate danger, so they are vulnerable. They are the ones who die first. If a worker or a porter is seriously ill, he is left behind in the jungle. If he can't crawl to his village, he usually dies. If he has a fracture of the thigh or leg, so he can't work, he is bayoneted to death.' I asked her if she knew why she had

165

been forced to work in this way. 'We were told nothing,' she said. 'We overheard we were building a railway so that a French oil company could run a pipeline through; and foreigners came to look over the site.'

The oil company is Total, which is owned in part by the French Government, and has its headquarters in Paris. With the American Unocal company, Total is building a $1 billion pipeline that will carry Burma's natural gas from beneath the Andaman Sea into Thailand. The deal will give the Rangoon generals an estimated $400 million a year over thirty years. According to Simon Billiness of the Boston-based Coalition for Corporate Withdrawal from Burma, the oil companies have paid $200–$300 million just in 'signing bonuses' – 'straight gravy for the generals'.[13] Since 1990, the year they cancelled the election result, it is estimated that the SLORC has received more than two-thirds of its foreign financial backing from oil companies.[14]

The companies deny that the railway is linked to the pipeline project; and while it is true that most supplies are likely to arrive by sea, there can be no doubt that the railway will allow the generals to protect their and the companies' investment. More than 5,000 Burmese troops have already been shipped to the pipeline area and army patrols protect Total personnel.

A former student leader from Rangoon, Koe Soe Naing (an alias), is one of a Thai-based group who have gathered evidence about human-rights abuses during the building of the railway and the pipeline. In February 1995, they travelled to where a section of the pipeline is being built. 'The army was so panicky,' he said, 'they deployed l,500 soldiers to try and find us. The villager who showed us the way [to the pipeline area] didn't know what he was doing. He was innocent. But his wife was arrested; they were newly married and had a child. She was tied and beaten in front of the other villagers for three days. On the last day both her hands were cut off by an army captain. I don't know what happened to her after that.'[15]

The pipeline will carry gas from two major offshore natural-gas fields whose discovery in 1994 promised a bonanza. Apart from Total and Unocal, the British company Premier Oil is part of a consortium with Nippon Oil and Texaco exploring the Andaman Sea. In 1993, Total was contacted by the National Coalition Government of the Union of Burma, the government-in-exile representing Aung San Suu Kyi's party. NCGUB officials provided the oil company with extensive evidence of slave labour along the route of the pipeline. They also described how the profits from the project would invariably buy the arms and ammunition to which more than half of Burma's budget is devoted, thus helping to underwrite the repression of the population.[16] Total has denied all knowledge of and complicity with slave labour – without answering the specific criticisms raised by Burma's democratic government in exile.[17]

The pipeline deal would not be possible without the collaboration of the Thai Government, whose Petroleum Authority is the single importer and consumer of the gas. The deal is little different from the logging, mining and fishing concessions which Thai companies have negotiated with Rangoon since 'development' in their own country decimated its natural resources. In return, the Thai military sends back refugees. In 1993, Thai troops burned down two vast refugee camps, reported the Bangkok *Nation*, in an operation 'probably related to the gas pipeline'.[18] Thousands of ethnic Mon refugees have since been forced back into Burma, many of them into the hands of SLORC troops. On the border, where the pipeline will enter Thailand, Burmese soldiers display Total pens in the pockets of their uniforms. 'Total is coming,' said one of them, with a broad smile.[19]

Human rights organisations have attempted to estimate the scale of the tragedy for the Burmese people. According to one study, some 60,000 people every day are forced into slave labour on the railway; in the eighteen months to April 1994, up to 300 had died. This is widely regarded as a conservative figure.[20]

'Look here,' said Pat James, Texas entrepreneur and important friend of the SLORC, 'the cost of labour is very low by international standards and that makes Myanmar a *very* attractive location. As for the human rights violations, the government here, on the inside, behind closed doors, is concerned about this. This is something they're truly concerned about. I'm not here to condemn or justify it. I'm in Myanmar because I *love* the tradition and the values, and the *passiveness* of the people. I mean the acceptance. That's it. They're learning, you see. They're begging, too – literally begging for the foreigners to come in and teach them.'[21]

Pat James is the doyen of the entrepreneurs now descending on Burma. His office in Rangoon has Country and Western Muzak and framed pictures of him signing deals with SLORC generals. He describes himself as 'a player in the New Myanmar' and, as such, has 'a lot of balls up in the air'. These balls are held aloft by his Eagle Group, named after the two eagles he keeps chained to his front balcony. There is an Eagle company to 'open doors for foreigners', another for 'financial advice', another 'for individually tailored tours', another for promoting 'luxury resorts on unspoilt beaches' and another for the soon-to-be opened Eagle Café, 'offering American food and ambience'.

James estimates that foreign investment in Burma has multiplied tenfold since 1992. 'It's not so much a gradual pick-up', he said, 'as a skyrocket.' This is disputed by the World Bank and the International Monetary Fund, which have yet to lend the generals a penny. What has begun is a familiar process in which a dictatorship's crimes against its people are unmentioned and 'forgotten' as foreign businessmen seek to justify what their governments call 'positive engagement' and 'critical dialogue'.

This is what happened in Indonesia in the mid-1960s when a bloody 'pro-business' military coup was followed by oppression and foreign investment; tourists were unaware that the car-parks of their new hotels on the 'paradise isle' of Bali covered the mass graves of their host government's victims. This allowed the Indonesian generals to show that it was possible to encourage mass tourism by isolating 'problem areas'. Even as they extinguished a third of East Timor's population, they could note that the growth in investment and tourism did not falter; for that 'problem area' was also quickly 'forgotten'.

When Burma's General Khin Nyunt, the head of Military Intelligence and the most powerful member of the SLORC, boasted that 'tourism will replace criticism from abroad', he is said to have had the Indonesian model in mind.[22]

There are striking similarities between the Indonesian and Burmese juntas. In 1993, the Burmese generals established a new mass political party, USDA, which resembles the Indonesian military front party, GOLKAR. And while the generals in Rangoon are groomed for membership of the 'international community', like their counterparts in Jakarta their principal role as oppressor is overshadowed by their new role as guarantor of foreign plunder.

The only real obstacle to the economy becoming a 'skyrocket', says Pat James, is the SLORC's 'image problem'. 'Right now,' he said, 'a lot of the British company funding is actually coming through companies from Singapore and Thailand. Projects you see are British and American, but other countries will be receiving credit on the ledger sheet.'

The SLORC regularly produces figures that show that Britain is by far the biggest foreign investor with $634 million, well ahead of France with its pipeline.[23] The British Government claims the actual investment is only a fraction of this, leaving some half a billion dollars apparently unaccounted for. The explanation may be that most British investment is channelled through secretive 'back doors' like the Virgin Islands, a British colony and tax haven. The American oil company Unocal pumps millions of dollars into Burma through the Virgin Islands, thus much of its pipeline investment is accounted for as 'British'.

Singapore is by far the most important 'back door'. The business autocracy which runs the island has long provided a conduit for deals between the West and regimes with an 'image problem'. The arms industry is a Singaporean speciality. European arms have been made under licence for, among others, Pol Pot and Saddam Hussein, while British-manufactured arms have been passed on to their buyers with phoney end-user certificates.

In 1995, the *Independent* disclosed that the British

company BMARC was able to conceal the fact that it supplied arms to Iran by sending them via Singapore, thereby circumventing a British Government embargo. What was not revealed was that in 1990 BMARC secretly supplied arms and ammunition to the Burmese generals through Singapore and in defiance of another British Government ban – on arms licences to Rangoon.[24]

Although most of its arms have come from China, it was not surprising that the SLORC should look to Singapore in its hour of need. In 1988, at the height of the popular uprising against the regime that saw most of the country on the streets, the Burmese Army was running out of bullets. A rushed delivery of ammunition from Singapore probably saved the junta. Two years later, as the country erupted again, Singapore once again came to the rescue, this time with ammunition supplied by BMARC, a subsidiary of the now bankrupt British multinational, Astra.

Gerald James, the former chairman of Astra, maintains his company and its shadowy subsidiaries were all but taken over by British intelligence, which ran a 'secret order book'. James told me he discovered the Burma sales order in a box of papers returned by Astra's receivers in 1995, following a demand for documents from the inquiry led by Sir Richard Scott into the arms-for-Iraq scandals. 'Until I found this,' he said, 'I wasn't aware we were supplying Burma. It became apparent, as we investigated BMARC's affairs, that they were running a secret order book. They would have supplied [the junta] with up to 30 and 35 millimetre ammunition and the relevant guns. I would imagine it [before the elections] was very significant.'[25]

On the surface, Western governments have been hostile to Burma since the military coup in 1962. While the official reason has been the regime's human rights record, a more plausible explanation is that the dictator Ne Win nationalised everything when he came to power, effectively closing Burma to Western capital. This changed in 1989 when the generals reinvented themselves as the SLORC and declared Burma 'open to free enterprise'.

The British were quick to respond. Richard Needham, Britain's Trade Minister in 1993, told Parliament, 'The government's policy is to provide no specific encouragement to British firms to trade or invest in Burma in view of the current political and economic situation there.' In the same breath he said, 'British business visitors to Rangoon can of course look to our embassy there for advice and support.' In written parliamentary replies, the government admitted that it had appointed four new trade promotion staff to the Rangoon Embassy and was organising British trade missions and helping to fund them.[26]

By 1995, most veils had been dropped. The Department of Trade and the London Chamber of Commerce funded a seminar in London called 'An introduction to Burma – the latest Tiger Cub'. The organiser was Peter Godwin, a merchant banker and government adviser on trade in south-east Asia. 'To be a Briton in Burma', he told the delegates, 'is a privilege.' He said he had been assured by the senior general in SLORC 'openly and categorically' that Burma's 'socialism' had been 'a mistake' and that this mistake had caused the upheavals in 1988. He made no reference to the generals murdering thousands of unarmed civilians, then throwing most of the elected government into prison. The 'good news', he said, 'is that economic growth is picking up.'[27]

Godwin had just returned from leading a government-backed trade mission to Burma when I met him in March 1996. Companies of the size and importance of GEC, Powergen and Rolls-Royce were represented. I asked him how he felt about doing business with some of the world's worst violators of human rights. He replied that he had gone to Burma 'to have the opportunity of addressing some of these [human rights] issues'. Then why did he not see Aung San Suu Kyi, the elected leader?

'The general context of such a call', he said, 'would not be ideal.'

I pointed out that there was documented evidence that some 2 million people were being forced to build the infrastructure of Burma in brutal conditions so that foreign investment might get off the ground. 'Isn't that a factor to you and your business colleagues?' I asked.

'I suppose it is, but the involvement of foreign companies is going to improve conditions quite substantially. No foreign company is likely to employ labour under those terms.'

'But you've got to use the roads and railways.'

'Indeed.'

'Well, the railways are being built with forced labour.'

'I've not been outside Rangoon . . .'

For arriving foreign businessmen and tourists the drive to their hotel from Rangoon airport inevitably includes a short detour along University Avenue. To the uninitiated, this has a *frisson* of the forbidden and seditious. Number 54 is the home of Aung San Suu Kyi, the 1991 Nobel Peace Prize winner. Here, she spent six years under house arrest until her release in July 1995.

For almost a year she was allowed to speak every Sunday from over her garden gate to several thousand supporters corralled behind barbed-wire barriers. This was not so much a concession by the regime as a showcase for the new 'openness' of 'Visit Myanmar Year'. When I first drove past her home, a coachload of Taiwanese tourists was just ahead of me, snapping through the tinted glass. What struck me, apart from the steely courage of the Burmese who came to listen to her and, in so doing, branded themselves opponents of the regime, was the Kafka-like absurdity of Burma's leader having to address her people standing on a chair behind her back fence.

Since her 'unconditional' release, Aung San Suu Kyi has been denied freedom of movement, so that today she is effectively again under house arrest. When she tried to travel to Mandalay to hold a meeting, the carriage of her train was uncoupled and left standing as the train pulled out. She cannot freely associate with anyone. Those Burmese who are allowed to pass through her gate take a huge risk: at the very least their names are noted and they can expect a call in the night. These days it is more likely they face arrest as soon as they leave.

Shortly before I interviewed her, eight members of a dance

troupe, who had celebrated Independence Day with her, 'disappeared'. They include the popular comedians U Pa Pa Lay and Lu Zaw, who are believed to have satirised the generals. Both have since been sentenced to seven years' hard labour and have been sent to a labour camp, where they are shackled day and night, and their health has deteriorated.[28]

Aung San Suu Kyi's immediate family are in England; her husband, Michael Aris, is an Oxford don, and the younger of their two sons is still at school. The regime has refused Dr Aris a visa. The ban, which appears to be indefinite, also applies to the two boys, who have been stripped of their Burmese citizenship. Every day, the official English-language newspaper, the *New Light of Myanmar*, mounts a vicious attack on Aung San Suu Kyi. She is 'obsessed by lust and superstition'; she 'swings around a bamboo pole brushed with cess'; she is 'drowning in conceit' and 'it is pitiable and at once disgusting to see a person [like her] suffering from insanity . . . now at a demented stage'.

The intimidation quickened as she defiantly called a congress of her party, the National League for Democracy, at her home in 1996. The junta's reaction was to arrest and imprison more than 250 party members. This did not stop 400 NLD members eluding the police and getting through her gate. Like delegates of a normal political party with democratic support, they discussed tactics, passed resolutions and debated a new constitution for Burma, almost as if the guns outside were not aimed at them.

The congress was an inspired manoeuvre by Aung San Suu Kyi; by demonstrating the illegitimacy of the regime, she evoked the unbroken spirit of democracy in Burma and the right of her party to govern, while outside a peaceful crowd of 10,000 converged on the house in defiance of the guns and a ban on gatherings of more than fifty.

Furious, the generals passed a law banning all further meetings at Aung San Suu Kyi's back gate and threatening a ten-year prison sentence for anyone who came. They decreed 'Law No. 5/96', which makes automatic a twenty-year sentence for anyone who advocates an 'unauthorised' state constitution or who 'commits acts disturbing public order': in other words, anyone who expresses political views different from those of the government.

One of those arrested was James Leander (Leo) Nichols, a well-known businessman of Greek and Burmese parentage. Known as 'Uncle Leo', he was the godfather and close confidant of Aung San Suu Kyi. He had helped her in numerous ways: by lending her his car, finding people to repair her dilapidated house, seeing that her words reached the outside world. After her release from house arrest, he had breakfast with her every Friday, providing his usual reassuring voice.

Seized at his home in the early hours of the morning, he was taken to Insein prison, where he was kept in solitary confinement on Death Row. According to the *New Light of Myanmar*, he was accused of 'providing general expenses for the democratic stunt actress'. He was summarily sentenced to three years for possessing two fax machines and nine telephones 'in contravention of the Burma Wireless Act'.

The charge was bogus; Nichols had made no secret of his professional life, and was the honorary consul for several Scandinavian countries and Switzerland. He was not an actively political person, more the kind of entrepreneur the SLORC might have enlisted to build bridges to the democracy movement. Aged sixty-five and diabetic, and suffering high blood pressure, he was interrogated by officers of MI14, the unit that deals with political prisoners and uses both physical and mental torture. He died after having reportedly been denied sleep for four nights. Officially, he suffered a stroke. His family had been prevented from seeing him.[29]

A memorial service was promptly banned by the regime (though an Australian friend managed to slip a bottle of whisky into his grave). The Danish Government, which Nichols represented, called on the European Union and the United Nations to impose trade sanctions on Burma. In spite of objections from the British Foreign Secretary, Malcolm Rifkind, the European Commission recommended the suspension of preferential tariffs to Burma.[30]

In the week that Nichols died, Rifkind's ministerial number two, Jeremy Hanley, told the House of Commons that Britain's Ambassador in Rangoon had been instructed to demand the release of the arrested NLD members and the restoration of rights under the United Nations Charter. 'We have made it clear to SLORC', he said, 'that the resumption of normal relations is conditional on progress in those key areas.' He added that the government had 'pulled the plug' on a forthcoming trade mission to Rangoon.[31]

As he spoke, a senior British official was flying into Rangoon in order to prepare for the next trade mission. Indeed, on the day Aung San Suu Kyi appealed to foreign governments not to do business with the SLORC, Mike Cohen, the Head of Exports to Asia and the Pacific at the Department of Trade and Industry, was meeting a senior official of the regime's investment agency. 'He was assessing the market in Burma for UK companies,' a Department of Trade press officer told me. But what about the ambassador's demands for democratic reform and the protection of human rights?

'Before financing other trade missions we want to evaluate the commercial prospects.'

But what about the minister's statement in Parliament about 'pulling the plug'?

'At this stage,' he said, 'there are to be no further trade missions . . .'

Then why did the DTI bother to send the Head of Export Sales all the way to Rangoon to assess the 'commercial prospects'?

'It's to see if further trade missions require consideration . . .'

This was the week, ironically, that another Nobel Peace Prize winner, Nelson Mandela, was in London, being given an effusive welcome by a British establishment which had done everything in its power to undercut him and to preserve the apartheid regime in Pretoria through investment and trade.

Shortly afterwards, the Labour Party made a strong call for sanctions against Burma. 'The government has argued that

175

such measures ultimately hurt the ordinary Burmese citizen more than the ruling elite,' said Shadow Foreign Office Minister Derek Fatchett. 'This argument was wrong when it was used to justify continued trade with the apartheid regime in South Africa, and it is still wrong today in regard to Burma.'

A year later, with Labour in power and Derek Fatchett elevated to the Foreign Office, he said the government 'will continue to provide British companies with routine advice about doing business in Burma'. This advice 'wherever possible' would 'draw to businessmen's attention statements by Daw Aung San Suu Kyi discouraging trade and investment in Burma'. There was no mention of sanctions. Nothing had changed.[32]

Unlike Britain's lucrative business with apartheid South Africa, actual British trade with Burma is small. What the Blair Government fears, as did its predecessor, is the animosity of the SLORC's allies, the dictatorships in China and Indonesia, which have human rights difficulties of their own and where British 'prospects', according to the *Financial Times*, 'have never been more exciting'. The hidden agenda of the British is not exclusive. The Western democracies, and Japan, are all betraying democracy in Burma and its leader while simultaneously honouring her with warm words and prizes.

In spite of studied sound and fury directed at the SLORC by the Clinton administration and Congress, a ban on 'new' investments to Burma exempts Unocal's pipeline project with Total, which will provide the generals with revenue for life. In 1996, the White House dispatched two 'special Burma envoys' to Asia: William Brown, a former US Ambassador to Thailand, and Stanley Roth, a former aide to Congressman Stephen Solarz, an enthusiastic supporter of the Khmer Rouge-dominated coalition which terrorised Cambodia during the 1980s.

After 'conferring' with the SLORC in Rangoon, Brown announced that 'contrary to what we read in the media, we found large areas of consensus in Burma'. He said, 'the issue of forced labour has diminished', apparently unaware that two days earlier the International Labour Organisation had reported that forced labour in Burma had 'increased markedly' and was now imposed 'on a massive scale and under the cruellest of conditions'.[33] Brown also praised the SLORC's allies in the governments that make up the Association of South East Asian Nations, ASEAN, referring to 'that noble organisation'.[34]

Although the Japanese Foreign Minister claims to have 'privately criticised' his Burmese counterpart on human rights, his government gives $48·7 million a year in aid to the SLORC, when even Western aid remains suspended. Meanwhile the great *zaibatsu*, Japan's corporate brotherhood of Mitsui, Mitsubishi, Honda and Nippon Steel, are all doing business in Rangoon, 'furthering our national interest', as one of its executives put it candidly to me.

Playing its part in this important cause is the Japanese national broadcaster, NHK, which is proud of its 'impartiality'. NHK owns some of the only television film of the Burmese Army shooting down people in 1988. During the making of my film *Inside Burma: Land of Fear*, Carlton Television asked NHK about buying it. This reply was received from Fumiko Chiba, Assistant Manager of NHK International Inc: 'Unfortunately it is NHK's policy that the footage showing the Burmese army shooting citizens who demonstrated in a street cannot be used in any programmes. This scoop material is still prohibited for use by anybody in the world, even by NHK in Japan, because it's too delicate and might threaten Myanmar's stability . . . Please erase the material in your library. I appreciate your understanding the situation.'[35]

For all the European Union's pronouncements on human rights, European companies, often secretly backed by their governments, are among the SLORC's most loyal underwriters. By far the biggest is the Total oil company. The German firm Fritz Werner has long supplied the junta with weapons-grade machine tools. The German electronics conglomerate Siemens is a major investor. So too is the Dutch multinational Philips, along with Britain's Premier Oil and Ireland's Dragon Oil.

In 1997, the governments of ASEAN granted Burma full membership. This was not unexpected. ASEAN is devoted to making money, has minimal interest in human rights and democracy and, of course, has its own hidden agendas, such as the enriching drugs trade. One of Burma's biggest investors is Singapore, whose 'elder statesman', Lee Kuan Yew, has said Aung San Suu Kyi 'should remain behind her fence'.[36] The sanctimonious Lee often lectures the world on the moral purity of what he calls 'Asian values' and on the need for 'constructive engagement' with oppressive regimes like Burma's. In 1996, the Bangkok *Nation* reported that the powerful drug lords Ling Ming-xian and Lo Hsing-han, who run most of the multi-million-dollar drugs trade in upper Burma, frequently visited Singapore and had established companies there 'as a way of possibly laundering drug money'.[37] The Singapore authorities have done nothing to deter him.

In recent years the Australian Government has directed its foreign policy to a 'regional role' in Asia. This is the child of the former Foreign Minister in the Labor Government, Gareth Evans, whose public enthusiasms have translated into uncritical support for the region's dictators, notably Suharto of Indonesia. While condemning publicly the Burmese regime and demanding that it meet 'a series of [human rights] benchmarks', Evans at the same time refused to discourage trade and investment with the SLORC. He called this 'diplomatic common sense'.[38]

Even while Aung San Suu Kyi was held under house arrest, the Australian Government quietly gave its support to ASEAN's 'constructive engagement' with the Burmese dictatorship. At ASEAN's conference in 1994, Evans told the Burmese Foreign Minister that, although Australia had an 'extreme concern about the continuing human rights situation', it also had 'a desire to find ways of moving the situation productively forward'.[39]

One way was to increase Australian investment in Burma.

In 1995, the number of Australian business delegations visiting Rangoon doubled. The giant BHP, Transfield, Pacific Arc Exploration and South Pacific Oil are either 'exploring opportunities' or have negotiated 'joint ventures' with the SLORC. The biggest Foster's beer hoarding in Burma shields an army watchtower from the gaze of passing tourists, many of them brought to Burma by the Melbourne company Intrepid.

One Australian business group was led by the former Prime Minister, Bob Hawke, who lauded the regime as having a 'genuine commitment to improving the economic condition of the country and its people'. Hawke's host was Lieutenant-General Khin Nyunt, 'Secretary One' of the SLORC and head of the secret police. Hawke said he had not raised the issue of human rights or the detention of Aung San Suu Kyi, then in her sixth year of house arrest. 'Constructive engagement' with the SLORC, he said, was 'justifiable and desirable' because the generals did not display the 'incompetence and self-aggrandisement' of other military dictators.[40]

The current Coalition (Tory) Government in Canberra, elected in 1996, heartily agrees with Hawke's assessment. The Deputy Prime Minister, Tim Fischer, visited Burma while in opposition and went to see Aung San Suu Kyi when it was still possible to call on her. He took her gifts of chocolates, woollen clothing, cosmetics chosen by his wife and a cuddly, stuffed wombat. She may now be studying the wombat with suspicion. On his return to Australia Fischer wrote that, under the SLORC, 'Burma is headed for democracy.' He based this remarkable conclusion on 'the small print of the objectives laid down in the Myanmar National Convention [that provide for] the establishment of multi-party democracy'.[41]

I read Fischer's remarks out to Aung San Suu Kyi when I met her in Rangoon. She laughed wearily and pointed out that the 'convention' Fischer was lauding was merely a front for the SLORC, and a farce, as it excluded Burma's largest and most popular party, the National League for Democracy, and herself, its leader.

Once in office, Fischer announced that Australia should 'show flexibility' in its dealings with Burma in order to help its 'democratic progress'.[42] In the same week four members of the National League for Democracy, the party elected by a landslide vote in 1988, were brought before a secret 'court' in Mandalay prison and each sentenced to seven years' imprisonment for their 'lack of respect' for the regime. Fischer later denied his own words. When my film was shown in Australia, he demanded that the Australian Broadcasting Corporation attach a disclaimer, denying he supported the SLORC. He had not seen the film, which accused him of nothing and merely quoted his words. The ABC rejected his demand.

When Burma's Prime Minister-in-exile, Dr Sein Wein, visited Australia, he impressed all who met him as a figure of dignity and courage, with a sense of moral purpose. A first cousin of Aung San Suu Kyi, he was forced to leave Burma soon after the 1990 election, leaving behind his pregnant wife. He has never met his daughter or spoken again to his wife. In the week that he was called to the office of the Australian Foreign Minister, Alexander Downer, he heard that his brother had been sentenced to a long term in prison and almost certainly had been tortured. Downer, a politician with no experience of a life and death struggle for democracy, lectured him on 'the principle of quiet diplomacy'. He never mentioned his government's deference to ASEAN or the principle of Australian companies making money and told Dr Sein Wein forcibly that sanctions against the oppressors of his people were 'unacceptable'.[43]

Burma's most profitable export to the West is drugs. More than half the heroin reaching the streets of American and Australian cities originates in the poppy fields of the 'Golden Triangle', where the borders of Burma, Laos and Thailand meet. Since the SLORC came to power, heroin production has doubled. Two researchers, Dr Chris Beyrer and Faith Doherty, conclude from a long investigation that the SLORC has allowed heroin to circulate freely and cheaply in Burma in the hope that it 'pacifies' the rebellious young. They also point to 400,000 HIV/AIDS cases recognised by the World Health Organisation and reveal that an unpublished UN report estimates that 70 per cent of addicts in Burma are HIV positive.

'The introduction of the HIV virus into this resource and information-poor country', says their report, *Out of Control*, 'is inherently political.' They quote a student veteran of the 1988 uprising: 'If you put up a poster about democracy at Rangoon University you get fifteen years in jail, if you hold a meeting to discuss human rights you get fifteen years in jail, but you can sell heroin in the college dormitory and nobody will bother you.'

Condoms were illegal in Burma until 1992 and syringes are still banned, except for medical purposes. A young doctor who agreed to speak to me in Mandalay said, 'AIDS is everywhere. We can't tell how much. People can't afford the HIV test, which costs a month's wages. You only have to visit one of the shooting galleries to grasp the size of the problem.'

Faith Doherty visited a 'shooting gallery', where addicts are injected with the same needle. 'While I was there a shooter used a needle five times,' she told me. 'He didn't clean the needle at all; he just wiped it with a rag. When it was blunt he sharpened it on a stone. The SLORC's anti-AIDS campaign is cosmetic and designed to appease the outside world and, like so many things in Burma, to conceal the truth. The statistics on AIDS are related directly to the amount of heroin that was made available during 1988 – which I have been told again and again, by doctors and nurses, was used to suppress the democracy movement ... From the knowledge gained after four years investigating heroin distribution in Burma, I must ask: how else, in a country that is run from top to bottom by the army, is heroin distributed?'[44]

The much-publicised 'surrender' of the drugs lord Khun Sa to the SLORC in 1995 was no more than another chapter in his long connivance with the regime. Now living comfortably in a house on Inya Lake in the centre of Rangoon, Khun Sa is served and protected by military intelligence officers. Eight Cabinet ministers attended the wedding of his son. According to the American Embassy in Rangoon, the textile industry, which supplies cheap clothes made-to-order to Western retail companies, is partly owned by the heroin lords.

Many of the hotels being built for Western tourists are financed by drugs. The US Assistant Secretary of State for Narcotics, Robert Gelbard, says the SLORC's 'lawless and authoritarian rule not only harms dissidents; it results in the criminalisation of the state . . . Burma's most important drug traffickers are no longer holed up in the jungle. The drug trade is entrenched in Burma's economic life.'[45] The Australian Federal Police, who estimate that three-quarters of the heroin entering Australia originates in Burma, say that Australian and other foreign companies investing in the country, as Burmese 'joint ventures', are awash with 'laundered' drug money.[46]

'At last the doors to Myanmar, the magic golden land, are open,' enthuses Dr Naw Angelene, the Director of Tourism. 'Roads will be wider, lights will be brighter, tours will be cleaner, grass will be greener and, with more job opportunities, people will be happier.'[47] In 1996, 'Visit Myanmar Year' was the centrepiece of the SLORC's campaign for foreign currency and membership of ASEAN. Tourism, calculated the generals, would bring half a million visitors a year and a veritable treasury of foreign exchange, along with a certain respectability. This did not happen, and the start of 'Visit Myanmar Year' was put back to October, then hardly heard of again.

For most Burmese the tourist 'development' offered little, apart from a few menial jobs. The new high-rise hotels are owned and managed by foreigners and, because there is virtually no manufacturing base, almost everything they need is imported, from hair-dryers to bed linen. Their air conditioners, generators and water purifiers are unknown in most Burmese homes. Most of the foreign exchange that the regime says 'the nation earns' goes abroad. According to one estimate, 70 per cent of the profits from tourism leave Burma, which is about the same proportion that leaves other very poor countries, such as those in the Caribbean.[48]

Burma has a beautiful, unspoilt southern coast, where scuba-diving resorts are planned. This is 'Myanmar's forgotten paradise', according to the regime's literature, where 'customised' tours are available – and the prime land is owned by SLORC officers from the rank of colonel up. Foreign investors here get generous 'tax holidays' and their 'partners' in the SLORC get rake-offs known as 'signature fees'. As for the local people, they provide, according to the Singapore-owned Air Mandalay flight magazine, 'some of the most inexpensive labour in the world'.

Mandalay, Burma's second city, is described as 'the Golden Land's Tourist Paradise City'. The view from Mandalay Hill offers an instructive panorama. On one side is the Novotel Hotel, a white concrete box whose brochure boasts of 'a computer socket, multi-channel in-house music and TV, a fitness centre and an 18-hole golf course'. The nightly rate for a room ranges from $200 to $650. Facing it across a landscape of pagodas is another white concrete box, this one a maximum security prison in which there are people serving ten years for writing poetry and singing songs about freedom.

I explained this to an Australian tourist enjoying the golden sunset, and he told his wife, who took a photograph of him smiling with the prison in the background. They asked if I knew of other 'off-beat sights'. I said that at the bottom of the hill was a shrine said to contain a replica of Buddha's tooth, which was being hurriedly built by 'volunteers'. They thanked me and gave me a wave from down below.

The principal British tour operator in Burma is the Oriental Express Group, which operates 'The Road to Mandalay', a 'champagne-style cruise' on the Irrawaddy River between Mandalay and Pagan in a converted Rhine cruiser. The company is owned by Sea Containers, a London-based company with worldwide shipping and transport interests, whose American chairman, James B. Sherwood, 'really gets a buzz out of going into those countries where others fear to tread', his public relations manager told me. 'He's also pretty outspoken, I can tell you,' she said. Sherwood demonstrated this on the day he was announced as a successful bidder for a chunk of Britain's newly privatised railway, the East Coast Main Line. 'We have to try and break', he declared, 'the communist approach to running a railway.'[49]

In the 1980s, Sherwood revived a tourist version of the Orient Express train, described in the company literature as 'the very, very last word in pampered luxury'. With air fares, his cruise up the Irrawaddy can cost more than £2,000 for eleven days – or twenty times the annual income of most Burmese. The cabins, says the brochure, 'are not *simply* luxurious'. There is a Kipling Bar and a swimming pool.

When I found her at anchor in the heat and mosquitoes, the *Road to Mandalay* looked squat and sturdy rather than luxurious. Once on board, however, she seemed the perfect vehicle for pampering fashionable tourism in one of the world's ten poorest countries. Like an air-conditioned bubble, she is constantly cleansed of the smells and noise and dust of the country through which she glides. The Burmese waiters and cabin attendants are graduates in physics and history. 'The beauty of this place', said Captain Brian Hills, 'is that you don't have to pay an arm and a leg for an educated bloke; they'll do anything for a job.'

Captain Hills said the company had 'tried to think of everything and be sensitive'. The Victorian etchings in the Kipling Bar are 'discreet'. That is to say, 'they don't show the British lording it over the natives'. In the 'staterooms' the television rises at the foot of the bed and, hey presto, there is Rupert Murdoch's satellite TV and a BBC cookery programme beamed straight to the Irrawaddy. 'Just let the aroma of *this* coffee waft through the house you're trying to sell,' oozed the posh presenter, 'and you'll have no trouble at all. The buyers will close there and then.'

In the distance, through a porthole, I noticed a woman and two small children in the doorway of a shack, whose rusted roof seemed to have been made of flattened beer cans and the walls of hessian bags. She was scrubbing her clothes on a rock surrounded by silt from the river.

In one of the side tours on offer, the passengers of the *Road to Mandalay* are taken to picturesque Buffalo Point, where they watch floating logs dragged ashore by yoked buffalo, urged on by whooping children. The people here are among the most wretched on earth. They have traditionally rented a patch of mud on the riverbank, where they cut and weave bamboo for thirty pence a day. Since tourism got under way, their children earn ten times that by begging from the foreigners. Ten-year-olds paint themselves with lipstick and sing 'Frère Jacques' with the result that the few who went to school now refuse to go. Infants have become the bread-winners, locking their families into a cycle of dependency seldom understood by tourists.

Captain Hills was preparing the *Road to Mandalay* for its maiden voyage. 'We've got some VVIPs coming for a party,' he said. 'We've invited the generals, but I don't think those chaps like to be all in the one place together. Tricky for them. Anything could happen.'

A few weeks later Captain Hills and James Sherwood were at the top of the gangplank to welcome their inaugural guests. 'They might have been', wrote *The Times* travel writer Peter Hughes, who was there, 'the cast from an Edwardian novel: a prince and two princesses from the Endsleigh League of European Royalty, our own Princess Michael of Kent among them; a duke; a *marchese* and *marchesa*; a film star, Helena Bonham-Carter; and assorted lords and ladies whose names tended to be the same as their addresses. Those without titles merely had money. A woman with a parcel of Burmese lacquerware explained where it might go: "This is not for Monaco or Barbados or London, but it could be perfect for Hong Kong or Majorca." '[50]

I met James Sherwood in his mock-Art Deco boardroom on the top floor of Sea Containers House on London's South Bank. A fan of Baroness Thatcher, he had dined with her a few days earlier when they had discussed the Gulf War. ('Mr Sherwood,' she had said to him, 'did you know I wanted to go all the way to Baghdad?') As for Burma, he was enthusiastic, with $35 million invested in the *Road to Mandalay* project. He described the investment policies of the SLORC as 'forward looking', compared with the Philippines, 'where foreigners are limited to only 40 per cent ownership'.

As for the regime's appalling human rights record, he was philosophic. 'You know,' he said shaking his head, 'I've tried to investigate these allegations about human rights infringements and it's very hard to pin them down.'

I read him part of the latest UN General Assembly resolution on Burma, which described as 'commonplace' torture, summary executions, forced labour, abuse of women, forced displacement. 'I just can't comment on these allegations,' he replied, 'because I don't have any evidence.'

I said they were not allegations and I read aloud from reports by Amnesty, Human Rights Watch and the US State Department. 'Your own government', I said, 'describes slave labour in Burma as routine and absolutely integral to tourism.'

'You know,' he said, 'I heard these allegations about forced labour, so I went to Mandalay Palace to see what the situation was, and I found a team of convicts [who] all seemed very cheerful. They were doing a job trying to prepare the palace. I accept I cannot visit all of Burma . . .'

'Isn't any of this a cause for concern for a company like yours?'

'No, not at all . . . I've met a number of the generals running the government and they seem to be rather bright, well educated, dedicated people who are trying to improve the country . . . and you mustn't forget this is a Buddhist nation and the people are very soft and, er, nice and they're not aggressive, they're not unpleasant in any way. You know, at any one time a third of the country is in the church and that means that their attitude is positive and welcoming, and we shouldn't be too hard on them . . .'

I said we had filmed people working as slaves on the railway, including children. 'My business', he said, 'is transport and I would say the upgrade of Burmese railways is a high priority. Now as to the use of child labour, I mean, obviously, no one could condone that unless it was volunteered labour . . .'

I said I didn't quite understand his remark about voluntary child labour.

'I can't comment on that.'

'Did you make any attempt to find out about this other side of Burma before you invested?'

'Sure. I contacted the CIA and the senior representative for Burma [sic] confirmed to me that these allegations were all untrue.'

'You think the CIA is a good source?'

'I think so, yes.'

'Didn't it strike you as grotesque', I asked him, 'that very rich people were toasting themselves in the Kipling Bar on your boat, while on the riverbank were people who could not afford clean running water or to immunise their children from preventable disease?'

'No, those who travel bring their money to help improve the economy and the standard of living of the people. I consider that a very high priority.'

The real road to Mandalay is being converted into an expressway for tourists. For the local people forced to labour on it, including children, who work in twelve-day stretches, it is known as 'the road of no return'. According to Amnesty, two workers who tried to escape were executed by soldiers on the spot. Another eight were beaten until they were severely injured; one was hacked to death with a hoe.

The Minister for Hotels and Tourism is General Kyaw Ba, formerly the SLORC commander of the Second Division in the south of the country. When I inquired about him, I heard the same story, over and again: that when General Ba's men were beaten back by guerrillas of the Karen National Union, they took their revenge for this humiliation by imprisoning 500 villagers and executing community leaders. To get to General Ba's office you go past three armed sentries, a curious sight in a ministry whose sole responsibility is tourism. Decked out in his medals and ribbons, the General grants interviews about tourism only. Clearly concerned that the tourists were not turning up in the droves anticipated, he assured a travel writer from the *Bangkok Post* that the 'pervasive military presence would ensure tourists' safety and security'.[51]

General Ba was not available, but I did talk to his director of tourism, Dr Naw Angelene, who told me that all the stories of forced labour were false: that the 'volunteers' I had seen were happily earning merit points to speed their passage to Nirvana in the afterlife. 'Please always remember', she said, 'Burma is a happy land. That is General Ba's message. Burma is a *very* happy land.'

In November 1995, Brian Whittaker, an Australian lawyer with an interest in human rights, flew to Burma with his wife, Jacqualine, an academic researching the SLORC's role in forest destruction. They travelled as tourists to the northern town of Putao. 'The first thing we heard was the clinking of chains,' he told me. 'There were thirty people working on an airport extension, crushing rock by hand. They were manacled; and it was clear that with every tourist flight that arrived the guards tried to hide the prisoners behind piles of rock.

'We waved at them and they reciprocated with one or two of them lifting their prison uniform to display their chains around their waist as well as their ankles. We also showed our anger and disgust; and among the Burmese Government officials accompanying us was one man who spoke good English and was clearly sympathetic. He told us they were political prisoners. I think he felt a little braver in the circumstances. I am familiar with the Universal Declaration of Human Rights and what I observed was a clear breach of the articles relating to slavery.'

The Whittakers also witnessed something of the 'selling' of Burma's vulnerable ethnic minorities as a tourist attraction. 'We went to a Kachin [minority people's] village,' he said, 'and it was clear that it was being prepared as a human zoo. The people there hadn't been visited by white people for thirty-five years, since missionaries were there, and when we arrived, the children were running around screaming. They were frightened of us. That night we slept in the village and were woken up by our guide asking if I could show the people what a US dollar looked like! The influence of tourism would be devastating on them.'

In Mytkina, another region being 'opened' to tourism, the Whittakers made contact with the Kachin Liberation Front, which had just signed a ceasefire with the SLORC. 'We were made aware that a major factor in the Kachin agreeing to sign', he said, 'was the systematic genocide by government forces. Burmese soldiers were using villagers as human shields, forcing them into active service where they believed there were land-mines; and we met a man who had lost a leg that enabled me to substantiate this. He had been made to walk across a field at gunpoint, and a mine went off. We were told about Burmese soldiers who were being forcibly married to Kachin women. The concept behind that is that the children born of that marriage are taught in such a way that breaks down the Kachin culture. It's a form of cultural genocide. I made great efforts to try and find these things out. But a foreigner staying within the designated tourist routes will not be aware of this. On the whole, people are too frightened to talk.'

Whittaker wrote to the then Australian Foreign Minister, Gareth Evans, enclosing a copy of an eye-witness statement he had sent to Amnesty International in London.[52] He got no reply.

WE SHALL HAVE OUR TIME

VISITORS ARE OFTEN struck by the apparent normality of Rangoon, the traffic, the markets, people thronging to a cinema, waiting for a bus. This is a façade. Even on the *maidan*, where many congregate on a Sunday, the pleasure of people with their families has a certain furtiveness. The young man seated on a bench next to me waited half an hour for the courage to speak, then looked away as he did. Strangely, he began each sentence with a verb, making our conversation at times hilarious, which attracted attention. 'Permitting us never English,' he said, as he described the long ban, now lifted, on learning English. The sight of a face in sunglasses peering through the iron railings, silently moving his lips through a half-smile, caused my friend to hurry away without saying goodbye. Prague used to feel like this.

On the White Bridge on Inya Lake it was just after sunrise and, even at that hour, I was conscious of being watched. Along this causeway on March 18, 1988 hundreds of schoolchildren and students marched, singing the national anthem. It was as joyful as it was defiant. Then suddenly they saw behind them the steel helmets of the Lon Htein, the 'special force', and knew they were trapped.

The soldiers systematically beat many of them to death, singling out the girls. 'A soldier reached down to his victim', an eye-witness told me, 'and ripped the gold chain from her neck.' A few managed to escape into the lake, where they were caught, beaten and drowned, one by one. Of those who survived, forty-two were locked in a waiting van, parked in the noonday heat outside Insein prison, where they suffocated to death. At the White Bridge fire engines washed away the blood.

The epic events of 1988 had their genesis in Burma's imperial past. The dethronement of their last king in the mid-nineteenth century freed the Burmese from the monarchical tradition, leaving the great spiritual force of Buddhism to blend easily with modern ideas, especially socialism. In the early part of the twentieth century Burma had one of the highest literacy rates in the world. Every boy was sent to the monastery to learn to read and write, and girls were educated too; this is the value that Buddhism places on education.

'The young nationalists', wrote the historian Bertil Lintner, 'were avid readers and the authors whose works they studied included Karl Marx, Lenin, Nehru, Sun Yat Sen, Mazzini, Garibaldi, Voltaire, Rousseau, Upton Sinclair, John Strachey, John Reed and various writers from Ireland's Sinn Fein movement.'[1] With divine certainty Marx was transformed into a disciple of Buddha. By the 1930s the Burmese had begun their struggle for independence and for the 'utopia', as some called it, of an 'equitable, spiritual, peaceful society'.

To the British, who had ruled Burma as a province of India, the golden land was merely an outpost of its imperial jewel. Myths familiar to Indian nationalists applied across the mountains in the Irrawaddy valley; the British were bringing civilisation, not empire building. Rudyard Kipling wrote a famous popular song that romanticised Mandalay, a town he never saw and which was then being stripped bare of its teak by British companies, leaving the dustbowl of today. Fortunes were earned by the British exporters of rice and precious stones. Companies made profits at the turn of the century of up to £12 million, a huge amount then. By 1939 British banks and Indian money-lenders controlled three-quarters of Burma's land.[2]

A Policy of divide and rule favoured certain ethnic minorities in a country with seven distinct groups and a multiplicity of sub-groups, speaking more than 100 languages. The Burmans were the majority, and the Karen and Shan the largest minorities. During the Second World War many died in communal strife, with hundreds of thousands of Indians driven across the border.

The British encouraged one group against another; and the arrival of British and American missionaries had an enduring influence on the Karen and the Kachin, and although today only a sixth of the Karen are Christian, Christian education had such a powerful effect that it promoted a coherent Karen nationalism for the first time, often to the detriment of the Burman majority. It was not surprising that the Karen sided with the British during the Second World War and that the Burman nationalists at first saw the Japanese invasion as the way to independence. The resulting bitterness and distrust survive today.

For the British, it was an article of colonial faith that those at the top of Burmese society were expatriots. 'The old type of servant is disappearing,' lamented Orwell's character Macgregor, in *Burmese Days*, written in 1934 following the author's stint as a policeman in Burma. 'In my young days, when one's butler was disrespectful, one sent him along to the jail with a chit saying, "Please give the bearer fifteen lashes." Ah well, *eheu fugaces!* Those days are gone forever, I am afraid.'[3]

In 1930, the poor farmers of southern Burma, impoverished by high taxation, revolted. Put down by British-led Karen forces, their rebellion was followed by a strike by the students of Rangoon University, whose leader was a gaunt young man called Aung San.

On the eve of the Second World War Burma was racked by insurrection. Aung San, now Secretary-General of the Burmese Communist Party, regarded the war as 'colonialism's difficulty [and] freedom's opportunity'. After trying unsuccessfully to make contact with the Chinese communists, he turned to the Japanese and in 1940 secretly led the 'Thirty Comrades', representing the various nationalist groups, to Tokyo, where he established the Burma Independence Army. With the British in retreat to India, he and his men marched into Rangoon behind the Japanese in December 1941.

Disenchantment with their benefactors soon set in; and in 1945 Aung San contacted the Allied commander, Lord Mountbatten, in India, and turned his guerrillas on the Japanese. For this he was allowed to march back into Rangoon with the British. Two years later, shortly before independence, he was assassinated. His daughter, Suu Kyi, was two years old.

The movement he founded sought to apply a union of Buddhism, socialism and democracy to freely-elected governments in the post-war years. And although this period is often seen as a time of turmoil and score-settling between the Burmans and the minorities who had sided with the British, it was also an extraordinary flowering of democratic socialism in a country left bereft by war and post-colonial upheaval. What had distinguished the Burmese anti-imperialist movement was its anti-fascism and socialism. Burma, wrote the historian Martin Smith, 'is that rarity of a country in which successive governments have been regarded as left-wing, but in which the principal political opposition has come from the left'.[4]

The root of anti-imperialism lay in the students' movement, also unique in the colonial world. For many Burmese, their nationalism's most significant date is December 5, 1920, when the students of Rangoon University boycotted their studies after the colonial administration had passed a law that tied Burmese education to British interests and the English language. The popularity of their stand was soon demonstrated by supportive crowds in the streets of Rangoon and the principal towns. 'We believe', declared a statement by the Students' Boycott Council, 'nothing can save the nation but a proud and indomitable stand on the part of Young Burma, with the whole-hearted cooperation of the Burmese people.'[5]

These stirring sentiments would be echoed more than forty years later when the students again led the country against an oppressor. On March 2, 1962, the hope of an independent Burma ended when the army seized power, inaugurating more than three decades of military dictatorship.

The new leader was General Ne Win, who proclaimed

another version of totalitarianism, called 'the Burmese Way to Socialism'. A Stalin-like figure, Ne Win concentrated power in himself and his court. 'Although he was an absolute ruler,' wrote Bertil Lintner, 'he never created a personality cult around himself like Mao Zedong, Chiang Kai-shek or Kim Il-Sung. [Yet] he established at his luxurious Ady Road residence on a peninsula in Inya Lake in Rangoon an almost absurd replica of the old Burmese monarchy. One of the few men he trusted was his old Indian cook, Raju, who had served him since his 4th Burma Rifles days. Fearful of being poisoned, he entrusted only Raju with the task of preparing his food. But even Raju had to taste it first, in Ne Win's presence.'[6]

For one who married seven times, Ne Win's public *diktats* were puritanical in the extreme. A devoted gambler, he banned horse racing 'to uplift public morals' – reportedly after a bookie cheated him at Ascot. When his daughter defied him and stayed out late dancing, he sent his bodyguards to stop a band playing where he suspected she was (she wasn't). Thereafter ballroom dancing was banned throughout Burma. Following a row with a brother-in-law called Georgie, who had taken American citizenship, he decreed that no Burmese with a foreign passport was to be allowed back in the country. Thus, he never saw Georgie again.

Martin Morland, who was British Ambassador to Burma during the 1980s, describes him as 'a control maniac'.[7] Like Stalin, Ne Win displaced whole populations, built labour camps and filled the prisons with his enemies, real and imagined. His wars against the ethnic peoples were un-relenting and vengeful; and along the way he made himself extremely rich. In 1984, the *Far Eastern Economic Review* reported that the privately chartered jet taking him to a Swiss health clinic 'was delayed because chests of jade and precious stones carried on board had been stacked incorrectly and had to be reloaded'.[8] Three years later Burma, a naturally rich country, applied for Least Developed Nation status so that it might seek relief on its massive foreign debt.

Ne Win gave himself the sobriquet 'Brilliant as the Sun'. The Burmese, who often likened him to Ferdinand Marcos, preferred to call his reign 'the madhouse dynasty'. In 1987, he produced his *coup de grâce*. Without warning, he withdrew most of the country's banknotes, replacing them with new denominations that included or added up to the number nine. According to his chief astrologer, nine was his lucky number. The people of Burma did not share his luck. As most of them kept their savings in cash, they were ruined.

It was this instant impoverishment that lit the touchpaper. Penniless farmers, forced at gunpoint to plant rice for export, rebelled; and by March 1988 the regime was at war with the principal political force, the students. Following the White Bridge massacre, 10,000 people joined the students as they marched into the centre of Rangoon. As the rains came, all schools and colleges were ordered closed and the country prepared for turmoil, with the army dominating the streets, ambushing demonstrators, then vanishing.

In a typically Machiavellian move, Ne Win called a special conference of his ruling party, announced his resignation and proposed multi-party elections. The conference promptly 'accepted' his feigned departure, rejected elections and named his successor as Sein Lwin, a man known to most Burmese simply as 'the butcher', whose record of bloody repression had few equals.

The moment of uprising came precisely at eight minutes past eight on the eighth morning of the eighth month of 1988. This was the auspicious time the dockworkers, the 'first wave', chose to strike. Other workers followed; and in the subsequent days and weeks almost everyone in the cities and towns, it seemed, showed a defiance and courage comparable with those who stormed the Berlin Wall the following year.

'It was unforgettable and moving,' said Martin Morland, who was Ambassador at the time. 'All you could see were people and all you could hear was *Do-a-ye! Do-a-ye!* ... "Our country is our business." I had seven years of experience in Burma and I have to say I was astonished by the events of 1988. There was a degree of repression in the Burmese system which I thought the Burmese people took for granted and I discovered in 1988 they did nothing of the kind. My earlier assumptions were wrong. They want the same human rights, broadly speaking, that we want in the West. The lesson of 1988 was that, like everyone else, they wanted the government off their backs. They wanted freedom.'[9]

People were now constantly on the streets. In Mandalay the imperial palace and its military barracks were surrounded by a human wall. The common enemy inspired co-operation and generosity across ethnic and religious lines. Joint committees of Buddhists, Muslims and Christians were set up to ensure that food supplies reached the poorest. Tribal peoples sent delegations of support. In the southern port of Moulmein 100,000 people marched from the Kyaiktouk pagoda to the *maidan*: monks, students and peasants, who arrived from the countryside in bullock carts.[10]

Without guns, ordinary people reclaimed town after town, village after village. Independent trade unions were formed for the first time in twenty-six years. Railwaymen refused to supply trains for 'dictators of the one-party system'.[11] Weather forecasters refused to forecast for the army. Grave-diggers refused to bury members of the ruling party and, according to a newspaper, the ghosts were now chanting: 'Corpses of [party] members are not allowed to be buried in our cemetery! Stay out!'[12]

Journalists on the state-run Burma Broadcasting Service struck, saying they would 'no longer broadcast propaganda'. 'After twenty-six years of silence,' wrote Lintner, 'Rangoon alone had almost forty independent newspapers and magazines, full of political commentaries, witty cartoons, biting satires and cartoons ridiculing the ruling elite.'[13] The new papers had stirring titles reminiscent of the free press in the post-war years: *Light of Dawn*, *Liberation Daily*, *Scoop*, *New Victory*. Some were printed, others photocopied, mimeographed or handwritten, and most were distributed free. 'Day after day,' said a journalist, now exiled, 'we created a parliament in the streets. Everyone had their say.'

By the end of August, prison warders and policemen had joined the demonstrators, as had customs and immigration officials and members of the air force. With their arms linked, and old people holding the hands of children, they marched behind giant portraits of Aung San and red flags enscribed with a yellow fighting peacock: the symbol of Burmese nationalism.

Ko Htun Oo was then eighteen. 'We thought we had won,' he told me. 'On August 23 an amazing thing happened; soldiers barred our way and an officer told us that if we passed the barricades, they would shoot. He threw down a challenge to us. He said, "If seven brave men advance towards us, then seven soldiers will be chosen to shoot them. If you think what you are doing is right, then do it." Seven people from our group, including three young ladies, advanced. When we passed the first barricade the soldiers cocked their guns. At the second barricade they took aim at us. At the third, when we were very close, the officer ordered his soldiers to put their guns down. Then he put his arm around me and said what we had done was right and that he was proud of us. He said he knew what was happening in the country but he was under orders. "I shall now have to face the consequences," he said. Then he withdrew his troops.'

But they had not won, and the killing began. Taking their lead from the Lon Htein, the army fired point-blank at the crowds and bayoneted those who fell. A group of schoolchildren were told to kneel, then were shot. 'One of my friends was shot in the head right there, in front of me,' said Ko Htun Oo. 'Two girls and a monk were shot next to him.'

Jeeps mounted with machine-guns roared into the side streets, rapid-firing into people's homes, markets and teashops. Truck-loads of dead and wounded were dumped at the gates of Rangoon General Hospital. They included the naked bodies of young men with shaven heads: monks whose identity the troops had attempted to disguise. 'The staff at the hospital had a Red Cross banner hung out the front,' said Aye Chan, a former student. 'It said, "Please stop the shooting." The nurses and doctors came out and were calling for an end to the violence when an army truck stopped in front of them and the soldiers started shooting into the crowd. Nurses, doctors, patients were killed.'

Thida, another former student, said she remembered, as the

killing went on, 'the soldiers continuously washing the blood off the streets'. Aye Chan said, 'A lot of flame was coming out of the crematorium which was surrounded by troops. They weren't even identifying bodies, so the parents would never know. The dead and wounded were all mixed up. They just burned them alive.'

Naing Oo, now exiled in Thailand, told me, 'I was at the cemetery on the night of 18th August. At about two a.m., between thirty and forty soldiers arrived in two trucks with a lot of wounded people. They asked the caretaker to bury the bodies. Only three holes were dug and nineteen bodies were buried in these three holes. The age of them ranged from thirteen to twenty-five. Some were wearing high-school uniforms – white shirts and green *longhi*. One of them was shouting. He was asking for his mother and he was fully conscious and said that he didn't want to be buried alive. The caretaker and his staff didn't want to bury the boy alive, but the soldiers forced him. The caretaker told me he felt very sorry about it.'

Those who survived were taken mostly to Insein prison, where they were greeted by the screams of the tortured. A former student, Maung, told me, 'I was kept in a room filled with mosquitoes. I was made to hold a half-sitting position while a lighted candle was held under my scrotum. Then they made me drink a lot of water, but I wasn't allowed to pass urine. If I did, I was beaten. I had to wear headphones and the most piercing noise was playing through them. Later I was made to crawl along a path littered with pieces of broken brick. This was called "The Crocodile". My registration number was 4,000. I knew the numbers of the new prisoners went up to 7,000.'

The people fought back with swords, clubs, Molotov cocktails and a lethal catapult called a *jinglee*. Even the monks joined the counter-attack. But they had no hope against the army, which also took care to minimise the international reporting of its ferocity. '[The] orders were to shoot any-one with a camera,' wrote Lintner. 'A Burmese cameraman freelancing for a Japanese TV company was killed by a sniper;

a bullet hit him through his right eye, which was closed as he held the camera to the other.' When two other cameramen were spotted by soldiers one of them concealed the camera with his body. On the tape that was later smuggled out, a voice could be heard saying in Burmese, 'What shall we do? What shall we do?' The other voice replied calmly, 'Keep on filming until they shoot at us.'

In Thailand, I met the Burmese popular singer Yuzana Khin who was then a student. 'One girl was just fifteen,' she said. 'She was shot right in front of me. I could not help her. I was only thinking of running. Now I am talking to you outside Burma, but since then my heart has been in prison...' Yuzana wrote a song called 'How Can I Forget', which she has sung abroad, making it into something of an anthem among her fellow exiles. I asked her if she had a tape of it with her. 'No,' she said, 'but I can give you the words.' I asked her to sing it. With her eyes closed she began...

> How can I forget, the 8th of August 1988
> The 8th of August
> I still remember everything
> Downtown Rangoon, the people came to
> demonstrate and sing,
> Students, lawyers, monks, workers everywhere
> How the sounds of freedom reached the air...

Then the tears ran down her cheeks, and she stopped.

On September 18, 1988, the regime announced that it had 'assumed power' following a 'coup' that never was. It had merely changed its name to SLORC, with the Army Chief of Staff, General Saw Maung, doing Ne Win's bidding. The 'new' ruling body immediately abolished all state institutions, purged the Civil Service and banned gatherings of more than four. Troops with photographs and lists went from door to door, looking for any opponent of the regime. The prisons now overflowed.

But the generals faced an opponent whose unforeseen presence in Burma Ne Win had not reckoned on. Aung San Suu Kyi, daughter of a man whose memory was revered both by the people and the army, had returned from

England in April to care for her dying mother.

'It was a quiet evening in Oxford, like many others, the last day of March 1988,' wrote Michael Aris, her husband. 'Our sons were already in bed and we were reading when the telephone rang. Suu picked up the phone to learn that her mother had suffered a severe stroke. She put the phone down and at once started to pack. I had a premonition that our lives would change for ever.'

Thus, Michael Aris begins his moving introduction to *Freedom from Fear*, a collection of essays by and about Aung San Suu Kyi, his wife. They had met in their student days at Oxford, she having originally left Burma for India in 1960 when her mother was made ambassador to Delhi. 'From her early childhood,' he wrote,

Suu has been deeply preoccupied with the question of what she might do to help her people. She never forgot for a minute that she was the daughter of Burma's national hero, Aung San ... There is a certain inevitability in the way she, like him, has now become an icon of popular hope and longing. In the daughter as in the father there seems an extraordinary coincidence of legend and reality, of word and deed. And yet prior to 1988 it had never been her intention to strive for anything quite so momentous ... Recently I read again the 187 letters she sent me in Bhutan from New York in the eight months before we were married on 1 January 1972. Again and again she expressed her worry that her family and people might misinterpret our marriage and see it as a lessening of her devotion to them. She constantly reminded me that one day she would have to return to Burma, that she counted on my support at that time, not as her due, but as a favour ...

'I only ask one thing [she wrote], that should my people need me, you would help me to do my duty by them ... Sometimes I am beset by fears that circumstances and national considerations might tear us apart just when we are so happy in each other that separation would be a torment. And yet such fears are so futile and inconsequential: if we love and cherish each other as much as we can while we can, I am sure love and compassion will triumph in the end.'

Aris described her departure for Burma that March day in 1988 as 'a day of reckoning'. He wrote the words I have quoted while Aung San Suu Kyi was in her third year of house arrest in Rangoon, an arbitrary sentence imposed by the SLORC and which lasted until July 1995. During most of that time she was completely alone and prevented from seeing her husband and sons. In *Freedom from Fear* there is this postscript: 'I was informed today that my dear wife Suu has been awarded the Nobel Peace Prize . . . It is my earnest hope and prayer that the Peace Prize will somehow lead to what she has always strived for – a process of dialogue aimed at achieving lasting peace in her country. Selfishly, I also hope our family's situation will be eased as a result of this supreme gesture of recognition for her moral and physical courage, and that we may at last be allowed to pay her visits again. We miss her very much.'[14]

On August 26, 1988, Aung San Suu Kyi made her first public appearance, addressing more than half a million people in front of Rangoon's ancient Shwe Dagon pagoda. 'I could not, as my father's daughter,' she said, 'remain indifferent to all that was going on. This national crisis could be called the second struggle for independence.'

The people now had a leader of national stature. Aung San Suu Kyi toured more than fifty towns that year, enlisting support for the National League for Democracy which she and others founded. At first, the SLORC seemed powerless as to how to handle her. They tried vilifying her, calling into question her loyalty to Burma because she had spent so many years abroad married to a foreigner. The greater the abuse, the more popular she became. People were ordered not to attend her meetings, but still they went. At one rally an army captain ordered six soldiers to aim and get ready to shoot her; only the intervention of a superior officer prevented her assassination.[15]

By mid-1989 the streets were filling again, but this time the crowds were more disciplined. Aung San Suu Kyi had made the restoration of democracy the issue; and the SLORC knew they could not easily renege on the promise, held out by Ne

Win, of multi-party elections. However, her popularity now deeply alarmed them.

Known as 'the lady' to the mass of Burmese, she was 'that woman', and no doubt worse, to Ne Win. Perhaps her great crime in his eyes was to dare to attack him by name and to call on the army to get rid of him. 'Ne Win is the one who caused this country to suffer for twenty-six years,' she said. 'Ne Win is the one who lowered the prestige of the armed forces. Officials of the armed forces . . . be loyal to the people. You don't have to be loyal to Ne Win.'[16]

Less than a month later, on July 20, 1989, she was placed under house arrest, accused of 'nurturing public hatred for the army'. At the same time, according to Amnesty, 3,000 of her party workers were arrested and more than a hundred sentenced to death. With the opposition weakened, so they thought, the generals called elections for May 27, 1990, the fourth Sunday of the fifth month on a date that added up to nine, Ne Win's lucky number. Canvassing was made illegal and Aung San Suu Kyi barred from standing as a candidate. The regime confidently expected its front party, the NUP, to win the biggest bloc of votes.

Instead, the National League for Democracy won an overwhelming victory with 82 per cent of the vote, including majorities in military cantonments. Most of the NLD candidates were unknown; the people were voting for 'the lady' and against Ne Win. Flabbergasted, the generals refused to hand over power. Newly elected MPs went underground or fled to the border areas. More than 200 were caught and given prison sentences of up to twenty-five years. A lawyer and writer, Un Tin Shwe, one of the masterminds of the 'Gandhi Document' which had called for a parliamentary democracy, was one of those never released and he died in prison nine years later.

In 1991, the award to Aung San Suu Kyi of the Nobel Peace Prize was made while she was a prisoner in her own home. Still the regime feared her. In the street outside, soldiers were ordered to lie with their ears to the ground to detect her 'tunnelling' to the house next door. As the weeks and months passed, it dawned on them that she had no intention of escaping.

Outside, in the crooked streets and ramshackle markets, her whispered name became a byword; and people would pass her house on University Avenue just to be reassured by the sound of her playing the piano. At one stage she did not have enough to eat and became terribly ill, her weight dropping to ninety pounds; she told me how she would lie awake listening to the thumping of her heart.

When Michael Aris was informed by the Burmese Embassy that his sons' Burmese nationality had been withdrawn and that they were refused visas on their British passports, he wrote, 'Very obviously, the plan was to break Suu's spirit by separating her from her children in the hope she would accept permanent exile. I myself was allowed to return once to be with her for a fortnight during the following Christmas. It seems the authorities had hoped I would try to persuade her to leave with me. In fact, knowing the strength of Suu's determination, I had not even thought of doing this.' He added, 'The days I spent alone with her that last time, completely isolated from the world, are among my happiest memories of our many years of marriage.'[17]

Completely alone, she rose at four o'clock every morning and sat at the foot of her bed, meditating. At five thirty she switched on her Grundig short-wave radio and listened to the BBC World Service news. She ate little, treating herself to a boiled egg at the weekend. She read biographies of those who had also suffered through isolation: Mandela, Sakharov. After four-and-a-half years she was allowed an occasional visitor, including an American Congressman, Bill Richardson, a friend of President Clinton.

The US Congress was then considering a bill of comprehensive sanctions against Burma, similar to that which had proved effective against apartheid South Africa. As the SLORC's need for foreign exchange became more desperate, so the usefulness of modifying their pariah status became apparent even to the xenophobic General Khin Nyunt, Ne Win's man. On July 10, 1995, ten days short of six years since her arrest, Aung San Suu Kyi was released 'unconditionally'.

I had arranged through the underground to interview her; it was the eve of our departure from Burma, and David Munro and I had ensured that our videotape was already in Bangkok on its way to London. The taxi dropped us far from the long green fence of Number 54. The cameras were in shoulder bags. We peered through a hole in the corrugated iron gate and a face asked our names. In the street a figure in sunglasses watched us. The gate swung ajar and there was a sort of checkpoint. Another sunglasses told us to write down our names, occupations and passport details. We wrote 'specialists in exotic travel' and gave false details.

From there we seemed to cross a line into another country. We were greeted by Aung San Suu Kyi's assistant, Win Htein, a man who had spent six years in prison, five of them in solitary confinement. Yet his face was soft and open and his handshake warm. He led us into the house, a stately pile fallen on hard times. The garden with its ragged palms falls down to Inya Lake and to a trip wire, a reminder that this was one woman's prison.

Aung San Suu Kyi wore silk and had orchids in her hair. She is a striking, glamorous figure who looked very much younger than her fifty years and appeared at first to carry her suffering lightly. It was only later when I looked at film of her taken just before her arrest that I realised her face had changed considerably and, in repose, offered a glimpse of the resolve that has seen her through. When she laughs this vanishes; it is like a blind closed and then opened.

For someone so famous there has been precious little written about her that strays from the known. In *Freedom from Fear*, an irreverent and affectionate chapter by Ann Pasternak Slater, a contemporary at Oxford, comes close to reaching behind the screen erected by a very private and strong person. She describes St Hugh's all-female college in 1964 as 'a warren of nervous adolescent virgins and a few sexually liberated sophisticates [which] made for an atmosphere airless and prickly as a hot railway compartment'. In this setting, she wrote, 'Suu was delightfully antithetical, an original who was at once laughably naïve, and genuinely innocent. All my memories of her at that time have certain recurring elements: cleanliness, determination, curiosity, a fierce purity. How do I see her? Eyebrows furrowed under a heavy fringe, shocked incredulity and disapproval: "*But Ann!* . . ." Yet it is Suu's kindness that is most sharply present to me now.'[18]

I talked to Aung San Suu Kyi in a room surrounded by pictures of her family, dominated by a wall-length portrait of the father she never knew, painted by the artist Soe Moe at the height of the 1988 uprising. 'I often look at it,' she said, 'and think it's like an Andy Warhol, done in the same style as his Marilyn Monroe.' It reminded me of something from the 1960s, whose true spirit was called up by the Burmese students in the late 1980s.

She sat perfectly still for an hour and a half on a straight-backed chair. I have not seen anyone else hold themselves like that, without a twitch. This was our conversation:

'What can I call you?' I asked.

'Well, you can't manage the whole thing? Friends call me Suu.'

I said, 'Three years ago an official of the regime announced, "You can forget about Suu Kyi; she's finished." And here you are, hardly finished. How do you explain that?'

'I think it's because democracy is not finished in Burma and until we finish the course for democracy none of us who are involved in it will be finished. [Consider] the courage of the people who go on working for democracy, those who have already been in prison. They know that any day they are likely to be put back there and yet they do not give up. Even if only five such people remain we shall get democracy, and there are many, many more than five.'

'What *is* the democracy you're striving for?'

'Well, it's very simple. We want security under the law, the kind of system where we can put our grievances right. For example, the farmers are suffering because they are forced to sow at a certain time and reap at a certain time, *and* to sow a second crop, which ruins a lot of them. Now they want to talk over their grievances. This is what most people want. They will tell you, "I don't want to be worried all the time." '

'But how do you reclaim the power you won at the ballot box with brute power confronting you?'

'In Buddhism we are taught there are four basic ingredients for success. The first is the will to want it, then you must have the right kind of attitude, then perseverance, then wisdom . . .'

'But it still comes down to power, doesn't it? They've got all the guns.'

'I think it's getting more difficult to resolve problems through military means. It's no longer acceptable. That's why they attack us in their newspapers. They've got the guns, but they use the pen.'

'Isn't it fair to describe your release from house arrest as a cynical decision by the regime to give itself a human face in order to encourage foreign investment?'

'They may have miscalculated that my release was not going to make any difference.'

'Should foreign businessmen come to Burma?'

'They should not come. [Investment] shores up the regime.'

'The former Australian Prime Minister Bob Hawke has said that the regime is "deeply committed" to the advancement of its people and [the present Deputy Prime Minister] Tim Fischer has been here and said Burma is heading towards democracy . . .'

She laughed. 'Oh, really? What *they* must understand is that Burma is heading for democracy not because of investment but *in spite* of it.'

I read out another pearl, this time from Britain. 'A Foreign Office minister said, "Through commercial contacts with democratic nations such as Britain, the Burmese people will gain experience of democratic principles." '

'Not in the least bit, because the so-called market economy that exists at this moment is only open to some and not to everybody. New investments will help a small elite to get richer and richer. This works against the very idea of democracy because the gap between rich and poor is growing all the time.'

'Should tourists stay away?'

'It's not a good idea to come. Burma will always be here and one day, when it's a democratic Burma, this will be a place that tourists will enjoy.'

'How has forced labour been used?'

'Forced labour goes on all over the country and a lot of the projects are aimed at the tourist trade. It's very painful. Roads and bridges are built at the expense of the people. If you cannot provide one labourer per family, then you are fined. They can't afford the fine so children are sent to work on these forced labour projects.'

'Your fellow Nobel Laureate Desmond Tutu said, "International pressure can change the situation in Burma. Tough sanctions, not so-called constructive engagement, finally brought about a new South Africa." He was saying: "Be tough with tyrants." Do you agree with that?'

'I'm certainly not going to argue with that!'

'But you have spoken of compromise, and he is saying it doesn't work.'

'What I'm saying is that if there is going to be constructive engagement it should be with both sides in Burma: the regime and those of us who represent democracy.'

'You have become an icon of hope. Is that a burden?'

'I don't take myself that seriously.'

'I've spoken to people here who regard you as something of a saint, a miracle worker.'

'I'm not a saint and you'd better tell the world that!'

'What are your sinful qualities then?'

'Er, I've got a short temper. And I'd rather sit and read than go to public meetings and things like that.'

'Looking into the future, how would an independent, democratic Burma deal with all the pressures that come from so-called friendly forces, like the World Bank, the IMF, multinational companies: the pressures of those who appear to run the world?'

'Well, first of all by not thinking of them as pressures. I wouldn't like to think of the IMF and the World Bank as bringing pressure. We would always be open to advice ...

and perhaps as Buddhists we think of these pressures as part of the trappings of the world which we have to take in our stride.'

'Yes, they are trappings but they are pressures, too. Look at Cory Aquino in the Philippines. She ran a campaign similar to yours, then she ended up having to pay half her country's budget in debt repayments. And her plans for her people were shelved.'

'I don't think debt payment is imposed on you from outside. After all, if you borrow, then you have to pay back. It's inner pressures that have forced you to borrow in the first place.'

'Your husband Michael has written movingly of his early commitment to you: that if you felt destiny calling you back to Burma, he would understand. Can you tell me about that?'

'I just said to him there may come a time when I have to go back, and I'd expect him to be sympathetic. It was very simple. It was not a big, complicated negotiating process.'

'Could you tell me about the day you were placed under house arrest?'

'There were a lot of people with me and we were all in good humour. There wasn't a scurry to burn incriminating material or anything like that, because we didn't have any! My two sons were here and I remember them playing Monopoly. Some people made phone-calls to their families while the phone was still usable. Then we had to arrange lunch for all the people who were caught up here. Everybody was very cheerful and very calm. It was not unexpected. We just thought, "Yes, this is it."'

'Did you ever, during all those years alone, waver in your resolve not to accept exile?'

'No, of course I didn't. There was no question . . .'

'It would have been very human for you to have doubts, wouldn't it?'

'I had promised the people I would do everything I could to get democracy. I didn't promise them a paradise on earth, just that I would do my best . . .'

'What were the most difficult times for you personally?'

'I worried for our people out there when they were enduring a lot of repression. I missed my family, and I worried about my sons very much because the young one was only twelve and he had to be put into boarding school. But then I'd remind myself that the families of my colleagues [in prison] were far worse off.'

'Were you able to stay in touch with Michael?'

'There were times when we were out of touch . . . two years and four months was the longest.'

'No letters or anything during that time?'

'No.'

'No letters from the children got through?'

'No.'

'That must have been hard.'

'You do everything you can to adjust . . .'

'You and Michael had a commitment, but were you concerned with the impact it would have on the boys?'

'Yes . . . I worried about them. I do not think it was easy for them. As I said, my youngest had to be sent to boarding school and he's a very home-loving child. He's not the sort who enjoys boarding-school life at all. But these things had to be done.'

'They must have been very proud of you. When they did write, what were the sort of things they wrote to you about?'

'Oh, children always write in a very practical way. They'd write about what they were doing, their pets, their friends at school.'

'I believe you didn't have enough to eat. Is that correct?'

'Yes, but I don't think of that as a tremendous suffering . . .'

'It's a pretty basic suffering!'

'I generally don't eat very much anyway . . . well, yes it is pretty basic. One does get very weak and, er, it's inconvenient.'

'You were ill and you worried about your heart.'

'Yes, I had difficulty breathing and I thought, perhaps, how shall I put it? . . . You see, I couldn't lie flat because I found it difficult to breathe lying flat on my back after I became very weak.'

'You were worried about your spine, too . . .'

'I had spondylitis [which] is rather painful.'

'Weren't there times when, surrounded by a hostile force, cut off from your family and friends, you were actually terrified?'

'No, because I didn't feel hostile towards the guards surrounding me. Fear comes out of hostility and I felt none towards them.'

'But it must have produced an aloneness that itself is frightening?'

'Oh, I had a radio, and I listened to it about five or six hours a day, and I had my books. And loneliness comes from inside, you know. People who are free and who live in big cities suffer from it, because it comes from inside.'

'You've written a great deal about fear and fearlessness. Was there a point when you actually had to conquer fear?'

'When I was small it was in this house that I conquered my fear of the dark.'

'How did you?'

'Just by wandering around in the darkness. I did that for about two weeks and by the end . . .'

'You knew where all the demons might be . . .'

'Yes.'

'And they weren't there?'

'They weren't there.'

'During those days of house arrest what were the small pleasures you looked forward to?'

'I'd look forward to a good book being read on *Off the Shelf* on the BBC and of course my meditation, which was always very calming and very strengthening. I didn't enjoy my exercises so much; I've never been a very athletic type and I did it out of a sense of duty.'

'Did you do aerobics?'

'Yes, then Michael was allowed to come and see me and brought me an exercise machine and it did seem to help my back. It was always a *great* pleasure to look forward to when I'd got it over and done with!'

'And music?'

'Yes, it was a comfort to me. I'm afraid my tastes are very conventional. I like Bach and Mozart and Vivaldi, but I did become fonder of more modern music, like Vaughan Williams.'

'What happened to your piano?'

'You mean when the string broke?'

'Yes.'

'In this climate pianos *do* deteriorate and some of the keys were getting stuck, so I broke a string because I was pumping the pedal too hard.'

'That temper you described . . . you lost it?'

'I did.'

'It's a very moving scene. Here you are all alone and you get so angry you break the piano.'

'I told you, I have a hot temper.'

'And you had nobody to take it out on.'

'I took it out on the piano.'

'Your friend at Oxford, Ann Pasternak Slater, wrote that you were a pure Oriental traditionalist. Is that a fair description?'

'Well, I grew up in Burma at a time when the Burmese could afford to be proud of themselves. If your country is doing well, which it was when I was young – we were a democracy – then you naturally feel you can hold your head up when it comes to traditional values and your culture, so it's very natural for me to be proud of Burmese values and culture. This is probably why she saw me like that.'

'She wrote it admiringly. She admired the way you dressed and held yourself, although I have to say she gave the impression you were rather strait-laced. Is that fair?'

'Compared to a lot of people, I am strait-laced. We were brought up strictly because my mother was a disciplinarian.'

'Are you also a product of the English upper-class environment you knew growing up in England and at Oxford?'

'When I think of Oxford I think of intellectual liberalism . . .' (She avoided that one.)

'Are you a feminist?'

211

'Not in the sense that the term is understood in the West. I'd rather be known as a humanist. The men in Burma have no rights either and under the circumstances I feel that first of all we have to get basic human rights for everybody and then we'd have to attack the areas where women are discriminated against, such as the Civil Service.'

(The Burmese scholar Josef Silverstein says Burmese society has unusual features in its attitudes to women. 'There are no real cultural impediments to a woman as a leader,' he wrote. 'Throughout its history, women have enjoyed equality with men in the household and the economy. Marriage was and is a civil act; women retain their own names during marriage, and divorce is a simple procedure with no stigma attached to either party. More important, women have always had the right of inheritance. Only in Buddhist religious terms were they considered inferior.')[19]

'Will Burma be free in the foreseeable future?'

'This is my belief, yes.'

'That's not just a dream?'

'No. I calculate it from the will of the people and the current of world opinion.'

'What can people outside Burma do to help?'

'People can ask their governments to implement the UN General Assembly Resolution on Burma which calls for democracy and human rights.'

'You know, when you were completely isolated, I never thought I'd be sitting in this room having this conversation with you. Do you sometimes wonder how your fortunes have changed in a way you yourself didn't expect?'

'No, I knew I'd be free. Some day.'

This last remark was especially poignant. Not only are her husband and sons prevented from seeing her, but anyone letting it be known they intend to visit Aung San Suu Kyi is refused entry to Burma. When it became known that the head of the World Health Organisation had an appointment with her, his plane from Mandalay was inexplicably delayed for two hours and he was forced to remain on board without being allowed even to telephone her.

The individual who inspires her torment and intimidation is still Ne Win, who is not as tired and ill as 'observers' claim. In 1997, he met General Suharto and so ensured Burma's membership of ASEAN. However, it is General Khin Nyunt, the head of Military Intelligence and Ne Win's protégé, who is responsible for making Suu Kyi's life as miserable as possible.

Although he wears a fixed smile behind the obligatory sunglasses, Khin Nyunt has one of those faces from which you divine nothing. When I was in Rangoon, a headline in the *New Light of Myanmar* reminded readers of the 'blood and sweat' that the military had sacrificed for the country: a noble sentiment accompanied, unfortunately, by a photograph of General Khin Nyunt and his fellow generals teeing off on a golf range.

His seminal work goes under the catchy title, *The Conspiracy of Treasonous Minions Within the Myanmar Naing-Ngan and Traitorous Cohorts Abroad*. Basically, this is about the generals' refined paranoia and is reminiscent of the ranting, conspiracy-laden tracts turned out by Pol Pot. There are pages of mug shots of foreign 'instigative' (sic) journalists, who are abused as 'fabricators' and 'slanderers'. Alas, I was left out. Elsewhere, Burmese recant their accounts of torture 'to stop the bitterness against the nation', and writers promise to 'write correctly' in future.

One wonders how many of the gallery are dead. Khin Nyunt is the man who ensures that 'certain matters' are 'forgotten' and heretics are silenced: those like the lawyer Nay Min, serving fourteen years for 'spreading rumours' to the BBC; the UNICEF researcher Khin Zaw Win, serving fifteen years for sending 'fabricated news' to the UN Special Rapporteur on Burma; and the writer San San Nwe, sentenced to ten years for 'spreading false information injurious to the state'.[20]

In 1995, Khin Nyunt subjected a senior American senator, John McCain, to an hour-long harangue about how the SLORC were holding back the 'red tide'. He then played him a videotape showing 'communists' beheading villagers with machetes: footage so sickening that McCain's wife had to leave the room. The aim apparently was to convince the senator that Aung San Suu Kyi was a front for 'Red subversives'.[21] This is the man to whom the jet-lagged businessmen from PowerGen and Rolls-Royce, Total and Unocal, Pepsi and Fun Tours, Mitsui and Honda, pay their respects. Napoleon in Orwell's *Animal Farm* comes to mind.

Khin Nyunt's appearances lately in the *New Light of Myanmar* have taken on a religious quality. With his fellow SLORC members he is often photographed at a shrine, on his knees, head bowed before Lord Buddha. It is clear that, as none of them is getting any younger, the generals are keen to pile up merit points to ensure their speedy passage to the afterlife and Nirvana. Without merit points and considering their record so far they could be in difficulty, returning as frogs or rats. It is said they have taken ecclesiastical guidance from Ne Win, now an octogenarian and in urgent need of all the merit points he can get.

In order to crunch the vital numbers, Ne Win has built in the centre of Rangoon the biggest Buddhist temple of its kind in the world; its gold leaf alone reportedly weighs sixty tons. The people of Rangoon pointedly have ignored it as a place of worship. One night recently, according to reliable rumour, the top fell off: the worst kind of omen.

As I left Aung San Suu Kyi's house, the gentle Win Htein bade us farewell. 'Be careful in the street,' he said. Three months later he was arrested and sentenced to fourteen years' imprisonment. His crime was 'conspiracy' to smuggle abroad a videotape which purported to show the failure of the summer rice crop in the region of Henzada. This, said the prosecutor, was 'defamatory' and 'heinous'.[22]

Outside in the street a sunglasses followed us. He had located our driver and interrogated him, only to be told we were tourists. The next day, Sunday, we joined the officially permitted crowd outside her gate waiting for her to speak. The people were different from any I had seen; they were smiling, talking freely with each other, as if waiting for a gig to start. There were betel-nut sellers and cheroot sellers and a man with a block of ice ingeniously suspended in a red sock, selling cups of cold water. With the grace and courtesy that are never deferential and are part of the Burmese character, people made way for the foreign Gulliver, offering news-papers, even a cushion, for me to sit on.

When Aung San Suu Kyi appeared she was flanked by two other figures of principle and courage: General Tin Oo and U Kyi Maung, a former colonel, the vice-chairmen of the NLD, both of whom have spent years in prison. The clapping and whooping lasted minutes. She looked not at all glamorous, but grey and drawn. Yet she had people laughing uproariously as she mocked the dictatorship, using irony and parable.

As they laughed, I turned and counted the sunglasses, filming and photographing, watching. Their arbitrary power is a presence. A week earlier, a young man had tried to ease the crush by moving the barrier and was bundled away and given a two-year sentence. A former SLORC chairman, General Saw Maing, put it nicely: 'Today our country is ruled by martial law. Martial law means no law at all.'[23]

At the end of her speech people asked questions. She leaned over the spikes in the fence and listened intently, replying expressively. An old monk pushed through and asked her if she would join him in prayer; and she did. Most did not linger, knowing that they are often followed. A man told me he never goes home the night of a meeting. 'If they track you,' he said, 'things start to happen. The power goes off; the kids are sent home crying from school.'

When I asked him if 1988 could happen again, this time successfully, he said, 'Imagine a zebra crossing. The traffic never seems to stop for the pedestrians. One or two dart across. The majority wait impatiently at the kerb, then they surge across, until the traffic has lost all its power. Well, we are all back at the kerb now, waiting impatiently.' At that, he looked over his shoulder and walked away.

In its report on Burma, the World Bank thanks the regime for its 'invaluable help'. Although it is the size of a telephone book, the report includes not a single reference to the regime's crimes. They are not the bank's business. The bank does not yet want to give the SLORC money, neither does the International Monetary Fund. But like the Asian Development Bank, they will in time. Burma is too great a 'prize' to ignore. The unseen side of the 'Asian economic miracle' is the establishment of a vast, expanding pool of cheap labour extending from China to Indo-China to Indonesia, and now with the prospect of Burma undercutting them all.

Burma's economy will 'grow' as multinational companies exercise their prerogative under the rules of the World Trade Organisation to plunder its resources, markets and labour, free from local interference and international accountability. The 'investment' of the oil companies in Burma, the SLORC's biggest single source of hard currency, is a model of 'globalisation'.

After I had interviewed Aung San Suu Kyi, I crossed the border into Thailand. Here the future is laid out like an Asian *Silent Spring*: birdless, treeless, jerry-built, polluted, the traffic policemen in their face masks, the tourists in their deodorised rooms, the rich in their Mercedes, the poor in their fire-risk factories and their rubbish vats, the economy at the mercy of speculators. It is this 'economic' devastation that poses to a vulnerable society like Burma an even greater long-term threat than the barbarities of the dictatorship. Perhaps understandably, Suu Kyi skirted questions about it: her dilemma, about how she faces up to the power of the SLORC without providing an excuse for more bloodshed, and how she establishes a 'dialogue' without compromising her concept of democracy, is presently an overwhelming one. She is a Mandela without a de Klerk.

What is hopeful is the promise of sanctions in a remarkable disinvestment campaign spreading across the United States and Europe. Inspired by the boycott of apartheid South Africa, selective purchasing laws have been enacted by a number of American cities, including San Francisco, and the state of Massachusetts.These make illegal any state or city contracts with companies that trade with or invest in Burma. The Massachusetts law prohibits the state from commerce with Texaco, Federal Express, Johnson & Johnson, British Airways and other major firms.

Elsewhere in the United States, firms that have withdrawn from Burma include Reebok, the oil company Amoco and Levi-Strauss. Until January 1997, Pepsi-Cola, with a multi-million-dollar 'joint venture' in Rangoon, justified its collusion with the SLORC as missionary work. Louise Hoppe Finnerty, Vice President of Pepsico Government Affairs, explained that the company was in Burma 'to build bridges of understanding between people – bridges which open lines of communication, find common ground, stimulate dialogue and thus bring people and their nations closer together and towards world peace'. This was how, she said, Pepsi helped bring down communism in Eastern Europe where 'our presence [was] a positive force for change'.[24]

Pepsi has its world headquarters in Purchase, New York, whose state legislature is considering its own Burma sanctions. Pepsi products have been subjected to a worldwide student-led boycott. In announcing the company's withdrawal from Burma, a spokesman said, 'Pepsi still believes that free trade leads to free societies.'[25]

The brewers Heineken of Holland and Carlsberg of Denmark have also withdrawn. Heineken, the biggest-selling foreign beer in the American market, scrapped a proposed £20 million investment in order to guard its 'corporate reputation', admitted its chief executive.[26] After a picket of its main store in London, Oxford Street, British Home Stores said it would no longer buy Burmese-made clothes. The Burton Group has followed suit.

A Massachusetts Representative, Byron Rushing, who wrote the successful legislation for his own state, told me, 'In the case of South Africa, we were able to put pressure on a whole range of companies, and most eventually withdrew. That really added to the pressure on the white government. That was a victory. As for Burma, it's not going to happen overnight, but we've started. The civilised world should follow.'

In Britain, the United States, Canada, Australia and other

countries, a growing number of travel agents no longer sell tours to Burma. Some travel writers have dropped Burma from their itinerary. They do not include the author of the best-selling *Lonely Planet* guide, Joe Cummings, who wrote that those who claimed Burma was not 'better off' today were 'deliberately delivering misleading information to serve a political agenda'. Although the SLORC were 'abominable', 'political imprisonment, torture' and what he described as 'involuntary civilian service to the state' were not new and 'have been around for centuries'. Indeed, 'human rights abuses have decreased in the face of increased tourism'.[27]

His reassurances contrast with a current report by Amnesty International, which called the period of tourist promotion leading up to 'Visit Myanmar 1996' the 'worst year for human rights in Burma this decade'. This continued in 1997, said Amnesty, 'in an escalation in political repression un-equalled since the violent suppression by the army of the 1988–89 popular uprising. More than 2,000 people were arrested for calling for human rights reforms [and] severe restrictions were placed on Daw Aung San Suu Kyi's freedom of movement and speech ... While the world talks about "constructive engagement", things are going backwards in Burma. We call on the international communities to redouble pressure on the Burmese authorities.'[28]

Aung San Suu Kyi can no longer appear at her back gate, and people approaching her house are menaced by armed troops. Whenever she is allowed to leave, it must be by car and she is preceded and followed by vehicles of the secret police. The image is bizarre: one slight woman amidst a motorcade of gun-toting state goons.

Most of the time her phone at home is dead. If Michael and her sons manage to get through they are often cut off. Early one morning, at a pre-arranged time, and in circumstances contribed by the underground, I phoned her.

'Thank you so much for the books,' she said. 'It has been a joy to read widely again.' I had sent her an eclectic lot, including poetry – her favourite is T. S. Eliot – and Jonathan Coe's acclaimed political novel, *What a Carve Up!*

I asked what was happening outside her house.

'Oh, the road is blocked and they're all over the street . . . for my own security, of course!'

'You sound in good spirits.'

'Oh, I'm not doing too badly. But I *am* distressed at the way everyone is being treated. Twenty NLD people have been sentenced to seven years under what the SLORC calls the Public Order Preservation Act. There are secret trials going on all the time in Insein prison. The accused are hooded throughout these travesties, so the lawyers can't identify them. They are even hooded when their families visit: the few who are allowed to visit. People are arrested for no reason whatsoever.'

'What is the resistance like now?'

'Pretty good. Indignation is increasing, and defiance. Students were on the streets [in December 1996] demanding democracy. And you may have heard that the rice farmers in Shwebo district held a rally, and joined up with the students.'

'Are there similarities with 1988?'

'There is certainly the same anger and resentment; and the state of the people is dreadful. I mean the nutritional level. Everything costs more now. Only the super rich are protected.'

'How is "Visit Myanmar Year" doing?'

'There were six people in the largest hotel in Rangoon last week, and another one boasts two guests. This is definitely not a flying start!' She described how trade and tourism with Burma 'benefits only those at the top' and said that 'if Western governments want to stop the drugs trade, they should support democracy in Burma'.

'Are they still abusing you in the press?'

'Do you know anybody at the *Guinness Book of Records*? At the moment, they're building up to a crescendo. I just wonder how long they can remain on a high C!'

'How is that affecting you personally?'

'Look, they can't get through to me . . .'

'Do you not worry that you are trapped in a terrible stalemate?'

'I'm really not fond of that expression,' she said rather sternly. 'Students have been on the streets. That's not a stalemate. Ethnic people, like the Karen, are fighting back. That's not a stalemate. The defiance is there in people's lives, day after day. You know, even when things seem still on the surface, there's always movement underneath. It's like a frozen lake; and beneath our lake, we are progressing: bit by bit.'

'What do you mean exactly?'

'What I am saying is, that no matter the regime's oppression and its physical power, in the end they can't stop the people; they can't stop freedom. Who would have imagined a few short years ago that the people of Czechoslovakia would be free, and Vaclav Havel would be President, and Nelson Mandela would be free ... They couldn't be stopped, and neither can we. We shall have our time.'

IV

AUSTRALIA

Secret Waters

The porpoises pick their partners and dance, and go up in the air. It's the most glorious thing to watch. Just like the surfers, they ride the waves and everything. It's a real picture.

Jack Platt, Bondi Beach shark catcher

Genocide is the attempt to destroy a people, a culture. The first act was the dispossession of Aboriginal people of their land. The second act was the dispossession of Aboriginal people of their children. The land was stolen. The children were stolen. What is the third act going to be?

Sir Ronald Wilson, President, Australian Human Rights and Equal Opportunities Commission

THE SKIES HAVE sulked for days and now, through the blinds, there are the first shafts of diamond light, said to give us our laconic squint, and by rush-hour on the Harbour Bridge the temperature is thirty degrees. Thereafter, the massed bands of locusts strike up; strangers exchange the Australian salute, which is a windscreen-wiper motion conducted with one or both hands to ward off the flies; Nick the Bondi fruitologist brings out his first plums and apricots, while the magpies watch from the huge cross of the Catholic church opposite, and the convent playground turns to liquorice. By the evening a southerly breeze has delivered a cocktail of salt spray, dogshit and other seasonal fragrances. Summer has arrived.

223

Down at the beach, the first of the tidal swells known as bombaras are rising like pyramids and breaking into steep rolling surf. Everyone is on the beach. Or I like to think so. Like all Bondi kids, I learned to swim the crawl, which is known as freestyle here. My coach was Reg Clark, who lived two doors along in Moore Street. Reg was a freckled, silent man who expressed himself in the relentless grace of his swimming stroke. He swam every day just after dawn, summer and winter, his long arms reaching out and hardly stirring the surface of the water, head turning every now and then. He taught me to keep swimming, to 'reach out', even when it seemed the giant hand of a wave would snatch us away.

When I began to race for the Bondi Amateur Swimming Club, Reg passed me on to Sep Prosser. Sep was a swimming king, with his throne on the whitewashed rock overlooking Bondi Ocean Baths. He wore extra Brylcreem, a deep tan and the prototype of Ray-Bans. He was a matinée idol, permanently garlanded in females and not taking a lot of notice, I thought, of us kids tadpoling up and down in front of him. I was wrong. Sep was one of those who produced an Australian swimming generation once described as 'Don Bradman's equivalent in the water'.

There were so many kids who were to perform feats in the water, some of them in their teens establishing Olympic and world records that would stand for years. Theirs was an amateurism that expressed a love of swimming and Herculean selflessness; and what was thrilling about them was that they were all from 'down the street': from the faded Art Deco flats with stairwells that smelt of cabbage and beer, and the dark semis, and the backyards fenced in rusted corrugated iron.

Bondi's races were held in the early hot dazzle of a Saturday morning. Afterwards we would walk along the great crescent of white sand to where the best surf was running. I still do this. Then, as now, rollers not dumpers were the waves to catch. No matter how steep, they are exhilarating for a body surfer. Strength is needed to get to the crest but, once you feel the power of it, you become a human catamaran with your feet the rudder. Dipping your head as you move down the face of the wave, you can ride all the way to the sandcastles. The walk up the beach is almost as good as the sun on your back when you hit the hot sand and listen to the rhythm of your heart.

Lying near the heart of Sydney, Bondi, where I grew up, is not a resort but part of the city. This is unusually Australian and puzzling to outsiders. A travel brochure I picked up described Sydney's beaches as its 'tiaras'. I agree, although tourists might be disappointed; the charm of the most famous beach is its fine ordinariness. Indeed, Bondi has remained defiantly down at heel since I grew up on the tram route that joined its most famous pubs, the Astra on the beach and Billy the Pig's up at the Junction.

Then much of Sydney was down-at-heel, with crooked streets of Edwardian slums, long since gentrified. In Bondi, the 'battlers' often had jobs and stayed loyal to the beach; and that remains true. My father and mother, when they first married, had a room for a few shillings a week with a view beyond the lace curtains like none on earth. Framed between the chimneys and the dunnies, the Pacific was always there, deepest green to the first breaker and deepest blue to the horizon. The dunnies have gone, but the great sheet of green-blue endures.

On the other side of Sydney Harbour was a place that almost stole my swimmer's heart from Bondi. At the age of thirteen I was selected to swim for Sydney High School in a pool that advertised itself as 'the finest swimming baths on earth'. The North Sydney Olympic Pool was built in 1935 in Lavender Bay, three years after the Harbour Bridge that towers over it. With the mighty coat-hanger on one side and the white sails of the Opera House beyond, it is one of the three symbols of Sydney, if not Australia.

The first of its kind, the salt-water pool was lavished with glazed Roman tiles and arcades of tapestry brickwork inset with motifs of shells, dolphins and seagulls, and decorative glass which ensured that light always played on the water. It was known as the 'wonder pool'. On opening day, Alderman

C. C. Faulkner described its innovations as follows: 'No dead fish will ever float into this pool, and the man who drowns his cat in the harbour can bathe here in the certainty that the corpse will not confront him.'

During its first twenty-five years, the Olympic Pool saw the golden days of Australian swimming. Although it was never used for the Olympics (Melbourne took that honour in 1956), some of the greatest swimmers of the century set their records there. Until recently, life-sized black-and-white photographs of them lined the entrance tunnel. Beside the turnstiles there is a list headed, 'World records created at the North Sydney Olympic Pool'. I still count them – eighty-six in all. No pool on earth can match it.

(In 1938, the only time a boat was allowed into the pool was for a duel between the world champion sculler, C. Pearce, and the Australian champion swimmer, J. R. Wilshire, over one lap. Pearce only just won.)

These champions were of my era: John Devitt, who swam 110 yards in just over fifty-five seconds in 1959, an incredible performance in those days; John Konrads, who had set twenty-three world records at the pool while still a teenager, and his sister Ilsa, who set seven records by the time she turned fifteen; Murray Rose, who dominated 440 and 800 yards (at the age of twelve, I prided myself in being runner-up to him, almost a pool's length behind); the amazing Steven Holland, the 'super fish', who broke three world records in the Olympic trials of 1976; and Dawn Fraser and Lorraine Crapp, whose style and courage made them our heroines.

Coached by friends and fathers, training at sunrise and at night, none of them made money out of swimming. That such a small population (fewer than ten million then) could produce so many fine swimmers was affirmation of the way we Australians liked to think we were. It had something to do with our origins: the strong sense of being a nation of underdogs, which is still there and is probably related, by blood and myth, to the historical fact that a number of our great-great-grandparents, like my own, had arrived in leg-irons.

Unlike the United States, our first white inhabitants were

not on a mission from God but were Godforsaken. We clung to the foreshores of an ancient continent whose mysteries and harshness made us, so we thought, innocent bystanders in our own country. We liked to think that we were the poor who had got away: 'an entire continent peopled by the lower orders', as Mark Twain once observed of Australia.

He was not that far out; and the proof is there still in the unpatronising celebration of working-class culture. Bondi people were the Irish who ran the politics, and Jewish refugees – known as reffos – and others known as Eyeties, Chinks, Balts and Boongs. There were numerous Little Belfasts and Little Cypruses and Little Lebanons; and there was no blood on the streets. It did not matter that people got on by default; most agreed there was nowhere better a battler could go. We did not know it and could not imagine it, but this was the prototype of what was to become the most culturally diverse society on earth (after Israel).

That Bondi belonged to a people excluded from this melting pot was never mentioned. Their secrets remained beneath the concrete and asphalt on the ocean promenade, in the workshops and armouries where they made the weapons and tools with which they had endeavoured to defend their homeland against the white-skinned invaders. All but a few of the original people of Bondi died in the invasion: from diseases brought by the English, or they were shot or poisoned.

Something similar happened over at Lavender Bay, on the site of the Olympic Pool. This side of Sydney belonged to the Waddermedegal and Cammeraygal peoples until they, too, were exterminated. This happened all over the continent. It was our secret life; and that has not changed.

In the 1960s, when a generation of young Australians (including myself) was leaving Australia to discover the 'swinging' England of squalid bedsits and missing bathrooms, the majority of Australians could boast the most equitable spread of personal income in the world. The myth of an egalitarian or 'fair go' society was at least half true. 'What sort of peculiar capitalist country is this', V. I. Lenin was moved to ask half a century earlier, 'in which the workers' representatives predominate in the *Upper* House?'[1] The inheritors of the 'living hell' of the penal colonies, the children of the Chartists and Fenians and those who simply survived, wanted 'Utopia under the Southern Cross'. They were denied that; but their achievements were considerable.

Although times were often hard for a nation of wage-earners, long before the rest of the Western world, Australians gained a legal basic wage, an eight-hour working day, pensions, maternity allowance, child benefits and the vote for women. In 1920 the silver and zinc miners of Broken Hill, New South Wales, won the world's first thirty-five-hour week. The secret ballot was invented in the state of Victoria and became known as the 'Australian ballot'. The world's first Labour Government was formed in Queensland; and the Australian Labor Party formed governments twenty years before any comparable socialist or social democratic party took office in Europe.[2] 'To Europeans', wrote the historian Jill Roe, 'the state in Australia appeared to be a boldly experimental agent.'[3]

In fact, the state was an orthodox Keynesian social democracy, with a strong sense of class. The colonial establishment was made up of landed and commercial conservatives, while the great majority were wage-earners. Although they consistently won majorities, a preferential system of voting and gerrymandered electoral boundaries kept the Labor Party out of office for twenty-three years. Elected in 1972, the Labor Government of Gough Whitlam sought to use the state as an experimental agent, extending education, welfare and health care. When he was deposed three years later in a 'constitutional *coup d'état*' led by the Governor-General, the Labour Party never recovered its radical mythology.[4]

More than that, Labor remade itself as a truly conservative party and, re-elected in 1983, launched the most spectacular redistribution of wealth in living memory – in favour of a new elite. The Prime Minister, Bob Hawke, called this an 'historic transformation' that would lead to a 'golden age'. When Labor came to power, the combined wealth of the top 200 richest Australians was less than $A5 billion. After six years, it was $A25 billion.[5] Having begun the decade with one of the smallest public debts in the world, Australia became one of the most indebted countries in the world, as the newly rich reaped the bonanza of a deregulated, anything-goes financial system.

The corporate crook Alan Bond built a paper empire that ended up owing $A14 billion, or 10 per cent of the national debt. 'Bondy', as Hawke liked to call him, is now in prison serving three years, with another five years a possibility, for illegally siphoning off a billion dollars from within his corporate group: what the *Australian Financial Review* called 'the biggest robbery in Australia's history'.[6]

The redistribution was carried out by Paul Keating, Hawke's Treasurer and later his successor. Keating asked Australians to look at what he called 'the big picture'. This included a 'republicanism' he promoted assiduously while transferring the country's economic sovereignty to foreigners with more power than the Queen of England could imagine. Rupert Murdoch, for one, owns two-thirds of the Australian metropolitan press – thanks to a Media Bill introduced by Keating in 1986. According to the financial analysts, County Securities Australia, the Labor Government's deregulation of the television industry gave Murdoch and Kerry Packer 'a one billion dollar gift entirely free of tax'.[7] Next to Canada, Australia is now the most foreign-owned country in the world.

At the same time, wage-earners saw their incomes cut by 25 per cent, with millions of dollars in wage and tax cuts transferred into profits. When Keating's reign ended in 1996, structural unemployment stood at 8·6 per cent, although the real figure is much higher. A United Nations Human Development report concluded that the gap between rich and poor in Australia was one of the widest in the developed world and greater than in many Third World countries. Today, almost one Australian in four is born into poverty. In Sydney alone, there are an estimated 200,000 homeless young people. One wintry Sunday, I watched many of them converge on Bondi Beach and build bonfires on the fine white sand of the national icon as a demonstration of what had happened to their 'fair go' society.[8]

While I swam in my wonder pool, Aboriginal children were barred from entering public swimming pools all over Australia. In 1966, Charlie Perkins, an Aborigine, chained himself to the turnstile of the municipal pool at Moree, in western New South Wales, and after enduring threats and violence, he and his fellow 'freedom riders' saw the black kids in.

Three years later, Charlie and I smashed down the gate of the Aboriginal reserve at Jay Creek in the Northern Territory by driving a Ford Falcon at it. The other way was to get permission and fill out forms with the certainty of refusal. Heddy, Charlie's mother and a queen of the Aranda people, was in the back seat wearing her best black hat. 'Do it,' she said.

Moree and Jay Creek were part of the Australian Gulag. At Jay Creek, in the red heart of the country, 300 people lived in administered squalor, often without water in 40-degree summer temperatures and with the pipes frozen in winter. In exchange for the 'security' of the reserve, they were subjected to a series of arbitrary, petty and often brutal punishments, such as enforced separation from family members. The children had distended bellies, stick limbs: the obvious symptoms of malnutrition. They were shooed into the bush when, every other Thursday, tourists came to watch the people throw boomerangs and ride a camel. Aborigines on a camel? 'Yanks don't know the difference,' said the white manager. 'We need the money for those little extras.'

Times have changed, though not altogether. Nearly thirty years later, I was travelling in northern Queensland and happened on 'Wild World', a tourist attraction. Twice a day, between 'wombat feeds' and a 'toad and snakes show', Aborigines performed a 'cultural show'. That is, three young men blew didgeridoos and cavorted unconvincingly while a Japanese tour guide stood in front of them, interpreting for her non-plussed package tour. Tourism, not sheep, is now Australia's biggest export earner.

Aborigines are counted in the census and have the vote and can administer many of their own affairs through land councils, several of which have done shrewd deals with mining companies. Yet, says one government study, 40 per cent of the indigenous people are so poor they still lack 'the most basic needs imaginable'.[9]

That was the situation when I was growing up, when now and then I would glimpse the ragged kids with flies on their eyes, many half-blind from trachoma, a Third World scourge. They went barefoot then; they wear trainers now. Their life expectancy, says the Australian Bureau of Statistics, is lower than that of most countries in the world and is matched only in India and Central Africa.[10] Aboriginal infant mortality is three times higher than that of white children, higher in Western Australia than in Bangladesh. The health of Aboriginal women has so deteriorated that the death rate is now up to six times that of white women.[11]

In 1983, two researchers made a discovery in the records of the Queensland Health Department: Aboriginal deaths from infectious, preventable diseases were as much as 300 times higher than that of the white average in the state and among the highest in the world.[12] In 1997, the Federal Health Minister, Michael Wooldridge, made an extraordinary admission. 'In my area of health,' he said, 'there is no evidence of any improvement whatsoever in the last decade ... the gap [between Aboriginal and white health] has actually widened.'[13]

What used to be regarded by establishment voices as conveniently contentious is now stated as fact. 'Much of the poverty and disease in Aboriginal communities', said the President of the Australian Medical Association, Dr Keith Woollard, 'is a result of the dispossession of their lands.'[14]

This was also the view of expert witnesses giving evidence to a Royal Commission into Aboriginal deaths in custody in the late 1980s. The Commission heard that Aborigines were sixty times more likely to be arrested than whites in Western Australia, and Aboriginal children made up 2·7 per cent of the state's youth and 58 per cent of the juveniles in detention. There was evidence of beatings and, by any definition, torture; neglect was established as standard police procedure. After sitting for two years at a cost of $A30 million, the Commission made 339 recommendations. Not one of them called for criminal charges against police or prison officers. Not a single one alleged foul play.[15]

The Royal Commission recommended the blindingly obvious: that Aborigines should be imprisoned as a last resort. Since then, Aborigines have been sent to prison at a rate higher than ever before and the number dying behind bars has doubled.[16] The former chief psychiatrist at Bargwanarth Hospital in Soweto wrote to the *Sydney Morning Herald* to point out that the rate of black deaths in custody in Australia was thirteen times higher than in South Africa.[17]

There is no mystery why. In 1996, newspapers published a series of photographs of New South Wales policemen at a party with blackened faces and mock nooses around their necks, meant to depict Aborigines who had died in police custody. No disciplinary action was taken against them.

When the Liberal and National Party coalition defeated Labor in 1996, largely as a result of the electorate's bitterness towards Keating personally, the new Prime Minister, John Howard, picked up smoothly where his predecessor had left off. Whereas Labor's Thatcherism had been veiled, Howard's was not. He took two significant steps.

The first was to attack the very concept of justice for and 'reconciliation' with the first Australians by slashing more than $A400 million from the Aboriginal affairs budget – what he contemptuously referred to as the 'Aboriginal industry'. The second was to undercut immigration, which had been the basis of Australia's economic development for half a century.

For those encouraged to make their lives far from their ancestral homes, the family reunion programme had been an article of faith. Now this, too, was decimated – together with the funding of the Human Rights and Equal Opportunity

Commission, whose responsibility is to protect minorities and raise awareness about racism. 'Political correctness', as the new Prime Minister put it, had 'gone too far' . . . there should be 'a new spirit of freedom of expression'.

No one was in any doubt what he really meant. He was speaking in Queensland, a state whose racist history had recently demonstrated its resilience in the election of a Federal Independent, Pauline Hanson, on a provocative anti-Aboriginal, anti-immigration platform.[18] Her electorate has one of the highest unemployment rates in Australia. More than half the young people cannot find work. Having identified the scapegoats, she made the time-honoured connections.

She is a female, Antipodean version of George Wallace, the Alabama Governor who ran for the American presidency in the late 1960s and spoke for 'the little folks the system don't care about any more'. She emphasises her ordinariness. She is in her early forties, a single mother and a former manager of a fish and chip shop. She says she is 'not a politician, just a naïve mother' who speaks 'on behalf of the ordinary, average person who's fed up with the pollies [politicians]'. That refrain has a resonance in a country where cynicism about dissembling politicians and their rich and bent 'mates' may be more prevalent than in any Western democracy.

She says that Aborigines are 'privileged', and a book written for her, *Pauline Hanson, the Truth*, says they 'killed and ate their women and children and occasionally their men'. All that is false. Describing Aboriginal women, the book uses the word 'gin': the equivalent of 'nigger'. She 'warns' that by 2050 Australia will be part of the 'United States of Asia' and that the 'new class elites have deliberately earmarked Anglo-Saxon Australia for destruction'.[19]

Her apocalyptic message echoes in a political vacuum left by a Labor Party which no longer pretends to defend ordinary Australians. In 1997, Australia's largest corporation, BHP, the 'big Australian', announced that it was closing down all steel production in the working-class city of Newcastle, New South Wales, with other closures to come. More than 8,000 jobs are expected to be lost.[20] At the same time, a poll revealed that one in four voters would consider supporting Hanson's 'One Nation Party'.[21]

Apart from calling her an 'empty populist', Prime Minister Howard pointedly refused to criticise Hanson, who had become a lightning rod, frightening Aborigines and ethnic groups. In fact, the immediate threat to them came not from her but from the Prime Minister himself. The message of Hanson's 'One Nation Party' bore a close resemblance to Howard's 'One Australia Policy' which, he had declared in 1988, would be pursued by a future government led by him. He, too, 'warned' about the rise of 'social tension' and 'a lack of social cohesion'. He was, in effect, calling for a version of the former White Australian Policy, which had been openly racist and inspired by apartheid South Africa.[22]

Once in office, Howard began to reverse the most significant gain made by the Aboriginal people. This is the Native Title Act, passed by Federal Parliament in 1993. Based on a landmark ruling by the Australian High Court the year before, it removed from common law the fiction that Australia was uninhabited when Captain James Cook planted the Union Flag in 1770. Known as *Terra Nullius*, it was used for most of two centuries to justify the dispossession of the indigenous population.

Unlike Australia's sheep, the Aborigines were not counted until the late 1960s. 'We occupied the land, but we were fauna,' said Aboriginal lawyer Noel Pearson.[23] When British atomic scientists were given permission by Prime Minister Robert Menzies to test nuclear weapons on Aboriginal land at Maralinga in the 1950s, they used site maps marked 'Uninhabited'. Patrick Connolly, who served with the RAF at Maralinga, was threatened with prosecution by the security services after he had revealed that 'during the two and a half years I was there, I would have seen 400 to 500 Aborigines in contaminated areas. Occasionally, we would bring them in for decontamination. Other times we just shooed them off like rabbits.'[24]

The 1993 High Court judgement, known as the 'Mabo

decision' after a successful land rights claimant, Eddie Mabo, was not the victory it was hailed as at the time. It was a 'historic compromise' in the classic liberal mould, between the powerful and the powerless. The judges did not order stolen land to be handed back to the indigenous inhabitants. In deciding that Aborigines *might* have title to 'crown land' where they had lived continuously, the judges added an escape clause. Land rights could be 'extinguished' by the existence of freehold and leasehold of the huge pastoral estates, many of which were acquired by the sons of nineteenth-century English aristocrats simply by 'squatting' on them.

The Native Title legislation that followed the judgement became the 'personal mission', as he put it, of the then Prime Minister, Paul Keating, whose speeches about 'reconciliation' reached rhetorical peaks unscaled by his predecessors. Keating's achievement was to sell the critical ambiguity of the Mabo decision to 'moderate' Aboriginal leaders. It was, he told them, the best deal they would ever get from the white man. One of the Aboriginal negotiators, Noel Pearson, said ruefully, 'To refuse to play the game no longer seemed smart.'[25]

Keating lost no time in demonstrating how the game was played. In accepting his assurances, Aborigines gave up the right of veto over 'development' on much of their land, a fundamental principle of land rights. The Keating Government's unspoken agenda was to confirm the 'land rights' of the mining lobby, promising to hand back to the states the right to 'validate' all Aboriginal land claims. This all but ensured the failure of claims against mining companies whose political power in the huge states of Queensland and Western Australia was undisputed. Prime Minister Howard went further. He demanded they give up even the right to negotiate land development. His adviser, Senator Nick Minchen, used code familiar to black Australians and which Pauline Hanson echoed. If Aborigines got 'too much', he said, the 'community' would resent their 'special rights' and this would 'undermine the reconciliation process'.[26]

In the meantime, the 'pastoralists' and their lobbyists clamoured for the new legislation to be tested. They did not have to wait long. In 1996, the High Court found that in an appeal case involving the Wik people in Queensland, Native Title was not necessarily cancelled by a pastoralist's leasehold. In other words, a lease was a lease: it granted possession only for a specific period of time. Thunderous abuse rained down upon the 'radical' and 'politically motivated' judges, from Cabinet ministers, agribusiness and mining groups.

'In other circumstances', wrote the historian Henry Reynolds, 'conservative politicians and business leaders would have flocked to the opposite side of the argument. They would normally applaud the centuries-old battle of the common law to protect property rights against the state. The problem in the Wik case was that the wrong people had acquired rights to the land. What they baulk at is that they will have to deal with indigenous Australians as equals for the first time in 200 years.'[27]

This is the heart of the issue. 'Most Aborigines', said the *Canberra Times*, 'gain no legal rights from the Mabo or Wik decisions. What they did gain was a significant moral victory . . . Aboriginal groups have [since] behaved with more dignity and more reason, and more willingness to discuss, negotiate and compromise, than some of the groups still unable to get over their outrage that Aborigines have any rights to land at all.'[28]

The outrage includes an element of guilt. Farmers are more aware than any that the land is not 'theirs': that the indigenous people have a unique relationship with it. There is a secret history here. Many farmers and their pioneer forebears could not have held or managed the land, especially during periods of environmental hardship, such as prolonged drought, without the support of the Aboriginal community. 'Aboriginal labour', wrote Henry Reynolds, 'was an indispensable component of the economic success of open-range grazing . . . The pastoral industry has a debt to Aboriginal people as the beneficiary of unpaid labour, on land that was taken by force.'[29]

Nor is the debt simply a moral one. Without Aboriginal stockmen, some of the largest and most profitable pastoral properties would not have survived. These men were paid half the wages of white workers, plus 'rations'. Their pay went into savings accounts held by the state-owned Commonwealth Bank. The men were issued with passbooks, which were held by the local Aboriginal 'protector', usually a 'reserve' manager, mission superintendent or policeman. They could not withdraw even the smallest amount without the custodian's agreement, and because many were illiterate they were unable to read the amounts deposited and withdrawn.

Rodney Hall, who was the editor of an Aboriginal newsletter in Queensland in the 1960s, estimates that the sums owed to Aborigines, after a lifetime's work, could amount to millions of dollars. 'These stockmen quite reasonably expected their savings to be accumulating,' he wrote, 'but the balance seldom amounted to more than a few thousand dollars. Sometimes, just a few hundred ... [I] alerted the media, [but there was] never an answer. Never a single letter or phone call from a mainstream newspaper, radio or television station. Not one. The issue was not allowed to exist in the national forum. Somebody's pockets were lined. Are we to believe it was the protectors? Or the holders of the pastoral leases? Once this has been cleared up, we can revisit the subject of the scale of reparations Aboriginal people may legitimately expect.'[30]

Howard was having none of it. He produced a 'ten-point plan' for legislation that would convert leasehold to freehold and thereby wipe out Native Title in all but name. The beneficiaries will not be small farmers, but some of the richest and most powerful companies and individuals in white Australia. Effectively, 42 per cent of Australia will pass from leasehold to freehold controlled by fewer than 20,000 people. 'The influence of this group', wrote Kenneth Davidson, 'is magnified by the media and political connections of some of the biggest players.'

They include Kerry Packer, owner of the Nine television network and most of Australia's magazines, who is the seventh largest landholder in the country, and Rupert Murdoch, who controls 70 per cent of the major newspapers and owns nine vast properties. The top private landholder,

Hugh McLachlan, is the cousin of the Defence Minister in the Howard Government. The second largest holding is controlled by the McDonald family, notably the Federal President of the National Party, Howard's coalition partner. Twenty-six major landholders are government MPs.[31]

Nothing like it has been proposed in a modern society; it means the reintroduction of race into the political mainstream and the expropriation from one group of Australians, the indigenous people, of property rights that the High Court has said are theirs, the object being to advantage another group, almost all of whom happen to be white and wealthy. The legislation, regardless of its obfuscating 'complexities', is straight out of the fascist ideology called apartheid. It may well transpire that around the date this book is published, Australians are called upon to vote in their first modern election whose central theme, shamefully, is race.

During the 1980s, the historian Geoffrey Blainey, who had gained respect for popularising the Australian past, made a series of inflammatory public statements with race as the subtext. Like Pauline Hanson, he warned of a conspiracy, this time between an 'alliance of academics and ethnics' who met in a 'secret room' in the Department of Immigration. He referred to 'front-line' suburbs in the cities and said he was speaking up for those Australians whose dissent was confined to 'graffiti on the café lavatory'. He quoted complaints about spitting foreigners and their stinking cooking, the sort of people who dry 'noodles on the clothes line in the backyard' and 'fly around in flash cars while I walk all the time'.[32]

Aborigines, by any stretch of the imagination, fail to qualify for these categories, but an expression coined by Blainey includes them, their history and legacy: indeed, it covers all those who seek and document the truth about Australia's rapacious past. He calls this the 'black armband' view of history.

The 'black armband' records the dispossession and violence that took place during the invasion and occupation of territory where an indigenous people had lived continuously for thousands of years. It contradicts the version I was taught at school. This was that the story of the 'settlement' of Australia was a faintly heroic and sublime tale of white men tackling the frontier and bringing civilisation to an untamed continent.

In this 'white blindfold' version, blacks played almost no part. In the textbooks I studied, they were 'tribesmen who live in practically the same way as their forefathers did . . . They are people who know almost no history. We are civilised and they are not'; or they were 'an animal of prey . . . more ferocious than the lynx, the leopard, or the hyena'; or they were totally beyond the pale. A 1970 reprint of *The Squatting Age* by Professor Stephen Roberts concluded, 'It was quite useless to treat them [the Aborigines] fairly, since they were completely amoral and usually incapable of sincere and prolonged gratitude.' This was a departure for Roberts, whose *History of Australian Land Settlement*, regarded as a classic account, included not a single reference to the indigenous population.[33]

Many years later, this was explained by the doyen of a new wave of Australian historians, Henry Reynolds, in his 1981 book, *The Other Side of the Frontier*. 'The barriers which for so long kept Aboriginal experience out of our history books', he wrote, 'were not principally those of source material', which had been 'available to scholars for a century or more. But black cries of anger and anguish were out of place in works that celebrated national achievement or catalogued peaceful progress in a quiet continent, while deft scholarly feet avoided the embarrassment of bloodied billabongs.'[34]

For John Howard, things had gone too far. As an anti-black-armband man, he launched his own campaign, criticising schools that taught that Australia had a 'racist, bigoted past'. Was he suggesting that teachers should falsify history? Here was the equivalent of President Clinton attacking schools for teaching that slavery was a product of racism and bigotry. The incredulity and anger of the reaction to his inanities forced him to retreat, but not for long.[35]

Howard, now joined by Hanson, was stoking this fatuous 'debate' when the Human Rights and Equal Opportunity

Commission, the body he had tried to destroy, released the most damning and painful report on perhaps the darkest chapter in the nation's history: that of the 'stolen generations'. Entitled *Bringing Them Home*, the report concluded that up to a third of Aboriginal children were forcibly removed from their families between 1910 and 1970, making a total of 100,000 stolen children. Placed in white missions, institutions and foster homes, the children were forced into a form of slavery, often physically and sexually abused and denied protection by the state.[36]

Police were used to find and steal children. They had orders not to tell the children or their parents where they were being taken. The following is a typical case, reported in the *Sydney Morning Herald* of January 10, 1925:

ABORIGINALS
Children Removed from Parents' Control
Heartrending Scene

Grafton, Thursday. The circumstances under which four aboriginal children, whose ages ranged from four to thirteen years, were separated from their parents have aroused much indignation locally.

The separation occurred just before Christmas ... It appeared that a police officer's instructions were to meet the parents at the ferry, and thither [the children] went accompanied by their parents, who did not know that their little ones were to be taken away from them. The scene at the parting was heartrending, but the children were taken, despite protests and tears ... The parents were in a terrible state about it ...

As previously suppressed files now reveal, there was often no pretence of taking into care 'neglected' children, who were stolen from loving two-parent families. Robert T. Donaldson, an inspector of the perversely-named Aborigines Protection Board, became infamous as the 'kids' collector', a gaunt figure who roamed New South Wales, appearing with sweets and disappearing with children.

The policy was fascist and stemmed from the eugenics

movement, which was fashionable in the first two decades of the century and which promoted fears that white women were not breeding fast enough and the 'white' race would be 'swamped'. During the 1930s this was known as 'assimilation' and was inspired by the Professor of Anthropology at Sydney University, A. P. Elkin, who speculated that Aborigines were the 'lowest race' and 'parasites' that should be 'absorbed'.[37]

The stolen boys were sent to sheep and cattle stations as labourers and paid in rations and pennies. The girls, who were the majority, were sent mostly to the Cootamundra Training Home for Aboriginal Girls, where they were made into domestic servants, then 'indentured' to 'masters' in white middle-class homes.

There is a historic parallel with the use of black slave girls as domestics in the American southern states before Emancipation. While books, plays and laments have been written about the dispossession and suffering of black Americans, there has been no such outpouring in Australia. Until recently, there was a belief that the children were being 'saved' from the horrors of a 'primitive' upbringing, in particular the 'half-castes'. Mostly there was indifference and silence.

Whenever word of the horror leaked out there was, at first, disbelief, then extreme discomfort and censorship. It took the film-maker Alec Morgan almost two years to convince the Australian Broadcasting Corporation to show his searing documentary, *Lousy Little Sixpence*, the first film to tell the full story of the stolen children; and that was as recently as the early 1980s.

When my own television series about Australia, *The Last Dream* (made with Alan Lowery and Alec Morgan) was shown on the ABC in 1988, the year that whites celebrated the bicentenary of their 'settlement', it elicited fury from establishment commentators, incensed at the suggestion by witnesses in the films that genocide had taken place in Australia. Nine years later, the President of the Human Rights Commission, Sir Ronald Wilson, stood up at the National

Reconciliation Convention in Melbourne and said, 'We as a committee have decided that what was done meets the international definition of genocide.'[38]

Sir Ronald explained that fifty years ago the United Nations ruled that the forced transfer of children to a group where they were given a different education, religion and language equated to the destruction of a race. 'Genocide is the attempt to destroy a people, a culture,' he said. 'The first act was the tragic dispossession of Aboriginal people of their land. The second act was the dispossession of Aboriginal people of their children. The land was stolen. The children were stolen. What is the third act going to be? Are we now witnessing in the betrayal that the Wik legislation represents, the completion of the first act, the dispossession of land?'

The Commission's report called for an apology from the government and for reparations. John Howard refused to make an official apology and made clear that there would be no reparations. During that week, Federal Parliament spent an hour debating a proposal for a levy on the slaughter of emus for human consumption. Sir Ronald Wilson's report describing genocide in Australia was given half an hour, during which the Prime Minister, the members of his Cabinet and most government MPs left before the 'debate' was over.

I have interviewed many of the stolen children – men and women now in their middle age. Perhaps it is because I too am an Australian, but I can think of few situations in which I have been so moved and angered by what I have heard.

There was Joy. 'People would hide their kids,' she told me. 'A truck would pull up outside and the officers would get out a bag of boiled lollies, give the kids one, then snatch them. It was kidnapping. I knew one woman who was waiting for her son to come back from the dentist. He'd be fifty-three now, and they snatched him when he was nine on the way back from the dentist; and he never saw his mother again.

'My Mum was snatched . . . Later, when I came along, of course I was taken away. Mum was given a hysterectomy at the age of eighteen. She didn't know anything about it.'

'Was that unusual?' I asked.

'For Aboriginal women? No ... Western Australia was notorious for it.'

Joy grew up believing she was an orphan. When she asked repeatedly, she was told her mother was 'bad' because 'she didn't want you'. And when, years later, her search ended and she found her mother, there was a terrible moment. 'The first thing she did was hit me,' she said. 'Afterwards I found out that she'd come to visit me at the home and they'd reassured her I would be coming back to her. But they were lying; it wasn't true; and she blamed me for not coming back to her.'

Joy herself had a daughter, who was adopted while she was in hospital. 'I was sedated on that day,' she said. 'I wasn't aware I was signing the papers. I found out last year she was married. Not a day passes when I don't think about her.'

Rob Riley was an Aboriginal friend of mine who died. Beneath the headline in the *Canberra Times* of May 11, 1996, 'Freedom Fighter's Farewell', Jan Mayman, another of his friends, wrote this:

> The sad, troubled spirit of Robert Riley will be healed at last next week when he is buried with his people in the Noongar Aboriginal heartland of Western Australia. He was a brilliant and charismatic indigenous leader who died at 41, burned out by a lifelong struggle with racism, injustice and dirty politics. On May Day, with the nation still stunned by the Tasmanian massacre, he ended his life in a lonely hotel room.
>
> As former head of the Western Australian Aboriginal Legal Service, Rob Riley was a leading player in the Mabo land rights debate. With direct access to Paul Keating, he sat down to negotiate with Cabinet ministers and senior bureaucrats. Eloquent, witty and thoughtful, he spoke hard truths in a gentle voice ... His high public profile enraged the redneck tribes. They sent him frequent death threats.
>
> His downward spiral began when he decided to speak out publicly about a secret that had haunted his life – his pack rape, at the age of eight. It happened in a Perth orphanage, Sister Kate's ... Riley described years of torment, and his final rescue as a 12-year-old by an uncle, who helped him find his

mother, Violet, and his shearer father, Bill. He had always believed his parents were dead. This was what his good Christian jailers had told him as they sent him to church every day to pray for forgiveness for his sins. He said his reunion with his family was the happiest, then the saddest day of his life . . .

[At the motel] he paid in advance, in cash, and left a carefully written note, in blood-red ink. There were farewells, apologies – and a final, passionate appeal to white Australia to act on the findings of the Stolen Children inquiry, so no one would ever have to suffer as he had . . . As advice to a friend he wrote, 'Remember two important things: you can't be wrong if you're right, and you don't stop fighting for justice simply because those around you don't like it. You keep on fighting.'

On May 27, 1967, white Australians voted in a national referendum which produced an astonishing result. More than 90 per cent gave the Federal Government the constitutional right to legislate justice for the Aboriginal people. No referendum in modern times anywhere has reflected such an expression of good faith.

The pessimistic view of the result today is that white Australians then perceived no threat from the indigenous people, whom they believed would remain out of sight and out of mind. There may be some truth in that; but it is also true that there is 'a whispering in our hearts', as Henry Reynolds described it to me. For me, it means that until we white Australians give back to the first Australians their nationhood, we can never claim our own.

First of all, we shall have to give up our self-given role of innocent bystanders. White Australia was, and still is, an imperial power in its relationship with the indigenous people. The crime committed against them was the logical consequence of imperialism. What happened in Australia was no different from cataclysmic events all over the imperial world. The historical parallels are the British invasion and occupation of southern Africa; the Spanish invasion of the Americas; the French invasion of Cochin China; the Dutch invasion of the East Indies; the US invasion of Central America. The same theft of land, resources and human identity took place. In some countries, such as New Zealand, the inhabitants were able to negotiate a treaty with the invaders. There was no *Terra Nullius*; there was recognition, at least, that they existed and had certain rights. The first Australians were never given that chance.

Of course, this may seem too abstract for politicians without the moral imagination, let alone the political will and spine, to interrupt Australia's imperial story of betrayal of the Aboriginal people. Certainly, balmy summer days, fine beaches and wonder pools do not make a modern, civilised state; and one hopeful sign is that a great many Australians know that to be true.

In 1997, research commissioned by the Council for Aboriginal Reconciliation showed a clear majority of the population was deeply concerned about relations with the indigenous people. Even in the conservative outback, 64 per cent said that the nation must recognise Aborigines' rights as the original occupants; and 95 per cent believed that every child should learn 'the true history of Australia, including Aboriginal history and culture'.[39]

In my experience, few contemporary young Australians are in doubt that 'their' country belonged to others, from whom it was taken violently. Visiting my old school, Sydney High, I was told, 'We teach that Australia was invaded. That is the historical truth. There is no equivocation.' Seldom a year passes without the publication of a clutch of histories of the kind John Howard, his spirit moored in the 1950s, would deride as espousing a 'black armband' view; David Day's *Claiming a Continent: A History of Australia* comes to mind.[40]

The same can be said of the Australian film industry, whose pioneering works like *The Chant of Jimmy Blacksmith* have informed and helped to change attitudes. In the Australian media, times have changed since genocide was reported on page 16 of the *Sydney Morning Herald* by the paper's 'Environmental Writer'.[41] Among Australia's best journalists are those who have confronted bigotry and apathy in the newsroom: Jan Mayman and Diana Plater in Western

Australia; Graham Williams, Tony Hewett and David Marr in Sydney, and others.

Above all, it is those among the first Australians, the Aboriginal men and women of the Koori renaissance, the writers, teachers, elders, historians, broadcasters, artists and activists who have brought the beginning of real change. As Primo Levi wrote of the Holocaust survivors, 'only they, by their unique experience, are immersed in the truth'. They are, to name only a few, Faith Bandler, Geraldine Briggs, Paul Coe, Mick Dodson, Pat Dodson, Eve Fesl, Gary Foley, Marcia Langton, Arthur and Leila Murray, Pat O'Shane, Noel Pearson, Charles Perkins, the late Rob Riley, Roberta Sykes and Galarrway Yunupingu.

As Prime Minister Howard tears up the Native Title Act, and drains the seemingly endless reserves of Aboriginal patience and generosity, he might reflect on the determination of those of the calibre I have listed. The Olympic Games in Sydney in 2000 are being spoken of as 'Australia's greatest showcase in the modern era'. The Aborigines will use it to show the world a side of Australia many had not imagined. However glittering the Olympic ceremonies and the gold medals won by Australian athletes, these will diminish alongside a shame so richly deserved – unless most Australians show their government now whose side they are on.

The late Kevin Gilbert was a renaissance man. I last saw him in the book shop at the Australian National University in Canberra. The publication of my book, *A Secret Country*, was being launched by Manning Clark, the historian, who described the omission of the Aboriginal story from earlier Australian texts as the result of a 'terrible indifference . . .'

'Killing and indifference are the same thing,' shouted a voice from the back. 'Don't you people understand that?'

There was a hush, the kind that white Australians dread.

'If you do nothing and you *know*,' said the angry, lean man with a mane of jet black hair, 'you're in on the bloody murder!'

'Kevin Gilbert?' I called out.

'Yeah, mate . . .'

Kevin Gilbert was the first Aboriginal author and playwright to be acknowledged by white Australia at a time when they were counting the sheep and not him. His *Living Black* was searing oral history; all his work, his writing and art, was precise and unsentimental, yet open-hearted and mystical.[42] The superb collection, *Breath of Life*, edited by his partner Eleanor Williams, is a tribute to a spirit that embodied the struggle of his people. When he won the Human Rights Award for Literature for his anthology of Aboriginal poetry, he refused to accept it because his people were still denied their human rights.[43]

And he had the courage to address his own people unsparingly. In his book, *Because a White Man'll Never Do It*, he described the degradation of Aboriginal Man: 'He bowed to the fact of his women having to prostitute themselves for the food that would allow the children to survive, or for the alcohol that would yield the oblivion that was so much more desirable than the daily reality.'[44]

Kevin was born in 1933 on the banks of the great Lachlan River at Condobolin in New South Wales. His mother was a Wiradjuri-Kamilaroi woman, his father Irish. He was stolen at the age of seven and sent as an 'orphan' to a 'reserve' like the one at Jay Creek. He was meant to grow up with Christianity; like so many, he grew up with violence and alcoholism. In a drunken craze he murdered his wife, for which he was imprisoned for fourteen years. At Bathurst gaol, one of Australia's toughest, he spent years in the 'intractable yards' where he was often beaten senseless.

Yet he came back from the abyss; he taught himself to paint and to read and write; and his appetite for books was voracious. His first play, *The Cherry Pickers*, was performed in 1971 while he was still in prison. On his release, he became one of the most eloquent of the land rights activists.

Typically, he once stood in the main street of a New South Wales country town, facing the cenotaph, and made a speech. It was cold and windswept, and he had on a big knitted pullover with the collar drawn up. A single page flapped in his hand. It was his poem 'Memorials', which he read aloud in his rasping voice:

> Our history is carved
> in the heart of the country
> our milestone memorials
> named Slaughter House creek
> the Coniston Massacre, Death
> Gully and Durranurrijah
> the place on the clifftops called
> Massacre Leap
> where the mouth of the valley
> filled up with
> our murdered dead bodies
> the place where our blood flowed
> the river ran red
> all the way to the sea . . .

When he had finished, those who had gathered said nothing. 'The silence was like almost a hurt,' he recalled. 'You could feel it.' Then he reminded them that in a land littered with cenotaphs to the white dead in foreign wars, not one stood for the Aboriginal people who had fought and fallen defending their own country.

'We are not defeated,' he said. 'By the strength of our spirit and our resilience, we have survived on this earth longer than anyone, so they say, and we have come through. You know what that means? It means we have won.'

Then he walked away.

ANZAC DAY

The battle for Australia and the battle for the Pacific was something that our nation should never forget and [we] should rejoice in our victory and appreciate the people who were involved in it.

Paul Keating, Australian Prime Minister

IN 1987, I SPENT Anzac Day in the village of Villers-Bretonneux in France. It was here that Australian troops broke through the German advance in April and May 1918. On the brow of the hill, overlooking the town and its surrounding fields wild with mustard flower, stands the Australian war memorial, white and clean, its lawns manicured and headstones paraded in perfect symmetry. There are only 772 headstones; the other dead, 11,000 in all, have no known grave. In the 'Great War' men tended to be blown to small pieces.

'Are you Australian?' a man said outside the church, where an Anzac Day ceremony would be held that evening. He produced a brown-paper package, carefully wrapped with string, which held a sepia photograph of two 'diggers' (as Australians call their soldiers) in their poncho capes, the rain coursing down their 'slouch hats' with the brims turned down all round. Both men were beaming, one with his single tooth and large freckled forehead, the other with his bony hands on his hips, the way Australians stand.

'My grandfather took this picture the day they came,' he said. 'Look, he wrote on the back of it, "men of honour".'

When the war was over, Australian money rebuilt Villers-Bretonneux and children from the state of Victoria donated the funds which raised a new school; among them were those whose fathers had fallen here. On the day I was there, the local children sang 'Waltzing Matilda' and displayed drawings of kangaroos and the Sydney Opera House. That evening there was a ceremony, during which the Australian Ambassador described the 'spirit of Anzac' as 'always doing your best to come to the help of people in need' and 'more than anything, when you owe a mate something, you never forget it'.

It was a moving occasion, the way many Australians like to commemorate Anzac Day, April 25, the day in 1915 when Australian and New Zealand troops landed on the Gallipoli peninsula and were cut down by Turks dug into the cliff-face. Although a typically pointless blood sacrifice – for every 500 yards gained, at least 1,000 Australians were lost – the landing inspired stories of selflessness and loyalty, of 'never forgetting a mate', which became the 'spirit of Anzac'.

Ten years later, in 1997, I took part in another ceremony on the eve of Anzac Day, in Canberra, the national capital. There were about a dozen of us on the steps of the War Memorial on a cloudless autumn day. The first to speak was Paddy Keneally, a former commando in the Second Independent Company of the Australian Army.

In December 1941, the commandos landed in the neutral Portuguese colony of East Timor, hoping to prevent the advancing Japanese troops from building airfields from which they could invade Australia. Unfortunately, the presence of the Australians had the effect of drawing the Japanese to areas of the island they might otherwise have bypassed. Fighting a guerrilla campaign against a numerically superior Japanese force, the men of 'Sparrow Force' were later dramatised in Damien Parer's film, *Men of Timor*, and their exploits joined the Anzac legend. In the film, the East Timorese are 'the natives'.

'We wouldn't have achieved a thing, we wouldn't have survived a day without the heroism of the Timorese,' said

Paddy, now eighty-one, in his speech on the steps of the War Memorial. 'They supplied and protected us. We slept in their houses; and when the chips were down, they fought alongside us, displaying the kind of bravery we Australians like to admire. Because of them, we lost only forty men. And because of us, they lost at least 60,000 of their people, many of them tortured to death by the Japanese after we pulled out – and after we gave our word that we'd stay right to the end.

'I tell you, that night on the beach, when we withdrew, broke my heart. We were all crying our eyes out, the Australians and the Timorese. We went to their country and we brought nothing but misery down on those people. They sacrificed their lives to prevent the Japanese invading Australia and we deserted them.'

Paddy described how, when the commandos had gone, Royal Australian Air Force planes flew low over the villages, dropping leaflets that promised, in Portuguese: *Os vossos amigos nao vos esquecem* – 'Your friends do not forget you.' He paused to collect his emotions. A group of Japanese tourists watched from the perfect lawn that spills down to Anzac Parade. 'We completely betrayed them,' he said. 'Every Australian Government since 1975 [when Indonesia invaded East Timor] is guilty of standing by while Indonesians have murdered, starved and ill-treated a people we owe everything to . . .'

By now, our audience had grown to include the curious, many looking as if they were hearing this for the first time. When Paddy had finished, I spoke next. I said that I was speaking on behalf of Steve Stevenson, a digger who, shortly before he died in 1992, had led me along a trail of inquiry that eventually took me to East Timor, and a terrible discovery.

Sitting on a park bench overlooking Sydney's Parramatta River, Steve had told me the story of Celestino dos Anjos, a Timorese trained by the Australian Army, a man whose ingenuity and courage behind Japanese lines had saved his and other Australian lives. He had shown me a treasured snapshot of himself and Celestino. They were airborne and swathed in parachutes, heading for Timor. 'I'm the terrified one,' he said, 'whereas Celestino was a calm, thoughtful bloke. He had fine, square shoulders and powerful arms; you felt it in his handshake. He was always thinking ahead and could see trouble coming. He was the sort of bloke every soldier dropping into unfamiliar territory should have with him.'

Steve returned to East Timor in 1970 and had an emotional reunion with Celestino. 'I stayed in his village,' he told me. 'We had sons the same age.' Back in Australia, he wrote to the Defence Department in Canberra and asked for campaign ribbons and 'proper military recognition' for his friend, only to be told that 'native troops' were never officially part of the Australian Army, even though they wore Australian uniforms.

'I managed eventually to squeeze out of the pen-pushers what they called a "loyalty medal",' he said, 'after they'd assured me it had no value in the pecking order of war gongs.' Steve flew back to East Timor and arranged for the Portuguese Governor to pin it on Celestino. 'That was in 1972,' he said. 'I was there beside him.' He produced a photograph of the two of them, bemedalled, grinning, standing self-consciously to attention in front of the white colonial buildings and bougainvillaea on the seafront at Dili.

Three years later the Indonesians invaded. Steve wrote anxious letters, but heard nothing for almost eleven years. In 1986, a letter arrived from Celestino's son, Vigilio, dated two years earlier. It told of Celestino's murder. Indonesian forces had entered their village of Kraras in August 1983, he wrote, and 'looted, burned and devastated everything and massacred over 200 people inside their huts, including old people, the sick and babies . . . four battalions encircled Bibileo and fighter aircraft bombed the area intensively during the following weeks'.

The Indonesians, he wrote, had 'captured about 800 people' who were 'massacred by machine-gun fire . . . on 27/9/83 they called my father and my wife, and not far from the camp, they told my father to dig his own grave and when they saw it was deep enough to receive him, they machine-gunned him into the grave. They next told my pregnant wife to dig her own grave, but she insisted that she preferred to share my father's grave. They then pushed her into the grave and killed her in the same manner as my father.' Soon after writing that letter, Vigilio and his brother, who had escaped and joined the resistance movement Fretilin, were captured and killed.[1]

When I went to East Timor in 1993, I heard Kraras described as the 'village of the widows', because of the massacre there. My colleague Max Stahl obtained a remarkable handwritten list of all the dead. Written in Portuguese by a priest, it records the name, age, cause of death and date and place of death, and in the last column, the battalion responsible. Celestino's name is there, as are those of his immediate family, including his daughter-in-law and infant grandson: 'Cacildo dos Anjos, aged 2 . . . shot.'

Steve told me, 'When Celestino and I were reunited in 1970, he didn't ask me why Australia let him and his people down, why we deserted them. He felt that was a consequence of war. It was as if the Japanese reprisals hadn't happened! But for us, a free people, to let the Timorese down, to watch while the Indonesians mark their boots on them is intolerable.'

After I had related this, and others had spoken, we went inside the War Memorial, each of us with a rose for the Timorese defenders of Australia. The next day, Anzac Day, some 25,000 ex-servicemen and their families marched along Anzac Parade, past the line of cenotaphs, one after the other, that makes this a unique route of war remembrance; none of them remembers the East Timorese. As Paddy pointed out, there is only one such memorial in Australia: tucked away in a small park in Marrickville, Sydney, inscribed, 'In memory of the men of Sparrow Force and the people of East Timor who died in World War Two'.

When the great march reached the War Memorial, the Last Post was sounded and there were speeches celebrating how Australians had defended the homeland 'with honour and sacrifice'. There was reference to the Anzac legacy: its 'generosity of spirit'. Just then, a small aircraft flew over the march, trailing a banner saying, 'We will never forget you':

the words on the leaflets dropped by Australian pilots on East Timor in 1943. The plane, which had been arranged by the campaigner Jim Aubrey of Australians for a Free East Timor, was immediately ordered to land by the Federal police, even though it had been given Civil Aviation Authority clearance. Superintendent Anthony Curtis said he 'deemed it necessary because of the interference with the dignity of the occasion'. The pilot, John Hogan, said, 'I was astounded. I have flown exactly the same Anzac Day sorties for more than six years with no hassles. There's no doubt that this has to do with the East Timor issue.'[2]

Historically, the Australian self-image is of a nation that stands up for the underdog and 'never forgets its mates'. In truth, the betrayal of the people of East Timor is the antithetic expression of the Australian establishment's relationship with foreign power: one of service and deference.

There is a history to this. When the Australian colonies federated as states in 1901, it was not as a proud act of independence, but in the hope that a unified nation might persuade the Royal Navy to stay on as protector. With the demise of Britain as the dominant imperial power, Australian obsequiousness was transferred to Washington. 'It's like the British having the Gurkhas,' an American colonel said during the Vietnam War. 'We have the Australians.'[3] In this almost mercenary role, Australians served America's disaster in Indo-China; and the man who arranged it, Robert Menzies, was, like all Australian prime ministers who serve foreigners, ordained a 'statesman'.

At the root of this lies an enduring, subliminal fear of Asia: that one day the 'hordes' to the north will fall down on under-populated Australia as if by the force of gravity. This is not admitted, of course, and often disguised by a constant stream of pseudo-academic literature obsessed with whether or not 'we' are 'in Asia'. Most Australians, in my view, do not share these anxieties, having made the transformation peacefully from a second-hand Anglo-Irish society to one of the most culturally diverse countries in the world, and a semi-Asian society at that.

After all, there is no external threat, or the remote possibility of one. This does not deter the inflated defence establishment and its Vietnam-era staff officers from producing spurious 'strategic reviews' which continue to explore ways of saying there is a threat. There is one in progress at the time of writing, which, according to the *Sydney Morning Herald*, 'is likely to warn the Federal Government that Australia faces an increasingly unpredictable and more dangerous security situation'.[4] Of course, the language of these 'warnings' is suitably tempered so as not to offend Asia's dictators and autocrats; for not offending them is the basis of an unerring and frequently bizarre policy of appeasement, highlighted by the abandonment by Australian politicians of fundamental principles of civilised international behaviour.

The appeasement of the Suharto military dictatorship in Indonesia stands at the centre of this, like a canker in the body politic that has begun to affect the way Australians view their national identity. It began in the mid-1960s, in the wake of the coup that weakened, then deposed the populist President Achmed Sukarno. Ignoring the machinations of General Suharto and his coterie, who in seizing power killed more than half a million Indonesians, the Australian establishment rushed to reward the new regime with its support for a consortium of Western 'aid'.

The most influential Australian Indonesia specialist of the day, Professor J. A. C. Mackie, eulogised the regime's 'moderate' character. The new government in Jakarta, he declared, was 'clearly anti-communist and committed to a low-key, unassertive foreign policy, with a new stress on regionalism and "good neighbourly" relations with nearby countries.' The stage was set for Australia to work out 'a new and more constructive, enduring set of links'.[5]

The 'good neighbourly relations' were tested on December 7, 1975 when Suharto invaded East Timor and set about an ethnic cleansing which, according to an authoritative report by the Foreign Affairs Committee of the Australian Parliament, wiped out 'at least 200,000' East Timorese.[6] Just over a year earlier, Prime Minister Gough Whitlam had met

Suharto and agreed that 'the best and most realistic future for Timor was association with Indonesia'.[7] Neither he, nor anyone else in the Australian Government, consulted or spoke up for the East Timorese.

Delighted by the demise of the non-aligned nationalist Sukarno and the rise of the 'pro-West' Suharto, the Department of Foreign Affairs in Canberra launched a policy which, with the passing of the years, has grown ever more evangelical in its pursuit of the immoral. To the Australian Suharto apologists, the expendability of East Timor was explicable in two ways.

First the tiny Portuguese colony, they argued, was 'an unviable state'. They saw no contradiction in Australia's support for the independence of other small, 'unviable' states in the region: Nauru, Tonga, Samoa and Papua New Guinea. Second, the integration of East Timor into Indonesia was 'geographically natural': as 'natural' as the integration of Australia into its northern neighbour. Whereas most Indonesians are Muslim or Hindu, the East Timorese are animist or Roman Catholic. Even their colonial experience was different, with the Portuguese latinising the eastern half of the island and insulating it from the upheavals of the Dutch colonies, including West Timor, which became Indonesia in 1949.

There was a third, secret Australian reason for pushing East Timor into the arms of the Indonesians. They wanted to plunder it.[8] Richard Woolcott, the Australian Ambassador in Jakarta in 1975, who was tipped off by the Indonesians that the invasion was coming, secretly cabled the Department of Foreign Affairs, proposing that '[we] leave events to take their course . . . and act in a way which would be designed to minimise the public impact in Australia and show private understanding to Indonesia of their problems'. He described this as a 'pragmatic rather than a principled stand' and added, 'It would seem to me the Department [of Minerals and Energy] might well have an interest in closing the present gap in the agreed sea border and this could be much more readily negotiated with Indonesia . . . than with Portugal or independent East Timor.'[9]

Woolcott was referring to the exploitation of East Timor's

oil and gas resources, which were subsequently divided up between Australia and Indonesia in the piratical Timor Gap Treaty, signed by Foreign Ministers Gareth Evans and Ali Alatas in 1989 while flying over the Timor Sea and toasting each other in champagne. The ultimate prize to be gained from 'unviable' East Timor was estimated at seven billion barrels of oil or, as Evans put it, 'zillions of dollars'.[10]

The Australian Government not only had advance warning of the invasion and of the tragedy about to befall those to whom, as Steve Stevenson said, 'Australia owes the debt of life', it did nothing to stop or moderate the bloody outcome. On the contrary, there is abundant evidence that Australian officials conspired with the Indonesians. Based largely on information collected by the Australian Defence Signals Directorate (DSD) at its base near Darwin, Central Intelligence Agency files describe in detail Indonesia's preparations for the invasion. On September 17, 1975, the CIA reported, 'Jakarta is now sending guerrilla units into the Portuguese half of the island in order to . . . provoke incidents that would provide the Indonesians with an excuse to invade.'[11]

By the time the invasion came, Gough Whitlam had been dismissed by the Governor-General in a constitutional *coup d'état* and replaced by Malcolm Fraser's Liberal (Tory) Government. For the East Timorese, there was no change. Fraser took Woolcott's 'pragmatic' advice that 'what Indonesia now looks to from Australia . . . is some possible action to assist public understanding in Australia rather than action on our part which could contribute to criticism of Indonesia.'[12] Although the Fraser Government voted for the UN Security Council resolution which called upon the Indonesians to withdraw, by the time the matter came up again before the United Nations, Australia's diplomats, according to a senior UN official, 'seemed preoccupied not with the act of aggression against East Timor but with providing a plausible explanation to other delegations of why Indonesia had felt it necessary to take such action.'[13]

This was significant because the Western Group of Governments at the UN often looked to Australia for guidance on the region. 'It was precisely in this context', wrote James Dunn, 'that the Australian position may have had a decisive influence on the United Nations' response.'[14] Shortly afterwards, in the critical year of 1976 when Fretilin almost gained the upper hand over the invaders, the Fraser Government closed down a radio transmitter in Darwin that had become a lifeline for the resistance. Prime Minister Fraser then flew to Jakarta, where he left Suharto in no doubt.

Addressing the rubber-stamp Indonesian 'parliament', he gave the first public *de jure* recognition of the occupation of Portuguese Timor. At a press conference, he said his government now 'acknowledged the merger' with Indonesia, but 'only for purely humanitarian reasons'.[15] He was accompanied by J. B. Reid, managing director of the Broken Hill Proprietary Company (BHP), Australia's biggest corporation. BHP had recently acquired a controlling share in the Woodside-Burmah company, which had been drilling for oil on and offshore from East Timor before the invasion.

However, it was under Fraser's successor, the Labor Party Prime Minister Bob Hawke, that the betrayal got into its stride. It was Hawke who cried in public for the victims of the Tiananmen Square massacre and, when Saddam Hussein invaded Iraq, said that 'big countries cannot invade little countries and expect to get away with it'; and it was Hawke, his Foreign Minister, Gareth Evans, and his successor, Paul Keating, who did everything in their power to ensure that Suharto did get away with it.

Hawke's first Foreign Minister was Bill Hayden, a capricious figure who had shown some deftness in trying to end the American-led blockade of post-war Vietnam and post-Pol Pot Cambodia. Although he had spoken up for East Timor in opposition, Hayden reversed his position once in office. Under pressure from his party to take advantage of a ceasefire between the Indonesians and Fretilin, Hayden dispatched to East Timor a 'mission of inquiry' headed by a former Labor minister, Bill Morrison – an extraordinary choice, renowned for his support for Suharto.

Morrison accepted most of the Indonesian conditions for his

visit, including travel by Indonesian helicopters and Indonesian military interpreters – which guaranteed that none but stooges would speak to his team. A letter smuggled to the delegation from the Fretilin leader, Xanana Gusmao, suggesting ways of making contact, was ignored. 'In all the villages visited by the delegation,' wrote the historian John Taylor, 'the contrast between its commentary [in its subsequent report] and evidence from refugee and resistance accounts was stark. In all cases, the delegation concurred with the military perspective, whether it be concerning reasons for resettlement, empty villages or malnutrition. No other view was presented or sought, even when the explanation seemed vacuous.'[16]

When he came upon Fretilin troops by the roadside, taking advantage of the ceasefire, Morrison was told by one of them about conditions in an Indonesian concentration camp. This was deleted by the interpreter. Leaving them with the promise that he would get a message to them about how their commander could meet him, Morrison returned to his hotel in Baucau. 'No attempt', wrote Taylor, 'was made to contact the Fretilin representatives.' That evening, notes Morrison in his report, he settled down to 'a night of bridge'.[17]

On his return to Australia, Morrison was asked about Fretilin reports that the Indonesians were planning to break the ceasefire in August with a major offensive. He replied, 'Nothing we saw, nothing we were told gives any credence to that report.' On August 17, 1983, the Indonesian military commander, General Benni Murdani, a crony of Suharto, unilaterally broke the ceasefire. Heartened by the Australian delegation's support, Murdani had begun the military build-up less than two days after Morrison's departure. 'This time, no fooling around,' he said. 'We are going to hit them without mercy.'[18]

Hayden's successor as foreign minister, Gareth Evans, brought another dimension to the appeasement. Evans saw himself as a sort of Australian Kissinger, a worldly-wise navigator around the 'international community', opening up new horizons for Australian diplomacy and for himself. He made no secret of his ambition to be the next United Nations

Secretary-General. He got up very early to learn French (a requirement for the UN job) and he published vacuous books with grandiose titles, such as *Co-operating for Peace: The Global Agenda for the 1990s and Beyond*. One article, partly drafted for Evans by an unacknowledged academic, was modestly described by the Foreign Minister as having been 'extremely influential in determining the shape of the whole debate about the peace and security agenda of the United Nations'.[19]

In fact, he merely paid homage to the American-dominated orthodoxy. In *Co-operating for Peace*, written after the Indonesian massacre of up to 400 East Timorese in Dili in 1991, there is not a single reference to the genocide in East Timor – which, as Michael McKinley pointed out, in a work of such pretensions, is the moral equivalent of denying the Holocaust.[20]

Although he frequently lectured the press on 'understanding the cultural sensitivities of Asia' (meaning not upsetting regimes like Indonesia's) and was an advocate of press censorship under the 'D Notice' system, Evans was clever with journalists. He created a media court in Canberra, flattering selected insiders, who reported him uncritically and collaborated in the fiction that the Australian Foreign Minister was a rising star in the corridors of world power.[21]

Most of Evans's reputation (in Australia; abroad, he was little known) stemmed from his claim that he had brought peace to Cambodia. His real talents, as a functionary of a superpower and an appeaser of regional power, were demonstrated at the first international conference on Cambodia in Paris in 1989. American delegates had made clear that they wanted to rehabilitate China and, if necessary, its Khmer Rouge client. Western diplomats entertained Chinese and Khmer Rouge representatives in private, and the word 'genocide' was declared 'impolitic'. In a conference briefing document bearing the handwriting of the Australian Foreign Minister, a 'specific stumbling block' is 'identified' as 'whether it is appropriate or not to refer specifically to the non-return of the "genocidal" practices of the past'.[22]

In announcing his 'UN plan' for Cambodia in November 1989, Evans said his aim was to exclude the Khmer Rouge – even though he had faithfully followed the American and Chinese line by calling for the Khmer Rouge to be included in the government in Phnom Penh. In the Australian Government's 'working paper' on Cambodia, all mention of Pol Pot's slaughter of up to 2 million people was left out, replaced by 'human rights abuses of a recent past', a euphemism coined in Washington.[23]

Evans was not as successful in his promotion of the dictatorship in Jakarta. Indeed, so keen was his apparent appeasement of East Timor's mass murderers that it probably put paid to Australia's application for a temporary seat on the Security Council, from which Evans had hoped to improve his prospects for the Secretary-General's job.

'The human rights situation [in East Timor]', said Evans in February 1991, 'has, in our judgement, conspicuously improved, particularly under the present military arrangements . . .'[24] Nine months later, the Indonesian military killed at least 400 people in a massacre in the Santa Cruz cemetery in Dili. Evans described it as 'an aberration, not an act of state policy'.[25] The Indonesians agreed. A 'special commission of inquiry' set up by Suharto blamed a few soldiers, but found that the real culprits were the unarmed demonstrators themselves, whose 'provocations' had been too much for the military to bear. Foreign journalists, who witnessed the massacre, were also to blame.

This was virtually the Australian Government's line. When I interviewed the former Ambassador, Richard Woolcott, in 1993, he had not long retired as head of the Department of Foreign Affairs under Gareth Evans. I was struck by the way he answered my questions from the perspective of the Jakarta regime. The Indonesians, he said, 'are highly sensitive and feel that journalists may well cause further trouble, as happened, of course, after the [Santa Cruz] massacre of 1991'. I suggested that the 'trouble' had been caused by Indonesian troops who had murdered hundreds of unarmed people. 'I don't know the truth of this,' he said. 'Some of the journalists were on tourist visas and had played a part in the stirring up of the trouble . . .' He added quickly, 'That doesn't justify what happened.'

When the 'special commission of inquiry' was set up, Evans congratulated the Jakarta regime for such a 'positive and helpful' reaction, and said he was 'reasonably happy' with the commission's finding that only nineteen people had been killed, a figure it later revised to fifty following the outraged reaction of foreign witnesses to the massacre.[26]

When witnesses in my film, *Death of a Nation: The Timor Conspiracy*, disclosed that the true figure was at least 270 dead, and that 150 wounded had been killed through the night, Evans's response was that 'whether he likes it or not, the balance of available evidence is against this'. He said his sources were 'senior churchmen' and 'human rights organisations'. I asked him to name them, but he offered no details.[27] So what had happened to those young people who had been in the Santa Cruz cemetery and were now missing? 'They might have simply gone bush,' said Evans.[28]

Lacking evidence, Evans and Paul Keating, who had succeeded Hawke as Prime Minister, publicly attacked my 'credibility'.[29] This was a propaganda gift for the Jakarta regime, which published what it called the Australian Prime Minister's 'official judgement' on my film, and released it to the press wherever it was shown around the world. I doubt if there has been another time when an Australian prime minister and a senior Cabinet minister have used their high office vehemently to deny evidence, in a work neither had seen, of murderous violence carried out by a ruthless dictatorship in an illegally occupied territory. It was a shameful episode, as was their silence when the United Nations Commission on Human Rights confirmed the testimony of the film's witnesses and Amnesty International reported that not only were they 'credible', but their 'allegations that civilians were deliberately killed or "disappeared" after the massacre have been corroborated by other reliable sources'.

Amnesty cited a number of its own witnesses, such as 'José'. 'This witness', said its report, 'told Amnesty International how four soldiers beat him on the head and chest with the butts of automatic weapons after he had been felled by a bullet near the entrance to the cemetery. As he lay on the ground he could also see soldiers assaulting his friend Simplico de Deus. He said the soldiers cut off one of Simplico's ears and slashed the other deeply with a knife. About fifteen minutes later both José and Simplico were thrown on to the back of a military truck, together with dozens of others. Most were already dead and the floor of the truck was wet with blood. José told Amnesty International that, while in the truck, he saw soldiers stab at least one person who was still alive.'[30]

Moreover, said Amnesty, the 'special commission of inquiry' which Evans had praised was 'totally lacking in credibility' and 'principally directed at the appeasement of domestic and international critics and the suppression of further political dissent in the territory'.[31]

Amnesty said, 'We feel compelled to break with tradition [and] to address our remarks ... to [those] who have effectively turned their backs on the reality of systematic human rights violations in East Timor. [They] have accepted uncritically Indonesian government promises of commitment to human rights [which] are empty ... The lack of concerted pressure from the international community [has] contributed to the perpetuation of a pattern of systematic human rights abuses in East Timor.'[32]

In a subsequent report, Amnesty all but declared the Suharto regime criminal, saying it had displayed an 'increasing contempt' for the basic civil and political rights of people.[33] Evans dismissed this as 'not a measured, objective, systematic, balanced analysis'. He told Parliament that Amnesty had failed to recognise that 'there have been significant [human rights] improvements in East Timor'.[34] Two months later, a United Nations Rapporteur sent to East Timor by the UN Commission on Human Rights to investigate, concluded that the massacre in the cemetery was 'a planned military operation' by the Indonesian authorities and that those responsible 'continue to enjoy virtual immunity'.[35]

The Special Rapporteur interviewed the head of the Catholic Church in East Timor, Bishop Carlos Felipe Belo, who had cared for survivors. When I asked Bishop Belo about the discrepancy between the UN findings and the Australian Government's view, he replied, 'Unfortunately, I don't have a good impression of this Mr Evans, because of the extraordinary statements he makes. This massacre was well prepared; it was a deliberate operation to teach us a lesson . . . It is [those who question it] who are lying.'[36]

On Evans's recommendation, Ali Alatas, Jakarta's Foreign Minister and the principal apologist for the massacre, who had described East Timor's agony as 'a pebble in our shoe', was awarded the Order of Australia, the country's highest honour.

In 1994, Prime Minister Paul Keating spoke at the opening of an Australia–Indonesia trade promotion in Sydney. Without a trace of irony, he described Australia's relationship with Indonesia as 'a model for partnerships between developed and developing countries'. He said the 'stability' of the Suharto regime was 'the single most beneficial strategic development to have affected Australia and its region in the past thirty years', and he chastised 'Australian ignorance' of its neighbour. Keating made no mention of East Timor, the slaughter that had brought Suharto to power, or the murderous repression that underpinned Indonesia's so-called 'stability'.[37]

Keating discovered Indonesia late in his career. Essentially a Tammany Hall-style operator, or 'number cruncher' as the breed is known in the political wards of Sydney, he had shown scant interest in international affairs. On his first trip to Jakarta, however, he was flattered by Suharto. An attachment was formed, with Keating conceding that the Indonesian dictator had become 'something of a father figure'. In Suharto's presence, reported the *Canberra Times*, Keating grasped Suharto's hand and wore his 'affection' for the man he regards as an 'elder statesman, shamelessly on his sleeve'.[38]

In 1993, he astonished the US Senate Foreign Relations Committee, which had just voted unanimously to end arms sales to Indonesia unless it improved its human rights record in East Timor, by turning up on its doorstep and haranguing the Congress for not taking a 'more balanced' view of human rights in Indonesia and his mentor's problems.[39] Keating reportedly told President Clinton, 'You've got to look after Suharto.'[40]

This roar of the Australian mouse was greeted by Suharto's weapons chief, B. J. Habibie, as 'music to my ears'.[41] Later, Keating sent Suharto a videotape of his more theatrically pugnacious performances in Parliament, during which he abused the Opposition with terms like 'sleazebags', 'pieces of criminal garbage' and 'piss-ants'. The *Sydney Morning Herald* reported that the dictator was 'mightily impressed'.[42]

As for 'Australian ignorance' of Indonesia, which Keating had complained about, his own record suggests prime examples. At the height of the genocide in East Timor, he suggested that the East Timorese would have voted 'for incorporation into Indonesia'.[43] There is no evidence to support this assertion. On the contrary, there is abundant evidence that they opposed incorporation. Speaking on the subject of Indonesian history, Keating said he was 'fascinated' to 'discover' that Labor governments in the 1940s had supported Indonesian independence from the Dutch. 'Most people suffering this degree of ignorance of modern Indonesian/Australian history', wrote the commentator Brian Toohey, 'would be reluctant to assume they were nonetheless qualified to personally set the parameters for a dangerous exercise in treaty-making.'[44]

Toohey was referring to a much-vaunted 'historic security treaty' with Indonesia which Keating had negotiated in high secrecy, without consulting Parliament or the Australian public. Keating made no attempt to explain the secrecy, which was reminiscent of the veiled circumstances in which Australians had been drawn into the American war in Vietnam. A government spokesman said the Prime Minister had not wished to give the 'Timor lobby a chance to exploit the situation'. The 'Timor lobby', according to a survey in the *Age* newspaper, is 70 per cent of the Australian population.

The treaty states that Australia and Indonesia 'undertake to consult each other in the case of adverse challenges to either party or their common security interests'.[45] What exactly were these 'common security interests'? Neither Keating nor Evans would say. Did it mean, for example, if Indonesia objected to China building a naval installation in the Andaman Sea, Australia would end up as the junior partner in a confrontation with Asia's most powerful nation? Other equally dangerous possibilities came to mind.

Significantly, most of the treaty was drafted by an Australian general and his Indonesian counterparts. The 'military component' of the treaty was revealed to include plans for joint Indonesian-Australian operations in 'counter-terrorism', as well as intelligence exchange and arms sales.[46] The proud heirs of Anzac were joining forces with a fascist military organisation which could not even claim to be a properly constituted defence force. In its 1994 study, Amnesty says the Indonesian military is 'organised to deal with domestic rather than international threats. Troops are deployed throughout the country, down to village level. At each level, the military has wide-ranging authority over political, social and economic matters. [These] are complemented by a range of elite units . . . All are responsible for grave human rights violations. The most powerful are Kopassus units which have been responsible for grave human rights violations.'[47]

The treaty formally integrates the Australian military into Indonesia's war effort against the people of East Timor and supports its suppression of the pro-democracy and trade union movements in Indonesia itself. For years, Australia has sold Suharto millions of dollars' worth of weapons, such as automatic rifles, and the Australian Strategic Air Services (SAS) have trained his torturers and assassins at bases in Australia.

Kopassus, which spearheaded the invasion of East Timor and has since been responsible for the worst atrocities of the occupation, sends its troops to an SAS base near Perth, Western Australia, where they take courses such as 'hostile interrogation'. Commanded by Suharto's son-in-law, Kopassus is a glorified death squad, not unlike Hitler's Waffen SS.

Kopassus soldiers almost certainly murdered the five Australian, British and New Zealand TV newsmen killed at Balibo in East Timor in 1975.

'Units of Kopassus crawl like ants around the scenic countryside,' wrote the Oxford historian Peter Carey following a visit to East Timor. 'Patrolling in civilian dress in unmarked Toyota landcruisers, they are armed with Heckler and Koch automatic weapons supplied by British Aerospace ... The hours of darkness are the Kopassus's favourite time as I discovered, nearly to my cost. At eight o'clock on a moonless night, I was travelling with my son and a priest. Lights appeared to the left of our vehicle and a moustached figure dressed in black loomed out of the darkness, powerful halogen torch in hand. Up in front, hidden by a large palm tree, another Kopassus soldier was covering our pick-up truck with his automatic rifle.'

Because the priest was a well-known figure, Carey was finally allowed to proceed. 'In conversation,' he wrote, '[the Kopassus leader] let slip an interesting fact. He had received training in the Kangaroo 95 [a code-name] joint exercises with the Australian army and commando units ... Our conversation ended with handshakes all round, but it is quite different for the Timorese who fall into Kopassus clutches. In the same area where I met the commandos, two Timorese suspects had been tied to a post and starved to death. Many [of their victims] are buried in shallow graves right under their camps. At the same time, Kopassus interrogation methods are often designed to leave few traces of torture: black plastic bags drawn tight over the head to induce temporary suffocation are a favourite, with water sometimes being poured over the outside to give the impression of drowning.'[48]

In 1995, Major-General Sintog Panjaitan, the senior Indonesian officer responsible for the Santa Cruz massacre, was invited to Canberra as guest of honour of the Australian Defence Department. Five months earlier, the US District Court in Boston had awarded a New Zealand woman, Helen Todd, $14 million in damages against General Panjaitan for the murder of her son, Kamal, aged twenty, at Santa Cruz. She was able to bring the action in Boston because Panjaitan was briefly a resident there; as 'punishment' for Santa Cruz, he had been sent to 'study' at the Harvard Business School, where he never enrolled. The judge ruled that the general 'oversaw and implemented a program of terror and systematic violence in East Timor' and that Santa Cruz was a 'premeditated attack'. Before he could be served with a summons, Panjaitan flew back to Jakarta, where he was appointed a senior adviser at the Ministry of Technology. Today, his job is to deal with important foreigners, such as Australian Defence Department officials, who want to sell arms to Indonesia.[49]

While the general was being entertained in Canberra, Foreign Minister Evans publicly defended him. He said that Panjaitan personally had not given the order to fire. 'He received his punishment', said Evans, 'by having to leave the military and I don't think that should be permanently held against him.'[50]

Pedro Batista, an East Timorese refugee whose family has been decimated by the Indonesian military, ran into Gareth Evans outside a shopping mall in Melbourne. 'I asked him', he wrote in the local newspaper, 'how the Australian Government could sign a security alliance with one of the worst military dictatorships in the world. He told me that we had to see the "big picture" and that Paul Keating would help solve the problems of my country. Actually, I think President Suharto should feel very uneasy about an alliance with Australia. After all, Australia and East Timor were once allies. We Timorese sheltered, saved and fought with Australian soldiers during World War Two. We did not receive the Order of Australia, but were given all sorts of assurances as a favoured ally. With fatalities rising to 50,000, we believed in these assurances . . . If the victims of President Suharto and his regime were Australian children, then perhaps this country would shake off its apathy and its cowardice. Is there no limit to this government's shame?'[51]

Flying to Jakarta on one of their pilgrimages, Paul Keating and Gareth Evans were informed that violent unrest awaited them. Journalists had marched on the Ministry of Information to protest against the banning of three publications, including the popular *Tempo* magazine. Confronted by riot police who beat and gassed them, they rallied thousands of supporters. Meanwhile, up in the air, Keating and Evans agonised with their advisers as to how the Prime Minister might respond. Surely, they complained, 'elder statesman' Suharto could have waited until his 'son' had been and gone before cracking down.

On arrival, they chose to say nothing, except the usual platitudes about 'quiet diplomacy'.[52] Whether it occurred to them that Suharto might have been demonstrating how *little* he cared about the Australian Prime Minister's embarrassment is not known. Certainly, the courage shown by Indonesian journalists in the streets offered a salutary example to their Australian colleagues, who have known no such onerous conditions.

After years of media silence, East Timor is now reported widely in Australia. Among political commentators and Jakarta-based reporters, however, there is limited challenge to the government's collusions and, from some journalists, a great deal of important support. When the 'security treaty' with Indonesia was announced, ironically it was a former Defence Department official, Alan Wrigley, who called into question the lack of critical analysis in the press. 'Look', he wrote, 'at the performance of those proud guardians of democracy, the newspapers [whose] editorials gushed their admiration of Keating's skill at keeping them in the dark. The tone overall has been one of rapturous adoration for the Prime Minister for having persuaded those stand-offish Indonesians to sign up with little old us. There have been no demands to see enough to be able to weigh up the pluses and minuses.'[53]

A prominent commentator on Asia, Milton Osborne, explained, as he often does, the dictatorship's point of view. 'What Australians see as the often brutal acts of an occupying force,' he wrote, 'the Indonesian army sees as the latest example of its longstanding and special role as the protector of Indonesia's territorial integrity.' He made no mention of the fact that a third of the population has been extinguished as part of this 'protection'.[54]

For others, Indonesia is the victim. 'JAKARTA WAKES UP TO THE NIGHTMARE OF EAST TIMOR', said Rupert Murdoch's *Australian* on the twentieth anniversary of the Indonesian invasion.[55] 'In a sense,' wrote the paper's Jakarta correspondent, Patrick Walters, 'Suharto is a victim of his own success.' Walters described the dictator's insecure childhood and how he 'stepped into the limelight in 1965': a novel way of describing his extermination of more than half a million Indonesians.[56]

In 1993, Walters went on a government-guided tour of East Timor and wrote that 'no one is now arrested without proper legal procedure'.[57] Two years later, Australian Jakarta-based journalists, Walters included, accompanied Australian Ambassador Allan Taylor on another shepherded tour of the occupied territory. They ran into a fellow countryman, Simon De Faux, who was working as a volunteer health worker with the Catholic Church. De Faux had treated people who had been tortured, raped and beaten almost to death by Indonesian soldiers. He described men who had been tied naked to a metal bed with electric wires attached to their penises. He also discovered that the so-called 'civil development', such as clinics and basic medical equipment – which Jakarta and Australian officials boast about, and Australian journalists often write about – did not exist for the majority of people.

De Faux tried to speak to Ambassador Taylor and others in the Australian group. 'They weren't interested,' he told me. 'An official took me aside and told me to keep quiet about it and not to speak to the media.'[58] It was Taylor who, as Embassy counsellor in 1976, conducted an inquiry into the deaths of five Australia-based newsmen killed by the Indonesians. The 'evidence' they gathered was largely based on interviews with Indonesian soldiers dressed up as East Timorese 'witnesses', and with known agents and collaborators.

Among cynics in the Department of Foreign Affairs, the Australian Embassy in Jakarta is known as the 'good news post'. The 'good news' is that the Kopassus gestapo is adopting a 'hearts and minds' approach' in East Timor, that repression is easing, the resistance is 'finished' and the territory is being 'opened up' to 'development': meaning military roads and bridges are being built, and commercial life is being monopolised by 'transmigrants' from Indonesia.

On the eve of a visit by the Pope to East Timor in 1989, the Embassy held a cocktail party at which a senior Australian diplomat announced that the Vatican was about to recognise Indonesian sovereignty over East Timor. With an unfortunate choice of words, he said the Pope's visit was 'the last nail in Portugal's coffin'. This was duly reflected in correspondents' reports. The fact that he was wrong, and the press reporting that depended on the Embassy as a primary source was wrong, was revealed when a group of very brave East Timorese demonstrated at the papal mass in Dili, and the army reacted with its usual brutality – but this time there were foreign television cameras present, and the videotape showed the regime's thugs beating demonstrators viciously. This alarmed Australian Embassy officials, who pleaded with journalists not to send the tape, arguing that such 'a small demonstration is hardly news'. Similar pressure was applied following the Santa Cruz massacre, when Australian diplomats tracked down two Australian witnesses to the massacre and subjected them to offensive questioning, clearly looking for inconsistencies in their stories that might discredit their evidence.

Generally speaking, the reporting from Jakarta strains to be 'fair' to the regime and to strike a 'balance' between the dictators and their victims; going 'too far', as one journalist put it, can endanger the renewal of the all-important journalist's visa.

In 1981, the Australian Broadcasting Corporation office in Jakarta was closed down after Radio Australia reported a famine in East Timor, a consequence of the occupation. When the office was re-opened nine years later, the Department of

Foreign Affairs in Canberra had insisted that its officials meet regularly with ABC executives to discuss 'problems that might arise'. When the ABC correspondent reporting a human rights conference in Vienna pointed out the hypocrisy of a speech by Ali Alatas, the Indonesian Foreign Minister, he was told to desist.[59]

These days, former Ambassador Richard Woolcott is frequently in print, damning, with particular chutzpah, the 'East Timor lobby' and the 'anti-Indonesian lobby'. Having once advised his government to 'assist public opinion' in 'understanding' the point of view of the invader, Woolcott now describes himself unashamedly as a consultant 'on sea-bed matters' to BHP, one of the companies exploiting East Timor's oil and gas reserves against the wishes of the East Timorese. He also runs the Indonesia–Australia Institute, a propaganda body funded partly by the Australian Government.[60]

In a paper entitled *Pathways to Diplomacy*, Woolcott complained that television reporting 'can lead to disproportionate public reactions against a state, as the frequent repetition of TV clips of the tragic Tiananmen Square and Dili incidents have done [in Australia] in respect of China and Indonesia'. By 'tragic incidents' he meant massacres.[61]

Paul Kelly, until 1996 editor-in-chief of the *Australian*, Australia's only national newspaper, is a member of Woolcott's institute. In the week that the Suharto dictatorship was accused of murdering the wounded survivors of Santa Cruz, he published an editorial evocative of *The Times* editor Geoffrey Dawson's efforts to appease the Germans in the 1930s, which said that the regime now 'can be declared moderate'.[62]

Under the influence of its foreign editor, Greg Sheridan, the *Australian* has been a reliable ally of the dictatorship. A few dissenting voices provide the paper with a minimal respectability; but whenever the clouds roll over his friends in Jakarta, Sheridan is there to protect them and take the offensive. Among his targets are President Clinton's administration for raising human rights with Suharto, the

Foreign Affairs Committee of the Australian Parliament for publishing a study that confirmed the genocide and eye-witnesses to the massacre of survivors of Santa Cruz. 'The sad truth', he wrote, 'is that even genuine victims frequently concoct stories . . .'[63]

Sheridan travels frequently to south-east Asia, where he lectures the Australian press that it ought to be more 'responsible' in its reporting of Asia. The cardinal rule is that journalists should never spread news that can 'aggravate a situation', because 'some truths are better left unspoken.'[64] In any case things are not so bad. In Indonesia, 'citizens are free to do anything they like, except for the things that are banned . . .'[65] During Indonesia's rigged elections in 1997, when there was an open, popular rebellion in response to the regime's violence, Sheridan fell silent, publishing not a word.

Occasionally, his hagiographies reveal more about his relationship with the dictatorship than he may intend. Writing about a visit to Jakarta immediately following the Santa Cruz massacre, he boasted about being invited to an exclusive dinner party for top officials of the regime where he 'enjoyed one of the most fascinating evenings of my life'. Among the guests was the notorious General Benni Murdani, the man who led the invasion of East Timor and whose troops committed one atrocity after the other. According to Sheridan, the 'hot topic' of the dinner, to which presumably he contributed, was how the blood-soaked regime should 'handle' its public relations response to the massacre.[66]

In contrast, a group of Australian journalists have distinguished their craft by their efforts to keep the record straight on East Timor and their government's complicity. *The Timor Papers*, the work of Brian Toohey and Marian Wilkinson, exposed Richard Woolcott's secret cables in 1975 and the rest of the duplicitous overture to the Australian betrayal. The late Michele Turner, Bill Pinwill and Denis Freney, Bruce Juddery, Wendy Bacon and Peter Cronau also shone torches in dark corners, along with documentary film-makers of the distinction of Gil Scrine. Above all, there was the sacrifice of Greg Shackleton, Tony Stewart, Malcolm

Rennie, Brian Peters, Gary Cunningham and Roger East.

Every time I watch Greg Shackleton's plea on behalf of the East Timorese, filmed on the eve of his murder in East Timor, I am struck by the power of his words. 'Something happened here last night that moved us very deeply,' said Shackleton, a Melbourne television journalist. 'It was so far outside our experience as Australians, and so inextricably interwoven with the atmosphere of this place, that we find it very difficult to convey to you watching in an Australian living-room . . . Why, they ask, are the Australians not helping us? . . . At that, the second in charge rose to his feet, exclaimed, "*Commerado* journalist", and shook my hand, the rest shook my hand and we were applauded because we were Australians . . . The emotion here last night was so strong that we felt we should be able to reach out into the warm air and touch it. This is Greg Shackleton at an unnamed village which we'll remember for ever, in Portuguese Timor.'

Australia's betrayal of the East Timorese is reflected in the enduring cover-up of the murder by Suharto's troops of Greg Shackleton and two Australian television crews in East Timor on October 16, 1975. As Australian and US intelligence were well aware, Indonesian special forces had already secretly invaded by that date. The Australian public knew nothing of this, although journalists had heard rumours; and Shackleton, a reporter with Channel Seven, Melbourne, set out with a camera crew to look for evidence. He was followed by Malcolm Rennie, a reporter for the rival Channel Nine. They met up in East Timor and decided to join forces, heading for Balibo on the coast near the border with Indonesian West Timor, the most likely invasion point.

On October 16, they witnessed and filmed the landing of Indonesian troops in the bay, beneath the town. Had they lived, their 'scoop' undoubtedly would have had a significant impact on Australian public opinion and might have altered the course of the great tragedy to come. Instead, it cost them their lives and called into question the Australian Government's responsibility towards and concern for the safety of its own nationals, let alone its former allies.

Greg Shackleton was twenty-nine. Tony Stewart, his sound recordist, was twenty-one, and also Australian. Malcolm Rennie, a British citizen, was twenty-eight. Cameraman Brian Peters, also British, was twenty-nine. Gary Cunningham, a New Zealander and the second cameraman, was twenty-seven. A sixth journalist, Roger East, who went to East Timor to investigate the killings, was himself murdered the day after Indonesian paratroopers landed in Dili six weeks later.

Shackleton and his colleagues were unarmed and dressed in civilian clothes. They had painted 'Australia' in large letters on the side of the house where they were staying. All the reliable evidence suggests that they were put up against a wall and shot and stabbed to death. 'They were screaming, "Australians, Australians!" with their hands up,' said a retreating Fretilin guerrilla. 'The [Indonesian] soldiers circled them and made them face the wall of the house . . . then there was a burst of automatic fire.' The Indonesians dressed the bodies in Fretilin military uniforms and burned them.[67]

There is plenty of evidence that Australian officials knew the journalists were in danger and failed to warn them. James Dunn, the last Australian consul in East Timor, says the Australian Government knew about the Balibo invasion twelve days before it took place. The warning was contained in Australian and American intelligence summaries circulated around the government, including an advisory committee on East Timor of which he was a member. 'There was no excuse for not taking stronger action to advise the journalists,' he said.[68] Informed of the murders, the Whitlam Government made no formal protest to Jakarta, thus giving Suharto yet another sign of approval as he began the slaughter in East Timor. (The Foreign Office in London, which shared the same intelligence, also remained silent on the murder of the two Britons.)

'The reaction of the Australian Government and its diplomats to the wanton killing of five members of the nation's press corps', wrote Dunn, who investigated the murders and interviewed witnesses, 'was consistent with the other aspects of its dismal record in relation to the annexation of East Timor. What is particularly disturbing is that the Whitlam Government knew about the impending attack.' Dunn was personally warned about it 'by a sensitively placed senior official'.[69]

Ambassador Woolcott later claimed that he had sent warnings to Canberra. 'I would be truly amazed', he wrote, 'if that information was not passed to the proprietors of Channel Seven and Nine.'[70] Cyril Jones, who was Greg Shackleton's Chief of Staff and News Producer at Channel Seven, Melbourne, replied, 'I can state categorically that at no time was the news department warned by any government agency of the imminent danger in Balibo ... the DSD [Defence Signals Directorate] office in Melbourne, which received the signals at the time, was situated less than 100m away from Channel Seven in Melbourne.'[71]

Six months passed before the Australian Embassy sent an investigation team to the scene of the murders. Led by the Councillor, Allan Taylor, their inquiries were directed almost entirely by senior Indonesian officials. Witnesses to the murders had already been moved well away from Balibo by the Indonesians. The 'Timorese' the Australians met were Indonesian soldiers 'specially selected from among the troops originating from neighbouring islands where the people resemble the Quemac of the Balibo area'.[72] Others were trusted agents working for the Indonesians and well-known collaborators who went on to occupy high positions in the puppet administration of East Timor, including the 'governor' and the 'vice-governor'.

'It seems incredible', wrote James Dunn, 'that the members of the Australian team were not aware that their reception and the testimony they received were being orchestrated by an Indonesian intelligence operation. Presumably Allan Taylor had been informed of what really transpired at Balibo . . .' To no one's surprise, their subsequent report, tabled in Parliament, suggested the journalists had been killed 'in crossfire' and was 'inconclusive'.[73]

After a long campaign led by Greg Shackleton's widow, Shirley, the Australian Government set up an inquiry in 1996 conducted by Tom Sherman, the former head of the National Crime Authority. Given the narrowest of briefs and with no power to subpoena witnesses, his conclusion was ambiguous. He found that the five newsmen had been killed by 'irregulars' in an 'invading force of the Indonesian army'. Roger East, however, was 'more likely than not summarily executed by an unidentified soldier'. He said nothing about a cover-up. Shirley Shackleton immediately called for 'a full judicial inquiry'.[74]

Her protests were reinforced in January 1997 when the Melbourne *Herald-Sun* published photographs of a secret funeral, purporting to be that of the five journalists, in Jakarta in 1975. In attendance, wearing dark glasses, was Ambassador Woolcott. There was only one coffin. None of the journalists' families was invited or informed and, when it later emerged there were photographs, they were refused copies despite repeated requests.[75]

'Why weren't we paid the most basic civilised respect?' said Shirley Shackleton. 'Why weren't we allowed to say goodbye to our loved ones? What was in the coffin? Was it their remains? Why was there only one coffin? Who paid for the cemetery plot, the coffin and the headstone?'[76] In 1975 Shirley received a telegram from an official of the Australian Embassy. It read, 'The most I can say about the remains of the journalists is that they are possibly human.'[77] Breaking its silence after twenty-one years, the Department of Foreign Affairs said in 1996 that the families had not been informed 'on the grounds of compassion'.[78]

The Indonesian regime, which persisted with the 'crossfire' story, dismissed the findings of the Sherman report. Prime Minister John Howard excused their reaction. He said Australians should understand that 'you can't always expect countries with whom you want to have good relations to have the same value system as we have'.[79]

The work of campaigners like Shirley Shackleton, Jim Aubrey, Stephen Langford, Jim Dunn, Pat Walsh, Max Lane, Andrew McNaughton, Kath O'Connor and Josephine Mitchell may help to salvage something of Australia's reputation when

East Timor is free, and democracy returns to Indonesia and their liberated peoples examine the record of governments which aided their oppressors. With each change of government in Canberra, there is hope; and hope is routinely dashed. When Keating and Evans were buried in an electoral avalanche in 1996, the East Timorese looked to Evans's successor, Alexander Downer, who in opposition had murmured something about 'upholding human rights'.

Once in office, Downer flew to Jakarta, saying he would never 'lecture' Indonesia or be 'rude and self-righteous'. The new Deputy Prime Minister, Tim Fischer, a former army man, described Suharto as 'perhaps the world's greatest figure in the latter half of the twentieth century'.[80] Fischer confirmed that his government was backing bids by Australian companies to win contracts with Indonesian conglomerates controlled by the Suharto family. Through a corrupt network of favourites and bribers, the Suhartos are poised to benefit from $53 billion worth of infrastructure projects.[81]

At the same time, the Australian Government signed a new maritime treaty with Indonesia, which 'upgraded' the 1989 Timor Gap Treaty, under which Indonesia and Australia stole East Timor's oil. They would now steal East Timor's fisheries and other maritime resources.

When President Clinton visited Australia in 1996 and held a joint press conference with Prime Minister Howard, he voiced the mildest of criticisms of Indonesia for its occupation of East Timor. When it was Howard's turn to comment, he said he would not allow East Timor 'to contaminate or undermine the broader relationship'.[82]

The contrast between American and Australian policies was made even clearer following the Indonesian 'elections' in 1997. 'We believe Indonesia should move towards a political system in which the will of the people can be heard,' said a State Department spokesman. The translation of this was that Washington had lost patience with the corrupt and intransigent Suharto and the embarrassments of his dynasty, and was searching around for a less offensive, more malleable alternative.[83] As for Australia's response to the violence and vote-rigging during the election, Downer said it was important to understand 'the difficulty of administering a country with so many islands'.[84]

Hypocrisy has found a firm ally in Downer. In opposition in 1995, he attacked Paul Keating for claiming that East Timorese refugees had Portuguese citizenship and therefore could not be given refugee status in Australia. 'The fact is', he said, 'Australia has never considered the people of East Timor as anything but Indonesian since 1979. This latest claim by Mr Keating is simply absurd and hypocritical.'[85]

The absurd and hypocritical is now the policy of Downer's Government, which wants to send 1,360 East Timorese in Australia, seeking refugee status, to Portugal, even though the Portuguese Government will not accept them unless they want to go to Portugal – which none of them does. 'So determined is Australia not to offend Indonesia by sheltering the refugees', wrote Mike Steketee, 'that it has left them in limbo, their futures unresolved for up to seven years.' Many of them are torture victims.

In 1997, the Federal Court declared the government's policy illegal when it overturned a decision that a refugee could not stay in Australia because he had Portuguese as well as Indonesian nationality. As the Refugee Review Tribunal prepared to follow the legal judgement, it was instructed by the government to suspend consideration of other East Timorese cases while 'a new policy [is prepared] to deal with them'.[86]

Like the ghost of Hamlet's father, Australia's betrayal of its ally keeps coming back. At the ceremony in Oslo honouring the 1996 Nobel Peace Prize winners, the East Timorese José Ramos-Horta and Bishop Carlos Felipe Belo, it was pointed out that Australia had refused to accept a human rights clause in a proposed treaty with the European Union – because the Indonesians might object. 'Nineteen years of such acquiescence have produced nothing, only misery,' said José Ramos-Horta. 'Australia could do so much. It could work with Portugal. It could enlist the support of New Zealand, Canada, the United States and the Europeans for a strategy in dealing with Indonesia. It could regain its self-respect . . .'[87]

A start could be made on Anzac Day, when the symbolism is like a presence all over Australia. But perhaps the true symbolism is that of rejection and betrayal.

On Anzac Day 1997, an exhibition of photographs ought to have been held in Parliament House, entitled 'East Timor: World War Two to the present'. It contained 170 pictures, including those of Indonesian atrocities and the victims of the Santa Cruz massacre. But the President and the Speaker of the Australian Senate decided to limit the exhibition to the period when Australians fought in Timor. Photographs taken after 1941 were considered 'offensive' and the exhibition was withdrawn.[88]

'I am angry at you Australians,' said Amandio Da Costa Gomes, a survivor of East Timor's holocaust, who was at my side on the steps of the War Memorial. 'I am so angry because of your cowardice and because my people are very much like the Jews of Germany. To be fair, the German people had the very real fear of a swift and brutal retaliation from the Nazis if they interfered. You have had no such fear.'

V

WE RESIST TO WIN

XANANA

These are the times that try men's souls. The summer soldier and the summer patriot will, in this crisis, shrink from the service of their country; but he that stands it *now*, deserves the love and thanks of men and women.

Thomas Paine

THE CROSSES CROWD the eye as much as they litter the earth: great black crosses etched against the sky, crosses on peaks, crosses in tiers on hillsides, crosses beside the road. Commanding all before them, they march in legions all the way from Tata Mai Lau, the highest peak of East Timor, 10,000 feet above sea level, down to Lake Tacitolu, where a Calvary line of them begins above a crescent of hard salty sand. On the edge of the sand is a mass grave.

The inscriptions on some are normal: those of generations departed in proper time and sequence. But look at the dates of these, and you see they are all prior to December 7, 1975, when the Indonesian invasion began and proper time and sequence ended. Look at the dates on most of them and they reveal the extinction of whole families, wiped out in the space of a year, a month, a day.

In the twenty years since then, at least 200,000 people have died under the Indonesian dictatorship's illegal occupation. That figure, which represents about a third of the population, has been verified by Amnesty International, the Roman Catholic Church, the Foreign Affairs Committee of the Australian Parliament and numerous other sources. A study by the French demographer, Gabriel Defert, concludes that the 'real figure is more than 300,000'. Considered as a proportion of the population, either estimate is far greater than the number of people who died in Cambodia under Pol Pot.[1]

These crosses are etched on my memory of East Timor, along with a single recurring sound that accompanies them and which is quite different, being a sound of life. It can interrupt the silence of the night and the early morning, even though it is barely a whisper, a name spoken under the breath: '*Shananaa* . . .'

Once, watching the sun rise over the town of Suai, I was approached by a man who, without looking at me, held a furtive conversation ending with, 'Shananaa . . .' On the veranda of a hotel in Dili, the capital, an old man nervously asked me to phone his daughter in Darwin, then offered the familiar whisper and departed.

What was remarkable about these encounters was not only the raw courage they involved – just to be seen talking to a foreigner was to invite arrest – but the name whispered as a password of hope belonged to a man who has been locked away, perhaps for the rest of his life. Kay Rala Xanana Gusmao, known as Xanana (the 'X' is pronounced 'Sh'), Commander of the Forces of the East Timorese National Liberation Front, known as Falantil, has been the symbol of East Timorese resistance since 1981, and remains so in his cell in Cipiang prison near Jakarta.

If a people's history of the twentieth century is ever written, recording the true distinction of those who led ordinary people against the onslaughts of power and greed, at the risk of their own survival, Xanana's name will join those of Mandela, Gandhi and Ho Chi Minh. At fifty-two, his own life mirrors a national struggle and suffering which, until a few years ago, were consigned to historical oblivion by the 'international community' and most of Western journalism.

In the age of television, few images and reported words reached the outside world when Indonesian paratroopers landed in East Timor on December 7, 1975. Special forces had already landed secretly in the port of Balibo and executed two Australian television teams. The only foreign journalist to remain behind on the invasion day was Roger East, another Australian, who was dragged to the wharf in Dili, his thumbs bound with wire, and told to face the sea. He refused and was shot in the eyes. His body fell into what the Timorese were to call the 'sea of blood'.

The one link with the outside world was a radio voice, picked up in Darwin 300 miles to the south. Rising and falling in the static, it said: 'The Indonesian soldiers are killing indiscriminately. Women and children are being shot in the streets. We are all going to be killed. I repeat, we are all going to be killed ... This is an appeal for international help. This is an SOS. We appeal to the Australian People ... and to all the people of the world. Please help us ...'

No help came. More than 60,000 people were slaughtered in the first three months of the invasion. Or they died in concentration camps into which Indonesian troops herded peasants whose villages they had razed. 'I was the CIA desk officer in Jakarta,' Philip Liechty, now retired, told me. 'I saw intelligence that came from hard, firm sources in East Timor. There were people being herded into school buildings and buildings set on fire. There were people herded into fields and machine-gunned, and hunted in the mountains simply because they were there. We knew the place was a free-fire zone and that Suharto was given the green light by the United States to do what he did. We sent the Indonesian generals everything that you need to fight a major war against somebody who doesn't have any guns. We sent them rifles, ammunition, mortars, grenades, food, helicopters. You name it; they got it. And they got it direct.

'Without continued, heavy US logistical military support, the Indonesians might not have been able to pull it off. None of that got out in the media. No one cared. No one gave a damn. It is something that I will be forever ashamed of. The only justification I ever heard for what we were doing was there was concern that East Timor was on the verge of being accepted as a new member of the United Nations and there was a chance that the country was going to be either leftist or neutralist and not likely to vote [with the United States] at the UN.'

East Timor, which its colonial master Portugal had effectively abandoned and few people anywhere could find on a map, was expendable. Alone, Fretilin, the resistance movement, fought on. In 1981, Xanana Gusmao was made its leader. With his beard and beret, he bore a striking resemblance to Che Guevara and, like him, became a Pimpernel figure, eluding capture for more than a decade.

The East Timorese paid dearly for the skill and daring of Xanana's guerrillas. In their frustration, the Indonesians deployed a tactic known as 'the fence of legs'. They forced tens of thousands of old people, women and children to march through the jungle in all conditions, 'sweeping' the undergrowth for guerrillas and calling on them to surrender.

However, what Xanana and his men heard were voices warning them in the Timorese language, Tetum, which the Indonesians did not understand. 'You are in danger,' they shouted into the jungle. 'Quick. Run now. We will cover for you.'

Xanana wrote in his diary: 'The old men embraced me. They cried out, "Son, carry on the fight! Don't ever surrender!" We were moved by this and swore to die for the homeland.'

Thousands of civilians were caught and punished, often with death, for aiding the guerrillas; and their sacrifice demonstrated that which the Indonesians failed, and still fail, to understand: that the armed resistance is at one with the people and thus has been able to regenerate itself. Many of the resistance fighters today were not born when the Indonesians invaded.

On November 20, 1992, Xanana was captured in a 'safe' house on the outskirts of Dili after one of his drivers was tortured. He was found in a concealed room beneath the floorboards. Interrogated day after day, he was confined in a small cell with a convicted criminal suffering from highly infectious hepatitis B who, on pain of death, was to report everything Xanana said. At the same time, hundreds of young East Timorese were rounded up and forced to declare their allegiance to Indonesia by drinking each other's blood, which was taken from them with a single syringe, squirted into a bowl and mixed with wine. Such public acts of humiliation, often conducted near a church with a priest made to attend, were turned into rituals of defiance, with people quietly chanting, in their own language, Xanana's words: 'We resist to win.'

In July 1995, I made contact with Xanana in prison through an underground which, since his 'trial' in an Indonesian kangaroo court four years ago, has ensured that he continues as chairman of the National Council of Maubere [Timorese] Resistance. Strategy documents, poetry and Christmas cards have all been smuggled out. In messages sent from London in code, I proposed an interview on videotape. Within a fortnight, I received a handwritten note: 'Dear J.P. I agree . . .' It was signed 'X'. I had said in my message that I was concerned about what might happen to him when the interview was made public, that we could be under no illusions about the Jakarta regime's vindictiveness.

His reply echoed the statement he had read out at his 'trial' until the judge ordered him silenced. 'As a political prisoner in the hands of the occupiers of my country,' he had told the court, 'it is of no consequence at all to me if they pass a death sentence here today. They are killing my people and I am not worth more than [their] heroic struggle . . .'

He told me that any risk was his right to take and his responsibility alone. Just as that message arrived in London, he was moved to solitary confinement, completely cut off from other political prisoners. The previous occupant of his new cell, Indonesia's former Foreign Minister Subandrio, spent almost thirty years there. Smuggling in a video camera was now out of the question. Instead, a miniature tape recorder reached him, along with my coded questions.

His response is a personal record of the East Timorese holocaust and of a resistance movement that has survived solely on its popular base, without any outside help. It is also a document of defiance; he calls Suharto, his gaoler, a murderer and warns prophetically that unless the question of East Timor's self-determination is resolved, it will ignite an uprising in Indonesia itself. And that, as pages 325–7 describe, has since happened.

He is generous, offering to Indonesia terms of reconciliation that would allow the current regime of the world's fourth largest nation to reclaim some of the international respect worthy of Indonesia's own struggle for independence against the Dutch. His anger is directed against 'complicit foreign governments', notably the British and the 'cynical' government in Australia.

Listening to the tape, an hour in duration, it is clear he is speaking in a small and empty space. Towards the end, he is rushing and slightly breathless, and speaking more closely to the microphone, presumably for fear of being caught. He ends with a personal message to me – '*un grande abraco*': a big hug – and signs off with his title, 'Commandante'. The following is our conversation, conducted literally a world apart.

'What was it like growing up in East Timor?' I asked. 'What memories do you have of peace?'

'I was born in Manatuto one year after the Japanese withdrawal. My father was a primary school teacher, and I had to enter the [Catholic] seminary. I worked as a fisherman, wharfside worker and draftsman until I finally got a job in the Civil Service, which was the ambition of all the *assimilados* [those regarded as 'assimilated' with the Portuguese]. My entire youth was a difficult experience which I tolerated by virtue of a will to win in life.

'The Portuguese legacy was a strong part of our cultural identity. But for some of the "educated", as those who had spent time behind a school desk were called, the struggle to uproot ourselves from our native culture often caused a crisis of conscience.'

'How do you remember the day of the Indonesian invasion and the weeks and months that followed?'

'I was on the Lois River with our troops, who were trying to stop the advance of the Indonesians after their assault on

Balibo and their murder of five Australian TV journalists. We were stunned by the sheer number of aircraft. Dili was under attack from the air and naval ships. Three days later we witnessed the sacking of the city, the plundering of everything from taps and bathtubs to window-panes and floors. In the cemeteries they desecrated tombs, ripping from them gold rings and crucifixes. Everything was loaded on to cargo vessels while frigates shelled the coast.

'The killing was indiscriminate. They murdered hundreds of people on the first day, including the Australian journalist, Roger East. Like him, many people were brought to the harbour, where they were shot one by one, as the Nazis did. Anyone, women, children, the elderly, anyone who dared venture outside their homes was shot down. They smashed down doors, firing their weapons inside at anybody and anything. They smashed up churches, leaving them full of urine and faeces.'

'What happened as the months turned into years and the world remained silent?'

'Between 1977 and 1978, large numbers of people surrendered. Their able men had been murdered, their scanty possessions pillaged and their women raped. In Uatu-Lan, for instance, all those who could read and write were massacred, and in some villages only women remained. In those years the Indonesian troops would tie people up and leave them outdoors, naked and exposed to the harsh heat and the cold of the night while, little by little, they would cut pieces from their skin, their arms and legs. They often cut off their penises or their ears, which the victims were then forced to eat. Each village had a detention centre which held the able-bodied men and women. At night their bodies were disposed of. From 1980, we tried to tell the world about this, but no one was listening. It is this which the murderer Suharto calls "returning to the people of East Timor their human rights"!'

'What were the conditions you and your men had to endure during the eighteen years you were in the mountains?'

'We were constantly on the move and exposed to heat and heavy rains. We suffered from a lack of food, medicine and clothing, as we stayed just ahead of the enemy. It was not uncommon to be on the march for three weeks, sleeping two hours a night and chewing on dried meat and coconut.'

In his diary (which was previously smuggled out), Xanana wrote: 'One day I climbed a hill. Sad, silence, desolation, grass spreading its cover over short-cuts and paths, struggling to smother the cabbage and potatoes, the only sign a human hand had ever been there. Every ridge, every stone, every brook and tree had witnessed such tremendous suffering. The seven of us marched in silence. All the scenes of past months rushed back into mind. We could feel the voices of the dead . . .

'Another journey to the west of Matebian. Six weeks of pain in my kidneys, and daily fighting. I couldn't sit down, I couldn't stay standing up and I couldn't bear to lie down. I used to roll around on the ground as if possessed. How I cried! Many is the time I wanted to commit suicide. I couldn't stand that terrible kidney pain. I used to drink huge amounts of tea made from leaves, peelings and roots. The sympathy in the eyes of the warriors offended me! I would avoid the ineffectiveness of their words. I tried all possible and imaginary cures. I put up with the boiling steam and leaves heating my arms. I was vanquished, beaten . . . I just needed to believe something in order to keep me going.'

For most of his eighteen years in the jungle, Xanana was unable to see his family. In 1970 he had married Emilia, 'in a registry office, after insulting the priests!' he wrote in his diary. They have a son, Nito, and a daughter, Zeni, now both in their twenties and living in Australia. Nito's only childhood memory of his father is riding on his shoulders, each of them with an ice-cream. While Xanana was in the mountains, Emilia was terribly abused; once, with the children watching, an empty pistol was rammed into her mouth and the trigger pulled.

In 1990, after long negotiations, she was allowed to leave for Australia. On the day she was driven to the airport, hundreds of schoolchildren suddenly appeared out of the fields along the route and stood with their heads bowed in a defiant gesture of respect for her. When her plane landed in Bali, she found a crumpled note in her pocket. It read:

You leave us not for ever
We do not forget,
You have helped the Timorese
women keep their dignity and hope,
Xanana remains with us and is not alone,
So you can leave us. Go!
Shout like Winnie Mandela!

I had asked Xanana to send me some of his poetry, knowing that this had helped to sustain him during his years in the mountains. Although he replied that 'I consider myself neither a poet nor a writer', the verse he sent is spine-tingling. I asked him if there was one poem that expressed something of the East Timorese struggle. He sent the following, entitled 'Generations'.

Names without faces
Hearts stabbed
with memories
of the tears of children
shed for their parents . . .

More than death
made them utter their last word
in every tear the cruel spectacle . . .
the whimpering of a mother
without energy
upon her body are etched
the blemishes of anguish
depleted

The rags
which cover her
in tatters
in the dim of her own flesh
cruelly scorned
by the Indonesian soldiers
one by one
on top of her

Inert, the body of a woman
becomes a corpse
insensitive to the justice

of the dagger
which has liberated her from life

and in the meantime . . .
blows of the rifle butt
resound
in the tear drops
of the very same children

A father pays the price
for the last 'no' of his life
and . . .

the tears dried
in the memories of the children
replaced by the sweat of the struggle . . .

Xanana has often made the link between his people's suffering and the West's supply of arms to Indonesia, which prolongs it. I asked him about the 'reassurances' that suppliers, like Britain, get from Jakarta.

'In the early years,' he said, 'American Bronco and Skyhawk aircraft relentlessly bombed and machine-gunned the camps and wells of the refugee population. And the new [batch of] aircraft sold by Britain will inevitably be used in East Timor. As for the denials that the Hawks will be used against us, the Western powers, concerned primarily with profits, have made these lies the condition for the continuing sale of arms and ammunition. The British Government must accept its share of moral responsibility for the war in East Timor. The [latest] sale of twenty-four Hawks provides Jakarta with precisely the approval it requires that it may continue to persecute and murder with impunity.'

'What do you say to Indonesia's Australian backers: to [then] Prime Minister Paul Keating and Foreign Minister Gareth Evans when they argue that there is, in Evans's words, "no turning back on East Timor"?'

'Never have I encountered in the whole world two more cynical and insensitive Labor Party politicians as Messrs Evans and Keating. The Australian Labor Government has shown itself to be without principles. To the point where—

Canberra has even stooped to kow-towing to the Suharto regime, this is truly a disgrace. They are traitors of the conscience of the Australian people.'

'But what about the historical debt that Australians are said to owe the East Timorese, who stood with them in the Second World War?'

'I belong to the generation which grew up immediately following the Japanese occupation. As a child, I knew that East Timor fought to ward off Japan's invasion of the Australian continent. Yet Australia claimed victory! If there is a military threat to Australia today, it comes from Indonesia. Logically, East Timor would serve as a bulwark against Indonesia in the defence of Australia. But no! Due to its fear of an Indonesian invasion, every Australian Government since 1975 has given its approval to the taking by force of the small territory which fifty years ago saved Australian soil . . . and it recognises the criminal twenty-year occupation as the best option for us.'

'What do you propose as a solution?'

'We propose a process that gives everyone the right to debate integration [with Indonesia], autonomy or independence, based on the UN's understanding of East Timor's legal-political status. After a period of time we propose a plebiscite to be carried out under international supervision. If the East Timorese freely opt for integration, we will make every effort to maintain a climate of peace and understanding. But if the people decide upon independence, Indonesia must be prepared to respect this. The regime is now aware that the case of East Timor is a far greater threat to its credibility than any other domestic problem. Until a few years ago Indonesian society was closed. Now human rights are better understood, thanks to the revelation of their violation in my country.

'There are also signs that Suharto is no longer sure of who his friends are. Not all his old guard can be made ministers; the most they can hope for is to be appointed to large firms or as ambassadors. In the meantime, the regime has begun to promote the idea of Suharto's mortality – while the new generation of generals grow more and more anxious for their share of "benefits" from the regime. If the Indonesian opposition fails to [exploit this] and recognise that the time has come for mass mobilisation and risk-taking, it will die out.'

'What can people all over the world do to help bring about freedom in East Timor?'

'Go out on the streets and protest in front of the nearest Indonesian Embassy, as they do in Australia. Put the lie to Indonesian claims that the problem of East Timor is a domestic one for Indonesia. During the African colonial wars, [the Portuguese dictator] Marcelo Caetano was mobbed in the streets of London and forced to return to Portugal like a bandit fleeing from the police. Actions such as these are worth more than a million letters written to Suharto . . . This is what the British people should do. Show the regime that it will never be free of public displays of repudiation for as long as the question of East Timor remains unresolved.'

'You are now in solitary confinement. Could you describe your cell and the possessions you are allowed to have?'

'I am under the supervision of Military Intelligence. Everything I do is recorded every day, everything: the hour I wake up, what I do then, and the hour I go to bed. I am not permitted to mix with other East Timorese prisoners or with other so-called subversive inmates. I am only allowed to receive Red Cross visits twice a year. If members of my family wish to visit me at other times, they are not allowed. [Emilia and Nito have since been allowed to see him.] Intelligence officers visit me regularly and ask me stupid questions. I am in a cell three metres by four metres with an outside area ten metres long. I can see the sun through the iron bars . . . I don't have a lot of possessions, as you appreciate.'

'Like any human being in such confinement, your spirit must ebb and flow. When you are not at your strongest, what restores you?'

'The memory of my people's sacrifices [and] an awareness that no sacrifice I could make could compare with the sea of blood that has washed over my homeland. And so I do my best to overcome my own difficulties . . .'

'For those who have never been to East Timor, could you

describe its beauty and the particular memory you have in your mind and heart?'

'Would I say my country is beautiful? Perhaps yes and perhaps no. The thing that enchants me is the primitive harmony of the relationship which exists between human beings and the natural world. And how beautiful it is to feel an instinctive fondness for the cool of the mountains which are not blue; no, they are not blue. It is the fragrance that hangs in the air, close to the earth, that is blue. And how beautiful it is to feel the peace which invades the soul as the body brushes through the dense foliage of the woods, the sensation of a concealed freedom.'

JOSÉ RAMOS-HORTA

Exile is strangely compelling to think about but terrible to experience. It is the unhealable rift forced between a human being and a native place, between the self and its true home; its essential sadness can never be surmounted.

Edward Said

NATALINA HORTA, IN her seventies, lives in a small flat above a pizza shop in Fairfield, one of Sydney's less-well-off suburbs. She escaped from East Timor only recently and her warmth at receiving visitors is occasionally interrupted by an anger she expresses in a rich flow of Portuguese, Tetum (the Timorese *lingua franca*) and English.

I asked her, 'Can you ever laugh?'

'Yes,' she replied. 'I have laughed, we all have laughed, because we had to. We put on happy faces, because if we didn't, the Indonesians would want to know why; and if we told them why, we'd be punished. Some would disappear into prison for months, even years. We laughed, we smiled, but I have to say there were times when that wasn't possible . . .

'Maria Ortensia was my daughter. She was twenty-one years old. She was too close to the Indonesian bombs and the shrapnel caught her, and she died. That same year, 1978, I lost two sons, Nuno and Guiherme, also killed by the Indonesians. Now if I say the Indonesians are bastards, you may wonder; but bastards they were, and they are.

'Let me give you another example. I used to go to the hospital in Dili, and I knew what happened there. When the

296

babies were born, many had diarrhoea and vomiting and the Indonesian authorities made sure they went on suffering and were not cured, because they wanted them to die. They wanted all of us to die, to vanish.

'I have something else to tell you. My grandson had a motorbike and the police grabbed it and took it to the police station, where it stayed for three or four months. The boy didn't have the courage to talk to the authorities to get it back; you must understand that anything can happen when you approach them. So I went to the station and demanded it, only to find it had parts missing. I looked at those men and said, "I see the rats don't just eat the rice and millet in Timor; they eat motorbike parts as well." Maybe I frightened *them*; but I got it back with new parts. You learn not to be afraid . . .

'I have something else to say. It is that I am proud of my son, José, who is here in Australia, sometimes. He wanted to have a family, but he can't, because he fights for his country. If one marries, one has the responsibility of a wife and children, and the problems are greater, whereas on his own he can go where he must, anywhere in the world, for the sake of our freedom. This is hard for him; he must sacrifice and he smiles and laughs, too, when he doesn't want to. Do I make sense? Like the best of us, he has the courage to keep going, never faltering. Like he says, we shall all get there soon . . .'

Before I met José Ramos-Horta, I read that whenever he felt defeated, he tried 'to think about those in the mountains, the women, the old people, the kids as young as seven who have the courage to smuggle information out, to travel from one resistance group to another, to monitor the international radio, to pass on hope and encouragement to the villages. Before she came to Australia, my mother kept me going this way; I once received a message from her asking *me* not to give up. "Your comrades are still fighting," she wrote. "Fight on . . ."'

José has been fighting on since three days before Indonesian paratroopers dropped into Dili on December 7, 1975. As the spokesman for Fretilin, he was chosen to leave and seek international help. Within two days, the shivering twenty-five-year-old with an Afro hairstyle was standing in United Nations Plaza in the depths of a New York winter. 'I had never seen real snow before,' he wrote, 'I had never imagined a world like this. Where I was born and grew up, in the mountains, there were no cars except for the yearly arrival of the Chinese merchant in his old truck ... A very nice American couple took me to a nearby store to buy cutlery. I bought only one of each: one fork, one spoon, and they were amused that I didn't buy a set, which would have been cheaper. But I wanted to hang on to the illusion that I was just passing by New York and I was going back to Timor soon.'[1]

I asked him about the effect of separation from a society which is virtually an extended family and which, in his absence, more than twenty-two years now, has been subjected to genocide. He spoke about the 'extraordinary resilience and courage' of those like his mother, Natalina: 'a natural rebel against injustice who survived the Japanese occupation, losing all her relatives but one sister. She lived through the first ten years of the Indonesian occupation of East Timor and cared for the freedom fighters in the mountains, and looked after civilians behind enemy lines. She was captured in the mountains in 1978 by Indonesian troops and taken to Dili, where she was imprisoned and interrogated. She has influenced me greatly.'

He listed many names, including those of his dead sister and brothers; and his stubbled face and mischievous eyes, so often given over to the black humour of having to deal with governments, were consumed by tears. 'We are a nation born in tears' is an expression I often heard when I was travelling clandestinely in East Timor; I did not meet a single family or community there that had not lost most of its principal members to the Indonesian slaughter.

It is José Ramos-Horta who has told the world about this, travelling thousands of miles every year to petition ministers, raise awareness and lobby support for the Timorese cause. Based in, yet always passing through, Sydney and Lisbon, New York and Geneva, Macau and Brussels and elsewhere, he has no real home, no furniture, no car, no driver's licence.

His bed is a sofa or a mattress in a friend's front room or an economy-class seat on an international flight. His 'head-quarters' has been a cupboard-sized room in the wrong end of Manhattan, where the phone was frequently cut off when he could not afford to pay the bills; and a $54-a-week address amid the strip clubs of Sydney's King's Cross, two floors up from a shop called Condom Kingdom displaying, he recalls, a variety that glowed in the dark.

He carries the fatigue and aloneness of a man permanently in transit. His homesickness for the places he grew up in – tin-roofed and palm-fringed places called Laklubar, Soibada, Barike, Atsabe and Laga – is often desperate. He once put to me a scheme to hire a small aircraft and fly home. Fortunately, I was able to talk him out of it, as 'home' would have been an Indonesian cell; only an exile has what Edward Said called the 'essential sadness' to contemplate such an adventure.

In this, he is his father's son. Francisco Horta was a Portuguese *deportado*, a Portuguese political dissident exiled in East Timor by the Salazar dictatorship. In 1936, as a sergeant in the Portuguese Navy, he had taken part in what became known as 'the mutiny of the Tagus River warships'. He and other sailors detained their officers, took control of two ships and attempted to sail off to Spain to help the Republicans in the Spanish Civil War. Intercepted at the mouth of the Tagus River, they were bombarded from the mainland and surrendered. Francisco was deport-ed to East Timor just before the outbreak of the Second World War.

Although Portugal was neutral, he teamed up with Australian commandos fighting on the island against the Japanese and never returned to Portugal. He died in 1970, the year that his son José was himself sent into exile to Mozambique by the Portuguese authorities for anti-colonial views. There José met his wife, Ana Pessoa, a lawyer. They have a son, Loro Sae, who is eighteen. They are divorced now, Ana has since remarried and José seldom sees Loro. 'We are good friends,' he said. 'Both are very supportive of my work.'

Following the 1974 'Carnation Revolution', which ended fascism in Portugal and began decolonising its empire, José was home again as a founder of the Timorese Social Democratic Association (ASDT), one of the two main fledgling political parties. ASDT changed its name to Fretilin, the Revolutionary Front for an Independent East Timor. It included Christian socialists, Marxists, social democrats and others who were simply nationalist; José's political model was Sweden.

After winning a clear majority in local elections, and with the Indonesian invasion looming, Fretilin declared independence. Today, the Foreign Minister-in-exile, minus his Afro and flares, ought to be looking out from the white colonial administration buildings on the Dili waterfront, where the view sweeps from Timor's oldest church, the Motael, and four ancient cannon with the Portuguese royal seal across a polished sea to Atauro Island.

In his book, *Funu: The Unfinished Saga of East Timor*, José wrote, 'We criss-crossed the country. Our theme was simple. We spoke the language of the people: "Are we human beings or a sack of potatoes to be sold to another country?" The people responded enthusiastically. A literacy campaign was launched; we taught children and adults to read and write in their own language for the first time ever. We helped the people build schools and health centres; paramedics were mobilised for a vaccination campaign ... co-operative schemes were launched.'[2] Such is the honoured, now unfashionable language of people on the cusp of freedom, about to claim their right to build their society as they alone would wish.

'I have never lost this faith in what we set out to do,' he told me. 'I have learned more: that's the only difference.' As his plane landed in New York in 1975, the Indonesians invaded his homeland. 'I felt every emotion,' he wrote. 'I was shy, intimidated, excited, euphoric and fearful. As the exiled representative of an extinguished government, I was allowed to address the UN Security Council: the youngest ever ... I had never addressed any formal forum apart from the mass meetings in my beloved island and a few meetings with students and labour unions in Australia.

'I learned quickly about diplomacy. To my surprise, I found China was our main ally. Relations between Jakarta and Beijing had been broken following the 1965–6 *coup* in Indonesia and the subsequent slaughter of almost a million civilians, many of them innocent Chinese merchants. Beijing had waited in the wings for an opportunity to settle the score with Jakarta. [The Chinese Ambassador] called the invasion of East Timor a "naked act of aggression" . . . I found myself plied with a never-ending supply of the finest Chinese cuisine.

'It was obvious to all that the invasion was a clear breach of the UN Charter, but what was remarkable was that, at the height of the Cold War, the Security Council handed down a rare unanimous resolution by December 22, calling on Indonesia to withdraw all its troops from East Timor "without delay". It was a grand moment! There I was, the youngest Foreign Minister in the world, holding in my hands Security Council Resolution 382, which affirmed the right of my people to self-determination . . . and I couldn't take it home, as I had promised, and so I waited. I waited for the world community to fulfil its pledges. Twenty-two years later I am still waiting.

'My schooling in international hypocrisy began in that first year. As a teenager back in East Timor, I was nicknamed "O Americano", the American, because of my admiration for everything American. America stood for freedom, power and wealth. No other world figures impressed me more than JFK or his brother, Robert. I dreamed of one day studying in the US . . . In December 1975, the US voted for the Security Council resolution. This, in my innocent reading, meant that the minimum the US and the rest of the Security Council would do would be to withdraw delivery of new weapons to the country that was in breach of the council's ruling. Instead, US arms deliveries to Indonesia continued unabated.

'Three years later, my young sister was killed by a Bronco aircraft, the pride of the American Rockwell Corporation. Then my brother was killed by fire from an American-supplied M16 rifle, then another brother in an assault on a village by a Bell helicopter.*

'But the big powers are not the only hypocrites. The nicest countries play the same double game. David Lange, the former Prime Minister of New Zealand, recently wrote, "What has happened in Bosnia is a powerful message to the world that countries which don't have oil, don't block an international trade route or don't have nuclear secrets, hold no real interest for the Great Powers." This is the same man whose government consistently voted on the side of Indonesia at every UN General Assembly resolution on the issue of East Timor. Even the mildest resolution, the one that mandated the

---

* In a secret cable to US Secretary of State Henry Kissinger on January 23, 1976, the United States Ambassador to the UN, Daniel Patrick Moynihan, boasted about the 'considerable progress' he had made in blocking UN action on a number of issues related to the developing world, and he mentioned East Timor. This, he explained, was part of 'a basic foreign policy goal, that of breaking up the massive blocs of nations, mostly new nations, which for so long had been arrayed against us in international forums'.[3] Later Moynihan wrote, 'The United States wished things to turn out as they did [in East Timor], and worked to bring this about. The Department of State desired that the United Nations prove utterly ineffective in whatever measures it undertook. This task was given to me and I carried it forward with no inconsiderable success.'[4]

During his first year in office, President Jimmy Carter, who, like the current British Foreign Secretary, Robin Cook, professed to link human rights to foreign policy, ordered a 79 per cent increase in military aid to Indonesia, including deliveries of 'counter-insurgency' aircraft that allowed the Indonesians to expand dramatically the air war, with devastating consequences. When asked about the US law that banned the arming of aggressor states, a Carter State Department official said that since Indonesia had 'annexed' East Timor, there was no longer aggression, merely 'internal rebellion'.[5]

Since then, the United States has repeatedly voted with a minority of countries in the United Nations to oppose self-determination for East Timor, and arms shipments have continued to Indonesia. At the time of writing, and following the announcement of the 1996 Nobel Peace Prize, the US State Department says it will go ahead with the delivery of F-16 fighter aircraft to Jakarta. During the 1996 election campaign, it was disclosed that President Clinton and the Democratic Party received hundreds of thousands of dollars in contributions from Indonesian businessmen with close ties to the dictator, Suharto.[6]

UN Secretary-General to open a dialogue between Portugal and Indonesia to resolve the conflict in East Timor, met with strong opposition from friendly New Zealand. Don't get me wrong. David Lange is a nice guy . . . You learn; you keep on learning. I have even been approached for a bribe from a Commonwealth ambassador in order to secure a favourable vote for East Timor. The going rate is $2,000.'[7]

José has been attacked, slandered and smeared, not surprisingly in Indonesia, but also in Australia, where his motives have been questioned by journalists fed lies by officials of the government in Canberra seeking to justify its appeasement of Jakarta and recognition of the annexation of East Timor. To José Ramos-Horta, they, too, can be 'nice guys'. It is no wonder he helps to pay the bills by teaching a university summer school in diplomacy.

This generosity has even been extended to the Indonesians. With Xanana Gusmao, he has put forward a three-phase peace plan. In phase one, lasting about two years, the East Timorese, Indonesians and Portuguese (East Timor is still, in international law, a Portuguese colony) would meet at the United Nations to implement a range of what diplomats call 'confidence-building measures'. These would include 'a drastic reduction in Indonesian troops and weaponry in East Timor and a significant UN presence'. Phase two would last five to ten years, with political autonomy and an elected People's Assembly. Finally, a referendum would determine the sovereign status of the territory.

Designed in part to save the face of the generals in Jakarta, it is a risk. As the regime sends more and more Indonesian migrants to East Timor, thus altering the population balance (as the French succeeded in doing in New Caledonia), it is not inconceivable that the indigenous Timorese may lose their majority, just as they have lost control over their economy.

On October 10, 1996, the Nobel Committee in Oslo tried and failed to get in touch with José. Like the rest of us, they had no permanent address for him. Two Australian friends, Ken and Audrey Fry, heard the news on the radio and drove the five hours to Sydney, to where they thought Natalina lived. They found the pizza shop and asked a lad, who was hanging about, if he had heard of the Horta family. No, he said, although he lived next door. Had he heard of the man who had just won a famous prize: José Ramos-Horta? 'No,' said the boy. 'What's it for, soc-car?'

It was only when they spotted a van with an 'Indonesia Out Now' sticker that they knew they had come to the right place. They found José upstairs, asleep on his mum's bed, trying to recover from his disbelief. A Portuguese radio reporter had traced him and informed him that, together with his country-man Bishop Carlos Felipe Ximenes Belo, he had been awarded the Nobel Peace Prize. No one had forewarned him. 'Why me?' he had said. 'It is for Xanana; I dedicate it to him . . .'

When I phoned him that evening from London, he was still incredulous. 'Why me? I can't tell you, John, the shock is getting to me . . .'

Behind him, there was a party going on. The radio was up full volume; I could hear Timorese songs, and laughing people. Among them was Natalina.

BISHOP BELO

> I urge you to defend human rights, to guarantee that your government will not intervene directly or indirectly with military, economic, diplomatic or other pressure to undermine the fate of my people.
>
> *Archbishop Oscar Romero of El Salvador, in his appeal to President Jimmy Carter, two weeks before he was assassinated*

I NEVER MET Carlos Belo in East Timor. A 'guard' stood at the gate to his church and home whenever I drove by; as people entered, their names were noted. On my return to London, I sent him a message. He replied that I should try to phone him just before midnight his time. At every attempt his number was 'out of order', then one night it rang and he answered. 'We have a little time before they pick it up,' he said. Later he paused and said, 'We are being listened to ... please continue.'

Our conversations spanned several months, always at the same late hour. 'The other voice likes to sleep,' he quipped. Not only are his phone tapped and his movements monitored, there are spies in his household, 'right inside my own circle'.[1] Yet he spoke unhesitatingly about the 'hell' the Indonesian regime had created in his country: the atrocities committed around him and the dangers he himself faced.

He disclosed for the first time that there had been at least two attempts to assassinate him. 'They tried in 1989,' he said. 'I had just written a letter to the Secretary-General of the

United Nations [in which he appealed for international help, saying, 'We are dying as a nation']. Soon after that, they prepared an ambush for me while I was travelling; but I got away. In 1991, they tried again when I went to the site of a massacre near Viqueque, where more than 1,000 people were killed in 1983. It was after I had seen the graves, the evidence of the massacre, that they tried again. But they were unsuccessful and I escaped . . . yes, there is this pressure on me all the time.'

In awarding Carlos Felipe Ximenes Belo the 1996 Nobel Peace Prize (with José Ramos-Horta), the Nobel Committee said of East Timor's Bishop: 'At the risk of his own life, he has tried to protect his own people from infringement by those in power. In his efforts to create a just settlement based on his people's right to self-determination, he has been a constant spokesman for non-violence and dialogue with the Indonesian authorities.'

He has also perplexed and frustrated both the Suharto regime and, no doubt, the Vatican. When he was appointed apostolic administrator of Dili in 1983, he was seen as the Vatican's 'amenable' appointment, much to the relief of the dictatorship in Jakarta. Like the United Nations, the Vatican does not recognise Indonesia's sovereignty over East Timor, so Belo is independent of the Indonesian bishops and reports directly to Rome.

His predecessor, Martinho da Costa Lopes, a passionate and outspoken nationalist, exercised this power to the full. He gave support and refuge to the resistance and was among the first to provide demographic evidence of genocide. For this, he paid a price. The regime complained to the Vatican, which withdrew him. Unable to break the international silence surrounding his people's suffering, he died in exile, wrote Carmel Budiardjo, 'of neglect and a broken heart'.[2]

Belo is a very different man. Having left East Timor in 1969 and trained abroad, he had never spoken publicly about the condition of his people. The thirty-nine priests in the East Timorese diocese made their feelings plain by boycotting the ceremony to mark his appointment as bishop: a snub unheard of in the Catholic world and a demonstration of the radically changing nature of the East Timorese Church under the occupation.

Under Costa Lopes, the Church, the one institution free of Indonesian control, had become the centre of the civilian resistance. Before the invasion, 33 per cent of East Timorese counted themselves Catholic; since 1975 this has risen to at least 90 per cent. For pious, scholarly Carlos Belo, it seemed that circumstances were about to make the man.

In defiance of the expectations of him, in his first year he sent a comprehensive report on Indonesian atrocities to Lisbon, providing graphic first-hand evidence for Portuguese Catholics and eventually the rest of the world. At the same time, he published a pastoral letter which implicitly accused the Indonesians of forcing sterilisation on East Timorese women under cover of a birth-control programme sponsored by the World Bank.

This was too much for Indonesia's Suharto-supporting bishops, who withdrew their endorsement of him, inadvertently honouring him in East Timorese eyes. His next target was the official ban on the Timorese language, Tetum. By adopting it as the liturgical language of the Church, he sanctified it and perhaps rescued it from oblivion.[3]

Those who have seen him emerge as a heroic figure liken him to Latin American clergy who established in the heart of tyrannies a 'people's church', defying the state and its murderous forces (and the Vatican), while often paying for their popularity with their lives. Oscar Romero, assassinated in his cathedral in El Salvador in 1981, also began as an orthodox, cautious priest. Today, Belo is revered by his people and called 'Ramelau', after the towering peak that dominates the Matebian range.

He will still insist he wants only a pastoral role, but this is now his diplomatic language. Ironically, he is at his most circumspect when he travels abroad, aware that a controversial headline might give the Indonesians a reason for preventing his return. Once, when called on to deliver a prepared speech in Sydney, he remained in his chair; moments before he left his hotel, he had received a phone call from the Indonesian Embassy, threatening him.

These pressures make his outspokenness all the more astonishing. A turning point is believed to have been the massacre of up to 400 peaceful demonstrators at the Santa Cruz cemetery in Dili on November 12, 1991. That day, and the next, he walked among the gravestones on the massacre site, his flowing white soutane dragging in the blood and dust.

When witnesses filmed for my documentary, *Death of a Nation*, revealed how Indonesian troops had deliberately killed survivors of the shooting, including wounded taken to the morgue where their heads were crushed, it was Belo who largely substantiated this and so speeded the discrediting of the Suharto regime.

'You seemed to speak out more after that,' I said to him down the line.

'I don't agree. There were massacres before that, many of them, and I spoke about them. But there was no international interest, no documentary film; no one listened.'

I said that the British and Australian Governments had described Santa Cruz as an 'incident'.

'They are covering up the truth for economic reasons,' he said. 'This was no incident; it was a real massacre. It was well prepared. It was a deliberate operation to teach us a lesson. To say otherwise is to deny the evidence of our ears and eyes ... After the first massacre, there were more killings [of the wounded]. Some of the killings happened near my house. When I visited the [military] hospital at 11 a.m. on the day of the first massacre, November 12, there were hundreds of wounded. When I came back the next day, there were only ninety. Witnesses have told me the killing of the wounded began at eight o'clock that night, and that most deaths occurred between two and three in the morning of the 13th when the lights suddenly went out in the city. I don't know what happened to these people. Maybe they were put into the sea. I told all I knew to the commission of inquiry sent by Jakarta, but they weren't interested.'

(He has since said, 'I have a list of 271 names, but I was told by Timorese intelligence people working with Indonesia that there were more than 400 killed. And now we have the problem of justice because the families are still waiting for the bodies of their children. And we don't know where they are buried.')[4]

I said that Western governments often claimed that Indonesian rule in East Timor was no longer harsh. I read to him a statement by the British Foreign Office that it was 'wrong to suggest that the widespread abuses of human rights persist in East Timor'.

He laughed wearily. 'I cannot believe they mean that,' he said. 'They *know* it isn't true. It has never been worse here. There are more restrictions than ever before. No one can speak. No one can demonstrate. People disappear . . . it never stops.'

What of Jakarta's claims that East Timor was now so 'peaceful' that the Indonesian military was beginning to withdraw?

The laugh again. 'I don't believe it. Please do not believe it . . . you must understand that we are undergoing a second colonisation. If I am asked for one description, I would say we live as if under the old Soviet Union regime. For the ordinary people, there is no freedom, only a continuing nightmare.'

I said, 'The regime insists that it has brought great material benefit to East Timor in the building of roads, schools –' He stopped me.

'Who is this development for? Who enjoys it? Not us, the Timorese. It is for the immigrants they are bringing in from Java and Sumatra, while our young people find it impossible to get a job. Actually, they are using this so-called development to change our society, to destroy it . . . Look at the compulsory methods of birth control. Women are given drugs to sterilise them when they are not aware. I saw nine women in the hospital at Suai, who were there for sterilisation they didn't understand. This is a policy that is being enforced. This is what they call development . . . it is the same with the creeping Islamisation . . . Indonesian soldiers have come into our churches apparently to take communion, then have spat the communion wafers out in order to humiliate us. Is this what they call development?'

I asked him if he was afraid that the outside world would again forget East Timor.

'Yes, yes,' he replied. 'There is a real fear that, if one day the issue of East Timor is finished, then we are all finished . . . Contact with the world is very, very important for us . . . it gives us hope and some of us protection.'

'What can outsiders do to help?'

'More documentaries please, more international conferences, more letters, more voices . . . keep speaking, everyone must keep speaking about us.'

In 1989, Bishop Belo sent a letter to UN Secretary-General Pérez de Cuéllar, in which he appealed for help from the world. He received a reply five years later from the then incumbent in New York, Boutros Boutros-Ghali. He read it to me: 'The United Nations is committed to make every effort for a final, just, comprehensive and internationally acceptable solution.'

'How do you feel about that?' I asked.

'At least', he said drily, 'after five years I got a reply.'

When I heard he had won the Nobel Prize, I tried to call his number, but it was unobtainable. Suharto calculated and let him go to Oslo to receive the prize, sending Indonesian agents to watch his every movement and hear his every word. On his return, an orchestrated mob demonstrated against him at Jakarta airport.

However, on the day he flew back to Dili, he was greeted by an estimated 100,000 people, cheering and calling his name: 'Viva Belo!' According to one of his confidants, the Australian Bishop Hilton Deakin, an assassin was waiting for him at the cathedral. 'A group of supporters decided they would provide a bodyguard for him,' Deakin said. 'We had the most reliable advice that an Indonesian soldier had been paid to kill him. When the Bishop arrived at the cathedral there was a scuffle and in the violence that followed, he was protected, and a soldier was killed and others were injured.'[5]

At times Belo's acute sense of his own position can cause

even the leaders of the resistance privately to shake their heads. He has talked about East Timor being granted 'special status' within Indonesia, which is anathema to those who have fought for twenty-three years for the right of self-determination and independence. He never uses the word 'independence', preferring 'dialogue' and 'reconciliation', even though there is no evidence that his people have any desire to be 'reconciled' with Suharto's mass murderers. Lately, he has referred to the East Timorese having the right of 'consultation', which probably means a plebiscite.

He is unambiguous, however, on human rights. When the United Nations Commission on Human Rights convened in Geneva in March 1997, one of the most powerful submissions it received was from Carlos Belo. He described in detail the 'routine' use of torture in East Timor, with prisoners held under water in tanks and burned with cigarettes. He wrote that families of young people suspected of being 'anti-Indonesia' ... 'know no peace at night. Their houses are searched in the middle of the night [and] showered with stones ... In the name of all Timorese, I wish to make a plea for greater respect of human dignity in East Timor.'

I met him two months later when he was briefly in London. He looked drawn. 'You will have to forgive me,' he said. 'I was more energetic when we last spoke. Now I admit I am exhausted.' He had just addressed a Catholic gathering in London's Westminster Theatre, attended by at least two furtive spies from the Indonesian Embassy. They had cause for concern. At the end of a careful, diplomatic speech, he lifted his eyes and said, 'The problem is whether East Timor survives as a nation or is integrated into another country ...'

He then addressed one of the main agents of this 'integration', the British Government, Indonesia's biggest single arms supplier. 'Arms can never be treated like ordinary commercial goods,' he said. 'Similarly no economic interest can of itself justify their production or transfer [where] the law of profit is supreme ... As a bishop and as pastor of East Timor, whose people have suffered terribly from the effects of armaments made in countries far from our shores, I appeal to the

Government of the United Kingdom, and to its allies, whose factories make a variety of weapons, to consider the dreadful consequences of this so-called defence industry. Please, I beg you, restrict still further the conditions under which trade is permitted. Do not sustain any longer a conflict which without these sales could never have been pursued in the first place, nor for so very long . . .'[6]

JO, ANDREA, LOTTA AND ANGIE

I first saw the Hawks in action [in East Timor] in 1984.
They have a terrible sound when they are coming in to
bomb, like a voice wailing. They fly in low and attack
civilians hiding in the mountains. Four of my cousins were
killed in Hawk attacks near Los Palos.

José Amorin

JO WILSON PHONED me at home at five in the morning of
January 29, 1996. She was in a mood to celebrate. 'Guess
what?' she said into my answering machine, 'we've just put a
Hawk out of action [singing and laughter in the background]
and no one's come to arrest us. Any suggestions? We've done
just about everything we can do; it looks good with holes in it
... Anyway, thanks for helping to get us started ... Surely,
they must arrest us *soon*. Bye for now.'

Two hours earlier Jo, Andrea Needham and Lotta Kronlid
had cut through the perimeter fence surrounding the British
Aerospace military site at Warton in Lancashire, climbed an
icy embankment, waited for a security patrol to pass and, in
clear view of closed-circuit cameras, prised open the doors of
a hangar.

They headed straight for Hawk jet ZH955, one of twenty-
four due to be delivered to the Indonesian dictatorship. 'We
had secretly watched this particular aircraft in test flights,'
said Jo. 'It was ready for delivery.' Using household hammers
they went to work on the nose, surprising themselves at how
quickly they punctured it.

'Jo had a smaller hammer which had been a gift from a friend,' wrote Andrea, 'and Lotta had two hammers, which had both been used in previous Ploughshares actions. For me, one of the beautiful things about Ploughshares actions is that anyone can do them. You don't need to be a technical genius or an engineer; you don't need to be physically strong; you don't need any expensive equipment or special skills. All you need is a hammer and a functioning arm. We each had both of those things. We started hammering.'[1]

Within half an hour, they had caused what British Aerospace claimed was £1.5 million's worth of damage to the aircraft, including its radar and missile guidance system. They did such a thorough job that the Indonesians demanded a brand-new aircraft.

Still no one disturbed them. So they plastered the Hawk with photographs of the victims of the 1991 Santa Cruz massacre in East Timor; and they placed a videotape on the pilot's seat, which explained their 'act of disarmament' and which included Max Stahl's footage of the Santa Cruz atrocity and sections of my film *Death of a Nation: The Timor Conspiracy*.

After trying unsuccessfully to attract the attention of another security patrol and dancing in a circle in front of the closed-circuit cameras, they called me from a company phone in the hangar (I was abroad). They then phoned the Press Association and asked a journalist to inform the British Aerospace management. When the security guards finally arrived, the women had been in the hangar more than two hours. Charged with burglary and criminal damage, they were sent to Risley prison to await trial. A week later, Angie Zelter was arrested after announcing that she intended to break into the same factory and continue the damage.

Jo, Andrea, Lotta and Angie belong to 'Seeds of Hope – East Timor Ploughshares', a direct-action group inspired by the biblical injunction to 'beat swords into ploughshares'. The Ploughshares Movement began in the United States in 1980 when eight people disarmed two nuclear warheads in Pennsylvania. They, too, used ordinary hammers in what they and their successors pithily describe as an 'an act of military conversion'. In sixteen years, 'hammerers' have 'converted' more than £4 million's worth of 'swords into ploughshares'. Warton was the fifty-sixth 'conversion' and the first by an all-woman team, though not the first in Britain in defence of East Timor.

In 1993, Chris Cole broke into the British Aerospace plant at Stevenage in Hertfordshire and caused £90,000's worth of damage to aircraft. In court, he invoked the Criminal Law Act of 1967 to argue that he was acting with reasonable force to prevent a crime, namely genocide. The judge, Stephen Sedley, unusually instructed the jury to use their conscience, common sense and common humanity in reaching a verdict. 'If what Mr Cole says is happening in East Timor,' he said, 'it may amount to genocide, which is a crime under British and international law.' There was a hung jury and a second trial, resulting in Cole receiving an eight-month prison sentence.

The women prepared their case on similar lines, adding the Nuremberg Principle that, under international law, all of us have a duty to refuse any part in war crimes. Convincing the jury that Hawk aircraft were not merely 'trainers', as British Aerospace claimed, but part of Indonesia's assault on a civilian population, needed careful preparation and expert witnesses.

None of the four had legal training. Jo was a tutor in further education and a borough councillor in Kirkby, near Liverpool. Andrea trained as a physiotherapist and nurse and was attracted to Ploughshares in the United States after working with the homeless in Washington. Lotta, the youngest at twenty-eight, is Swedish and has worked as a gardener and cleaner in Oxford. Angie, who lives in East Runton on the Norfolk coast, is a Green Party member and a long-standing peace and environmental activist.

Although Andrea is a Christian, religion is not the dominant influence. All four share a straightforward morality that demands that democratic governments reflect the common decency of those they claim to represent. It is the moral gulf between established power and the people that their actions brilliantly illuminate, especially the cynicism and lies of decision-makers whose actions leave no blood on their own hands, but in distant, 'expendable' societies (as a British diplomat once described Cambodia).

British-made Hawk aircraft are highly effective instruments of East Timor's expendability. Sold with kits that enable them to be converted to anything but trainers, 'these British aircraft', noted the Center for Defense Information in Washington, 'are designed to be used against guerrillas who come from and move among the civilian populations . . . they shoot high velocity cannon and deliver ordnance at low levels against unprotected human beings.'[2]

Like thousands of others, the women wrote letters to the government, lobbied their MPs and took part in peaceful demonstrations to protest at the sale of the Hawks to Indonesia. 'For over three years,' wrote Andrea, 'I have written letters, held vigils and street stalls, signed and asked others to sign petitions, talked at public meetings . . . and asked the police to investigate British Aerospace for contravening the Genocide Act. Despite this, the sale is going ahead . . . I have no option but to disarm these planes myself.'

Support for the women came from across the country and the world, mostly by word of mouth. In Kirkby, where Jo and Andrea live in one of Britain's poorest towns, Keith Hassell, chairman of a residents' and shopkeepers' association, said even children on the estates were aware of the issues raised by the case. When they were not arguing about sport, he said, 'there's a good chance they'll be going on about this tiny tropical island thousands of miles away where people are being killed by the government and the army. And Britain is selling them weapons by the lorryload. How do you explain that to your kids?'[3]

José Ramos-Horta wrote to the women: 'In twenty years of resistance, we were never able to shoot down an aircraft. You did it without even firing a single shot and without hurting the pilot. Keep up your courage. A big hug to you all.'[4]

Andrea provided a glimpse of their courage when she later wrote about their action and its personal consequences:

As the searchlight swept over the frozen fields towards us, I dived into a ditch whilst Jo and Lotta flattened themselves on the ground. We hardly dared breathe as the light – more powerful than any we'd ever seen during our night visits to the site – came closer and closer to where we were lying. But then it was gone and we were once again plunged into a cold darkness relieved only by a little moonlight and the distant floodlights around the huge hangar within which we hoped we'd find the Indonesian Hawk. A moment's panic ensued; did the powerful searchlight mean that British Aerospace had discovered our plans, and were just waiting for us to make a move? Or was it merely coincidence? . . .

We wanted to see two security patrols before we went in, so that we'd know roughly how frequently they were passing and we wouldn't be taken by surprise as we cut through the fence. We passed the time watching the site through binoculars, looking for any signs of movement, and jumping around trying to keep warm. But mostly we sat in silence, each deep in our own thoughts about what was ahead of us – not just the next few hours, but possibly the next few years. I tried to focus my mind on why we were there; I'd spent nearly a year thinking about prison and coming to terms with my fears of it, and now I wanted to concentrate on the action at hand.

Finally, we heard the sound of an engine and another patrol drove into sight. We flattened ourselves against the sides of the newly-dug ditch in which we were standing; the lights swept over our head and were gone. The time had come. We stood in a circle, held hands and had a minute's silence to think about why we were there. Images came flooding into my mind; young people, covered in blood, screaming in terror as Indonesian soldiers opened fire on them in the Santa Cruz cemetery in Dili after a peaceful procession. A young boy in front of a banner showing the East Timorese resistance leader, Xanana Gusmao. Both of his arms are raised; one fist is clenched in a gesture of defiance, whilst with his other hand he is making a victory sign. His face is set, determined. Shortly after the picture was taken, he was shot dead by the Indonesian military, one more death in a bloody occupation which has claimed the lives of one-third of the Timorese population.

I thought also of the promotional video we had recently watched about Hawk aircraft. Along with much gloating over the attack capability of the plane – the narrator almost salivating as he declares that the Hawk 'packs a healthy wallop' – there are shots of a Hawk flying in low and firing a missile into a tank, which explodes in a ball of fire. Although it was obviously a scene created for the camera, it was impossible to watch it without thinking about the outcome if, instead of a tank, the target was a house or a hut in East Timor. Standing in that ditch, many thousands of miles from East Timor, a country I had never even visited, I felt a great connection with the people who would be at the receiving end of these British weapons, and a great sense that what we were about to do was right and necessary . . .

For several weeks I had been having panic attacks. They would swoop on me out of nowhere; walking down the street, not even thinking about the action, my legs would suddenly turn to jelly and waves of panic would engulf me. One of the books I took with me – to the great amusement of the police officers who listed my property after arrest – was *Crime and Punishment*. In it, Dostoyevsky describes the panic attacks suffered by the protagonist, Raskolnikov, in the days before he puts into action his plan of murdering the moneylender. Reading this book in my cell after our arrest, I was struck by how the feelings he describes mirrored exactly what I had been going through for several weeks. Raskolnikov's aim was murder; ours was to prevent murder, but the feelings of fear and panic beforehand were just the same.

But on this occasion, to my surprise, I felt very calm and focussed. We'd spent nearly a year in planning, and had talked through every last detail of what we were to do, right down to the configuration in which we'd cut the fence and who would wield each tool as we broke into the hangar. I think we all needed reassurance that we could carry off this action, and such detailed planning gave us a sense of security; there were to be, we hoped, no surprises.

We finished the minute's silence, gave each other a last hug, and headed for the fence. Lotta and I were carrying bolt-cutters, Jo had in her hand the Japanese peace cranes we'd made to tie on the fence as a symbol of our peaceful intentions. As we approached, the hangar seemed to loom larger in front of us, and the lights to glow brighter. I could feel my heart thumping, and my legs started to shake, but I felt quite calm.[5]

In a letter from Risley prison, Jo asked me to be an expert witness at the trial and to send her all the evidence I had of Hawks in East Timor. I sent her a dossier and offered to bring a Timorese eye-witness to England. Although three of them were representing themselves, they were advised by the distinguished solicitor Gareth Peirce, who had helped free the Birmingham Six and Guildford Four. Jo wrote, 'Whatever else happens, I feel strangely content.'

In our correspondence, I was struck by her calm and dry wit. 'You will be pleased to hear we have been classified a high-security risk,' she wrote. 'We've been told that we can no longer attend the lower-supervision education block [because] there is not enough staffing to supervise us adequately – given the serious nature of our crime! The Governor has agreed that we've behaved ourselves perfectly (I shamefully admit!); and we have explained that we are totally non-violent and have no intention of escaping . . .

'But logic is a stranger here. We've been told that we must not *run* around the "exercise" yard during "exercise" sessions, as we might hurt ourselves and attempt to sue the prison. We tried hopping and skipping, only to be rebuffed with a new ruling that the only permissible form of movement is walking! Perhaps we could sue them for increased flab instead?'[6]

By now the burglary charges had been dropped, and replaced by conspiracy charges, presumably to lessen the acute embarrassment for British Aerospace, which had failed to stop three women gaining access to aircraft worth £13 million each. At the committal hearing before magistrates, the prosecution introduced the videotape left in the Hawk's cockpit as evidence of conspiracy, because it showed the four women explaining their intentions before the action. Although conspiracy was indeed evident – something the defendants were only too happy to admit – so, too, was the evidence of genocide, with scenes of Indonesian soldiers murdering unarmed East Timorese. The tape ended with a plea by an East Timorese woman: 'Please stop your commercial relations with Indonesia if you are really human.' The prosecution had made their first serious blunder. As the video ended, the court was hushed and obviously moved.[7]

Almost nothing about the case was reported in the national media. When asked why, journalists replied that it was *sub judice*. The environmental campaigner George Monbiot commented that 'such delicate scruples seem inapplicable to the reporting of gruesome rapes or murders, whose circumstances are divulged in meticulous detail long before the jury reaches its verdict. When ordinary people have taken the law into their own hands to disable not machines but other people – burglars or intruders – the papers have bellyached so loudly in their defence that the Home Secretary was persuaded to review the law.'[8]

The trial was set for July 22, 1996 at Liverpool Crown Court. The women were delighted; Merseyside was the centre of their support. Other supporters arrived from all over the world and were accommodated in people's homes, church halls and scout huts. A local priest, Father Arthur Fitzgerald, hung a banner across the front of his church: 'Stop the Hawks, Set Free the Doves of Peace.'

The women pleaded not guilty on the grounds that they were acting to prevent a crime. Because they admitted their action, they all but cancelled the prosecution's role and were able to concentrate on explaining to the court why they had done it. Surprisingly, the judge allowed them to call witnesses who could describe the horror in East Timor.

José Ramos-Horta recalled numerous instances of Hawks bombing villages. 'They are a constant threat to us,' he said, 'and we fear their supply.' Paul Rogers, Professor of Peace Studies at Bradford University, said that Hawks were an integral part of the Indonesian Air Force's 'Bandung Squadron', which was dedicated to counter-insurgency, which meant crushing the East Timorese resistance. Carmel Budiardjo, the founder of Tapol, the Indonesian human rights organisation and a former political prisoner of the Indonesians, described the years she and her husband, an Indonesian, were locked away by Suharto without trial and Tapol's documentation of the crimes of the regime. I described my clandestine visit to

East Timor and my shock at seeing the lines of headstones sil-houetted on the horizon: the sense of arriving at a vast death camp.

Appearing for the prosecution, the British Aerospace site manager at Warton, Christopher Foster, said that the Hawk was primarily a training aircraft and he was confident that it could not take part in genocide. Cross-examined by Andrea, he admitted that the 'trainer' could carry 'anti-personnel' cluster bombs.

'Did you', she asked, 'have any concern for the people who might be killed when it was delivered?'

'No,' he replied, 'I had no concern.'[9]

'When the time came for summing up,' wrote Bernadette Meaden in her study of the trial, 'Vera Baird [the defence counsel] used a simple but telling analogy. Imagine if a person slashes the tyres of a car, she said. Under normal circum-stances that would be a crime. But suppose they knew the car was carrying a bomb which would devastate Manchester city centre? In that case, slashing the tyres would not be a crime, it would be a responsible and public-spirited act.'[10]

On July 30, the jury retired, leaving Jo, Andrea, Lotta and Angie in their cell with their lawyers planning speeches of mitigation. There had never been an acquittal at a Ploughshares trial and over the years the movement's activists had received a collective total of 156 years in prison. After four hours the jury announced it could not reach a unanimous decision. The judge said he would accept a majority verdict. The jury returned an hour later to announce: 'Not guilty on all charges.'

The court became an instant carnival, with people clapping, singing, dancing and embracing. The judge left so quickly few noticed he had gone. Father Fitzgerald led a group in prayer around placards with the names of East Timorese dead. Somehow maintaining her composure, Jo said, 'This is a victory for justice. This is a victory for the people of East Timor. This is a victory for the people of Liverpool.' Outside the court, British Aerospace served injunctions on the women, barring them from their establishments. These were torn up.

A few Tory MPs 'demanded' the Attorney-General 'do something' about the jury system, which once again had been proved to be a bastion of justice. Alan Clark, who as Defence Minister under Margaret Thatcher approved the biggest sale of Hawks to Jakarta and who had told me that he was 'curiously not concerned' by whether or not British arms killed people, fulminated in his 'disgust' at the verdict. It was 'almost unprecedented', he said, for a court to excuse 'such criminal conduct'.[11] The Labour MP Bruce George, a member of the Commons' Defence Select Committee, said that the women 'should have found some legitimate way of airing their gripe' – perhaps the first time that opposition to genocide has been described as a 'gripe'.[12]

Most newspapers, having ignored the case, recorded their astonishment. The BBC's Michael Buerk, chairing a *Moral Maze* radio discussion of the verdict, simply ignored the evidence presented at the trial and echoed the government line that 'there is no evidence' that Hawks were being used in East Timor;[13] Jeremy Paxman said as much on *Newsnight* some months later. The *Guardian*'s legal correspondent, Clare Dyer, described the verdict as 'the latest in a catalogue of "perverse" decisions by juries who sympathise with a stand taken by defendants, despite the strict letter of the law . . . The four Hawk women [argued] that they had acted to prevent a greater crime, a defence [that is] intended to cover cases such as committing an assault to stop a burglary.'[14]

Jo, Andrea, Lotta and Angie replied, 'This was not a perverse decision, but one based on law . . . Is it any less legitimate to use force to prevent murder and genocide? The law is being broken, but not by us. The law against genocide is being broken by British Aerospace selling Hawks to the brutal Indonesian dictatorship. We have been held accountable by the courts for our actions, but British Aerospace and the British Government are flouting the law with impunity. We took full responsibility for our actions, but British Aerospace and the British Government are ignoring theirs. Now that we've been acquitted, it is time to bring the real criminals to account.'[15]

THE INVISIBLE REVOLUTION

> Now we must begin all over again. Step by step, with no
> shields but those born of our own bodies. It is necessary
> to discover, create, imagine. And today, more than ever,
> it is necessary to dream . . . together.
>
> *Eduardo Galeano*

> The last few weeks have been turbulent. They are but a
> precursor of the turbulence to come.
>
> Financial Times, *on the strikes sweeping Europe*

AN UPRISING ENGULFED East Timor in November 1994.
Crowds beat back police and soldiers; for more than a week,
the Indonesian military machine seemed to lose control of its
colony. At the same time, in the Indonesian capital, Jakarta,
twenty-seven young East Timorese scaled the twenty-foot
spiked railings of the American Embassy. As an evocation of
incorrigible bravery, the silhouette of a slight young man
poised defiantly on the spikes joins those who stood against
the tanks in Tiananmen Square.

If 'the struggle for freedom is the struggle of memory
against forgetting', as Milan Kundera wrote, events such as
this have a universal meaning.[1] Until recently, few Indonesians knew about the resistance in East Timor; families of
soldiers killed there regarded it uncomprehendingly as their
'Vietnam'. The government-controlled media maintained an
effective news blackout. That changed in 1994 when heads of

state of Asian and 'Pacific Rim' countries came to Jakarta for a meeting of the Asia Pacific Economic Conference, APEC. The East Timorese stole the show.

Outwitting Suharto's Western-armed riot troops, they occupied embassy after embassy, giving interviews to foreign reporters through the railings, and electrifying Indonesians, with whom they had in common memories of the regime's barbarities. This was a critical point for Indonesia. Waking up after almost two decades of a dictatorship which, in the mid-1960s, oversaw the extermination of more than half a million people, many Indonesians had not forgotten their country's rich history of popular resistance.[2]

'A frequent argument heard from the current Indonesian Government and its defenders internationally', wrote the Australian academic Max Lane, 'is that it is inappropriate to judge its human rights record using so-called Western values. But since the beginning of the twentieth century a fundamental aspect of Indonesian history has been the struggle for freedom and human rights.'[3]

The first mass organisations, such as Sarekat Islam (Islamic Union), were followed by the Indonesian National Party, the Indonesian Communist Party and other great popular parties. Before the Second World War, thousands of Indonesian workers went to prison to defend a vision of what their country might look like after independence from the Dutch. And when independence was won in 1949, millions demonstrated their desire for political democracy and social justice, regardless of whether they were Islamic or Christian or communist.

Between 1945 and 1959, Indonesia had one of the freest parliamentary democracies in the world. In 1955, there were general elections with more than thirty parties competing. But the military's exploitation of the often chaotic populism of President Sukarno put an end to that. The subsequent extermination campaign led by Major-General Suharto against 'communists' and his denial of democracy were hailed in the Western media as a 'gleam of light in Asia ... the West's best news for years in Asia' and the opening to 'an investors' paradise'.[4]

As Indonesia industrialised, intolerable conditions in the investors' paradise speeded the awakening. Jeremy Seabrook, author of *In the Cities of the South*, described a 'free-market' slavery. 'There are factories', he wrote, 'where the only jobs available are sex with management, others where the drinking water is polluted and metal roofs intensify the tropical heat so they are sometimes working in temperatures of 50 degrees centigrade. There are factories where accidents are commonplace but medical treatment is sketchy or unavailable, where exhaustion and malnutrition are part of the uncounted daily cost of the production of those familiar trademarks and logos that form part of the landscape of our lives.'[5]

Today, for wages of less than $2 a day, most Indonesian workers can barely afford a subsistence diet. Labour accounts for less than 10 per cent of production costs, compared with up to 30 per cent in 'enlightened' Thailand. The role of the military in the factories is sinister and pervasive: it is to spy, manipulate and crush disputes and prosecute trade unions not approved by the regime. In 1993, the mutilated body of a female worker called Marsinah, who had played a leading part in a strike at a watch-making factory in East Java, was found in a forest three days after she had dared to complain to the local military command.

Marsinah's courage was an inspiration to tens of thousands of workers, and her murder provided a spark. Rolling strikes ensued; and support for the recently formed Indonesian Prosperous Labour Union, known by its initials, SBSI, grew rapidly. In 1995, the union took over the factory town of Medan, in Sumatra, with 50,000 workers demanding the right to form free trade unions.

The regime was horrified; the SBSI chairman, Muchtar Pakpahan, was arrested and charged with 'incitement'. This led to other occupations and illegal mass meetings. At many of them there would be a speaker from East Timor, who would describe the fate of Indonesia's 'twenty-seventh province': the killings, the disappearances, the forced sterilisations. The audience would listen, shocked and the link would be made.

In 1995, the PPBI trade union was formed. One of its

leaders was a 23-year-old female worker, Dita Sari, who distinguished herself by organising a strike by 14,000 workers at a textile factory owned by Suharto's wife. She then brought out 12,000 workers at Cibinong, in Java, and 15,000 people at ten factories in Bogor, before she was arrested. She has since been re-arrested and interrogated many times.

I met Dita Sari when she made a brief, anxious visit to Australia to seek support. It was difficult to believe that such a tiny, nervous, self-effacing individual had done what she had. 'I should not be amazed,' she told me, 'but I am always amazed at the way people give their heart and soul, and their courage, in facing up to the military. Every day now there is a strike, or a stop-work, or a continuing action against the regime. Maybe things look normal to businessmen and tourists and journalists, who see us as teeming and passive and don't see the truth about us. This is our invisible revolution.'

On her return, Dita Sari was sentenced to six years in prison for 'subversion'. Shortly afterwards, some 300 prisoners fought their way out of Medaeng prison in Surabaya, and the rest followed, setting fire to one wing. Armed troops took two days to regain control. The authorities accused an 'element' in F Block; Dita Sari was the element.

By June 1996, a broadly based democracy movement had emerged in Indonesia, centred on the Indonesian Democratic Party, the PDI, a coalition of nationalist and Christian parties led by Megawati Sukarnoputri, daughter of the late President Sukarno. Within weeks, the PDI had become a mass movement, with thousands demonstrating on the streets of Jakarta. On July 27, troops mounted a full-scale assault on the PDI headquarters. People fought back, most of them for the first time in their lives. Building after building in the centre of Jakarta was torched. Forty-seven people are known to have been shot or stabbed to death by the army. Although Megawati was forced to stand down, an underground People's Assembly was quickly formed to defend her party. The popular liberal Muslim leader Abdurrahman Wahid publicly challenged the regime; academics and others spoke out for the first time.

In the weeks before the rubber-stamp elections in May 1997, there was a rash of show trials. The leader of the People's Democratic Party (PRD), Budiman Sujatmiko, shrugged off his guards and, turning away from the judges, spoke words almost identical to Franz Kafka's in *The Trial*: 'You may object that it is not a trial at all; you are quite right, for it is only a trial if I recognise it as such.'

Having been sentenced to thirteen years, he leapt on to the vehicle about to take him to prison and, clutching a flag and the flowers his parents had given him, he spoke about democracy until soldiers dragged him down.

The regime's fear of this new party, which has attracted large numbers of young people, ensured that most of the country knows about it. The army newspaper, *Berita Yudha* (News of War), described the PRD as 'an operation among students and workers, forming public opinion through leaflets and publications. They are very intelligent and clever young people. They are not only theoretically brilliant, rivalling any scholar, but also throw themselves into the field. They are not only brilliant orators casting a spell over the people, but also understand the people in great detail. That's the PRD.'[6] The mass-circulation weekly magazine *Forum Keadilan* published an eight-page supplement on the PRD 'threat' and newsboys shouted, 'PRD! PRD!' as their papers were snapped up.

As the regime prepared for its elections, hundreds of thousands of people took to the streets, factories and shopping centres were burned down, police stations were attacked, the offices of district authorities were ransacked and pro-government mullahs were seized and stripped of their yellow Golkar shirts. Golkar is Suharto's party, which, on cue, was awarded two-thirds of the 'vote'. Independent monitors reported 'multiple voting, intimidation of party scrutineers ... a systematic violation of the rules.'[7] Documents showed that district officials had already worked out the results in the *kampungs* (hamlets) before voting started.[8]

What was authentic was the boycott of the election and spoiling of ballot papers. In East Timor, this was almost total outside the capital, Dili. On election eve, the resistance ambushed a patrol, killing seventeen soldiers; and on a hill overlooking the fortress town of Baucau their flag flew briefly.

On the same day, in Hong Kong, the building that houses the official Chinese news agency, the headquarters of mainland power on the island, was enveloped in a banner depicting the Goddess of Democracy; some 7,000 people stood silently in the street outside. They were protesting against what one of the speakers described as 'the union of totalitarianism and capitalism, and the stillbirth of democracy'.

During that week, on the eighth anniversary of the massacre in Tiananmen Square, a sea of defiance flooded Victoria Park. Dismissing appeals by Beijing's leader-in-waiting, Tung Chee-hwa, to 'set aside the burden of June 4', more than 50,000 people converged on five football pitches. They gathered around the 'Pillar of Shame', a memorial to 1989 depicting fifty mangled bodies. Banned from public display during the period of transition to Chinese rule, it was carried into the park all the same. At its base is the legend: 'The old cannot kill the young for ever.'[9]

The same spirit is abroad in South Korea. On Boxing Day 1996, the Government of Kim Young Sam convened Parliament in the early hours of the morning in order secretly to enact laws that struck at the country's tenuous democracy. These laws increase the powers of the secret police, the Korean CIA, and impose sweeping restrictions on trade unions. Workers in this, the leading 'tiger' economy, now face prison if they go on strike, or even object to conditions. This is the Korean version of the deity of work 'flexibility' worshipped by Western Thatcherites. It means unemployment or part-time employment, long hours, unsafe conditions and insecurity.

The response was immediate. In the first general strike for half a century, some 800,000 people stopped most of Korea's industry, transport, universities and schools, with overwhelming public support. Evoking the *minjung* movement, which had forced open democratic doors in the 1970s (the literal meaning is 'popular masses'), trade unionists and students were joined by tens of thousands of middle-class people opposed to what they call the 'new authoritarianism'. In 1998, as the IMF sought to take control of the Korean economy and its diminished currency, the trade unions and popular organisations became the nationalist opposition.

There is the same spirit in West Papua, where Asia ends and the Pacific begins. In 1969, this magnificent wilderness, rich in its diversity of people and natural resources, was annexed by Indonesia with the connivance of the United Nations. The Dutch-trained militia went into the mountains and, calling themselves the guerrillas of the Organisasi Papua Merdeka or OPM/Free Papua movement, have fought on for independence. Like East Timor's, theirs has been an epic struggle ignored; and just as East Timor has come out of the shadows, so West Papua has begun to draw the outside world's attention to its need for freedom.

West Papua (the Indonesians renamed it Irian Jaya) has one of the most lucrative copper mines in the world, earning more than $1.4 billion a year and contributing a fifth of Indonesia's Gross National Product. Part-owned by the British minerals giant Rio Tinto Zinc, the mine's expansion has cut through communities and their environment, dispossessing ancient tribes which have nurtured the forests and causing 'rivers of pollution'.[10]

OPM guerrillas and tribal people have attacked the mine, and have paid dearly in Indonesian reprisals. On Christmas Day 1994, thousands of people came down from the mountains and the OPM flag was raised audaciously between two Indonesian bases. When the Indonesian troops arrived, their officer shouted, 'Are you Christians or communists?' and opened fire. As attacks by the Indonesians have increased, the movement has grown and today is stronger than ever.

All these are fragments of the 'invisible revolution' Dita Sari spoke about. They are seen by turning the media telescope around: by observing the unchanging phenomenon of struggle all over the world, not over the shoulders of the managers of

329

power, but from the perspective of the majority. No matter how humble or isolated or 'developed', people everywhere share the same aspirations and many share the same consciousness: freedom, security and equity. These are the most basic human rights.

The 'invisible revolution' is universal. It is in Latin America and Africa, in the Indian sub-continent and right across the steppes of the former Soviet Union. It is the independence movement in Bougainville, the Zapatistas in Mexico, the landless workers' movement in Brazil, the endurance of people in Cuba. There is an ebb and flow; for some societies it is their turn, for others not. What is not in doubt is that the phenomenon continues, in spite of its consignment to oblivion by the Western media, whose propaganda of organised forgetting says that imperial capitalism has 'succeeded' and socialism has 'failed'. Defeats at the hands of raw power, as in Chile, Nicaragua, Guatemala and those many other countries subjected to Western economic and military terrorism, have not been failures of their economic experience. On the contrary, popular democracy, health and education under Salvador Allende and the Sandinistas were extraordinarily successful. To say that these alternatives 'failed' is like saying that Hitler's destruction of Western European democracies was a 'failure of democracy'.[11]

During the old Cold War, confusing Soviet Communism with democratic socialism was a propaganda standard that corrupted much of Western journalism. Today, the dominant propaganda aims to discredit *any* alternative to the 'triumphant market', including historical truths. Thus, it is fashionable to confuse the aims and morality of the October Revolution in Russia in 1917 with the totalitarianism that followed it. But even now there is a regeneration. With a third of the Russian people deeply impoverished by the consequences of bandit capitalism, there is, wrote the independent journalist Renfrey Clarke, 'the sense that the October Revolution was morally right, and that a present-day analogue of it would be a good thing'. Although people are more desperate than militant, 'a fight-back is occurring, and in order to stage it, Russian workers are having to re-invent many of the methods of organisation and struggle in which their forebears were expert eighty years ago.'[12]

The new iconography of the rich and privileged is temporary. Russians are again beginning to build their own popular assemblies in place of the eunuch institutions of the new 'democracy'. In the vast Siberian coalfields, miners and other workers have formed themselves into labour collectives and set up a 'Trade Union Centre with Emergency Powers', which is pledged to fight for the just distribution of state funds. The number of strikes and acts of civil disobedience across Russia has tripled. 'The point about titanic social collisions', wrote Clarke, 'is that they develop swiftly, educate masses of people almost overnight in the realities of their social existence and thrust them into action in ways they could not have possibly anticipated. Such collisions are guaranteed to happen again in Russia.'[13]

The 'invisible revolution' is under way in Western Europe. Its objective is to overturn the Maastricht Treaty, under which European governments agreed to implement a single European currency. This means the sacrifice of jobs and public services in order to 'achieve' low inflation and a reduced national deficit: the same 'macro-economic' or 'neo-liberal' refrain heard across the world.

French working people are having none of it. In the winter of 1995–6, most of France stopped in protest against the conservative government's plans to implement the first stage of Maastricht. Nothing like it has been seen since 1968. Direct action has since convulsed Germany, Belgium, Spain, Italy and Greece. In 1997, the French Socialist Party was voted back into office and, although originally one of the midwives of the Maastricht Treaty, it has been forced to reflect people's anger and to consider abandoning Monetary Union.

There are many battles to win. One of the most hopeful is the growing resistance to the racist political force led by Jean-Marie Le Pen. In April 1997, some 70,000 anti-racists from all over France converged on Strasbourg, where Le Pen's National Front was holding its national conference. They included many who had never made such a commitment before. On roads into the city the street signs were each tied with a black band, symbolising that Le Pen's presence had made Strasbourg a city in mourning. In the main square a cinema screen was erected and some 5,000 people, of all colours, watched Charlie Chaplin's anti-Nazi film *The Great Dictator*. No attempt was made directly to confront Le Pen and his people; there was no violence.

But the action at Strasbourg marked a significant change of mood; and the divide appears to be narrowing between French working people who filled freezing streets in 1995 in defence of jobs and a decent standard of living, and those who have long opposed the rise of racism and the scapegoating of immigrants. For the first time in years, the main trade union confederation, the CGT, has launched a national debate on racism among its member unions, sweeping aside what was something of a taboo.

'In turn,' wrote Peter Morgan from Paris, 'the anti-fascist movement has given confidence to groups of workers to raise other demands ... Junior doctors, a group not normally associated with militant action, blocked roads and railway stations in protest against government plans to cut spending on health care. Air France pilots grounded all flights to and from Paris protesting against a plan to pay new pilots lower salaries – and they were supported by mechanics and cabin crew. Bank workers across the country have protested against the drive to "flexible labour" ... Postal workers and printers have all been involved in strike action, and lorry drivers are threatening to reimpose blockades ... The question of Europe is like a timebomb. You can suddenly see how the thing can explode.'[14]

The spirit was the same when, in 1989, a determined Australian woman, Shirley Shackleton, managed to reach Balibo, the Timorese town where the Indonesians murdered her husband, Greg, with four other television newsmen. She had wanted to plant a tree in Greg's memory. A priest offered the yard behind his church; and Shirley planted the sapling with Indonesian troops surrounding her.

'They had not allowed any Timorese to be present,' she said. 'But the organised resistance was there. You couldn't see them, of course; but their presence was such that the soldiers hung grimly on to their weapons and looked very nervous. As I knelt, saying a few words to Greg, the most wonderful singing washed over me. On the other side of the road, a young people's choir started up. They had timed their practice to my being there. I shall never forget those voices. They came through the barrier the Indonesians had set between us, and they comforted me. They will never be defeated.'[15]

THE DOCKERS

> The efforts of ordinary people to improve their standard
> of life and to secure greater dignity and recognition of
> their role in society have been evident in British history
> since at least the Peasants' Revolt of 1381.
>
> *Eric Taplin, Liverpool historian*

LIVERPOOL DOES NOT suffer from historical amnesia. Although its pantheons of the slave trade and the industrial age have been made fit for tourists, the cobbles restored and swept litter free, the past remains defiantly the present. As a keeper of the secrets of the blood, sweat and tears of ordinary people, Liverpool has few equals. That is why it excites such prejudice, even hatred, and why the unfashionable resistance of its people endures.

Under Margaret Thatcher, the people of Toxteth rose against a newly politicised police force. Thatcher's assault on local democracy almost came to grief in Liverpool. 'Self-pity city,' Rupert Murdoch's *Sunday Times* abused it when a thousand people publicly mourned the murder of James Bulger; Liverpool was 'a paranoia theme park' that 'refuses to listen to criticism'.[1] That came after Murdoch's *Sun* had lied that Liverpool football fans had robbed and molested the dead in the Hillsborough stadium. Today, a widespread boycott of the *Sun* on Merseyside holds after more than seven years, which would be remarkable anywhere else.

Liverpool was my first assignment as a young reporter in England more than thirty years ago. Dockers and their

334

families were then being 'decanted' into 'new towns': lunar landscapes of jerry-built boxes where window-frames had already burst free and the damp had already risen by the time the first key turned in the door.

On my first day I walked along the miles of docks my grandfather had described as 'a man-made wonder worked by stoic men'. In his sailor's log, which he called *With Folly on My Lips*, young Richard Pilger was in no doubt of Liverpool's place of honour in a people's history. He was a Cape Horner, who took the fully-rigged tall-ships around the Horn and into the gales of the roaring forties. Born in Germany, he regarded English ships as his own and Liverpool was his home port, which he loved and probably hated, too.

'My stock of sovereigns had become exhausted,' he wrote in September 1889. 'It was a Saturday night and into the barroom burst Old Tom [a local scout for crews], shouting, "Do you want to ship in a four-masted barque going to Sydney? If you do, you'll have to go straight away. She is lying out in the stream and the tug is waiting at the pier head. It will be a pier head jump.' I said goodbye hurriedly to Lottie [his Liverpool love], and made haste for the docks.'

The ship was the fully rigged *Province*, laden to the Plimsoll line with locomotive boilers for the new railways of New South Wales. They had been loaded, he wrote, 'by fully subscribed members of one of the world's first trade unions, the National Union of Dock Labourers'. Formed in February of that year, and supported by his own fledgling union of seamen, the first union of the Liverpool dockers barely survived the shipping companies' efforts to destroy it. 'Christian gentlemen', he wrote in 1890, 'had made fortunes from the trade in slaves, headquartered in Liverpool, so it was not at all surprising when they objected to us paid slaves at sea and on the docks wanting our fair rights.'

The leading seaport of the world's greatest maritime nation had worse poverty and generated greater profit than almost anywhere in Britain. An incredible £237 million's worth of cargo passed through Liverpool in 1905 – the equivalent of several billion pounds today – in a city of rampant, preventable disease and shoeless children.[2]

In 1911, the General Transport Strike was the long-awaited popular explosion, so alarming the government that a gunboat, HMS *Antrim*, was sent to the Mersey estuary. Initiated by the seafarers and with the dockers the last to go back, it was, wrote Philip Gibbs, *The Times*'s correspondent, 'as near to a revolution as anything I have seen in England'.[3] The employers had wanted more work for less pay under worse conditions: an unchanging demand whose trademark was casual labour, known as 'the evil'. People in Liverpool still call it that.

For the docker, the ritual was unrelenting: you went to the waterfront before dawn every morning where you were put in a pen and waited for a man in a bowler hat to pick you out. 'You'd be fighting and climbing over each other's backs to get the boss to take your book and hire you,' one of them remembers. If you were picked, you worked that day for a pittance. If not, your family went hungry. Exclusion was often due to age or religion, or a reluctance to endanger your life or grease the boss's palm. Men worked from seven in the morning often until ten at night and in all weathers; many slept on the docks rather than miss 'getting first on the stand'.

'I was brought up with it,' said Doreen MacNally. 'My dad was a docker. My husband's dad was a docker. So casual work, and everything it stood for, is within living memory. I remember it as a child. I'd be playing out on the street and Tommy, my dad, would come home and say to my mum, "Nothing on today"; and I'd remember other days when my mum would say, "Oh Tommy's all right for a job today, because Ernie Roberts up the road is the ship's boss and he'll pick Tommy because he knows he's a grafter."

'Once when my dad was being hoisted up by the crane, the belt snapped and he fell into the ship, on to railway lines. He was off two years, then when he returned four bales of cotton smashed into his back. Experience like that ought to be known today, because it's come back, in different forms and with different names, but it's back, and not only on the docks but all over this country. Working lives are being impoverished everywhere, and it's time once again to do something about it.'[4]

Doreen did something about it. She went to the local Job Centre, known as 'the joke shop'. A strike-breaking man-power firm, contracted by Mersey Docks and Harbour Company, had advertised vacancies on the docks a year after it had sacked the entire workforce of almost 500 dockers, many with a lifetime of service.

'I waited outside until I saw these young lads going in,' she told me, 'then I spoke to them: "Excuse me, those jobs on offer already belong to men who've put their whole lives into the docks. My Charlie was sacked after twenty-nine years' loyal service. These jobs on offer were fought for by our fathers and uncles and grandfathers. Look, I'm a picket line, just me.' They said, "Don't worry; we won't pass your picket line; we understand." '

I first saw Doreen doing something about it one Saturday in September 1996 at the Pierhead. The heroic architecture of the Liver Building reared up behind her to a watery sun; a flock of seagulls rose and fell until a hooter sent them flapping back to the Mersey. On the spot where my grandfather had leapt on to his clipper bound for Sydney, an unusual crowd gathered to hear her and the others speak.

'It's one year today,' she said. 'We've had our hearts wrenched when a son tells his mother to sell his bike to pay the electricity bill; and we've disguised our feelings with laughter. We've shared the feeling of soaring spirits when we've looked around and seen the support from com-passionate working people all over the world. We know we are telling the truth, but *where* is the union, *where* is the Trades Union Congress?'

On September 25, 1995, dockers working for a private contractor, Torside, were ordered to work overtime for a disputed rate. They protested and were sacked on the spot. Within a day the entire work force of eighty men had been sacked. Three days later, they mounted a picket line and all 329 men employed by the Mersey Docks and Harbour Company, including fathers and uncles of the Torside men, refused to cross it. They, too, were summarily dismissed.

They were got rid of so quickly that within twenty-four hours their jobs were being advertised in the local press. It was the end of the bloodline. Men like Jimmy Campbell, whose father was killed on the docks, had almost forty years' service. Shockwaves hit more than 8,500 men, women and children. 'When my husband received his P45 after twenty-eight years' working in the port,' said Pat Dooley, 'it was like someone had died in our house.'[5]

Few of them doubted that they had walked into a trap. Because the overtime dispute was not theirs, the dockers' refusal to cross the Torside picket line was illegal under Margaret Thatcher's anti-trade-union laws. Mersey Docks and Harbour Company claimed that it was 'entirely independent' of Torside.

This meant that the dockers could be sacked for 'secondary' picketing. But to those who knew the life of the port, there was no doubt that Torside was merely a device set up to enable the principal company to disassociate itself from labour practices that echoed the discredited past.

In a study of the dispute, Liverpool University sociologists Michael Lavalette and Jane Kennedy conclude that 'one of the more distasteful aspects of the company's campaign against the dockers has been to deny any responsibility for the Torside dockers or to include them in any discussions aimed at resolving the dispute.' The Torside workforce 'were part and parcel of Mersey Docks' labour force: they were recruited at interviews held in Mersey Docks' premises, were trained at Mersey Docks' training sessions, worked on ships brought to the port by Mersey Dock . . .' The evidence, they say, clearly indicates that the company wanted to get rid of the old, secure workforce and to introduce casualisation.[6]

The company denies this. 'We have never employed casual labour and have no intention of doing so,' said Eric Leatherbarrow, the public relations director.[7] Yet, when the dockers tried to return to work ten days after they were sacked they found a contractor had filled their jobs with cheap, casual labour. The scab workers' contract stipulated an hourly rate of £4 for 'all hours'. Employment could be terminated 'when the contractor determines'. There was 'no obligation on the contractor to provide the worker with a guaranteed number of working hours in any day or week. There would be periods when no work is available . . .'[8]

According to Eric Leatherbarrow, this contractor 'is no longer on the docks'. What he did not say was that it had been replaced by other contractors of casual labourers. A bundle of documents passed to the dockers reveal a web of employment agencies employing scab labour behind picket lines. The case of 'Eddie' is typical. Employed on a day-by-day basis, he was given no training, nor was he issued with a safety helmet, a standard high visibility vest, overalls or safety boots. Customs officers who happened to be scouring the ship he was working on were so shocked by the lack of attention to Health and Safety regulations that they complained to the supervisor on deck and have since reported the company.[9]

The company blames the dispute on 'a small group' of dockers who 'intimidated' the rest: a charge that becomes laughable when you spend time with dockers and their families. When I asked Leatherbarrow if he understood the historical resonance of casual labour, and the fear it pro-voked, I was told, 'That's a red herring. We're protecting a major employer and wealth creator in the region [whose] presence created as many as 80,000 jobs.'

On the contrary, long-term unemployment has increased dramatically in Liverpool and on its waterfront, where the number of dockers' jobs has spiralled down to fewer than 600, a tiny fraction of the figure a few years ago. As for 'wealth creation', profits have certainly soared from less than £9 million in 1989 to more than £31 million in 1995, the year the company jettisoned its dockers.

Mersey Docks and Harbour Company is the very model of a Thatcher-era 'enterprise'. Having grown out of a public body, the company has been the beneficiary of the Thatcher Government's abolition in 1989 of the National Dock Labour Scheme, which was meant to end the scourge of casualisation for ever by giving dockers the legal right to minimum work, holidays, sick pay and pensions. Uniquely, the docks are the only public utility still partly in public ownership and – if you discount the arms industry – still prospering on a cushion of public subsidy.

Mersey Docks and Harbour Group was a public trust which, like the nation's water resources and so much else, was not the government's to sell. Still, in 1970 the government used taxpayers' money to write off £112 million in loans, to fund up to £200 million's worth of redundancies, and to pay out £37.5 million for the regeneration of the docks area. The company has also received £76 million of City Challenge funding and, since 1989, some £13.3 million in European Regional Development Funds. According to the *Liverpool Echo*, 'directors of Mersey Docks have received phenomenal grants to create employment' during a period when unemployment has gone up. Inexplicably, the company's literature boasts about its success in the 'free market'.[10]

During the heyday of this 'free market', in the 1980s, hundreds of miles of waterfront and docks were handed over to bankers, financiers and speculators. On the River Medway in Kent, Medway Ports, a newly privatised company, sacked all its dockers and replaced them with casual and contract labour. The Medway dockers, said the company, had 'sacked themselves' by objecting to new contracts that meant longer hours and harsh and regressive conditions.

This was a workforce that had not been involved in industrial action for twenty-five years, an exemplary record. When the Medway ports were privatised, the dockers were persuaded to join a management-employee buy-out. However, when they lost their jobs the terms of their contract obliged them to sell back their shares – for just £2.50 each.

Speedily on the scene was the Mersey Docks and Harbour Company, which bid for Medway Ports, paying £37.25 a share.[11] Medway's chief executive, Peter Vincent, who had bought the ports from the government eighteen months earlier for one-seventh the price, scooped up his sacked dockers' shares at their old knock-down price and made £12 million on the deal. Vincent described the sale as 'a very

"Here you are—don't lose it again!"

The front page of the *Daily Mirror* on the day of the general election, July 5, 1945, when the paper called on its readers to 'Vote for Them': meaning those who had fought and died for a land 'fit for heroes'. The Labour Party won by a landslide.

Above: Phil Hammond with a photograph of his son, Philip, aged 14, who was killed in the Hillsborough Stadium tragedy on April 15, 1989. *The Sun* falsely blamed the Liverpool fans in a notorious front page written by the editor, Kelvin MacKenzie. *(Photograph: Drew Gardner)*

Left: Kelvin MacKenzie, editor of *The Sun*, 1981–1990. As head of L!ve TV, a cable channel owned by the Mirror Group, one of his innovations was a 'News Bunny' which gave the thumbs up or down to each news item. He is now the Mirror's managing director. *(Photograph: David Sillitoe)*

Above: Steve Bell's metamorphosis of Tony Blair into Margaret Thatcher.

Opposite: Mrs. Thai Thi Tinh, with photographs of her husband and two sons killed in the Vietnam War. She lost five of her eight children in the war and wears some of their medals. *(Photograph: Nic Dunlop)*

Below: Leaders of the Liverpool dockers' epic two-year struggle for jobs and social justice: (clockwise from top left) Terry Teague, Jimmy Davies, Mike Carden, Jimmy Nolan, Tony Nelson and Bobby Morton. *(Photograph: John Garrett)*

Above: Children of East Timor, where more than 200,000 men, women and children, a third of the population, have died as a result of Indonesia's illegal occupation since 1975. *(Photograph: Steve Cox)*

Opposite: An East Timorese boy and Indonesian occupying troops, 1991. *(Photograph: Steve Cox)*

Below: Aung San Suu Kyi, elected democratic leader of Burma in 1990 and prevented from holding office by a military dictatorship; with the author, Rangoon, 1996. *(Photograph: David Munro)*

Above: Bobby Muller, a former US Marine who lost the use of both his legs in Vietnam, returns to China Beach, where the first Marines came ashore in 1965.   *(Photograph: Nic Dunlop)*

Below left: A child slave labourer in Burma, a country ruled by a military dictatorship for 36 years.   *(Photograph: Nic Dunlop)*

Below right: Xanana Gusmao, leader of the East Timorese resistance from 1982 to 1992 when he was captured by Indonesian troops. He was sentenced to life imprisonment.

fair deal'. The sacked dockers sued the accountants who had put such a low value on their shares, and won an out-of-court settlement.[12]

In the meantime, the government, which owned 20 per cent of Mersey Docks, stood by while the value of its 'gold share' – the taxpayers' stake in the company – fell to less than 14 per cent. 'It was odd', mused chairman Gordon Waddell, at the time, 'that a company with a government shareholder should be buying a privatised port.'[13]

When I suggested to Mersey Docks' spokesman, Eric Leatherbarrow, that this was a striking example of 'wealth creation', he said, 'We're not in the business of calming prejudices of individuals against what other individuals may achieve in their lives.' One such achiever is his colleague, Mersey Docks' managing director Trevor Furlong, who took an £87,000 pay rise just before the company sent an entire workforce to the dole. Furlong's 38 per cent increase brought his earnings to £316,000 a year. He also has a £293,000 share option.[14]

Leatherbarrow said directors' salaries were decided by a 'remuneration committee' – of other directors, the non-executive variety. If Furlong required such a generous reward, the dockers' remarkable productivity clearly did not. Last July a House of Commons Employment Committee was told that in September 1995, the month they were sacked, the dockers handled the highest tonnages ever recorded in the Port of Liverpool.[15]

The shipping industry newspaper *Lloyd's List* described them as 'the most productive work force in Europe'. Three years earlier, in the *Liverpool Handbook and Directory*, Trevor Furlong himself eulogised the dockers he was soon to sack as 'men who appreciate the value of cargo' and contrasted their 'professionalism and performance' with the 'lack of professional commitment' in other British ports now operating casual labour.[16]

After they were sacked, some of the men were offered individual contracts which imposed new, harsh conditions and effectively cut wages. They were all balloted on a 'final offer' of £25,000 redundancy pay and just forty jobs – which they rejected overwhelmingly. Men with only months to go before they retired voted no and stood to lose everything. 'Our fathers and grandfathers fought and died for jobs that we could be proud of,' said Jimmy Campbell, aged sixty. 'I did it for the young ones.'[17]

The dockers were represented by the Transport and General Workers' Union, Britain's second largest union, whose leaders maintained that because the dockers' action was technically against the law, the union could not make the dispute official. But had the TGWU launched a national campaign challenging the sinister circumstances and the injustice of the dockers' dismissal, along with the issue of casualisation, the battle could have been won there and then. As it turned out, the union's failure to act unceremoniously closed a chapter of struggle to achieve civilised working conditions in Britain's docks. Moreover, the company is delighted with its 'good relationship' with the union and boasts that it runs 'the only unionised port in the country'. 'We show the TGWU far more respect than the [sacked] men,' said Leatherbarrow.

It is hardly surprising that, at Transport House, the TGWU headquarters in Liverpool, the dockers use a bust of Ernest Bevin, the union's pre-war General-Secretary and pillar of the right wing of the Labour Party, as a coat-stand. For much of its history the TGWU has been, as one labour historian wrote, 'an encrusted, complacent, bureaucracy' which, in containing the anger of its ordinary members at the injustices imposed on their working lives, has served the aims of the British establishment.[18]

An unchanging attitude of union officialdom was summed up by John Magginnis, who started on the Liverpool docks in 1951. 'We worked in dirty, unhealthy, dangerous conditions,' he said. 'But if the men had a grievance and sent for the delegate [trade union official] he would walk round the sheds, straight into the office, come out, walk past the men without saying a word and you would find out later from the employer's representative that nothing had changed. The favourite phrase of delegates was, "My hands are tied. What can I do?" '[19]

The 'unofficial strikes' for which the docks became notorious in the 1960s and 1970s more often than not reflected workers' frustration with the union leadership's seemingly instinctive willingness to collaborate, however indirectly, with employers and hostile politicians. Ironically, just before he was sacked, a Liverpool docker, Mike Carden, had just completed a masters' degree in philosophy on how trade unions are 'incorporated' in the establishment.

Big unions like the TGWU are still absurdly portrayed by the Tories, New Labour and much of the media as a potentially dangerous fifth column in the body politic. Yet, without the timidity and inaction of some of the famous union 'barons', the legislative attack on trade union rights in the 1980s probably would have failed, along with the devastation of the steel and mining industries, and the privatising of the docks.

This perspective on the unions has always been something of a taboo. It was considered so threatening during the early part of Thatcher's reign that a 1982 television series by Ken Loach, *Questions of Leadership*, for Channel 4, was withdrawn then drastically cut. Consider the opening sequence of the Loach films. Over archive film of a mass meeting of trade unionists during the 1930s Depression the soundtrack begins to play the chorus from Gilbert and Sullivan's *Iolanthe*:

> Bow low ye lower middle classes;
> Bow, bow ye tradesmen;
> Bow ye masses . . .

As the mockery continues, the pictures dissolve to a parade of earnest young men, standing on platforms, exhorting the masses. Then they grow older, florid, comfortable, and become portraits of self-satisfaction, dressed in the ermine of the House of Lords. They are Joe Gormley, Vic Feather, Richard Marsh, all former trade union leaders (soon to be joined by Lord Len Murray). The commentary says, 'There are some trade union leaders who are so prosperous that they have in their own person achieved the harmony of the classes.' Rank-and-file trade unionists speak about the meaning of 'democracy' within the big unions, referring to 'small, bureaucratic, centralised groups of people ... that prevent individual members from playing a role within the union and the general direction the union is going'. Were these not the familiar media words of right-wingers complaining about the 'militants' infiltrating their 'democratic' institutions? Yes, but in the Loach films the voices came from ordinary trade unionists who were analysing the hold of the trade union establishment on the organisations and fortunes of millions of ordinary people.[20]

The fate of the Liverpool dockers and their community exemplifies this. When the National Dock Labour Scheme, regarded as the last protection against 'the evil' of casual labour, was abolished in 1989, the response of the TGWU was craven. While three readings of the abolitionist bill went through Parliament, there was no sustained attempt to challenge it. Two ballots for a national strike were approved overwhelmingly by the membership of the union, but when the strike was finally called by the leadership it was too late. The employers could now use non-registered dockers in the ports. Not surprisingly, the strike, when it finally came, collapsed.

The Liverpool dockers were the last to go back. Taking their cue from the miners four years earlier, they marched back. Throughout the country the scale of the defeat was all too evident. An independent study four years later found that most of the docks had fallen to casual labour. More than 5,000 jobs had been lost nationally, with a 41 per cent saving on wages going straight into profits. Hourly rates had fallen to as low as £2.50 on the east coast. The accident rate had leapt by more than a third, because, said the report, training for the new-style 'temporary dockers' was now 'rare'.[21]

With the Dock Labour Scheme scrapped, relations between Mersey Docks and its men deteriorated – although, as Eric Leatherbarrow points out, relations with officials of the TGWU hardly missed a beat. A campaign of demoralisation followed, similar to that waged against the miners following the coal strike. Hours lengthened, work loads increased and a gruelling 12-hour shift rota was introduced. As Jimmy Nolan, the chairman of the shop stewards, remembers, he had fought thirty years ago to end ten-hour shifts and now it was 'twelve hours or the sack'.[22]

Men were placed 'on call' during their days off. 'The company intruded in our family lives with daily phone calls and changing shifts,' wrote the dockers' wives. 'Sometimes they had only been home four or five hours. If the company couldn't contact them by phone, they'd send them hand-delivered messages, ordering them to return to work. The men were quizzed about their whereabouts twenty-four hours a day.' Discipline for petty offences became common; men with a lifetime of service found themselves under constant threat of dismissal, including 'a final warning for life'. Others were disciplined for not answering the phone on their days off.

'Jimmy's sixty now,' said Irene Campbell. 'Almost forty of those years were spent as a loyal, hard worker. Not long ago he could run marathons. But when they increased the intensity of work, with the men there all hours, seven days a week, I watched the deterioration in him. Before he was sacked, he'd be working from seven in the morning to ten at night, at the age of fifty-nine, when his shift should have ended three hours earlier. All he could eat for dinner was a sandwich. Like all of them, he felt the job had to be done regardless of the reduced workforce and the lack of holiday relief. You see, those jobs had been fought for and you couldn't give the company the excuse to abolish them. Men like Jimmy were given no choice but to look out for each other and work themselves half to death.'[23]

Five years ago, the company began to 'de-recognise' those elected TGWU stewards who refused to sign loyalty pledges to the company. Bizarrely, Mersey Docks demanded that the workforce vote on the issue in a secret ballot. When the dockers voted with the stewards, the company took out advertisements in the *Liverpool Echo* calling for applicants to replace the entire workforce. In a city with 13 per cent unemployment, some 2,000 unemployed young people thronged the company offices in a chaotic scene reminiscent of pre-war days when men begged for work at the port gates. None was offered a job.

Their hopes had been raised by what the dockers saw clearly as a ploy to force them to accept new draconian contracts under which 'all existing jobs including your own are to be eliminated with new jobs being created which fit into the new working system'. An editorial in *Lloyd's List* commented, 'One does not have to be left-wing to have sympathy for the sacked dockers of Liverpool, who now find themselves effectively the victims of a markedly macho management.'[24]

What the Liverpool University study reveals is that the company's 'macho management' and the TGWU's determination to maintain a presence on the docks at times converged. The unspoken arrangement gave the company a certain respectability and the union continued to recruit. 'This led union officials to act as "industrial policemen",' says the study, 'dissipating workers' anger, refusing to take industrial action and threatening the dockers that if they did not comply with management they would be sacked.' Shop stewards who did not 'keep the lid on' – as a service to the company – were out.

The sacked dockers called on the TGWU to investigate why an offer to the union by the Torside managing director, Bernard Bradley, was not passed on to them. Bradley told the Commons Employment Committee in July 1996 that he had made the offer to a regional official of the union.[25] The men say that, had they been told, they would have returned to work immediately, and there would have been no picket and no pretext to sack the workforce. A union inquiry into this episode was 'referred up', then the Executive Committee voted to do nothing about it. In his speech to the Labour Conference at Blackpool in 1996, Tony Blair said, 'No more bosses versus workers. We are on the same side, the same team.' The dockers understood the unintended irony.

Five months after the dockers were sacked, TGWU General-Secretary Bill Morris, who consistently refused to make the dispute official, came to Liverpool and made an emotional speech. 'I am proud to be with you,' he told the men and their families. 'Your struggle is so important that our grandchildren will ask, "Where were you at the great moment?" and you will either stand up with pride and say, "I was there," or you'll hang your head in shame, without an answer.' He went on, 'There can be no turning back and no backsliding until victory is won.' He pledged that the union would 'keep going . . . until we get this company to understand that a negotiated settlement which gives people their jobs back is the only way.' He added, 'God is on our side.' The dockers cheered him.

In November 1996, Morris called the dockers' committee to London and told them that they would have to abandon the principle of getting their jobs back – the same principle that Morris had said in his speech was 'the only way'.

I tried repeatedly to elicit a comment from Morris, or from anyone at TGWU headquarters. When I phoned Morris's office and asked for an interview, his assistant discussed a time and place. But when I said that it was about the dockers, I was passed to a press officer, Andrew Murray, who said, 'Bill Morris cannot legally speak to you.'

I asked him for the names of the lawyers advising Morris not to speak. 'They don't want to be bothered by journalists,' he said.

'What law prevents the leader of one of Britain's biggest unions from speaking out on an industrial dispute concerning his members?'

'This is not a fruitful line to take . . .'

'Doesn't this secrecy strike you as ridiculous?'

No answer.

Finally he agreed to take questions from me in writing. So I wrote to Morris reminding him of his 'God is on our side' speech and the 'extra mile' he had pledged to walk on the dockers' behalf and asked him what he had done to honour this. I got no reply. Inexplicably, Morris later wrote to a colleague, 'It was I who asked Mr Pilger to submit written questions, a request that he refused.'[26]

I phoned the Trades Union Congress. As it happened, John Monks, the General-Secretary, had made a ringing speech in

Liverpool that weekend about moral values. 'You cannot have a moral society', he had said, 'when people feel they can be treated like dirt by their employers.'[27]

I asked to speak to John Monks. 'What's it about?' said a TUC press officer.

'The Liverpool dockers . . . As Mr Monks was in Liverpool and talking about the morality of treating working people badly, I thought . . .'

'Sorry, John never comments on disputes, and that one is far too sensitive for him to be involved in.'

Britain was a founder member of the International Labour Organisation, an arm of the United Nations. Year upon year the ILO has condemned the British Government for Thatcher's laws which deny working people 'the most basic right' to defend each other by refusing to cross a picket line without endangering their own jobs. The government refused an ILO challenge to have this resolved at the International Court of Justice, where it would surely lose. Put another way, most of the democratic world regards the Thatcher laws as a disgrace in a free country.

This is hardly surprising as the struggle of working people for the right to defend each other is probably the oldest in labour history, preceding even the Peasants' Revolt. In 1306, the Trades Union of Journeymen Shoemakers of London drew up the following charter: 'If there is any dispute between a master of our trade and his man, such a man is wont to go to all the men within the city of the same trade, and then by covin and conspiracy between them made, they will order that no one among them shall work or serve his own master, until the aforesaid master and his servant or man have come to an agreement; by reason whereof the master of the said trade have been in great trouble and the public is left unserved.'[28]

'You've got to ask', Jim Donovan, President of the Australian Maritime Union, told me, 'why a powerful union like the TGWU is not challenging anything? They should be saying, "We've had enough of this. We're standing up to bad laws. Come and sequester our funds." They've had plenty of time to get them away. We face the same attacks on jobs, and our funds are no longer in Australia. If you wait for Blair to be elected, you'll find nothing will change. We've been through that here. Only the will is needed. The public will support it: they know it's gone too far now.'

At six o'clock every morning, regardless of the weather, the pickets were huddled outside the port gates around the traditional brazier. Those on duty were often grey-haired and could count more than a century of service between them. The ritual, however, was not as familiar as it appeared. Every day the picket moved, covering the three main gates of the port, unannounced, so that the company and the police, working together, were never quite sure where they would turn up.

An innovation was all-women pickets, some of them with young children. These were organised by WOW, which was short for Women on the Waterfront: partners, mothers, sisters, aunts and cousins, and mostly from traditional households. 'The young men were never a problem,' said Doreen MacNally. 'You could say they were already socialised. At first the older men used to laugh: "Oh them bloody WOWs." I think the men expected us to organise the Christmas party, you know, women's things, but we soon changed that. We have our own mass meeting every Wednesday; we lobby with the men or instead of them, while they mind the home.' Doreen's husband, Charlie, says, 'Now I ask her about what's going on in the dispute.'

Fourteen months ago Doreen had never made a speech. At her first rally on the steps of Liverpool's massive neo-classical pile, St George's Hall, she said, 'I am Doreen MacNally. I have red hair, blue eyes, flesh and blood and as much right to shelter and nourish my family as you.' She has since made hundreds of speeches, all over the country. She and others were at the TUC and Labour Party conferences. 'Bill Morris', she said, 'told us his hands were tied. I told him he should get out of the job if he's afraid to confront bad laws.'

'The women', said Mike Carden, 'have been like a hurricane of fresh air blowing through the union.' They have been to 10 Downing Street and occupied the London boardroom of one of the firms providing scab labour on the docks. One of their specialities was candlelit vigils outside the homes of the directors of Mersey Docks. 'We sang,' said Doreen, 'and the kids sang. We found out it was Trevor Furlong's birthday. He's the one who got an £87,000 pay*rise* the other day. He was sixty something. He's the one who said a docker was too old to work at the age of fifty. We had a birthday card and everyone signed it, and a cake made by one of the girls – not too nice a one – in the shape of one of the ships that were then staying away from the port because of the dispute, just to remind him; and we knocked on his door and sang happy birthday, Trevor. So what did he do? With a lot of women and kids singing away outside around a birthday cake, he phoned the police.'

On the day that longshoremen on America's east coast refused to handle ships from Liverpool the women went from director's house to house, singing, 'New York, New York, it's a wonderful town . . .' The most spectacular innovation was the way the dockers internationalised the dispute. 'It was clear very early on', said Mike Carden, 'that one-sided labour laws in this country made it extremely difficult for other workers to join us. So we set out to build a dockers' network abroad, from Australia, to Canada, to the US and Europe. What we discovered was that dockers everywhere faced the same threat of casual labour. But we also live in an age of "just-in-time" deliveries where exporters and importers expect cargo to be moved efficiently and rapidly across the continents, and if a ship is delayed for twelve hours – which is the case every week in Gothenburg as a show of support for us – then the Port of Liverpool has problems.'

At Newark, New Jersey, they set up a picket line where the Port of Liverpool's biggest customer, the American shipping company Atlantic Container Line, had just docked one of its ships. 'It was six o'clock on a December morning in the fiercest blizzard for seventy years,' said Bobby Morton, one of the Liverpool dockers. 'We didn't know what to expect. But the longshoremen coming to work knew instinctively. When we told them what it was about, they turned their cars around. We were dancing on the picket line, we were intoxicated, even though we hadn't been drinking.'[29] They maintained the picket line for a week, and as ACL began to lose serious money in delays it brought pressure on Mersey Docks, eventually suspending its Liverpool operations for a month.

At a longshoremen's meeting in Florida, Bobby Morton came away with $50,000 in a carrier bag. In Los Angeles, they set up a picket line at the port and among those who refused to cross it were a convoy of Mexican truck drivers who had no union and were among the lowest paid in the country. In Canada, four Liverpool dockers walked in with a morning shift at the Port of Montreal, climbed a gantry and unfurled a banner announcing that the Canadian Pacific-owned container firm CAST was employing scab labour in Liverpool. When police tried to arrest them, a ring of Canadian dockers protected them until they met the management to explain their case.

Jim Donovan, the Australian Maritime Union leader, told me from Sydney: 'In a lifetime as a union official I have never seen anything like the Liverpool campaign. It's a phenomenon. They've gone to every corner of the earth to seek support, to places they've never been before, and they've done it on their own, with no backing from their union. They've held two international conferences in Liverpool, I've been to both, and they've had eighteen countries represented. I took over $A60,000 for them last time. Over a hundred years ago support from Australian wharfies helped to keep the great dock strike going in London, that really gave birth to modern trade unionism; and we'll do everything we can this time. We've blacked a major Liverpool customer, the ABC Line, and the pressure added to its financial difficulties. There is a fundamental human right at issue here: the right of ordinary people to secure work at decent rates and conditions.'

In August 1996, the dockers came close to their biggest coup: a blockade of Liverpool ships in Europe. They needed the support of the German and Belgian unions, which had promised to send officials to Liverpool. They failed to turn up, dissuaded, it was said, by the International Transport

Federation (ITF), which worried that the dockers were setting up a parallel world organisation that would challenge the dominance of the ITF. The dockers are bemused by the suggestion, a back-handed tribute to what they have achieved virtually alone.

Up until 1997, the ITF, the maritime unions' world body, had supported the dockers only 'within legal bounds'. This is changing dramatically. In a scathing open letter to the ITF, one of its senior inspectors, Jack Heyman, wrote that a victory for the Liverpool dockers 'would offer an alternative to the defeatist strategy [of the British trade union establishment] that has so far lost every port save Liverpool, much to the dismay of maritime workers around the globe ... This aristocracy of labour, while bemoaning draconian Thatcherite anti-labour laws – which their darling Tony Blair has vowed to uphold! – actually use them as an excuse for inaction.' Heyman reminded the ITF that it was 'launched in 1896 when British seamen sailing into the strikebound ports in Holland joined striking Dutch workers. They didn't fax their union for official authorisation or check to verify if it was legal ... They just did it.'[30]

On January 20, 1997, they just did it. From a room in Transport House, Liverpool, with one phone, one fax line and a tea urn, they triggered a show of international labour solidarity believed to be without precedent this century. 'It was as if the planet skipped a heartbeat,' wrote Chris Knight. Workers in 105 ports across the world took action in support of the Liverpool dockers.

'Pacific Rim trade sputtered to a halt', reported the *Los Angeles Times*, 'as dozens of mammoth cargo ships sat idle in their ports as union dockworkers from Los Angeles to Seattle stayed off the job in a one-day show of support for striking longshoremen in Liverpool, England ... At the Los Angeles–Long Beach harbour complex, the nation's busiest, 33 ships were either stranded in berths with no one to handle their cargo or were anchored in the San Pedro Bay with nowhere to go.'[31]

The American West Coast and much of the East Coast were

stopped for twenty-four hours. 'Dear Bobby,' faxed Ray Familathe, an ITF West Coast inspector, to Bobby Morton in Liverpool, 'this morning over 100 gantry cranes are standing idle along with nearly 50 ships ... I just want you to know that I have called British Airways to book my flight to the UK for the victory party as soon as I hear from you that everyone has been reinstated.'[32] 'This is going to cost us millions of dollars in delays,' bemoaned an American shipping executive. 'Half a billion dollars in commerce is shot, down the drain.'[33]

The breakthrough had come ten days earlier when the Liverpool dockers received a letter from David Cockcroft, General Secretary of the ITF. 'I have requested', he wrote, 'that all ITF affiliates take ... if possible, direct action aimed at ships currently using the port facilities in Liverpool affected by the dispute during the week commencing January 20, 1997.'

In Japan, 40,000 members of the National Council of Dockworkers stopped 'in solidarity with Liverpool while fighting deregulation in Japan'. Fifty Japanese ports were affected. In Canada, the important port of St John, New Brunswick, shut completely, and all ships in and out of Montreal were delayed. In Sweden and Denmark, all ships using Liverpool were left idle for twenty-four hours. In Holland, the key port of Rotterdam was stopped for twelve hours. In Greece, dockers stopped for three days. In France and Germany, all ships were delayed. In Australia, the *Zim Australia*, which trades with Liverpool, was turned away from Sydney Harbour. In New Zealand, dockers, seafarers and truck drivers set up pickets at the ports of Auckland, Wellington and Lyttleton. On September 8–9, 1997, the maritime world stopped again, this time with the South African unions defying legal action and closing all the ports 'in solidarity with the Liverpool dockers who stood by us during the years of apartheid'. Such was the spectacular return of an internationalism that was said to have died with the 'end of history'.

In Britain, few people knew anything about it. Nothing was reported in the national press, or on national television and radio. But then few people had been told anything about an industrial dispute that had now lasted longer than the 1984–5 coal strike.

One of the first references to the dockers in the national press came more than two months after they had been sacked, in a letter to several national newspapers from four Scottish writers, including the Booker Prize-winner James Kelman. They alleged 'a conspiracy of silence' and a 'gentlemen's agreement' between John Major and Tony Blair. It was, they suggested, less the dispute Britain forgot than one that Parliament and the media simply did not want people to hear about.

The media blackout – with a very few honourable exceptions – of what, by normal journalistic criteria, is an important and dramatic story demonstrates a significant change in the selection and reporting of national events. Because the myths of the 'market' have become received wisdom throughout the media, with millions of trade unionists dismissed as 'dinosaurs', the dockers' story has been seen as a flickering curiosity of a bygone era. That their struggle represented more than half of all working people caught up in the iniquities of casual or part-time labour, making Britain the sweatshop of Europe, was not considered real news.

Kevin Bocquet, who covers Liverpool for the BBC, told me he had done only four pieces for television and four for radio in the fourteen months since the dispute began. 'Great pictures . . .', he said, 'you know, the men against the docks in the early morning light, but editors say, "Who's suffering? How does it affect the economy?"'

But was not the spread of poorly paid casual work a critical issue facing millions of people? 'They're casualising at the BBC,' he said. 'That's life.'

On Liverpool's famous Albert Dock, amidst the tasteful renovation and museums, stands an odd Graeco-Roman façade boldly announcing Granada TV. Until autumn 1996, the networked programme *This Morning* was broadcast from here. Not once has it mentioned the struggle of the dockers, genuine local heroes, just a few miles away. 'People just don't want to know,' said the producer, Jo Taylor.

'But how do you determine that?' I asked. She could not say, except that 'it's really embarrassing . . . you see, we go for the female at home. We're tabloid, though we did starving children in Rwanda when Sally Gunnell went out there.'

In spite of the absence of publicity, the dockers say they have had public support they could never have imagined. 'Either it's a bag of groceries on the doorstep,' said Bobby Morton, 'or someone pays your bill at the supermarket checkout. We need around £30,000 a week to keep going, mostly to pay something to the families. We've had hardship money from the union, but most of what keeps us and our families going comes from people who can least afford it. They send us postal orders and fivers in an envelope. There's a pensioner, Mrs Burns, who refuses to give us her address. She has given us literally almost everything she has. The other day she wrote to say she'd sold her fridge for a fiver, for us.' However, like the miners, the dockers can sustain only so much on fivers; in 1997 more than ninety of their homes were under repossession orders.

On the first anniversary of the dispute another kind of support was vividly demonstrated. Thousands of youthful activists from 'Reclaim the Future' converged on Liverpool: environmentalists and direct-action campaigners. At first sight, the disaffected young in woolly hats, dreadlocks and pierced noses, accompanied by drums, fire-eaters and street theatre, seemed a world away from the dockers. But many are sophisticated activists, veterans of anti-road and other environmental campaigns who, having come up against repressive laws such as the Criminal Justice Act, understand well the dockers' struggle.

Their alignment with the unofficial labour movement could influence the direction of grassroots action – especially as more and more young people are alienated from the 'gentlemen's agreement', as James Kelman put it, of mainstream politics. Unimaginable not long ago, their banners, alongside the dockers' traditional union banners, carried messages such as, 'New Labour, new wage slavery'.

Such common cause with the dockers began in 1988 when they stopped the import of uranium hexafluoride from South African-occupied Namibia. The following year, when the waste disposal company Rechem won a contract to dispose of 3,000 tonnes of highly toxic chemical waste from Canada, the dockers refused to unload it, forcing the ship to return to Montreal. This was considered a major victory by environmentalists; and the dockers are in little doubt that their refusal to handle hazardous waste contributed to their sacking. Liverpool, they say, is marked down as the future waste disposal capital of Europe.

There is big money in toxic waste. Rechem is owned by a company called Shanks & McEwan, whose non-executive chairman is Gordon Waddell – who happens also to be chairman of Mersey Docks and Harbour Company. In the first year of the dispute, the amount of waste passing through Liverpool increased by more than a third, to 19,500 tonnes. In 1997, it doubled.[34]

Before the sun was up on the anniversary morning, the Reclaim the Future activists had outsmarted the police and occupied gantries in the docks and the roof of the company headquarters, watched with admiration by snowy-haired dockers and their wives. 'We saw their banners fluttering over the occupied docks,' said Jimmy Davies. 'We didn't see the TGWU, whose officers should have been there. Now we know who our friends are; we welcome the young people's support and idealism.'

Bill Morris, in Blackpool for the Labour Party Conference, had another view. 'We deplore the violence and unlawful action that has taken place,' he said. 'The dockers must disassociate themselves [from the environmentalists].'[35] In fact, as I witnessed it, the violence came almost exclusively from the Liverpool police, especially the rubber-suited Robocops of the Operation Support Division (OSD). I found it moving to see dockers shielding the young activists, leading them to safe houses and guarding them until their buses and trains had left.

At the TGWU's 1997 conference, Morris made a ringing speech in defence of law and order and insisted that a delegates' vote, supporting the dockers, had been defeated. There was uproar on the floor and a second ballot was demanded. The delegate from Rover Cars at Cowley spoke of how 'the dockers' strike of 1889 sowed the seeds for the creation of our union ... We owe the dockers everything. I can remember how they blacked cars for us in the 1980s and made a victory for us possible.'

The second vote was a decisive victory for the dockers, and for a moment it seemed that Britain's second biggest trade union would pay its historical dues to the men. But Morris and the national executive still refused to back them. He said the union would be breaking the law and its funds would be sequestrated. 'We would be impotent,' he said, almost as self-parody. Morris claimed he had written to the government, asking it to intervene on behalf of the dockers. Trade and Industry Minister Ian McCartney said no such request had been received.[36]

Britain's trade union establishment could not have made its position, and contempt, clearer at the 1997 Trades Union Congress annual conference. Dockers who had inspired the support of 50,000 trade unionists on every continent were told that the only place for them was on the pavement outside the hall, with a collection bucket.

On October 13, 1997, Mersey Docks' Chief Executive Trevor Furlong threatened to withdraw the company's 'final offer' if it was not put to a postal ballot. The terms were £28,000 severance pay, thirty-eight jobs and 'interviews' for forty unspecified jobs. The Torside men, whose action precipitated the dispute, were excluded. Without consulting the dockers, the TGWU imposed a ballot. Seventy per cent voted against; had the Torside men been balloted, the result would have been at least 80 per cent. It was a decisive rebuttal by men and their families now deeply impoverished by two years of fighting for the right of them all to work.

Having done everything the trade union establishment demanded of them, the dockers now called on Bill Morris to put the TGWU behind them, to seek for the support of other unions and to insist that the company negotiate on jobs., They waited; the response was silence.

During Christmas 1997, there was the spectre of aloneness and desertion during freezing winter days on the picket line, as if a harsh and uncertain journey lay ahead for the men and their families. Then Bill Rooney had a heart attack and died and a week later, Jimmy McUmiskey, who seemed a fit man in his fifties, followed. 'Jimmy lived and breathed the dispute,' said a member of his family. 'He couldn't sleep at nights; the struggle killed him.' He was the fourth docker to die since they made their stand.

It was now clear the families could no longer survive on the £12 a week the union gave them. (Had the dispute been official, strike pay would have been more than treble that.) Mersey Docks and Harbour Company left the offer of £28,000 'on the table' for each man to pick up if he wanted to; for impoverished men watching their families suffer, it was an excrutiating enticement. Desperate men picked it up. With characteristic resolve, the stewards told their regular Friday meeting that, for their sake of the lives of comrades and their families, they had decided to recommend an end to the dispute; understandably, they incurred the wrath of a few. The *Guardian* described their decision as a 'climbdown'. It was nothing of the kind; it was the end of one battle of the most critical struggle of the late twentieth century.

At both anniverary rallies, in the warmth of the crowds who came to cheer them, there was also an atmosphere of shared purpose and solidarity which, after my years in this country, I recognised as British society at its best. At the Pierhead rally the final speech was made by eleven-year-old Neil Fox, a docker's son. 'I always thought my dad was very brave,' he said. 'He drove a gantry crane. He was so high up in the air, working that massive machine. He sometimes worked fifteen hours a day. Our families will not give in; we have been through too much. Thank you for coming to Liverpool.'

VI
ON THE FAMINE ROAD

THE ROOTS OF WAR

The only way to prevent the people from becoming habitually dependent on Government is to bring operations to a close.

Lord Trevelyan, ending Irish famine relief, 1846

IN COUNTY MAYO, in the west of Ireland, there is a stretch where Mweelrea rises steeply on one side of the great lake and the Sheeffry Hills on the other, where clouds tumble in silent avalanches down slopes of iron grass and scabrous rock and the sound of birds carries across the water. Without knowledge of the past, there is no doubting its special beauty. This is especially true out along the coastline, where the beaches at low tide string a necklace of islets that become fire-red silhouettes at dusk.

Yet all of this is a burial ground; beneath a single pyramid of rocks there are said to be hundreds of skeletons. Discussion of precisely how many are buried in this place or that becomes a disrespectful irrelevance once you walk past them and over them and feel something of the enormity of what was done in Ireland.

The other day I took part in the annual Famine Walk organised by the human rights body, Action from Ireland (AFrI), which has marked the 150th anniversary of the Irish Famine, or the 'Great Hunger' as it is still known in those places that bear its scars. With people from all over Ireland and the world, I walked the ten miles from Doo Lough to Louisburgh, where hundreds of starving people arrived on the night of March 30, 1849, seeking relief and workhouse shelter. The local Poor Law guardians were to 'inspect' them in order to certify them as 'official paupers'. This would then entitle them to a ration of three pounds of meal each. Instead, the people were told to be at Delphi Lodge, the fishing lodge of the Marquess of Sligo, ten miles away, at seven the next morning.

Setting out in snow and gale, some were blown from the road to their deaths; others died from exposure and starvation. When they reached Delphi Lodge, they found the guardians eating their dinner and refusing to be disturbed. They waited, only to be refused relief. Many more died on the homeward journey, with the bodies remaining where they fell.

Such tragedies were common in Ireland then. Previously, the population had stood at 8·2 million. By 1871, it had almost halved, with at least 1·5 million dead in the famine and two million fled to America, many of them dying during the voyage or on arrival. The historian and critic Terry Eagleton, author of *Heathcliff and the Great Hunger*, describes the famine as 'the greatest social disaster of 19th century Europe, an event with something of the characteristics of a low-level nuclear attack'.[1]

When Don Mullan, then with AFrI, first took me to Mayo, he recommended I read *Paddy's Lament, Ireland 1846–1847: Prelude to Hatred* by Thomas Gallagher. I pass on the recommendation, for it provides a vivid appreciation of the roots of the current war in the north of Ireland. Gallagher gives a meticulous description of the 'hollow of the blood', a designated place where a 'bleeder' would take blood from animals and distribute it as food; and of caves containing the skeletons of people who had died agonising deaths, clinging to each other, after eating seaweed and poisonous shellfish; and of evictions, with people dragged from homes where the few bits of furniture had already been sold for food; and of abundant grain and animals being delivered to ports for export to England, 'always with an escort of armed constabulary to prevent an attack by the few Irishmen still strong enough to lift a stick or throw a stone . . .'[2]

Many more grain ships left Irish ports during the famine than delivered food. Although the immediate cause of the famine was a crop disease, the potato 'blight', Ireland continued to produce enough food to feed its population twice over; it was known as the 'granary of Britain'. Writing at the time, Dr Dominic Corrigan described how 'the poor starve in the midst of plenty, as literally as if bars separated them from a granary'. Forced to pay exorbitant rents to landlords, farmers of what these days would be called 'cash crops' were left dependent on potatoes for their own food. When rents went unpaid, landlords, helped by British troops and police, evicted the people and demolished their houses.[3]

In 1847, the Liberal Government in London set up soup kitchens in Ireland, but this one and only concerted attempt to relieve the hunger was soon abandoned; and market forces reasserted their power of life and death over the Irish colony. The 'relief effort' was controlled by the Chancellor of the Exchequer, Charles Trevelyan, a 'free enterprise' zealot. Like most of the ruling class, Trevelyan was devoted to 'Manchester economics', which was a fashionable version of the *laissez-faire* that is today's catechism.

'The great evil with which we have to contend', said Trevelyan, 'is not the physical evil of the famine, but the moral evil of the selfish, perverse and turbulent character of the [Irish] people.'[4]

Trevelyan's casual racism towards the Irish was common and, of course, still exists. 'The moment the very name of Ireland is mentioned', wrote Sydney Smith, 'the English seem to bid adieu to common feeling, common prudence and common sense, and to act with the barbarity of tyrants and the fatuity of idiots.'[5]

The tone of British press coverage of Ireland is also familiar. According to the editor of *The Economist* in 1847, a benign consequence of 'the great sacrifice' which England had made to help the starving, was that 'of convincing every reasonable Irishman, and the world at large, of the deep interest which is felt by the Government and the people of this country for the welfare of Ireland'.[6]

As the Famine Walk set out, our voices echoed across the lake and its treeless landscape, a legacy of a colonialism that left Ireland one of the most deforested countries in Europe. Led by the balladeer Derek Worfield, people sang into the valley:

No ears could hear the crying and the powerful men were deaf
And eyes that seen the dying saw seeds of hate were left.

The actor and film-maker Gabriel Byrne said, 'People think the Irish famine has no relevance to our lives today and that the famines in Ethiopia or Rwanda or elsewhere are isolated events. The truth is that the same conditions designed to enrich a very few and deprive the majority of their rightful wealth, and not just their right to their land, but to their identity and culture – this is happening all over the world today. The famine was a symptom of social and economic policies that continue.'

This was supported by Gary White Deer from Oklahoma, whose Chocktaw Indian people sent $710 to Ireland as famine relief: a huge amount at the time. Juana Vasquez and Dano Caal, representing the Mayan people of Guatemala, the survivors of the Spanish invasion of their country, lit candles, including black for the famine victims and yellow, the symbol of light.

At the first stop along the road a children's choir from Derry, led by Richard Moore who was blinded by a rubber bullet when he was eleven, sang Charlie McGettigan's 'The Famine Roads'. Overlooking us, crouched on a rock, was a ragged and barefoot woman, gently rocking a baby back and forth. One of a theatre group called the Galloping Cat, she appeared like a phantom from 150 years ago.

But then this was Ireland, and the whole event, the shared act of bearing witness, could not happen across the water, where actors seldom perform politically and children are not encouraged to sing the laments of a people's history, and the links between old and new colonialism are suppressed. It is not at all surprising that issues like the terror in far away East Timor become national concerns here. (When the former

Australian Prime Minister, Paul Keating, arrived in Dublin to pay the obligatory homage to his Irish roots, he was greeted with full-page newspaper advertisements damning Australia's complicity with the Indonesian regime.) Dick Spring, the Foreign Minister, was prepared to spend an hour around midnight with me discussing East Timor, whose freedom he has championed in Europe. 'We have the *experience*,' he said. 'We can start every sentence with, "Historically speaking..."'

Yet the Irish Government now appears to be moving away from the neutrality born of its own bitter colonial experience towards some sort of relationship with the expanding NATO, the modern colonisers' club. Historically speaking, as Spring would say, what a tragedy if that happens. In Dublin, official commemoration of the Great Famine is related to this shift. Until 1997, the government did little; the famine and the passions it arouses are apparently not part of modern 'free-market' Ireland, which, beneath the consumerist gloss, is beset by growing divisions between rich and poor similar to those across the water.

Related to this is what the historian Christine Kinealy, author of *The Great Calamity*, calls the 'strong revisionist tradition of Irish writing on the Famine, which plays down the negative role of the British Government'. What has emerged, she wrote, is 'a sanitised alternative that has endeavoured to remove the patina of blame from the authorities involved in providing direct relief, while minimising the suffering of those who were most directly affected by the loss of the potato crop'.[7]

The revisionists say that the causes of the famine were 'too complex' to blame on Britain. They maintain that the famine was part of an historical pattern in Ireland, notably in immigration. 'The caricature', wrote Kevin Myers in the *Irish Times*, 'of starving, cringing peasant and haughty, horse-backed landlord has become too attractive for the Poor Us school of political theory to dispense with.'[8]

From Oxford, the historian Stephen Howe pronounced British Government ministers of the 1840s 'well meaning', though 'hobbled by free market dogma', adding, almost as an after-thought, 'of course, a longer history of exploitation helped make the disaster possible'. He dismissed as 'false' the description by Joe Murray, the Famine Walk organiser, of a 'holocaust in Ireland'. Moreover, he wrote, 'There's something deeply sordid about trying to establish hierarchies of historical suffering, elbowing for places in the front row of victimhood.' It was all just 'a natural disaster'.[9]

Not according to Lord Clarendon, Britain's main representative in Ireland, it wasn't. Pleading with the Liberal Prime Minister Lord Russell to intervene, he wrote, 'Surely this is a state of things to justify you asking the House of Commons for an advance. For I don't think there is another legislature in Europe that would disregard such suffering as now exists in the west of Ireland, or coldly persist in such a policy of extermination.'[10]

The hidden agenda of this revisionism, one of many in the representation of Irish affairs, draws on a traditional silence over the famine. The historian Brendan Bradshaw has described how 'the central event of the 19th century' has been 'simply ignored, written out of history, omitted from the agenda of Irish historical research'. Others have suggested this has much to do with the 'shame' implanted by colonialism. 'Colonialism is an insidious process,' wrote John Waters of the *Irish Times*, Ireland's most eloquent columnist. 'Its victims recognise themselves in the coloniser's descriptions. And when the coloniser leaves, unless there is a coherent project to restore national consciousness, the liberated colony internalises the colonial condition in manifold ways.'[11]

Coming from a profoundly colonised society, I recognise the truth of this. My own family on my mother's side regarded our Irish convict forebears as a 'stain' upon us, not to be revealed under any circumstances. When I wrote about my great-great-grandfather's conviction at Cork for 'uttering unlawful oaths' and his transportation to Sydney in leg-irons, I was not readily forgiven.

In June 1997, Prime Minister Tony Blair commemorated the 150th anniversary with an 'apology' to the Irish. This was not as it seemed. In a carefully constructed statement, clearly designed to draw the Dublin Government into his 'peace process' in the north, Blair assumed no retrospective responsibility and made no apology. He merely regretted the failure of his predecessors to act 'while a crop failure turned into a massive human tragedy'.[12]

There are fine historical ironies here. Lord Trevelyan, in charge of famine relief, was an early opponent of 'welfare dependency'. At the height of the famine he argued, 'The only way to prevent the people from becoming habitually dependent on Government is to bring operations to a close.' Relative to the times, his thinking compares with the 'new thinking' of New Labour's Social Security Minister, Frank Field, who regards welfare 'dependency' as a social evil and has moralised about single motherhood. Strikingly similar attacks on the 'able-bodied poor' led to the introduction of the Poor Law in Britain in the 1830s, which replaced relief with the hated regimes of the workhouses.

A few days before we set out on the Famine Walk, the World Health Organisation published the most damning report in its history. Poverty, it said, was the leading cause of premature death and sickness across the planet and the gap between rich and poor was widening as never before in recorded history. Almost a third of the world's children suffer hunger and half of humanity is denied access to decent medical care. Indebted countries are forced to export food as a 'free market' commodity while the producers are denied their own produce and many of them go hungry, and their children starve. That is what happened in Ireland.

In Lord Trevelyan's day, it was known as Liberalism. Today, it is known as 'neo-liberalism', although there is a range of euphemisms. 'England made the famine,' wrote the Irish socialist James Connolly, 'by a rigid application of the economic principles that lie at the base of capitalist society.' In essence, nothing has changed; and the truth to be found on the road from Doo Lough to Louisburgh cannot be revised.

VII

THE RISE AND FALL
OF POPULAR JOURNALISM

FORWARD WITH THE PEOPLE

> There are shining victories to be won in the cause of peace and social justice. We shall reach the new freedom by not submitting to economic slavery ... Forward with the People.
>
> Daily Mirror, *editorial 1945*

> The *Daily Mirror* gave an indication as never before of what ordinary people were thinking. The English people at last found their voice.
>
> A. J. P. *Taylor,* English History, 1914–45

I ARRIVED AT the *Daily Mirror* in January 1963, during the second harshest winter since the Middle Ages. My bus got as far as a snowdrift in Trafalgar Square, where its decanted passengers joined a conga line along the Strand and Fleet Street. It was the first snow I had seen. I had never owned a coat; I wore a velvet jacket and a Magic Drip-Dry shirt, purchased from Pineapple Joe's in Sydney, and a tie. This was a tie day. The £100 my father's bookie had lent me had almost gone. Freelancing for *Tit-bits* paid less than waiting tables at the Golden Egg in Earls Court Road. I needed serious employment.

I had with me what these days is called a portfolio. Mine was in a red plastic envelope embossed with the name Ferrari, the car maker, a memento of the nine months I had just spent in Italy, where I had written numerous stories for Australian

371

publications, and had been paid, as yet, for none of them. They included pieces on Ferrari, the fountains of Rome, the health properties of pasta and an interview with the Australian sheep-shearing champion, a Greek-Australian I had met on the ship to Genoa, whose achievement was all the more remarkable because he was not much taller than a sheep on its hind-legs. (*Tit-bits* bought the shearer for £20.)

I had a few precious clippings from my first days on the Sydney *Telegraph*, where I had served my apprenticeship before joining the great moving belt of Australians bound for Europe. My immediate ambition was to earn enough money to buy a Burton's coat, then to leave England for somewhere, anywhere, that was warm. A sub-editor's job was on offer at the *Mirror*, and I had an interview arranged with Michael Christiansen, the assistant editor responsible for features, and son of the famous *Daily Express* editor, Arthur Christiansen.

'Good grief, an Australian! You're just what we want!' he said, bowling an imaginary ball. 'And what do you do best, Pilger?'

'I've done production . . .'

'No, cricket!'

'Er, I bowl, I *spin* bowl . . .'

'Splendid,' said Christiansen. 'You start on the *Mirror* tomorrow.'

'What as?'

'Oh, we'll work that out . . .'

Surreal. With snow falling outside, I was recruited into the *Daily Mirror* cricket team as the means of defeating its old and bitter rival, the *Daily Express* XI. My qualifications were my place of birth and a skill I did not possess and had never possessed. Journalism was not an issue. My rehearsed *spiel* was not heard; my red portfolio remained closed. People appeared to shake my hand and talk cricket. It was true: England was populated by eccentrics.

Christiansen led me to the news chief sub-editor, who had no job available, then to the features chief sub-editor, who had nothing available but was a Yorkshireman and enquired, 'What does he *do*?'

'He's a spin bowler,' said Christiansen.

'Smashing!' said the chief sub-editor, whose name was Denis Futrell and who without delay appointed me assistant to the sub-editor in charge of television programmes, gardening, fishing and the Pets' Club. My career in Fleet Street had begun.

On my first day I was in luck; I was given Xenia Field's copy. Xenia was the *Mirror*'s septuagenarian gardening writer, who had a considerable public following and, most important, the ear of Cecil King, the chairman. I was not aware of this, or that it bestowed a sanctity on her copy. Above all, I could not understand a word of what she had written – the subject that week was hydrangeas. Furthermore, I made the capital mistake of rewriting her column.

Later that day Xenia arrived, waving a proof of her page like a chequered flag. She was incensed and demanded to know who had besmirched her hydrangeas. However, my act of subversion had made me so popular with my long-suffering fellow sub-editors that they closed ranks and declared me indispensable to their routine. A deputation to Derek Dale, the features editor, included dark talk of 'going to the chapel' (the union).

So Xenia was duly placated and I was promoted to TV programmes. I confessed to Christiansen that I had swum, not bowled. 'An Australian who *can't play cricket!*' he harrumphed. '*Disgraceful!*' and proceeded on his way, rather like the hare in *Alice*. We remained good friends until he died, too young. He had fitted the *Mirror* perfectly: at once benign and mischievous, tolerant and unpredictable and a craftsman.

I had grown up with plenty of characters at the *Telegraph* in Sydney: the Chandleresque crime reporters and the Runyonesque racing writers, the great fire-engine chasers, the creative idlers, poets and drinkers. The surprise was to find that Fleet Street was not as tough as Sydney. In Sydney journalists were used and menaced by a breed of newspaper proprietors immortalised by Cyril Pearl in his book called *Wild Men of Sydney*.

I worked for one of them, Frank Packer, an ex-boxer and

racehorse owner who ran his publishing empire like a *mafioso*, firing when he felt like it or when your face did not fit. (He once 'fired' a Post Office telegram boy in a lift for answering back.) His chief courtiers were frightened men; his journalists survived behind a thinly veiled servility. They referred to him as 'Frank', even 'Uncle Frank'. (This may help to explain why Rupert Murdoch is called 'Rupert'.)

The *Mirror* was very different. Irreverence and a certain anarchy were encouraged. When I joined the features department, it was administered by Freddie Wills, a former RAF ace who had also distinguished himself by dive-bombing the outcrop Rockall, believing it to be, through the mist, the conning tower of a German U-boat. He had a gloriously insane rule that in a newspaper office you did not read newspapers. The reasoning behind this was that you were supposed to have read all the papers before you arrived in the office. Those caught infringing this rule would find themselves stalked by Freddie, who, creeping on hands and knees, would whip out a match and set fire to the pages.

Freddie was a most likeable man, as well as a fine journalist, and there was much affection for his manic ways. When he fell ill with tuberculosis, he was sent by the *Mirror* to a sanatorium, where he learned Russian. Thereafter he became the *Mirror*'s Kremlinologist, arriving early every morning to pore over the Soviet press in order to supply the news desk with an erudite digest of that day's events and machinations in Moscow. Years later I occupied an office next to Fred's and relished his wild phone conversations in Russian, often ending in English with: 'KGB bastard!'

There was one empty desk where the feature writers sat. It belonged to Eric Wainwright, a Canadian who had assumed the *persona* of an English toff. Impeccably turned out in tweed, sometimes in a bowler, a furled umbrella striding ahead of him, Eric made his name with death-defying stunts, such as free-falling from aircraft, setting fire to himself and joining a Teddy Boys' gang. His most famous stunt was locking himself in a cage with a lion, which tore off his trousers.

One day Eric decided he had had enough of this and never wrote another word for the *Mirror*. There was no question of the paper getting rid of him. On the contrary, as Mike Molloy, who later became editor, told me, 'Everyone loved Eric, so he continued drawing his salary. Indeed, it was only after we had not seen him for several months that we began to worry that a story would come out that he'd been found dead in a hostel and people would ask, "Weren't his employers ever concerned about him?" Fortunately, a check with the cashiers revealed that he'd drawn an advance on expenses the day before, so we were much relieved to know he was still alive. Of course, this sort of thing would send someone from the Harvard Business School berserk, but it was typical of the *Mirror*'s tolerance, which was part of the paper's character.'

The same qualities were extended to the readers. Every letter, every phone call, no matter how cranky, was taken seriously. During the Second World War the Daily Mirror Readers' Service was set up to help families while the breadwinner was away at war. Guiding people through bureaucracy was a speciality. Anybody could use the Readers' Service, which after the war gained a reputation for extracting 'justice' from the system and became something of an ombudsman for countless thousands of powerless people: the elderly, the handicapped, single parents, people in urgent need of legal advice.

It was entirely free of charge and what the *Mirror* got in return was good will, loyalty and affection. The *Mirror* was the first popular paper to encourage working-class people to express themselves, for whatever reason, to *their* newspaper. When someone came to reception and asked to see the editor, it was assumed that a reporter would be sent down to sit and listen, and help, regardless of whether a story was in the offing.

There was a code of ethics long before the National Union of Journalists wrote one. This left the staff in no doubt that if they knowingly submitted false or distorted stories, they would be dismissed. The same was true of 'foot-in-the-door' and other forms of harassment against ordinary people, although a dispensation was available in seeking information from the privileged and the criminal.

When I first went on the road for the *Mirror*, in the north of England, knocking on doors in mining and steel villages and railway towns and on council estates, I found myself welcomed inside once I had said I was from the *Daily Mirror*. Like most of my colleagues, I became immensely proud to be a journalist on a paper so respected by working men and women. I have never known a newspaper to enjoy such an abiding relationship with its readers.

We were also proud of the enmity of those who feared the *Mirror*'s political power. In preparing a series of articles on the 'public' schools, I found myself courted by the head-masters of Eton, Marlborough and similar institutions. With a Labour Government newly in power and making hostile (and, as it turned out, innocuous) murmurings about the evils of private education, the *Mirror*'s influence was not under-estimated. On Headmaster Chenevix-Trench's desk at Eton were copies of *The Times* and the *Mirror* with the latter ostentatiously on top. 'I much prefer the *Mirror*,' he lied. 'It reminds me of the great democracy we live in.'

I shall always remember one campaign in my first year on the *Mirror*, 1963. It was a series of 'shock issues' on behalf of the elderly. This was remarkable because it ran every day during the week that saw one of the great celebrations of youth: the Beatles' first appearance at the London Palladium.

To the *Mirror* there was no contradiction. Carefully and boldly, it brought together the needs and hopes of both young and old. On the front page of the issue of October 14, beneath the single-word banner, ALONE, was an almost three-dimensional photograph of the clasped hands of 94-year-old Kate Malone, who, said the caption, lived alone in a top-floor flat in Bristol. Cicero was invoked: 'No one is so old to think he cannot live one more year.'

Over the page was a news report of the Beatles 'under siege' at the Palladium the night before. 'Fifty girls managed to break down the emergency doors,' it said. 'The manager, Mr.

David Willmot, dialled 999. And as the police ran into the theatre, the girls ran out . . .' On the next page, the headline said, 'In this room a man lay dead for six months'. The story told how James Dunn, aged sixty-five, had died alone in a bare, freezing room on an estate in Liverpool, 'the city of the Beatles'. He had fought in two world wars, his hearing ruined by gunblast, yet he received no pension.

The *Mirror* was in no doubt that he had died from poverty. Over the page the government and the local authority were called to account for their slowness in rehousing Liverpool's 90,000 pensioners. The paper questioned 'the seldom-spoken fact that old people are placed at the bottom of the priorities list [behind] child welfare'. Then it told of a group of teenagers who cared for old people living on their own. There was a picture of Sally Hock, seventy-three, with her friend and helper, Pat Connolly, nineteen, a black Liverpudlian described as a 'teen-angel'.

'We know', said an editorial, 'that the people who can consistently show the great kindness to old folk are the young. Old people know it as well. Ask them. The people they like having around are youngsters. In a curious but very real way, old and young speak the same language and have much to give each other . . .'

Finally, the columnist Cassandra (William Connor) described the 'silent tragedy' facing the increasing number of old people. 'As science grapples successfully with the enemy of early death,' he wrote, 'a paradoxical blight of new unhappiness descends. Life, propped up by new skills, resurrected by new medical research and by new drugs, finds new and implacable enemies. You come to a point where all your contemporaries, good or bad, are your friends [because] poverty is often your last companion. When [the writer] O'Henry lay dying, he was credited with saying, "Turn up the light, I am afraid to go home in the dark." For those who will help, there is still time to rescue the aged before it is dark.'

The composition of this campaign epitomised the *Mirror*: the shocking and shaming story of the death of one lonely man, the eloquent glimpse of ageing in the modern world, the appeal to youthful idealism and the celebration of those building social democracy and bridges between disparate groups, right down to the deliberate use of a positive image of a black person, Pat the typist, at a time when black faces were rare in the press. Not a word was wasted and hardly a cliché used.[1]

It is salutary to compare that *Daily Mirror* with the paper today. When in 1995 and 1996 Britain's pensioners held their national conference, called the pensioners' parliament, more than 2,400 delegates attended, representing a quarter of the population. With the lone exception of the *Morning Star*, no newspaper reported a word of it. After the first conference was ignored, the organisers wrote to the editor of the *Mirror*, Piers Morgan, to protest, pointing out that more than fourteen million people surely had a right to expect the debates and decisions of their representatives to be news in the *Daily Mirror*, especially as pensioners were probably the paper's most loyal constituency. They asked for their second conference to be covered.

When that was ignored, the pensioners finally received a contemptuous computerised standard reply to their letter. 'We have decided not to pursue this matter with you any further,' it said, 'but would like to thank you for taking the trouble to write to us.' It was signed the 'Readers' Service Department', thus misrepresenting one of the *Mirror*'s honourable institutions, which, in fact, had been axed by Robert Maxwell so that he could save a paltry £25,000.[2]

'The history of the *Daily Mirror* is the history of our times,' wrote Maurice Edelman.[3] Edelman wrote his history of the *Mirror* in the mid-1960s when there was a great deal of hope, expectation and social change in Britain, which the *Mirror* reflected. However, the contrast with its origins could not have been greater, as the paper had begun life as a reflection of the unreality of its times.

Owned by Alfred Harmsworth, later to become Lord Northcliffe, the first *Mirror* was published on November 3, 1903 as 'a paper for gentlewomen'. The front page was a collection of advertisements for 'Dressmakers, Milliners and

Furriers to the Courts of Europe' and Tiffany & Co in Regent Street ('precious stones, jewellery and silverware'). Inside, the owner assured his readers that the *Daily Mirror* would be 'feminine, but not effeminate'. The promise was tantalising. The main story was the Court Circular and the main news that the King was motoring to Windsor for lunch. There was a list of 'Distinguished Invalids' ('Sir J. Blundell Maple maintaining improvement') and 'Social News of Town and Country', notably the 'good many cheery luncheon parties', the guest list for a party for the Grand Duke Michael of Russia and Countess Torby, and 'where Notable People Spent the Weekend'.

Under 'Entertainment', there was a magnificent tract of bitchiness entitled 'Other People's Uncomfortable Houses', by 'A Veteran Visitor'. The male writer complained about 'the tipping nuisance that has been growing of late in country houses'. He was especially miffed at having to tip the chauffeur. On one occasion, he wrote, 'I debated in my mind whether I would give him anything at all, for I really detest the new form of locomotion' (cars). Listing 'Insufferable Annoyances' he complained about his hosts' barking dogs, 'the various domestic sounds that disturb visitors', not to mention that 'in some guest chambers, the bed is pointed towards the window'. The writer's purpose was clear: 'I have taken the opportunity of venting these grumbles in the hope that they will reach the eyes of some of the charming people with whom I shall stay within the next few months.'

Meanwhile, the 'in town' news recorded that 'yesterday Claridge's was exceptionally full'. On the food page, and beneath the motto 'A good dinner brings out the softer side of a man', the recommended 'time-saver' dishes for the day included oysters *au gratin*, cold pheasant, cold grouse and sole *à la Savoy*. Within two months, after a print run of more than 265,000 on its first day, the *Mirror* was selling fewer than 26,000.

The editor was an apparent innocent called Mary Howarth, who instituted a Paris column originally called 'Our French Letter'. Determined to cut his losses, Northcliffe declared the

Mirror a picture paper and jettisoned the 'gentlewomen'. A new editor, Hamilton Fyfe, was appointed and told to sack the female staff. 'They begged to be allowed to stay,' he wrote. 'They left little presents on my desk. They waylaid me tearfully in the corridors. It was a horrid experience, like drowning kittens.'[4] Northcliffe's epitaph to his failed project was: 'Women can't write and they don't want to read': words he presumably later choked on, as women became the larger part of newspaper readership.

By 1913 the new *Mirror* claimed it had 'the world's largest circulation' with an unprovable 800,000. Now popular for its photographs (it was briefly the *Daily Illustrated Mirror*), it had some memorable scoops, such as the famous picture of the bodies of Captain Scott and his companions after their doomed expedition in Antarctica.

On May 1, 1910, the front page was devoted to another exclusive picture of a corpse: that of Edward VII lying in state. No *paparazzo* had snapped it. Queen Alexandra had given the court photograph to the *Mirror* 'because that's my favourite'. Thus began a relationship with the royal family that would end, much later, in tears.[5]

In 1914, Northcliffe sold his shares in the *Mirror* to his brother, Lord Rothermere, who controlled it until he sold most of his interest in 1931. However, three years later the Rothermeres still held enough sway for the paper to publish a fascist apologia written and signed by Rothermere himself. 'Give the Blackshirts a Helping Hand', said the headline, beneath which His Lordship railed against anti-Nazi 'panic mongerers' who had not been to Germany and Italy 'as I have done, travelling around and observing the national life in all its aspects'.

British fascists were not anti-Semites, he wrote, because Jews did not dominate industry and were therefore not the danger they were in Germany. He called on British youth 'to work for national reconstruction like that which has transformed and revitalised Italy and Germany'.[6]

Lord Rothermere went on to poison his *Daily Mail* with his fascism while leaving the *Mirror* without a single owner, a highly unusual position for a national daily then, and now. Although Rothermere's chairman, John Cowley, remained in charge, on the board was Cecil Harmsworth King, Rothermere's nephew, an extraordinarily able individualist.

Aged thirty-two, a towering tree-trunk of a man, he was an aloof and yet curiously diffident standard bearer for his family of aristocrats. 'The *Mirror* was a paradox,' said Mike Molloy, who was editor for ten years from 1975. 'The defender of ordinary people was controlled essentially by one of the grandest human beings you could ever imagine. He had grown up in the purple. He made the royal family seem quite common.'[7] As advertising director, King, the grandee, set in train changes on the *Mirror* that turned it into a campaigning 'paper of the Left', as the *Mirror* was to proclaim itself.

His first 'representative on earth' was Harry Guy Bartholomew, the editorial director, known as 'Bart', who was the diametric opposite of the bookish and cultured King. He drank a lot, was relentlessly foul-mouthed and often hit his editor, Cecil Thomas, over the head with an eight-foot balsa-wood plank. The *New Statesman* at the time described him as a 'rough, erratic genius'. Charles Wintour in his history of Fleet Street called him 'a petty tyrant of the worst kind [who] liked spying on his colleagues, opened their letters and listened to their phone calls [but who] gave the paper brilliant pictures and strips, short punchy stories . . . vitality, heart, toughness and an instinctive affinity with the reader'.[8] He transformed the *Daily Mirror* into the first modern tabloid.

The assistant features editor then was a young Welshman called Hugh Cudlipp. 'Bart was a journalist who couldn't write,' Cudlipp told me in 1996. 'It may sound ferocious, but his letters were illiterate: full of mis-spellings, that sort of thing. He was simply and solely a picture man, who used pictures in a way they had never been used before. He invented the big splash and the centre spread. At the same time the *Mirror* was becoming a crusader, the voice of the underdog. The staff had a bond with the readers. We came from ordinary backgrounds. I came from South Wales, which was a distressed area. Then I worked in Lancashire where I used to cover the cotton strikes. If you've been through that, you don't forget it. It was not surprising that we set out down the road of an entirely new kind of journalism.'

Hired by Cecil King in 1935, Cudlipp joined the *Mirror* on the same day as Cassandra and the great sports writer Peter Wilson. It was Cudlipp who would eventually take over from Bart and remake the *Mirror* as a paper of its times, and, to many, an inspiration for them. Self-educated and highly literate, he says with pride, 'I was a journalist at fourteen.' His high forehead, shock of hair, jutting jaw and hunched shoulders marked him as a pugnacious character, which sometimes belied his real distinction as a pioneer, even a visionary.

Politically, Cudlipp was a maverick. That is to say, he was unlike most journalists who rise to power and become either seriously right wing or highly skilled at second-guessing their paymasters. Although, on retirement, he became Lord Cudlipp and joined David Owen's SDP, he was a true radical and something of a moralist, in the sense that he believed that popular journalism should reflect the 'decency of ordinary folk', as he put it, and stand up for its readers and fight their battles, and that it should warn them when they were being deceived. Of course such a newspaper also had to sustain itself financially; but these were its *moral* responsibilities.

Apart from C. P. Scott, founder of the *Guardian* – which did not aspire to a mass readership – no leading popular journalist had ever thought and acted in these terms. Cudlipp gives much of the credit to his mentor, Cecil King, who rose to be chairman and, following Bartholomew's retirement, appointed Cudlipp as editor-in-chief. Certainly, King's peculiar brands of humanism and internationalism were a presence at the *Mirror*. Alas, he was to succumb to the ultimate temptation of the powerful; but more of that later.

The 'entirely new kind of journalism' that came with King, Bart and Cudlipp allowed millions of Britons their first glimpse inside the British establishment. An early example was the Abdication crisis of 1936. Edward VIII planned to marry the American divorcee Wallis Simpson, which meant he would have to give up the throne. The country stood at the edge of a constitutional crisis; yet Fleet Street reported not a word of it and conspired to suppress it. 'The proprietors, Lords Rothermere and Beaverbrook (who owned the *Express*), held a private meeting,' said Cudlipp. 'They guaranteed not to reveal the king's liaison with Mrs Simpson, even though the story was published in every newspaper in the world.'

The arch-monarchist Rothermere the Second still had a financial interest in the *Mirror*. He also had a big influence over the *Mirror*'s board and its chairman, John Cowley, who had viewed the Bartholomew tabloid revolution with hostility, partly because it raised the eyebrows of his establishment friends. To circumvent these difficulties, subversion was required.

As Cudlipp told me, 'Bartholomew lived in a flat near by and came in late one night in his pyjamas and a black hat and said, "We're going to break this story tonight, but we're not running it until the final edition, so that the board doesn't find out." At that time there were various relatives of directors lurking about the place, and we waited for them to go home before we did the front page. It said simply, "The King wants to marry Mrs Simpson." And that did it. The impact was colossal, because every other paper had to do it. At the time it wasn't looked upon as a great scoop, but as a piece of courageous journalism. The *Mirror* had the courage to tell the British public what was going on.'

Shortly afterwards, the *Mirror* broke another of the century's great conspiracies of silence when it warned its readers about the true menace of Adolf Hitler. It was 1938, Prime Minister Neville Chamberlain had been to Munich, returning with his fluttering piece of paper and his speech seeking to justify his 'peace with honour' with the Nazis. Appeasement bloomed. The British establishment's and Fleet Street's links with fascism were well forged. In 1937, the editor of *The Times*, Geoffrey Dawson, wrote to his correspondent in Berlin, 'It would interest me greatly to know what it is in *The Times* that has produced this antagonism in Germany. I did my utmost, night after night, to keep out of the paper anything that might hurt their [the Nazis'] susceptibilities.'⁹

The British public was not fooled, but there was a great deal of confusion about where and how Hitler might strike and whether Britain might 'stand aside'. The very notion of 'peace with honour' not surprisingly appealed to many who remembered the slaughter of the Great War as if it were yesterday, and wanted to believe that, whatever the domestic political fate of the Germans, peace *was* possible. It was to these people that the *Mirror* spoke with care.

'Our voice', recalled Cudlipp, 'was a fussy old gentleman called Richard Jennings, who wrote our leaders and who used to walk around the office in furry slippers. He was a highly intelligent character who used to write with a very wicked, pungent pen, and if he didn't appear one day, Winston Churchill, who was in the political wilderness at that time, would ring up and ask, "What has happened to Mr. Jennings?" It was then that the *Mirror* began to matter.'

When Churchill first warned Britain in 1932 of the menace of a rearmed Germany, it was a Jennings editorial that offered him support. Signing himself 'W.M.' – possibly as a tribute to William Morris, though no one was quite sure – this tall, thin, sardonic man, a collector of first editions and patron of poets, a socialist who often wrote by allusion and in parable, or about roses, became a lion on the subject of appeasement. 'The dictators mean war,' he wrote. 'Be strong. Re-arm. Seek allies. Appeasement will not save us; it is leading to disaster.'¹⁰

When Chamberlain called on 'all concerned' to continue their efforts towards peace, Jennings replied, 'Does this include Hitler or Goebbels or the pale spy Ribbentrop, so recently the darling of the treacherous upper-crust riff-raff in this country? Mr. Chamberlain must be aware of the hardening of opinion here ... If it weakens among "those concerned" in the Government we had better stop handing out gas masks and hand round swastikas instead for use a few months hence.'¹¹

On Chamberlain's return from Munich, Jennings addressed himself to the millions who not only yearned for peace but believed it was still possible. With irony and subtlety, he wrote:

> Yesterday, all over the world, the mood was one of immense relief. Even in Berlin! There, English newspaper correspondents heard the cry, 'Thank God that the danger of war is averted!' ... Today we do not ask you to plunge back into gloom, but we ask you to agree that the mood ought to be one of confidence with caution. Therefore (again) the mood of resolute preparedness ...
>
> Do not relax your defence efforts. Redouble them. Bear in mind that we have gained this respite, not because we plaintively argued, reasoned, and explained how right we are, or even how we long for peace. We gained this reprieve because we stood firm.
>
> A great pity that it had to be sought that way – this peace which is our passionate desire and our real aim. But the world isn't a nice place, ruled by kind men and old ladies who wouldn't hurt a fly. Large parts of it are ruled by men who have proved they stop at nothing to gain their ends. At nothing but the certainty that if they strike, they will be struck.[12]

When war came, the *Mirror* described its leader writer as 'The Man Who Made All England Sit Up'. This was justified; but he was hardly 'the one voice', as the *Mirror* boasted. There was also Churchill, who had been hired by King and Cudlipp to write a fortnightly column which became a series of prophetic warnings, such as the one published the day after the Nazi-Soviet Pact was announced. Wake up, was its message: war was on the way, whatever the appeasers said.[13]

And there was William Connor, Cassandra, who, on the day that war was declared, wrote one of the most successful polemics of the period. This was a full page in the style of a 'Wanted!' poster. Hitler's mug shots, full face and profile, stared out from beneath charges of murder, kidnapping, theft and arson. He was alias 'Adolf Schicklgruber, Adolf Hittler or Hidler ... known to be suffering from acute monomania, with periodic fits of melancholia. Frequently bursts into tears when crossed. Harsh guttural voice, and a habit of raising right hand to shoulder level. DANGEROUS! . . . THIS RECKLESS CRIMINAL IS WANTED – DEAD OR ALIVE!'[14]

Connor had come to the *Mirror* via the advertising agency J. Walter Thompson, where he had devised a campaign to promote Harpic, the lavatory cleaner. Guests in your home, he wrote, 'would judge the hostess in the only room where she could not be present', and where 'the old-fashioned brush-work is out of date'. From Harpic to Hitler. The lavatory cleaner sold and sold, as did the *Mirror*.[15]

Hitler had long complained about the paper, as Lord Halifax, Chamberlain's Foreign Secretary, bemoaned. 'With this page by Cassandra', wrote Hugh Cudlipp in his history, *Publish and Be Damned*, 'the *Mirror* declared war on Nazi Germany. An order was issued by the German High Command that all *Mirror* directors were to be immediately arrested when London was occupied.'[16] On May 10, 1941 the *Daily Mirror* office was bombed: a direct hit. 'I wouldn't go so far as to say that this was Hitler's reply,' said Cudlipp, 'or his aim was that good, but nevertheless, it was the *Daily Mirror* that got the first bomb in Fleet Street.'

During the war the *Mirror* was the only paper to make enemies on both sides, the most formidable being its former columnist, Winston Churchill. Together, Jennings and Cassandra relentlessly attacked the retention of Chamberlain and other 'Municheers' in the Coalition Cabinet, now led by Churchill. 'The *Mirror* deflated the notion', wrote Cudlipp, 'that criticism in war is cloaked defeatism.' Churchill called Cecil King to Downing Street and protested bitterly; King replied that 'a popular newspaper had within limits to reflect popular opinion'.[17]

Jennings continued his assault, describing Churchill's first Cabinet reshuffle as 'the sifting and shunting of mediocrities', while Cassandra warmed to his campaign against 'the encrusted barnacles [at the War Office] in obsolete brass hats' and the petty disciplines they imposed on soldiers, as if Britain's fighting men were children. This made him instantly into a hero in the barracks.

When Cudlipp, then editor of the *Sunday Pictorial*, the *Mirror*'s companion paper, wrote a signed piece dismissing the new Cabinet as the same bunch of Tory Party-servers who had misled the nation under Chamberlain, his article was damned by Churchill as 'vicious and malignant' and the *Mirror* papers as part of a fifth-column movement. Farce was approaching.

The Cabinet authorised a search of the *Mirror*'s financial background: perhaps Goebbels or even Hitler was pulling the strings at the *Mirror*'s HQ in Fetter Lane. Censorship was threatened, and worse. Under the government's emergency powers, the communist *Daily Worker* had already been suppressed for suggesting the war should never have been fought. The *Mirror* papers were now under threat, wrote Cudlipp, 'for insisting that the war be fought efficiently'.

Jennings replied to Churchill with his usual esoteric logic: 'It is not "subversive" to criticise the weaknesses of a Government ... Again and again, it has been seen that criticism, at first resented by the Government, is later accepted and acted upon'.[18] The stand-off was now reaching its finale, not with words but a single cartoon. Drawn by Philip Zec, 'the people's artist', it showed a shipwrecked merchant sailor clinging to a raft in the dark U-boat-infested Atlantic. The caption read, 'The price of petrol has been raised by a penny (Official)'. An enraged Home Secretary, Herbert Morrison, told Parliament, 'The cartoon in question is a particularly evil example of the policy and methods of a newspaper with a reckless indifference to the national interest'; for had not the same issue carried an editorial that referred to certain generals as 'brass-buttoned boneheads, socially prejudiced, arrogant and fussy ...'?[19]

Morrison's, and Churchill's, interpretation of Zec's cartoon was that merchant seamen were endangering their lives while the oil companies profiteered. Zec maintained it meant nothing of the kind; that it was a call to preserve fuel because importing it cost lives. That hundreds of readers wrote to the *Mirror* for copies of what they saw as a vivid, patriotic symbol seemed to confirm this. The paper was formally warned; but the government never acted. Cassandra and Cudlipp went to the army soon afterwards, and, although remaining a watchdog for readers in and out of the Services, the paper concentrated on morale-raising.

This was achieved largely by Jane, the star of a cartoon strip about an apparently coy young woman who took her clothes off a great deal and wore the kind of frilly knickers that ordinary males, and females, could only dream about in wartime. Her popularity in bleak times was extraordinary. Cudlipp described her as 'the daily aphrodisiac', yet one survey disclosed that the strip was read mostly by women.

What was certain was that Jane became a cult among the troops. She decorated barrack walls, tanks and the fuselages of aircraft. Was she, I asked Cudlipp, the forerunner of the Page Three Girl? 'A vital difference', he said, 'was that Jane was two and a half inches high, therefore in utter nakedness, her breasts would appear to be a small stop in a very small type. She could adorn a postcard any son would send to his mother for her birthday. She was also fun – an ingredient lacking from the tabloids today. The American Services thought she was wonderful because there was nothing like that in the States; and the legend grew that if she took her clothes off again, there was going to be another push forward against the Germans. One British general said that Jane was worth two divisions. Wonderful nonsense like that.'

When the war was over, Cudlipp killed off the strip. 'It became old-fashioned,' he said. 'With the royal family walking round in split skirts, there's not much fun having Jane do the same. Somebody had to have the nerve to say, "It's been nice, Jane, but goodbye." '

George Greenwell's famous *Mirror* photograph of St Paul's, still standing amid the fire and smoke of the Blitz, became as much an image of England, defiant, as Churchill's V-sign. It was not as simple as that, of course, just as the evacuation from Dunkirk was not entirely 'bloody marvellous', as the *Mirror* had proclaimed it. But the *Daily Mirror*'s own survival during the war, the fact that it did not lose a single issue written and printed at the height of the Blitz, often with fires raging around it, and that it understood and expressed clearly the importance of democratic dissent even during a national emergency, was as powerful a wartime symbol as any.

As Cecil King's correspondence with Churchill in the first year of the war reveals, the *Mirror*'s attacks on the government had not come from a tabloid's scatter-gun. The *Mirror* now saw itself as a keeper of working-class memories of the horror of unemployment and class war in the 1930s. On the eve of war, and in the phoney first months of war, its writers had not only called for the sacking of discredited Tory ministers and the democratisation of the Services as essential to victory, but also for a post-war plan for the reconstruction of a 'New Britain'. For ignoring the latter, Churchill was to pay a political price he never expected.

On May 11, 1945, ten days after the death of Hitler in the Berlin Chancellery, the *Mirror* included on its front-page masthead the words, 'Forward with the people'. 'There are shining victories to be won in the cause of peace and social justice,' said the paper. 'We shall reach the new freedom not by submitting to economic slavery ... We stand for equal opportunities for all children, good homes and robust health for everyone, a high standard of living for all. And we challenge every vested interest that obstructs the realisation of that idea.'[20]

Since its inception in 1903, the *Mirror* had supported the Liberals, led Lord Rothermere's assaults on the Labour Party and backed the Tory 'National' Government in 1935. In the decade since the last general election, the *Mirror* had changed out of all recognition. Britain now had a mass-circulation newspaper challenging received wisdom. In parliamentary terms, the *Mirror* was the first popular paper speaking for socialists, as Labourites then were proud to call themselves, although the new force it represented was not socialism, but social democracy. Certainly, the 'Old Gang', as the *Mirror* characterised the pre-war Tories, now had a formidable adversary as the 1945 election approached.

The *Mirror* then had a daily circulation of 2,400,000; the

Daily Express sold almost a million more. The *Express* was, as ever, histrionically right wing and its proprietor, Lord Beaverbrook, was Churchill's closest friend and ally. Churchill's popularity as a war leader was at its peak, but he was also the leader of the Tory Party. The *Mirror*'s postbag had long given notice that people were prepared to be brutally schizoid about their hero and vote him out; yet the *Mirror*'s electioneering was uncharacteristically obscure, 'skilfully subliminal', as Cudlipp described it.[21] Addressing itself primarily to women, to the wives, mothers and sisters of servicemen still abroad, many of them fighting the Japanese, the *Mirror* asked them to imagine how their men would want them to vote on their behalf.

'Why', I asked Cudlipp, 'didn't the *Mirror* simply say, "Vote Labour"?'

'Because half the directors would have dropped dead.'

'But the readers knew what you meant.'

'They knew exactly what we meant . . .'

On the eve of the poll, the *Mirror* told its readers, 'For five long years the lusty youth of this great land has bled and died. From Berlin to Burma, through desert and jungle, on the seas and in the air, they have fought and are fighting still for *you*. Vote for *them*.'

On election day, the front page was given over mostly to Philip Zec's celebrated VE Day cartoon of a wounded soldier handing over a laurel representing victory and peace in Europe. The caption read, 'Here you are – don't lose it again!' The spirit of this was echoed in the following: 'As you, the electors, go to the poll, there will be a gap in your ranks. The men who fought and died that their homeland and yours might live will not be there. You must vote for *them* . . . Vote on behalf of the men who won the victory for you. You failed to do this in 1918. The result is known to all. The land "fit for heroes" did not come into existence. The dole did. Short-lived prosperity gave way to long, tragic years of poverty and unemployment. Make sure that history does not repeat itself. Let no one turn your gaze to the past. The call of the men who have gone comes to you. Pay heed to it. Vote for *them*.'[22]

And they did. Labour won by a landslide; and even political opponents granted the *Mirror* an important role in the victory. A Tory Cabinet minister said the *Mirror*'s campaign had given Labour an extra 100 seats. *The Economist* credited the *Mirror* with having reached 'an unconverted public'.[23] Could a newspaper have exercised this influence? Had the *Mirror* at least countermanded the vicious anti-Labour campaign led by the *Daily Express*, Britain's biggest selling paper? ('This is terrible,' a famously anonymous woman in the Savoy is supposed to have said. '*They've* elected a Labour Government and *the country* will never stand for that!')[24]

However, Cudlipp believes that newspapers do not win elections and points to Franklin D. Roosevelt's first presidential victory when every major paper in the United States opposed him. The *Mirror*, he wrote, merely spoke the minds of its readers, allowing himself that 'Churchill was wrong and the *Mirror* was right'.[25]

Although Lord Rothermere had sold his *Mirror* shares in 1936, it was not until 1947 that the *Mirror* and the *Daily Mail* were financially separated. As the paper entered the 1950s, no shareholding was larger than 4 per cent. 'The *Daily Mirror*', wrote A. J. P. Taylor in his *English History, 1914–45*, 'was popular in a special sense. Previous popular newspapers, the *Daily Mail* and the *Daily Express*, were created by their proprietors, Northcliffe and Beaverbrook – men not at all ordinary. The *Mirror* had no proprietor. It was created by its staff . . . it gave an indication as never before of what ordinary people were thinking. The English people at last found their voice . . .'

By 1951, the *Mirror* was selling well over 4 million copies and was about to pass the *Express* as the world's biggest-selling newspaper. This did not help Labour in the election that year; and the *Mirror*'s campaign this time was anything but oblique. The front page on polling day carried a drawing of a huge revolver beneath the headline, 'WHOSE FINGER?' This was a repeat of a front page eight months earlier when the paper had asked, 'WHOSE FINGER DO YOU WANT ON THE

TRIGGER WHEN THE WORLD SITUATION IS SO DELICATE?' The implication was that Churchill, if not a warmonger, was trigger-happy and loath to pursue peace. By contrast, 'Labour's level-headed and independent judgement has probably saved us from world war over Korea'.[26]

Having won the election (with fewer votes than Labour), Churchill sued. The case never came to court and the *Mirror* eventually apologised and paid £1,250 to a charity. Two years later the *Mirror* returned to the scrap when it suggested it was time the old warhorse retired. And when the paper proposed that the young Prince Charles 'spend more time with ordinary children', Churchill was apoplectic, wrote his biographer, Lord Moran, and hurled the *Mirror* across the room in disgust. 'I wish we could buy that rag,' he said. 'It is doing so much harm.'[27]

During the 1950s with 'Forward with the People, Greatest Sale on Earth' on its masthead, the *Mirror*'s confidence continued to grow. In 1956 it was the only popular paper to reject the jingoism whipped up over Suez and to oppose Prime Minister Anthony Eden's invasion of Egypt. ('Today, the *Mirror* earnestly warns Sir Anthony Eden to rid his mind of the dangerous delusions from which he is suffering . . .') This cost some 90,000 readers.[28]

Three years later, inexplicably, 'Forward with the People' was dropped. Jane had already gone, but Andy Capp, whose melancholy life seemed mired in the 1930s, was retained, and went on to become the most syndicated cartoon strip on earth. Among its usual fare of mischief and the respectably raunchy, the *Mirror*'s idiosyncratic use of fine writing increased.

One of its sharpest and wittiest writers, Donald Zec, brother of the cartoonist Philip, specialised in what is now called the entertainment industry with a panache and honesty that shame his successors. Zec's puncturing wit and irony owed nothing to PR men; he never paid for a story. 'There was a *respect* for the newspaper I represented,' he told me. In this case, there was also affection for the writer; one of my favourite *Mirror* pictures is of Zec and Marilyn Monroe, arm in arm, laughing boisterously. Zec was close friends with the stars (Richard Burton, Sophia Loren, among many), while maintaining his reputation as an uncompromising critic.

When the director Carl Foreman objected to something Zec had written about one of his films, he phoned Hugh Cudlipp to complain. 'I know, Carl . . .' said Cudlipp in mock elegiac tones. 'There's nothing I can do about him.' When Diana Dors's marriage broke up in a burst of ballyhoo, Zec wrote, 'The tear-stained gap between Diana Dors and her husband Dennis ("The Menace") Hamilton gets smaller and smaller. They spent yesterday, the second day of their much-proclaimed parting, just like the first, together . . . so Mr. Hamilton was asked, "Does this mean a happy ending?" He shrugged and replied, "Who knows?" They ought to decide pretty fast before their ever-lovin' public begins to ask, "*Who cares?*"'

In 1954, the *Mirror* published the first Marje Proops column. It began, 'Funny the way, when a marriage breaks up, it's so often the little things that bring it to an end . . .' In this case, a man had allowed his macaroni cheese to go cold while he talked on the phone. For his wife, wrote Proops, 'it was the last soggy straw . . .'

Proops told me she disliked her first columns intensely. She had been a fashion artist, whose writing experience had been limited to captions. 'I wrote awful stuff,' she said, 'silly and trivial, but it gradually got better as I matured and felt I could broach personal subjects that newspapers never touched. I decided to pick off the taboos, one by one. One morning Hugh [Cudlipp] rang me up and said, "Congratulations, you've made history today. You're the first journalist to use the word masturbation in a national newspaper." I wasn't sure that this was worthy of congratulations, but he thought it was.

'In those days most of my letters were about matrimonial problems, because marriage was quite fashionable then. Women would write me sad letters saying, "I submit to my husband three times a week," or three times a month, or three times a year if they were lucky. They regarded themselves as fortunate if it wasn't too often. Now if I get a letter about submission I know immediately it's someone having fun with S and M!

'The most harrowing letters were from women who'd survived the horrors of a back-street abortion, and my column began to grow more serious as I was influenced by the women's movement; I teamed up with MPs like David Steel and Leo Abse and I championed reform of laws affecting abortion, divorce, homosexuals. Like Dr Spock in America, I took some of the blame here for the so-called permissive society, which of course is the civilised society.'

Marje Proops's reputation as the voice of whimsical common sense often belied her support for political direct action. In 1969 she wrote one of her most influential pieces, about equal pay, which began with the words of a motion moved by Clementia Black at the Trades Union Council of 1888: 'That in the opinion of this congress it is desirable, in the interests both of men and women, that in trades where women do the same work as men, they shall receive the same payments'. The article occupied a full page and was headlined, 'WOMEN ARE TIRED OF THE SOUND OF DRAGGING FEET'.

What was clever about this piece was that it was aimed simultaneously at employers, politicians, males with traditional attitudes and women who had reservations about militancy. One by one, she reasoned away the shibboleths: 'A woman, doing an interesting job for the same interesting salary earned by an interested man, is just as interested [in the job] . . . It is monstrous that the present-day equivalent of the employer of 100 years ago should still have the power to make the decision as to whether or not women have *responsibilities* [outside the job]'. Her message was that feminists and the majority of women had everything in common and that militancy was almost certainly the only course. 'If peace-loving women join in the battle with their vociferous sisters', she wrote, 'they could bring industry to a standstill.'[29]

In the 1960s, when there was a tendentious press 'debate' about whether or not those with 'vocations' should strike,

Proops helped to educate public opinion. 'The nurses are fast getting militant,' she wrote. 'I daresay a good many people will be deeply shocked at the idea of nurses on the march [but] unless the nurses make their voices heard, they'll just go on being put upon, no matter their long hours and grim conditions. So long as the rest of us can say, "Oh well, they're dedicated to their vocation," we needn't, we reckon, feel guilty. But guilty is just what we should feel. And the only way to assuage guilt is to do something practical to get rid of it, like making sure we support the nurses. I know you're going to say, "They're not all saints, they can be darned tough." True enough. They can be and it's a wonder to me they're not tougher. They are going to be from now on. They're contemplating forming a [breakaway] Nurses' Trade Union.'[30]

Proops's postbag was probably as reliable a social weather vane of Britain as any issue of *Social Trends*. In the 1990s, as the trivialisation of the British press accelerated, her post reflected very different concerns among *Mirror* readers. 'My postbag has changed out of all recognition,' she said. 'Today it's filled with letters about basic gut economics. They're mainly from people getting into debt: people worried about money, anxious about their jobs, about whether or not to take redundancy, and how their kids will cope in the future. If I get a letter about a relationship it's very likely related in some way to the shocking economic state of this country. The readers are right, as usual.'

My most vivid memory of Marje Proops was in 1974 when I happened to be in the deputy editor's office, protesting along with others about the *Mirror*'s first topless pin-up, which was a desperate attempt to match the soft-porn Page Three of Rupert Murdoch's *Sun*. Proops arrived, cigarette holder clenched between her famous gappy teeth, and the room fell silent for her. 'I'll be brief,' she said. 'What we published today was a disgrace, a *bloody* disgrace. Either the nipples go, or I go!'

The gallery was silenced. Proops usually reserved her sharpness for the private manoeuvre of seeing off a potential rival on the paper, a symptom of what some called her 'ambition', but which sprang from a little-known side to the nation's leading agony aunt: her nagging insecurity. She seldom criticised the paper to those who ran it and controlled it. She regarded her compliance as loyalty to the paper she loved. But nipples in the *Daily Mirror* went beyond that and demanded the direct action she so often advised. Coming from one whose name was synonymous with the paper, it had the desired effect. Opposing the invasion of Suez was one thing, letting Marje Proops go was quite unthinkable. Coyness returned, albeit temporarily.

'They'd sneak them back in,' she said, 'usually, it was when someone who was standing in as editor had this idiotic belief that the *Sun* was our standard. I was quite nervous when I made the threat. I couldn't imagine leaving the *Mirror*, but at least I would have let them work bloody hard at persuading me not to go!'

Proops told me this in September 1996, forty-two years after she had joined the paper and a fortnight before she died suddenly, on a day we had arranged to meet for lunch. When I last saw her, she was an elegant eighty-odd-year-old, funny and feisty and ever loyal to a *Mirror* which had long abandoned the standards for which she had made her stand. On her office wall was a collection of self-portraits that used to illustrate her column, together with a photograph of her friend Germaine Greer and a framed *Mirror* front page: '40 Glorious Years'. She was the longest-serving, and the last, *Mirror* name.

After six months on TV programmes, gardening, fishing and the Pets' Club, I was told I could write features if I agreed to go 'north of Watford', a land many of my colleagues seemed reluctant to visit. My rusting, Italian-registered Fiat was given a petrol allowance, which meant that it might go on for ever; and for almost two years the two of us discovered an England I had never imagined.

From Lancashire to Tyneside, to the Border, across the Pennines, to the Mersey, here was another nation with a different history, different loyalties, different humour, even different values. In a series of 'on the road' pieces published at first in the northern editions, I wrote about communities, and their industrial and social history, on the edge of change that was invested with considerable hope and expectation.

I would find a street, virtually any street, and knock on doors; what intrigued me and intrigues me still was that such human warmth, tolerance and forbearance could survive the treadmill of English industrial cities and the hypnotic routine of working lives. In the autumn and winter months, smoke would seize the mist and congeal into night, which would 'settle' like fine silt, on lace curtains and in the lungs of those who as silhouettes passed along the ribbon of black barracks to and from a steelworks or a brickworks or a pit.

I formed many friendships, especially on the coalfields of the north-east. My first encounter with Durham miners was as a boy growing up in New South Wales where both my grandfathers and my father worked in the deep-shaft coal-mines. There was a 'Durham pit' (and a 'Welsh pit' and a 'Scottish pit'). The miners there had emigrated *en masse* from several villages and spoke a dialect that owed as much to Norway and Ireland as England; it was in Australia that I had first heard the word 'marra' (friend) and 'craic', meaning comradely chat. On the other side of the world they preserved and expressed a sense of community that was the strength of working-class England, and which was, within a few years, to be declared politically expendable.

Murton was the archetypal pit village. With its Democratic Club, Colliery Inn, ribbons of allotments producing champion leeks and pigeons, there were relatively few 'travellers', as pit men from closed mines were called. Everybody knew everybody and looked out for each other. Long before governments thought seriously about providing 'welfare', the miners of Murton were looking after their most vulnerable, building homes for the old, providing for pensions and convalescence for the ill and injured, and recreation for their families. All this was paid for by a levy at the pit. There has always been an ambiguity among miners about the nature of their job, but there was none about their loyalty and pride. This is not a romantic notion; in the cemeteries the inscriptions speak about 'respect' for those who died, men who 'rest appreciated by all [their] friends'.

Standing at the heart of the town, the mine was both provider and enemy, a Hell's Kitchen into which men went like troops. In my first report from Murton, I spent a night shift in the pit, led by the miners down a difficult seam called F32, a third of a mile beneath the town and extending under the sea. Here contorted bodies 'titillated' the roof to test for a fall and moved the hydraulic chocks, as heavy as cannons, which propped up the roof. They were like troops bringing up artillery under fire. With the clipped commands of the deputy, the filthy wet trench and the spirit of comradeship, of watching out for each other, the coalface was a kind of front line. And up at the pithead you found the wounded: men without fingers, and men with scars the length of their backs, and men who lifted their ribcage, as others might hitch up their trousers, in order to clear their lungs of 'the muck'.

The first piece I wrote from Murton was headlined simply, 'THE MINERS'. Designed by Mike Molloy, the three pages allotted were models of newspaper understatement, allowing the full power to the people speaking about the pit and their community. At another time I wrote about three generations of the Herd family of Baildon, Yorkshire: the pitman who had survived terrible conditions, his son the trade unionist and his grandson, the pub owner, a jovial type suspected of voting Tory. The trade unionist, Les Herd, is still a friend. The *Mirror* devoted eight pages, over three issues, to the epic story of their working lives.

This, for me, was the paper's strength, its true distinction, which made me feel I had found a journalistic home. Unlike the stereotypes and the pompous establishment respectability that were the stock-in-trade of most of Fleet Street, the *Mirror* gave expression to the views and hopes of ordinary people which were authentic, powerful and dignified. Jack Walker, who worked in the filth in a dyeworks in Keighley, Yorkshire, described eloquently how he survived the tedium of factory routine. 'I think about my garden in summer, the big leeks and marrows, and the cricket, the strategies of the game,' he said, 'and I think about the joy, and it is a joy, of going home.'

The expectation of a better life was now urgent in Britain. Thirteen years of Tory rule were coming to an end; the new Labour Government of Harold Wilson would complete the project begun in the immediate post-war years. The *Mirror*'s front page on the eve of the election in 1964 expressed the popular mood. 'IS THIS THE PROMISED LAND?' it asked, above a picture of a woman hanging out her washing in her squalid back yard, six feet by nine feet.[31]

However, instead of change, the Wilson Government invested people's optimism in something called the 'consensus'. Brian Walden, then a Labour MP who was to make a smooth transition to Thatcherite broadcaster, later explained what 'consensus' really meant. 'The two front benches [in Parliament] liked each other and disliked their back benches,' he wrote. 'We were children of the famous consensus ... we were spoiled, of course, because the electorate was even more irresponsible than we were, could be relied upon to grow bored or disenchanted and turn the opposition into the government. It made little difference, for we believed much the same things.'[32]

For working people, the 'consensus' did not represent the same cosiness. At best, it meant that, in exchange for their acceptance of low wages and the acquiescence of their trade union leaders, they were granted affordable, if sub-standard, housing, clothing and food, as well as basic services such as nationalised health care and the hope of a 'new start' for at least one child. One of the profound effects of the Second World War was that the compliance, the 'flat cappery', of working people was no longer assured, and so the generation of 'hope for the future', however illusory, was the most important element of the 'consensus' arrangement.

The *Daily Mirror* in the early 1960s was an important bearer of this optimism and a mouthpiece for the Wilson Government's hidden agenda. The paper backed Wilson's plans to 'modernise' Britain in the 'white heat of the technological revolution'. 'In all our plans for the future, we are re-defining and we are re-stating our Socialism in terms of the scientific revolution ... The Britain that is going to be forged in the white heat of this revolution will be no place for restrictive practices or for outdated methods on either side of industry ...'[33]

These words, 'the white heat of the technological revolution', which became a rallying cry to embrace 'the hi-tech future', were coined by Hugh Cudlipp. He denied this at the time, even writing to *The Times*, probably because he did not want the *Mirror* and the Labour Government to be seen as one. 'I hadn't the slightest idea,' he later wrote, 'and still haven't, what the seven words actually meant.' [34]

Wilson's attack on 'restrictive practices' was one-sided, it quickly became clear, and the precursor of the Tories' anti-trade union laws, just as the 'revolution' his government and the *Mirror* promoted led to the scrapping of millions of working lives once its Robespierre came to power in the person of Margaret Thatcher. It is something of a tragedy that the *Mirror* did not foresee this. By tying itself to the conservative, Gaitskellite wing of the Labour Party, the *Mirror* often depleted its greatest power, its genuine, often unpredictable popular radicalism, which had been demonstrated so effectively before and immediately after the war.

In the early 1960s, the Great and the Good were frequent visitors to the *Mirror* building in Holborn Circus, the lunch and dinner guests of Cecil King in his ninth-floor suite. Labour ministers and trade union 'barons' one day, high Tories and the 'captains of industry' the next – all were meant to keep the chairman and his deputy, Hugh Cudlipp, 'in the know': a vital necessity, King had declared, after the Baldwin Government had denied the *Mirror* inside knowledge of the Abdication.

That the *Mirror* had scooped Fleet Street on the Abdication was not seen, strangely, as the advantageous result of being left outside the charmed circle. Indeed, being 'in the know' could mean the opposite. The *Mirror* never described

Wilson's 'modernising' society for what it was: the buttressing of the country's social and economic divisions. Behind a façade of new-found egalitarianism, such as the lionising of working-class pop stars, fashion designers and actors, 'modernising' society meant bringing poverty up to date, as in moving people from old slums to modern wastelands. The message was that these were swinging times and progress was progress.

'People's faces', announced a page in the *Mirror*, 'wear none of the despair that the North's myths say they should. [In Sheffield] street decks connect the ground with the fourteenth floor so that people can meet and chat, and the milkman can drive straight up to your door and no child need sit forlorn in his boxed isolation, but instead play all around and up and down . . .'[35]

Alas, I wrote that.

In keeping with the new optimism, the *Mirror* launched 'Boom Cities 1967', which was meant to coincide with one of Wilson's periodic lectures to 'the industrial partnership of boardroom and unions'. A 'Boom Cities *Mirror*' was produced in the regional centres of England, and on the eve of publication a spectacular banquet was held in the poshest hotels, attended by at least one Cabinet member, various 'captains of industry', local politicians and assorted 'dignitaries'. In Liverpool it was held on a ship fully dressed for the occasion, complete with Harold Wilson as guest of honour and a large sculpture of a Liver bird. In Newcastle, guests were startled to find a 'tableau' of real steel-plate riveters in their midst. In Birmingham, a motorcycle burst through a screen, knocking over a tray of prawn cocktails.

All represented grand illusions. In Liverpool the docks were falling silent. In Newcastle, shipyard orders were being lost to the Japanese. In Birmingham, the motorcycle industry was in its death throes. The suspicion that it was all a terrible mistake hung over the festivities; black jokes about 'Doom Cities' crept into speeches.

However, once the applause of its bemused guests had died away, the *Mirror* typically allowed its writers to prick the bubble it had blown. I produced a series about the struggle of the workforce at the Norton Villiers motorcycle factory to keep the bankrupt firm going as a co-operative. Others highlighted the rapidly rising unemployment, and the misery of people trapped in the new high-rises.

By the end of the 1960s, the *Mirror* had recovered what Hugh Cudlipp later called its 'understanding of the reality of the times it existed in'. Quite apart from some mild editorial criticisms of the Wilson and Callaghan Governments (almost always from the right), the paper itself began to change dramatically, arguably as no British popular newspaper had tried to or wanted to or dared to. Under Cudlipp, Harry Guy Bartholomew's brash and crusading paper retained its brashness, but now began to spread a map of the world before its readers, estimated in 1967 at a quarter of the population.[36]

'The first thing that happened', said Cudlipp, 'was that Cecil King set out to educate me about the world, so he claimed. He was the Wykehamist and I was the uncivilised Welshman. He sent me almost everywhere: to Japan, India, the Soviet Union, including Siberia, eastern Europe, the United States. Cecil would say, "We shall know what is going on in the world, and so will our readers." We had no blacklist of people we didn't mention or places we wouldn't go to. King was a completely honest man. He could be challenged, and successfully challenged, and expected to be. And because of that, the paper attracted writers who knew they would not be told they couldn't say this or that. The *Mirror* set out to cover *all* the world; it was one of the greatest adventures in journalism.'

Thus, Cudlipp, who was effectively editor-in-chief, invented Britain's first popular quality newspaper. During the political upheavals of the late 1960s – Paris, Prague, Chicago, Saigon – the coverage and presentation by the *Mirror* were frequently more incisive and better written than the quality broadsheets. Reporters were encouraged to abandon stereotypes and clichés, along with what Dr Johnson called 'the tyranny of the stock response'.

Not only was the *Mirror* the newspaper of most working

people but its readership soon included more so-called 'A' readers than the entire readership of *The Times*. According to a survey by the National Union of Students, the *Mirror* in 1968 was the most widely read national newspaper in the universities. This breadth of readership – the fact that the *Mirror* was read by more people of every social class than any other newspaper – represented an achievement unprecedented in the history of the British press.

One of the myths about the quality *Mirror* was that it produced worthy sermons few wanted to read. In fact, its skill was to integrate stories offering a window on the world with the humour, mischief and common sense of fine writers like Cassandra, Keith Waterhouse and Donald Zec. 'Shock Issues' continued to dissect issues that the other papers had barely begun to contemplate, such as the environment, child abuse and the financial starvation of state education. 'Divided Britain', a Shock Issue from April 1973 about class, its privileges, subtleties and economics, could be published today, with minimal change.[37]

Much of this enterprise fell to two young Cudlipp-bred executives, Tony Miles and Mike Molloy, both of whom rose to be editor. Miles, an exceptionally skilled journalist, started 'Mirrorscope', a twice-weekly, four-page feature of background news, profiles and analysis. Molloy, a talented artist, produced on his layout sheets *Mirror*s that remain exemplars of tabloid newspaper design and the antithesis of today's mutations. He gives the credit to Hugh Cudlipp.

'I first met Cudlipp', he told me, 'when I was called up to his office to do a Shock Issue for him. I didn't do it; he did it. I was his runner. He was a terrific teacher and quite dazzling to watch. Here was the very stuff of legends, and I was barely twenty-one years old. He gave me a cigar, a huge Havana; I didn't even know how to clench it in my teeth, let alone smoke it. He went through everything, explaining the layout, why he was doing it, why he was writing the headline in a particular way, why he was cutting a picture in a particular way, what the emphasis would be and the pace of it. It was like watching a master craftsman.'

These were exhilarating days for me. When I returned from the north of England, I was told that Cassandra had recommended me to Cudlipp. I was called to his office.

'How old are you?' said Cudlipp.

'Twenty-four.'

'Good. I want you to write a series called *Youth in Action* that will show how young people can put their ideals and hopes into practice and, if possible, change the world. That sort of thing. They can be anywhere in the world . . .'

'Anywhere . . .?'

'Anywhere. We'll run it for a year. Give me a list of ten ideas in the morning.'

In the *Mirror* library I discovered an organisation called Voluntary Service Overseas, which sent volunteers throughout the world and on which President Kennedy had based the American Peace Corps. That night, aided by the *Daily Telegraph* map of the world, I charted a journey that would take me across every continent, from Rio de Janeiro to Lake Titicaca in the Andes, from the islands of Polynesia to Papua, Laos, India, the Levant, Africa, and included almost everywhere on earth I had wanted to go before my father's bookie's loan had run out.

I regarded the memorandum I sent the next day as an exercise in the audacious, if not the implausible. It came back with 'Yes!' scrawled on it. During the journeys I made over the next year, I was able, in a series of dispatches (on average about 1,500 words in length), to describe something of the nature of the political and economic divisions across the world, as seen through the eyes of intelligent young Britons who, in a variety of ways, wanted to change it for the better. That greatly sharpened my own political senses.

Thereafter I was sent to South Africa. Peter Wilson, the *Mirror*'s greatest sports writer (an old Harrovian who was billed as 'The Man They Can't Gag'), had waged a personal campaign against apartheid, and more than anyone had forced the MCC to boycott South Africa. 'This colour bar just doesn't make sense,' he wrote in 1963. 'You cannot shoot or wrench away ideas of freedom.' Contrary to the timidity on race elsewhere in Fleet Street, or downright racism, Wilson's sustained and principled stand received overwhelming support from *Mirror* readers. Moreover, many of its editorials on apartheid were written or inspired by Basil Davidson, the acclaimed author of many books on Africa's post-imperial struggle for freedom.

The *Mirror*'s reputation meant that my arrival in Johannesburg did not go unnoticed. My illegal journey on a 'non-whites only' train to Soweto brought a polite warning. It was when I bribed my way into one of the secret hearings of the Race Classification Board in Cape Town and reported what I saw that trouble beckoned.

A theatre of the absurd was performed in Room 33 every Thursday. Here was apartheid's horrific quackery on display, its moral and intellectual mutation made to appear normal, with forms and regulations and decision-making based on 'criteria'. Suited officials, models of respectability, took evidence, scribbling, nodding sagely and now and then leaning down from their magistrates' bench in order to touch a human head of hair and peer at the whites of human eyes. After due consideration, 'racially borderline' people were classified or reclassified 'according to appearance and acceptance', which meant a ticket to a lifetime of either privilege or humiliation. Black-skinned people need not apply. I was banned from returning to South Africa.

Subsequently, I became the *Mirror*'s special correspondent, and during the next twenty years I reported from all over the world: the Middle East, the revolution in Cuba, the rise of Japan as a manufacturing power. In December 1971, the future Prime Minister of Bangladesh, Moudud Ahmed, held aloft the *Daily Mirror* before a crowd of new citizens of the world's newest state. The front page carried the banner headline, 'BIRTH OF A NATION'. I made numerous trips to the Soviet Union, recording dissident voices; and for that I was banned. I reported the birth of the 'Charter 77' democracy movement in Czechoslovakia, and the *Mirror* and its correspondent were honoured with a sustained denunciation on Prague Radio. These acknowledgements were proudly received.

In 1968, I went to live and travel in the United States, to write about an America beyond Hollywood, especially the political awakening of black and poor people in a civil rights movement that became a second civil war. None of these momentous times was presented in the *Mirror* as a sensational morsel; advertisements were moved or jettisoned to allow the words to run.

In September 1966 Cudlipp handed me a copy of that morning's *Guardian*. 'Have you read the Martha Gellhorn piece?' he asked. I had. One of the greatest war correspondents, she had written a series from Vietnam for the *St Louis Post-Dispatch*, which had refused to print her final piece. This had raised the forbidden question about American motives in Vietnam. The *Guardian* published the banned article, in which she described a refugee camp, a 'dump heap' she called it, where she found some of the million people made homeless since the American land invasion. Cudlipp had ringed the following passage:

> These peasants had survived the Vietcong since 1957, on whatever terms hostile or friendly, and the war however it came to them. But they cannot survive our bombs. Even the Catholic refugees did not leave their hamlets until the bombs fell. We are uprooting the people from the lovely land where they have lived for generations; and the uprooted are given not bread but stone. Is this an honourable way for a great nation to fight a war 8,000 miles from its safe homeland?[38]

The *Mirror* became the only British newspaper to oppose outright the American war. My first dispatches were carried over three issues of the *Sunday Mirror*. The front-page headline read, 'HOW CAN BRITAIN SUPPORT A WAR LIKE THIS?' (Harold Wilson was then ingratiating himself with Lyndon Johnson.) During the next eight years, up to the last day of the war on April 30, 1975, I was sent on frequent assignments to Vietnam, often when the rest of the popular media had grown bored with a war in which Americans had ceased to die and American bombers were killing more Vietnamese than ever before.

I was censored once. On my return from the Biafran War in Nigeria, I wrote that the Wilson Government, as the principal supplier of arms to the military government in Lagos, bore much of the responsibility for the dead and dying Biafran children whose suffering the *Mirror* had so graphically displayed. Britain, I pointed out, was a major customer for Nigeria's oil. Lee Howard, the Buddha-shaped editor, a benign man who called people 'Duckie', summoned me.

The page-proof of my piece was on his desk. He offered me a Scotch and suggested I was being 'rather harsh' on the government 'at a difficult time'. He was sure I would agree to hold over the piece until I had more time to think about it. Still in my twenties, I was in considerable awe of the editor of the *Daily Mirror*. Assisted by the Scotch, I said I would prefer to choose another form of words there and then so that the piece could run that night.

He no longer looked benign. 'You have fifteen minutes,' he said, handing me the proof. Outside, I rearranged my criticism of the government to include a sprinkling of the vacuous words of sympathy which government ministers had offered the Biafrans. I returned and watched the editor brood over it. No Scotch was offered.

'Shall we dispense with the reference to *oil*, Duckie?' he asked, though more as a statement of invincible authority. I remained silent, watching his fountain pen career across my words.

'There we are, Duckie . . .' He had taken out virtually all mention of the government's complicity. 'I'll tell the sub-editors we're all agreed . . .'

Oil probably came under the heading of 'national interest' and the *Mirror* was being protective towards the government on this issue. But the unusual sensitivity almost certainly was linked to events of the previous year when Cecil King had succumbed to a disease common among those who own, or come to think they own, newspapers. This was megalomania.

King had decided that Harold Wilson, the elected leader of the country, 'had to go'. For his part, Wilson had tried his best to win over King after the *Mirror* had helped him to victory in 1964. He had offered him a life peerage and a job at the Board of Trade 'with responsibility for the export drive'. He had made him a director of the Bank of England, vice-chairman of the National Parks Commission and a director of the National Coal Board. King turned away these overtures, believing that his abilities for high public service, if not recognition, were being passed over.

King became more and more convinced that the Wilson Government was leading the nation to economic disaster. This was criticism not from the point of view of many *Mirror* readers, whose hopes had been so comprehensively dashed by the Labour Government, but from the maverick right. King was an intensely complex man. He had been the driving force behind the *Mirror*'s move to the left. His instinctive 'support for the underdog' was sincere. He had backed every *Mirror* campaign to expose the social disparities wrought by the class into which he had been born and of which he was such an outstanding beneficiary.

Now King was talking about a 'disintegrating government', and the prospect of troops in the streets to put down rioters. He wanted a 'national government of businessmen', including himself. Tony Benn, then Minister of Technology, wrote in his diaries after a lunch at the *Mirror* that he found the chairman 'slightly unbalanced'.[39]

King took his plans forward and had two meetings with Lord Mountbatten, the Queen's uncle. He proposed 'something like the emergency committee that he [Mountbatten] ran in India during the war'.[40] At a second meeting with Mountbatten also present was Sir Solly Zuckerman, Scientific Adviser to the Cabinet. The budding *coup d'état* now dissolved into farce, with Zuckerman storming out, exclaiming 'This is rank treachery,' and Mountbatten following him.[41]

Two days later, on May 10, 1968, the *Mirror*'s front page was dominated by 'ENOUGH IS ENOUGH BY CECIL H. KING, CHAIRMAN . . .' Next to a photograph of King, his words got quickly to the point: 'Mr Wilson and his government have lost all credibility and all authority ... We are now threatened with the greatest financial crisis in our history. It is not to be removed by lies about our reserves, but only by a fresh start under a fresh leader.'

I asked Cudlipp about this. After all, King had been his mentor and the two men had worked closely together for thirty years. He said, 'Meeting all those politicians and telling them what to do and what not to do, King came to believe he had a higher duty than serving his readers. He believed, to use his words, that the economic crisis of the day would lead to blood in the streets and that a government of businessmen should be imposed on the country. He wasn't a plotter. He couldn't have marshalled a troop of cubs. By a vote of the board, he was sacked. It was the saddest episode of my career.'

I met King only once. He seemed a most unlikely dictator of Britain. After we had been introduced, he said nothing at all while I muttered pleasantries at his six and a half feet. This was typical, I was assured, of his acute shyness. When he died, I remembered him with some affection. It was he who had urged Cudlipp to give my first pieces from Vietnam such prominence; he later sent me an entire collection of first editions of the Crimean War diaries of *The Times* correspondent William Howard Russell. Enclosed, in a spidery hand, was a note: 'Dear Pilger, These are precious to me. Thank you for your work. I think the great Russell could have fitted comfortably into the *Mirror*, don't you?'

Breaking the Mirror

Those who aim to give the public what the public wants begin by under-estimating the public taste [and] end by debauching it.

T. S. Eliot

On Monday November 17, 1969, Hugh Cudlipp held a dinner at his favourite restaurant, the Ivy, in the West End of London. Among those present were his close friend Sydney Jacobson, the *Mirror*'s former political editor, Lee Howard, the *Mirror*'s editor, Tony Miles, the assistant editor, Marje Proops, Peter Wilson, Donald Zec and myself. It was the launch day of Rupert Murdoch's *Sun*. Lee Howard, who disliked such occasions, spoke dutifully about the *Sun* sinking without trace in a few months' time, then sat down looking decidedly unwell.

Cudlipp's performance was vintage. Holding up the new tabloid, he mocked the 'dirty digger' by listing the features the *Sun* had stolen from the *Mirror*: 'liveliest letters' from the *Mirror*'s 'live letters', a cartoon strip called Scarth similar to the *Mirror*'s Garth, and 'Wack', a version of the *Mirror*'s national institution, Andy Capp. The *Mirror*'s old masthead slogan, 'Forward with the People', now announced the new Murdoch paper, which included a column called 'Son of Cassandra', written by Bob Connor, son of the *Mirror*'s most famous columnist.

Cudlipp went on to denigrate the *Sun*'s 'downmarket' character and its pornographic appeal, which exploited the climate of the 'permissive society'. Before he had finished he had defined the threat which his scorn barely concealed. He had done it so well that when he had finished speaking there was silence. Donald Zec finally broke it with a joke, which was funny but hardly raised a laugh. Lee Howard looked as if he was about to have a cardiac arrest, his pallor a perfect reflection of the foreboding most of us felt, but did not express. 'A few of us went back to the editor's office for a drink,' Marje Proops later recalled. 'By that time the mood had changed; we'd persuaded ourselves there was nothing to worry about.'[1]

With Cecil King's dethronement in 1968, Cudlipp took over as chairman of the International Publishing Corporation, an empire of newspapers and magazines built on the profits of the *Daily Mirror*. In 1961, King had bought Odhams Press, which included the *Daily Herald*, a broadsheet with a declining circulation of a million and a half, 49 per cent owned by the Trades Union Congress and committed to supporting the Labour Party line. Cudlipp had promised the TUC the paper would be kept alive for a minimum of seven years.

After the unions sold their holding in the *Herald* to IPC, Cudlipp re-launched it as the *Sun*, a paper that seemed to fall between a number of stools. Neither tabloid nor broadsheet, it was designed to appeal to a new consumer class, 'educated and left-wing'. Once again, the overriding concern was to prevent it from becoming a direct competitor of the *Mirror*.

'We had a dilemma,' Cudlipp told me. 'If we ourselves had started the *Sun* as a tabloid and made it a success, it would have ruined the *Daily Mirror*. Cecil King once suggested to me we set up a rival to the *Mirror*. I thought that would have been an overt act of cynicism, which I could not go along with. But now we had a paper that was hardly a threat to the *Mirror*, but which was losing readers and money. Once the seven-year commitment was up, I had no choice but to sell the title, or close it down.'

In the meantime IPC had merged with Reed International, the paper manufacturer, whose board did not share the same interest in the joys and mysteries of newspapers. The *Sun*, whose circulation was now fast declining, was a liability. There were two bidders for the title: Robert Maxwell, a successful specialist publisher and Labour MP, and Rupert Murdoch, who had arrived from Australia a year earlier and had bought the *News of the World*. The unions did not want Maxwell, who was demanding redundancies and seemed the more ruthless of the two. They believed Murdoch's wealth, based on his family and press holdings in Australia, would guarantee jobs: an irony left for newspaper historians to savour. The title was sold to Murdoch for a knock-down £800,000.

In the last issue of the old *Sun*, November 15, 1969, an editorial urged its readers to 'reach for the new *Sun*' which 'will be different on Monday. Very different. But the most important thing to remember is that the new *Sun* will be the paper that CARES. The paper that cares – passionately – about truth, and beauty and justice. The paper that cares about people. About the kind of world we live in. And about the kind of world we would like our children to live in.'[2]

The *Sun*'s description of itself was not a parody, rather an accurate reflection of the cynicism and fabrication that were to become its hallmarks. Contrary to Fleet Street lore, the *Sun*, although it made off with the *Mirror*'s artefacts, did not plagiarise the successful post-war *Mirror*. It mined little of the *Mirror*'s populism, which was founded on its humanity: its sympathy for the ordinary person and its crusading tradition.

The *Sun* was a new invention, a hybrid. At a glance it looked like a tabloid newspaper, even at times like the *Mirror*, but most of it was drawn from the past: from the English 'penny dreadful' and the American 'yellowback', whose believe-it-or-not tales were thought to have expired with the death of *John Bull* in the 1960s and *Reveille* in the 1970s. The new *Sun* was an exhumation, with the lurid now dressed up to look like news, along with made-up gossip, cheap fantasy (the centre pages of the first issue displayed a naked female in the midst of the Rolling Stones pop group) and fake moral outrage. Racism and smear were to come.

Initially, critics of the *Sun* dismissed it as a comic. They were wrong; it was a great deal cleverer than that. Following the pattern he had set in Australia, Murdoch offered the politics he believed would appeal to his readers while they inspected the cleavages. At first he backed Labour, believing, as many did, that Harold Wilson was certain to be returned at the next general election.

The Prime Minister came several times to lunch at the *Sun*, perhaps recognising something of his own opportunism in the new Fleet Street proprietor. Wilson had much to offer: he knew how to make deals with the union 'barons' and his government ran the Monopolies and Mergers Commission. The *Sun* backed Wilson in the 1970 election, which he lost to Edward Heath. Murdoch dumped Labour and the *Sun* began to foretell the world of Thatcherism.

The *Sun*'s then editor was Larry Lamb, a former *Mirror* chief sub-editor and trade union enthusiast known, at one time, as 'Red Larry'. Disaffected at the *Mirror* by his lack of progress towards the editor's chair, Lamb had moved on to be northern editor of the *Daily Mail*, where Murdoch found him. One of his attractions to Murdoch was his contempt for the *Mirror*'s development as a quality paper, which he regarded as 'out of touch with the punters'. From the beginning of his editorship of the *Sun* Lamb and his team astutely identified the constituency that would one day vote for Thatcher – 'Maggie' – and buy the *Sun*. The two were indivisible.

The *Sun*'s readers belonged to a social group the market researchers were calling the 'C2s'. They had previously voted Labour with little commitment, which was hardly surprising as the Labour Party had long traded on the 'flat-cappery', or passivity, of much of its working-class support. They were, wrote the Conservative historian Lord Blake, 'fairly young . . . largely belonging to the skilled working class, primarily concerned with problems of housing, coloured immigration and the economy (prices and costs) rather than the condition of old-age pensioners. Only one in six bothered about international affairs.'[3] Lamb believed they were Labour's and the *Mirror*'s 'soft under-belly'.

It is probably true that the people who deserted Labour for Thatcher included the same people who stopped reading the *Mirror* and started taking the *Sun*. Whether or not it looked like an adult comic, the *Sun* represented a coherent, world view of Thatcher's ideology and the political and cultural impact of her 'revolution', notably her systematic assault on 'society'. Thatcherism's cause, the power of money, was the *Sun*'s message, whereas Thatcherism's effect, the redistribution of billions of pounds from ordinary people to the rich, was never mentioned.

The spicing was titillation, offered by bare-breasted pin-ups, and the sport of public vilification and the gleeful fly-posting of misfortune. The true messages of the 'permissive society' – humanity, anti-authoritarianism and anti-sexism – were understandably of no interest. In successfully casting itself as 'anti-establishment', the *Sun* echoed Murdoch's own specious claim.

There was another critical element. Thanks to Murdoch's direct influence, the *Sun* also anticipated a media world dominated for the first time by television – which, in 1968, the year Murdoch arrived in Fleet Street, overtook the press as the principal source of information in Britain. ITV, with its news, entertainment and current affairs programmes like *World in Action* and *This Week*, began to fulfil the role of the *Mirror* in its more confident days. Many people stopped buying popular newspapers altogether; indeed, circulation figures of mass circulation papers have been falling ever since. Others, however, turned to the *Sun*, which had become a scandal sheet for television, a salacious appendage to the new 'soaps'.

As the *Sun*'s circulation leapt in the first year to more than 1·5 million, the *Mirror* found itself in another dilemma. In competing with its new rival, was it to maintain its standards and character or was it to become more like the *Sun*? Every night on the editorial 'back bench' there was an almost breathless wait for the arrival of the first edition of the *Sun*. Mike Molloy was assistant editor at the time. 'We developed a split personality,' he said. 'There were two camps: those who wanted to keep standards up, and those who wanted to stick anything in the paper and make it like the *Sun*.' The latter group had already started to refer to the readers as 'punters'.

As the columns of non-news and non-features in the *Mirror* increased, 'the punters' became part of a vocabulary of justification. 'The punters' were no longer interested in real news or issues that touched their lives; these were 'pretentious' and 'pompous'; 'the punters' wanted 'fun', the euphemism for patronising junk, which in any case was not as sharp as the *Sun*'s junk. A series about 'the world's great photographers' was really a series of pictures of naked women. I well remember waiting to see the editor while the theatrical Cockney tones of a senior editorial executive ahead of me could be heard bellowing, 'If we have another spread on the fucking Health Service, we've fucking well had it!'

Few had their hearts in the plunge downmarket; mostly, when the subject arose, an embarrassed silence would hang in the editor's office. At the same time few acknowledged that fighting Murdoch on his own, low ground, then justifying it by saying that it was what the readers wanted, was a disaster.

The circulation continued to dive. In the second year the *Sun* put on another million sales. Hugh Cudlipp held a series of unhappy staff seminars in his ninth-floor suite during which he attempted, not always successfully, to explain the Murdoch effect on the paper he had created. He retired suddenly in 1973. The *Mirror*'s spectacular coverage of the Yom Kippur War, with staff correspondents reporting from throughout the Middle East, often ahead of their rivals, was a fitting tribute as he left.

'There was a terrible irony about our early struggles against Murdoch,' said Molloy. 'Larry Lamb told me later he was just waiting for the *Mirror* to swat him with all the marketing resources we had at our disposal; he couldn't understand why that didn't happen. The truth is that the new *Mirror* board, which was then dominated by Reed International, wouldn't allow it. They had no particular love for newspapers, only the bottom line. And we were bleeding to death.

'The *Mirror* was kept consistently more expensive than the

Sun. We carried more advertising than the *Sun*, which meant that there was actually more editorial content in the *Sun*, whatever you thought of it; and it was better printed. What's more, Murdoch was spending £4 for every pound we spent on television promotion. He was aggressively offering the public a new product that was bigger and cheaper than its rival, and he was prepared to invest money in doing it. Purely in marketing terms he was destroying us; if the *Mirror* had been a breakfast cereal, it would have vanished out of sight.

'When the *Sun* finally raised its cover price to equal the *Mirror*'s, we passed it in circulation. Murdoch was so alarmed he hurried back to England and replaced Larry Lamb with Kelvin MacKenzie, cut the price by twopence and introduced bingo, which was the equivalent of the lottery! Within six weeks the *Sun* had put on 600,000 circulation. It's an extraordinary tribute to *Mirror* readers that they stayed with us during those years.'

I asked, 'What would have happened had the *Mirror* kept its nerve?'

'We wouldn't have seen off the *Sun*, but the sales of the two papers would have remained about the same. People would have had a clear choice. Our circulation actually stabilised just below four million when we held our nerve and became again a *quality* popular newspaper; in fact, we were increasing sales slightly. This didn't last because there was now a powerful received wisdom that tabloids *had* to be a certain way. Once this was accepted, bad journalism drove out good journalism and the *Mirror* became an imitator.'

With hindsight, what is astonishing is that the *Mirror* was able to retain so much of its former self. Some of its most powerful Shock Issues were published in the 1970s and early 1980s: 'Divided Britain' on class, 'This Green and Poisoned Land' on the environment. The thalidomide campaign, which had been fought originally by the pre-Murdoch *Sunday Times*, was pursued for five years by the *Mirror*, seeking justice for working-class children damaged by the drug who had been left out of the original cash settlement because their mothers or their doctors had mislaid the actual prescription.

416

After the *Mirror* published on the front page photographs of two children with almost identical deformities, pointing out that only one had been compensated, all the children were included in a final settlement.[4]

During the late 1970s, a group of more than a hundred consultants working in the Health Service secretly supplied the *Mirror* with the first expert evidence of the human cost of government cuts to the NHS. 'THIS HOSPITAL IS DYING', read the banner headline over a ghostly, almost surreal picture of a closed children's ward.[5] A maternity ward in the East End of London was so deprived of resources that it was regarded by doctors as highly dangerous. Thatcherism had already begun, under a Labour Government.

In 1978, the year the *Sun*'s circulation finally triumphed over the *Mirror*'s, a series of mine about the low paid was published in the face of stiff editorial opposition. I had wanted to demystify the so-called 'winter of discontent', laying the blame not with hospital workers, ambulance drivers, grave-diggers and dustmen, but with the economic policies of the Callaghan Government. A passionate debate raged over days; and the series was published.

In 1979, only the *Mirror* could have had the nerve to devote eleven pages, 6,000 words and fifteen photographs to events in a far-away country, Cambodia. Every copy was sold. Unsolicited, *Mirror* readers sent more than £500,000 for Pol Pot's victims in Cambodia, most of it in small amounts, including whole pay packets and pensions. The first relief flight was funded entirely by them.[6]

In the same year, the *Mirror* took on to the staff a journalist who, alone at times, distinguished the paper during some of its most difficult times – Paul Foot. 'I was overjoyed, and very nervous, the day I was shown up to this little office on the fourth floor,' he told me. 'All I had was a telephone; I didn't even have a telephone directory and had a job getting one. I sat there the whole afternoon thinking this can't be true. No one told me what I had to write . . . I had this idea of making millions of ordinary people informants, of establishing a network of readers who felt they could trust me.

'I was on the *Mirror* for fourteen years and I had well over 150,000 letters and innumerable telephone calls, all of which were dealt with. It was the most extraordinary time for me. The atmosphere was something I had never expected: the feeling of respect and self-respect, and the democracy. I don't want to exaggerate that. It was hierarchical; but the sort of things the *Mirror* publishes now would never have seen the light then, because people in the office would have spoken out.

'There was a continuous discussion about what should appear in the paper and what shouldn't. There was an instinctive solidarity with the poor and the dispossessed. As a socialist, I had started basically hostile to the capitalist press, but found [the *Mirror*] a place where all the things that I wanted to do as a journalist – finding things out, challenging the powerful, tackling the government – were possible.'

In 1980, Foot received a letter from Ann Whelan, mother of Michael Hickey, one of four men accused of murdering a thirteen-year-old newspaper boy, Carl Bridgewater. She wrote, 'No one has looked into this case because everyone assumes they are guilty. I can assure you they're not.' Foot went on to amass critical evidence that the confession of one of the four, Patrick Molloy, was beaten out of him and was false, and that the others were also innocent. In 1997, thanks to him, Ann Whelan and others who never gave up, the men were finally released by the Court of Appeal.

The Bridgewater case is typical of the many campaigns this remarkable journalist fought in the *Mirror*. In 1981 an elderly working-class woman from Derby, Florence Siddons, told Foot that her granddaughter, Lyn, aged sixteen, had been murdered by her stepfather, Michael Brookes. His son had been tried and acquitted in a trial which left little doubt that the evidence against Brookes senior was overwhelming. But the police, as Foot put it, 'sulked and did nothing': a pattern in miscarriages of justice. For seventeen years Foot campaigned for Brookes to be brought to trial. In August 1996 the real murderer was finally convicted.

In 1982, at the height of the Falklands War, Foot flew to

Lima, the capital of Peru, and was shown documents which confirmed that the Peruvian Government had brokered a peace agreement between Britain and Argentina. On the day the ambassadors of both countries were due to sign it, a British submarine sank the Argentine cruiser *Belgrano* – on orders which Prime Minister Thatcher had made no attempt to countermand. Foot's investigations reinforced the evidence about how far Thatcher would go to continue the war, regardless of the willingness of the Argentinians to compromise. He also disclosed that her government had been arming the Argentine junta.

'Every time I hear Margaret Thatcher going on about the cruel military dictatorship in Argentina,' he wrote during the war, 'I am bound to repeat that no government in Europe has snuggled closer to the junta than hers has. From the moment it came to office, Mrs Thatcher's Government set out to make friends with South American tyrannies, especially in Chile and Argentina. The first victims of this policy were the political prisoners in both countries. In 1974, the Labour Government had set up a special programme for refugees from the right-wing terror in Chile. Political prisoners were "adopted" by union branches and other groups, and granted visas to come to Britain. These prisoners were allowed to choose between staying in prison and going into exile. In 1978, the scheme was extended to Argentina. Altogether, nearly 3,000 people were rescued from Chilean and Argentine concentration camps . . . In October 1979, the Tories abruptly cancelled the entire special programme, and the following year, cut off all its funds.' Thus Foot illuminated the other side of Thatcher, the Falklands heroine.[7]

The coverage of the Falklands War was one of the last high points at the *Mirror*. In a perverse way, the *Mirror* was blessed by a change of editor at the *Sun*. Having been knighted for his devotion to 'Maggie' in the 1979 election – 'services to journalism', the citation said – Larry Lamb's establishment affirmation loosened his links to 'the punters', which is why Murdoch replaced him with Kelvin MacKenzie.

Unlike Lamb, wrote Peter Chippendale and Chris Horrie in

their splendid history, *Stick It Up Your Punter*, 'MacKenzie was a social diver rather than a social climber, playing to the gallery of the rougher end and absorbing the code of the cocky, macho soccer fan personified by Millwall, the club he purported to support.' Although he came from a solidly middle-class background and had gone to an elite grammar school in Dulwich, he affected a 'sarf London accent' and 'enthusiastically embraced the two-fingers-to-society-I-don't-give-a-fuck mentality'. MacKenzie was exactly what Murdoch wanted: someone with 'the knack . . . an incisive and intelligent mind, quick to exploit the weaknesses in others and with a hard edge of cruelty which gave no quarter'.[8]

MacKenzie's behaviour during the Falklands War left Murdoch in no doubt that he had found a star. The front page headline, 'GOTCHA', which gloated over the news of the sinking of the ancient cruiser *Belgrano* with more than 1,200 conscripted young sailors on board, is infamous. Changed after the first edition because even MacKenzie thought he had gone too far, it was approved by Murdoch. 'I rather like it,' said the proprietor.[9]

Far from 'backing up our lads', the *Sun*'s stunts and lies during the war dismayed the troops in the field who, like most soldiers faced with the reality of war, are contemptuous of crude propaganda. A prime example was the outrage that followed the *Sun*'s fabricated interview with Marcia McKay, the widow of Ian McKay, who had been awarded the Victoria Cross posthumously.

Before and during the war, the *Mirror* had counselled scepticism at Thatcher's mounting jingoism – which the *Sun* merely aped. A typical *Mirror* editorial headlined 'MIGHT ISN'T RIGHT' warned against hysteria and the cost in lives. 'The killing has got to stop,' it concluded. 'If that means Britain and Argentina need to compromise, then compromise they must.'[10]

The next day the *Sun* replied, 'What is it but treason for this timorous, whining publication to plead day after day for appeasing the Argentinian dictators . . . We are truly sorry for the *Daily Mirror*'s readers. They are buying a newspaper which again and again demonstrates it has no faith in its country and no respect for her people.'[11]

The *Mirror* responded with a long leader entitled, 'THE HARLOT OF FLEET STREET'. 'There have been lying newspapers before,' it said, 'but in the past month [the *Sun*] has broken all records. From behind the safety of its typewriters it has called for battle to commence to satisfy its bloodlust. The *Sun* today is to journalism what Dr Joseph Goebbels was to truth . . .'[12]

During 1982 the *Mirror*'s circulation rose slightly and the *Sun*'s fell, although the *Sun* remained well ahead. Although factors other than the war influenced this, it is reasonable to assume that the *Mirror* had captured a popular mood that did not show itself in newspaper circulation figures. It was a mood of misgiving and ambiguity, exacerbated by the Prime Minister's bellicosity. Millions of Britons, while opposing the Argentine invasion of the Falklands and wanting to support the troops, were not pleased to see young men go blindly to yet another war on the other side of the world, against an adversary who offered no threat to the homeland. The *Mirror* reflected these grave doubts, thus taking a position that was as courageous as its warnings, in the 1930s, of the consequences of true appeasement.

Perhaps the coming of Robert Maxwell was inevitable. He and Rupert Murdoch, their voraciousness feeding off the secret deals and loans of the new 'market opportunities', exemplified the Thatcher years. Between them, they hijacked popular journalism. Yet even that truth is denied, no doubt because there remain so many consorts and acolytes to deny and distort it. Consider, for example, the headline, 'THE MAN WHO SAVED THE MIRROR', written by the *Mirror*'s Maxwell-appointed editor, Richard Stott, and splashed across the front page the day after the great embezzler's death in November 1991.[13]

To understand the falsity of this claim, one need only look at the period immediately before Maxwell took over in 1984. Not only was the circulation stable, but there was now the prospect of a new kind of ownership that had every chance of guaranteeing the independence of the paper for many years to come. The chief executive of the Abbey National Building Society, Clive Thornton, was appointed chairman of the Mirror Group with a brief from the owner, Reed International, to prepare the company for flotation on the stock market. On October 13, 1983, the Reed chairman, Sir Alex Jarratt, gave the following 'binding pledge': 'The Reed board ... is not seeking, nor will it seek, offers for Mirror Group which would result in its coming under the control of a single individual or corporation since the Board believes such offers would not be conducive to maintaining the traditions, character and independence of the newspapers.'[14]

Thornton was an interesting maverick who had grown up in poverty on Tyneside, left school at fourteen, and studied law the hard way. While at the Abbey National, he broke the building societies' cartel and financed inner-city housing. He drew up a 'protective structure' for the *Mirror* in which no single shareholder could own more than 15 per cent of the company; and he began to assemble a portfolio of solid, institutional capital. On top of this, he intended to give the workforce a substantial share of the company. He had no airs. He shunned the executive lift. He ate in the office canteen.

Reed was taken aback. Thornton had been hired on the implicit understanding that he would 'cut the unions down to size' and instead he was winning them over. He found the unions co-operative, a mood undoubtedly reinforced by fear of Murdoch, and a management suspicious, if not contemptuous, of his ideas. In the boardroom an atmosphere prevailed that made it clear the new man was 'not one of us'.

Thornton had many ideas, some of them excellent, others impractical. He proposed that the company launch a 'serious left-wing tabloid' in addition to the *Mirror*, together with a second London evening paper. For this, he was criticised as 'naïve' by managers and journalists alike. He also had to suffer the presence of an editorial 'Maxwell mole', who, as it transpired, was passing his best-laid plans to the waiting predator.

When Alex Jarratt broke his 'binding pledge' not to sell the company to 'a single individual' and looked like selling to

Maxwell, the print unions gave Thornton a pledge of industrial peace for a year: a commitment unprecedented in British newspapers. The journalists quickly joined them. I well remember the passion expressed at the *Mirror* 'chapel' (union branch) meeting at which we voted for Thornton. A red-faced Joe Haines, the talented leader writer and former press secretary to Harold Wilson, said he would have to be 'dragged through the door to work for a crook and a monster like Robert Maxwell'. Haines was one of those who all that week had been warning us that Maxwell might plunder the pension fund – which he subsequently did to the tune of £526 million.

Within forty-eight hours, Thornton was thrown out of the *Mirror* building by Maxwell, and Haines accepted instant promotion from Maxwell to assistant editor, later rising to 'Mirror Group Political Editor' with a seat on Maxwell's rubber-stamp board and an assured place at his side. After a month of accommodating himself with the man he had called 'a crook and a monster', Haines said on television, 'Mr Maxwell doesn't believe in doing things by half.'[15]

Such a wise, prophetic observation certainly applied to the *Mirror*'s circulation. In June 1984 the *Mirror* under Thornton was selling 3,487,721 copies daily. After eighteen months under Maxwell, this had dropped a record low of 2,900,000 and was still falling.[16] Calculating readership figures, at least a million people stopped reading the *Daily Mirror* in the wake of Maxwell's takeover. 'Whatever else might be said about Maxwell,' noted a trade observer quoted in *Marketing Week*, 'it takes something close to genius to lose so much circulation so quickly.'[17]

During the first few days under Maxwell there was speculation elsewhere in the press that Paul Foot and I might no longer be welcome at the *Mirror*. We decided to find out and went to see the new owner. On the ninth floor we were greeted by Ian Maxwell, one of the sons, a slight, pale, diffident young man. 'Oh, you're the one your father sacked,' said Foot, setting the tone. The father appeared. 'He's a good boy,' said Maxwell, 'everybody deserves one more chance.' Hollow laughter all round.

Maxwell then played a little power game with us. He ordered either of us to cross his vast office and get a drink for him 'and something for yourselves'. Neither Foot nor I budged while the human pyramid in front of us glowed crimson.

'You occupy a lot of space in the paper,' he said to Foot. 'You're a space imperialist!'

More hollow laughter.

'I hear you're thinking of sacking us,' I said.

'Good God, no,' said Maxwell, feigning hurt. 'Furthermore, I can guarantee that your work will never be interfered with while I'm here. Your jobs are secure!'

Eighteen months later, after relentless interference from Maxwell, I was sacked.

'Solemn commitments' flowed out of Maxwell at the rate that food flowed in. (A partition in his suite ensured that he could host two lunches simultaneously, devouring two meals as he moved from one to the other.) On taking over the *Mirror* he announced that 'under my management editors in the Group will be free to produce their newspapers without interference with their journalistic skills and judgement.' So false was this that at one stage an acting editor was ordered to move into Maxwell's suite so he could more efficiently translate the owner's whims into commands.

Maxwell's first indulgence was to turn the *Mirror* into a family album. There were Maxwell and/or various members of his family celebrating this or that, and Maxwell with the President of Sudan and the President of Bulgaria and Chairman Gorbachev, and Maxwell getting an honorary degree in New York, and 'saving' this and 'rescuing' that. There were days when most of the photographic staff were unavailable for news assignments because they were either in Maxwell's suite taking pictures of 'The Publisher' (his favourite title) with 'visiting dignitaries' or elsewhere in the Maxwell empire, such as the Oxford United Football Club, which he owned, taking pictures of him surrounded by grateful fans.

His favourite photographer was Mike Maloney, an affable,

smart-suited operator with one famous possession. In a book entitled *Flash! Splash! Crash! All at Sea with Cap'n Bob*, Maloney recalled,

> I had been summoned unexpectedly to meet the great man himself. Why, I had no idea. 'Call him R.M. [I was told] when you want to be formal, and when other people are in the room. Call him Publisher when the other people in the room are VIPs or when he is in a bad mood . . . Call him Boss. Or Chief. Or Chairman. He likes all of these. On a good day, with care, you may eventually be allowed to call him Bob.'
>
> Unknown to me, the new Chairman had arrived at the company's underground car park, sitting in the back of his maroon Silver Shadow Rolls-Royce. Now the limousine nosed past the barrier and searched for a bay. There was one space left. By chance it happened to be next to a gleaming green and white Silver Shadow Rolls-Royce already parked there, complete with the personalised number plate 914 MM emblazoned on it. My number. My Roller.
>
> The Chairman stepped out, and surveyed my car in silence. At last he said [to chief executive Douglas Long], 'Which one of my executives drives a Rolls-Royce, Douglas?'
>
> 'Er, it's not one of your executives, Chairman. It's the *Mirror*'s junior photographer.'
>
> 'You'd better send this boy up to me . . .'[18]

During the rest of his career at the *Mirror*, Maloney saw Maxwell through his lens. 'Are you ready, Mr Snapper?' Maxwell would shout, snapping his fingers, when a 'visiting dignitary' hove into view. Mr Snapper was required twenty-four-hours a day as life at the *Mirror* became one stunt after another for the greater glory of 'Cap'n Bob'.

One of the first was Maxwell's flight to Ethiopia at the height of the 1984–5 famine. He had hired a British Airways airliner and filled a container with relief supplies, with the intention that Mr Snapper and I would record his great act of generosity. I disappeared. He flew off.

He did not give up easily. He began to phone me at home late at night with 'assignments'. 'Bulgaria!' he boomed. 'You will write what a wonderful place Bulgaria is and you will say that the Bulgarian Government did not try to kill the Pope.' Again, I vanished.

Another journalist accompanied Cap'n Bob to Bulgaria. The *Mirror* published a large photograph of him toasting President Zhirkov, and a fawning story that described the dictator as the enlightened head of 'a tourist top-spot, a go-ahead place with one of East Europe's successful econo-mies . . .' Then it got to the point: 'The President's special guest, Robert Maxwell, had just struck a huge deal with the Bulgarian Government to help update the country's printing and packaging industries.'[19]

'Poland!' boomed the late-night voice. I croaked with fake 'flu. Thereafter I became the Houdini of Fleet Street, narrowly missing China, to which he took Julia Langdon, the political editor. Reporting in the *Mirror* that Maxwell had been given 'an exclusive interview with Deng Xiaoping, leader of a quarter of mankind', Langdon described 'the successful negotiations between Robert Maxwell's printing and publishing interests and a number of Chinese Government printing organisations'.[20]

Meanwhile, at home there was a '*Mirror* train' with 'Forward with Britain' emblazoned on the engine, which bore the great man on a kind of royal tour. At each stop Maxwell demanded to be met by the stationmaster, and to be photographed with celebrities. This provided a challenge for the harassed organisers as few, if any, famous names wanted to be part of the charade. Linda Lusardi, a *Sun* Page Three Girl, was hired to greet the *Mirror* owner, suitably clad in a bikini.

The train was part of a 'Tell-the-*Mirror* campaign'. The plan was that Maxwell and his court would travel to public meetings where, according to the *Mirror*'s front page, he 'wants to know from YOU what is right and what has gone wrong with the country – and how the *Mirror* should reflect it'. Next to this was another 'Special Announcement' which said, 'It's guaranteed. It's tax free. Win £1 million in our new Lucky Dip game which starts on Monday.' The illustration was the nearly naked form of Jane Warner, another *Sun* Page Three Girl.[21]

Almost everything went wonderfully wrong. Stooge audiences being as difficult to find as celebrities, the people at the public meetings were genuine readers who wasted no time in telling Maxwell what they thought of his influence on *their* newspaper.

'How dare you treat women like pieces of meat in the *Mirror*!' said a woman at the meeting in Newcastle. 'It's disgusting what you've done to it . . .'

'Madam,' intoned Maxwell, 'you don't seem to understand that it's just a bit of fun and we've had very few objections from the lads . . .'

With that, the hall exploded with female, and some male, wrath. Maxwell held his arms in the air, as if to calm his troubled subjects, thereby intensifying the fire directed at him.

'You're just a big fat dictator,' said a Geordie voice from the back.

'There's no need to get personal . . .' said Maxwell.

'Why not?' said a woman in the front row. 'When does the *Mirror* do anything about young people any more, like the youngsters who are unemployed. My son is one of them, so I know . . .'

'Send him to me,' said Maxwell, 'and I'll give him something. Take the lady's name . . .'

Having avoided the train, I used Maxwell's presence on Tyneside and his stated interest in youth unemployment to inquire into a common complaint of the *Mirror*'s young readers: that the government's Youth Training Scheme was little more than a cover for cheap labour. The piece I subsequently wrote was delayed for two months, then published only after Maxwell had instructed an editorial executive to deliver a copy to the Employment Secretary, Tom King, who was responsible for the YTS. King's not surprisingly hostile remarks about the piece were published prominently on the page: the first time in my experience that a government minister was shown an investigative article prior to publication.

The response from readers to this innovation was overwelmingly hostile. But the letters page did not reflect the ratio of those for and against, which had always been a rule at the *Mirror*. Instead, it was dominated by a second letter from the minister – the kind of small corruption that became routine under Maxwell. Similarly, a piece suggesting that the origins of the coal strike lay more in Thatcher's determination to 'get' the miners than in the issue of 'uneconomic pits' was doctored by Maxwell himself after the editor had gone home.

The coal strike, one of the longest industrial strikes this century, began shortly before Maxwell took over, and the *Mirror*'s new owner left no doubt that its outcome 'is of deep and abiding concern to me'. This deep concern was to lead the *Mirror* down to its lowest ebb. At first Maxwell appeared charitable towards the miners, launching an appeal for their families, 'who are not to blame for this conflict'. He asked people to send their donations 'directly to me, Robert Maxwell'. Money did arrive; *Mirror* readers had already made clear their support, but what was unexpected was a torrent of letters attacking Maxwell for playing fund-raiser instead of fund-giver. It was, in effect, a vote of no-confidence in the new proprietor.

In August that year, the booming voice was on my phone again, instructing me to arrange a 'secret meeting' with the President of the miners' union, Arthur Scargill. Maxwell had assumed I knew Scargill, but I had never met him. Believing the miners needed all the help they could get in the press, I agreed; and a *Mirror* 'team' led by Maxwell met Scargill and Peter Heathfield, the NUM General-Secretary, in the penthouse of the Hallam Tower Hotel near Sheffield.

Scargill was clearly bemused by this minor politburo sitting across the table from him, with Maxwell fulfilling the twin roles Eric Heffer once attributed to him: that of a Mafia Godfather and an Eastern European dictator. On the table was that morning's *Daily Mirror*, with the front page given over to a picture of a beaming Maxwell and a million pounds in banknotes. 'I'm itching to give it to one of our readers,' said the caption. His daughter, Ghislaine, twenty-two, was quoted as saying how pleased she was that 'it will make one of our readers happy'.[22]

Scargill and Heathfield laid out the miners' case. They had also come with evidence of the Coal Board's manipulation of the Colliery Review Procedure and of repeated attempts by the NUM to reach a compromise. Little of this had received national publicity. Maxwell was not interested. He harangued the two men about 'my fears for the country' and of 'a breakdown of law and order and civilised values in Britain'. He reminded them of what communism had done to other countries. They struggled to contain their laughter until eventually Scargill stood up. 'Excuse me,' he said, 'may I have a cup of tea?'

A *Sun* photographer was waiting outside to record the 'secret meeting'. This prompted the spectacle of the massive Maxwell being bundled out of a side door to avoid having his picture taken with Scargill. He and Joe Haines were delivered to the safety of his helicopter. The next day I went over the documents Scargill had given us and realised we had an important story of Coal Board deceit. Maxwell killed it.

In the ensuing months Maxwell mounted a series of vitriolic attacks on Scargill, blaming him for almost everything to do with the strike. The assumption was that more than 100,000 miners were sheep, too dull to understand for themselves the issues involved and too craven not to revolt against their leader. Returning frequently to the coalfields, I did manage to get published a piece on police paramilitary tactics and the intimidation of pit villages. The story was initially killed, then revived when I demanded to see Maxwell and argued almost every line of it with him.

I saw a lot of my friends in the pit town of Murton, County Durham. Impoverished but seldom dispirited, they remained solid until the end. The trade union establishment, spurred on by the *Mirror*, had hoisted the white flag long before that. In February 1985, I was in the Murton Miners' Institute when the television news showed the recently retired TUC leader Len Murray doffing his cap to Lord Hailsham, as 'Lord Murray of Epping Forest' took his seat in the unelected upper chamber. Before departing for the Lords, Murray had called for an 'attitude of reality' from the miners, as had the leader of the Labour Party, as had Margaret Thatcher, as had the banks that foreclosed on their homes, as had the *Daily Mirror*.

On the bitter morning a month later when the Murton miners went back to the pit, their prize-winning brass band emerged from the mist with the women marching first. I cannot recall a moment quite as moving.

The Murton pit closed in 1991, regardless of the miners' increased productivity and the mine's profitability: so much for the government's rationale about 'uneconomic pits'. Within two years the industry mining Britain's greatest sustainable resource was decimated, as Scargill had predicted, along with mass trade-union resistance to growing unemployment and poverty. The crushing of the miners' union, and its leader, was essential to this result.

In March 1990, the *Mirror* published what Maxwell called his 'scoop of the decade'. 'SCARGILL'S WATERLOO', said the headline over an editorial signed by Maxwell himself. The *Mirror*, in company with Central Television's *Cook Report*, accused Scargill and Peter Heathfield of using Libyan money donated to the union during the strike to pay off their mortgages. The story was totally false; Scargill did not have a mortgage; Heathfield did not own his own home.

Maxwell had paid £130,000 to three 'sources', former associates of Scargill, two with a personal grievance. The main 'source', Roger Windsor, former chief executive of the NUM, was subsequently named in Parliament by fifty MPs as an MI5 agent. An official inquiry conducted by Gavin Lightman, QC, now a High Court judge, found that 'Mr Windsor's allegation that the cash he had brought in was used to repay Mr Scargill £25,000 is entirely untrue ... No such monies were used to repay any home loan of Mr Scargill or Mr Heathfield. Mr Heathfield never had a home loan until much later and Mr Scargill had some time before repaid his home loan out of his own monies.'[23]

Apart from the unsubstantiated word of 'unnamed intelligences sources' and of Windsor, there was not a shred of evidence that the union had received any money from

Libya. Windsor subsequently abandoned two libel actions against Scargill, and all costs were awarded against him. An allegation that Scargill had diverted millions of pounds in donations from Soviet miners to a secret trust fund to further his personal political ambitions was also found to be false; an Inland Revenue investigation cleared the NUM and its leaders of all charges of misapplication of union funds and breaches of duty.

In his definitive book on the episode, *The Enemy Within*, Seamus Milne of the *Guardian* wrote, 'Of the legal actions, prosecutions and investigations launched [against Scargill], all were abandoned, dismissed or found in favour of the miners' leaders. All charges brought in a Certification Office prosecution were dismissed, with costs paid by the government. A Fraud Squad investigation was dropped; the Commissioner for Trade Unions' investigation never got anywhere, and the Inland Revenue found unequivocally in the NUM leaders' favour.'[24]

Moreover, in November 1994, three years after Maxwell's death, the *Mirror* itself reported, under the headline 'MI5 TRIED TO "FIX" SCARGILL' that 'MI5 is said to have inspired newspaper investigations four years ago – first printed by the *Daily Mirror* – which accused Mr Scargill of using Libyan cash to repay a home loan. That allegation has since been discredited.'[25]

The *Mirror* editor who published the smear against Scargill was Roy Greenslade. He had been an assistant editor to Kelvin MacKenzie on the *Sun* and had come to the *Mirror* from the *Sunday Times*. He is now a commentator on the media. Greenslade describes his fourteen months as editor under Maxwell as 'horrendous' and says he was 'presented' with the Scargill story on his first day. 'It was a *fait accompli* which disheartened me,' he told me. 'I thought it would probably be a great *Sun* story, but not a great *Mirror* story . . . I've never been under any illusion that we may have, in fact, been the victims ourselves of a probable MI5 plot. I've never myself worked out quite what Mr Roger Windsor was up to . . .'

In his book, *Maxwell's Fall*, Greenslade acknowledges that the *Mirror* never put the central allegation to Scargill – that the miners' leader had paid off a mortgage with Libyan money – because he did not want to give Scargill a chance to cover up. He was also worried about an injunction because he was 'deficient in documents'.[26]

Greenslade told me, 'I wasn't convinced by the reporter that ran the story from the beginning . . . so I put two more reporters on it and with more experience and slightly more scepticism . . .' In *The Enemy Within*, Seamus Milne describes Greenslade as keen to publish the smear: 'He decided to run [the story] immediately – without consulting Maxwell about the date. The *Mirror*'s proprietor was "apoplectic" when he discovered that Greenslade had pressed ahead . . .'[27]

As each allegation was knocked down, the *Mirror* came up with another, to the point where the front page carried a ludicrous, 'GADDAFI TO SUE SCARGILL'.

'Why didn't you call a halt to it?' I asked Greenslade. 'After all, you were the editor.'

'I think I got carried away with it. I thought if Scargill was telling the truth, he would simply sue . . . let's face it, this is not an exact science, being an editor. You make mistakes [and] this was probably a great mistake to make.'

I asked him, 'Do you ever reflect on the irony that here was Maxwell, one of the great embezzlers of our time, running a campaign against the head of the Mineworkers' Union, accusing him of the very dishonesty of which he himself was guilty?'

'No one is more struck by that than me . . . of course we didn't know at the time that Maxwell was a con man.'

'Knowing that now, have you ever apologised to Scargill?'

'I haven't apologised to Arthur Scargill . . .'

'Is it something you would like to do?'

'That's an interesting question . . .'

Greenslade and the *Mirror*'s 'Scargill team' were not alone in their treatment of Scargill. Edward Pearce in the *Guardian* described Scargill as a 'despicable braggart who has squeezed the miners dry'.[28] The *Observer*, the *New Statesman* and the

Independent all attacked him on the basis of the *Mirror/Cook Report* allegations. There was even speculation about how many years in prison Scargill might get.

It was two years before the press acknowledged that Scargill had been exonerated. The *Daily Express*, like the *Mirror* eventually, described the allegations as discredited. The *Independent* dismissed them as 'untrue'. *The Economist* said that Scargill had been 'subjected to a succession of smears and that these culminated in an entirely false allegation'.[29]

With the honourable exception of the *Guardian*, thanks mainly to Seamus Milne and other investigative reporters who revealed how Scargill had been 'set up' by MI5, no newspaper has since reflected on the culpability of the press as the willing dupe of a malevolent government determined to destroy a trade union, its leader and a whole industry. Milne wrote in a postscript to his book: 'The British mining industry is now privatised, most of it sold to Richard Budge, a man identified in a confidential 1994 report for the Trade and Industry Department by the accountants Coopers & Lybrand as "unfit to be concerned in the management of a company". The words echoed those used by DTI [Department of Trade and Industry] inspectors in 1971 about Robert Maxwell . . .'[30]

Why did so many journalists fall under Maxwell's spell? The *Mirror* feature writer Mary Riddell wrote that 'behind the glittering career – the yacht, the Rolls-Royces, the gloss and glory and influence – lay his unswerving crusade to better the lot of the ordinary man'. The *Mirror* columnist Anne Robinson described his 'sense of daring and fearlessness that was truly astounding . . . He was, in truth, part monster, part magic . . . He enriched many lives. Mine was one of them.'[31]

Peter Jay had been a well-connected broadcaster and British Ambassador to the United States when he went to work for Maxwell as his chief of staff. Maxwell consumed him, even paying for his honeymoon to Venice, allowing him 'a weekend and no more'. Jay told me he saw himself as a senior civil servant meeting the challenge of ordering Maxwell's chaotic life. Life with 'Bob' was exciting. 'He was a primitive,' Jay said, 'stalking about, a sort of pre-moral entity, both horrific and magnificent. He lived from minute to minute in a state of whirling chaos. He had no personal interests, he had no personal hobbies, he had no personal friends. His driving motive was not money or power or fame, but fear of boredom. On a Saturday morning he would have a fantastic scheme to save the world from whatever horror he imagined, then by the Sunday all that would be forgotten. To relieve his boredom he would call me at four in the morning, just to say, "What time is it?" '

When Maxwell drowned, the *Mirror* devoted eleven pages to a eulogy of a kind the paper had never before given to a public figure, including two kings and numerous prime ministers. No issue of the *Mirror* lauded Winston Churchill to the degree that it praised Robert Maxwell. The editor, Richard Stott, wrote on the front page, 'In one of our late-night conversations I asked him [Maxwell] what he would like to be remembered for when he died. "As the man who saved the *Mirror*," he said without hesitation. It's true. He did . . .' Over the page, an editorial called him 'The giant with a vision . . . under him our commitment to social justice and political decency was strengthened. [Because of him] the *Daily Mirror* you are reading today is strong *editorially*, strong *financially*, strong technologically and strong on *integrity*' (my italics).

True, Maxwell had computerised the *Mirror* without the upheaval that Rupert Murdoch's 'Wapping revolution' caused – so 'technologically strong' was probably correct. The rest was demonstrably false, though no less astonishing than the posthumous grovelling offered on other pages.

A feature writer, Barry Wigmore, was even given a page to pay tribute to Maxwell's yacht, a £12 million gin-palace called the *Lady Ghislaine*. 'Bob would think nothing of sending her 3,000 miles across the Atlantic to St Martin, his favourite Caribbean island. On board, life was mostly very casual . . . Business or pleasure, Bob loved his *Lady*

Ghislaine.' Clearly writing in a personal capacity, Joe Haines completed the parody. 'There are those', he wrote, 'who started off hating him and ended up loving him or at least standing in awe.'[32]

Less than a month later the real reason to stand in awe of him was revealed. In place of the tear-stained *Mirror* was this front-page headline: 'MILLIONS MISSING FROM THE MIRROR'.[33] The following day it got worse: 'MAXWELL: £526 MILLION IS MISSING'. The money, said the *Mirror*, had 'vanished' in the week before Maxwell died and it 'includes £526 million from the pension fund'. Secretly and systematically, Maxwell had stolen this fortune from the *Mirror*'s pensioners, including those who had given their working lives to the paper.

Today's *Mirror* is produced at Canary Wharf, the pyramid-topped building in London's Docklands and symbol of the Thatcher years. Just along the river from Murdoch's Fortress Wapping, Canary Wharf is a sort of vertical Fleet Street, with the *Mirror* offices occupying the top floors. Here the spirit of Murdoch rules as a coterie of his acolytes ensures that his model for the popular press is adhered to, at times surpassed.

The banks which took over the *Mirror* following Maxwell's looting appointed David Montgomery as the new chief executive. Montgomery is the quintessential Murdoch man. He was editor of the *News of the World*, then *Today*. The managing director of the Mirror Group is Charles Wilson, who is credited with 'rescuing' *The Times* for Murdoch. The current *Mirror* editor is Piers Morgan, who made his name running the *Sun*'s 'Bizarre' column and having his photograph taken with the 'celebrities' he featured. Thereafter he was appointed editor of the *News of the World* at the age of twenty-eight, the youngest editor of a national newspaper for half a century. His other distinction is that he is the only Murdoch editor to have been publicly rebuked by the proprietor on a matter related to journalistic standards. He was said to have 'gone too far' in publishing photographs of

Countess Spencer, the sister-in-law of the Princess of Wales, when she was ill with anorexia.

Morgan's mentor at Canary Wharf is Kelvin MacKenzie, his old editor at the *Sun* and Murdoch's 'favourite editor'. MacKenzie joined the Mirror Group as the managing director of the cable television company, L!ve TV, which has introduced the 'News Bunny' to the broadcasting of news. 'News Bunny', a person dressed in a rabbit costume, sits beside the newscaster and comments on the news of the day. In 1998, he was appointed managing director of all the company's newspapers.

David Montgomery shares Murdoch's Thatcherite world view, particularly his hostility to trade unions. His mission at the *Mirror* has been to make a profit and he has achieved this largely by cutting the wages bill. He began by sacking 100 journalists, who were turned away when they arrived for work. He then rounded on the National Union of Journalists, whose 'chapel' officials were told they must resign or be sacked. They went.

The entire chapel committee was forced out, and for the first time in the *Mirror*'s history its journalists passed a vote of no confidence in its editor, the Montgomery-appointed David Banks. After fourteen years, Paul Foot went, though not before he had devoted his last, unpublished column to the upheavals at the *Mirror* and distributed it on the steps of the old *Mirror* building in Holborn Circus.

When Foot's colleague, Margaret Renn, took over as senior NUJ official, she watched as her desk was removed from her office while she was sitting at it. She was informed she had been sacked a fortnight earlier; no one had bothered to tell her at the time. The entire security staff, including a number of *Mirror* veterans, were told to leave the building immediately. As they went, replacements from a low-wage private company arrived. They had been waiting outside in a van.

This did not inhibit the *Mirror* from declaring itself 'The paper that fights for a fairer Britain'. A series of articles purporting to 'speak up for the rights of part-timers' was blessed by the TUC General-Secretary, John Monks, who made no mention of the many part-timers Montgomery had sacked. Similarly, a 'Rolling Rose' recruitment drive by the Labour Party was launched in the *Mirror* by the deputy leader, John Prescott, without reference to the sackings. New party members received the *Mirror* free for a week and drew lots for the privilege of taking tea with Tony Blair. In 1996, Blair called for an easing of the legal limits on the ambitions of newspaper companies to buy into television. This would benefit both the Mirror Group and Murdoch.

Perhaps the most important loss has been the *Mirror*'s coverage of politics. *Mirror* editorials retain none of the power, knowledge and acerbic wit of former leader writers, such as Richard Jennings, Basil Davidson and Alan Fairclough. Under its chief executive, Montgomery, a Tory, and editor, Piers Morgan, a Tory, the paper's backing for New Labour has been slavish. Blair's words and deeds are reported adoringly. The political editor, John Williams, spent the first morning of the party conference at a 'How to promote Labour's message' session run by Peter Mandelson. The *Mirror*'s front page that week was filled with a picture of Cherie Blair kissing her dewy-eyed husband. An artist had tastefully framed them in chintz red curtains. Blair's speech to the conference was described as 'Labour coming home' when the truth was that he had abandoned the party's traditional base and beliefs. During the election campaign, the paper became a Tony-and-Cherie pamphlet. Following the election, John Williams published a hagiography entitled *Victory!*

During this important episode in British political history, when the single-ideology state was consolidated, completing the 'project' of Thatcherism, the *Mirror* explained none of these developments. The paper declared that Blair, within weeks of his election, had already kept his promise to 'make things better . . . So make the most of it. Get up this morning, smile, give a little cheer and do something positive. The Great is back in Britain.' With Hong Kong's return to China, *Mirror* readers could 'feel proud to be British'. Who deserved this credit? 'Under the leadership of Tony Blair, it could be the start of a new respect for Britain in the world.'[34]

Fortunately, the ridiculous is never far away. In November 1996, the *Mirror* was handed the political scoop of the year: a leak of the Budget papers. Morgan immediately handed these back to the government, then published 'tributes' from establishment figures for his 'act of responsibility'. The Tory Chancellor, Kenneth Clarke, was the first to pay 'tribute'. A Downing Street spokesman told the paper the whistle-blower would face 'very severe disciplinary measures'. In his message of congratulations to the *Mirror*, the disgraced former government minister David Mellor said, 'Serious economic damage could have been done to this country.' The then Shadow Chancellor, Gordon Brown, said, 'I hail you for giving the papers back.'

At a stroke, the *Mirror*'s proudest tradition was destroyed and the British secret state had enlisted a new, if obtuse, ally. The veteran freelance journalist Peter Hounman, whose hard work had secured the 'leak', was not consulted. The most charitable explanation for these absurd machinations was that, having for so long published non-news and debased 'exclusives', the *Mirror* had lost altogether the ability to recognise a genuine story.[35]

I met Piers Morgan soon after an earlier controversy. On the day England played Germany at soccer in the Euro 96 competition, he had published a front page which said, 'ACHTUNG! SURRENDER'. *Mirror* readers, angered by the insult to visitors in the host country, complained in record numbers. I asked him for an interview, but he declined. 'I'm keeping a low profile,' he said. 'The Achtung thing was a joke that people didn't get, that's all. We did it to get the youth on side. We've got droves of readers over sixty-five. We've gotta get the youth.' Allegedly with the youth readership in mind, Morgan had printed an entire issue of the *Mirror* in blue as a stunt to advertise the new colour of a can of Pepsi-Cola. He also devoted four pages, including the front page, to a street brawl involving the pop star Brian Harvey.[36]

I told Morgan I had been at Pimlico School in London the day before, talking to sixth-formers about popular newspapers. 'Are they the sort of readers you want?' I asked.

'Absolutely. Spot on. What did they say about the *Mirror*?'

'They said it was crap.'

'Really? What didn't they like?'

'Five pages devoted to a priest who ran away with a woman . . .'

'What else?'

'Another five pages devoted to Fergie . . . They said everything in it insults their intelligence.'

'What about our campaigns?'

'What campaigns?'

'Come off it. What about the knives amnesty campaign? What about *that* front page – the bloke with a knife through his head? Credit where it's due . . .'

One of these campaigns saw the *Mirror*'s front page dominated by a representation of a man's face half-transmogrified into that of a pig. This was meant to be Tim Holley, chief executive of Camelot, which runs the National Lottery. In the man-pig's mouth was a wad of cash. The headline said, 'LICENSED TO SWILL'. In the story the pig becomes a 'fat cat' for paying himself the 'whopping' sum of £725,000 including bonuses.[37] The *Mirror* had already attacked 'fat cat' Cedric Brown on his retirement as head of British Gas, where his salary had been £475,000 and his pension £250,000.[38] The chief executives of the water companies and the National Grid were also singled out as 'greedy bosses'.

Mysteriously, some of the fattest cats were left out. These are David Montgomery, chief executive of the Mirror Group, whose salary, at the time of writing, is £581,000 a year and who in two years has cashed in shares worth £2.4 million; and Mirror Group managing director (and deputy chief executive) Kelvin MacKenzie, who is paid more than £400,000, together with the usual fortune in share options.

I phoned Montgomery about this and he seemed agitated. 'I've made this company profitable, efficient and got rid of dead wood,' he said. I asked him if he would be interviewed for a film I was making about the *Mirror* and Fleet Street. 'I couldn't possibly take part in something', he said, 'that might disturb the public's reverence for the *Daily Mirror*.'

In 1997, the *Daily Mirror* was 'relaunched' at a cost of £16 million, although how this money was spent remains difficult to discern. 'Daily' was dropped from the masthead and replaced by '*The Mirror ... The paper for the new millennium*'. The lavish use of colour suggests a 'free sheet' of the kind that invites rapid passage from the doormat to the bin. Pin-ups are now on the front page. Morgan's announcement that the *Mirror* would be different from the 'mysogynist' *Sun* needs further clarification. There is a column called 'Mad for It'. The rest is a dog's breakfast of the usual television gossip, 'love-cheat' stories and warmed-over indignation. The Maxwell *Mirror*, by comparison, looked staid. The appointment in 1998 of Kelvin MacKenzie as editor-in-chief is to put things right. He believes, wrote a friend not as a joke, 'that the tabloids have gone too downmarket'.[39]

The truth is that a few years from its centenary, the *Daily Mirror* gives the powerful impression that it is dying. Death throes may continue for several years, but all the terminal symptoms are evident. The circulation is below 2·5 million and falling. This is lower even than the lowest Maxwell-era figure. If the trend continues, the mass-market *Mirror* will be overtaken ignominiously by the middle-market *Daily Mail*.

The question arises: could a mass-circulation *Mirror*, restored to its former glory, succeed today? Probably not: too much has changed. But that is not to say that a bold, quality tabloid, with the same values as the old *Mirror* and a radical mind of its own, could not take the so-called middle ground by storm, challenging the supremacy of the *Daily Mail*. Such a paper, I believe, could prosper if it broke from the present sameness and cynicism that pervade the British press and spoke, once again, as a true agent of people.

Pete Hamill, one of America's last great nonconformist journalists, was until recently editor of the New York *Daily News*, a paper that has suffered a succession of British Murdoch-inspired editors and the ownership of Robert Maxwell. Hamill tried another way. There were no *Sun*-style sound bites, no pin-ups, 'no cheap emotion and no fraudulent stories', as he had promised. 'You have to trust the readers,' he said. 'You don't have to hit them over the head and say, "This is tragic, this is shocking" – they can make the moral point themselves. Sensationalism expresses a shock or a horror that is not felt. You don't have to treat people as if there is only one way to look at a story. You don't have to treat them like morons. It's about respect and real journalism.'[40]

VIII
THE MEDIA AGE

A CULTURAL CHERNOBYL

> There is only one thing in this world, and that is to keep
> acquiring money and more money, power and more
> power. All the rest is meaningless.
>
> *Napoleon Bonaparte*

EDDIE SPEARITT AND his son, Adam, went to a football
game in Sheffield on April 15, 1989. They had been caught in
traffic and had just enough time to find places in the allotted
Liverpool terraces at Hillsborough stadium. Adam was
fourteen and a devoted Liverpool supporter; and this was a
critical FA Cup semi-final against Nottingham Forest. 'We
were so excited,' said Eddie. 'It was only when the crowd in
the pen really began to build up that I got frightened.'

The ancient turnstiles became a bottle-neck as 5,000
Liverpool fans sought to gain entrance before the kick-off.
When the police eventually opened the main gates, instead
of directing the fans to the open terraces they sent them into
the crowded pen. Eddie and Adam were crushed in each
other's arms. Adam was one of ninety-six fans who died.
The subsequent inquiry by Lord Justice Taylor left no
doubt where the blame lay. 'The real cause of the Hillsborough disaster', he said in his report, 'was overcrowding
. . . the main reason for the disaster was the failure of police
control.'[1]

By the following Tuesday, the editor of the *Sun*, Kelvin
MacKenzie, had convinced himself that the tragedy had been
caused by Liverpool 'football hooligans'. When he sat down

to design his front page, he scribbled 'THE TRUTH' in huge letters. Beneath it he wrote three subsidiary headlines: 'Some fans picked pockets of victims' . . . 'Some fans urinated on the brave cops' . . . 'Some fans beat up PC giving kiss of life'. The story described how 'drunken Liverpool fans viciously attacked rescue workers as they tried to revive victims' and 'police officers, firemen and ambulance crew were punched, kicked and urinated upon'. A dead girl was abused and fans, said an unnamed policeman, 'were openly urinating on us and the bodies of the dead'. A Tory MP, whose sole source was the police, was quoted.[2]

None of it was true. There was no hooliganism. People were vomiting and behaving strangely because they had been crushed and traumatised. Others died because senior police officers failed to understand that the fans inside the pen were fighting for their lives, not trying to 'invade' the pitch. 'THE TRUTH' was the opposite. Like much in MacKenzie's *Sun*, it was clearly intended to pander to prejudice. Other journalists on the *Sun* appeared to know this instinctively. 'As MacKenzie's layout was seen by more and more people,' wrote Peter Chippendale and Chris Horrie in their history of the *Sun*, 'a collective shudder ran through the office [but] MacKenzie's dominance was so total there was nobody left in the organisation who could rein him in except Murdoch. [Everyone] seemed paralysed, "looking like rabbits in the headlights", as one hack described them. The error staring them in the face was too glaring . . . It obviously wasn't a silly mistake; nor was it a simple oversight. Nobody really had any comment on it – they just took one look and went away shaking their heads in wonder at the enormity of it . . . It was a "classic smear".'[3]

I met Eddie Spearitt and two other Hillsborough parents: Phil Raymond, whose son Philip, also aged fourteen, died, and Joan Traynor, who lost two sons, Christopher, twenty-six, and Kevin, sixteen. We sat with coffee and sandwiches in a large sunlit room in the Philharmonic pub, which overlooks Liverpool. Those who try to justify the substitution of a free press with a circus press that speaks to prejudice and 'gives people what they want', might listen to Eddie and Phil and Joan.

'As I lay in my hospital bed,' Eddie said, 'the hospital staff kept the *Sun* away from me. It's bad enough when you lose your fourteen-year-old son because you're treating him to a football match. Nothing can be worse than that. But since then I've had to defend him against all the rubbish printed by the *Sun* about everyone there being a hooligan and drinking. There was no hooliganism. During thirty-one days of Lord Justice Taylor's inquiry no blame was attributed because of alcohol. Adam never touched it in his life.'

Joan Traynor said that ITN had asked permission to film the funeral of her two sons. She refused and asked for her family's privacy to be respected. The *Sun* invaded the funeral, with photographers shooting from a wall. The picture of her sons' coffins on the front page of a paper that had lied about the circumstances of their death so deeply upset her that, eight years later, she has difficulty speaking about it. 'Is that what a newspaper is meant to do?' she asked.

Phil Hammond said, 'Like Eddie, the family kept the papers away from me. I've still got the papers in a white nylon bag in the loft. Take one of the *Sun*'s lies; they said fans were robbing watches and money from the dead laid out on the pitch. I'm the secretary of the Family Support Group and every family has been in touch with me about that accusation. All of them have accounted for the possessions of their loved ones. Nothing was stolen.

'[The *Sun* said] that fans were urinating on the bodies. We got all the clothes back; they hadn't been washed; none of them smelt of urine. But some mud sticks, doesn't it, and there is always someone willing to pass it on. The *Sun* hurt us, and hurt us badly. We've had to defend the name of our loved ones when all they did was go to a football match and never come back.'

In the days that followed the tragedy, Billy Butler, a popular Radio Merseyside disc jockey, became a voice for Liverpool's grief and anger. 'There were newsagents calling in,' he told me, 'assuring people they would not stock the *Sun*.

They were writing on their windows, "We do not have the *Sun* here". There was a public burning of the *Sun* in Kirkby. Caller after caller said they were boycotting the paper, and the boycott is still going on today. It's a marvellous way that ordinary people have to show their power, and this city used it.'

Unlike the homes of the Hillsborough families, Kelvin MacKenzie's suburban home was not 'staked out' by a press mob. His chauffeured Jaguar routinely collected him every morning and took him to the Murdoch fortress at Wapping, east London, where, surrounded by razor wire and guards, he caught the lift to his windowless office and did not leave until the Jaguar took him home again.

However, sales of the *Sun* on Merseyside were falling fast, down by almost 40 per cent, a loss that would cost News International an estimated £10 million a year. When the Press Council subsequently condemned the *Sun*'s lies, and the boycott intensified, Murdoch ordered MacKenzie to respond publicly. BBC Radio 4's *The World This Weekend* was chosen as his platform. The 'sarf London' accent that was integral to MacKenzie's persona as an 'ordinary punter' was now a contrite middle-class voice that fitted Radio 4.

'It was my decision', said MacKenzie, 'and my decision alone to do that front page in that way, and I made a rather serious error.'[4] In 1996 MacKenzie was back on Radio 4, this time in a very different mood. 'The *Sun* did not accuse anybody of anything,' he said aggressively. 'We were the vehicle for others . . .'[5]

The *Sun*'s treatment of the Hillsborough tragedy was typical not only of its record of distortion, but of its cruelty. The rich and famous have been able to defend themselves with expensive libel actions; the singer Elton John won damages, before appeal, of £1 million following a series of character assassinations. But most of the *Sun*'s victims are people like the Hillsborough parents, who have had to suffer without recourse. Turn the pages of back copies of the *Sun* and the pattern is clear. Here are a few examples taken at random.

A man who had undergone a heart transplant operation was vilified across several pages for having left his wife fifteen years earlier. This was published while his recovery was in the balance. People who perform exceptional public duty and are celebrated as popular heroes for rescuing somebody or tackling a criminal are ritually 'knocked down' when something in their private lives is revealed. They are then branded 'love cheats' and 'rats'.[6]

Minorities are a favourite target. A bishop was vilified for being gay, a lesbian for being 'unfit' to care for children.[7] Racial stereotypes are routinely promoted; an Asian in the 'soap' *EastEnders* was defamed as 'small, greasy and cheap'.[8] A *Sun* editorial about Australia's bicentenary celebrations, headlined, 'THE ABOS: BRUTAL AND TREACHEROUS', was described by the Press Council as 'inaccurate, unjustified and unacceptably racist'.[9] The disabled are mawkishly pitied; Simon Weston, the soldier who suffered terrible burns in the Falklands War, was the subject of a faked 'interview', which invited readers' revulsion for his disfigurement.[10]

Unlike journalists, politicians are said to be 'fair game' if they are found to be hypocrites. The Labour politician Tony Benn is not a hypocrite, but his principles are anathema to Murdoch. Benn was declared 'insane' in a malicious *Sun* story whose 'authority', an American psychologist, described the false quotations attributed to him as 'absurd'.[11] The Thatcher Government's campaign against 'loony' London councils, which probably helped turn the Labour Party in on itself and away from progressive policies, was based substantially on a long-running series of inventions and distortions in the *Sun*.

The person ultimately responsible for this is Rupert Murdoch. More than any proprietor since Lord Beaverbrook, Murdoch prides himself on his ability to choose the right people to edit his newspapers. He remains in close contact with all of them. Kelvin MacKenzie was his 'favourite editor'. Under MacKenzie, the profits from the *Sun* allowed Murdoch to build his television empire. Murdoch personally approved, or approved of, much of MacKenzie's unscrupulous behaviour, such as the 'GOTCHA' headline.

When journalists on *The Times*, sister paper to the *Sun*, expressed their concern about the damage done to the paper's reputation by the publication of the bogus Hitler Diaries, Murdoch replied, 'After all, we are in the entertainment business.'[12]

The ethos Murdoch wanted to build in his papers was demonstrated early in his career. In 1964, his Sydney tabloid, the *Daily Mirror*, published the diary of a fourteen-year-old schoolgirl under the headline, 'WE HAVE SCHOOLGIRL'S ORGY DIARY'. A thirteen-year-old boy, who was identified, was expelled from the same school. Shortly afterwards, he hanged himself from his mother's clothesline. The girl was subsequently examined by a doctor from the Child Welfare Department and found to be a virgin. The 'diary' was the product of a fertile adolescent imagination.

Richard Neville, one of the editors of *Oz*, went to see the boy's family and was moved by their grief, and angered by the circumstances of his death. 'It seemed', he wrote in his autobiography, '[that some] publishers could get away with murder . . . or almost.'[13] Neville later confronted Murdoch with the consequence of his newspaper's behaviour and was told, 'Everybody makes mistakes.'[14]

In the very few interviews he allows, Murdoch is often defensive about the product that has built his multi-billion-dollar empire. In 1967, on the eve of his departure for Fleet Street, he told ABC Television in Sydney, 'I'm not ashamed of any of my newspapers at all, and I'm rather sick of snobs who tell us they're bad papers, snobs who only read papers that no one else wants, who call themselves liberals or radicals and want to impose *their* taste on the community.'[15] In London, Murdoch encouraged this view of himself as an 'outsider' persecuted by 'snobs'. These 'snobs' would later include the House of Commons and the broadcasting regulatory authorities, which consistently denied him access to British television.

Murdoch himself came from an Anglocentric elite. He went to the most exclusive 'public school' in Australia, Geelong Grammar (Prince Charles was sent there), then to Oxford.

His parents' numerous establishment connections were available to him. His mother, Dame Elisabeth, a wealthy dowager, has long bestowed her patronage on a range of cultural interests. There can be little doubt that she would find a paper like the *Sun* abhorrent, as would Murdoch's wife, Anna, a devout Roman Catholic.

Murdoch's American biographer, Thomas Kiernan, is one of the few outside his circle who has known him personally. His book *Citizen Murdoch*, was written with the co-operation of Murdoch and his family and friends.[16] 'The contrast between the private Murdoch and the business Murdoch is quite astounding,' Kiernan told me. 'I used to play tennis with him quite often and for someone who publicly is so anti-elite, he is very elitist in his manner. In his office, he is like a field-marshal: demanding, abrupt, short-tempered. But in his private life he maintains very high standards and has rigid values, high values, and demands that his children and his friends keep to these. On the other hand, in the media, he destroys standards. This has long been true of his newspapers. The infection is insidious. Even the *New York Times* will quote the *Star*, a supermarket tabloid he started, and one of America's two main sleaze merchants. The *Star* may well have got the story from the *Sun*, and around the Murdoch circuit it will go, and before you know it, some awful fiction becomes received truth. Now it's television's turn and the danger is already there.

'In the United States he has a lot of direct influence in the programming of his Fox network, which relies on sleaze. He already has turned news into entertainment, with *paparazzi* with video cameras chasing celebrities down the street: that's basically a Murdoch invention in the US. Those who run TV news fear they're going to have to go downmarket even more than they have, just to keep up with Murdoch. It's as if everything he touches becomes desensitised, like the horror displayed every day on his front pages; after a while, we get used to it.

'Now set that against his private life where the influence of his wife, Anna, is very important. When I was close to both of them, she was very critical of what he was doing. When he turned the *New York Post* into a version of the *Sun*, he did so without Page Three Girls, because his wife put her foot down and told him she didn't want their three young children walking past news-stands and seeing the topless girls on their dad's paper. She didn't want them to suffer at school or the family to have social disapprobation as they established themselves in New York.'

Reiner Luyken, a prize-winning journalist on the respected German newspaper *Die Zeit*, has reported from Britain for almost twenty years. He is the author of a series of perceptive articles about Murdoch's impact in Britain, entitled 'A Cultural Chernobyl'. 'The most striking effect of Murdoch is self-censorship,' he wrote. 'Self-censorship is now so commonplace in the British media, that journalists admit to it without blushing.'

We met outside the gates of Murdoch's headquarters at Wapping, which Luyken called 'a journalistic penitentiary' and a 'new brave new world'. 'If you look closely at this place,' he said, 'if you look at the electronic bars, the wire on the perimeter, the patrolling guards, you must ask yourself, "How can information and ideas flow freely in such a place?" Wapping is a factory for making money, yet it has become a kind of media model. Whether you read the *Daily Mirror* or the *Telegraph* or turn on the BBC, you get the feeling that the purpose of the enterprise of journalism has been turned on its head and the new ethic is that journalism is a commodity, purely to generate money. This is the Murdoch effect. Wapping is a cultural Chernobyl, spewing its poison across the whole journalistic landscape.'

The experience of Murdoch's 'new brave new world' leaves many of the journalists on his papers with an abiding ambivalence about him. Some will insist they were never told what to do, that there was never a 'line' – when the truth is that it was never necessary to tell them: they *knew* and accepted what was required of them.

Roy Greenslade, a critic of Murdoch, was Kelvin MacKenzie's number two on the *Sun*. 'As a young man,' wrote

Peter Chippendale and Chris Horrie, '[Greenslade] had embraced revolutionary Maoism. In his early days he had been a militant in the National Union of Journalists Chapel . . . But he had watered down his politics to the point where he could take a senior job on the avowedly Thatcherite *Sun* with few qualms.'[17]

Greenslade was a witness to many of MacKenzie's 'triumphs', such as his jingoistic fabrication of much of the Falklands War coverage. When MacKenzie called on his staff to cross the picket line representing the 5,900 printers, secretaries, librarians and cleaners sacked by Murdoch in 1986, Greenslade crossed it.

In 1995, no longer employed by Murdoch, Greenslade mounted a devastating attack on the ethos of Wapping, writing one of the most cogent explanations for the success of the *Sun*:

> Murdoch had seized the time [he wrote], the old values of a discredited Establishment were crumbling. An energetic working class had cast off deference as an aberration of generations past. Television was god . . . What was once said only in the pub or the intimacy of your bedroom would be published in your soaraway *Sun* [which] latched on to the permissiveness of the age.
>
> Then, as the years passed, it perverted that ethos of liberalism for its own ends. It cultivated sex, yet decried sexual licence in its leading articles. It lured readers to play bingo for huge prizes while lecturing them on the vice of a something-for-nothing society. It encouraged people to sell their sexual secrets while holding them up to ridicule. It cultivated the shallow world of celebrity as a cynical circulation device. It pushed back the boundaries of taste and decency while wringing its hands at the decline of standards. It employed the language of the lager lout while lambasting the growth of youth culture. Its politics were opportunistic, conjoining the radical and the reactionary to extol the virtues of Margaret Thatcher, the supreme mistress of cultural philistinism.

Greenslade called this 'the degradation of the newspaper form [in which] the old notion of a public service press was replaced by newspapers as machines of private profit'. He described the scramble among broadsheets as well as tabloids, to ape the 'sales-winning formula . . . accommodating the cult of celebrity, games and television promotions [in which] sleaze is a national pastime, tackiness is stylish, the lowest common denominator is the bottom line. And the bottom line is all that counts . . .'[18]

Greenslade told me his article (in the *Literary Review*) was 'a recognition that much of what I took part in was wrong'. 'You're fired up by taking part in the technical process of producing a newspaper,' he said. 'It's like the way [Nazi] Germany was . . . when you're taking part in the technical process, you are blinded in many ways to what you're actually doing. You're so worried about the next story, the next feature, filling that page and so on, that the overall thing eludes you . . . It isn't as bad as Germany was, but I do think that you divide labour in the way they did and you do your own little bit . . .'

Greenslade met Murdoch on several occasions. 'He's not the Dirty Digger figure he's painted,' he said. 'He's an educated person. I found him to be a totally rational person, not just in financial terms but in the sort of questions he asked: "Will this sell? Should we give them more sports? Have we any sex surveys?" He asked questions in such a way that you didn't actually think of the connotations . . . but when it got to politics, *well* . . .

'There was a dinner in London around the time the Berlin Wall came down, and Murdoch was utterly defiant, saying we in the West must keep a grip on the nuclear weaponry. You had right-wing executives of the *Sunday Times* arguing that there ought to be some kind of peace dividend, and he was saying, "No, no" and all the time quoting someone he called his "political adviser . . ." When he was asked who this was, he replied, "Richard Nixon . . ." '

In David Hare's play about the press, *Pravda*, the Murdoch figure, Lambert Le Roux, comments, 'Upmarket, down-market, it's all the same stuff!' In the play's final line, Le Roux is clearly referring to Wapping when he says, 'Welcome to the foundry of lies.' One of Murdoch's achievements has been to instil the same values throughout most of his organisation, in Britain and across the world, especially in his tabloid and broadsheet newspapers which are produced side by side at Wapping.

Murdoch acquired *The Times* and the *Sunday Times* in 1981 after long and agonised negotiations during which he agreed to the appointment of 'independent directors' on the board of Times Newspapers. He also gave 'personal guarantees' that he would not interfere in the editorial content of either paper. The whole performance lacked only the arrival of the March Hare.

While dispensing these 'guarantees' to politicians and the Great and the Good, Murdoch told Thomas Kiernan, 'One thing you must understand, Tom. You tell these bloody politicians whatever they want to hear, and once the deal is done you don't worry about it. They're not going to chase after you later if they suddenly decide what you said was not what they wanted to hear. Otherwise they're made to look bad, and they can't abide that. So they just stick their heads up their asses and wait for the blow to pass.'[19]

And so it came to pass. John Biffen, Secretary of State for Trade and Industry in the Thatcher Government, decided not to refer Murdoch's bid to the Monopolies and Mergers Commission, despite the commission's rule that a company owning a newspaper with a circulation of more than half a million had to be thoroughly investigated before it could acquire another paper. An exception could be made only if it looked like the newspaper up for sale might otherwise close down. Certainly *The Times* was not financially secure, but the *Sunday Times* was profitable and had the prospect of making a lot of money. However, Biffen accepted highly contentious figures that 'proved' the *Sunday Times* was a loss-maker. His decision was made all the more remarkable by the fortune the paper has since delivered unerringly to Murdoch.[20]

Just as this was about to be contested in court, Murdoch offered further 'guarantees' of editorial independence, this time to the journalists. He accompanied this with a 'warning' that the present owners would close the papers unless he bought them. 'At one stage during the battle for Times Newspapers,' wrote Christopher Hird and his co-authors in *Murdoch: The Great Escape*, 'a member of the staff consortium trying to buy the *Sunday Times* rang an old friend working as an adviser to Thatcher at 10 Downing Street. Playing on the government's apparent commitment to competition, he urged a halt to the Murdoch takeover. He was told to stop wasting his time. "You don't realise, she likes the guy." '

When the takeover came to be discussed by a Cabinet committee, Thatcher chaired the meeting. Murdoch was, in effect, being rewarded for his papers' 'years of loyal support'. The result, as Michael Leapman wrote, 'was a no-contest takeover [with] all the external appearances of an establishment "fix" of the kind Murdoch affects to despise.'[21] His mother, Dame Elisabeth, told the BBC, 'Britain will perhaps learn to know that he's a pretty good chap.'[22]

Unlike the unpretentious *Sun*, the *Sunday Times* from time to time carries serious journalism, even genuine scoops, although these are sometimes difficult to discern from journalism that *appears* serious. Since Murdoch acquired it, the *Sunday Times* has borne much of the burden of the promotion of his interests and ambitions. In the 1980s, the paper consistently attacked the BBC and ITV, which were seen as obstacles to Murdoch's frustrated television plans in Britain. He made the editor, Andrew Neil, head of his satellite television company, Sky. Described as 'cross-fertilising' by a Murdoch executive, this has long been a feature of the Murdoch press all over the world.

In Neil's 470-page book, *Full Disclosure*, arguably one of the most sustained boasts in autobiographical history, the author devotes fewer than thirty words to the *Sunday Times*'s most notorious, scurrilous and destructive smear campaign – against the journalists and broadcasters who made the 1988 current affairs programme, *Death on the Rock*, for Thames Television.

This investigation was highly significant because it lifted a veil on the British secret state and revealed its ruthlessness under Thatcher. In describing how an SAS team had gone to Gilbraltar and murdered four unarmed members of the IRA, the message was clear: the British Government was willing to use death squads abroad in its pursuit of the war in Ireland. *Death on the Rock* also posed a threat to the political and media consensus on the war in the north of Ireland, and Margaret Thatcher did not forgive Thames Television for its transgression. Having frequently attacked the ITV 'monopoly' in commercial television, her echoes of Murdoch were vociferously covered in the *Sunday Times*. When the government rounded on Thames for what it called the 'distortions' of *Death on the Rock*, the *Sunday Times* appeared only too willing to give vast amounts of space to a series of wholly spurious, politically motivated charges.

An eye-witness to the murders, Carmen Proetta, who appeared in the programme, described how she saw two unarmed people shot at close range and offering no resistance. They had their hands in the air, either in an act of surrender or in reaction to the shootings. She heard no warning. The Murdoch press, in company with most of Fleet Street, subjected her to a torrent of lies and personal abuse. She was falsely accused of being involved in vice and drugs and of being 'anti-British'. The *Sun* described her as 'The Tart of Gib'. The *Sunday Times* coverage was different in one respect only: there was more of it.

Of over £300,000 in libel damages eventually paid to Carmen Proetta, more than half was paid by the *Sunday Times* in an out-of-court settlement. According to the producer of *Death on the Rock*, Roger Bolton, one of the reasons Andrew Neil decided to settle was that 'on the first day in court a former journalist for the *Sunday Times* was ready to give evidence about the way her copy, sent from Gibraltar, was misrepresented by Mr Neil's editors'.[23] In a memorandum sent to the features editor Robin Morgan, the reporter, Rosie Waterhouse, accused her own paper of being 'wide open to accusations that we had set out to prove one point of view and misrepresented and misquoted interviews to fit – the very accusations we were levelling at Thames'. She later resigned.[24]

An inquiry conducted by a former Tory minister, Lord Windlesham, vindicated the programme's accuracy and integrity. The Sunday Times's branch of the National Union of Journalists called for an inquiry into the paper's role in the affair, specifically Andrew Neil's. There was none. Under the new system of allocating ITV franchises instituted by Thatcher, Thames, one of the most innovative of the major companies, lost its licence to broadcast.

'From the start,' wrote Hugo Young, political editor of the Sunday Times when Murdoch took it over, 'the omens were bad. During their first visits to the building, Murdoch and his associates made clear their hostility to Sunday Times journalism and their contempt for those who practised it. The journalists collectively were stigmatised as lead-swinging, expense-padding, layabout Trotskyites. Each of these epithets was uttered in my hearing by senior Murdoch executives. The political label was especially emphatic, wholly removed though it was from reality. Reports from El Salvador which allowed for any possibility that US foreign policy was in error were clearly potent evidence that the Commies had the Sunday Times in their grip.'[25]

Once acclaimed for its journalistic and political independence, the Sunday Times was quick to reflect its master's world view. The largest rally ever staged by the Campaign for Nuclear Disarmament, which drew as many as half a million people, was dismissed beneath the headline, 'SUNSET FOR CND'. Coverage of the 1984–5 coal strike was crudely slanted to depict the miners as violent, intransigent and at odds with their leaders, an 'enemy within': the essential elements of the government's propaganda.

To the Sunday Times, wrote Hugo Young, 'the strike was a Marxist plot'. The paper's international coverage was reduced to that of 'a mid-Atlantic cheerleader'.[26] A published interview with Ronald Reagan bore striking similarity to a Sun 'exclusive': that is, it never took place. Salman Rushdie, in hiding and threatened with assassination by an Iranian fatwa, was subjected to a front-page, personalised, one-sided, Sun-style attack by his estranged wife.

Michael Foot, the former leader of the Labour Party, was accused, across the front page, of being a 'KGB spy', an 'exclusive' which was followed by the announcement that Foot was to be paid 'substantial damages': a familiar post-script to 'investigations' that had once been the paper's pride. No corner of the *Sunday Times* has escaped contamination. In a section entitled 'Culture', a television reviewer, Adrian Gill, unleashed a stream of gratuitous abuse about a documentary I had made on the Murdoch effect on Fleet Street and the *Daily Mirror* in particular. As part of his 'review', Murdoch's man viciously attacked the retired *Daily Mirror* writer and critic Donald Zec, whom he accused of breaking into Marilyn Monroe's home in the 1950s. Soon afterwards, Gill's page was dominated by the standard *Sunday Times* apology and retraction.[27]

In the 'Style' section there was a regular feature, 'Relationship of the Week', in which Chrissy Iley, photo-graphed in a shiny black coat, sneered and speculated about a chosen couple, quoting hearsay about them. Mysteriously, it disappeared one Sunday and never came back. In the same week, Murdoch was named 'Humanitarian of the Year' by the United Jewish Appeal Foundation in New York. His award was presented to him by Henry Kissinger. When Kissinger was awarded the Nobel Peace Prize for his contri-bution to 'peace' in Vietnam, the great American satirist Tom Lehrer said he was retiring because, clearly, satire was now obsolete. The 'Humanitarian of the Year' reaffirmed this.[28]

Murdoch's move to the 'new brave new world' at Wapping took place on January 24, 1986. Virtually overnight, more than 5,000 employees were abandoned. The print unions, Kelvin MacKenzie told *Sun* journalists, 'haven't got us by the balls any more'.[29]

In exploiting resentment of the unions' power and abuses, such as the 'wildcat' stoppages that had lost millions of newspapers, and the 'Spanish practices' that allowed some people to pick up two pay packets, Murdoch was able to persuade most of his journalists to go to Wapping. For many, this came as a welcome justification; for while there was truth in many of the stories about the unions, it was also true that newspaper managements operated their own corruption – on perks alone – and it suited them to look the other way.

In my experience, the majority of compositors, linotype operators, machine-room workers and others were honest people who worked hard in antiquated, filthy and often dangerous conditions, especially in the old *Sun* and *News of the World* headquarters in Bouverie Street. They were paid well compared with other workers; and in scandalously low-paid Britain that fact was enough to make them enemies.

In 1985, Brenda Dean was appointed General-Secretary of SOGAT, representing the industry's clerical and ancillary workers. 'It's time the myths surrounding Wapping were swept away,' she told me. 'The first thing Murdoch made clear to me was that if I could deliver an agreement on new levels of manning, he could do business with the unions. Of course there was some resistance to new technology. But this came from people who had worked in the industry all their lives and were not permanent employees. Quite a few had no pension provision. If they lost their jobs they wouldn't get other employment. They wanted to know what was in it for them. But there is a world of difference between that view and saying we couldn't conclude a deal. We could. The great majority wanted agreement. There is no doubt about that.'

The unions had already successfully negotiated a comprehensive agreement with the new chief executive of the *Daily Mirror*, Clive Thornton. Staffing would be reduced, new technology introduced and no strike action would be taken for three years. In seeking a similar deal with Murdoch, the unions were told that News International planned to produce a new paper, the *London Post*, at Wapping. The unions by and large welcomed this and put forward their proposals for an 'all-in new technology deal'.

On January 2, 1986, Tony Britton, the assistant general manager of News Group Newspapers Limited, publishers of the *Sun* and the *News of the World*, wrote to Tony Isaacs, the senior machine-room union official, 'The company has agreed [to the union's proposals] . . . and has given assurances that no regular employee need make himself available for voluntary redundancy.' To which Isaacs replied, 'It is with pleasure that I can advise you that my Chapel [has] accepted Management's proposals that embrace the [Wapping] plant.'[30]

Unknown to Dean, Isaacs or any other union official, Murdoch had been secretly moving non-union staff into Wapping for months and was discussing with his senior executives how they could sack the thousands who had been given 'assurances' that their jobs were secure. In a letter to News International managing director Bruce Mathews, Geoffrey Richards, the senior solicitor advising Murdoch, proposed precisely how they might 'dispense with the workforces'. 'The cheapest way', he wrote, 'would be to dismiss employees while participating in a strike . . . The idea is to catch as many employees in the net as possible and it seems to me this will be done best if the dismissals take place at the weekend . . .'[31]

What he was saying was that, under Thatcher's new anti-trade union laws, workers who struck during 'negotiations' could be sacked instantly and would lose their redundancy entitlements: a huge saving to the company. There was no longer any mention of the *London Post*, which began to sound more and more mythical, a ploy for the 'real game', as Murdoch insiders called the trap being set.

'We were tricked,' said Brenda Dean. 'We had agreements that were at the point of being signed and the management suddenly were holding off signing them. We had even agreed to a third redundancies in some areas.' In fact, Dean had conceded more than any Fleet Street General-Secretary previously had dared to. Tony Dubbins, of the National Graphical Association, which represented typesetters, had gone even further by agreeing the principle of direct computerised typesetting by journalists at Wapping, although it effectively undermined the very existence of his union.

Only signatures were needed. The stalling continued as Murdoch's men waited for the signal to implement 'Project 800', a top-secret plan described by Murdoch at a meeting of his executives in New York as 'our dash for freedom'.[32] When the unions finally realised they had been tricked and their agreements were worthless, they called a ballot and went on strike. 'We had given him an olive branch', said Dubbins, 'and he'd broken it in two and beat us around the head with it.'[33]

As 'negotiations' technically were still in progress, the workforce could be dismissed without compensation. Thus, almost 5,500 people were sacked, many of them lifelong employees. 'I feel deeply and personally bitter', said Dean, 'on behalf of the thousands of our people who stood on the picket line at Wapping for more than a year and have since been forgotten. The dimension of the unseen human tragedy was shocking. We had people who came with their families, their children; they wanted to take part in a peaceful demonstration. They wanted to say to Murdoch, "You've not only done this to me, you've done it to my wife and kids." But the Metropolitan Police clearly had other instructions. They were there to protect the newspapers, to see that Murdoch got the *Sun* out, and the rest of his publications. We called them "paper boys", and that was exactly what they were.

'To achieve this, they acted in a most brutal way – as the subsequent inquiries confirmed. I saw many people deliberately beaten up by the so-called riot police. The journalists who came along were shocked by what they saw. The police went for decent, straightforward trade unionists as if it was a civil war situation. One of our people was killed by one of Murdoch's lorries, and the lorry didn't even bother to stop. There were several nervous breakdowns. Marriages broke up. Strong men I knew, and I don't mean physically strong, but men with leadership, turned bitter. It broke them. People entitled to unemployment benefit didn't receive it. I'm not only talking just about the relatively well paid, but cleaners, canteen workers, who outnumbered the printers four to one . . . It was as if the British state had joined forces with Murdoch against us . . .'

In the days and weeks that followed the 'dash for freedom', the television news showed surreal images of journalists alighting from Murdoch company buses. They queued to show the security guards their new identification cards, which described them ignominiously as 'consultants'. They passed through ten-foot electronically operated steel gates, set in spiked walls topped with coils of barbed razor wire. Several would try to run inside, squinting into searchlights that covered the perimeter of their new workplace. These were journalists on publications which, between them, commanded the greatest newspaper readership in the English language. They had been ordered to go to Wapping or be sacked. They were not consulted; and all their agreements with the management were dishonoured.

'I used to think how intimidated they looked,' said Dean. 'One always regarded the journalists as the thinking people; and if they'd thought for half a moment, they actually had a power that weekend they'd never had before. Without them, those newspapers would not have come out. Journalists lost a lot of their pride then, and their self-confidence. They came and went, with many having to lie face down on the floor of the coaches with the blinds drawn. It was not an image that sat comfortably with journalists when you read that there were others who risked their lives to get the story and tell the truth.'

Thirty-eight journalists refused to go to Wapping. Among the handful from the *Sun* was Eric Butler, a crusty sports sub-editor whose nickname was 'Scoop'. After forty-two years in Fleet Street, he was less than three years from retirement. 'I knew it meant the end of my career,' he said, 'but there was no alternative for me. What Murdoch did was industrial gangsterism; the people he sacked had given him loyal service and helped him make a lot of money. He offered the journalists £2,000 to cross the picket line. For that they could keep their job, but not their self-respect.

'Ellen, my wife, took a call one night and it was one of my mates, who said, "Eric will change his mind, won't he?" and she said, "No he won't. More to the point, I don't want him to change his mind." I thought it was strange so many journalists were suddenly saying they had no time for the printers. Yes, we had our disagreements, but it was on both sides; they were blokes making a living just like us. There were a lot of good people among them. We had a great office football team: the journalists and the printers together. Then out of the blue my mates were saying they hated the printers. Did they? Or were they trying to excuse what they were doing?

'I stood on that picket line for a year, in freezing cold a lot of the time, and I watched my old mates go in and out in the coaches, and I never saw one of them again. And yet later on so many of them were disillusioned, or were kicked out by Murdoch. They'd served their purpose. It must have been sad for them.'

David Banks was assistant editor of the *Sun* at the time of Wapping. 'We lived on adrenaline', he said, 'and on defiance . . . the defiance of the moment and the fact that the mob were at the gates, that it was us or them.'

I asked him if he had lain on the floor of the coaches that took the scab journalists through the picket line.

'Oh, I did, I did . . .' he replied. 'It wasn't pleasant. You knew the bottles and the bricks coming against the side of the coach were meant for you; and the fact that the driver then had to race through miles of darkened docklands, just to escape the anger. All of that had its effect . . . After a while it dawned on me that I wasn't part of a cavalcade of knights on white horses: that there was a serious anti-social side to what I was doing. In the end, I decided on balance that, despite the fact that little people were being hurt, it was all worth while to save a great industry.'

Murdoch, who slept on a campbed at Wapping for almost two weeks, tried to engender the spirit of a 'crusade' against the infidels at the gates. Andrew Neil contributed to this by waving his champagne glass at the pickets, although in a television interview he compared the appearance of his new offices to that of 'a concentration camp'.

Sun journalists at first enjoyed a view of the Thames. This was soon closed down, apparently for security reasons, then there was no view at all. This hermetically sealed atmosphere contributed to what John Murray, Murdoch's 'personal counsellor', described as a 'certain mental uncertainty among the more sensitive members of the staff'.

Murray, an Australian and confidant of Murdoch, was flown to London to 'help with the transition'. I asked him about Murdoch's reputation for ruthlessness. 'Look,' he said, 'at that high level business principles can come across as ruthlessness. But let me give you another picture of the man. There was one day when a group of people were retiring – they hadn't been sacked, I hasten to add – and I asked Rupert to come down and say a few words to them. "Certainly, John," was his immediate reply. Well, he thanked them for their work and their contribution and when he was finished, one of the union leaders put his hand up and said, "Mr Murdoch, we know about your great kindness in looking after your chauffeur, who died recently, and I want to express on behalf of the unions, our appreciation for that." As he and I left the room, he said, "John, I've got a feeling they were surprised: that they don't really think I'm a kind man." '

In 1989, Murdoch disclosed that he was a born-again Christian. He said he foresaw a major religious revival in Britain in which his papers would play their part by maintaining 'high moral values'.[34] A few months earlier the *Sun* had devastated the lives of the Hillsborough families.

'I'm very much aware of Rupert's Christian values,' said John Murray. 'Actually the move to Wapping was like the crossing through the Red Sea, and Rupert was like our biblical leader . . . it was the passage from the old Fleet Street, from Egypt through to the formation of a new people. It was a bit like the Holocaust. I mean, the state of Israel was born out of the Red Sea and the passage of the Holocaust . . . and so the whole newspaper world has been revolutionised here in the UK since that crossing. Even today I don't think journalists want to hark back to the flesh pots, if you like, of Egypt . . . to the old Fleet Street. They know that's over and now we've got the promise of the modern world.'[35]

What Murdoch got from Wapping was money. He saved millions of pounds in the redundancy payments the new Thatcher laws ensured he did not have to pay the people he sacked. His wages bill was instantly cut by £45 million. Using cheap, non-union labour – many of them unemployed and unskilled teenagers bussed secretly to Wapping from Southampton – he increased his profits from £39.1 million in 1985, the year before the move, to £98.3 million two years later and £675 million in 1990.

This gave him the money to pay the interest on loans he had borrowed in March 1985. Had his 'dash for freedom' failed, it is highly unlikely he would have been able to pay these debts. He had gambled hugely. With borrowed money he had bought six Metromedia television stations in the United States. These formed the basis of a new network, Fox, with which he planned to challenge the primacy of the great American TV networks.

With his 'Wapping revolution' won, he folded his campbed and took Concorde to Washington to collect his American citizenship, which he needed to own both newspapers and television stations. This had been 'fast-tracked' by the Reagan administration, the President having expressed his 'deepest appreciation' to Murdoch for his newspapers' support.[36] 'It is almost impossible to underestimate the importance of Wapping in the history of the Murdoch business,' said Christopher Hird, one of the authors of *Murdoch: The Great Escape*. 'If Murdoch hadn't moved to Wapping, he probably would have gone bust. It's as simple as that.'[37]

Murdoch boasted that his 'revolution' would bring what he called 'a new dawn of freedom' to the British press, a flowering of independent newspapers. The opposite happened. Of four national newspapers launched in the mid-1980s, *Today*, the *Correspondent*, *News on Sunday* and the *Independent*, only the *Independent* barely survives, its independence circumscribed by its majority shareholder, the Mirror Group. There is now less diversity and less independence in the British press than ever before, while Murdoch's power has never been greater.

At the time of Wapping, Alf Parish was the senior London official of the printing union SLADE, which has since merged with the NGA. He negotiated directly with Murdoch. 'I smile at the irony,' he told me. 'Many of the corporate people who supported Murdoch are now the recipients of his aggressiveness, based on the tremendous financial power he acquired as a direct result of Wapping. Breaking the unions was just the first step. He's now wielding a big stick in a price-cutting war against his old allies. Think of the provincial newspaper owners who supported him and how he shows his gratitude. Every time he cuts the price of one of his national newspapers, so the circulation of the major provincial papers is affected.'

Today, Rupert Murdoch controls 34 per cent of the national daily press and 37 per cent of the Sunday market. In cutting the cover price of his newspapers, and absorbing the losses in his global empire, he controls effectively a rigged market, in which those rivals without his sources of cash are likely to fail.

'It is clear to me', Andrew Marr, the then editor of the *Independent*, told me, 'that Murdoch is engaged in a process of trying to create a *de facto* newspaper monopoly in Britain and that the politicians are well aware of it and are not prepared to do anything about it. Murdoch told Sir David English that he believed there would be three surviving newspapers – the *Daily Mail*, *The Times* and the *Sun*, and that would be it. The price war is his way, in part, of achieving that. It was designed to destroy the *Independent* and to cripple the Hollinger Group that owns the *Telegraph*, and after that he'll go after the rest. The reason he can do it is that he has enormous profits pouring in from satellite TV. Everyone I know in politics and the media understands this. Everyone knows the dangers . . . and I have no faith in the politicians doing anything about it.'[38]

If Murdoch's prediction is correct, two of the three remaining national newspapers will be owned by him. It is a prospect diligently attended by establishment silence. In the 'debate' about Europe in Parliament and the media, it is significant that there has been none about the press. Yet the structure of much of the European press offers alternatives.

In France, anti-trust media laws prohibit any individual or group from owning newspapers with more than 30 per cent of combined national and regional sales. In Germany, a cartel office sees that minority shareholders in newspapers have rights to veto the decision of a block majority. In Sweden, a Press Support Board, independent of government, ensures the health of a range of newspapers. In none of these countries does the existence of specific legislation restrict the freedom of the press.

The source of this information is a Labour Party discussion document, *Freeing the Press*, published in 1988. It called for a right of reply and legal aid on libel cases. It proposed a Right to Distribution, similar to that in France which allows small imprints to reach the bookstalls – in contrast to Britain, where small-circulation papers like *Tribune* have been excluded. Most important, it recommended the establishment of a Media Enterprise Board similar to the Swedish Press Subsidies Board, which provides 'seed' funds for new newspapers committed to protecting editorial independence. (Of 165 newspapers in Sweden, 70 receive direct subsidy from the board.)

The inclusion of such proposals on a legislative agenda of the Blair Government is inconceivable. Tony Blair's New Labour is in many respects a creation of the Murdoch press and the rest of the right-wing media. The dedication of the Blair leadership to appeasing the Labour Party's traditional enemies has been unprecedented. From the day he became leader, Blair, ghosted by his press secretary, Alistair Campbell, has written frequently for the *Sun* and the *News of the World*. A common strand in these articles has been Blair's respect for Thatcher's legacy and his determination, in effect, to carry on her work.

Shortly after the death of his predecessor, John Smith, Blair and his wife Cherie were invited to dinner by Murdoch and his wife Anna. Two dinners followed. Then, in July 1995, the Blairs flew to Australia, their first-class fares paid for by Murdoch. Blair was the principal speaker at a News Corporation conference at the Hayman Island resort, which is owned by Murdoch.

From the blue Newscorp lectern Blair spoke about 'the

need for a new moral purpose in politics' that would meet the 'moral challenge' facing the British people. Murdoch nodded his approval; the two men, after all, are Christians. This 'moral challenge', Blair went on, 'is every bit as pressing as the economic challenge – the two are linked.' He named two politicians who had met the 'economic challenge'. They were Ronald Reagan and Margaret Thatcher, who had put 'a greater emphasis on enterprise' and had rewarded 'success'. Murdoch clapped enthusiastically. After all, Reagan and Thatcher had been his favourites, and he had helped to elect them.

Blair then got to the point. This 'economic challenge', he said, also applied to the owners of the press, whose 'enterprise' was challenged by government regulations. He was referring to the 'cross-ownership' rules that prevent very powerful individuals and interests from controlling both newspapers and television companies. 'There is an obvious requirement', he said, 'to keep the system of regulation [of the media] under constant review. The revolution taking place makes much of it obsolete. This is the mass multi-media society [and] we have real concerns about the role of the new media regulator, which is to be given immense power under the [then Tory Government's] proposals.'

Murdoch greeted his guest as he stepped down, shaking his hand warmly. The next day the *Sun* commented, 'Mr Blair has vision, he has purpose and he speaks our language on morality and family life.'[39]

Long before its election, the Labour leadership exchanged roles with the Tories as the supporter of media monopolies. A frequent sideshow in the House of Commons was provided by a bemused Tory minister responsible for the media, whose plea for a modest threshold of cross-ownership was routinely opposed by Labour. 'The whole point', wrote Labour's broadcasting spokesman, Dr Lewis Moonie, in Murdoch's *Sunday Times*, 'is to ensure the creation of bigger companies.' Moonie told me he regarded Murdoch as a 'visionary'.[40]

'The extent of the ties that developed between New Labour and News Corp has never been fully revealed,' wrote Andrew

Neil in his autobiography. 'In addition to regular meetings between the two top men, a network of contacts has been established between senior company executives and Labour front benchers. Even the Murdoch family was brought into the act. Lachlan, the son Murdoch has been grooming as an heir apparent, met Blair and got on well with him, as [did] his father. Elisabeth, the daughter Murdoch thinks Lachlan should have to compete with for the succession, was also introduced to senior Labour figures ... She took to calling Peter Mandelson "my dear friend". More serious contacts were established in regular meetings between Rupert's top managers and advisers and Blair's men ... Blair in power has so far exceeded Rupert's expectations.'[41]

'What'll it be,' an Australian politician was once famously asked, 'a headline a day or a bucket of shit a day?' When Tony Blair landed at Sydney on his way to meet Murdoch on Hayman Island, he was met by Paul Keating, then Labor Prime Minister, who owed much of his rise to power to Murdoch. Keating coached Blair on what Murdoch liked to hear: 'deregulation' was his favourite hymn.

The state of the Australian media provides a model for and a glimpse of the future in Britain. Of twelve daily newspapers in the various capital cities, Murdoch controls seven. Of ten Sunday papers, Murdoch has seven. In Adelaide, Murdoch has a complete monopoly. He owns the daily, Sunday and local papers and all the printing presses. In Brisbane he controls all but some suburban papers. In other words, of the daily papers published in the capital cities, where the great majority of the population lives, two of every three copies sold are Murdoch papers. Three of every four Sunday papers sold are Murdoch's.

The only comparable media baron is Kerry Packer, who owns most of the magazines Australians read and the dominant television network among the three commercials. Until December 1996, the Canadian Conrad Black, in controlling the Fairfax Group, controlled most of the rest of the city press. With his departure from the Australian scene, the

Howard Government tried at first to steer the Fairfax papers into the eager arms of Packer, then backed away after a backbenchers' revolt. At the same time Murdoch was seeking control of a commercial television channel by way of compensation. Pay TV is still in its infancy, but Murdoch and Packer look set to dominate it.

This is largely due to the Labor Governments of Bob Hawke and Paul Keating, whose Thatcherite policies offered inspiration to 'new' Labour in Britain. As Treasurer, then Prime Minister, Keating was the architect of media deregulation. In November 1986, Keating announced legislation to 'restructure' commercial television. Under the old regulations no one could own more than two television stations. Now the government proposed that one owner could command an 'audience reach' of 75 per cent of the population. This would mean that the nation's fifty television stations, which had been spread among 25 owners, would be taken over by a handful of conglomerates, notably those with numerous and often conflicting commercial interests. Not since the dawn of the television age had there been such a contraction of ownership.

At the same time, with Wapping out of the way and a foothold gained in American television, Rupert Murdoch was turning his attention to his native land. He had long wanted to fulfil a 'dream' and buy the country's biggest newspaper group, the Herald and Weekly Times, which would allow him to dominate the press. However, Murdoch faced the twin obstacles of the Foreign Takeovers Act and the Australian constitution. Having recently renounced his Australian citizenship in order to further his American ambitions, he faced the obstacle of a law that restricted foreign ownership of the press. Moreover, Section 51 of the constitution gives Parliament the authority to prevent concentrated ownership of any section of Australia's small and often fragile economy. Clearly, as the Australian saying goes, he needed a 'mate'.

On November 13, 1986, three weeks before he flew to Melbourne to make his bid for the Herald and Weekly Times, Murdoch's *Australian* newspaper unexpectedly attacked the

471

conservative opposition to Hawke's Labor Government. Shortly before that editorial appeared, Murdoch met Paul Keating in the United States, where they discussed the problems of media ownership. On their return to Australia, they met again, this time with Bob Hawke, the Prime Minister, present. Within days, Murdoch's senior executives were left in no doubt that his papers now supported the Labor Government.[42]

Murdoch exuded a new public confidence. When it was pointed out to him at a press conference that the chairman of the Trade Practices Commission, a regulatory body, had said that his takeover of the Herald and Weekly Times might contravene the law, he said, 'That is not an insurmountable problem.' Neither was the Foreign Takeovers Act nor the constitutional safeguard a 'problem' any more.

The only remaining 'problem' was a law that prevented Murdoch from owning television and radio stations which were part of the Herald and Weekly Times empire. Murdoch dealt with this by vanishing. His Australian company, News Limited, announced his disappearance in the following press release:

1 Although Mr Murdoch was formerly a director of News Ltd, he is no longer a director and he holds no office in the company.

2 Mr Murdoch has no authority to speak on behalf of or to bind News Ltd . . .

The ruse beckoned endless court action, so Murdoch tried another. Now in *de facto* control of the Herald and Weekly Times, he arranged the sale of its television and radio interests *before* he took it over officially. That one worked. The Australian Broadcasting Tribunal, although pressed by the Australian Journalists' Association to investigate the deal, was outmanoeuvred and, with no encouragement from the government to do otherwise, simply gave up.[43]

For his part, Prime Minister Hawke had only to remain silent to acquiesce. The Minister of Foreign Affairs, Bill Hayden, and the Opposition spokesman on communications, Ian Macphee, called for a public inquiry into the Murdoch bid, to no avail; Hayden was silenced by the Cabinet and

Macphee was visited on a Sunday morning by his frantic leader, John Howard, who had interrupted a holiday to tell him that under no circumstances was Murdoch to be offended. On both sides of the Australian Parliament the silence was contagious. One MP told me at the time, 'The hostility of Murdoch would mean my political death. So I shut up and I'm not proud of it.'

Elsewhere few dogs barked. Coverage by the non-Murdoch media of such an historic shift in power was primarily of the isn't-Rupert-clever-school. The Australian Press Council all but disintegrated as a result of the Murdoch takeover. With seven of its members representing the proprietors, their vote blocked a proposal for an inquiry. The chairman, Hal Wootten, a former judge, resigned in protest, saying bitterly, 'Allowing Murdoch to assume control of Australian newspapers was unparalleled outside totalitarian countries. The Federal Treasurer [Keating] could stop the takeover if he wanted to . . . in this case it is a man who has renounced his citizenship to further his worldwide power, and who makes no secret of the fact that he intends to make personal use of his control of newspapers.'[44]

When Hawke finally spoke about the sale, he and Keating had been entertained by Murdoch on his estate a short drive from Canberra. Ian Macphee refused to accept the government's silence and, under the Freedom of Information Act, requisitioned from Keating's office the Foreign Investment Review Board's recommendations. Six of the eight pages he received were blacked out and stamped 'Commercial. In confidence'. One paragraph, released two years later, indicated that the Board had opposed the takeover. Hawke denied this, and Keating still refused to release the full report, declaring the episode 'over'.[45]

At the root of Murdoch's financial power is his talent for manipulating tax laws. At the beginning of the 1990s his Australian parent company, News Corporation, paid tax of less than two cents in the dollar. In 1996, the *Australian Financial Review* calculated that Murdoch's tax bill was $A300 million less than the amount he would have paid had he been taxed at the statutory rate of 33 per cent.[46] However, this pales against his savings in Britain, where, in the decade to 1996, Murdoch's News International paid virtually no tax on recorded profits of almost a billion pounds.[47]

None of this is against the law. Murdoch's great skill lies in the way he moves capital and profits around the world, specifically to and from the books of 'letter-box companies' in tax havens like the Cayman Islands, the Virgin Islands and the Netherlands Antilles. This is his secret empire: an ever-changing number of subsidiary companies that trade in circumstances bewildering to all but the most creative accountants.

In 1994, for example, an 'off-the-shelf' Murdoch subsidiary, News Times Holdings, paid almost a billion and a half pounds for News Publishers, a Bermuda-registered shell company also owned by Murdoch's News International. Why was this unheard-of company worth so much money? Why should a Murdoch subsidiary buy a Bermuda-registered company owned by its parent company? The answers lie in the now standard practice by multinational corporations of creating 'virtual companies' in order to avoid tax.

Murdoch is reputedly the cleverest of them all. Although in 1997 his companies were being investigated by tax authorities in Britain, Australia and Israel, it was unlikely that any action would be taken against him. 'This government will not tolerate any action by companies which rip off the rest of the community,' said Paul Keating in 1987: a year in which the Australian Tax Office estimated that, by shifting profits to tax havens, News Corporation and other Australia-based companies had cost Australian taxpayers $A1.2 billion in lost revenue.[48]

'Murdoch is not like you and me,' said Christopher Hird, one of the few journalists to have investigated Murdoch's tax affairs. 'We work, we pay our taxes. Murdoch lives by different rules. His companies use the services that we provide, they use the roads to carry their newspapers around, they use the health service for their employees to use when they're ill. They benefit from all the things that our society provides, but they feel no sense of obligation to make a contribution to that. On the contrary, they see it as a challenge to avoid paying taxes. They are a different class of people. They are the over-class, the ones who want to rule the world, and they don't want to pay us for the privilege of doing so.'[49]

It is the scale of the hypocrisy that is difficult to grasp. Murdoch's newspapers incessantly attack people who are not meeting the 'moral challenge': that is, those who do not speak the *Sun*'s language on 'morality and family life'. These are mainly the minority among the poor who, usually out of desperation, 'fiddle' the social security system out of a few extra pounds.

Impoverished single mothers are a frequent target. They are labelled 'scroungers'. The *Sun* has campaigned for their child support to be cut, arguing that the saving would allow a five pence cut in taxes.[50] No mention is made of the fact that big business in Britain owes £23 billion in uncollected tax. Because Murdoch's companies pay so little tax, papers like the *Sun* are, in effect, subsidised by the public purse and are scroungers on a grand scale.

In 1996, the *Independent* asked the Labour Party leadership what it planned to do about Murdoch's taxes, or lack of them. Gordon Brown, then Shadow Chancellor, had frequently denounced 'fat cats' and promised they would be taxed 'fairly'. When asked about Murdoch's taxes, neither he nor other members of the Labour front bench were available for comment. Alistair Darling MP was eventually put forward as spokesman. 'You can't be subjective,' he said. 'You must never design a tax system to get at one person. It is a matter of fundamental principle.'[51]

The fear of offending Murdoch was evident early in 1997 as Murdoch began to take control of the 'digital revolution' in television. He has monopoly ownership of the 'black box' technology which you buy and put on the top of your TV set. If you have a satellite dish, this will eventually bring in 200 digital channels. At the very least, it will provide a further thirty terrestrial channels.

Murdoch formed British Digital Broadcasting in partnership with the two biggest ITV companies, Carlton and Granada. The Independent Television Commission (ITC) subsequently granted the consortium the franchise to broadcast the first digital channels, even though it said it was 'more attracted by the innovative programme proposals' of the rival bidder, Digital Television Network. The group got the licence because it promised to buy movies and sports coverage from Murdoch's BSkyB and so draw more viewers.

The twist was that Murdoch himself was ordered by the ITC to sell his shares – a curiously coy demonstration of the regulator's power as Murdoch will still be effectively in charge. He will draw 70 per cent of the revenues, control the electronic programme guide and, most important, he will have gained the foothold so long denied him in British terrestrial television.

The political reaction in Britain has been silence, or fatuities about the ineluctable nature of progress. 'The consumer can sit back', said a *Guardian* editorial, 'and wait to be positively spoilt for choice.'[52] The 'choice' was demonstrated in the programming offered by the new consortium. There is 'tele-shopping', 'Animal Planet', sport and old movies and old costume dramas and old sitcoms. The current affairs and documentaries planned are, says the prospectus, 'linked to law and order, and to Sky News in the morning'.

The remains of the eclectic range of British television are to be replaced by the equivalent of a shopping mall, where, beneath the bright packaging, most of the goods are the same. There is nothing adventurous and little that has not been seen before, over and again, in one form or another. The words of Murdoch's rival, Ted Turner, owner of the 24-hour Cable News Network, come to mind. 'We're a lot like the modern chicken farmer,' he said. 'They grind up the feet to make fertiliser, they grind up the intestines to make dog food. The feathers go into the pillows. Even the chicken manure is made into fertiliser. They use every bit of the chicken. Well, that's what we try to do with the television product.'[53]

In Doug Lucie's play *The Shallow End*, inspired by the

Murdochising of the *Sunday Times*, one of the reporters rails against the Murdoch figure who is about to devour the one last decent newspaper: 'Pollute the market, distort it, drag the quality and the price as low as they can go, and then, if there is still a market left after that, fine, because you're the major player, and if there isn't . . . another outmoded product becomes history, and anyway, you control the alternatives.'

The putrescence of the 'cultural Chernobyl' now flows through most of the media. Switch on *Independent Television News* and hear the following: 'Hello. The teddy bears he loved so much sat side by side in church today. The day of the funeral of James Bulger. The toys were propped up on a seat that had been specially made for James by his father. It was placed a few inches from James's coffin . . .'

This is 'newszak' according to Bob Franklin, author of *Newszak and News Media*. 'It seems unthinkable', he wrote, 'that this could be the transcript of a *genuine* news bulletin rather than some grotesque parody of the cynical antics of the fictional journalist Damien Day from the satirical television series *Drop the Dead Donkey*. This report of the death of a young child, with its insensitive conjoining of the sentimental and the sensational, the prurient and the populist [is the] exploitation of personal tragedy for public spectacle [and] constitutes little more than pornography.' Franklin defines newszak as 'news converted into entertainment' and says that 'the shifting balance in favour of entertainment in news media content has rarely, if ever, been so apparent [and] accompanied by a related decline in news, especially foreign and investigative news journalism [which] have virtually disappeared from some news media . . .'[54]

The growing acceptance of newszak was evident at a satellite and cable media conference in London in 1996 organised by the *Financial Times*. One of the speakers was Kelvin MacKenzie, in his capacity as head of L!ve TV, a cable channel owned by the Mirror Group and the home of the 'News Bunny', which gives the thumbs up or down to each news item.

MacKenzie began his speech by telling a joke about oral sex

and another about news bulletins read by stammerers. He then said that television news should follow the tabloids and 'with more channels there will be more TV, from more points of view'. He described the main television news programmes as 'dull and regimented clones of each other, working to news values light years away from the interests of the great swathes of the population'. He was not challenged on either of these statements.

Yet when MacKenzie was its editor, the *Sun* discouraged 'great swathes of the population' from defending their 'interests'. In the world of the *Sun* and the News Bunny, ordinary people are merely passive consumers of the trifling, the puerile, the trashy and the pornographic. They are never a political force; for the only 'politics' permitted is specious indignation about false demons and worship of the consumer gods and their priests. Old people are of no account, unless they serve as victims. Young people are morons or drug-dealers. The solidarity of working people seeking their rights is redundant – like them.

MacKenzie's audience of fashionably suited marketing men listened attentively to his aggressive banalities. It was clear they did not regard him as a buffoon in a dirty mac. They made a point of calling him 'Kelvin'; this, after all, was the man who made the *Sun* a 'success': a term whose boundaries are determined by profit and naturally exclude the likes of Hillsborough. Indeed, a certain respect was in the air. Mark Damazer, the editor of BBC TV News, was almost deferential in conceding that 'Kelvin has certainly got a point, in the narrow sense. Certainly, as the spectrum expands, there is no reason for all the news programmes to be pitched quite so high up the scale, there is a case for different approaches.' He hastened to add that the BBC was not heading downmarket.

Such assertions rarely suggest that all the population – old people as well as young people, disabled people as well as able people, earnest people as well as the light-hearted – have a right, under the charter of the corporation *they* own, to expect a truly representative service. At the same time, regulated, commercial television has a vital place; my own television career has been spent entirely in the commercial sector. Some of the best drama, current affairs, documentaries and children's programmes in the world have been produced by Britain's ITV network. That, too, is now threatened.

A former executive of the American National Broadcasting Company, Sonny Fox, put it bluntly. 'The salient fact today', he said, 'is that commercial television is primarily a marketing medium and secondarily an entertainment medium.' The former vice-president of the Columbia Broadcasting System, Arnold Becker, was even more forthright. 'I'm not interested in culture,' he said. 'I'm not interested in pro-social values. I have only one interest. That's whether people watch the program. That's my definition of good, that's my definition of bad.'[55] As Thomas Kiernan points out, the undisputed 'pacesetter' of this view is Murdoch's Fox network in the United States, whose transmission began with the 'live' broadcast of the voice of a woman about to die in a blazing building.

The Thatcher Government's Broadcasting Act of 1990 brought about a television 'revolution' as significant as Wapping. By introducing market ideology directly into ITN's gathering and presentation of news, 'for the first time in British broadcasting', wrote Franklin, 'news had to make a profit'.[56] Jon Snow, the presenter of Channel 4 News, called this 'news under siege'. 'Ratings will be the determinants', he wrote, 'because the money comes from advertisers. Within a couple of years, there could be no serious analytical news programmes on American TV and that is the way we are heading.'[57]

Something similar has happened in radio. The Broadcasting Acts of 1990 and 1996 almost doubled the number of Independent Local Radio (ILR) stations. The government's stated aim was that 'market forces' would trigger greater choice and diversity. 'In reality,' wrote Franklin, 'the policy outcome has been precisely the opposite. The market penalises those who stray too far from the mainstream; ILR stations offer a dull, homogeneous and predictable output ... a rather unwholesome diet of muzak seasoned with newszak.'[58]

Again, mostly silence has greeted these radical changes in the

way millions of people are to be allowed to perceive and inter-
pret their world. Media sections in the broadsheet newspapers
occasionally allow dissenting voices, but that is not their purpose. Like the media itself, they are essentially marketing vehicles, whose primary interest is not serious journalistic scrutiny
of the industry, but formulaic 'media village' tittle-tattle, something on circulation figures, something from the what-I-had-for-
breakfast school of journalism and perhaps a 'controversial'
interview with a wily political 'spin doctor'. The reason why
journalists are so malleable is rarely discussed.

Media stories, no matter how incestuous and trivial, are now
so popular with editors they are no longer confined to their
specialist section. The *Guardian* filled three pages of its tabloid
section with a 'profile' of Tina Brown, editor of the *New
Yorker*. This was 'market' or 'shopping mall journalism', written largely in American marketspeak. 'As new-broom editor of
the fusty *New Yorker*', it began, 'Britain's Tina Brown has had
both brickbats and bouquets. Held in awe by some as a very big
cheese in the Big Apple, to others she is Stalin in high heels . . .
Tina is what marketing men call a breakout star [who] can
command a table in any New York restaurant at any time.'
However, her 'commitment curve' is 'brutal'. And so on.
Market ideology's division of humanity into 'new' people
(good) and 'old guard' (bad) was duly honoured. The performance would not have been out of place in the tabloids.[59]

Tabloid stories now appear often on the news pages of the
broadsheets. The front page of the *Observer* carried, in large
type, Lynn Barber's gratuitous abuse of the actress Felicity
Kendal – 'IF A MAN SAYS HE FANCIES HER, I TAKE IT AS A SIGN
HE IS SEXUALLY DEFUNCT'. Inside, in her 'interview', Barber
noted that Kendal's 'hands are hideous knotted bony claws
with crimson talons'. What her subject had done to deserve
such cruelty was never explained. It would have fitted
comfortably into the *News of the World*.[60]

Some journalists have been mesmerised by Murdoch and
his ethos. There is widespread admiration for the *Sun*, the
sort that comes from vicarious middle-class flirtation with
low-life. Murdoch's semi-official biographer and faithful

defender, William Shawcross, described the *Sun*'s fatuous sound-bites as 'witty'. Forget the lies and the devastation of people's lives: this is the sensibility of the late 1990s, the way of the reactionary tide.[61]

A 1996 history of the popular press, *Tickle the Public* by Matthew Engel, exemplifies this. The author describes the infamous *Sun* headline 'GOTCHA' as 'a cultural reference point' and exudes an almost missionary zeal in persuading us that Kelvin MacKenzie has been misunderstood. Although MacKenzie 'behaved obnoxiously', he wrote, 'he is not an obnoxious man'. On the contrary, he can be 'endearingly vulnerable'. Indeed, he only abused people because his own journalistic 'standards were very high'. For here was an editor with 'a natural, instinctive flair for turning raw information into highly readable stories . . .' Endearing anecdotes about the great man follow, the sort that 'cling . . . to all really great journalists'. Here Engel can barely contain himself. 'MacKenzie was a sort of genius,' he effuses. 'No other word will do.' As for Murdoch's 'revolution' at Wapping, this 'did indeed give journalists new freedom'.

Freedom to do what? Engel does not say. Freedom certainly to carry on falsifying and pillorying while suppressing the truth of the most sustained political attack on ordinary people in modern times? He does not say.[62]

In 1975, Murdoch's *Australian* conducted a campaign resembling a vendetta against the reformist Prime Minister of Australia, Gough Whitlam. The conservative Opposition, led by Malcolm Fraser, had paralysed the Australian Senate, blocking bills providing legislative authority for the government's annual spending. The Governor-General, Sir John Kerr, was on the verge of sacking Whitlam and triggering a constitutional *coup d'état*. The *Australian* urged on Fraser and Kerr during the critical period before Kerr finally acted. Journalists' copy was slanted and rewritten as the country's only national newspaper clearly assisted in the despatch of the elected government.

The journalists rebelled, and seventy on the *Australian*'s staff wrote to Murdoch: 'The *Australian* has become a laughing stock. Reporters who were once greeted with respect when they mentioned the *Australian* have had to face derisive harangues before they can get down to the job at hand.' They told him they could not be loyal to a 'propaganda sheet'.[63] Murdoch ignored their letter, and Kerr dismissed Whitlam. The journalists went into the streets and burned copies of their newspaper in the centre of Sydney. They were joined by hundreds of passers-by. Nothing like this had ever happened before in Australia.

'Since when did any democrat admire great power used for private advantage?' wrote David Bowman, a former editor-in-chief of the *Sydney Morning Herald* and one of the few Australian journalists publicly critical of Murdoch today. 'The danger is that the media of the future, the channels of mass communication, will be dominated locally and world-wide by the values – social, cultural and political – of a few individuals and their huge corporations. Democrats ought to fight to the last ditch against what Murdoch and the other media giants represent.'[64]

Like any emperor, Murdoch is clearly anxious to establish his dynasty, especially in the land of his birth. When age has finally caught up with him, his heirs will still need to manipulate politicians in order to bypass laws so that the empire continues to prosper. So the 'grooming' of his offspring, has begun in earnest.

In 1996, a 'Sir Keith Murdoch Memorial Lecture' was instituted, honouring Lachlan's grandfather, a famous journalist. The first lecture was given by Lachlan, who emphasised that his parents were Australian and that he was the product of both Australian and American cultures. In fact, he was born in Britain and brought up in the United States. As part of an accompanying propaganda drive to establish both acceptance and respectability for the heir, pictures of Lachlan and his father appeared, Maxwell style, in the Adelaide *Advertiser*. They looked out from the front page, from the sports pages (Murdoch owns the TV rights of Super League football) and from the business pages.

'The danger for the Murdochs', wrote David Bowman, 'is

that [Rupert Murdoch's] disappearance will stiffen the back-bone of the politicians in Canberra. Only Canberra can break the Murdoch grip on the Australian press . . . His special place of power and privilege in Australia, arranged for him by Paul Keating, was made possible to a large extent by the rose-tinted view the public held of Murdoch personally. With time, reality is sinking in and he is increasingly viewed not as the Aussie who took on the world and won, but as a foreigner-by-choice who is in this country for what he can get out of it.'[65]

With his son at his side, Murdoch described himself as an Australian. He seemed not to understand that in an immi-grant society the renunciation of citizenship is not viewed kindly, particularly when the reason is the circumvention of laws in the country of adoption. He also had the audacity to call for 'tax reform' in a country where he pays minimal tax. The letters pages of the *Age* and the *Sydney Morning Herald* (which he does not yet own) lit up with anger.

'How dare Rupert Murdoch use the term "us" and "we" when referring to Australia?' was a typical response. Another was: 'Will somebody please remind Mr Rupert Murdoch that he is no longer an Australian. He sold his birthright, for money, and therefore renounced his right to a say in how this country is run.'[66] Public opinion can be a bewildering phenomenon, even to powerful individuals who believe they understand it, even own it.

In his seminal book about journalism, *The Captive Press*, David Bowman compares Murdoch's growing power, and its accompanying silence among politicians, with the rise of Alfred Hugenberg in Germany in the 1920s. 'Hugenberg is reliably estimated to have enjoyed control or influence over nearly half the German press by 1930,' he wrote. 'His philosophy was right-wing nationalist, and accordingly he helped block the spread of democratic ideas in Germany, to that extent weakening the Weimar republic and paving the way for the triumph of the Nazis.'[67]

This theme is taken up by Reiner Luyken, the *Die Zeit* journalist who coined the expression 'cultural Chernobyl'. 'The laws of supply and demand worked well for Hitler,' he told me. 'He no doubt gave many people what they wanted. Does that mean that supply and demand is an immutable law? Does that mean that, as journalists, we listen to the Murdochs and always look over our shoulders, wondering if we are giving the readers what they want, regardless of the demands of principle and of honest journalism? Of course not. As a German I know that Britain not only won the war, but brought freedom back to Germany. This freedom allowed us to establish newspapers whose main concern was not what the readers wanted, but truth and contributing to democracy. Not to further this objective, not to cling to it as if it were life itself, is surely an abuse of something that has been created with the deaths of tens of thousands of soldiers.'

Hugh Cudlipp went further. 'I look to the journalists on the lousiest of our newspapers', he wrote, 'not to do the dirty work.'[68]

GUARDIANS OF THE FAITH

> At any given moment, there is a sort of all pervading
> orthodoxy, a general tacit agreement not to discuss large
> and uncomfortable facts.
>
> *George Orwell*

THE SIXTIETH ANNIVERSARY of television was
celebrated at the BBC in Shepherd's Bush, west London, with
a gala dinner and 'hall of fame' awards. In keeping with the
times, it was sponsored by a multinational corporation, the
electronics giant Philips. Everyone received a miniature model
of the first Philips' wireless set. Among the guests were
television's Great and Good – Sir Robin Day OBE, Sir Jeremy
Isaacs, Sir Christopher Bland, Sir Geoffrey Cox CBE, Lord
Thomson of Monifieth, Esther Rantzen OBE, Kate Adie OBE,
David Glencross CBE and others of similar distinction.

In a glossy booklet, the BBC described itself as a 'centre for
excellence'. There was a photograph of Robin Oakley, its
political editor, who, said the blurb, 'heads the political unit,
based at Millbank studios, Westminster, where staff have
rapid access to the main centres of power, Parliament and 10
Downing Street'. There were two pages on *Crimewatch UK*,
whose 'value can be gauged by the fact that nearly 300 people
have been convicted as a result of information given to the
police by viewers'.

The highlight of the evening was a celebratory video
produced by the Royal Television Society. This mentioned
only one programme which had questioned, indirectly, the

nature of the political and social system of which broadcast television is part. This was *Death on the Rock*, about four murders committed by an SAS death squad in Gibraltar, and which may well have cost Thames Television its licence to broadcast. When the congratulations petered out, a fleet of chauffeured cars collected the most important participants. Like a Guildhall dinner or the Trooping of the Colour, the ritual had celebrated the prerogative of power.

In 1968, television passed newspapers as Britain's primary source of information. 'Broadcasters', wrote the media historian Michael Tracey, 'had convinced the public that the words they spoke may have been few [compared with the press] but, by God, they had been touched by the beauty of truth.'[1]

Today, British television enjoys more credibility than television in most countries. This is partly because in other countries institutional bias in broadcasting is understood, if not always acknowledged. In the former Soviet bloc, as in other totalitarian states, many people regarded the bias of the state as implicit in all media and made a conscious or unconscious adjustment.

Since the birth of the BBC, the bias of the British state has operated through a 'consensus' created and fostered by a paternalistic order. The public has been groomed, rather than brainwashed. George Orwell, in his unpublished introduction to *Animal Farm*, described how censorship in free societies was infinitely more sophisticated and thorough than in dictatorships because 'unpopular ideas can be silenced, and inconvenient facts kept dark, without any need for an official ban'.[2]

In the fifty years since he wrote that, much has changed, but the essential message remains the same. This is not to suggest a conspiracy, which in any case is unnecessary. Journalists and broadcasters are no different from historians and teachers in internalising the priorities and fashions of established power. Like others with important establishment responsibilities, they are trained to set aside serious doubts. If scepticism is encouraged, it is directed not at the system but at the competence of its managers, or at popular attitudes as journalists perceive them.

Ambitious young journalists are often persuaded that a certain cynicism about ordinary people ordains them as journalists, while obedience to higher authority and deference to 'experts' is the correct career path. By this route, the myths and assumptions of power routinely enter the 'mainstream' unnoticed and unchallenged. 'I am still hanging on to my idealism,' a young graduate journalist wrote to me from Wales. 'But people I work with tend to think my belief in real democracy and the media's responsibility to question institutions and events is strange. I am repeatedly told I will grow out of it.'

Those who do question the nature of the system risk being eased out of the 'mainstream', a process described by one veteran journalist as 'a sort of gentle defenestration'.[3] Unless they navigate with care, they will find themselves exiled to the margins and stereotyped with a pejorative tag, such as 'committed journalist' – even though their commitment to an independence of mind may well pale against the surreptitious zeal of those who loyally serve the system.

Perhaps in no other country does broadcasting hold such a privileged position as an opinion leader as in Britain. When 'information' is conveyed on the BBC with such professional gravitas, it is more than likely to be believed. Possessing highly professional talent, the illusion of impartiality and an essentially liberal ethos, Britain's 'public service broadcasting' has become a finely crafted and infinitely adaptable instrument of state propaganda and censorship.

The much-admired BBC World Service is an outstanding example. When BBC Director-General John Birt announced his cost-cutting plans for the World Service, the vigorous opposition he triggered included not only journalists but impeccable establishment figures, such as the British commander in the Gulf War, General Sir Peter de la Billière, and the British naval commander in the Falklands War, Admiral Sir Sandy Woodward. The NATO general, Sir Anthony Farrar-Hockley, was another signatory to the campaign.

Originally the Empire Service, the World Service was funded by the Foreign Office and still is. After the Second World War, its role was to 'preserve and strengthen the Commonwealth and Empire' and 'increase our trade and protect our investments abroad'. In 1948, the Labour Cabinet directed the World Service to play its part in winning the Cold War by launching 'a vigorous, systematic attack' on communist ideology.

Criticism of 'free world' regimes was frowned upon. Since then the World Service has championed or counselled compromise with capitalism, and given both tacit and open approval to British and American policy from Vietnam to the Gulf War. General de la Billière and Admiral Woodward would not have been displeased with the BBC's presentation of their wars.

This is not to say the World Service's liberal image is unjustified or that it cannot claim to be the best national service of its kind. When it is compared with the overtly propagandist Voice of America, there is no contest. Foreign broadcasters employed by the BBC are allowed to criticise vicious regimes – that is, until 'Western interests' are directly threatened. Then the mood is likely to change.

The Indonesian dictatorship is a case in point. When the Indonesian democracy movement took to the streets of Jakarta in 1996 in the most momentous show of opposition to the Suharto regime for more than a generation, a World Service reporter summarised it as 'more a rampage: we have twenty million youths in this country, between seventeen and twenty-one, with an excess of testosterone'. He was not challenged by the interviewer in London. In the same report, he described the country's 'stability' in terms of the vagaries of the stock market index. That Suharto was increasingly isolated and a popular uprising had begun was not reported.[4]

Far from the independent 'fourth estate' envisaged by Lord Macauley, much of serious journalism in Britain, dominated by television, serves as a parallel arm of government, testing or 'floating' establishment planning, restricting political debate to the 'main centres of power', as outlined in the BBC's commemorative booklet, and, above all, promoting Western power in the wider world.

One of the most effective functions of 'communicators' is to minimise the culpability of this power in war and terrorism, the enforced impoverishment of large numbers of people and the theft of resources and the repression of human rights. This is achieved by omission on a grand scale, by the repetition of received truths and the obfuscation of causes.

'I have recently found mountains of evidence pointing to a radically revised understanding of post-war British foreign policy,' wrote the historian Mark Curtis in 1996, 'which has simply been sitting in the Public Record Office, apparently untouched.' He cited secret British backing for the denial of human rights in many countries, such as Indonesia, Turkey and Colombia, which are 'systematic and consistent rather than evidence of "double standards" ... Neither the conservative nor liberal media betray much interest in exposing [these] topical realities ...'[5]

On television, information about the many millions of people affected by these realities, indeed about most of the world, is meagre. According to one study of programming, it accounts for 3·4 per cent of peak viewing time, almost all of it confined to 'minority' channels.[6] The little news there is from most of humanity follows a predetermined pattern of stereotypes that is seldom questioned. Mobutu of the former Zaire is declared a figure of revulsion, as if he plundered his country alone, rather than as the West's hired crusader against communism. The Government of Sierra Leone, described as an 'infant democracy', is overthrown, plunging 'the long-suffering people of this former British colony' into 'anarchy'.

The message is a ubiquitous one: that it was better in the good old colonial days. Sierra Leone's post-colonial peonage to Western financial institutions, notably British banks, is not mentioned. There is space only for soundbites, which are frequently merely rhetoric, not so much 'concise' as sanctioned. Statements and assumptions that are part of a received wisdom are regarded as 'facts', whilst those that are critical are rejected as 'opinions'.[7]

Language plays a vital part; popular concepts like 'democracy', 'freedom', 'choice' and 'reform' are emptied of their dictionary meanings. This has long been standard practice, but in the late twentieth century it is reinforced by the facility of technology and the illusion of an 'information society' which, in reality, means more media owned by fewer and fewer conglomerates. There is minimal public discussion about this, although there is strong evidence that the public has intuitive concerns about the secret laws of media power and its influence over and intrusions in their lives.

In the respectable media, especially broadcasting, discussion of widespread voluntary and subliminal censorship is a taboo subject. A striking illustration of this was a public spat in 1997 between BBC senior management and the presenters of current affairs programmes. The issue was the appointment of five executives who would control all the programmes. The broadcasters argued that this would 'CNN-ise' the BBC, reducing it to one corporate voice. A BBC correspondent, Fergal Keane, spoke about the purity of an 'unalterable principle of journalism that is our heritage and our mission', and said he would 'rather sweep the streets of London than compromise on that'.[8] Like the revolt of the clergy against a modification of intonement, it was essentially an argument about form. There was no mention of the powerful, exclusive, almost instinctive shared assumptions which, with a handful of exceptions, already produce a corporate echo – as was illustrated by the coverage of great events like the Gulf War and the death of Diana Spencer.

It is this issue, its genesis and subtleties, that ought to be high on the curriculum of media studies courses seeking to turn out independent and critically minded journalists; but it is seldom even discussed. Students are taught, often by former practitioners, the collective responsibility of precepts that shade the bias of the state behind a veil of saintly 'principles'.

These include the 'three truths' laid down by Lord Reith, founder of the BBC: 'impartiality', 'objectivity' and 'balance'. There is something to be said for the stamina of the Reithian myths. As a propagandist, Reith was a true pioneer. His 'three truths' were to be adhered to at all times, except when the established order was threatened. Reith demonstrated this in 1926 by broadcasting Prime Minister Stanley Baldwin's propaganda during the General Strike – much of it scripted by Reith himself – while refusing to allow the union leaders to put their side until the strike was over.

'Reith emerged [from the strike] as a kind of hero,' wrote Patrick Renshaw in his study, *The General Strike*. '[Here was] a young man who had acted responsibly and yet preserved the precious independence of the BBC. But though this myth persisted, it had little basis in reality ... the price of that independence was in fact doing what the government wanted done ... Baldwin saw that if they preserved the BBC's appearance of impartiality, it would be much easier for them to get their way on important questions and use it to broadcast Government propaganda.'[9]

Even then, this was not a new concept. During the Boer War and the First World War, respectable journalists, who had promoted their impartiality above all other virtues, became little more than propagandists for the state. 'There was no need of censorship in our despatches,' wrote Sir Philip Gibbs, correspondent of *The Times*. 'We were our own censors.'[10] Prime Minister Lloyd George confided to C. P. Scott, the editor of the *Manchester Guardian*: 'If people really knew [the truth], the war would be stopped tomorrow. But of course they don't know and can't know.'[11] According to the historian Arthur Ponsonby, 'there was no more discreditable period in the history of journalism than the four years of the Great War'.[12]

The modern era has produced many such periods. In 1945, the Allied governments did their best to cover up the fact that the atom bombs dropped on Japan produced new, devastating effects from radiation. The media, including the BBC, reported the official line. The truth was left to a maverick, the Australian Wilfred Burchett, then working for the *Daily Express*, who was almost expelled from Japan by the Allies for giving them the slip and travelling to Hiroshima to find out for himself.

In 1952, at the height of the Korean War, the United Press correspondent, Robert C. Miller, echoed Philip Gibbs with this admission: 'There are certain facts and stories from Korea that editors and publishers have printed which were pure fabrication ... Many of us who sent the stories knew they were false, but we had to write them because they were official releases from responsible military headquarters and were released for publication even though the people responsible knew they were untrue.'[13]

Contrary to one of the most resilient myths of modern journalism, the first 'television war', fought in Vietnam, was reported largely from the point of view of the Americans. The competence of the foreign military 'involvement', as the US invasion was called, was questioned at times, but not American motives, which were judged to be essentially well-meaning, even 'noble', at worst wrong-headed (see pages 558–60).

Another 'noble cause' was the Falklands War in 1982. Leaked minutes of one of the BBC's Weekly Review Board meetings showed BBC executives directing that the reporting of the war should be concerned 'primarily with government statements of policy' while impartiality was felt to be 'an unnecessary irritation'.[14] This suppression was quite successful. As British Government statements barely mentioned it, a peace plan put forward by the Peruvian Government for a negotiated settlement between Britain and Argentina was barely reported. How close it came to success the public never knew.

On May 13, 1982, Edward Heath told ITN the Argentinians had requested three minor amendments to the peace plan. They were so minor, said Heath, that they could not possibly be rejected. But Prime Minister Thatcher rejected them out of hand – and that brief interview with Heath was the only occasion on television news that reference was made to the British Government having a case to answer. The story then died and the invasion went ahead.

When the war was over, the broadcasters gave the game away. Having once defended their objectivity as 'a matter of record', they were now almost truculent in their praise of their own subjectivity in the cause of Queen and Country, as if the war was a national emergency, which it was not. If they had any complaint, it was that they had not been allowed sufficient freedom to 'get on side' and to win the 'propaganda war'.

As in previous wars, it was risky to question this kind of coverage. A Channel 4 series, *The Friday Alternative*, was taken off the air following an episode based on research by the Glasgow Media Group, which showed how journalists had let the government use them during the Falklands War.[15] A subsequent study showed how the BBC and ITN had allowed themselves to be manipulated so that Thatcher could make a political connection between her 'victory' over the Argentinians and her 'struggles' against workers at home. 'We have found a new confidence,' she said unchallenged on ITN, 'born of the economic battles at home and tested and found true 8,000 miles away.'[16] When the BBC's industrial correspondent asked a minister, 'Is the government going to meet [the miners'] strike with the same resolve it showed over the Falklands?' he got the answer he expected.[17]

In covering the miners' strike of 1984–5 respectable journalism did not go as far as tabloids such as the *Daily Express*, which invented a secret 'confession' by the miners' leader, Arthur Scargill, that he had 'lied', or the *Sun*, which distorted a photograph to make Scargill appear like Hitler.[18] Instead, the miners were cast on the television news, night upon night, as violent and provocative, flouting and challenging law and order: an 'enemy within'. TV crews, who had not hesitated to film from both sides in Beirut, remained behind police lines. The pictures showed the faces of angry miners, seldom the police, and never the paramilitary-style attacks on miners' villages, and the suffering these caused.

When the strike was over, the National Council for Civil Liberties documented the scale of police violence. 'Contrary to the impression inevitably created by the media', said the NCCL report, 'most of the picketing during the strike had been orderly and on a modest scale.' This was reported only in the *Guardian*.[19]

The objective of the government's war against the miners – the destruction of the coal industry – was derided in the media as a 'myth'. Arthur Scargill's uncannily precise forecast of a mass closure of mines if the strike was lost was dismissed as propaganda. Although reporters on the coalfields were given reliable tip-offs about the intervention of the secret intelligence services in the strike, none disclosed the government's use of MI5 to subvert and crush the miners' union. It was ten years before the 'Get Scargill' campaign, conducted by a special task force in MI5 and personally authorised by Thatcher, was documented by Seamus Milne in his book, *The Enemy Within*.[20]

The getting of Scargill and the miners was not simply a vendetta by Robert Maxwell's *Mirror*, as already described (see pages 430–3); it could not have succeeded without the compliance of serious journalists throughout the media. Reporters from all branches of the media were known by the miners as 'Thatcher's frontline troops'. It was only when the strike was lost, and scores of bogus assault and riot charges against miners were thrown out by magistrates, that a few journalists realised the extent to which they had been used by the state. Many others continued to assume Arthur Scargill's guilt long after the trumped-up 'Libya-paid-his-mortgage' story peddled by Robert Maxwell's *Daily Mirror* and Central Television's *Cook Report* was demolished.

Without a shred of their own evidence, serious journalists casually attacked Scargill with 'a level of vituperation verging on the unhinged', wrote Milne. The efforts of Scargill's lawyers to establish his innocence were dismissed as 'classic Comintern stuff'. The miners' leader was compared to Nicolae Ceausescu, the Romanian tyrant who had been summarily shot a few months earlier. To this day, there has not been a single apology from any of the journalists who attacked a man Milne describes as 'ferociously principled'.

There was a resonance of this in the reaction to the disclosure in 1994 that the literary editor of the *Guardian*, Richard Gott, had accepted trips from the Soviet Embassy in London. Rival, respectable journalists had a field day. That the *Guardian* was then immersed in the early, seemingly arcane stages of a campaign that would bring down a senior establishment figure and pillar of the arms trade, Jonathan Aitken, was barely acknowledged.

The Times found Gott guilty of nothing less than 'treachery'. Certainly, Gott compromised his independence; but he had not provided the kind of service that is the everyday practice of journalists promoting and collaborating with rapacious Western interests. 'The Gott affair', declared *The Times* in a leader, 'has resurrected the pernicious doctrine of moral equivalence between the West and the Soviet Union. It has been suggested that Mr Gott's links with the KGB were no different to reporters' contacts with Western intelligence. The two are not the same. *Many British journalists benefited from CIA or MI6 largesse during the cold war*; none was supporting a totalitarian regime devoted to the overthrow of their own country . . .'.

My italics point up an astonishing admission. What exactly was this 'largesse'? What did these journalists have to do in order to 'benefit'? And who are they? Should they, like Richard Gott, be named? Surely, if there is no 'moral equivalence' with the agents of Stalinism, they have nothing to fear?

The 'largesse' came from, among others, the commissars who ran the Information Research Department in the Foreign Office (IRD), a secret political warfare agency, which in the 1950s and 1960s 'ran' dozens of Fleet Street journalists.[21] The IRD used 'white' (true), 'grey' (partially true) and 'black' (false) propaganda, planting forged official documents, smear stories and outright fabrications in the media. In the anti-colonial struggles in Kenya, Malaya and Cyprus, IRD was so successful that the journalism served up as a record of those episodes was a cocktail of the distorted and false, in which the real aims and often atrocious behaviour of the British were suppressed. Thus the bloodshed in Malaya was and still is misrepresented as a 'model' of counter-insurgency; the anti-imperial uprising in Kenya was and still is distorted as a Mau Mau terror campaign against whites; and the struggle for basic human rights in the north of Ireland became and remains a noble defence of order and stability against IRA terror (see pages 514–19). The common denominator of British political and military terror was deemed non-existent: a brilliant illusion that brought 'disinformation' to the language.

The most enduring success for the IRD and its 'contacts' in the media was in misrepresenting the Soviet Union as a threat and the source of a global conspiracy. This gave legitimacy to the nuclear arms race initiated by the United States, thanks largely to the fictional 'missile gap' of the Kennedy era, a triumph of disinformation, and to nuclear provocations such as the siting in Western Europe of 'first strike' nuclear weapons. Had war broken out with the Soviet Union, those propagandist journalists absolved by *The Times* of any moral equivalence with Stalinism would have shared the responsibility.

In 1991, Richard Norton-Taylor of the *Guardian* disclosed the existence of some 500 prominent Britons who were paid by the CIA through the corrupt and now defunct Bank of Commerce and Credit International in London. They included ninety journalists and broadcasters, many in 'senior positions'. Journalists who worked directly for the intelligence services are not uncommon. One prominent journalist and author has served British and American intelligence in a parallel career shortly after graduating from Oxford.

This is surprising only because it has been so effectively suppressed. For forty years, from an office in Bush House in London, home of the BBC World Service, a brigadier passed on the names of applicants for editorial jobs in the BBC to MI5 for 'vetting'. Journalists with a reputation for independence were refused BBC posts because they were not considered 'safe'. The *Observer* exposed the secret process in 1985,[22] and senior management are still vetted by MI5. In any case, it was quite unnecessary. Many senior journalists and broadcasters are proud that they are 'safe' and willing to be influenced, at times flattered by the state, without any formalised intrigue or material favours. For them, it seems perfectly natural to receive the state's 'hospitality', 'contacts' and 'access' – and, most important, its blessing.

For example, a number of influential journalists in the BBC and the press belong, like those Cabinet members of the Blair Government already mentioned (see pages 95–97), to the 'Successor Generation' network. This is the British-American Project for the Successor Generation, set up in 1985 with money from a Philadelphia trust with a long record of supporting right-wing causes. Although the BAP does not publicly acknowledge it, the source of its inspiration was a call by President Reagan during the Cold War for 'successor generations' on both sides of the Atlantic to 'work together in the future on defence and security matters'.

Washington was then deeply anxious about opposition to nuclear weapons, specifically the stationing of Cruise missiles in Britain. Today the aims of the network are broader. They are, according to David Willetts, the former director of studies at the Thatcherite Centre for Policy Studies, to 'help reinforce Anglo-American links, especially if some members already do, or will occupy positions of influence'.

The British Ambassador to Washington, Sir John Kerr, was more direct. In a speech to Successor Generation members in 1997, he said the BAP's 'powerful combination of eminent Fellows and close Atlantic links threatened to put the embassy out of a job'. Indeed, the Successor Generation 'was clearly a threat to the very existence of diplomats'![23] An American BAP organiser described the BAP network as committed to 'grooming leaders' while promoting 'the leading global role that [Britain and the US] continue to play'.[24] Not surprisingly, the BAP has had little publicity in the mainstream media.

An instrument of the 'leading global role' is, of course, NATO. Reporting from the NATO summit in Madrid in 1997, Ian Black of the *Guardian* noted that, although critics at the conference had described the organisation's expansion into Eastern Europe as 'an error of historic proportions' that would 'encourage a £22 billion arms race and undercut democracy in Russia, strikingly, there has been little public debate about this'.[25]

Here again it should be emphasised that there is no

suggestion of a conspiracy, rather a shared world view based largely, though not exclusively, on class. 'The British class system', wrote Anthony Sampson, 'has always been like an onion, revealing yet more layers.'[26] The mutuality of class and aspiration is assured, unspoken, and the warm embrace of power memorable. For some, this is a noble connection which, although having nothing to do with journalism, has everything to do with the preservation of things. They are the guardians of the faith.

Guardians are often candid and proud. In his autobiography, *News from the Front*, the ITN correspondent and newscaster Sandy Gall boasted of his high government and MI6 contacts and the work he did for them. 'I received a call from a friend in British Intelligence,' he wrote, 'telling me that the Foreign Secretary remained particularly concerned about Afghanistan and was anxious to keep the war "in front of the British public"; how could this be done? Would I talk to someone from his office and give him, and Lord Carrington, the benefit of my advice? Feeling flattered, I agreed . . .'

Gall made Afghanistan his speciality. In the 1980s, he went on a number of trips with the mojahedin, the guerrillas fighting the Soviet occupiers. On the eve of one of these assignments, which began in Pakistan, he went to see the Pakistani dictator, General Zia, who clearly regarded Gall as an important ally. Both MI6 and the CIA were backing Zia as the ruler of a 'frontline' state in this important Cold War conflict with the Soviet Union. As they strolled through his garden, the General, one of the world's nastiest fundamentalist tyrants, asked Gall if there was anything he wanted.

' "Yes," [Gall] said, "would it be possible to have some SAM 7s with us?" Zia laughed. "SAM 7s? I don't see why not. But why?"

' "We're likely to come under attack by Mi24 gunships, I suppose, and it would make some spectacular pictures if one of them were to be shot down."

'Zia laughed again, seeing the point. "I'll see to it," he promised. "You'll get your SAMs." '

Gall got his missile, which, he wrote, 'we fired', but it malfunctioned. Back in London, he was invited to lunch by the head of MI6. 'It was very informal,' wrote Gall, 'the cook was off, so we had cold meat and salad, with plenty of wine.' Britain's leading spymaster wanted information about Afghanistan from Gall who, once again, was 'flattered, of course, and anxious to pass on what I could in terms of first-hand knowledge'.

Moreover, the man from ITN determined 'not to prise any information out of him in return', even though 'this is not normally how a journalist's mind works'. The reason for this journalistic reticence was that 'avuncularly charming' as the head of MI6 might be, 'he was far too experienced to let slip anything he did not wish to'.[27]

In 1992, an internal committee of the Central Intelligence Agency reported that the CIA now had excellent links with the media. 'We have relationships with reporters', it said, '[that] have helped us turn some intelligence failure stories into intelligence success stories. Some responses to the media can be handled in a one-shot phone call. Others, such as the BBC's six-part series, draw heavily on [CIA] sources.'[28]

The BBC series in question, *CIA*, was written by John Ranelagh, formerly of the Conservative Party's Research Department and a speech writer for Margaret Thatcher. In 'drawing heavily' on the CIA's 'sources', Ranelagh's films allowed the notorious organisation to 'correct allegations' about its role in the overthrow of numerous governments and in the 1962 Cuban missile crisis. Ranelagh wrote that '[of the] subjects which US intelligence was expected to address . . . none was more momentous than the growth of international terrorism, a subject of major concern to the Reagan administration'.[29]

Nowhere in his films did Ranelagh identify the CIA itself as arguably the most powerful instrument of international terrorism, notably under the Reagan administration. The record on this is, of course, voluminous. In Reagan's first term alone, wrote the CIA historian William Blum, 'CIA-led, trained and funded Contra terrorists murdered 8,000 Nicaraguan civilians.'[30]

In 1994, the United States invaded Haiti. Bill Neely of ITN described the invaded country as 'festering in America's backyard' and crying out to be 'saved'. The BBC reported that the Pentagon had 'brought democracy' to Haiti. A BBC correspondent added the rider that 'the days of America as Mr Nice Guy are over'.[31] On neither of these primary channels of news was there reference to Mr Nice Guy's murderous interventions in Haiti since 1849 which, as the American historian Hans Schmidt noted, 'have consistently suppressed local democratic institutions and denied elementary political liberties'. Currently, Mr Nice Guy's plan for Haiti, wrote another American historian, Amy Wilentz, 'achieves two strategic US goals – one, a restructured and dependent agriculture that exports to US markets and is open to American exploitation, and the other, a displaced rural population that not only can be employed in offshore US industries in the towns, but is more susceptible to army control'.[32]

British governments have generally supported American terror in the region. Margaret Thatcher's Foreign Secretary, Geoffrey Howe, said that Britain 'absolutely endorsed' US objectives in Central America. According to *The Times*, these objectives were to 'maintain and strengthen the forces of democracy in an area threatened with a communist takeover'. Examining the serious British press, Mark Curtis surveyed 500 articles that dealt with Nicaragua during the early Reagan and Thatcher years of 1981–3. He found an almost universal suppression of the achievements of the Sandinista Government in favour of the falsehood of the 'threat of a communist takeover'.

'It would take considerable intellectual acrobatics', he wrote, 'to designate Sandinista successes in alleviating poverty – remarkable by any standard – as unworthy of much comment by any objective indicators. This might particularly be the case when compared to the appalling conditions elsewhere in the region – surely well known to every reporter who had ever visited the area . . . The absence of significant press comment on the Sandinista achievements was even more remarkable in view of the sheer number of articles that appeared on the subject of Nicaragua in these years. One might reasonably conclude – and this is supported by the evidence – that reporting was conditioned by a different set of priorities, one that conformed to an ideological framework in which the facts about real development successes were ignored in favour of the stream of disinformation emanating from Washington and London.'[33]

While rejecting any notion of a conspiracy theory, Curtis found in the work of leading journalists and academics a slavish, if at times unconscious devotion to the myths that perpetrated the old Cold War, which have extended to the new Cold War. At times ideological support becomes parody. Professor Lawrence Freedman of King's College, London, who was called upon frequently by the BBC and the press as an 'expert', wrote in a major study of the Gulf War (with Efraim Karsh) that 'there seems little doubt that [President] Bush was influenced most of all by the need to uphold the principle of non-aggression'. He called Bush a 'crusader' for 'the cause of international norms of decency'.[34]

Soon after taking office, this crusader for non-aggression and decency attacked Panama, killing at least 2,000 civilians, more than the number estimated to have been killed by the Chinese army in Tiananmen Square. He then attacked Iraq, killing at least 200,000 people, the majority of them civilians. He then invaded Somalia, killing, according to CIA estimates, between 7,000 and 10,000 people. And Bush was a president who, like Richard Nixon, was frequently lauded in the British media for his expertise in foreign affairs.[35]

In the glory days following Mr Nice Guy's victory in the 1991 Gulf War, Peter Snow interviewed the chairman of the US Joint Chiefs of Staff, General Colin Powell, for the BBC's *Newsnight*. Snow began by asking, 'Do you now regard the United States as the world's policeman?' The General, softly lit from behind, his ribbons marching down his chest, smiled sagely.

'Sir,' he replied, 'what we provide is a presence, a stabilising influence. You see, we have power that people tend to trust.

[However] I would not say we have seen the end of wars, or the end of history.'

Snow then had some suggestions to make. What about putting American troops into Yugoslavia to 'sort out the situation'? And, 'Look, is it not practicable to conduct air strikes?' After all, Margaret Thatcher had said it was.

'I'm second to no man', replied the General, 'in my respect, indeed in my love for Margaret Thatcher. But, sir, I'm always nervous about proposals that say all you have to do is go bomb some folks and they will be deterred from action you don't like.'

Snow nodded his agreement. 'Thank you so much, General,' he said.[36]

In 1997, the BBC showed the last of its acclaimed *People's Century* series, which expertly marshalled archive film and interviews with witnesses to and participants in the closing century's stirring and apocalyptic events. A recurring technique was the merging of government propaganda film, from Britain, France, the Soviet Union and the United States, with documentary footage, all of it accompanied by a narration. After a while, it became difficult to tell one from the other.

The overall effect was quite unlike the propaganda of the *CIA* series. This was finely honed, at times subliminal and, above all, dependent on political airbrushing. In the pivotal episode, *Brave New World*, about the origins of the Cold War, Stalin's crimes were played against the West's post-war heroics, as in the Berlin air-lift. This was 'balanced' by the absurdities and cruelties of American anti-communist paranoia in the 1950s.

However, there was barely a hint of the massive post-war planning in the United States aimed at controlling and exploiting millions of people and their resources: a hegemony greater than the world had ever seen, dominating markets and trade, from food to oil; a *Pax Americana* under which, as the great American imperial planner George Kennan put it, the United States had 'a moral right to intervene' anywhere in the world – and did so relentlessly, subverting and destroying governments which dared to demonstrate independence, from Italy to Iran, Chile to Indonesia.[37]

In helping to bring the Indonesian tyrant Suharto to power, American imperial power ensured the deaths of more than half a million 'communists'. In Indo-China, the same fundamentalism oversaw at least five million dead and millions more dispossessed, their lands ruined and poisoned. Then known as the 'free world', the American empire rules today with ever-changing euphemisms. Perhaps its most brilliant, if unsung, victory has been in the field of media management, as the omission of its rapacity from *People's Century* demonstrated.

Guardians of the faith, the clerics of the established order, are most commonly found in the 'lobby system'. This is periodically attacked as a 'cosy club', even 'pernicious', but it never changes. 'Lobby correspondents' have their own rules, 'officers' and disciplinary procedures. Their 'privileges' include access to government statements before they are made public and to private briefings by ministerial press secretaries or senior Civil Servants, or even ministers themselves.

At the time of writing, the BBC employs thirteen national and nineteen regional political correspondents, all of them based at London's Millbank, close to Parliament and the other 'centres of power' covered by Robin Oakley and his team. On a clear day you can see the MPs queuing up to dispense their mostly predictable views. According to a former BBC reporter, Steve Richards, now the political editor of the *New Statesman*, some MPs go straight to Millbank in the morning, rather than to the House of Commons, 'in the hope that someone will interview them'.[38]

In an average week 'lobby' journalists churn out some 300 reports: most of them are on the same theme, adhering to the agenda put out by the two main political parties, which are themselves virtually the same. The truth that the British people are now denied the semblance of a democratic choice is not reported.

The message from the Millbank echo chamber is quite

straightforward. There is only one way now, the way of the triumphant 'market'; and no buts, let alone 'balance'. It shapes political news and commentary and it excludes genuine challengers – that is, those *outside* the collective responsibility of 'mainstream' journalists and politicians and their vested consorts. The influence of this parallel arm of government cannot be overestimated. 'MPs are giving up their capacity to set their own agenda in Parliament,' wrote Richards, 'and are accepting the journalists' power to shape the agenda, and to fit in to what the journalists decide they want the MPs to say.'[39]

What many journalists want them to say comes from an agenda that divides the world neatly between 'new' and 'old', rather like the pre-election division of the Labour Party. 'New' political issues are sustained by the media's unequivocal support for 'the market' – regardless of the fact that every reliable indication, such as the annual survey by the venerable *British Social Attitudes* survey, leaves little doubt that most of the public has 'old' priorities. Millions of people reject the Westminster parties' unwillingness to redistribute the national wealth from the rich to the poor and to spend on vital services like health, education and jobs. During the 1997 election campaign, to my knowledge, no journalist asked Tony Blair or John Major to justify this discrepancy.[40]

Following Labour's landslide victory, the media quickly sought reassurances on behalf of the status quo – what did it mean for the 'stability' of the pound, the stock market, interest rates? Was Tony Blair a 'safe pair of hands'? Of course he was; the share indexes had soared and the pound strengthened. The guardians may have changed; the faith had not.

British liberalism's three principal newspapers, the *Guardian, Observer* and *Independent*, along with the BBC, were, it is fair to say, beside themselves. The new government, rejoiced the *Guardian*, 'has set a breathless pace [as] the floodgates of change burst open . . .' The first floodgate was Chancellor Gordon Brown's surrender of vital economic powers to an unelected committee of financiers at the Bank of

England: something a Tory would never have dared. 'The Bold Chancellor', cooed the front page. 'How daring he is . . . clearly, the new government has hit the ground running.'

'GOODBYE XENOPHOBIA' was the *Observer*'s post-election front page, and 'THE FOREIGN OFFICE SAYS HELLO WORLD, REMEMBER US'. The government, said the paper, would sign the Social Chapter within weeks, push for 'new worldwide rules on human rights and the environment', ban land-mines, implement 'tough new limits on all other arms sales' and end 'the country house tradition of policy-making'. Apart from the land-mines ban, which was already effectively in place, none of the above happened. A week later it was 'WELFARE: THE NEW DEAL'. The Chancellor, said the paper, 'is preparing to announce the most radical welfare budget since the Second World War . . .' On the contrary, what he announced was a 'welfare-to-work' scheme that was a pale imitation of failed and reactionary schemes already tried by the Tories and the Clinton administration. There was no new deal.

When Blair went to Europe the crescendo rose again. 'Blair ready to fight for a People's Europe', announced the *Independent*, and the next day: 'Europe's leaders smitten by Blair'. In Amsterdam, said the *Guardian*, 'the Prime Minister charmed his way to a EU Treaty deal'. On the BBC's *Newsnight* Peter Snow declared it 'Blair's day as admiring delegates expressed their admiration . . .'

Like the old *Pravda*, most of it was simply untrue. Blair's 'triumph' in Europe, like that of his predecessor, had been to fudge the question of a single currency and to shore up Britain's inhuman refugee laws by demanding special border controls. 'Peace in our children's time', shouted the *Independent*. At last, irony? No, the signing of the NATO–Russia Security Pact, with Blair centre-stage, was another triumph. The alarming implications of NATO's expansion were of no interest.

'The New Special Relationship' was the next good news, with Tony Blair and Bill Clinton looking into each other's eyes in the garden at 10 Downing Street. 'What was it', asked

Rupert Cornwall on the front page of the *Independent*, 'one Jack Kennedy, exactly our Prime Minister's age, 43, when he came to power, said about torches being passed? Rub your eyes on a dazzling spring day in Downing Street, and it seemed to be happening – from a becalmed and aimless American presidency to the coltish omnipotence of Blairdom?' In the total absence of satire (Steve Bell excepted), journalism had become parody.

A mystical tone emerged. The new Prime Minister, wrote Hugo Young, 'wants to create a world none of us have known, where the laws of political gravity are overturned'. In the Age of Blair 'ideology has surrendered entirely to "values" . . . there are no sacred cows [and] no fossilised limits to the ground over which the mind might range in search of a better Britain, and very few that these values would not be able to accommodate.'

The besotted minds ranged far. In a prize-winning Tonier-than-thou piece, Martin Kettle declared Blair an honorary Australian. 'He is not in awe of the past,' he wrote. 'He is not intimidated by class. He is a meritocrat, a doer [and] he is not particular about where he gets his ideas from. He is simply happy making his own history . . . it would be nice to think that one day these would be thought of as British characteristics, too.'

I suppose I ought to have been grateful for this reappraisal of my heritage. Goodbye corks-around-the-hat and beer-swilling blokes, we Australian males were now the exemplars of post-modern man. Kettle's effusions were from the same well of patronising ignorance lampooned in the old Barry MacKenzie strip in *Private Eye*: such is Blair-love. The irony is that Australia, a class-based society like any other, is burdened with the same high unemployment and poverty as Britain, thanks to policies set in train by a Labor Government which has served as something of a Blair model.

By the time Foreign Secretary Robin Cook had made his famous 'mission statement', putting human rights at the 'heart' of British foreign policy and reviewing arms sales on 'ethical' grounds, scepticism remained dormant. Indeed, the

Guardian counselled him not to be too 'soft centred'. On *Newsnight* Jeremy Paxman assured his audience that even if the new 'ethical' policy stopped the sale of Hawk fighters to Indonesia, their presence in East Timor was 'not proved' – the Foreign Office lie. Alone on a panel of New Labour hagiographers, it was left to a man from the Body Shop to make the point that Cook's policy was a sham because British foreign policy was *institutionally* committed to the denial of human rights. As it turned out, Cook continued arms-dealing, as the Tories had done and Labour before them had done.

The next 'dynamic' change was Defence Secretary George Robertson's 'radical, wide-ranging review' of 'priorities'. His 'review' banned all discussion of the billions of pounds spent on the Eurofighter aircraft and Trident nuclear submarines. Setting the tone of the reporting, BBC radio news put it this way: 'The Government has become alarmed at continual delays by Germany in approving its share of funding for production of the multi-national aircraft. Thousands of British jobs depend on the project.' The fact that each job cost £1.1 million, which could create hundreds more jobs, as well as restore much of the nation's infrastructure, was simply left out.

One media-managed stunt followed another. 'POVERTY'S THE PROBLEM, WORK IS THE SOLUTION', said the Victorian headline in the *Independent* over a piece about a visit by Blair to the land of the 'underclass' on a battered London council estate. Surrounded by poverty, he pledged no resources and proposed no plan to alleviate it. 'Blair', wrote Donald Macintyre, 'was trying to teach the lesson that where the Sixties was the age of the state, the Eighties of the individual, the millennium ushered in the age of the community.' Thus, political journalism and a government's sloganeering merged.[41]

A not untypical example of the subversion of journalism by political public relations was on the front page of the first 'relaunched' issue of the *Independent*. This was pure *Baghdad Observer*, dominated by a back-lit, messianic image of the

Prime Minister, beneath the banner headline: 'BLAIR: MY VISION FOR THE YEAR 2000'. The 'interview' was mostly a series of slogans. 'Speaking from Chequers', The Leader declared that he would 'create a country that would hold its head high as the model of what a 21st century developed nation should be'. There were no details, simply 'hard choices ahead' in order to achieve 'proper levels of social provision'. 'The Prime Minister,' noted the political editor, Anthony Bevins, 'would not be drawn on the application of these principles.'

The next day, it was Harriet Harman's turn. Announcing its 'exclusive' interview with the Social Security Secretary, the paper celebrated the 'sensational early results [of] New Welfare ... giving the underclass an escape from a life on benefit'. 'With 1000 [single] mothers seen so far,' wrote Bevins, 'the hit-rate is beyond all expectations; without precedent.' What kind of work they were found he did not say. How much they were paid and how much they had to spend on child care he did not say.[42]

Nor did he refer to the fact that one of Harman's first decisions on coming to power was to abolish the single parents' welfare premium and benefit, in spite of her pledge to the House of Commons that Labour opposed these impoverishing Tory-inspired cuts. 'The way to get lone mothers out of poverty and cut spending on benefits for them', the future minister had said, 'is not by cutting the amount on which they have to live year by year and plunging them further into poverty. [Such cuts] will make hundreds of thousands of the poorer children worse off.'[43] Nor did the lobby writer make any mention of an independent report released that week by the Joseph Rowntree Foundation, which all but dismissed the Government's 'New Welfare Deal', concluding that 'welfare-to-work' schemes rarely helped the unemployed find lasting work and were poor value for money.[44] Instead, the *Independent* allowed the minister to say, unchallenged, that her sinister project 'is about real people, real lives. It is what government is for. It is very exciting; it's liberating people. This is part of the process of creating a new welfare state. And it works.'

Blair's invitation to Margaret Thatcher to visit him in Downing Street caused momentary confusion. Blair (who in 1987 described Thatcher as having an 'unchecked and unbalanced mind') was rescued by Hugo Young, once the scourge of Thatcher. Young wrote, 'It is entirely related to the kind of inclusiveness he sees as the philosophy with which any sensible leader should be running any country he happens to control. Into this frame Margaret Thatcher easily fits. She has a contribution to make.' This is the same woman who, Young once wrote, had an 'utterly insatiable desire for domination'.[45]

The new guardians briefly scratched their heads as to why ruthless *laissez-faire* capitalists like Alan Sugar and Lord Rothermere, owner of the *Daily Mail*, should embrace Blairdom. Oh, well, they were now One of Us. Let the celebrations continue *Hello!* style! Blairdom, wrote Sally Weale, 'already has an icon like Princess Diana'. It's Cherie Blair! 'Cherie is naturally brilliant,' Tony told Sally, who wrote that for the first time in 10 Downing Street, 'we have a brilliant professional whose salary (and talents, many say) far outstrip those of her husband'. *And* she is a 'brilliant working mother'. This is the same Cherie Booth, barrister, who in 1995 asked a magistrate to return a penniless poll tax defaulter to prison.[46]

'New York, New Labour, new opportunities . . .' sang the *Guardian* in its report of a 'celebrity fund-raising' party for the Blairs by a group of rich, corporate, expatriate Britons. The guest list had given Alistair Campbell, the Prime Minister's press secretary, 'a positive frisson of delight'. *Everybody* was there: Henry Kissinger, Bianca Jagger, Lauren Bacall, Barbara Walters. 'There was, however, one name that troubled him [John F. Kennedy Jr]. Ye Gods, he could see the headlines . . . "Blair Sups with IRA Sympathiser".' The late President's son 'had been spotted standing at the back of an IRA funeral'. So JFK Jr was out, and 'Campbell could not have planned it better himself . . . Everyone just loved Blair.'[47]

And they loved Gordon Brown, too – literally, it seemed. 'A BUDGET FOR THE PEOPLE' said the *Independent*'s front page over a drawing of Brown dressed as Oliver Cromwell. This was difficult to fathom. Apart from a few crumbs for the Health Service and education, and windfall taxes on the utilities, which their huge profits easily absorbed, the nature of Brown's budget was reflected the next day when the *Financial Times* Share Index rose a record 80 points and shares in all the utilities leapt, because the stock market had expected him to be tougher on them. Moreover, he reduced corporate tax to the lowest of any major industralised country. Most Labour voters had endured eighteen years of cuts in education, social security, disability and other benefits – yet Brown reversed not a single one of them; and there was not a word of protest from the mainstream media. As the Institute of Fiscal Studies mused, the new Labour Chancellor had imposed a squeeze 'far harsher than any during eighteen years of Conservative rule'.

'I, personally,' wrote the *Guardian*'s Emma Forrest of the Chancellor, 'am obsessed by his lounge suit and what exactly it might turn out to be. I keep picturing him playing Las Vegas in purple crushed velvet, or wandering the corridors of power in a romper suit ... Let's be honest: in the nineties, who doesn't want to be with a man who knows about money and how the markets are being played?'[48] In the *Independent*, Suzanne Moore wrote, 'When he smiled on election night it was so beautiful, like when Mandela smiles – you could poke him and there would be something there.' Moore is a zealous guardian. Before the election, she proposed 'a kind of political rehabilitation programme for those uncomfortable at these changes being brought on board [by New Labour].'

And as in the former Soviet Union, or down on Animal Farm, all those who fail to greet the 'new' establishment must be suffering a form of mental illness. According to Susie Orbach, the pop psychologist, not taking unquestioning plea-sure in the rise of Blairdom must be because 'there's something safe in negativity ... you often find [this state of mind] in someone who appears to be a fighter, who takes on external injustice and enemies, but who, on the other hand, is unable to recognise their own attachment to defeat'.

To be critical of New Labour at this historic and orgasmic moment was thus to be an emotional inadequate, someone to be pitied: 'a fighter who can only fight, who can never rest from battle ... trying to defeat inner demons, hopeless feelings, that are far too frightening to touch directly'. Thatcher's command to the nation to 'rejoice!' during the Falklands War comes to mind.[49]

Alas, those inner demons and hopeless feelings would not go away, but migrated to the rejoicing class itself. The *Guardian* tried its best to ignore them. 'HIGH IDEALS, HARD CHOICES', said the front page, 'Blair can be a beacon to the world ... Blair [is] turning leadership into an art form.' But it was not to be.[50]

Through the media looking-glass Bernie Ecclestone, for whom the notion of 'hard choices', unlike single parents and the unemployed, did not apply. Tony Blair had met Ecclestone, the billionaire controller of Formula One motor racing, when he visited the Silverstone track before the election. He had sat in a Formula One car; he had been very impressed, and Ecclestone, a lifelong benefactor of the Tory Party, had been impressed by him. Unfortunately, one of New Labour's 'promises' had been to ban tobacco advertising, including sports sponsorship. With Blair in 10 Downing Street, Ecclestone asked to see him. Twenty-four hours later the Prime Minister had sent a memorandum to the Secretary of State for Health, exempting Formula One from the sponsorship ban.

It was left to the Health Minister, Tessa Jowell, to tell the world what a good idea this was. Alas, it was discovered that Jowell's partner, David Mills, had been, until just after the election, a director of the Benetton Formula One racing company and remained its legal adviser. The minister derided suggestions of a conflict of interest. Then it was discovered that Ecclestone had given £1 million to New Labour. For his part, Blair claimed that he had already alerted Sir Patrick Neill, Chairman of the Committee on Standards in Public Life, as to the 'question of ethics' of accepting such a donation, long before the press had disclosed it. In fact, the letter to Neill was sent after the press published it. The government had not only acted in the interests of a powerful businessman and against the interests of the electorate, but had lied about it. Blair subsequently apologised, but his apology was really for a failure of public relations. If the public are to be fooled, they should be fooled efficiently. Of course, the only difference between New Labour's and the Tories' sleaze was that the New Labour variation involved more money.

'DID YOU LIE TO US, TONY?' pleaded the *Independent on Sunday*. 'We believed you when you promised sleaze-free politics. We shared in your electoral triumph. We thought you were different. But now we're not sure.'[51]

In 1983, during the Cold War, two colleagues and I were given a 'secret' briefing at the Ministry of Defence, presided over by Ian McDonald, who achieved fleeting fame during the Falklands War as the government's spokesman, or 'speaking clock' as journalists unkindly but concisely called him. We sat down with a senior Civil Servant, whose name and position I forget, and who was described as an expert on the 'nuclear deterrent'. He gave us a stream of low-grade Cold War propaganda of the kind you read in *Daily Telegraph* editorials.

I wondered if this was what defence correspondents swallowed regularly behind a screen of schoolboy secrecy. McDonald assured me it was. As we parted, he said, 'You realise none of this happened? ... what's more, you cannot even say that none of it happened.' It is not surprising that when the Berlin Wall came down and the old Cold War ended, those journalists on a strict diet of their government's propaganda were taken completely by surprise.

However, from the point of view of the state, the efficacy of the system cannot be denied. Between 1965 and 1980, Parliament did not once debate the nuclear arms race, arguably the most urgent and dangerous issue facing humanity. An almost parallel silence existed in the media. The 'lobby system' contributed to this. Journalists were either put off the scent of genuine stories of public interest, or they were given briefings that were spurious in their reassurance. Little has changed. The post-Cold War acceleration of the nuclear weapons programme in Britain and the United States, which Russia is again attempting to match, is a non-story.

This omission is part of the 'culture of lying', described by the former Foreign Office official Mark Higson at the Scott arms-to-Iraq inquiry.[52] It ensured the cover-up of a series of nuclear disasters in Britain spanning forty years, including nuclear fires, crashes, contamination and dropped and damaged weapons. In the most extreme case, reported the *Observer* belatedly in 1996, 'a United States nuclear bomber and its weapon burnt on the ground [at Greenham Common in Berkshire], contaminating the surrounding countryside with fissile material in its deadliest form.' A large part of Britain was almost turned into 'a nuclear desert'. Not a word of this was reported at the time.[53]

The silence and complicity on the nuclear issue were dramatised to remarkable effect in Peter Watkins's film, *The War Game*, which reconstructed the aftermath of an attack on London with a one-megaton nuclear bomb. The film's commentator said, 'On almost the entire subject of thermo-nuclear weapons, on problems of possession and effects of their use, there is now practically total silence in the press, official publications and on TV. There is hope in any unresolved or unpredictable situation. But is there real hope to be found in this silence?'

The irony of this statement equalled its accuracy. In 1965, the BBC banned *The War Game*. The official explanation was that 'the effect of the film has been judged by the BBC to be too horrifying for the medium of broadcasting'. The BBC insisted that the decision had been taken entirely on its own and 'not as a result of outside pressure of any kind'. Both these statements were false.

The chairman of the BBC Board of Governors was Lord Normanbrook, formerly Secretary to the Cabinet. In a letter to his successor at the Cabinet, Sir Burke Trend, Norman-brook revealed that the real reason for the ban was that the film 'might have a significant effect on public attitudes towards the policy of the nuclear deterrent'.[54]

The Director-General who concurred with this decision was Hugh Greene. A few months earlier, Greene, a distinguished liberal, had said in a speech, 'Censorship to my mind is the more to be condemned when we remember that, historically, the greatest risks have attached to the maintenance of what is right and honourable and true'.[55]

It was not until 1985 – twenty years after the film was made – that *The War Game* was finally shown by the BBC. In introducing 'this highly controversial film', Ludovic Kennedy said it had been kept off the screens all this time because it was 'too shocking and too disturbing to transmit'. To my knowledge, no one challenged this falsehood.

Peter Watkins never worked for the BBC again, becoming both bitter and wise. In 1980, he described 'the liberal repression which has been emerging as a phenomenon on TV ... Using the names of "quality" and "professionalism" and "objectivity" and "standard", the middle echelons of television are now exercising a repression which is even more severe than that of the political bosses who they like to claim are responsible, but in fact whose only guilt often is that they (the bosses) provide an excuse, or a front, for the middle echelon to carry out a wave of censorship and self-censorship unparalleled since the inception of public service broadcasting.'[56]

The war in the north of Ireland has been covered successfully and often courageously by a select band of journalists, notably Peter Taylor, John Ware, Robert Fisk, Eamonn McCann, Simon Winchester, Ronan Bennett and Paul Donovan. They and others are the honourable exceptions; for the nature of the conflict, its causes and likely solutions are seldom illuminated.

To British viewers, listeners and readers, 'northern Ireland' is synonymous with a cycle of malicious violence perpetrated exclusively by the IRA. Beyond that is an arcane struggle between two tribes, with the British authorities honourably in the middle. That is the official version, and attempts by British journalists and broadcasters to tell the truth about the state's pivotal part in the denial of human rights and justice in Ireland are likely to end up on a list of hundreds of programmes on Ireland that have been banned, doctored, delayed or neutered.[57]

I have reported from the north of Ireland, but I have never submitted a proposal for a documentary; and part of the reason is undoubtedly a self-censoring trepidation tied to the 'special difficulties' that lie ahead. The Independent Broadcasting Authority guidelines stated that 'para-militaries' could be interviewed anywhere in the world without prior reference to the Authority, *except in Ireland*. I could interview Pol Pot's genocidists without permission from London, but not members of the IRA.

In 1988, this attained the level of high farce when broadcasting institutions accepted a Home Office decree that the representatives of certain Irish political organisations, including those with MPs elected to Parliament, could not be heard on the public airwaves. Their faces could be seen on television, their lips could be seen moving, their words could be spoken by someone else, but their voices could not be broadcast.

Instead of opposing outright such an absurdity, the broadcasting organisations substituted actors' voices. This served to marginalise and demonise those like the Sinn Fein leader, Gerry Adams, who were to play, and could have then played, a part in bringing peace and justice to Ireland.

'Some journalists who have argued that the ban is counterproductive', wrote David Miller in his book *Don't Mention the War*, 'implicitly agree with supporters of the ban that the main object of covering Sinn Fein and the IRA is not to explain the conflict but to discredit the republicans as part of the campaign to defeat "terrorism". Their difference with supporters of the ban is that they see it as a means of "inhibiting" the exposure of Sinn Fein.'[58]

David Nicholas (later Sir David), the editor of ITN at the time, protested that a ban was unnecessary, 'because we all understand that what these extremist organisations stand for is abhorrent to many people. British public opinion has never been more resolute than it is now, in my opinion, in defeating terrorism and that owes a lot to [our] full and frank reporting . . .'[59]

What he did *not* say was that ITN (and the BBC) had seldom discussed British withdrawal from the north of Ireland, an issue on which public opinion had indeed been 'resolute'. 'In almost every poll since 1971', Miller pointed out, 'a majority has favoured some form of British withdrawal from Ireland.'[60]

Backed by the National Union of Journalists, I and five other journalists tried to have the ban declared illegal in the High Court, but we were unsuccessful. There is no doubt in my mind that had the BBC, ITN and Channel 4 mounted a concerted campaign against the ban they would have had it overturned. John Birt, then deputy Director-General of the BBC, wrote a number of hand-wringing articles in the press after he had failed to raise any objection to the ban when it was imposed. With ventriloquists on the evening news, Britain became a laughing stock until the ban was lifted after the IRA declared a ceasefire in 1994.

The paranoia felt by the British establishment over Ireland was described by Colin Wallace, the former British army psychological operations officer who was subsequently framed on a manslaughter charge. 'MI5's increased role in Northern Ireland from the early 1970s', he told Paul Donovan, 'coincided with growing industrial unrest in the rest of Britain. More extreme elements within the security service, aided by equally extreme associates in politics, industry and the media, projected the situation as part of a world-wide communist conspiracy. The intelligence community saw the Irish situation as the front line of the left's threat to the UK, and of a great conspiracy by the communist bloc to undermine the whole of the UK . . . Media operations played, and as far as I can judge, continue to play an important part in this psychological warfare.'[61]

In December 1996, Sean O'Callaghan, a former IRA commander claiming responsibility for more than seventy attacks on security targets, was suddenly released and pardoned. He was immediately put through a £10,000 'media training' course by MI5, and his former position in the IRA was rewritten to enhance his status. Thereafter the 'ex-IRA leader' was given extraordinary coverage in Britain. For his handlers in MI5 all went brilliantly. O'Callaghan was on the BBC's *World at One*, then the *Nine O'Clock News* and *Newsnight*. His message was straightforward: the IRA ceasefire 'was never genuine ... the Irish Government must admit they have been conned ... the IRA has to be politically and militarily defeated if there is ever going to be peace.' The SDLP leader and peace broker John Hume 'must be brought under control'.[62]

All this had a familiar ring to it. On the BBC and in the *Belfast Telegraph*, O'Callaghan opined that 'political isolation, security force attrition and broadcasting bans [were] the methods that had brought the IRA to the edge of defeat'. In the *Independent*, he wrote that 'the Prevention of Terrorism Act or something similar is absolutely necessary in the fight against terrorism'. O'Callaghan's 'insights' were, almost word for word, those of the British Government's propaganda model of the previous twenty-five years.[63]

The Irish press recognised this, including the conservative *Irish Times*, and O'Callaghan's pronouncements were treated with proper journalistic caution. In contrast, the British media, wrote David Miller, 'tend to accept the definition of the conflict in Ireland as "terrorism" versus "democracy"'. This has led to 'a souring of relations between the republican movement and the media', which has meant that journalists are frequently denied the kind of legitimate contacts that might allow them to assess more objectively the kind of 'insights' offered by O'Callaghan.[64]

In his 1969 book *Low Intensity Operations*, which is widely regarded as a propaganda blueprint for the war in Ireland, Brigadier Frank Kitson wrote that the government must, above all, 'promote its own cause and undermine that of the enemy by disseminating its view of the situation'. And what better way to achieve this than by the time-honoured use of a grateful collaborator and a malleable press?[65]

On December 29, 1996, the *Sunday Times* reported on its front page that 'Gerry Adams and Martin McGuinness, Sinn Fein's two most senior strategists, have been appointed to the IRA's army council, intelligence officials say'. There was no corroboration for what was an 'intelligence plant'. Ten days later, the *Observer* allowed Michael Mates, the former Northern Ireland Security Minister, to repeat this unsubstantiated claim, and to add that the two men 'are certainly orchestrating [terrorism]'. This, Mates assured the *Observer*, is 'all you need to know'.[66]

During the 1994–6 IRA ceasefire, both press and broadcast coverage adhered strictly to the British Government model. That is, it continued to concentrate on the IRA. 'Decommissioning' of IRA arms became a major issue, even though it was a non-issue, while minimal attention was paid to the Unionist paramilitaries and nothing was made of the extensive refortification of British military bases and of continuing British Army activity in nationalist communities, specifically the border town of Crossmaglen.

When a conference on demilitarisation was held in Crossmaglen, army helicopters hovered overhead. This spectacular intimidation was not reported in Britain. Throughout the ceasefire the Royal Ulster Constabulary continued to use plastic bullets, firing more than 100 in two days in Derry. This also went unreported in Britain.[67]

When the IRA renewed its bombing campaign in February 1996, the American liberal journal the *Nation* described it as 'an indefensible military response to the corruption and recklessness of a politician who was willing to torpedo peace to keep his job'. Similarly, the *Washington Post* described John Major as the 'saboteur' of the peace negotiations.[68] These were far from being pro-republican voices; and they reflected a body of opinion in the United States that appreciated why the bombers had returned. Such a perspective remains suppressed or obscured in Britain behind ritual denunciations of violence and a consensual media/ parliamentary silence.

With the release of Ken Loach's 1988 film, *Hidden Agenda*, which effectively broke the silence on the government's 'shoot-to-kill' policy, the cinema began to play a role forsaken by journalism. Certainly, the level of press hysteria directed at Loach's film suggested a shaming of journalism's record on Ireland. The writer Jim Sheridan told a London Film Festival audience that films like *Hidden Agenda*, *In the Name of the Father*, *Michael Collins* and *Some Mother's Son* were 'gradually bringing some glimpse of history to the British public'.[69]

In 1997, *Some Mother's Son*, about the hunger strikes in which IRA prisoners died, was routinely attacked as 'anti-British' and 'IRA propaganda'. The *Daily Mail* predicted that the film's effect would be to 'weaken the consensus which has kept Parliament united on the issue . . .' Helen Mirren, the star, was constantly asked to take a loyalty pledge to Queen and Country. 'Mirren is quick to stress', wrote Ian Katz in the *Guardian*, 'that one of the most sympathetic characters in the film is a Foreign Office official who tries – and fails – to broker an end to the stand-off, but it is hard to escape the impression that she too feels some unease about the film's transparent bias. She points out that she fought hard for her character to express her disapproval of the IRA and the hunger strike . . .'[70]

In fact, her character *is* disapproving of both the IRA and the hunger strike; and it is an irony that, contrary to its depiction in the film, in reality the IRA tried to stop the hunger strike. This fact eluded the film's critics, who also failed to question whether the 'sympathetic' Foreign Office official existed. 'Transparent bias' can be like a mirror.

'The paradoxes and dilemmas explored in *Some Mother's Son*', wrote Ronan Bennett, 'will undoubtedly unsettle some British audiences in much the same way other recent films on Ireland have. But if it encourages debate and speculation, if it drives people to question the assumptions on which British policy in Ireland continues to be based, where is the harm in this? The questions the film raises can either be answered, or they can't.'[71]

'Europe' is an enduring establishment concern, or obsession.

To the serious media, politicians are 'pro-European' or they are 'Euro-sceptics' or 'Little Englanders'; the 'debate' is conducted largely in jargon with frequent xenophobic outbursts. 'The terms of Maastricht' slips from the lips of interviewers and interviewees alike without the viewing or listening audience being granted a clue to what they are talking about.

Yet Britain's membership of the 'single market' and the European Monetary Union has grave implications for the majority of people. The issues have nothing to do with the joys of European togetherness, or with European notions of democracy and prosperity for all. 'Europe' is an economic cartel, dominated by Germany's conservative elite and the German central bank, which wants every member country's balance-of-payments deficit and rate of inflation wiped out so that the deutschmark can reign all-powerful, becoming the 'Euro' currency by another name. As governments strive to meet these conditions by cost-cutting on jobs, health, welfare, education and transport, economic and social disaster beckon throughout the European Union, especially in the poorer countries.

The consequences are well understood by millions of Europeans who have angrily demonstrated their opposition to 'Maastricht'. France has twice been paralysed by popular protest; at the time of writing, demonstrations are sweeping Germany, where the rate of unemployment has risen to 12 per cent, the highest since Hitler came to power in 1933.

The coverage in Britain has concentrated almost exclusively on effect rather than cause and on political careers. When French cities filled with protesters in 1995, the emphasis was on the 'survival' of the then French Prime Minister, Alain Juppé, and his deficit-cutting policies. A year later, during the French truckers' strike, the emphasis was on the inconvenience caused to British business and the alleged 'intimidation' of British truckers held up in France; typically, most of an item on the BBC *Nine O'Clock News* was about drivers who had tried to escape the blockade.[72] There was scant reference to why the truckers were blocking roads and ports. The newsreader referred to the 'industrial anarchy' of the French, implying a generic fault. The positive and moving spectacle of working people united, supported by the overwhelming majority of the French people, was minimised.[73]

On the day of the truckers' victory, the BBC's Paris correspondent, Hugh Schofield, reporting on *PM*, brushed over the issues before interviewing an employers' representative, whom he accused of a 'cave in' and 'giving in to blackmail'. Refusing to rise to the BBC man's level of indignation, she explained that the truckers were poorly paid and had every right to retire at the age of 55 'because it is such a hard job'. The irony of the employer having to put the truckers' side appeared to be lost on the broadcaster, who failed to explain why there was no union representative on the programme.[74]

I could find only one report that made the connection between the truckers' action and the pressure to install a single European currency. This was by Martin Woollacott in the *Guardian*. He explained how 'the policies necessary for the single currency are more and more against the grain in France. A majority of French people sympathised with the drivers and, in a choice between cutting deficits and creating jobs, or sustaining adequate wages, prefer the latter . . . The uncompleted single market is already a force driving down wages and conditions.'[75]

Similar mass action by workers elsewhere in Europe failed to qualify as 'mainstream' news in Britain. This included a long-running strike by 70,000 secondary-school teachers in Greece and strikes by bus and Métro workers in France and steelworkers in Belgium. The most newsworthy action of all was in Britain on January 20 and September 8–9, 1997, when dockers in 105 ports across the world stopped all shipping as an act of solidarity with 500 sacked dockers in Liverpool (see pages 352–3). This was both unprecedented in modern maritime history and ignored.

The consequences of 'market forces' are generally reported as if they are acts of God. To the BBC, the penury of some sixty million pensioners in Russia is a 'free market reform' and those who oppose it are 'hardliners' and 'crypto-commu-nists'. So it was not surprising that the first anniversary of Boris Yeltsin's military assault on Russia's democratically elected parliament should be celebrated on BBC radio as 'Yeltsin's courage that crushed the hardliners'.[76] Moreover, lamented the *Guardian*'s Moscow correspondent, David Hearst, there is no longer 'any faith that democratic values are the right ones for crisis-ridden Russia today . . . The question remains, did *we* win the East or are *we* about to lose it?' (My italics.) Who is 'we'? More to the point, why do journalists take refuge in what Orwell called 'the language of power'?[77]

This 'we' is an increasingly fashionable device, long used to represent the civilised West against dark forces, now used to great effect in the promotion of something called 'New Britain'. Born on the day Tony Blair took office, New Britain is the latest attempt to breathe life into the Victorian notion that 'we' are a single nation with a single identity. Class dis-tinctions that ensure whether or not you have a job and how long you live have no place in this 'kinder, gentler land', where, as Jeremy Hardy pointed out, 'Michael Heseltine and a former miner will embrace each other because they're both Welsh [and] people will have more say over their own lives so long as that doesn't mean selecting their own political candidates or cramping their employer's style.'[78] 'Culture' is everything; style and image 'make it happen'; populism is democracy. The self-promoting marketing agency Demos, a source of many New Britain stories, offers 'principles for culture changers'. 'Be distinctive,' it advises. 'Seventeen out of twenty new brands fail – usually because the brand doesn't offer the consumer anything new. In a world where countries have very little "brand recognition", it is vital to isolate a unique selling proposition.'[79]

Although it is not disputed that Blair is the major inspira-tion of New Britain, as Jonathan Freedland memorably wrote in the *Guardian*, 'it took the death of Princess Diana to inject real life into the idea'.[80] On the evening of Diana's funeral, the BBC broadcaster Gavin Eslar announced that we had 'come together as a people and learned who we are'.

With every maudlin cliché and platitude and crapulous homily, from 'Diana is at rest; the nation is not', to 'Things will never be the same again', those whose job is to keep the record straight, *especially* in challenging and emotionally try-ing circumstances, became little more than assistant pall-bear-ers, at worst cogs in a mighty public relations juggernaut. Like the Gulf War, few dared raise uncomfortable questions; those who did were heretics. Few dared to point out that a wealthy aristocrat and her playboy lover found speeding through a built-up area with a criminally intoxicated driver could have caused the deaths of innocent road users. Few dared to sug-gest that, given the infinite opportunities and privileges of her wealth and class, Diana Spencer had done little to advance the human condition, and that her principal achievement was her own media-constructed image. Most of her estimated fortune of £40 million did not go to the charities that were 'close to her heart'.[81]

Apart from 'our' grieving, the serious media's line was that the House of Windsor was somehow threatened by Diana's popularity in death. On the contrary, during the week of the funeral the British establishment demonstrated, yet again, its consummate skill at assimilating populism and drawing new life from it.

Ruling politicians can, of course, be counted on to arrange their own place in the assimilation. The 'spontaneous and utterly genuine' reaction of Prime Minister Blair to the news of Diana's death was, in fact, written for him in the early hours of the morning by one of his numerous 'spin doctors', who coined the mantra 'people's princess', the mantra of both politicians and media speaking as one.

As for the crowds, and without detracting from the decent responses of people and their support for a perceived 'underdog', few journalists dared to say that the numbers in the streets were as much a product of the new power of the media, particularly the global celebrity 'culture', as Diana's ephemeral reputation. This was demonstrated by the many people who repeated for the camera the rushed judgements and gossip served up to them as news and current affairs.

A sense of history is part of serious journalism, and history is marked by spectacles of 'grieving' and otherwise 'moved' crowds; I have been among my share of them. When the Pope visited the shrine of the Black Madonna in Poland in 1979, he was greeted by a million people; I shall not forget a landscape of green meadows lined with hundreds of portable confessionals. The Poles were also 'dignified' and threw flowers at their hero, just as people did at Diana's hearse. The funerals of the Egyptian nationalist Gamal Abdel Nasser and Iran's Ayatollah Khomeini drew millions to events of great shared emotion. This did not mean they held the key to the truth of the occasion. In my experience, the opposite is usually the case. Journalists who fail to recognise this let down the millions of people who did not lay tributes and did not watch the funeral (almost half 'the nation') and who still look to them for the truth.

In his book, *Joe McCarthy and the Press*, Edwin P. Bayley, a veteran reporter, reveals and regrets how he and the majority of his colleagues became the tools of McCarthyism in the United States by 'going along with the propaganda' and seldom challenging its assumptions or identifying the power that lay behind it. 'All the while we believed we were being objective,' he wrote.[82]

Forty years later the veteran BBC war reporter Martin Bell, now the MP for Tatton, announced his own revelations and regrets. Bell said he now regarded 'the notion of objectivity [as] something of an illusion' which belonged to 'bystander journalism'. He believed in 'the journalism of attachment' – 'a journalism that cares as well as knows; that is aware of its responsibilities; and will not stand neutrally between good and evil, right and wrong, victim and oppressor'.

What was striking about Bell's Damascene conversion – apart from his desire to have it both ways: he rejects BBC 'objectivity', while 'holding fast' to BBC 'impartiality' – was his failure to acknowledge the *inherent* propaganda role of the media, especially the BBC, as an extension of establishment power. When did these institutions *ever* 'stand neutrally between good and evil, right and wrong, victim and oppressor'?

Bell is, of course, right about the 'illusion of objectivity'; George Orwell dispensed with this long ago. 'The more one is aware of political bias', he wrote, 'the more one can be independent of it, and the more one claims to be impartial, the more one is biased.'[83] This can only be understood by looking behind the façades of benevolence and paternalism in the institution Martin Bell served and identifying its true 'language of power'. Instead, he paid fulsome tribute to the 'long and honourable BBC tradition of distance and detachment' and 'the culture of truthfulness [that] still prevails'.[84]

He might tell that to the miners, and the Irish, and the Liverpool dockers, and the French truckers, and the Nicaraguans, and the Vietnamese, and the Russians, to name just a few whose lives and struggles have been filtered, misrepresented and excluded by the same 'tradition' and 'culture'. And he might mention it to his blackballed former colleague, Peter Watkins, who did not concern himself so much with establishment myths about 'detachment' but simply strove to tell the truth.

It is time journalists and broadcasters abandoned these myths. The great American journalist T. D. Allman once defined 'genuinely objective journalism' as that which 'not only gets the facts right, it gets the meaning of events right. Objective journalism is compelling not only today. It stands the test of time. It is validated not only by "reliable sources" but by the unfolding of history. It is reporting that which not only seems right the day it is published. It is journalism that ten, twenty, fifty years after the fact still holds up a true and intelligent mirror to events.'[85]

THE LAST VOICE

First they came for the Jews
And I did not speak out –
Because I was not a Jew.
Then they came for the communists
And I did not speak out –
Because I was not a communist.
Then they came for the trade unionists
And I did not speak out –
Because I was not a trade unionist.
Then they came for me –
And there was no one left
To speak out for me.

Pastor Niemöller

NOT LONG AGO, I left for the last time a place where I had invested much of my working life. It was the home of Central Television's freelance documentary makers: a three-storey terrace you would easily pass by, in Charlotte Street, London. Except for the night bell it did not announce itself. This was put right when Michelle Hartree was at the reception desk and, in her wonderfully exuberant way, welcomed visitors into what must have seemed like a cell of elusive anarchists.

A string of camp followers came and went: homeless people, worried people with good and bad ideas for films, talented people wanting to work for nothing, shadowy Pimpernel people who had served the British state in nefarious ways, like the SAS renegade with part of his face missing. 'Charlotte Street', as our documentaries unit was known, was one of the very few places in British television, or any-where, where film-makers were encouraged to make the documentaries they wanted to make without institutional assumptions and *diktats*. They were films that reached behind the screens of power and fashion, as good journalism, in whatever form, should do.

The location was important. Charlotte Street itself is the spine of Fitzrovia, one of the last remaining villages in the heart of London, home to writers and poets such as Dylan Thomas. The lemming march of Oxford Street is nearby; but the eccentricities of Charlotte Street seemed somehow immune.

Our neighbouring iconoclasts, like the revolutionary Index Bookshop, would not have survived in less bohemian territory. Neither would the man in the woolly hat who shouted at cars and was looked after by the people at the Villa Carlotta and Camisa's deli opposite. Near where I sat, within frying distance of two restaurants, one Greek, one Italian, the *plats du jour* were announced at noon by the crackle of fresh food in great pans of oil and the smell of garlic and basil. In the summer we waved to people in their deckchairs next to the chimney pots.

We were so cramped that entry and exit were by single file. The flushing of a lavatory would be remarked upon at the other end of an international telephone line. Almost every phone call was overheard, with perhaps the exception of director Adrian Cowell whispering in Portuguese. Some calls were tapped, and the place was broken into during long-running investigative films which involved government secrecy. But in the end they got nothing: I think the clutter defeated them. When Michelle Hartree left for the third time (she was a brilliant dancer who had also worked in a circus as a knife-thrower's assistant), we knew the rest of us would not be far behind.

Charlotte Street was the inspired idea of Richard Creasey, a gentle, determined man who produced the first television series made for the disabled, called *Link*. As head of documentaries at Central's forerunner, ATV, in 1980, he looked for a place where, as he put it, 'film-makers could develop their ideas into films, with our support, occasionally turning up to tell us how it was going; we were seldom disappointed'. Richard was succeeded by Roger James, a talented film editor, who offered support and commissions to those who might have seemed to others like itinerants but who, given the chance and a bit of development cash, produced memorable films.

These included Adrian Cowell's *Decade of Destruction*, a series of visionary films that alerted the world to the destruction of the Amazon rain forests; Judy Jackson's *In Search of the Assassin*, which showed vividly the CIA at work in Central America; Chris Menges's *East 103rd Street*, a stunning portrait of New York lost and found; Brian Moser's lyrical series on Latin America, *Before Columbus*; Anthony Thomas's *Thy Kingdom Come and Thy Will Be Done on Earth*, which exposed the evangelical movement in the United States; the late Juris Podnik's raw glimpse of communist Europe in transition, *Hello, Can You Hear Us?*; and Michael Grigsby's *Living on the Edge*, which bared Thatcher's Britain.

Ken Loach made *Questions of Leadership* at Charlotte Street. This was the series of three films which revealed the collaboration between the trade union hierarchy and Thatcherism (see pages 343–4). With the connivance of lawyers, they were banned, then gutted. It was an inglorious episode. With Alan Lowery, I made a series on Australia called *The Last Dream*, which told something of the rapacious truth about the country of our birth. And, of the many films to come out of my long partnership with David Munro, five on Cambodia were planned, researched and made in the cramped fire hazard opposite the deli.

There was a myth the place did not pay; in fact, it gave Central a modest, steady profit, mainly because our films sold all over the world and because our audience in Britain would wait up, if necessary, to watch them. When *Death of a Nation*, a film I made with David Munro about an unheard-of place called East Timor, went to air on ITV, British Telecom recorded, after midnight, 4,000 calls per minute to the 'helpline' number.

The problem with Charlotte Street was that it did not fit the future corporate mould and so it had to go. The homeless were said to be turning up far too frequently and sleeping on our doorstep. When the order to vacate finally came from our new owners, Carlton, it seemed appropriate that moving day was the day that the Tory Government minister responsible for the media, Virginia Bottomley, announced her Broadcasting Bill, which allowed the biggest and richest in commercial television to swallow the smallest.

That is the trend. The biggest and richest are swallowing not just the minnows, like Charlotte Street, but most of the world's media: news, current affairs and documentaries, our primary sources of information. This began in the 1990s in the United States, where the Disney company has swallowed the American Broadcasting Company, Sumner Redstone has taken over Paramount Communications, Time-Warner and Turner (CNN) have merged to become the world's biggest media monopoly and Rupert Murdoch has become the largest owner of television stations in the United States. His friend John Malone now owns 23 per cent of all the cable television stations on the planet. In Britain, two companies, Granada and Carlton, dominate the ITV network; and the digital age of television belongs to Murdoch and his friends.

Writing in the *New Yorker*, Ken Auletta described the 'gameplan'. Above all, it was Murdoch, he wrote, who 'created the first global media network by investing in both software (movies, TV shows, sports franchises, publishing) and the distribution platforms (the Fox network, cable and the TV satellite systems) that disseminate the software. Within the next few years, the News Corporation's satellite system will blanket South America, in addition to Asia and Europe and parts of the Middle East and Africa. "Basically, we want to establish satellite platforms in major parts of the world", Murdoch explains.'[1]

Auletta described a 'summit' between Murdoch and John Malone, the 'king of cable'. 'Malone had several goals in this meeting,' he wrote. 'He wanted to see if there were areas where he and Murdoch could do business together, and he wanted to avoid conflicts.' Malone believed that 'between us' they could 'control' thirty-three million pay-TV subscribers. Change the names and they are Mafia godfathers, dividing turf.

The immediate aim for all of them, says Murdoch, is to keep 'technology galloping over the old regulatory machine, getting past politicians and regulators'.[2] He means everywhere. Take his remarkable relationship with the rulers of the world's most populous nation, China. In 1993, in a speech lauding the 'communications revolution', Murdoch said that advances in media technology posed 'an unambiguous threat to totalitarian regimes everywhere'.[3] The Chinese Government responded by banning individuals from owning a satellite dish, thus depriving Murdoch's Hong Kong-based Star TV of its biggest market.

Not one to make such a mistake twice, Murdoch set out to appease and court the regime. He started by 'removing' BBC World Service Television from his Asian satellite. The Beijing regime had objected to the BBC's reporting of the Tiananmen Square massacre and to a BBC documentary about Mao Tsetung. 'The BBC was driving them nuts,' said Murdoch. 'It's not worth it. [The Chinese government] is scared to death of what happened in Tiananmen Square. The truth is – and we Americans don't like to admit it – that authoritarian countries can work.'[4]

Murdoch proposed a 'joint venture' with the Communist Party mouthpiece, the *People's Daily*, to sell information technology. In 1996, Shao Huaze, the boss of the *People's Daily*, who is also head of the Central Committee of the Chinese Communist Party, was invited to Britain as a guest of *The Times*, which is owned by Murdoch. He stayed at the Ritz, where he was visited by Prime Minister John Major. Shortly afterwards, Murdoch's Star TV broadcast a documentary series, made by the regime, eulogising the life and times of the 'paramount ruler' Deng Xiaoping.

This was based on a hagiography of Deng written by his daughter, and published by Basic Books, a division of HarperCollins: owner Rupert Murdoch.[5] Ms Deng was flown

to America by Murdoch, who fêted her with private parties, put her up at his ranch and toasted her father as 'a man who brought China into the modern world'.[6] Like the events in Tiananmen Square in 1989, it was as if his earlier, unfortunate speech had never happened.

As part of his deal with the *People's Daily*, Murdoch reportedly offered the Chinese dictators 'smart card' technology that would allow television programmes to be vetted before they were broadcast, although his company denied this.[7] His aim is a 'joint venture' allowing him to 'wire' China for pay-TV, and consummation is at hand, if his latest deal with Beijing is an indicator. In 1997, with the *People's Daily*, he launched his 'Chinabyte' Internet service in English. Politics will be censored; the Chinese users' view of the West will be the Murdoch view.

Ninety per cent of all world news and current affairs now comes to us from fewer and richer and more powerful sources. Three agencies, Associated Press, Reuters and Agence France Presse, supply most of the world's 'wire service' news. One is American, one is British, the other is French. Reuters and AP make huge profits selling financial and corporate information; their newsrooms have become centres of the 'free market' crusade. AP gets most of its funding from American clients and devotes most of its coverage to events in the United States.

Africa accounts for less than 5 per cent of this coverage, most of it concentrated on disasters.[8] The former President of Tanzania, Julius Nyerere, has drily suggested that the people of his country should be allowed to take part in the elections for President of the United States because they are bombarded with as much information about the candidates as Americans are.[9]

In television there are just two agencies providing foreign news footage to all the world's newsrooms – Reuters Television, formerly Visnews, and World Television Network, WTN. Reuters supplies 400 broadcasters in eighty-five countries, reaching an audience of half a billion people. WTN

reaches an estimated three billion people. Another two Western broadcasters, CNN and BBC World, come second. And there is the Internet, which, for all its variety and potential, is essentially an elite operation as most people in the world do not own a telephone, let alone a computer.

At a media conference organised by the *Financial Times* in 1996, a man described as 'Rupert Murdoch's technology guru' declared that by the year 2000 'a newspaper could be sent around the world by digital satellite signal in ten seconds, compared to an hour on the Internet'. No one in the audience asked him what difference this made to the *content* of the newspaper. The *Sun* sent in ten seconds is still, alas, the *Sun*; the *Sunday Times* digitalised is still the *Sunday Times*. No one interjected, 'So what?'[10]

It is said, at gatherings like this, that something called 'technological determinism' has replaced something called 'economic determinism'. Both are euphemisms for the latest model of *laissez-faire* capitalism. This is never said. The social consequences of the rise of media technology are seldom an issue. When modern media managers discuss their calling, they celebrate the *chutzpah* of their godfathers. Michael Eisner of Disney gets $10 million a year! Murdoch rewards his immediate executives with 'packages' totalling $45 million! Michael Grade buys the key to his golden handcuffs!

In the meantime, production budgets for factual programmes are reduced; ITN's once proud news service is handicapped by cost-cutting and profiteering, the BBC is consumed by 'market' bureaucracy and the new Channel 5 introduces the equivalent of a television penny arcade. ('Tune in, or get out of the way,' says the continuity announcer.) As 'multi-skilling' becomes the doctrine, the deskilling of craft becomes the practice, with the untrained encouraged to believe that possession of a camcorder makes them a film-maker and pointing it at nothing in particular produces an 'observational' documentary.

The managers of Murdoch's BSkyB satellite channel offer the industry an hour of television for £2,000. By 1998, some 170 satellite and cable stations will be in service, with

minimal costs, maximum profits and a format described by David Montgomery, the boss of L!ve TV, as 'exciting, raw television' – i.e. spontaneous, meaningless trash.[11]

Murdoch says his growing control of sports broadcasting is 'a battering ram' aimed at destroying 'the old structure' and replacing it with pay-TV. The profits generated by Murdoch's empire, his ability to move capital from country to country without paying tax and the freedom of his cable and satellite companies from legal requirements to broadcast unprofitable in-depth public affairs programmes, allow him to outbid the BBC for exclusive rights to more and more sports events, and other forms of popular entertainment. These are drawing audiences away from the BBC, making increases in the licence fee seem increasingly difficult to justify.[12]

In order to compete, the BBC is becoming the worldwide commercial operation it was never meant to be. In 1997, the BBC signed a deal with John Malone's Discovery Channel to co-produce documentaries and share his cable and satellite facilities around the world. Discovery usually commissions on the basis of market research 'approval' and is never 'controversial'. It is a huge deal covering sixty-one separate agreements and conditions, which the BBC, a public broadcaster, says it will not publish.

The pressures are not always insidious. In an echo of Murdoch's appeasement of the Chinese regime, the *Nine O'Clock News* called off a reporter's assignment to China to investigate sweatshops producing cheap toys for the British Christmas market. *Newsnight* wanted to show secret film shot in Chinese-occupied Tibet, but dropped the idea after 'internal consultation'. The BBC has a growing trade with China, selling language courses, books and successful programmes, such as *Pride and Prejudice* and *The Secret Life of Plants*. 'Our programme makers', said a BBC executive, 'need to work in China and have access to decision-makers.'[13]

The same imperatives now apply to radio. Overseen by a new regulatory body with a 'lighter touch', the number of commercial radio stations in Britain has doubled in recent years. According to the Broadcasting Act of 1996, this will generate greater choice and diversity. 'In reality,' wrote Bob Franklin in *Newszak and the News Media*, 'the policy outcome has been precisely the opposite. The market penalises those who stray too far from the mainstream [resulting in] a dull, homogeneous and predictable output.'[14]

Marshall McLuhan was wrong. In the 1960s, the Canadian 'media intellectual' predicted that modern information technologies would create a 'global village', breaking down barriers of language and distance, bringing people a form of 'wired' socialism. He preached that technology was an extension of human consciousness, that 'the medium is the message'. McLuhan changed his mind shortly before his death in 1980. He saw technology spinning out of control and humans becoming 'servo mechanisms' of a technological order controlled by the few at the expense of the many.[15]

The American mathematician Norbert Wiener, the inventor of 'cybernetics', warned prophetically that the new technology would lead to 'an unemployment situation in comparison with which ... even the Depression of the 1930s will seem a pleasant joke'.[16] Those who express such views today are regarded in the 'mainstream' as dinosaurs. So they are seldom heard, except at 'alternative' conferences and in the pages of *samizdat* literature.

One of the most eloquent dissenters is the Indian social scientist Vandana Shiva, who has long attacked a Western-imposed 'monoculture of the mind' and called for an 'insurrection of subjugated knowledge' against the 'dominant knowledge' of capitalism. 'This [dominant knowledge] leaves out a plurality of paths to knowing nature and the universe,' she wrote. 'Ninety per cent of it could be stopped without any risk of human deprivation.'[17]

Media technology has become a wondrous tool. The speed at which pictures, voices and the printed word can be transmitted ought to invest news gathering with an excitement that those of us who struggled with the telegram and landline telephones can only envy and admire. Ironically, it is not only the traditional means of journalism that are becoming obsolete, but the honourable traditions.

Canary Wharf, the glass obelisk rising out of London's former docklands, where five national newspapers are produced, is known by journalists as 'the ministry of truth'. Journalism has turned inward here. Having penetrated the layers of 'security', you notice the silence: footsteps are unheard and voices distant. Eye-contact is with the banks of VDU screens. There are no smells, not of ink or wood panelling or carbolic on the stairs. A vertical airport comes to mind.

On the *Daily Mirror* floor there are spy cameras and guards patrolling the newsroom. A journalist was hauled before managers because video evidence showed he was 'not working hard enough'. 'You don't leave your desk without your smart card,' said one of the journalists. 'We are as isolated from our readers as it is possible to be.'[18]

The maverick humane reporter fades in places like these. The likes of Robert Fisk, Ed Vulliamy and Maggie O'Kane come to mind. Trained by experience to take time and listen to people, the best of them went to uncomfortable places, followed leads and gathered evidence Their scepticism was reserved for the powerful. They were 'investigative journalists', but that, after all, is what all journalists should be.

Today, isolation and depleted staffing have bred a new kind of 'multi-skilled' journalist, who is not multi-skilled at all, but a sad, Protean figure required to work for a range of very different publications in the group and be loyal to none. There is no time to investigate; lifting a phone and scanning 'cuttings files' require no apprenticeship and little expense. Partly as a consequence of this, newspapers have become 'viewspapers', as Julian Petley calls them, vehicles not of curiosity and inquiry but of narcissism.[19]

The so-called metropolitan journalist is concerned more with introspection than with finding out about others. For females, this means 'relationships', personal disclosure and exhibitionism, child-obsessed matters and other *angsts* of the middle class. It is rare to read a 'feminist' writer whose work fails to confirm the stereotypes of the 'women's magazines': what Indian middle-class women call 'sari talk' (tittle-tattle). This is another version of pack journalism. It lacks the basic courage expected of people with principled insights, as true feminists are meant to have. None, it seems, dares to reclaim the politics of feminism from the therapist's couch: to explain to both women and men that the interests and needs of a teenage single mother struggling to keep her family going in a high-rise flat and those of a redundant steelworker are not divisive: that only by making that *political* connection will society move towards a fairer relationship between the sexes. So narrow has 'women's' writing become in the respectable press that it is rare indeed to read a Western feminist celebrating the courage and independence of disadvantaged women around the world.

An exception is the writer Sheila Rowbotham. In 1997, she published a refreshing attack on a journalism obsessed with the 'personal dilemmas of the middle class' and 'excluding the experiences of the great majority'. The debate on feminist issues had become stuck in the narrowest of grooves, she argued, and went on to list inspiring examples of women's movements who were 'doing and thinking the unimaginable ... amidst adversity and in desperation they have developed the courage and conviction to challenge that dismal deification of "flexibility" and market forces which has threatened their livelihoods'.

One shining illustration she cites is the Self-Employed Women's Association of Ahmedabad, India. The SEWA acts as both campaign group and union for its impoverished members, who range from rubbish collectors and street vendors to agricultural and home workers. With the slogan 'dignity and daily bread', they now represent more than 200,000 poor women. In countries such as Peru, Mexico, Brazil, Nicaragua and South Africa, thousands of women have been active in campaigns around 'prices, rents and basic social needs, schools, health centres and sanitation'.

As Rowbotham reminds her readers, it is not just in the Third World that women are mobilising beyond the media lens. Poor black and native American women in the United States have protested against toxic dumping that has led to miscarriages and birth defects. The new 'militant mothers' include, for instance, Dolly Burwell, who has been in prison many times for protesting against the contamination of soil by transformer oil leaked down a rural road. Theirs is a feminism that embraces an infinitely wider range of women's concerns than those of the 'women's pages'. 'They have a great deal to teach those of us who see feminism as relevant to more than a privileged minority,' wrote Rowbotham, 'and indeed anyone concerned about the numbing acceptance of inequality and injustice which has left us with a society and a political system so manifestly out of joint.'[20]

Those words also apply to a male journalism limited to fellow travelling with established power: to the gamesmanship of politicians and spin doctors and 'media village' gossip, what F. Scott Fitzgerald in *The Great Gatsby* called 'bantering inconsequence'. Among these would-be opinion-leaders an 'ironic *hauteur*' is affected, exemplified by a political columnist devoting an entire piece to Tony Blair's 'iconoclasm' in allowing members of his Cabinet to call each other by their first names. False symbolism is all; political substance is obsolete.[21] As for the readers, like the readers of tabloids, their imagination is pacified, not primed, and the 'numbing acceptance of inequality and injustice' is left unchallenged. While corruption among the system's managers and supplicants is at times brilliantly exposed by a small group of exceptional journalists, the wider corruption is apparently unseen.

In 1988, the literary critic and novelist D. J. Taylor wrote a seminal piece entitled 'When the Pen Sleeps'. He expanded this into a book, *A Vain Conceit*, in which he wondered why the English novel so often degenerated into 'drawing room twitter' and why the great issues of the day were shunned by writers, unlike their counterparts in, say, Latin America, who felt an *obligation* to take on politics. Where, he asked, were the George Orwells, the Upton Sinclairs, the John Steinbecks of the modern age?

The same can be said about journalism. Reading Orwell again, I am struck by his genius at extracting the lies submerged just beneath the surface of the status quo. Yet the prizes awarded in his name to political writers and journalists rarely reflect this. Writing in the *Observer*, the chairman of the 1995 Orwell Prize for Political Writing, John Keane, attacked those who referred back to 'an imaginary golden past'. But if the past is imaginary, why have Orwell's name on a prize? Keane says those who 'hanker' after this illusory past fail to appreciate writers and journalists making sense of 'the collapse of the old left–right divide'.[22]

What collapse? The convergence of the Labour and Tory Parties, like the American Democrats with the Republicans, represents an historic meeting of essentially like minds. The real divisions between left and right are to be found outside Parliament and have never been greater. They reflect the unprecedented disparity between the poverty of the majority of humanity and the power and privilege of a tiny minority who control the world's resources.

Tell the people of Pollock in Glasgow that there is no longer a left–right divide. There, half the jobs available to working-class people have disappeared over the past dozen years and poverty is constant. 'It's like a blanket has been drawn over the place,' wrote Tommy Sheridan, the Socialist Party councillor who lives in Pollock. Where are the Orwells writing *The Road to Pollock*?[23]

In the United States, where scrutiny of the media is not confined to a spectator sport, as it is in Britain, the writer James Petras has traced the history of the 'collapse' of the left–right divide. He wrote:

During the 1980s the western mass media systematically appropriated basic ideas of the left, emptied them of their original content and refilled them. Politicians intent on restoring capitalism and stimulating inequalities were described as 'reformers' and 'revolutionaries' while their opponents were labelled 'conservatives'.

This reversal of the meaning of political language disoriented many, making them vulnerable to claims that the terms 'left' and 'right' had lost their significance, that ideologies no longer mattered. Global cultural manipulation is sustained by this corruption. In the Third World, the selling of national public enterprises is 'breaking up monopolies'. 'Reconversion' is the euphemism for the reversion to nineteenth-century conditions of labour stripped of all social benefits. 'Restructuring' is the transfer of income from production to speculation. 'Deregulation' is the shift of power from the national welfare to the international banking [and] corporate elite.

The examples that Petras cites come from the same lexicon as 'work makes you free' – *Arbeit Macht Frei* – the words over the gates at Auschwitz.[24]

Noam Chomsky often quotes the work of the late Alex Carey, the Australian social scientist who pioneered the investigation of corporate propaganda. 'The twentieth century has been characterised by three developments of great political importance,' wrote Carey in 1978, 'the growth of democracy; the growth of corporate power; and the growth of corporate propaganda against democracy.'[25]

Chomsky adds that, following the Second World War, American business looked to the public relations industry to deter the social democratic and socialist impulses of working people. 'By the early 1950s,' he wrote, 'twenty million people a week were watching business-sponsored films. The entertainment industry was enlisted for the cause, portraying unions as the enemy, the outsider disrupting the "harmony" of the "American way of life" and otherwise helping to "indoctrinate citizens with the capitalist story" ... Every aspect of social life was targeted and permeated schools and universities, churches, even recreational programs. By 1954, business propaganda in public [state] schools reached half the amount spent on textbooks.'[26]

The most dramatic illustration of the rise of corporate propaganda was in the late 1970s in the newly contested area of environmentalism. In response to gains achieved by 'green' campaigns, such as clean air and clean water legislation and the establishment of environmental regulatory agencies, corporate America struck back with its own 'activism'. By 1980, there were more lobbyists, 'public affairs consultants' and company-employed journalists in Washington than there were federal employers, including 8,000 public-relations 'environmental specialists'.

As Sharon Beder documents in her book *Global Spin*, the 'think tanks' that provided vehicles for the rise of the Reagan 'new' right in the United States (like Thatcherism in Britain) 'sought to cast doubt on the very features of the environmental crisis that had heightened public concerns ... including ozone depletion, greenhouse warming and industrial pollution'. By distorting the public perception of environmental dangers, they successfully campaigned for laws 'that would ensure regulatory efforts become too expensive and difficult to implement, through insisting on cost benefit analyses and compensation to state governments and property owners for the costs of complying with the legislation.' By 1992, '51 per cent of those surveyed agreed that environmentalists had "gone too far" compared with 17 per cent the year before.'[27]

Taking a lead from the United States, public relations in Britain and other Western countries, 'PR', has usurped much of journalism's proper work, becoming, as Tom Baistow warned in 1985, a 'fifth estate'.[28] Today, according to Max Clifford, the famous PR man who deals with the London tabloids, the function of PR is 'filling the role investigative reporters should fill but no longer can because cost cutting has hit journalism heavily'.[29]

As the staffs of newsrooms have contracted, the public relations industry has expanded. According to the editor of *PR Week*, the amount of 'PR generated material' in the media is '50 per cent in a broadsheet newspaper in every section apart from sport. In the local press and the mid-market and tabloid nationals, the figure would undoubtedly be higher. Music and fashion journalists and PRs work hand in hand in the editorial process. It is often a game of bluff and brinkmanship, but the relationship is utterly interdependent. PRs provide fodder, but the clever high-powered ones do a lot of journalists' thinking for them.'[30]

The same is true of the phenomenon of 'think tanks', also known as 'research institutes'. The oldest of these propaganda bodies are establishment arms, such as the Royal Institute for International Affairs. Others, with similar, scholarly sounding titles (such as the Institute for Strategic Studies), mushroomed in the 1970s and 1980s, at first to support and fund pro-business and pro-Cold War academics and counter the work of 'revisionist' and radical social scientists and historians. William Simon, head of the immensely rich Olin Foundation in the United States, called for a 'counter-intelligentsia' in the universities and the media that would 'regain ideological dominance for business'.[31]

During the Reagan and Thatcher years rich and well-connected think tanks like the Heritage Foundation in the United States propagated the notion of a post-Sixties conservatism sweeping the West. The media picked this up and, in an exemplary exercise of what Noam Chomsky calls 'manufacturing consent', deflected what had been a progressive trend on both sides of the Atlantic: on issues such as tax, welfare, race relations, environmental protection and military spending. 'By crediting conservative policies with a popular support they did not have,' wrote Michael Parenti in his study on the politics of the American media, 'the press did its part in shifting the political agenda in a rightward direction'.[32]

Today, it is common for think tanks to usurp the role of independent journalism. Accomplished at self-promotion and understanding editorial exigencies (and idleness), the leaders of the 'counter-intelligentsia' have no difficulty in finding public platforms for their reactionary *chic*. In Britain, just as the Thatcherite Centre for Policy Studies was a master at this, so too is the fashionable Demos, which serves the new Thatcherism.

Australia, with the narrowest base of media ownership of any Western democracy, has more than its share of think tanks. The best known is the Sydney Institute, formerly the Institute of Public Affairs. Modelled on the extreme-right American groups which spent the Reagan years monitoring and 'naming' liberal journalists, the 'institute' is the work of a one-man band, Gerard Henderson, an experienced clerical propagandist who was formerly a lobbyist for the conservative Prime Minister, John Howard. In 1987, Henderson attended a seminar in Washington entitled 'The Red Orchestra in the South-West Pacific'. Sponsored by the Reaganite Hoover Institution, the speakers described all manner of conspiracies, notably 'the left network and the Australian media' and Moscow's 'penetration' of the Australian press. (Most of the press was then, as now, owned by Rupert Murdoch.) Henderson began writing for Murdoch's *Australian* and now has regular columns syndicated in both the two principal non-Murdoch papers, the *Sydney Morning Herald* and the Melbourne *Age*. His targets include the often beleaguered Australian Broadcasting Corporation and virtually anyone who attempts to offer an alternative vision to the rampant forces that have destroyed Australia's proud claim to social equity.

The cry 'freedom of the press' was probably first heard around the time Wynkyn de Worde set up Caxton's printing press in the yard of St Bride's Church, off Fleet Street, in London. Twenty years later, in 1520, a weaver stood in the main square of the German city of Magdeburg and offered Martin Luther's printed work for sale. The mayor promptly ordered the weaver's arrest. A riot followed, then a revolt, which overturned the rule of the Catholic city council. Already aware of the power of the written and spoken word, the authorities now feared Gutenberg's revolution of mass printing – 'the press'.

The first great battle for the freedom of the press was fought by dissenters, dreamers and visionaries who begged to differ from the established guardians of society. They suffered terrible penalties. Thomas Hytton was executed for selling books by William Tyndale, who translated the Bible into English. Richard Bayfield, John Tewkesbury and other booksellers were burned at the stake. John Stubbs had his right hand cut off for writing a pamphlet on the possible marriage of Queen Elizabeth. William Carter, accused of printing a book that would encourage the women of the court to kill Elizabeth, was hanged, drawn and quartered. For the crime of printing Puritan books in Holland, John Lilburne, the Leveller, was given 500 lashes in the streets of London, pilloried and fined the fortune of £500.[33]

In the early nineteenth century, the law increasingly became the instrument of censorship and sanction. In Australia, Edward Smith Hall, publisher of the campaigning Sydney *Monitor*, was routinely convicted of criminal libel by military juries whose members were selected personally by the military governor of New South Wales. Hall spent more than a year in prison where, from a small cell lit through a single grate and beset by mosquitoes, he continued to edit the *Monitor* and to expose official venality.

Hall's vision was of a press that was 'a medley of competing voices'. When he died in 1861, there were some fifty independent newspaper titles in New South Wales alone. Within twenty years this had risen to 143 papers, many of which had a campaigning style and editors who regarded their newspapers as 'the voice of the people' and not of 'the trade of authority' or of vested mercantile interests.

By the beginning of the twentieth century there were twenty-one metropolitan newspapers in Australia owned by seventeen different proprietors. By 1997, Hall's 'medley of competing voices' had been reduced to sixteen principal newspapers, ten of them owned by Murdoch. Television, radio and computer software are in the hands of conglomerates. Free Australia now provides the model for the destruction of a 400-year-old freedom.

'What is deeply ironic', wrote David Bowman, 'is that, having thrown off one yoke, the press should now be falling under another, in the form of a tiny and ever-contracting band of businessmen-proprietors. Instead of developing as a diverse social institution, serving the needs of democratic society, the press, and now the media, have become or are becoming the property of a few, governed by whatever social, political and cultural values the few think tolerable . . . Looking at the thing historically, you could say that what we are facing now is the second great battle of the freedom of the press.'[34]

If Marshall McLuhan's 'global village' means anything, it is the power of the global media monopolies and their antipathy to a 'medley of competing voices'. 'It seems grotesque', wrote Bowman, 'that the press, or rather the media, should be allowed to abuse its social role fatally by rushing on down the road to monopoly ownership. That is a negation of press freedom.'

By falling silent, journalists and politicians both negate history; for the struggle for a free press was always part of the long journey towards universal suffrage and democratic government. It was a fight for opposing voices to be heard when those in authority considered themselves the custodians of truth: an enduring delusion.

By their acquiescence the journalists dishonour those like Edward Smith Hall, whose tenacity allowed the press to emerge from two centuries of repressive laws, corruption and political bribery; and William Howard Russell, whose dispatches from the Crimea revealed the truth of war, its sacrificial battles, waste and blunders; and Morgan Philips Price, the *Guardian* man in Moscow in 1917 who alone reported the Allied invasion and its grave implications for the future; and Ted Scott, the great *Guardian* leader writer (later editor), whose work included the following: 'If for any reason the right to strike is withdrawn it should be recognised as the deprivation of what is normally the most jealously guarded and most socially valuable means of progress.' That appeared in 1919. It could just as well appear today.[35]

Journalists ought not to stand outside the closed doors of the powerful waiting to be lied to. They are not functionaries, and they should not be charlatans: 'your sham impartialists', as Robert Louis Stevenson wrote, 'wolves in sheep's clothing, simpering loyally as they suppress'. They ought to be sceptical about the assumed and the acceptable, *especially* the legitimate and the respectable. ('Never believe anything', said Claud Cockburn, 'until it's officially denied.') Their job is not to stand idly by, but to speak for 'the true witnesses, those in full possession of the terrible truth', as Primo Levi described the victims of Nazism. At the least they ought to be the natural enemies of the authoritarianism that Rupert Murdoch says 'can work'.

In countries where the majority of humanity live, the efforts and sacrifice of journalists shame their quiescent colleagues. I have already mentioned my friend Ahmad Taufik, who had his prison sentence in Indonesia extended to three years. His crime was to write a mildly critical analysis of the Suharto dictatorship for *Independence*, a newspaper he and others dared to start. In Turkey, the regime has made something of a speciality of terrorising journalists. Metin Goktepe, a journalist for the daily *Evrensel*, was beaten to death on January 8, 1996, while in police custody in Istanbul. He was arrested under a law which classifies all reporting of the oppression and rebellion in Turkey as either propaganda or as 'incitement to racial hatred'.

The editor of *Ozgur Gundem* (Free Agenda), Ocak Isik Yurtcu, is serving fifteen years under the same law. 'I'm in prison', he said recently, 'because I tried to learn the truth and relay this truth to the public – in other words, to do my job – in the belief that it is impossible to have other freedoms in a country where there is no freedom of the press.'[36]

The Philippines has constitutionally the freest press in Asia and one of the highest death rates of journalists in the world. Edgar Cadagat, who runs the Cobra news agency on the island of Negros, works behind sand bags. He specialises in exposing official corruption. He has survived several assassination attempts, and one Christmas was sent a miniature coffin with a bullet and his photograph inside.[37]

In Russia, fifty journalists were killed in 1996, including the television commentator Oleg Slabynko, who spoke out against organised crime. In Algeria, sixty journalists have been killed for doing their job. In St Bride's, the journalists' church off London's Fleet Street, there are the names of others who have given journalism an almost Homeric pride. When I was last there, I lit a candle before a plaque for 'Veronica Guerin, aged 33, journalist, *Sunday Independent*, murdered in Dublin for writing the truth'.

This is not to suggest that journalists need to prove

themselves by facing physical danger – although in countries like Indonesia, Algeria, Russia, Nigeria, the Philippines and Turkey, they may have no choice. What all serious journalists ought to share is a certain *moral* courage. In the democracies, this means the courage to clear away the ideological rubble that smothers independence of mind and leads to self-censorship. This is not without risk. 'If one tells the truth,' wrote Oscar Wilde, 'one is sure sooner or later to be found out.'

In Britain, free-minded journalists might turn their attention to the repeal of legislation passed since 1979, which restricts and intimidates the right to report openly and without fear or favour: the 1981 Contempt of Court Act, the 1986 Police and Criminal Evidence Act and the 1994 Criminal Justice Act. Any authoritarian regime would be delighted to have these on its statute books. The libel laws should be abolished, too, or rewritten to provide a free service for ordinary people seeking redress. And there ought to be a law, similar to that in France, preventing huge companies like W. H. Smith and John Menzies, which have 53 per cent of the distribution market, from withdrawing small-circulation magazines and newspapers from sale. These are our *samizdat*.

A Freedom of Information Act unfettered by 'exemptions', the establishment of a public body to provide start-up funds for newspapers, journals and broadcasters independent of the monopolists, a new Broadcasting Act that stops the richest and biggest swallowing the smallest and requires an unfettered commitment to original drama and independent factual programmes – these would begin to win the second battle for the freedom of the press.

It is a freedom we are in danger of losing without even knowing it. For when there is no longer anyone speaking out, who will be the last voice?

IX
RETURN TO VIETNAM

STILL A NOBLE CAUSE

> You ask what we were doing over there all those years:
> what it was all about? I'll tell you pure and simple: it was
> a noble cause.
>
> *Ronald Reagan*

VIETNAM IS FASHIONABLE in the late 1990s. At Saigon
airport there are backpackers and conga lines of package
tourists, and Taiwanese businessmen watching *Mr Bean*.
They cancel nostalgia and the memory of fear, but not the
absurd. John Blake and his girlfriend have arrived from
Wolverhampton wearing black 'designer' combat fatigues,
like a two-person Swat team. 'The boots are *genuine*
American military,' he explained. At weekends he and his
friends dress as GIs, 'authentic down to the Zippo lighters',
and 'play Vietnam'. Johnny Rambo? 'No, that's rubbish.
More like *Platoon* . . . without the politics and the massacre
of civilians.'

At Cu Chi, a drive from the city, tourists descend on the
scene of one of the war's most remarkable chapters: the
tunnels where soldiers of the National Liberation Front
(Vietcong was an American term) crawled through a darkness
of insects and snakes with the technology of a 'free-fire zone'
rampant above them. Now teenage girls dress up as wartime
guerrillas, guiding tourists around the bomb craters and
shooing them off the new grass and in the direction of stalls
that sell toy helicopters made from Coke cans.

Like so much else in the new Vietnam, the People's Army

has turned itself into a business and runs the tunnels like a theme park. They have thoughtfully widened them for large tourists and set up a shooting range where, for a dollar a shot, Americans can relive all the fun of *Rambo* and *Platoon*. There is the choice of an American M-16 rifle or a Vietnamese AK-47, and should you hit a bull's-eye you win a genuine, black-and-white checked Vietcong scarf. People line up to do this.

There were no tourists at the American Embassy in Saigon when I returned, twenty years to the day after the Americans abandoned it. For most of this time it had stood empty, its six floors an echoing museum of fallen empire. A single fluorescent tube flickered; a time switch clicked on and off; a jammed lavatory flushed and flushed. The door of the embassy vault was open, and a sign read, 'This is US Government Security Vault Door Class 5. In case of radiological attack it will close for 20 man-hours'. On the stairwell leading to the helicopter pad on the roof, someone had smeared, 'Eat shit'. From up here, there is the view of a giant Vietnamese flag, red with a yellow star; looking down there is another, of the cesspool of the embassy swimming pool, the water unchanged for twenty years.

April 29, 1975: Another 'Jolly Green Giant' had just landed on the roof, the thudding syncopation and rhythm and whine of its rotaries invoking a menace I shall always associate with helicopters. From the courtyard I could just see it through smoke billowing from an incinerator on the roof attended by silhouetted figures running to and fro with sacks. The surreal seemed guaranteed on the last day of the longest war this century.

Now the sky rained money. Swept up in the draught of the rotary blades a snowstorm of dollar bills fluttered down: tens, twenties, fifties, one hundreds. Former ministers and generals of the disintegrating American-backed Saigon Government, a regime that once accounted for more than half of all the cases of torture in the world compiled by Amnesty International, scrambled for their severance pay from the sky or sent children to retrieve the notes. An Embassy official whispered,

'Every safe has been emptied and locked again, so as to fool the gooks when we're gone.'

The rumour was abroad that the Ambassador, Graham Martin, wanted to use the money to delay the evacuation further and buy time, literally, by bribing the fast-approaching People's Army of Vietnam into agreeing to a 'decent interval', so that the remnants of the old regime might be accepted into an interim government. This would give Washington, the Ambassador had argued, the fabled 'peace with honour' made famous by Richard Nixon and his Rasputin, Henry Kissinger.

From early morning the marine at the gates had a clipboard and a list. 'Look, it's me ... let me in ... thank you very much.' The shrill voice in the crowd laying siege to the embassy on April 29 belonged to Lieutenant-General Dang Van Quang, whose wealth was notorious. To his American mentors, who loathed him, he was 'Giggles' and 'General Fats'. He was on the list, and the marine helped him squeeze his bulk through, then retrieved his three Samsonite bags. Relieved to be on the inside, Giggles walked away, leaving his son in the crowd. Two packets of dollars sagged from his breast pocket; as he stuffed them back in, he joked that the Samsonites held more of the same.

Much of the drama of this gathering finale appeared not to invade Graham Martin's sound-proofed mahogany-panelled office on the sixth floor where the Ambassador sat, often alone, with Nitnoy, his poodle. Whether the bribery story was true or mischievous, it was clear that Martin could barely bring himself to contemplate the ignominy of the United States' departure from Indo-China. A few days earlier he had made an extraordinary appearance on Saigon television at his own request. 'I, the American Ambassador,' he said gravely, 'am not going to run away in the middle of the night. Anyone can come to my home and see I have not packed my bags ... I give you my word.' The camera panned to a pointedly empty suitcase beside him.

The last pro-consul was a private, strong-willed and complex man. His desk was dominated by a photograph of his son in uniform, who had died in the war nine years earlier. He was also sick; his skin was death-white after weeks of pneumonia. He chain-smoked, and conversations with him were frequently interrupted by bouts of coughing. For months he had tried in vain to convince Washington that its client state could survive with an 'iron ring' of bombs laid around Saigon by B-52s flying in relays. The war could still be won.

Graham Martin was the embodiment of the American mission in Vietnam; he was one of those who had, as the historian Gabriel Kolko wrote in his seminal *Anatomy of a War*, a 'penchant for illusions and symbolism that made them the only true ideologists of the war'.[1] Martin's symbol, as the end approached, was a tree: a great tamarind commanding the lawns of his Embassy. Unless it was cut down, the Jolly Green Giant pilots, flying in from carriers in the South China Sea, would be unable to land and a full-scale evacuation would not be possible.

The Ambassador had made it clear that once that tree fell, 'America's prestige will fall with it.' At a pre-dawn meeting in his office on April 29 he had berated the CIA Station Chief, Tom Polgar, who had argued for an orderly evacuation. When the meeting broke up without a decision on the tree, there was a sense that the pro-consul was planning to burn with Rome. At 6.30 a.m. someone, possibly Polgar, gave the order for the tree to be felled.

Within half an hour American Forces Radio broadcast the evacuation signal: Bing Crosby singing, 'I'm dreaming of a white Christmas'. (Evacuees had been advised in writing to 'bring along two changes of clothing, a raincoat, a sewing kit, an umbrella, a can opener, insect repellent, your marriage certificate, a power of attorney and your will ... Unfortunately, you must leave your automobile behind.') In the aerial Dunkirk that followed, some 7,000 people were lifted out of Saigon in less than eighteen hours.

At 2.30 a.m. on April 30, Kissinger phoned Martin and told him to be out by 3.45. Within half an hour, Martin emerged from his office with the Stars and Stripes folded in a carrier bag. He caught the lift to the roof and climbed the iron stairs to the tarmac. 'Lady Ace 09 in the air with Code Two,' crackled the marine radio. Code Two was the call sign for an American ambassador. As his helicopter banked over Highway One, he could see the silhouettes of the tanks and trucks of the People's Army of Vietnam, waiting for him to go. The war was over.

Ho Chi Minh's nationalists had fought for thirty years, first against the French, whose tree-lined boulevards, pink-washed villas and terraces were façades which concealed unrelenting plunder and cruelty; then against the Japanese, with whom the French *colons* collaborated and who, in 1944, starved to death two million Vietnamese in order to feed their own troops; then against the Americans, with whom Ho repeatedly tried to forge an alliance against China; then against Pol Pot's Khmer Rouge, who attacked from the west; then against the Chinese, who attacked from the north. All of them were seen off at immeasurable cost.

The story of Mrs Thai Thi Tinh is not untypical. A diminutive white-haired woman in her eighties, Mrs Thai lives in an area of Hanoi that might have been laid out in the Middle Ages. There are streets of workers in ivory, brass and leather, streets of tinsmiths and coffin-makers, hatters and herbalists. These streets, not the spacious, French-built centre of the city, were the targets of the B-52s that Nixon and Kissinger sent during Christmas 1972. Mrs Thai's house was not hit. She remembers only 'the great roar' in the sky and the ground above the shelter 'splitting open like an earthquake'.

Her life is the suffering and sacrifice of the Vietnamese in the twentieth century. She lost five of her eight children, the first two in a meningitis epidemic for which there were no drugs. Her eldest son, Lom, died at the Battle of Dien Bien Phu in 1954, which was decisive in driving the French out of Indo-China. Her next son, Khan, was killed shortly afterwards in the liberation of Hanoi. Her husband, a doctor in Ho Chi Minh's resistance, was killed evacuating the wounded from Hanoi. She had no idea then that America was to be 'the next enemy'.

Her youngest, Luong, was nineteen when he was called up in 1967. 'He wanted to be an engineer,' said Mrs Thai, holding a black-and-white picture of a handsome, smiling young man to her bosom. 'The day he said goodbye, he was concerned only that I watch out for the American bombing. "Always go to the shelter," he insisted. He loved me so much. When I saw him off at the station, I didn't know what to do; I couldn't let go of his hand. I made him take a pack of ginger sweets that would prevent him from catching cold. I had only two letters from him; in the first, he told me his job was to disarm bombs that didn't explode. In the second, he wrote that he had caught malaria and was getting ready to go to the tunnels at Cu Chi. I didn't hear any more. The records are destroyed. He is listed as missing.'

Twenty years later, Mrs Thai travelled to Cu Chi and erected a *dinh*, a shrine, and prayed for Luong and his brothers and their father, and wore their medals. When she greeted me on a Sunday morning, she was wearing a brilliant red silk *oi dai*, the traditional Vietnamese dress, and the medals, which must have weighed heavily on her tiny frame. Her only surviving son, Loc, and his wife, Tran Thi Ngoc, hovered nearby. After tea, we set out for the municipal cemetery to visit the grave of Lom, the eldest son. Mrs Thai carried a small plastic bag of water for the roses at the graveside, and a bundle of imitation money, whose offering, she said, 'will give his spirit a little wealth'.

Her dignity is mirrored by that of thousands of women with similar loss, who now and then appear on Vietnamese television to request information about the whereabouts of the remains of their missing sons: some 300,000 are still unaccounted for. Contrast this with the unseemly campaign in the United States, promoted by Ronald Reagan and taken up by Hollywood, which still mythologises a tiny number of American 'MIAs', most of them pilots shot down with their aircraft.[2]

My friend Thien Thi Tao has this dignity. I first met her in Saigon shortly after the end of the war. She was twenty-eight and wore the black of the National Liberation Front, and she beamed a smile in spite of a painful limp. When I asked her how she had felt the moment she heard it was all over, she said, 'My heart flies.' She had spent most of her youth in torture centres run by the Saigon regime's secret police, a terror organisation established and trained by teams from the CIA and Michigan State University. She was seventeen when she was first arrested. She was cycling home from school and was taken to a secret police villa, where she was accused of being a communist and a member of the National Liberation Front.

'I was neither,' she said. 'Like most students I hated the American-backed regime, especially for bringing a foreign army to Vietnam. It is true I did work for the NLF and I was prepared to fight for them. We all respected them. The police demanded that I hand over NLF names; when I refused I was strung upside down and electrocuted, and my head was held in a bucket of water. Then I was sent to Cong Son Island and put in what they called the tiger cages. You couldn't stand up in them and, anyway, my legs were shackled; and every day they threw quicklime down on me. They had a place that was full of cow and pig excrement, and for no reason they'd put you in it and leave you. This was known as the coffin.'

In 1988, Tao married an NLF cadre who had courted her for twenty years. They had lost touch during the war, each thinking the other was dead. 'Anyway, I couldn't be sure about him; he was a *communist*,' she said drily. 'As a child I was told to run away from communists!' She almost died during pregnancy, as her kidneys had been damaged by the years of torture. Her son, Huynh, was born prematurely with a blood disorder; and Tao was told he had a 'one per cent chance'.

When I met her again in 1995, on a bustling Saigon street outside a nursery school, she was dropping off a lad unusually well-built for a four-year-old. 'His name means golden spring,' she said.

At least three million people died during the Vietnam War, the great majority of them civilians. My own introduction to this war against civilians was at the hospital at Can Tho in the

Mekong Delta in 1967. During most of this week American aircraft had been attacking 'VC strongholds' nearby. This meant villages made of straw and tin.

'I guess he's around ten years old,' said the young American doctor, a volunteer. Before us was a child whose nose and chin had merged, whose eyes apparently could not close and whose skin, once brown, was now red and black and papery, like frayed cloth. 'Beats me how these kids live through all that shit out there,' said the doctor. 'This one's been burned with Napalm B. That's the stuff made from benzene, polystyrene and gasolene. It sticks to the body and is impossible to get off, and either burns the victim to death or suffocates him by using up all the oxygen.'

Seven years later I drove to the hamlet of My Lai, which then stood in a no man's land between NLF and Saigon Government lines. The people were still afraid to talk to anyone resembling Lieutenant William Calley and his killers. Calley's 'Charlie Company' had massacred more than 200 villagers, old men, women and children, on March 18, 1968. It took them four hours to kill everyone, and that included a break for lunch which they ate within a few yards of a pile of fresh corpses, mostly women and infants. There was one American casualty, Sergeant Herbert Carter, who shot himself in the foot.

What I had not realised on that first visit to My Lai was that the Americans had declared most of Quang Ngai province a 'free fire zone' and that 70 per cent of the hamlets and their villages had been razed. When it was My Lai's turn, civilians were being killed at a rate of 50,000 a year. This was known as 'collateral damage'.

It is a pity that very few foreign tourists bother to make the journey over unsurfaced roads into the hamlet, for there is much to learn. Again, the dignity of people is powerfully evident. There is a cenotaph of a woman and her child, and a mural that does not depict the Americans as monsters. Zippo lighters and the ubiquitous Coke-can helicopters are not available in the little museum.

There, in large fuzzy photographs, is bespectacled Colonel

Henderson, who could be an insurance salesman and who directed the Eleventh Brigade in its 'search and destroy' of the area; and there is Captain Medina, who ordered the village destroyed. On the wall he is wiping away a tear. And there is the famous almost three-dimensional colour photograph (taken by an army photographer attached to Charlie Company) of the piles of dead in the ditch.

Look closely at this, and you will see a shadow in the grass to the left. This was Mrs Truong Thi Le, who survived beneath the bodies of her mother, daughter and grandson. Now in her seventies, she bravely held the photograph and listed for me the others in the ditch who were her family: her brother, her nephew, aged one, four nieces, all of them under ten years of age, a total of nine people.

'It was six o'clock in the morning,' she said. 'Suddenly this helicopter was manoeuvring above the house, then we saw soldiers come across the fields. They ordered all the families out and told us to march towards the ditch. If we walked too slowly, they prodded us with their guns. We came to an assembly point and huddled together; then they shot us one by one. I saw a little boat and used it to cover my son, and dead bodies fell down on me. I kept telling my son, who was six years old, "Please don't cry. They will hear us if you do."

'When the Americans had finished and walked away, I waited, then stood up with my boy; I felt I was walking in the sky; I didn't have any kind of feelings. I was covered in blood and pieces of human brain, which smelt terrible. On the way back we had to walk in the field because the pathway was covered with bodies; I saw a mother die here, children there. They even killed the ox and buffaloes. When we reached our home, it was burned down. It was only then I realised a bullet had passed right through me, but I was still alive; I was alive.'

In 1970, little more than a year after My Lai, I went to the United States and interviewed a number of American soldiers who had taken part in other acts of mass murder in Vietnam. Seven of them had not been charged. Each was adamant that he had been under orders to 'kill everyone and everything'. 'A village was a designated playground,' one of them said.

Among those who were charged, and convicted, was Michael Schwarz, who grew up in a poor mining community in West Virginia and enlisted in the marines at the age of sixteen. At boot camp, the instructor yelled at him, 'Kill! Kill! Kill!' to which he and the others had to reply, 'Kill! Kill! Kill!' On the night of February 19, 1969, Private Schwarz was one of a five-man 'search and destroy' team which entered the village of Son Thang in the Mekong Delta. They killed eleven women and five children.

What was unusual was that they were all charged with various degrees of murder and court-martialled: a result of the belated publicity given to the massacre at My Lai. The prosecuting colonel said that a soldier was 'a reasoning agent who has a duty to exercise judgement in obeying orders . . .' Schwarz's defence lawyer reminded the court of the 'kill-kill-kill' routine. 'This was just a figure of speech,' said the prosecutor. Schwarz was sentenced to life imprisonment with hard labour. But after more than 750,000 people in West Virginia and Pennsylvania signed a petition demanding his release, and a legal fund was raised, his sentence was reduced to one year, and he was soon released. When I asked him why he had killed civilians, he held his neck straight and said theatrically, 'My country right or wrong,' as if he had just coined it. 'I just wish they'd send me back my Navy Commendation and Purple Heart,' he said.

The truth was that the dark side of the American system was exported to Vietnam. Homicide, not military tactics, was the means of conducting the war. For example, the US Ninth Infantry Division, the 'Glorious Ninth', was said to be 'notorious'. On the contrary, it did no more than carry out the orders of the military command at 'Dodge City' in Saigon: orders given by generals and colonels whose behaviour at times made Joseph Heller's *Catch-22* seem like an exemplary work of non-fiction.

In 1971, the Saigon command credited the 'Glorious Ninth' with a 'body count' of 11,000 of the enemy in a 'pacification' campaign known as 'Operation Speedy Express'. The flaw in this story was that only 700 weapons were found. Later an

American official admitted that 5,000 'non-combatants' had been killed. This was mass slaughter, condoned and covered up. The magazine *Newsweek* had the story for six months, but refused to publish it, describing it as a 'gratuitous attack' on President Nixon. When it was finally published, four years after the event, it bore little resemblance to the original.[3]

Suppression like this was routine. The walls of news organisations in Saigon had long been decorated with photographs of dismembered bodies: of GIs holding up severed ears and testicles and of torture in progress. In the office of Associated Press of America someone had written on one of these pictures: 'This is what happens when you speak to the press.' To the question why they had not been sent came the usual reply that the international agencies (mostly American) would not distribute them, because American newspapers would not publish them, because the public would not 'accept' them.

Yet Vietnam was said to be the first 'media war', in which there was no censorship and nothing escaped the scrutiny of reporters and especially the television camera. At the time of the My Lai massacre there were more than 600 reporters in Vietnam. None of them broke the story, even though it was widely known. For more than a year afterwards, a soldier who had heard about it tried to interest *Newsweek*, and others, without success. The story was finally written by a freelance reporter based in the United States, Seymour Hersh, who believed the murder of civilians by his country's soldiers was news.

My Lai eventually made the cover of *Newsweek* under the headline 'An American Tragedy'. This invited sympathy for America and deflected from the truth: that the massacre was, above all, a Vietnamese tragedy and that, far from being an 'aberration', as the army claimed, it accurately reflected the criminal and racist nature of the war. This was never spelt out. That the war was a series of 'blunders', or a 'quagmire' into which naïve politicians and generals were somehow 'drawn', even 'dragged', was the preferred media version, and still is. In a special issue of the *Observer* magazine to mark the

559

twentieth anniversary of the end of the war, the veteran correspondent Mark Frankland wrote that the lesson of the war was that 'the United States will never let itself be drawn into a long war abroad'.[4]

This myth endures alongside nonsense that reporters, by criticising the military effort, helped to 'lose' the war for the Americans. In my experience, most journalists had no objection to the 'noble crusade', only to the wisdom of its tactics and the competence of its executors. The war was almost never reported as an all-out American assault on the Vietnamese people, regardless of whether they were communist or non-communist, northerners or southerners; for that was the truth.

Instead the war was represented as a gladiators' contest between 'good' teams and 'bad' teams. The Americans were on the side of the good team, the 'South Vietnamese', who were defending themselves against several bad teams of 'communists'. Not surprisingly, this version excluded the fact that the Americans had killed tens of thousands of their South Vietnamese 'allies' and had levelled about half their forests, poisoned their environment and forced millions of them to leave their homes.

Neither did the news version ever come to terms with who exactly the 'communists' were. If the NLF, or Vietcong, were also South Vietnamese, how could they 'invade' their own country, as President Kennedy claimed? Words had to be found to make sense of this. So they became 'insurgents' who were guilty of 'internal aggression'.

The news version also had difficulty with the 'North Vietnamese', who were said to be attacking the south. There had been no North Vietnam and no South Vietnam until the Geneva Conference in 1954 'temporarily' divided the country to await national elections two years later. The record is now clear that the Americans, secretly egged on by the Chinese, who feared a confident Vietnam, sabotaged the prospect of elections for the good reason that they knew Ho Chi Minh would win hands down and unite the country.[5] 'I have never talked with a person knowledgeable in Indochinese affairs', wrote former President Eisenhower in his memoirs, 'who did not believe that 80 per cent of the population would have voted for Ho Chi Minh.'[6]

In 1968, the year of the My Lai massacre, the theme of the Vietnam War as a 'noble cause' was picked up by Hollywood in the spirit of previous noble causes, such as the slaughter of the North American Indians. This began with a letter written in 1965 to President Lyndon Johnson. 'Dear Mr President,' it said, 'When I was a little boy, my father always told me if you want to get anything done see the top man – so I am addressing this letter to you.'[7] The writer was John Wayne, the actor, who proposed a 'patriotic' movie about the United States in Vietnam, called *The Green Berets*.

The film was made, starring Wayne, and produced by his son, Michael, who later admitted that the script had been rewritten 'along the lines suggested by the Pentagon'.[8] I saw *The Green Berets* in a cinema in Montgomery, Alabama, in August 1968 with a friend from the civil rights movement. What struck us was its serious attempt to deflect from the homicidal nature of the American invasion, and to present reporters as naïve and the 'communists' as baby-killers. In one scene a reporter is lectured by a Green Beret (acted by a token black man): 'As soldiers . . .', he says, 'we can understand the killing of the military. But the intentional murder and torture of innocent women and children by the communists . . . I tell you these people need us, they want us.' The film ends with the sun setting in the South China Sea: that is, in the east – a memorable comment on the accuracy of all that had gone before.

My friend and I almost split our sides laughing, until he whispered that we should get away quickly. It was a Saturday night; the audience was mostly young white males, who had applauded every absurdity, every gook's zapping. Their attention was now drawn to us. We ran back to our hotel with a pack in hot pursuit. It was a salutary lesson in the celluloid power of the 'values' of John Wayne, a patriot who had distinguished himself during the Second World War by avoiding military service.

The Green Berets was dismissed as a black joke by the

critics, yet it made $8 million at the box office: a lot of money then. In any case, it was Wayne's influence over the course of thirty years, a generation, that mattered. All those good-guy/bad-guy films long before television made itself felt, all that 'standing tall' in and out of the saddle and always in defence of 'freedom' and America, all that *Americanism*, the only pure 'ism', undoubtedly left an impression. I saw too many American soldiers in Vietnam playing at being John Wayne not to believe this. Michael Schwarz, who took part in the killing of twelve people, was one of them. John Wayne was his hero. 'Like Big John,' he told me, 'I always enjoyed mixing it with people: you know, showing who's boss.'

In his book *Firing Line*, Richard Holmes describes the response the film director Delbert Mann elicited from a group of marines when he asked them, in 1960, why they had joined the Marine Corps. 'Half of them answered that it was because of the John Wayne films that they had seen,' he wrote. 'In *Sands of Iwo Jima* John Wayne played the classic firm-but-fair Sergeant Stryker, the archetypal role-model for young marines for the next twenty years ... Middle-ranking infantry officers in Vietnam in the late 1960s would have been in their early teens when *Sands of Iwo Jima* first appeared: it is, perhaps, not surprising that its impact was so tremendous. John Parrish [a former marine] endorsed these comments ... "I was John Wayne," he wrote, describing how he had helped wounded on to a helicopter under fire. "I was covering the retreat from the beaches of World War II. I was the star of the war comics." '[9]

After the American withdrawal from Vietnam, Hollywood shifted the emphasis to the war as 'an American tragedy' with a series of movies that pitied the invader: a potent blend of Rambo-and-angst: sometimes crude (*Rambo*) and sometimes subtle (*Platoon*). In all of them the Vietnamese flit across the screen as bit players. When they are not Oriental idiots and bar-barians (*The Deer Hunter*, which was wrongly received as an anti-war film), they are victims (*Coming Home* and *Platoon*) or sentimentalised (*Good Morning Vietnam*). The few films that have portrayed the Vietnamese as human beings have merely added credibility to the distortion and enriched the purgative.

The retrospectives that come and go with the war's anniversaries merely illustrate the stamina of these myths. The BBC, in displaying its formidable archives, congratulates itself on being 'more impartial' in its reporting of the war than the American media. There is never reference to the BBC's blacklisting of the reports by cameraman Malcolm Aird and journalist James Cameron of the bombing of civilian targets in North Vietnam: a rare glimpse of the longest aerial bombardment in history.

Familiar shorthand, such as the venerable catch-all, 'the communists', relegates to the shadows those, like Mrs Thai's sons, who fought and died not as Asian Prussians under the spell of some blind faith, but as nationalists who developed their ingenuity and patience to the extremes of human limits, who preserved their culture beneath the bombs and built underground schools and hospitals and were united in their sense of history.

Lately there has been some fine mock redemption. Former American Defense Secretary Robert McNamara used the twentieth anniversary of the end of the war to 'confess all'.[10] Well, not quite all. It was McNamara who bombed and bombed, then tried to build an electrified fence across Vietnam. He now says that his 'errors' were 'not of values and intentions, but of judgement and capabilities'. This would be laughable if only the language of Western power, and its devotion to minimising culpability, were not so insidious. Echoing McNamara, a BBC radio interviewer asked me, 'Well, how *does* an outside power impose order on a country that doesn't want it?'

Did the United States 'lose' in its disastrous war in Asia? I am not so sure. To American administrations, from Truman to Ford, the 'threat' posed by Vietnam was always long term: that of a development model which other states in the region and elsewhere in the world might emulate. Far from being vanquished in south-east Asia, the United States devastated, blockaded and isolated Vietnam and its 'virus'; today almost every regime in the region serves American interests in one way or another. Not even Hollywood appears to have understood the scope of this achievement.

THE FINAL BATTLE

> It should never be forgotten that the people must have priority.
>
> *Ho Chi Minh*

I RETURNED TO Vietnam in the winter of 1995. Hanoi presented a strange hybrid. The Odeon arcades, the avenues and villas and the replica of the Paris Opera, in which the French *colons* amused themselves with Berlioz and Bizet, were only slightly more decrepit. In the crowded Old Quarter, little had changed; there was still a sense of what Victorian England might have looked like: beneath the slate-grey skies diminutive houses huddled over open drains in crooked streets and the air was thick with sweet-smelling smoke from wood-burning braziers.

Tiny parlours were filled with people swathed in scarves, sipping green tea drawn from large floral-painted flasks while sepia figures in mandarin dress looked down from oval frames. Almost everywhere there was a cluster of military medals and a photograph of a lost loved one.

Normality graced with laughter has a certain excitement here. Laughter drew me to one house where a wedding party was in progress, and I was invited in by Thuan, aged twenty-eight, and his bride, Hong, twenty-four. He is a dog-meat salesman, she a 'flower girl': that is, she ekes out a living by selling single stems on the streets. They and their family and friends looked deceptively prosperous gathered in the small courtyard beneath a canopy made from an American parachute. There were pots of steaming noodles, sweets and betel nuts; and the bridesmaids wore shocking pink. The groom giggled, the bride cried, and we were all invited to inspect the marital bed.

Nearby, Nguyen The Khan, a venerable artist who speaks Chinese, French and English, sat like an old bird in his impossibly crowded loft, cigarette drooping, working on a series of lacquer panels. They show Hanoi in the mid-nineteenth century before the French built their scaled-down copies of Paris and destroyed the ancient landmarks: the Princess Huyen Tran Temple, the Jade Mountain Pagoda, the Subdued Waves Pavilion.

'What work would you like to do before you die?' I asked him.

'Something that announced true peace,' he said, 'A tranquil life . . . that's all. We are still not at peace; we are in a dilemma now.'

Rising above us were the symbols of this dilemma: some of the most spectacularly ugly buildings on earth, made from black glass and slab concrete, shaped like clothes pegs, the inspiration, clearly, of the same Thai school of 'architecture' whose monstrosities join up the powerlines in the deserts that have replaced Thailand's teak forests.

Nguyen The Khan and other residents of the old quarter had marched on the City Hall to complain about them and the corruption that often smoothed the way for planning permission. In these buildings reside the high commands of corporate Japan, Korea, Hong Kong, Singapore, the United States, Australia and the City of London, who are changing almost everything in Vietnam. As one American banker put it, 'The circus is back in town.'

To those who knew Vietnam during the war, the familiarity of the circus is almost other-worldly. In a bar on the corner of 'Duong Chien Thang B-52' (Avenue of the Victory over the B-52) was Joe, a former American helicopter pilot, who runs a fleet of corporate jets flying in American businessmen, many of them from companies which profited hugely from the war. Nearby are the new offices of a pillar of the war, the Bank of

America. When the bank's burglar alarm went off one evening, people gathered, wondering what it was. No one seemed to know, because no˙one robs banks in Hanoi. Not yet.

The teahouse opposite has been re-named the 'No Noodles Sandwich Bar'. The Marlboro Man covers its walls, and the old woman darting through the beaded curtain wore a red Marlboro baseball cap and a T-shirt with a picture of the Marlboro Man. At a stroke, she had surrendered her dignity: a metaphoric warning for her country.

Marlboro and Dunhill have claimed Vietnam, where the majority seem to smoke. Foreign tobacco companies were among the first to return, and now turn out cigarettes with a high tar content. Marlboro's advertising concentrates on its 'macho image', long discredited in the West. The cowboy with a cigarette in his mouth, the one who died from lung cancer, has been replaced by images of young, muscle-bound lads winning the girls, while real lads, with stick-thin arms and rotten teeth, are given red caps too big for them and lent a Honda and paid in cigarettes for selling Marlboros to teashops. Such is the reality of what is called 'Renovation'.

'Renovation', or *Doi Moi*, was conceived in collective desperation. The catastrophe wreaked in Vietnam by the American invasion was to be multiplied in the years that followed a ceasefire, signed in Paris in 1973 and which, said Secretary of State Henry Kissinger, would bring 'peace with honour'.

A cornerstone of the ceasefire agreement was a secret promise by President Nixon of $3.25 billion in reparations, contained in a letter to Pham Van Dong, Prime Minister of the Democratic Republic of Vietnam ('North Vietnam'). Dated February 1, 1973, the letter remained secret for more than two years, until after the war was finally over, when the Vietnamese showed it to a group of visiting American Congressmen.

The State Department confirmed its authenticity. Eight, single-spaced pages specified the forms that the American 'reconstruction grant' would take. Most of it would be spent in the United States; American firms would tender for contracts to build industrial plants and to restore bombed bridges, railway lines, dams and harbour facilities. 'We knew', a Vietnamese Government minister confided later, 'that without that minimum capital, we could never rebuild the country *and* remain independent.'[1]

Not a cent was paid. On April 30, 1975, the last day of the war, the US Treasury Department froze Vietnamese assets of $70 million. Two weeks later, the Commerce Department classified Vietnam a 'Category Z' country, requiring all exports to be approved by the State Department. This applied to foreign subsidiaries of American companies. The World Bank was frightened away, suspending a grant for an irrigation scheme which would have increased food capacity.

From 1981, under the Trading with the Enemy Act, a legacy of the First World War, American voluntary agencies were denied export licences for humanitarian aid to all of Indo-China: Vietnam, Cambodia and Laos. The first aid to be banned included modest amounts of seed-processing and storage equipment, which Oxfam America had promised to an agricultural co-operative in Vietnam, together with help in setting up a small bee-keeping co-operative designed to supply honey as a food supplement to pre-school children.

Revenge was the policy. Washington's allies joined in. In 1979, the new British Prime Minister, Margaret Thatcher, persuaded the European Community to halt its regular shipments of milk to Vietnamese children. As a consequence, the price of a kilo of milk powder in Vietnam rose to ten times the price of a kilo of meat. During visits in 1975 and 1978, I saw many children with distended bellies and fragile limbs in the towns as well as the countryside. According to World Health Organisation measurements, a third of all infants under five so deteriorated following the milk ban that the majority of them were stunted or likely to be, and a disproportionate number of the very youngest were reportedly going blind due to a lack of Vitamin A.[2]

In Hongai, a coal-mining community on the Gulf of

Tonkin, which claims the distinction of the most bombed town in Vietnam – during 1966, American carrier-based planes bombed it from seven in the morning until five in the evening – Dr Luu Van Hoat told me that 10 per cent of the children were deaf. 'Although they lost their hearing during the raids,' he said, 'they lived. It was a sign of hope. Now we are losing the next generation to malnutrition. The situation is straightforward; children need milk to live, and we don't have it.'

Among Washington's demons, not even Cuba was subjected to such a complete embargo. 'We have smashed the country to bits,' wrote Telford Taylor, chief United States prosecutor at the Nuremberg trials, 'and [we] will not even take the trouble to clean up the blood and rubble. Somehow we have failed to learn the lessons we undertook to teach at Nuremberg.'[3]

There seemed hope in 1978. The Vietnamese Government made contact with the Carter administration, seeking 'normalisation'. No conditions were sought; no mention was made of the $3.5 billion pledged by Nixon. The Foreign Minister at the time, Nguyen Co Thach, a humane and conciliatory man, flew to New York and waited a week in a room at the Holiday Inn on 42nd Street for a promised call from Richard Holbrooke, the Under-Secretary of State.

'He assured me our countries would have an "historic reconciliation",' Thach told me. 'Those were the words he used. But it never happened. I never got the phone call. Other developments were overtaking us. That summer China had become the big interest in Washington. Deng Xiaoping had been to the United States and worn a cowboy hat. No one seemed to be bothered that China was then backing Pol Pot in Cambodia, whose forces had been attacking us for over a year. On the contrary, when we counter-attacked (Christmas Day 1978) and drove the Khmer Rouge into Thailand, the new allies, China and America, made *us* the pariahs.'

In January 1979, the Chinese attacked Vietnam from the north. It was a massive assault by 600,000 troops, more than the Americans had deployed. China, said Peking Radio, was 'teaching Vietnam a lesson'. Before they were thrown back, the invaders destroyed dykes and canals that had withstood the American bombing, and most of the country's reserve stocks of rice.

A siege mentality now consumed the Communist Party leadership in Hanoi as the country descended deeper into isolation. Having cast Vietnam as an aggressor, the United States under Ronald Reagan sought to justify and redeem its 'noble cause' in Indo-China. A United Nations blockade, engineered by the United States, its Western allies and China, was mounted against Vietnamese-liberated Cambodia. At the United Nations and other world bodies, such as the World Health Organisation, Pol Pot's representatives continued to speak for their victims. Two American relief workers on the Thai border, Linda Mason and Roger Brown, wrote, 'The US Government insisted that the Khmer Rouge be fed . . . the US preferred that the Khmer Rouge operation benefit from the credibility of an internationally known relief operation.'[4] Under American pressure, the World Food Programme handed over $12 million worth of food to the Thai Army to pass on to the Khmer Rouge. '20,000 to 40,000 Pol Pot guerrillas benefited', according to Assistant Secretary of State Holbrooke.[5]

As the threat of Pol Pot's return effectively trapped the Vietnamese Army in Cambodia, the strain on Vietnam's war-ruined economy proved intolerable. For many Vietnamese, this meant austerity, hunger and repression: a time of bitterness. Although hundreds of thousands of war refugees were successfully returned to their land, and their villages rebuilt, many former soldiers and servants of the Saigon regime were imprisoned in extremely harsh 're-education camps', together with those who had owed no allegiance to either side. These were Vietnam's Gulags.

Liberty came to be measured by your standing in the Communist Party. Thousands of the newly impoverished took to the sea in boats, many of them Chinese-Vietnamese fearful of recrimination in the wake of China's invasion. They were followed by destitute farmers from the north. The Hanoi

Government had agreed to an 'orderly departure programme' in 1979, but without the co-operation of the United States this was all but impossible.

In 1986, faced with criticism from within the party and public discontent over shortages and rising prices, the old guard in the Politburo, who had led the country for forty years, resigned *en masse*. They were succeeded by a relatively youthful leadership, notably Nguyen Van Linh, 'Vietnam's Gorbachev', who had led the National Liberation Front ('Vietcong'). Linh saw himself as a 'pragmatist'; he had been dropped from the Politburo because of his opposition to the rapid 'socialisation' of the south in the late 1970s.

In December 1986, at the Sixth Congress of the Communist Party, the new leadership announced a far-reaching programme of economic and social change. This was *Doi Moi*: 'renovation'. The 'free market' was embraced as the means of breaking down the Western-led embargo. Since then, the Party line has been that 'all people in society and all Party members should strive to amass wealth for themselves and for the nation as a whole', thereby 'promoting economic growth'. Nervously, however, the leadership has warned that 'it will be difficult to avoid gaps between rich and poor', which if not controlled 'will lead to danger and social turmoil'.[6]

Within two years the World Bank had opened an office in Hanoi, along with the International Monetary Fund and the Asian Development Bank. They were joined by investors from Europe, Japan, Korea, Singapore and the other south-east Asian states. The 'prize', as Richard Nixon used to describe the countries of south-east Asia, was an abundance of natural resources: coal, oil, gas and timber. American companies, still legally prevented from trading, brought pressure on the White House. In 1994, President Clinton lifted the American embargo, and the first post-war ambassador arrived in Hanoi three years later. 'United States policy', said the Ambassador, 'is to help Vietnam [become] fully integrated into this dynamic region.'[7]

Alfonso L. DeMatteis, from Brooklyn, New York, is the founder of the American Chamber of Commerce in Hanoi.

When we met, he was sitting in front of a furled American flag and puzzling over why no one in Vietnam seemed to bear him a grudge. He reminded me of the old Hollywood comic Jerry Lewis, though his *bonhomie* was limited. I noticed on his desk a copy of a letter he had written to a ministry complaining about a proposed museum that would commemorate the American bombing of Hanoi.

Having made a fortune in the construction business, much of it in Saudi Arabia, DeMatteis is making another in Vietnam. After greeting me warmly he wanted to talk about Mother Teresa. 'Mother was recently in this very town,' he said. 'Mother was in this very office. She stood with me and was photographed next to the [American] flag.' He handed me a press release about 'Mother's movements' and how his company was 'accommodating Mother's local Sisters'.

He followed this with a fifteen-storey building he is building on Hanoi's West Lake, the Ho Tay, also known as the Lake of Mist. A place of beauty and the source of legends, like the rising of the Dragon King and the casting and ringing of a huge bell that can be heard all the way to China, it was once overlooked by grand pavilions and pagodas. A few pagodas rise out of the mist, still surrounded by the funerary monuments of twelfth-century monks.

People come here in the evenings and at weekends on their bicycles, pedalling all the way from the rickety streets that cling to the Red River dykes. On Sundays they hire ancient clinker-built rowing boats, and picnic in the public space soon to be occupied by the DeMatteis tower, and others like it.

'It will come complete with health club and running track,' said DeMatteis. 'We're fortunate; we got in early. All the prime sites have gone already.'

'Will the Vietnamese have use of it?'

'You've got to appreciate the rents are not cheap. In a word, John – unlikely.'

'Isn't it ironic', I said, 'that the foreigners Vietnam has been repelling all this century, the French, Japanese, Americans, might by other means end up gaining what they've been unable to achieve by war?'

'I don't quite get you.'

'Well, you're all back . . .'

'We sure are!'

'And you may well end up owning the place.'

'You know, I never thought of it like that. Thank you, John.'

Peter Purcell is an Australian version of DeMatteis. When we met, he was building the Hanoi Club, whose annual membership fees range from $6,500 to $15,000 and which, he says, 'will only work if it's exclusive'. 'I hate communism,' he said, 'but the socialism here is just right.'

As an illustration, he described how, with initial capital of $A14 million, he had already made $A50 million, and he still had a vacant lot. He told me a story about a senior Vietnamese Government official who had asked him, on the quiet, to teach him about stocks and shares. 'They're on the verge of being ripped off,' he said, 'as part of their necessary education programme converting them to the wonderful world of capitalism.'

A World Bank economist called David Dollar has predicted that Vietnam will end up as 'another Asian tiger'. 'They have made an excellent start with the necessary reforms,' he wrote.[8] These 'necessary reforms' were spelt out at a meeting in 1993 of the 'Paris Club' of donors, the richest Western states and Japan, which dispense 'aid' to countries with prospects of exploitation.

The Vietnamese were told that a total of £1·8 billion in 'grants' and loans would be forthcoming if they 'opened up' to the 'free market'. The state economy would have to be 'downsized', public enterprises would have to be scrapped or converted to 'joint ventures' with foreign firms, and tens of thousands of public employees sacked.

There would no longer be a place for public services, including health and education systems that were the envy of the Third World. These would be replaced by 'safety nets' dependent on 'macro-economic growth'. Foreign investors would be offered 'tax holidays' of five years or more, along with 'competitively priced' (cheap) labour. And before all this got under way, Hanoi would have to honour the bad debts of the defunct Saigon regime: in effect, pay back loans incurred by its enemy which had helped bankroll the American war.

It was as if the Vietnamese were finally being granted membership of the 'international community' as long as they first created a society based on divisions of wealth and poverty and exploited labour: a society in which social achievements were no longer valued: the kind of foreign-imposed system they had sacrificed so much to escape. It seemed, wrote Gabriel Kolko in *Anatomy of a War*, that the Vietnam War would finally end in 'the defeat of all who fought in it – and one of the greatest tragedies of modern history'.[9]

Few apart from Kolko have raised the alarm. In his subsequent book, *Vietnam: Anatomy of a Peace*, he pointed out that the new policies, in less than a decade, had destroyed the high degree of equity Vietnam had achieved by the end of the war, and created a class society with divisions of wealth greater than those of India, the United States and Britain under Thatcherism.[10]

The Canadian economist Michel Chossudovsky, a specialist in Third World issues, wrote in 1994, 'The achievements of past struggles and the aspirations of an entire nation are [being] undone and erased ... No Agent Orange or steel pellet bombs, no napalm, no toxic chemicals: a new phase of economic and social (rather than physical) destruction has unfolded. The seemingly neutral and scientific tools of macro-economic policy constitute a non-violent instrument of recolonisation and impoverishment.'[11]

The World Bank, together with the International Monetary Fund and the Asian Development Bank, are overseeing the implementation of these 'reforms'. The World Bank began by rewriting the land laws, affecting two-thirds of the population. Subsistence farming, which had kept famine at bay, is being replaced by cash-cropping for export, as Vietnam is 'fully integrated into the dynamic region'.

District co-operatives, which supported the elementary school system, ante-natal clinics and emergency food stores, are being phased out. These have no place in the new order. In order to be 'competitive', rice, the staple of more than seventy million people, is now linked to the depredations of the world market and sold below the world price. While the World Bank lauds Vietnam's 'rice surplus', buried in the jargon is the implicit acceptance that famine has returned.

Whereas farmers in difficulty could once depend on rural credit from the state ('interest' was unknown), they now must go to private lenders, the usurers who once plagued the peasantry. This was the system under the French; peonage was the result. In its report, *Viet Nam: Transition to the Market*, the World Bank welcomed this, explaining that it would cause the desired 'greater land concentration and landlessness'.[12] Other reforms followed, such as the abolition of pensions and social welfare measures that had supported the sick and disabled, widows, orphans and ex-servicemen.

After seven years of this 'restructuring', according to the World Bank's own estimates, poverty has increased, with up to 70 per cent of the population now in 'absolute poverty', half the adult population consuming considerably fewer than 2,100 calories a day and half the children severely malnourished.[13] At least a million people have been made unemployed, most of them in the health services. They, together with people thrown off their land, should be offered, says the World Bank, 'unskilled work at low wages'. (In the draft of this report I saw in the Bank's offices in Hanoi, someone had pencilled in the margins that the 'figure proposed by UNDP consultants is so low as to be virtually slave labour'.) [14]

Since these 'reforms' got under way, the Bank admits there is 'a higher proportion of underweight and stunted children than in any other country in south and south-east Asia with the exception of Bangladesh ... The magnitude of stunting and wasting among children appears to have increased significantly...' Unfortunately, 'the problem of food availability in the food deficit areas will not disappear overnight, since consumers in these areas do not have the purchasing power to bid up the price paid for foodgrains from the surplus regions. In fact, it is financially more rewarding to export rice outside Vietnam than to transfer it to the deficit regions within the country. Indeed, as private sector grain trade expands, the availability of food in the deficit regions may initially decline before it improves.' In other words, 'consumers without purchasing power' will have to go hungry.[15]

When I put these matters to Bradley Babson, an American economist who represents the World Bank in Hanoi, he was generous in his praise of the Vietnamese 'independence of mind' in 'defending their real achievements in the social arena'. He was also extraordinarily frank. 'I think it's fair to say', he said, 'that Vietnam in the past has had more equality than many other countries, and that the reforms necessary for economic growth will bring greater inequality.'

According to Michel Chossudovsky, 'the hidden agenda of the reforms is the destabilisation of Vietnam's industrial base: heavy industry, oil and gas, natural resources and mining, cement and steel production are to be reorganised and taken over by foreign capital with the Japanese conglomerates playing a decisive and dominant role ... the movement is towards the reintegration of Vietnam into the Japanese sphere of influence, a situation reminiscent of World War Two when Vietnam was part of Japan's "Great East Asia Co-Prosperity Sphere".'[16]

Japanese capital controls 80 per cent of the loans for investment projects and infrastructure, while the dollar has taken over from the Vietnamese dong, giving the US Reserve Bank effective control of the flow of currency. Singapore dominates the property market, and Taiwan and Korea the 'tax holiday' sweatshops. The French and the Australians are doing nicely, too, with the British not far behind.

In 1995, the then Chancellor of the Exchequer, Kenneth Clarke, visited Hanoi with a group of British businessmen, who had been given a briefing document by the Department of Trade and Industry. This was candid, almost ecstatic about the cheapness of people. 'Labour rates', it said, 'are as low as $35 a month.' Moreover, the Vietnamese 'can provide a new industrial home for ailing British products'. 'Take the long view,' advised the British Government, 'use Vietnam's weaknesses selfishly. Vietnam's open door invites you to take advantage of its low standard of living and low wages.'[17]

I showed this to Dr Nguyen Xuan Oanh, the economic adviser to Prime Minister Vo Van Kiet. 'We have *inexpensive* labour,' he said. 'I don't call it cheap labour. It allows us to be competitive on the international market.' Thereupon he extolled growth rates, 'tax holidays', diminished public services and the rest of the IMF deity.

What was interesting about this man was that not only was he an architect of Vietnam's 'market socialism', as he called it, but he used to be deputy Prime Minister in the old Saigon regime. Detained at the end of the war, he convinced the communists they would need him one day and, like a bending reed, he survived. Today, from his smart Saigon offices, with their black leather chairs and remote-controlled air-conditioning, he offers foreign businessmen silky 'personalised consulting' as they enter 'a paradise for your investment'.

'The regime you helped to run in the old days', I said, 'was pretty corrupt, wasn't it?'

'We had a bad administration,' he said.

'It was supported by a black market, drugs, prostitution and war profiteering.'

'It was not good . . .'

'You were number two . . .'

'I tried very hard to help, but not successfully.'

'Aren't you beginning to re-create that same kind of government?'

'No, we are harmoniously blending socialism with capitalism. That is not to deny that when you open the door for new winds to come in, the dust comes in, too.'

'That's an old Vietnamese saying?'

Laughter.

'I'm told Mrs Thatcher has been an inspiration.'

'We learned some things from her, but what we are doing is distinctively Vietnamese.'

'The Vietnamese kicked out the French, who forced the population to work for next to nothing in foreign-owned factories. Isn't that now happening again?'

'I told you our people are merely *inexpensive* . . .'

Although those like Dr Oanh, David Dollar and Bradley Babson speak publicly about Vietnam as 'the next tiger economy', the truth is that, as the current crop of Asian tigers – Korea, Hong Kong, Singapore, Malaysia – run out of steam, with their share markets collapsing and currencies devaluing, the last thing they want is a competitor the size of Vietnam. For this reason, Vietnam's 'integration' into the region is likely to be as an economic colony for the tigers, Japan and the West.

This is dramatically evident in the Export Processing Zones, known as EPZs. Run by a Taiwanese company on cleared land on the banks of the Saigon River, one of them announces itself as 'Saigon South . . . a Brave New World'. Inside, I was struck by the likeness to photographs of the cotton mills of Lancashire. Ancient looms imported from China, making towelling for export, were attended by mostly young women, who get a basic rate of £12 a month for a twelve-hour day. If they fall behind the target set by the manager, who secretly tags thread in their machine, they are sacked. One worker controls four machines. 'In Taiwan', said the Taiwanese manager, 'we'd have one worker on six, even eight machines. But the Vietnamese don't accept this: they object.'

The air was foul and filled with cotton dust, the noise unrelenting and the only protective clothing appeared to be hair curlers. One woman was struck in the eye while I was there. 'We've got a medical centre for that sort of thing,' said the manager, who told me he had a business diploma from a Californian college. Under Vietnamese law, there ought to be a union at the factory. 'We haven't got one of those yet,' he said. With 100,000 workers, many of them living in dormitories, 'Saigon South' is a city state, with its own stock exchange, police and customs. 'We calculate', said the manager, 'that this EPZ is what all Vietnamese cities will look like in the next century.'

Dr Le Thi Quy runs the Center for Scientific Studies of Women and the Family in Saigon. Her work lately has concentrated on the conditions of workers in the EPZs, which she inspects unannounced. In a report commissioned by the government she describes as 'commonplace' women forced to work from 7 a.m. to 9 p.m. every other day. 'They must never stop,' she wrote. 'They are given a "hygiene card" which allows them to do their personal hygiene only three times a day, each time taking no more than five minutes. The stress is something people have not known before, not even in war-time. It is systematic.'

She concluded, 'I have to report that something very serious is happening to our society. Traps are being laid at the gates of profits. As public service employment is drastically reduced, our families are being commercialised ... prosti-tution has emerged into the open and is growing.' She added eloquently, 'The market economy is about mechanism. I wish to speak for humanitarian values. If we affirm that develop-ment can only be achieved by sacrificing these values, which have been long pursued by mankind and give us hope for freedom, democracy and equality, it means that we reject the most basic factors that link people together as a community. It is an insult to our humanity to maintain that people only have economic demands, and therefore economic develop-ment must be made at all costs. To live is not enough. People must seek many things to make their lives significant.'[18]

If development was measured not by Gross National Product, but a society's success in meeting the basic needs of its people, Vietnam would have been a model. That was its real 'threat'. From the defeat of the French at Dien Bien Phu in 1954 to 1972, primary and secondary school enrolment in the North increased sevenfold, from 700,000 to almost five million. In 1980, UNESCO estimated a literacy rate of 90 per cent and school enrolment among the highest in Asia and throughout the Third World.[19]

Now that education has been transformed into a com-modity, 'consumers of [educational] services', says a consti-pated UN Development Programme report, '[are required] to pay increased amounts, encouraging institutions to become self-financing, and by using incentives to privatise delivery of education and training where appropriate.'[20] Teachers who have not been 'redeployed' on road gangs and other 'public projects' have had their salaries cut to as little as £5 a month. Most schools have been privatised, with the obligation to pay tuition fees now written into the constitution. By 1992, an estimated three-quarters of a million children had been pushed out of the education system, despite an increase in the population of children of school age.[21]

At a village in the Mekong Delta a woman and her twelve-year-old daughter sit in the shade making straw beach mats for export. A middle-man pays them a total of a dollar a day. They work from five in the morning until five in the evening. Ten years ago, the village had a co-operative that funded a primary school. Now that co-operatives have been abolished, the girl must work such grinding hours to pay for sporadic lessons at a near-by fee-paying school.

The Vietnamese health service was once famous. Primary care where people lived and worked raised life expectancy to among the highest in the developing world. Vaccination programmes reduced the spread of infectious diseases; in contrast to most of the Third World, preventable diseases were prevented. More babies survived birth and their first precarious years than in most countries in south-east Asia.[22] Now, under the tutelage of the foreign 'donor community', the government has abandoned direct support for all health services. Drugs are available only to those who can afford to buy them on the 'free market'. Diseases like malaria, dengue and cholera have returned.

In its inimitable way, the World Bank acknowledges this 'downside' of its 'reforms'. 'Despite its impressive performance in the past,' says the *Transition to the Market* report, 'the Vietnamese health sector is currently languishing ... there is a severe shortage of drugs and medical equipment ... The shortage of funds is so acute that it is unclear where the grass roots facilities are going to find the inputs to continue functioning in the future.'[23]

During the American carpet bombing of Hanoi at Christmas 1972, the Bach Mai hospital in the centre of the city became something of a symbol of resistance. A bomb destroyed a wing, including wards and laboratories; patients, doctors and nurses died. One of the survivors was Professor Nguyen Van Xang, a stooped man who could be Ho Chi Minh's brother and whose office is dominated by a picture of the rubble it was. 'I heard the bombs whistling towards us,' he said. 'I took the nearest patients and sheltered them over there, under the stairs. Everything seemed to collapse around us.'

As we talked, there was a power cut; the hospital's weary generator had failed yet again, turning the wispy-bearded figure seated in front of me into a silhouette in a Gothic setting, bathed in the thin, yellow light of early evening. The scene poignantly expressed the exhaustion of Vietnam.

Professor Xang explained that, under the new, privatised system, a patient had to put down a deposit of 7,000 dong (£4) and a bed cost the equivalent of £2.50 per day. This was a great deal of money for the majority, who were excluded, causing Professor Xang to put his socialist beliefs into practice by handing out free drugs to poor people at a pagoda every Sunday. 'The situation here', he said, 'is that we can no longer afford a filter for our one kidney machine. It costs $22. So we use the same filter several times, which is wrong and dangerous . . . If a patient has renal failure and cannot afford to pay a quarter of the cost of the treatment, we have no choice but to treat them by traditional means; and they die.'

In Saigon, I made an appointment to visit the Tu Du obstetrics and gynaecological hospital. Built by the French in the 1950s and extended by the Americans, it is one of the most modern in the country: in the circumstances, a handicap, for almost all the equipment is American, for which parts stopped coming in 1975. The last children's respirator had disintegrated a year earlier.

A former operating theatre is known as the 'collection room' and, unofficially, the 'room of horrors'. It has shelves of large bottles containing grotesquely deformed foetuses. In the late 1960s, the United States sprayed much of South Vietnam, which it said it had come to 'save', with defoliant herbicides. Intended to 'deny cover' to the National Liberation Front, this was code-named 'Operation Hades', later changed to the friendlier 'Operation Ranch Hand'. The defoliants included Agent Orange, containing an impurity called dioxin, which is a poison of such power that it causes foetal death, miscarriage, chromosomal damage, congenital defects and cancer.

In 1970, the US Government banned the use of Agent Orange on American farmlands, but continued to spray it in Vietnam, where a pattern of deformities began to emerge: babies born without eyes, with deformed hearts and small brains and stumps instead of legs. Occasionally I saw these children in contaminated villages in the Mekong Delta; and whenever I asked about them, people pointed to the sky; one man scratched in the dust a good likeness of a bulbous C-130 aircraft, spraying.

In August that year, in a report to the US Senate, Senator Gaylord Nelson wrote that 'the US has dumped [on South Vietnam] a quantity of toxic chemical amounting to six pounds per head of population, including women and children'.[24] When the new American Ambassador, Douglas Peterson, said that the 'exact consequences of Agent Orange' were not 'clarified', he was challenged by the Director of the War Crimes Investigation Department, Vu Trong Huong, who said, 'We have over 50,000 children that have been born with horrific deformities; the link is clear.'[25]

At the Tu Du hospital Dr Pham Viet Thanh showed me a group of recently born babies in incubators. They all had thalidomide-type deformities. 'These Agent Orange births are routine for us,' he said. 'Every now and then we have what we call a foetal catastrophe – when the number of mis-carriages and deformed babies, I am afraid to say, overwhelms us.' In one ward there were two women suffering from chorioncarcinoma – cancer of pregnancy, which is extremely rare in the West. 'We don't have the training to deal with this phenomenon,' said Dr Thanh. 'We have asked for scholarships in Japan, Germany, the US and the UK, but they say no, or they don't reply.'

The question begs: why is this being allowed to happen? Why are foreigners once again being permitted to dictate the future of Vietnam? One answer is that the Vietnamese Communist Party was never as ideological as it appeared. The original impetus was nationalist; initially, the communists were the only political group which opposed French imperialism. Once they gained power in the north in 1954, many people joined the Party for reasons of personal ambition. There was a similar influx in the south after 1975; party membership offered power and privilege. Another explanation is that, like other communist parties, with their hierarchy and disciplines and lack of internal democracy, they were best equipped to fight a protracted war, but not to govern and protect a society at peace.

Yet the Party was immensely popular. The great majority of Vietnamese 'provided its strength and often forced it to move in ways that broadened its popular appeal and, in turn, accepted and made monumental sacrifices,' wrote Gabriel Kolko. 'However elitist its top leadership, the Party's success as a social movement was based largely on its response to peasant desires.' And that, says Kolko, is at the root of its betrayal today, making 'the war a monumental tragedy and a vain sacrifice ... for the majority of Vietnam's peasants, veterans and genuine idealists'.[26]

I understand his disillusion, but I think the privations that the Vietnamese have endured during thirty years of war and twenty years of isolation made some things inevitable, such as the erosion of principle and ideology and the growth of corruption in a war-ruined economy, especially in a bureaucracy which, since the war, has operated substantially for the benefit of party cadres. Many of them had little interest or education in socialism and became, like those in Boris Yeltsin's Russia, the most visible and voracious members of the new urban consumer class.

As for the ones who refused to go this way, and who could legitimately claim to be the legatees of Ho Chi Minh, they, too, were both desperate and vulnerable – desperate to internationalise their country and fulfil a historic need for counterweights to the power of China, the ancient foe, and to lessen the dependency on a Soviet Union in its death throes. The most generous explanation for their embrace of *laissez-faire* capitalism is that they have been seduced, and as one destructive 'reform' follows another, the seduction is beginning to look like rape. In another sense, Vietnam is simply typical of poor countries denied an independent path for their economies and whose governments become more concerned, almost mesmerised, with satisfying their foreign creditors than with serving their people. The resolution of this is perhaps Vietnam's final battle and the most difficult one of all.

Certainly, the 'dangerous time' that the artist Nguyen The Khan and many others allude to has arrived. That is to say, the point is passing where the Communist Party leadership loses control and becomes a captive of the foreign impositions it has endorsed. When that happens, the pact between the Party and the peasants, which was probably unique to Vietnam, will be finally broken, and there will be a vacuum and trouble or, as Kolko calls it, 'a divorce'.

The signs are there. Every day very poor people and disabled ex-soldiers are swept from the centre of Saigon and taken to detention centres; and anti-government Buddhists, reminiscent of those who helped to topple the American-backed regimes in the 1960s, are again prisoners of conscience. The Vietnamese Army, having expended the nation's blood, sweat and tears, and built the co-operative system in the countryside, regards itself as the keeper of historical memories and legacies. That is why it has allowed its own journals to criticise their political masters and has made a subversive hero of the late General Tran Van Tra, the brilliant, nonconformist commander of the victorious army in South Vietnam in 1975, who later formed a dissident group, the Society of Resistance Fighters. Another war hero, Colonel Bui Tin, said from exile in France, 'I long for a humanist, modern and pluralist socialism in my country.'[27]

Unlike China, obedience requires consensus in Vietnam. In his biography, *Giap*, Peter MacDonald wrote that 'whereas in many nations there are thousands of family names, evolved over the centuries and added to by migrants, in the whole of Vietnam there are less than a hundred, based on tribal groupings such as the Ngo and the Nguyen: people are part of a big family'.[28] Tearing apart the fabric of this family will not be compensated for by Honda motorbikes, Pepsi-Cola and mobile phones.

In advocating an 'agricultural wage labour market' as a way of brutally disconnecting farm workers from their villages and making them 'flexible', meaning itinerant, Vietnam's new foreign managers and creditors ignore the resilience of rural life, with its *community* of labour, its village councils, mutual aid societies, craftsmen's guilds and emergency relief organisations. Much of this has lasted for 2,500 years: a model of natural socialism, you might say. Instead of trying to destroy it, genuine reform would build on its foundations and, with resources that eradicated poverty, create a modern, vibrant, agriculture-based economy that matched the needs of the majority.

The final battle has begun. Saigon's biggest strikes since the war have swept over the Korean-owned EPZs. The issues are slave wages, excessive hours and cruel managers. Although not reported in the press, they are widely supported in Saigon. Seldom a week now passes without a major 'wildcat' strike, which can be of such intensity that the civil authorities often choose to stand back: a clear sign that they are worried.

In 1997, Nike, the giant American running-shoe maker, which employs 35,000 mostly female workers in Vietnam, was hit by a series of rolling strikes. Illegal demonstrations were held outside the gates of the company's sub-contractors, and the police stood by. A study by the American-based Vietnam Labour Watch found that the workers' average wage was $1.60 for eight hours, whereas the shoes they made sold for up to $149 in the United States.

'Supervisors humiliate women,' reported the Vietnamese investigator. 'They force them to kneel, to stand in the hot sun, treating them like recruits in a boot camp. In one plant, workers were allowed to go to the lavatory only once during a shift and were limited to two drinks of water. The Taiwanese sub-contractor forced fifty-six women to run around the plant in the sun as punishment for wearing "non-regulation" shoes. Twelve fainted and were taken to hospital. The next day, the factory was attacked by local people.'[29]

In the countryside, the privatisation of land has brought administrative chaos and anger. This has been reported in the official press as 'hot spots' that are 'smouldering', 'tense' and 'very fierce'.[30] In Thai Binh province, south of Hanoi, government offices have been sacked and officials forced to flee for their lives. 'The military and police failed to halt the problem,' said one report.[31]

The biggest single foreign investor in Vietnam, the Korean multinational Daewoo, plans to build a £93 million EPZ near Hanoi, including an eighteen-hole golf course for its executives and customers. The golf course will destroy the rice fields and the way of life of the village of Tho Da. The government has offered the villagers compensation of £125 per family. Rejecting this, they erected barricades and a sign, 'Dangerous Area. Do not enter', over a skull and crossbones. Police attacked twice and were thrown back; one woman was killed. Daewoo's chairman flew in from Seoul with reassurances that the golf course was 'not just for golfers'. At the time of writing, there is a huge row involving the Prime Minister, the Hanoi People's Committee and the Korean Government. Meanwhile, the barricades remain, a symbol of a new popular resistance finding its natural leaders and confidence with every confrontation. Not only has the government admitted that this 'danger and social turmoil' is 'becoming more and more complex and serious', but the instigator of 'Renovation', Nguyen Van Linh, has warned that the 'gap between the classes needs to be solved promptly'.[32]

In Saigon, I stayed in the same room at the Caravelle Hotel that was my intermittent home thirty years ago. From the same balcony overlooking Lam Som Square, next to the

French playhouse, I used to watch people show immense courage in demonstrating against the vicious foreign-backed regimes that came and went. Here, too, I watched the dawn lit up by tracer bullets on the last day of April 1975, the last day of the longest war this century.

The hotel's cashier in those days, always a morbid man, had threatened to shoot himself that evening; but he chose not to, and he survived and retired on a cashier's pension. The door-opener, a laconic character from Bombay, was there until recently. 'I have ushered in victors and ushered out vanquished,' he would say. 'The good thing about this job is that, in hurrying in and hurrying out, they don't notice me.'

Coming back, I met Dr Nguyen Thi Oanh in the foyer. A gracious and wry person, she had trained as a sociologist in the United States in the 1950s. 'I was never a communist,' she said, 'but I was close to them because they expressed the nationalism I felt, and they were brave. The problem with the course we are taking now is that it flies in the face of the best of our history, which makes us proud and able to bear many privations. The real danger is that we shall lose our soul, and not realise it before it's too late.'

I told her that the Ministry of Culture had wanted to censor the documentary film my colleagues and I had shot at My Lai, because they were afraid it would offend the Americans and be bad for business. She shook her head. 'They know the Americans can never forget,' she said.

'Why', I asked, 'are the Vietnamese able to forget?'

'Because we didn't lose, we won. We lost materially speaking, but spiritually we *won*. We are losing a bit now, but we will win again.'

Apart from such pride, there are, for me, two outstanding attractions about Vietnam. The first is that the maxims of Ho Chi Minh, which inspired a great popular resistance, are still admired for their common wisdom and acted upon. When the bombing began in the mid-1960s, Ho travelled down Route One, which was then known as 'the Street of No Joy' by the American pilots who blitzed it and the Vietnamese convoys who depended on it. He made a speech along the way, in which he said that when the war was over, 'we shall make our country a thousand times more beautiful'.

I met a man who is the embodiment of this, Professor Vo Quy, a restless seventy-year-old whose office at Hanoi University is guarded by the ancient skeleton of an elephant. He has led one of the most dramatic environmental rescues in history. In 1974, while the war was still going on, he travelled south and found the environmental damage so great that he returned with the warning that, unless something was done, Vietnam in twenty years would look like the moon. 'The ecosystem was in a terrible way,' he said. 'The mangroves were largely ruined by bombing and herbicides. The wildlife was gone. The tigers, which had followed the sound of gunfire, were extinct. I found no water birds.'

The task of reforestation was enormous. In areas drenched in Agent Orange, not a single tree remained; the earth was thought to have solidified and 'died'. Professor Quy initiated a re-greening campaign, which involved almost everybody. Over the next five years millions of hectares of poisoned land were reclaimed. Every village planted a forest, every child a tree.

Today, in many parts of the country, the sound of birds and the rustle of wildlife are heard for the first time in two generations. 'We thought the stork and the ibis and certain types of crane were extinct,' said Professor Quy. 'But as each new tree encouraged the tropical organisms, and the mangroves began to grow back, we had exciting discoveries: we found great birds we thought we'd lost: twenty-five cranes *and* the rare milky stork. I myself saw an ibis on the Laos side of the border. *What a sight it was!* I immediately ordered a sanctuary to be marked out!' A pheasant which reappeared was named a 'Vo Quy'.

For me, the other compelling attraction of Vietnam is the spectacle of human reconciliation. Under a programme sponsored by the European Union, Vietnamese boat people scattered in refugee camps throughout Asia were asked if they wanted to go home. Tens of thousands said they did, but many were frightened. They were first reassured by videotaped interviews with their relatives and friends at home. A small nation has since returned. On arrival, they are lent enough money to start again; and their community is subsidised so that there is no talk of favouritism.

I was introduced to a fisherman, Mac Thi Nhan, who fled with his family to Hong Kong, and was now back in his village on Ha Long Bay, and with a new boat. 'I was afraid at first, but everyone has been thoughtful to us,' he said. His wife nodded agreement.

Michael Culligan, who runs the EU programme in Haiphong, said, 'I have travelled all over the country and met thousands of returnees, and I have not come across a single case of victimisation. The Vietnamese are a very kindly people. They were very sympathetic towards the boat people who came home, and they went out of their way to ensure they didn't lose face. That is a civilised society.'

CHINA BEACH

As the flight from Hanoi landed at Danang, Bobby fell silent. The last time he had seen this airport, with its rows of billets and blast-proof hangars, watchtowers and flags, was in 1968. 'Different flags,' he said softly.

It was his first and only tour of duty in Vietnam. Lieutenant Robert O. Muller, aged twenty-one, was what the US Marines call an 'honour man'. 'In 1967 I was top of my class; I could have had any job I wanted', he said, 'and I *chose* infantry. People forget what the mood was back then. Most of America was not on the streets, protesting. America was rah-rah, and it was very much expected that you'd go into the service.'

'What was it like', I asked, 'being trained as a real Marine, not a Hollywood Marine?'

'Is there a difference?' he replied. 'You remember the first half of the movie *Full Metal Jacket*? That's it. You even get told the atrocities! But here's the funny side. At college I was a business major and all my professors were telling me I really ought to go to Vietnam because I'd be welcomed on Wall Street. A year of war would look just great on a stockbroker's resumé.'

'When you landed here did you feel you were fighting the good fight against communism?'

'Absolutely. But on the day I arrived all these people in black pyjamas were running around the airport, and I said to myself, "Wait on a second. I thought people in black pyjamas were supposed to be the Vietcong and the enemy. What the hell are they doing all over this airport?" I'm serious. You've got to understand that Vietnam was a lie. It was a lie from the beginning, throughout the war and even today as they are trying to write it into the history books, it's a lie. Three million US servicemen came over here and confronted, in their own way, the lie. That was tragic.'

A total of 58,022 Americans were killed in Vietnam. Most of them were volunteers. According to Bobby Muller, almost as many have killed themselves since their return from the war.

On April 29, 1969, Lieutenant Muller was assigned to the Demilitarised Zone, the 'DeeEmZee'. Straddling the Seventeenth Parallel that arbitrarily divided North and South Vietnam, it was anything but demilitarised. For five years thousands of marines fought and died here, living in the mud or dust of 'fire bases' that today look like miniature extinct volcanoes.

Bobby was leading his men in an assault on a hill covered in cloud when he was shot through the chest. 'I remember every second of it,' he said. 'I felt the life going out of me. I was like a balloon deflating. I thought, "Oh shit, I'm going to die right here in the mud and rain."' He was saved only because a hospital ship happened to be in the vicinity of Danang. The bullet severed his spinal cord and he permanently lost the use of his legs.

Bobby Muller and I have been friends for eighteen years. When we first met, I realised I had seen him at the Republican Party's convention at Miami Beach in 1972. He and another disabled veteran had been thrown out, in their wheelchairs, having booed Richard Nixon during his acceptance speech as the party's presidential candidate. The other man was Ron Kovic, whose autobiography, *Born on the Fourth of July*, was made into a film by Oliver Stone.

Five years later I saw Bobby again, on the steps of City Hall, New York. It was Memorial Day, the day Americans remember their 'foreign wars'. There were medals and flags and dignitaries, then former Lieutenant Muller took the microphone and from his wheelchair brought even a construction site beyond the crowd to an attentive silence. 'There are 280,000 veterans of Vietnam just in New York

City', he began, 'and a third of them can't find jobs. Throughout America 60 per cent of all black veterans can't find jobs. Many veterans are dying right now from the chemicals we dumped on Vietnam . . .'

He continued in this vein to the mounting unease of his audience; and he ended by reminding them that the veterans held the secrets of the war. In other words, they understood its criminal nature.

I found him later in an almost bare office at the seedy end of Fifth Avenue, where he and a few friends, most of them disabled, had founded Vietnam Veterans of America. He is a slight, sometimes grey figure whose appearance belies a booming eloquence that comes in a stream of consciousness, much of it heavily ironic, and frequently interrupted by a laugh like a plane taking off. 'Read this,' he said, handing me a newspaper cutting reporting the results of a Harris Poll. 'The American public', it said, 'believes by a two to one margin that the veterans of the Vietnam War were suckers.'

Now, eighteen years later, we drove out from Danang towards the South China Sea. Silhouetted in the heat haze were small, neat peaks on the landscape. These were the remains of 'fire bases', which were built on the same principle that required covered wagons travelling in the American West to be drawn into a circle. The Vietcong were referred to as 'Indians'; Vietnamese civilians were 'gooks', 'dinks' and 'slopes'.

We drove past rows of war graves – not American graves; there are none in Vietnam, not even graves with human remains. At the end of the war, the Hanoi Government gave priority to a cosmetic operation that may have been unique in its intent and scope. Throughout the south, there are now hundreds of cemeteries which did not exist in 1975. They were prefabricated in the north and transported to old battlefields where the People's Army of Vietnam had fought and sustained great losses. Each new headstone has the name of the soldier purporting to be resting beneath it, but the grave itself is empty: a symbol of grief and defiance. We passed one of them, raised on a bulldozed American base, on what appeared to be a volleyball court.

591

I wheeled Bobby down to the seafront at China Beach and along the promenade, grass sprouting from the cracks in the concrete. Banyan trees leaned and provided shade; palms rustled in a light breeze that lifted off the sea. A distant figure stood framed between the trees and the sky. The only people on the beach were fishermen and a few French tourists. 'This is where it began,' he said softly, 'in this beautiful place.'

It was here that the first US Marines came ashore on March 6, 1965, and were greeted by a delegation from the Danang Chamber of Commerce and, of course, the media. A few weeks earlier, the American Congress had been presented with 'conclusive proof' of Hanoi's preparations to invade the south – a cache of weapons found floating in a North Vietnamese junk off China Beach. In 1983, Ralph McGehee, a former senior CIA specialist in 'black propaganda', told me that the junk and its 'proof' were a 'master illusion'. 'The CIA', he said, 'loaded up the junk with communist weapons, floated it off the coast, then brought in the international press. We got the headlines we wanted, and the marines followed.'[1]

The deceptions that sustained the American war left a historical amnesia. During the early 1980s, whenever Bobby spoke on college campuses, he was inevitably asked, 'Which side did you fight on?' Even from the best college history courses, which provide a large measure of truth, America emerges as victim, a subject for apparently limitless introspection about a 'failed crusade'. At the same time, recognition that Vietnamese nationalism had won an heroic and honourable victory was, and remains, withheld.

Unlike those veterans who simply craved a parade and public approval, Bobby and his comrades in the Vietnam Veterans of America set out to turn the prevailing liberal wisdom about the war inside out and show that it was not so much an American tragedy as a Vietnamese one. A VVA curriculum on the war is now taught in schools and colleges.

'We have a long way to go,' said Bobby. 'In the 1980s, we had a President, Reagan, who described the war as a noble cause, who made a concerted effort to rehabilitate the sense of US involvement in Vietnam, who rehabilitated the Vietnam veterans as heroes in a struggle against communism. It was fantasy and absurd, but in a significant way it shaped the nation's perception, and of course Hollywood took its cue and cleaned up on the screens. There were the Missing in Action films, which were outright lies, and all those images of the vile, evil Vietnamese holding our boys in bamboo cages. These were emotional buttons that were pushed very successfully. Now you mention Vietnam, and it's thought of in mythical terms: it's a war, a set of emotions; it's not a country of seventy-two million people.'

The VVA funds remarkable projects in Indo-China. In Vietnam, it runs a thriving clinic attached to the children's hospital in Hanoi. In Cambodia, it established a prosthetics centre that introduced the 'Jaipur limb' into a society blighted by land-mines. This is a simple aluminium leg with a latex foot that requires no hi-tech components. More than 150 limbs are fitted every month. Like Bobby, most of the veterans in charge bear the damage of the Indo-China war, including men who themselves stepped on mines. As the war correspondent Martha Gellhorn wrote, 'they are the people with a wakeful conscience, the best of America's citizens . . . they can be counted on, they are always there'.[2]

Irony intrudes here. 'I had a meeting at a state enterprise about medical equipment for the clinic we run,' said Bobby. 'I started off by saying we were a non-profit humanitarian organisation. The state director said, "Excuse me, do you mean you're not here to make money?" I said no. He then asked us to leave, saying what amounted to, "No profit, no deal." When I told people back in Washington that I was thrown out of a meeting in Hanoi, Vietnam, because I wasn't a capitalist, they didn't believe me.'

It was dusk when I drove with Bobby back to Danang. The clouds of an early monsoon capped the hills like wigs. 'It's a long time since I've seen that,' said Bobby.

'What does it remind you of?'

'It reminds me of the day I was shot, of how cold and lonely it is up there and how cold and sodden the ground is when you fall on it, and lie there in your shit and blood.'

593

X

EPILOGUE

THE VIEW FROM DIMBAZA

There is no evidence that the present model for monetary
policy, which has served the country well, should be
changed or abandoned.

*Chris Stahls, Governor of South Africa's Reserve Bank
under the apartheid regime, reappointed by the
ANC Government*

IT IS EARLY spring; the sun is warm through the wind-
screen, while the wind outside skids off the dry veld. Here,
climate changes dramatically with altitude; there are valleys
watered by perennial rivers, then a dozen miles further on a
dustbowl has made another country. Something about the
Eastern Cape reminds me of Palestine: beauty out of one eye,
a slum out of the other. Beneath the vast canopy of an African
sky, silhouettes of women file across the saddle of a hill to
draw water from a well where cattle drink and defecate. Most
rural people have no choice but to walk up to half a mile to
get water. Most have no sanitation, no electricity and no
telephone; and no work. The shadows on the road are those
of slight children and their mothers, walking, carrying,
enduring.[1]

Up to a million people were dumped here in the manner
that Stalin banished whole nations to Siberia and central Asia.
Officially known as 'redundant' or 'surplus', they were unable
to serve in the mines or the quarries or the foreign-owned
factories; and there were already too many sweepers,
gardeners and nannies. They were women and children and

the elderly, the infirm and the disabled. They were taken in trucks to places where there was nothing: some were left in the desert. Known as Bantustans and 'homelands', these were vast rural concentration camps, an inspiration of the Dutch-born fascist Hendrik Verwoerd.

'I was eleven years old,' said Stanley Mbalala. 'It was winter 1968 and I was in the second wave of children. The truck came for me and my mother and brothers at night. We were forced out of our home near Cape Town and never saw it again. The journey was mostly in darkness; I was wrapped in a thin blanket and still remember the cold. We didn't know where we were going. There was a line of trucks with people huddled together; we were like livestock on the move.'

The two 'homelands' in the Eastern Cape were the Transkei and the Ciskei. The 'Republic of Ciskei' was the poorer of the two, though the distinction was imperceptible. Like all of apartheid's creations, both were absurd as well as grotesque. The capital of the Ciskei was Bisho, which cost £60 million to build. It was given a parliament house, an 'independence stadium', government offices, a palace for the president and a casino to attract whites 'from across the border'. The apartheid regime understood the importance of a black elite. The Ciskei's 'president for life' was a tinpot autocrat called Lennox Sebe, known for his hangers-on and spies and his marble staircases. Today, weeds grow in the driveway of his palace, and the swimming pool is green with slime. A homeless family has camped in one of the watchtowers; their washing dries on the electric sensor fence.

Dimbaza is nearby, a symbol of the Ciskei and the deeply impoverished Eastern Cape. It was 'settled' in 1967 (the year of my last visit to South Africa; I was banned when my reporting was deemed 'embarrassing to the state'). Seventy families were dumped on a waterless, windswept hillside. Stanley remembers a forest, which became firewood during the first winter. They lived in tents and in wooden huts with zinc roofs and earthen floors. Later arrivals had boxes made from asbestos and cement; these, too, had neither floors nor ceilings and were so hot in summer and cold and damp in winter that the very young and old perished in them. 'When it rained', Stanley told me, 'our floor became mud.' Stanley was one of an 'influx' of 2,897 people, of whom 2,041 were children: 'apartheid orphans'. A government official explained the policy: 'We are housing redundant people [in Dimbaza]. The people could not render productive service in an urban area. The government will provide the children with one substantial meal a day . . .'[2]

Stanley cannot remember the substantial meal. 'In the hut next to mine there were thirteen children and one woman,' he said. 'They were all suffering from malnutrition. I went to sleep hungry most nights; it is a feeling you get used to, then one day you get sick; that's when the youngest used to die.'

Dimbaza today is still South Africa's secret heart. Physically, it is extraordinary. Whereas other towns are built around a civic square, a town hall, shops, Dimbaza's centre is a children's cemetery. The graves are mostly of infants aged under two. There are no headstones. There are plastic toys among the weeds and the broken glass of shattered flower holders; emaciated cattle graze here. Now and then, you trip over an aluminium pipe embedded in a piece of broken concrete. These were meant as headstones; on one is scratched, 'Dear Jack, aged 6 months, missed so bad, died 12 August, 1976' and on another: 'Rosie, bless her Lord, aged 10 months . . .'

The children died as a result of the conditions imposed in Dimbaza and places like it. Deliberately and systematically denied the essentials of life, they succumbed to tuberculosis and preventable diseases like measles. Across the 'homelands', thousands died like this: many from diarrhoea and starvation, so many that in all the available accounts there is reference to a shortage of coffins. In his classic book, *The Discarded People*, Cosmas Desmond disclosed that 40,000 infants starved to death in the Transkei in 1967 alone; in the Ciskei the figure almost certainly was higher.[3]

At least 500 children are buried at Dimbaza, or were. Stanley told me that in the 1970s heavy rains washed away many of them, and little skeletons appeared at the bottom of the hill. People came to look in grief and horror, and some tried to recover those they claimed as their own. 'Most of the families didn't have the money to bury them properly,' he said. 'I don't know why the cemetery has been left like this; it should be a place where we come to remember.'

In the 1970s, partly in response to an international outcry caused by Cosmas Desmond's book and a British film, Dimbaza and a few of apartheid's dumping grounds were 'industrialised'. That is to say, they were designated sources of cheap, subsidised labour as the government in Pretoria urgently sought Western capital to underwrite apartheid's parlous economy. Britain was the most enthusiastic backer. This was not surprising given that the British, long before the Boers, had laid the economic foundations of apartheid. As Prime Minister of the Cape in the late nineteenth century, Cecil Rhodes drove much of the black population into labour reserves. In 1960, when the South African police shot dead sixty-nine people at Sharpeville, they used weapons supplied by the British. This was a clear sign to British business that the population was being disciplined and opposition crushed. Capital poured in, with investments doubling by 1970. 'No major sector of British capitalism', wrote the South Africa specialist Geoff Berridge, 'was without substantial representation in these investments.'[4]

As the apartheid regime extended its terror to most of southern Africa, Britain became the biggest single investor, followed by the Americans, who saw their capital return 17 per cent profit, more than anywhere else in the world. In the two years prior to 1975, the year the South African military invaded Angola, igniting a war that devastated much of southern Africa, the International Monetary Fund's backing for the apartheid state was greater than that given to the rest of Africa combined.[5]

Twenty-two 'enterprises' were established in Dimbaza and the jargon of 'redundant' and 'surplus' was dropped; the rural concentration camp was now a 'showcase of investment opportunity'. Taiwanese and Israeli firms took over the new prefabricated factories, laid out like a vast grandstand overlooking the children's graveyard. Those employed in them were paid just enough to keep their families alive. The population grew; shops and a post office were built, and finally a school. Here, in April 1994, people queued to vote for South Africa's first black majority government. 'At last', said Nelson Mandela, 'the people can see their hopes and dreams about to be realised.'

Today, the Eastern Cape is officially a region of 'absolute poverty'. Almost half the people lack a proper roof over their heads. Teachers and civil servants are often not paid; the elderly wait outside government offices for pensions that seldom come. There are a few jobs in the white enclaves in the cities, while the majority have none and no visible means of support.

In Dimbaza, most of the factories have closed and un-employment is around 70 per cent or higher. Stanley Mbalala, the survivor, lost his last job a year ago. He guided me around the silent streets where the new factories stand empty except for a security guard. He explained how the few remaining foreign firms followed a pattern of closing down, then relocat-ing to Butterworth, a town so poor that people subsist by recycling scrap metal from wrecked cars on hundreds of tiny braziers; at dusk it looks like Dante's Inferno. 'In this way,' said Stanley, 'the foreign firms can force the wages down in both places. People count themselves lucky if they get 200 rands a month [about £30].'

One such firm is Malaysian and a model of globalisation, making T-shirts and other casual clothes for designer labels sold in the West. There is something symbolic about the position of this factory. Directly in front of it is the children's graveyard, a reminder of the price paid by the most vulnerable South Africans in their long journey to the 'new' globalised South Africa. On the edge of the graves, there is a narrow verge of brown grass, where people wait in the hope of a few hours' work.

At 50 St David's Road, Upper Houghton, the grass is green and manicured, glistening from the spray of sprinklers.

Houghton is the richest suburb of Johannesburg and one of the richest places on earth. Here, the houses are fortresses behind walls topped with razor wire and displaying pictures of salivating dogs and signs: YOU HAVE BEEN WARNED: 24-HOUR ARMED RESPONSE. The only people on the streets are members of the invisible population, the black domestics, walking to and from their homes in another world. Overlooking them is St John's School, modelled on an English public school; there are boys playing rugby behind a high fence.

St David's Road was busy on the night I was there. Chauffeur-driven Mercedes and BMW cars converged on Number 50, where an important garden party was in progress. The guests were multi-racial, mostly prosperous-looking men in business suits. They knew each other and affected an uncertain *bonhomie* across the old racial divide. The party was hosted by an organisation called BusinessMap, which, according to its brochure, gives 'guidance on . . . Black Economic Empowerment' and is to stage a 'Forum for the Globalisation of South African Business'.

The guest of honour was a famous black businessman, Cyril Ramaphosa, who was General-Secretary of the National Union of Mineworkers in the mid-1980s and the ANC's principal negotiator in the protracted talks with the De Klerk Government. It was, in great part, his efforts which led to elections and to the 'historic compromises' that left economic power in the hands of the corporate white elite. Five companies, dominated by the tentacular Anglo-American Corporation, then controlled three-quarters of the capitalisation of the Johannesburg Stock Exchange; and that is unchanged.

What has changed is the inclusion of a small group of blacks into this masonry, a process of co-option that was well under way during the later, 'reformist' years of apartheid. This has allowed foreign and South African companies to use black faces to gain access to the new political establishment. When a tender is proposed or a takeover announced, it is often a black executive at the top table who appears to be taking the initiative. 'It is impressive to note that there are about eighteen black-owned companies listed [on the

Johannesburg Stock Exchange],' observed an economics writer in the *Cape Times*, 'but these do not necessarily have majority black ownership where control can be exercised.'[6]

This is known as 'black economic empowerment', of which Cyril Ramaphosa is the embodiment. The chairman of a number of leading companies, he is a close ally of Thabo Mbeki, the next President of South Africa. Both men are admired by Margaret Thatcher for their 'commitment to the free market'. Ramaphosa, the former trade union leader whose fight against apartheid Thatcher did her best to under-cut, now refers to the 'integrity and compassion' of business associates who, like his erstwhile admirer, opposed every-thing he once stood for. His concern is with the need to build 'smart relationships and win-win situations'.[7]

At first, and in keeping with his Damascene conversion from workers' leader to millionaire corporate man, he preached 'black economic empowerment' as a philosophy for the 'new' South Africa. The majority would benefit from the ownership of shares in black businesses and from the 'trickle-down effect'. It was essentially Thatcher's message. Then in 1997, Ramaphosa admitted that 'all those [business] deals, ultimately, have a minuscule effect on empowerment'. These days, like other former ANC colleagues seeking 'empower-ment' in the boardroom, he prefers the term, 'black economic development'.[8]

On the surface and just below, much *has* changed in South Africa; for one thing, racists must hold their tongues. On the day I arrived in Johannesburg, a British expatriate business-man, David Cox, stood in front of a magistrate accused of sending an anonymous fax to the trade union leader Sam Shilowa, calling him a 'kaffir, arsehole and trash'. He was fined and publicly shamed: a normal act of justice in a civilised country, yet inconceivable until recently in South Africa.[9]

Among blacks, there is a renewed pride in who they are. Among those whites who opposed apartheid, there is genuine gratitude for the peaceful transformation, while other whites, perhaps the majority, continue to suffer, wrote David Beresford, 'from a collective delusion that they have done enough by "allowing" majority rule'.[10] They display a studied courtesy to the majority population when the two groups brush each other in public places. (This does not apply to the young, who have no memory.) Occasionally, a white will push in front of blacks in a queue, but disapproval of the new order is mostly unexpressed; the intelligent ones have measured the scale of their luck: that they, not the blacks, are the true beneficiaries of the 'Mandela factor'. No longer international pariahs, they can travel and play sport and do business wherever in the world they like.

With their privileges overseen by the first black President and his party, the inequalities of the past are perpetuated under cover of political 'reconciliation'. Complaints about 'crime' are permissible and unrelenting, crime being the code for the encroachment of unemployed blacks across the old dividing lines between rich and poor, white and black. The issue is quite useful to those who control the economy now and who controlled it under apartheid, for it reminds the black government that it must discipline those increasingly frustrated with the lack of change. Indeed, one of the ANC Government's most impressive achievements has been to restrain black people from protesting against the adaptation of apartheid's social injustices. Since democracy came to South Africa, the amount of public money spent on the police and prisons has risen by as much as a quarter in a country which already had one of the world's biggest internal security systems. Since 1995, deaths in police custody have doubled.[11]

Behind the often theatrical façade of 'reconciliation' between oppressed and oppressor, the absolutions dispensed by Desmond Tutu and the deifying of Nelson Mandela, the aspirations of the people of Dimbaza have been ignored, along with those of the majority whose humanity and courage forced the pace of change and brought down apartheid. The ANC has effectively scrapped its Reconstruction and Development Programme (RDP), which offered modest reforms in housing, land redistribution and jobs. Whenever the ANC's fine, liberal constitution is invoked, there is seldom mention of the fact that it guarantees the existing property rights of white farmers, whose disproportionate control of the land has its roots in the Land Act of 1913, which established a captive labour force and apartheid in all but name. It means that more than 80 per cent of the prime agricultural land remains in the hands of whites.

When I met President Mandela in Cape Town, I asked him about this. 'We have done something revolutionary,' he said, 'for which we have received no credit at all. There is no country where labour tenants have been given the security we have given them . . . where a farmer cannot just dismiss them.'

There is new legislation. However, I interviewed many farm labourers arbitrarily evicted as if nothing had changed. Voluntary organisations like the Border Relief Committee say most evictions are not reported. By one account there are more now than there were under apartheid.[12] A white farmer in the Eastern Cape had evicted five men and their families not long before I spoke to him. They included a man who had served the farmer's family for thirty years, for which he was paid in 1997 £30 a month. 'It's actually easier today [to evict people],' the farmer told me. 'If you get a good lawyer, you shouldn't have any complaints.'

For the majority, the one potentially radical change has been in health care. Clinics have been built in the rural areas where there were none and where young doctors must now spend a year's secondment. There is free health care for pregnant women and children under six; and the Health Minister, Dr Nkosazana Zuma, a courageous maverick, has stood up to the multinational drug companies in order to bring down the price of drugs to a level ordinary people can afford. Last year, on her initiative, abortion was legalised, and in the first six months of the new law, 45,000 women did not die, nor were they subjected to the indignity and pain of backstreet abortions, which were a feature of life and death under apartheid. This is only a beginning in a society where 87 per cent of children are in poor health. Unfortunately, there are few in the government like Dr Zuma, who state the obvious that there will be no change without the political will to redistribute the resources of a rich country. 'A humane society', she said, 'does not happen as a miracle.'

In the 'townships', the name given to African satellite 'settlements' that service the white cities and towns, little has changed materially. The government has built a fraction of the million houses it promised four years ago. A 15,000 rand (about £2,000) government grant is not enough to erect more than a room and a toilet and a corrugated iron roof; outside walls are 'extra'. At Ebony Park near Johannesburg these are known as 'kennels'. Most people who need homes cannot get bank credit and, anyway, cannot afford to pay interest rates of 19 per cent and more.

The government says that more than a million people have been supplied with water and this has been rightly acclaimed. Still, in the absence of a planned and properly funded reconstruction programme, the majority are fortunate if they can find a tap within walking distance – while the whites of wealthy Constantia in Cape Town consume on average 1,500 litres of water each a day, tending their gardens and swimming pools. Moreover, the privatisation of water is under way, with the British multinational Biwater leading the charge and with Margaret Thatcher on its board.

This was not what the ANC promised its people. Nelson Mandela did not stand before the expectant crowds in 1994 and say, as he said to me, 'You can say [our policy] is Thatcherite, but for this country, privatisation is the fundamental policy of the government.' Neither did he affect the part of an orthodox economist, as he appeared to do when we talked, quoting an array of statistics about the rate of inflation and the deficit and 'growth', while remaining silent on the loss of up to 100,000 jobs a year since the ANC came to power and the current curtailment of desperately needed public services.[13] Nor did he predict that 'black empowerment' and 'affirmative action' would serve to widen the wealth gap between his people as never before. In his valedictory speech to the ANC conference in December 1997, Mandela alluded darkly to 'enemies of change' without mentioning those within his own government.[14]

'We had to make the most significant compromises in order to attain power peacefully,' Thabo Mbeki, Mandela's successor, told me. Yet few South Africans were allowed to judge the truth of that statement because few were told what was being agreed in their name.

The most important 'historic compromise' was made not with the apartheid regime, but with the forces of Western and white South African capital, which changed their allegiance from P. W. Botha to Nelson Mandela on condition that their multinational corporations would not be obstructed as they 'opened up' the South African economy, and that the ANC would drop the foolish promises in its Freedom Charter about equity and the country's natural resources, such as minerals, 'belonging to all the people'. This meant the ANC agreeing to investment conditions that favoured big business, and to keeping on the apartheid-era Governor of the South African Reserve Bank, Chris Stahls, an arch monetarist, as the country's senior economic manager. 'At this juncture,' said Stahls in 1996, 'there is no evidence that the present model for monetary policy, which has served the country well over the past seven years, should be changed or abandoned.'

Since the ANC was unbanned and Nelson Mandela released, foreign investment capital, led by the United States, has surged into southern Africa, tripling to $11.7 billion.[15] US Secretary of Commerce William Daley has aggressively promoted American investment in South Africa, which he described, in 1997, as the 'launching point for exploring the other African markets'.[16] Most of it is not investment at all, but a shopping spree familiar in vulnerable Third World countries. A third of the state-owned phone company, Telkom, fell quickly to the Texas-based SBC Communications after seven other multinationals had vied for the prize. Foreign companies which continued doing business in the apartheid era—Coca-Cola, Siemens and Mercedes-Benz (which made military vehicles for the apartheid regime) – have prospered while those that stayed away have lost their place in the market. 'We are seeking to establish,' said Trevor Manuel, the Finance Minister, 'an environment in which winners flourish.'[17]

Today's South Africa provides a metaphor for much of the

human struggle described in this book. In the continent where the poorest people on earth live, the long march from the slave trade has not ended. More than 600 million people suffer from malnutrition and a lack of basic health care and education because the money that should be spent on them is being used to repay the interest on debt owed to Western financial institutions.[18] In other words, as Colin Ward pointed out, 'this is not a tragedy *sui generis* but the effect of a global logic from which no region of the world is immune. This is the logic of capitalism which breaks down all bonds between people.'[19]

Coming back to South Africa, I was surprised and delighted to find that apartheid had not destroyed these bonds: that even in Dimbaza, where the fabric of society was deliberately torn, African civilisation survived. This is *ubuntu*, a spirit and humanism expressed in a distinctly African notion that people are people through other people. It is not without the usual frailties, but the evidence of its resilience is everywhere in South Africa; and those seeking optimism about the human spirit need look no further than the African people of South Africa. 'How beautifully they have emerged from their nightmare,' Martha Gellhorn told me on her return from her first visit, and she is right. Treated for so long as sub-humans, they have somehow retained a generosity of heart and intellect, a grace and a fluency to which their oppressors can never aspire.

These qualities are sometimes mistaken for passivity. In the 1980s, South Africa came close to revolution; the day after the murder of Chris Hani, who carried the liberation movement's conscience, some two million angry people were in the streets and a general strike closed down 90 per cent of industry. Today, these people are beginning to say, as the Chartists said 150 years ago, that their vote will lose meaning unless their lives move forward. They ask if the goldminers voted to continue dying for wages kept indecently low, and if women voted to live in 'kennels' while serving in mansions. They ask if all that celebration took place in 1994 so that the 'new' South Africa might be slotted into a predetermined economic system.

Many are refusing to pay for water and electricity and other basic services that are intermittent or non-existent, or beyond their pocket. Once again, an often white-led militarised police force is being used against them, and this has stiffened resistance, as in the past. If apartheid left behind a positive legacy, it was the creation of arguably the most politicised population in the world; and it is in their renewed consciousness, especially in sections of the trade union movement, that the hope of South Africa resides.

In 1993, before he became president, Nelson Mandela said, 'How many times has the liberation movement worked together with the people and then at the moment of victory betrayed them? There are many examples of that in the world. If people relax their vigilance, they will find their sacrifices have been in vain. If the ANC does not deliver the goods, the people must do to it what they have done to the apartheid regime . . .'[20]

The 'economic growth' which Nelson Mandela now applauds was once described by Joseph Schumpeter, the doyen of Harvard economists, as 'creative destruction'. When the giant General Electric company in the United States closed down dozens of factories and sacked tens of thousands of employees, it achieved unprecedented 'growth'. 'Ahead of us,' said the Chairman, Jack Welch, 'are Darwinian shakeouts in every major marketplace, with no consolation prizes for the losing companies and nations.'[21]

The models of globalisation, the Asian 'tiger states', have been revealed as having been built on debt and corruption. Their 'Darwinian shakeouts' are in progress as these words are written. For the rest of us, especially those with the power of memory, the lessons of the Weimar Republic are writ large. Like the upheavals of capitalism in the 1930s and the rise of fascism, the crisis of the 'global economy' is set to become the most important issue of the first half of the twenty-first century.

As labour is cheapened and cast aside; as social legislation is eliminated and whole countries are transformed into one big plantation, one big mining camp, one big 'free trade' zone stripped of rights, sovereignty and wealth; as the rise of technology exacerbates class differences rather than abolishing them, increasing the vulnerability and tempo of work; as the guardians of this faith reduce 'free speech' to esoteric jargon, the warnings now come from within the new orthodoxy itself.

Beware 'the rumbling out there', says the President of the Federal Reserve Bank. 'People are dangerously suffering from globophobia,' says a senior floor trader in New York. 'The magnitude of change in the world economy since the end of the Cold War,' wrote the eminent American economist, David Hale, 'has been so dramatic it has given rise to a new political phenomenon ... voters now view trade issues in terms of domestic class struggle.'[22] In his book, *Has Globalisation Gone Too Far?* another Harvard high priest, Dano Rodrik, wrote 'The international integration of markets for goods, services and capital is pressuring societies to alter their traditional practices [so much that] in return, broad segments of these societies are putting up a fight.'[23]

The fight has only just begun.

NOTES

Introduction

1 Kiko Adatta, *Picture Perfect*, cited by Sharon Beder in *Global Spin: The Corporate Assault on Environmentalism*, Green Books, UK, 1997, p. 208.

2 Ibid., p. 183.

3 Third World and Environmental Broadcasting Project, *Watching the World* (c/o UNICEF), London, 1997.

4 *Independent*, March 1, 1991.

5 Numerous sources, including the Report of the Clark Commission referred to in my chapter 'Unpeople 1'; see Ian Lee, *Continuing Health Cost of the Gulf War*, Medical Educational Trust, London, 1991.

6 Food and Agricultural Organisation of the United Nations, *Evaluation of the Food and Nutrition Situation in Iraq*, Rome, 1995.

7 UNICEF, *State of the World's Children*, London, 1989, p. 1.

8 Dale Hildebrand, *To Pay is to Die: the Philippines' Foreign Debt Crisis*, Philippine International Forum, 1991.

9 *Guardian*, September 23, 1996.

10 Michael Parenti, *Inventing Reality: The Politics of the Mass Media*, 1986, p. 35, cited by Beder, *Global Spin*.

11 Thanks to Rob Brown for this insight, *Independent*, August 18, 1997.

12 Aelred Stubbs, *Steve Biko – I Write What I Like*, New York, 1978, cited by Allister Sparks, *The Mind of South Africa: The Rise and Fall of Apartheid*, Mandarin, London, reprinted 1997, p. 259.

13 *Labour Left Briefing*, October 1997.

14 Ibid., August 29, 1997; *Guardian*, October 9, 1997.

15 Estimate quoted by 1997 Nobel Peace Laureate, José Ramos-Horta, in his Wallace Wurth Memorial Lecture, University of New South Wales, Sydney, August 14, 1997.

16 *Guardian*, July 5, 1997.
17 *Time*, April 28, 1997.
18 *Resurgence*, no. 179.
19 Edward Said, *Culture and Imperialism*, Chatto & Windus, London, 1993, pp. 352–3.
20 *Guardian*, March 29, 1997.
21 *Daily Mirror*, September 6, 1996.
22 Nhu T. Le, 'Screaming Souls', *The Nation*, New York, November 3, 1997.
23 Cited by Noam Chomsky, *Index on Censorship*, 3, 1997.
24 Ibid.
25 *Financial Times*, May 3, 1997.
26 *British Social Attitudes*, 13th Report, edited by Roger Jowell, John Curtice, Alison Park, Lindsay Brook and Katarina Thomson, Dartmouth Press, London, December 1996. The 14th Report (1997) produced broadly the same conclusions. Gallup cited by John Rees, *Socialist Review*, July/August 1997; *General Household Survey*, cited by Anthony Gibbens, *Observer*, January 26, 1997; other surveys cited by Seamus Milne, *London Review of Books*, June 5, 1997.
27 Thanks to Vandana Shiva in *Resurgence*, no. 12.
28 Sparks, *The Mind of South Africa*, p. 341.
29 *War & Peace*, vol. 1, 1995.
30 Cited in *New Statesman and Society*, October 11, 1991, from *Nicaragua: A Decade of Revolution*, ed. Lou Dematteis, W. W. Norton, New York, 1991.

THE NEW COLD WAR

THE TERRORISTS

1 John Madeley, *Diego Garcia: A Contrast to the Falklands*, Report no. 54, Minority Rights Group, London, 1985.
2 Ibid.
3 *Independent*, September 8, 1996.
4 *Africa Research Bulletin*, vol. 28, no. 11, November 1, 1991. See Mark Curtis, *The Ambiguities of Power: British Foreign Policy Since 1945*, Zed Books, London, 1995, pp. 116–19.
5 *Guardian*, September 10, 1975.
6 Madeley, *Diego Garcia*.
7 Ibid.

8   British Government Cabinet Papers 1965, cited in *Guardian*, January 1, 1996.
9   Madeley, *Diego Garcia*.
10 *Financial Times*, April 5, 1982.
11 *Daily Telegraph*, April 19, 1982.
12 Curtis, *Ambiguities of Power*, pp. 116–19.
13 Richard Falk, 'The Terrorist Foundations of Recent US Policy', in *Western State Terrorism*, ed. Alexander George, Polity Press, London, 1991, pp. 107–8.
14 Robert O. Slater and Michael Stohl, *Current Perspectives on International Terrorism*, Macmillan, London, 1988, cited by Noam Chomsky in *Western State Terrorism*, p. 12. Thanks to Noam Chomsky for the postscript on Western power.
15 Falk, *Western State Terrorism*, p. 104.
16 See William Shawcross, *Sideshow: Kissinger, Nixon and the Destruction of Cambodia*, André Deutsch, London, 1979; Mark Hertsgaard, 'The Secret Life of Henry Kissinger', *Nation*, New York, November 29, 1990; William Blum, *The CIA, a Forgotten History*, Zed Books, London, 1986, pp. 275–8.
17 Cited by Chomsky, 'International Terrorism: Image and Reality', *Western State Terrorism*, p. 13.
18 'East Africa Political Intelligence Report', July–September 1948, cited by Frank Furedi, *The New Ideology of Imperialism*, Pluto Press, London, 1994, p. 44; Information Secretary, British Embassy, Teheran, to Eastern Dept, FO, June 16, 1952, cited ibid., p. 53.
19 Lord Hailey, 1943, cited ibid., p. 87.
20 Cited by Curtis, *Ambiguities of Power*, p. 57.
21 Foreign Office cable to Washington, October 26, 1950, cited ibid., pp. 57–8.
22 Cable from A. Humphrey, Federation of Malaya, to J. Higham, Colonial Office, January 19, 1953, cited ibid., p. 64.
23 Ibid., pp. 65–74.
24 See Blum, *The CIA*, pp. 117–23.
25 FO to UK Embassy, Jakarta, October 16, 1965, cited by Mark Curtis, *Ecologist*, vol. 26, no. 5, September/October 1996.
26 Curtis, *Ambiguities of Power*, pp. 16–24.
27 Dianna Melrose, *Nicaragua: The Threat of a Good Example*, Oxfam, Oxford, 1985, p. 26.
28 Cited by Chomsky, *Western State Terrorism*, p. 19.
29 Ibid., p. 16.

30   *Guardian*, September 22, 1996.
31   Jenny Pearce, *Under the Eagle: US Intervention in Central America and the Caribbean*, Latin America Bureau, London, 1981, pp. 58–9, 230–1.
32   Center for International Policy Aid memo, Washington, April 1981. See *New York Times*, April 1, 1981.
33   Rivera y Damas, quoted in Ray Bonner, *Weakness and Deceit*, Times Books, New York, 1984, p. 207.
34   *Links*, no. 6, January–April 1966.
35   Melrose, *Nicaragua*.
36   *Observer*, June 3, 1991.
37   *World Military and Social Expenditures*, World Priorities Inc., Washington, 1993, p. 20.
38   Ian Lee, *Continuing Health Costs of the Gulf War*, Medical Educational Trust, London, 1991.
39   Estimated by Mohamed Sahnoun, UN Representative in Somalia, *New Internationalist*, December, 1994.
40   *Guardian*, May 16, 1992.
41   *Red Pepper*, July 1994.
42   Ibid.
43   Alfred W. McCoy, *The Politics of Heroin: CIA Complicity in the Global Drug Trade*, rev. ed., Lawrence Hill, New York, 1991.
44   *Covert Action*, Winter 1996–7.
45   Report by the Sub-committee on Terrorism, Narcotics and International Operations of the Committee on Foreign Relations, US Senate, *Drugs, Law Enforcement and Foreign Policy*, December 1988, p. 36.
46   Translated by *Weekly News Update, Green Left Weekly*, August 27, 1997.
47   *Washington Post*, December 6, 1996.
48   *Efforts of Khmer Insurgents to Exploit for Propaganda Purposes Damage Done by Airstrikes in Kandal Province*, Intelligence Information Cable, May 2, 1973, declassified by the CIA on February 19, 1987.
49   John Pilger, *Distant Voices*, Vintage, London, 1992, pp. 411, 413, 439–40.
50   Linda Mason and Roger Brown, *Rice, Rivalry and Politics: Managing Cambodian Relief*, University of Notre Dame Press, Indiana, 1983, pp. 135, 159.
51   William Shawcross, *The Quality of Mercy: Cambodia, Holocaust and Modern Conscience*, André Deutsch, London, 1984, pp. 289,

345, 395.

52   Pilger, *Distant Voices*, pp. 414–17, 419, 421–4. 437–8, 444–50, 469–71.

53   Furedi, *New Ideology of Imperialism*, p. 116.

54   *Washington Post*, April 4, 1993.

55   Ibid., p. 117.

56   *Observer*, July 21, 1996.

57   Cited by Paul Rogers, *Observer*, June 28, 1992.

58   S. Zielonka, *International Affairs*, vol. 67, no. 1, p. 131.

59   *Foreign Affairs*, reprinted in the *Guardian*, November 23, 1996. Huntington's book, *The Clash*, is published by Simon & Schuster, New York, 1996.

60   *Guardian*, June 17, 1997.

61   Ibid., July 2, 1992.

62   Greenpeace and the Los Alamos Study Group, quoted by *Green Left Weekly*, Sydney, April 23, 1997.

63   Chomsky, *Western State Terrorism*, p. 35.

64   Thanks, for this press analysis, to Daya Kishan Thussu, *Economic and Political Weekly*, February 8, 1997.

65   Falk, 'The Terrorist Foundations of Recent US Policy', pp. 109–10.

66   Noam Chomsky, 'Israel, Lebanon and Peace Process', a circulated paper, April 23, 1996.

67   Letter from Harold Macmillan to Robert Menzies, February 9, 1952, cited by Furedi, *New Ideology of Imperialism*, p. 79.

68   Ibid.

69   *Daily Express*, October 21, 1949.

70   Furedi, *New Ideology of Imperialism*, p. 81.

71   M. Perham, 'African Facts and American Criticisms', *Foreign Affairs*, vol. 22, April 1944, p. 449; cited by Furedi, *New Ideology of Imperialism*, p. 88.

72   Ibid.

73   Ibid., p. 99.

74   *Evening Standard*, August 20, 1990.

75   *Financial Times*, November 1, 1990.

76   Phyllis Bennis, *Calling the Shots: How Washington Dominates Today's UN*, Olive Branch Press, New York, 1996, p. xv.

77   Ibid., p. xii.

78   *Covert Action Quarterly*, Summer 1997.

79   Thanks to R. Seymour, *Guardian*, November 11, 1997.

80   *Third World Resurgence*, no. 80, 1997.

81   US State Department daily briefing, July 10, 1997.

82   Eric Falt was interviewed on film for Central Television, *Return to Year Zero*, March 1993.

83   Charles William Maynes, editor of *Foreign Policy*, wrote, 'CIA officials privately concede that the US military may have killed between 7,000 and 10,000 Somalis'; cited by Noam Chomsky, *Z* magazine, Summer 1995.

84   *Guardian*, December 29, 1992.

UNPEOPLE 1

1   *Daily Star, Daily Mirror* and *Sun*, January 16, 1991.

2   BBC Short-wave Broadcasts, January 1991.

3   *Sun* and *Daily Express*, January 16, 1991.

4   Thanks to Greg Philo and Greg McLaughlin, Glasgow Media Group, *The British Media and the Gulf War*, Glasgow, 1993.

5   *Daily Mirror*, January 19, 1991.

6   Philo and McLaughlin, *British Media and the Gulf War*.

7   BBC TV, January 18, 1991.

8   Ibid.

9   *Sun*, February 14, 1991.

10   ITN, February 13, 1991.

11   Laurie Garrett, 'The Dead', *Columbia Journalism Review*, May/June, 1991.

12   Ramsey Clark, *The Fire This Time: US War Crimes in the Gulf*, Thunder's Mouth Press, New York, 1992, p. 71.

13   Miriam Martin, Gulf Peace Team, interviews submitted to the Clark Commission. Copyright 1992 Sati-Castek-Martin.

14   BBC TV, February 14, 1991.

15   Disclosed by Nik Gowing in a speech to Spectrum International Television Conference, 1991.

16   *International Herald Tribune*, February 23–4, 1991.

17   Ramsey Clark, *The Children Are Dying*, World View Forum, 1996, p. 109; *New York Times*, January 15, 1992.

18   *Independent on Sunday*, February 10, 1991.

19   Testimony of Paul William Roberts to the Commission of Inquiry in Montreal, November 16, 1992, pp. 54–8.

20   *Daily Mirror*, March 2, 1991; *Newsday*, New York, March 31, 1991.

21   *Newsday*, March 31, 1991.

22   *Daily Mirror*, March 2, 1991.

23   BBC Radio 4, FM, *Gulf Reports*, March 1, 1991.

24 BBC TV, March 1, 1991.
25 *Newsday*, September 12, 1991.
26 *The Late Show*, BBC TV, June 6, 1991.
27 Clark, *The Children Are Dying*, p. 109.
28 Stichting LAKA, Amsterdam, *Gulf War Fact Sheet*, no. 2, June 1994.
29 Clark, *The Fire This Time*, p. 42.
30 *New York Times*, January 26, 1992.
31 *Wall Street Journal*, March 22, 1991.
32 BBC TV, May 25, 1991.
33 Clark, *The Fire This Time*, p. 110.
34 *New York Times*, January 26, 1992.
35 Ian Lee, *Continuing Health Cost of the Gulf War*, Medical Educational Trust, London, 1991.
36 *The Times* and *Nouvelle Observateur*, March 3, 1991.
37 Memorandum to the Foreign Affairs Select Committee, *The Economic Impact of the Gulf Crisis on Third World Countries*, March 1991.
38 Clark, *The Fire This Time*.
39 Food and Agricultural Organisation of the United Nations, *Evaluation of the Food and Nutrition Situation in Iraq*, Rome, 1995.
40 *New Statesman and Society*, September 13, 1996.
41 *Guardian*, September 7, 1996.
42 Clark, *The Fire This Time*, p. 10.
43 UNICEF press release, November 22, 1996.
44 *Sydney Morning Herald*, August 7, 1996.
45 *Socialist Review*, January 1997.
46 Clark, *The Fire This Time*, p. 10.
47 Mark Curtis, *The Ambiguities of Power: British Foreign Policy Since 1945*, Zed Books, London, 1995.
48 Noam Chomsky, *Power and Prospects: Reflections on Human Nature and the Social Order*, South End Press, Boston, 1996, p. 35.
49 John Pilger, *Distant Voices*, Vintage Books, London, 1994, p. 132–90.
50 Chomsky, *Power and Prospects*.
51 *Covert Action*, Summer 1995.
52 Richard F. Grimmett, *Conventional Arms Transfers to the Third World*, 1986–93, Congressional Research Service, p. 6.
53 *New Yorker*, November 28, 1994.
54 ITN, September 1, 3, 1996.

55   Ibid., September 3, 1996.
56   Ibid., September 1, 1996.
57   'The Tiddler', *Observer*, vol. 1, no. 12, 1996.
58   Numerous media industry surveys have drawn this conclusion. The latest is MediaLab's, 1996.
59   David Morrison, *Television and the Gulf War*, John Libbey, London, 1992, pp. 41–62, 71–3.

THE CRUSADERS

1   *New Internationalist*, July 1997, ed. Chris Brazier, citing Martin Cottingham's report for Christian Aid, *A Sporting Chance*.
2   *Who Cares About Toys? The International Toy Industry, Transnational Corporations and Working Conditions in Asia*, a report by the Trades Union Congress in conjunction with the Catholic Institute for International Relations and the World Development Movement, cited in 'Toy Story – the Worker's Tale', *Labour Research*, December 1996.
3   *Time*, April 28, 1997, and speeches.
4   'Capitalism writ large' and the alliance of state terror and globalisation are developed by Frederic F. Clairmont in *The Rise and Fall of Economic Liberalism*, published jointly by Southbound and Third World Network, Penang, Malaysia, 1996.
5   Ibid., p. 12.
6   Noam Chomsky and Edward S. Herman, *After the Cataclysm: Postwar Indochina and the Reconstruction of Imperial Ideology*, South End Press, Boston, 1979, p. 71.
7   Clairmont, *Rise and Fall of Economic Liberalism*, p. 8.
8   Walden Bello with Shea Cunningham and Bill Rau, *Dark Victory: The United States, Structural Adjustment and Global Poverty*, Penang, Malaysia, 1994, pp. 42–5.
9   Ibid., p. 43.
10   *Los Angeles Times*, July 8, 1974, cited by Jenny Pearce in *Under the Eagle: US Intervention in Central America and the Caribbean*, Latin American Bureau, London, 1981.
11   Ibid., p. 93.
12   Research by the National Labor Committee, New York, cited in *Haiti Briefing*, no. 21, London, December 1996. See also World Development Movement, 'The True Face of Disney', October 1997.
13   Voice of America, Campaign Summary, September 1992.

14 *Nation*, New York, March 4, 1996.
15 BBC Short-wave Broadcasts, October 1994.
16 *Financial Times*, October 17, 1994.
17 Dee Brown, *Bury My Heart at Wounded Knee*, Vintage, London, 1995.
18 Jonathan Elliot (ed.), *The Debates in the Several State Conventions on the Adoption of the Federal Constitution*, 1787, Lippincott, p. 450.
19 Thanks to Clairmont, *Rise and Fall of Economic Liberalism*, p. 53.
20 *Red Pepper*, December 1996.
21 Cited by Sharon Beder, *Global Spin: The Corporate Assault on Environmentalism*, Green Books, UK, 1997, p. 161.
22 Ibid., p. 163.
23 Ibid., p. 166.
24 *Sun–Herald*, Sydney, May 4, 1997.
25 Speech to a seminar, 'A Free Press, Guardian of Democracy', held by the Bustamento Institute of Public and International Affairs, Barbados, April 1986.
26 Bello, Cunningham and Rau, *Dark Victory*, citing Lester Thurow, *Head to Head: The Coming Struggle among Japan, Europe and the United States*, William Morrow, New York, 1992; Lawrence Mishel and Jared Bernstein, *The State of Working America: 1992–3*, Economic Policy Institute, Washington, 1993; Priscilla Enriquez, *An Un-American Tragedy: Hunger and Economic Policy in the Reagan–Bush Era*, First Food Action Alert, Summer 1992.
27 Thanks to Danny Mack, *Loompanics Unlimited*, Spring 1997 supplement, republished in *Green Left Weekly*, May 21, 1997.
28 Thanks to Bobby Lee Daniels, a Georgia prisoner, cited in *Green Left Weekly*, July 16, 1997.
29 See Michel Chossudovsky, 'Crime Goes Global: The Criminalisation of the World Economy', *Third World Resurgence*, no. 80, April 1997.
30 Federal Reserve Board Statistics cited by Clairmont, *Rise and Fall of Economic Liberalism*, p. 52.
31 *Scotsman*, February 7, 1995.
32 Bello, Cunningham and Rau, *Dark Victory*, p. 77.
33 World Development Movement press release, November 2, 1996.
34 Human Development Report, United Nations, New York, 1996.
35 J. C. Louis and Harvey Yazijian, *The Cola Wars: The Story of the Global Corporate Battle Between the Coca-Cola Company and*

PepsiCo Inc., Everest House, New York, 1980, p. 58.

36 Richard Barnet, *The Crisis of the Corporations*, Washington DC, 1978, cited in Clairmont, *Rise and Fall of Economic Liberalism*.

37 World Development Movement, *Pulling Up the Drawbridge: The Multilateral Agreement on Investment*, June 1997.

38 Ibid.

39 *Observer*, September 14, 1997. Thanks to John Sweeney.

40 *Australian*, November 19–20, 1994; *Sydney Morning Herald*, January 15, 1997; B. A. Santamaria, *Australian*, August 30, 1997.

41 BBC Short-wave Broadcasts, July 1997.

42 *Guardian*, January 6, 1996.

43 As told to the author.

44 Southwark Council statistics, cited by the *Independent*, June 3, 1997.

45 *New Statesman and Society*, September 20, 1996.

46 United Nations Development Programme, *Human Development Report*, New York, 1997.

47 Cited in *Scottish Socialist Voice*, May 23, 1997.

48 *Guardian*, June 10, 1997.

49 'The Ideology of the Blairites', *Lobster*, Summer 1997; Peter Mandelson and Roger Liddle, *The Blair Revolution: Can New Labour Deliver?*, Faber & Faber, London, 1996.

50 Mandelson and Liddle, *The Blair Revolution*.

51 *Guardian*, August 15, 1997; *Socialist Worker*, August 23, 1997.

52 Amitai Etzioni, *The New Golden Rule: Community and Morality in a Democratic Society*, Profile Books, New York, 1997.

53 Cited by Joan Smith, *Independent on Sunday*, June 22, 1997.

54 Ibid.

55 Geoff Mulgan, *Connexity*, Chatto & Windus, London, 1997.

56 *Independent*, November 21, 1995.

57 *Independent on Sunday*, January 22, 29, 1995.

58 *Guardian*, May 14, 1997.

59 Ibid., May 9, 1997.

60 'BP's Secret Soldiers', *World in Action*, Granada Television, June 30, 1997; *Red Pepper*, June 1997.

61 *Red Pepper*, June 1997; *Independent*, February 17, 1997; *Guardian*, May 9, 1997.

62 *Tribune*, May 23, 1997.

63 *Sunday Times*, November 26, 1989; *The Times*, October 19, 31, 1994; *Guardian*, September 17, 1994; *Scotsman*, October 17, 1994.

64 *New Statesman and Society*, October 18, 1996; Frank Field, *Making Welfare Work: Reconstructing Welfare for the Millennium*, Institute of Community Studies, London, 1995.

65 *Independent on Sunday*, July 20, 1997.

66 For example, study by Harvard economist Richard Freedman, cited by B. A. Santamaria, *Australian*, August 30, 1997.

67 *Guardian*, July 22, 1997.

68 *Financial Times*, June 23, 1997.

69 *Guardian*, July 1, 1997.

70 *Socialist Worker*, July 19 and October 4, 1997.

71 Michael Barber, *The Learning Game*, Gollancz, London, 1997.

72 Peter Robinson, *Literacy, Numeracy and Economic Performance*, Centre for Economic Performance, London School of Economics, 1997.

73 R. H. Tawney, *Equality*, Allen & Unwin, London, 1931.

74 Pat Brewer, *Links*, Sydney, no. 7, July–October 1997.

75 *New Statesman and Society*, September 29, 1995.

76 Patricia Hewitt, *About Time: The Revolution of Work and Family Life*, IPPR, Rivers Oram Press, London, 1993. Hewitt's post-election contortions cited by Francis Wheen, *Guardian*, December 17, 1997.

77 *Independent*, June 7, 1997.

78 *Hansard*, May 11, 1994.

79 *Observer*, November 23, 1997. Thanks to Nick Cohen.

80 *Lobster*, Summer 1997. Thanks to Robin Ramsay for this perspective.

81 *New York Times*, May 5, 1986.

82 National Security Council papers submitted to the Report of the Congressional Committees investigating the Iran Contra affair. House Report no. 100–433/Senate Report no. 100–216, Washington, 1988. Thanks to Tom Easton and David Osler for their essays in *Lobster* 33.

83 *Guardian*, June 3, 1995.

84 Aneurin Bevan, *In Place of Fear*, Heinemann, London, 1952.

85 *Red Pepper*, November 1996.

Unpeople 2

1 United Nations Development Programme, *Human Development Report*, Oxford University Press, 1992.

2 Carey Oppenheim and Lisa Harker, *Poverty the Facts*, Child Poverty Action Group, 1996, pp. 1–2.

3 'Children in Statistics', *Index on Censorship*, February 1997.

4   United Nations Development Programme, cited in *Independent on Sunday*, July 21, 1996.
5   The School Milk Campaign, *The Hunger Within*, Stafford, January 1997.
6   Heather Mills, 'Breadline Britain', *Observer*, August 11, 1996.
7   Ibid.
8   Government statistics cited by *Socialist Worker*, November 8, 1997
9   As told to the author.
10 Government Statistical Service, *DSS Households Below Average Income: A Statistical Analysis, 1979–1992/3*, HMSO, 1995.
11 *Economic Trends, December 94*, HMSO, 1994.
12 CPAG analysis.
13 Nigel Lawson, *Views from No. 11: Memoirs of a Tory Radical*, Bantam Press, 1992.
14 *Guardian*, April 15, 1996.
15 Liverpool Public Health Report, 1996.
16 *Observer*, March 23, 1997.

FLYING THE FLAG

ARMING THE WORLD

1   Sir Hiram S. Maxim, *My Life*, Methuen, London, 1915, p. 182.
2   *Sunday Chronicle*, London, November 29, 1936.
3   Interviewed by Jonathan Dimbleby, 'Charles, the Private Man, the Public Role', a Dimbleby Martin production for Central TV, broadcast June 29, 1994.
4   Amnesty International, *Power and Impunity, Human Rights under the New Order*, London, 1994.
5   *Guardian*, July 21, 1995, November 19, 20, 1996; *Campaign Against the Arms Trade News*, March 1997; *Central America Report*, Summer 1996; *Flight International*, March 29–April 4, 1995.
6   World Development Movement, *Gunrunners' Gold: How the Public's Money Finances Arms Sales*, May 1995.
7   *Hansard*, July 21, 1993.
8   Overseas Development Administration statistics, cited in *Gunrunners' Gold*. See also analysis by Clare Fermont, *Socialist Review*, January 1997.
9   Central Television, *Flying the Flag, Arming the World*, 1994.

10 Campaign Against the Arms Trade, *Bread Not Bombs: The Arms Trade and Development*, London, 1992.

11 BBC Short-wave Broadcasts, August 1994.

12 *New Statesman and Society*, November 11, 1994.

13 Ibid.

14 Ibid.

15 BBC Short-wave Broadcasts, September 1980.

16 *Guardian*, July 17, 1981.

17 Ibid., February 18, 1996.

18 *Inquiry into the Export of Defence Equipment and Dual-Use Goods to Iraq and Related Prosecutions*, HMSO, London, 1996.

19 Ibid., p. 141–4 of evidence by Margaret Thatcher. Her Commons statement was in answer to a question by Harry Cohen MP on April 21, 1989. Cited by Michael Meacher, *Guardian*, December 14, 1993.

20 *New Statesman and Society*, February 23, 1996.

21 *Guardian*, February 16, 1996.

22 *Sunday Times*, October 9, 1994.

23 *Financial Times*, October 31, 1994.

24 Plaintiff's exhibit 26, March 3, 1992; Thomas F. Dooley *v.* United Technologies Corporation. Civ. no. 91–2599; 500C3272.

25 BBC Short-wave Broadcasts, July 1994.

26 *Red Pepper*, June 1997.

27 *Financial Times*, October 4, 1997. Thanks to Brian Rostron for his piece on Jack Straw's planned legislation on the prosecution of exiles. The quote is from a letter from Straw to the Board of Jewish Deputies, August 4, 1997. *Tribune*, November 21, 1997.

28 John Pilger, *Distant Voices*, Vintage Books, London, 1994, pp. 401–94. Margaret Thatcher made her remarks about the Khmer Rouge on *Blue Peter*, BBC TV, December 19, 1988.

29 *Hansard*, January 25, 1966.

30 Ibid.

31 Foreign Office cables cited by Mark Curtis, *Ecologist*, vol. 26, no. 5, September/October 1996.

32 Memo from Michael Stewart to Prime Minister Wilson, December 6, 1965, cited by Curtis, *Ecologist*.

33 Michael Stewart, *Life and Labour: An Autobiography*, Sidgwick & Jackson, London, 1980, p. 149.

34 *Sydney Morning Herald*, April 5, 1977.

35 Letter from David Owen to Lord Avebury, June 19, 1978.

36 *New Statesman and Society*, June 30, July 9, 1978.

37 *Hansard*, May 11, 1994.

38 Ibid., June 17, 1997.

39 Ibid., June 27, 1997.

40 A Martyn Gregory investigation for *World in Action*, Granada Television, June 9, 1997.

41 World Development Movement briefing, 'Will the Government Stop Arms Sales to Indonesia?', July 9, 1997.

42 Robin Cook, 'Human Rights into a New Century', Foreign and Commonwealth Office, July 17, 1997.

43 Stephen Cragg, 'Advice in the matter of the possible revocation of licences awarded by the Secretary of State pursuant to Article 7 of the Export of Goods (Control) Order 1994', June 6, 1997.

44 Admiral Eugene J. Carroll, Director, Center for Defense Information, Washington, as told to the author.

45 BBC Radio, May 23, 1997.

46 *Observer*, June 8, 1997.

47 Ibid.

48 TAPOL, *Bulletin*, April 1994, April 1996, April 1997.

49 *Financial Times*, July 1, 1997.

50 *Independent*, May 23, 1997; *Guardian*, October 9, 1997.

51 *Guardian*, October 7, 1997.

52 *Independent on Sunday*, June 1, 1997.

53 *Independent*, June 26, 1996.

54 *New Statesman and Society*, November 12, 1993.

55 *Hansard*, October 16, 1995.

56 Anthony Sampson, *The Arms Bazaar, the Companies, the Dealers, the Bribes: From Vickers to Lockheed*, Coronet, London, 1977, p. 26.

57 World Development Movement, *Biting the Bullet: Real Security in a New World*, London, 1993.

INSIDE BURMA

THE GOLDEN LAND

1 International Confederation of Free Trade Unions, *Burma's War Lords Dig In*, IFTU Press Office, February 1995.

2 Burma Action Group, *Burma: The Alternative Guide*, London, 1995, p. 17.

3 Geraldine Edith Mitton, *A Bachelor Girl in Burma*, 1907, cited by Nicholas Greenwood in his *Guide to Burma*, Bradt Publications, UK, 1995, p.v.

4   Cited in *Burma Alert*, vol. 6, no. 5, May 1995.

5   UN Commission on Human Rights, *Report on the Situation of Human Rights in Myanmar, by Yozo Yokota, Special Rapporteur, in Accordance with Commission Resolution 1993/73*, Geneva, February 16, 1994.

6   Amnesty International, *Myanmar: Conditions in Prisons and Labour Camps*, AI Index: ASA 16/22/95, September 22, 1995.

7   Ben Kiernan, *The Cambodian Genocide: Issues and Responses*, Yale University paper, New Haven, 1990, p. 11.

8   British Airways, *Free and Easy* (Executive Club brochure), November/December 1995. British Airways holiday brochure, Eastern & Oriental Express holiday, 1995. Confirmation letter from Michael Blunt, Head of Media, Public Affairs, British Airways, March 8, 1996.

9   Bertil Lintner, *Outrage*, White Lotus, UK, 1989, p. 88.

10   Milan Kundera, *The Book of Laughter and Forgetting*, Penguin, London, 1983, p. 5.

11   BBC Short-wave Broadcasts, March–December 1995.

12   George Orwell, *Burmese Days*, Penguin, London, 1989, first published 1934, p. 1.

13   As told to the author.

14   South-east Asia Information Network and the All Burma Students' Democratic Front, *Burma: Human Lives for Natural Resources, Oil & Natural Gas*, Chiangmai University, Thailand, 1994.

15   See report by Douglas Steele, who has investigated both Total and Unocal, *Bangkok Post*, May 7, 1995.

16   Ibid., December 18, 1992.

17   Communication to Carlton UK Television, February 27, 1996.

18   *Nation*, Bangkok, May 4, 1993. See also Pamela Wellner, 'A Pipeline Killing Field', *Ecologist*, vol. 24, no. 5, September/October 1994.

19   International Report, Radio Australia, February 12, 1996.

20   New Mon State Party, *Ye-Tavoy Railway Construction: A Report on Forced Labour in the Mon State and Tenasserim Division in Burma*, April 1994.

21   In an interview with the author.

22   *Burma: The Alternative Guide*, p. 4.

23   *Hansard*, March 19, 1996.

24   *Independent*, October 17, 1995.

25   Central Television, *Flying the Flag, Arming the World*, ITV, 1994.

26   *Hansard*, July 8, 1993.

27   Transcript of conference as recorded by David Boardman, Carlton

UK Television, 1995.

28 Amnesty International Report, 1997.

29 Ibid.

30 *Guardian*, July 17, 1996.

31 *Hansard,* June 12, 1996.

32 Labour Party news release, July 10, 1996. Foreign Office press statement, June 19, 1997.

33 Cited in letter to the *Far Eastern Economic Review* from John Shattuck, US Assistant Secretary for Human Rights and Labor, July 8, 1996.

34 Press conference, Foreign Correspondents' Club, Bangkok, June 16, 1966.

35 Letter to Janet Raynor, Film Librarian, Carlton UK Television, January 23, 1996.

36 *Australian*, July 31, 1996.

37 Cited by Dr Peter Hinton, ibid., July 7, 1996.

38 *Australian*, December 14, 1995. Letter from Evans to the *Sydney Morning Herald*, October 13, 1993.

39 *Australian Financial Review*, November 9, 1994.

40 *Age*, February 25, 1995.

41 *Australian*, January 2, 1996.

42 *Age*, March 6, 1996.

43 *Canberra Times*, August 25, 1996.

44 South-east Asia Information Network, *Out of Control*, Chiangmai University, Thailand, 1996.

45 *Observer*, January 29, 1997.

46 Janet Hunt, Australian Council for Overseas Aid, *Australian*, July 1, 1996.

47 Greenwood, *Guide to Burma*, p. xii.

48 *Burma: The Alternative Guide*, p. 20.

49 *Guardian*, March 30, 1996.

50 *The Times*, February 17, 1996.

51 *Bangkok Post*, February 9, 1996.

52 Letter from Brian Whittaker to Amnesty International, January 2, 1996.

WE SHALL HAVE OUR TIME

1 Bertil Lintner, *Outrage*, White Lotus, UK, 1989, p. 17.

2 Ibid., p. 19.

3 George Orwell, *Burmese Days*, Penguin, London, 1989, first

published 1934, p. 27.

4 Martin Smith, *Burma: Insurgency and the Politics of Ethnicity*, Zed Books, London, 1993, p. 48.

5 Ibid., p. 49.

6 Lintner, *Outrage*, pp. 60–1.

7 Interviewed by the author for Carlton UK Television's *Inside Burma: Land of Fear*, ITV, 1996.

8 *Far Eastern Economic Review*, October 18, 1984.

9 Interviewed by author for *Inside Burma*.

10 Lintner, *Outrage*, p. 96.

11 Ibid., p. 117.

12 Ibid., p. 118.

13 Ibid., p. 117.

14 Aung San Suu Kyi, *Freedom from Fear and Other Writings,* ed. with an introduction by Michael Aris, Penguin, London, 1992.

15 *Vanity Fair*, October 1995.

16 Ibid.

17 Aung San Suu Kyi, *Freedom from Fear*, p. xiii.

18 Ibid., pp. 259, 263–4.

19 Ibid., p. 268.

20 Amnesty International reports, 1995/6/7.

21 *Newsweek*, June 19, 1995.

22 Amnesty International Report, 1996.

23 Bertil Lintner, *Burma in Revolt: Opium and Insurgency since 1948*, White Lotus, Bangkok, 1994, p. 321.

24 Letter from Louise Hoppe Finnerty to David Boardman, January 3, 1996.

25 Burma Action Group press release, January 27, 1997.

26 *Financial Times*, July 11, 1996.

27 *Planet Talk* newsletter, October–December 1996.

28 Amnesty International press release, February 12, 1997.

AUSTRALIA

SECRET WATERS

1 *Pravda*, no. 134, June 13, 1913.

2 The Australian Labor Party was formed in Queensland in 1891, took office briefly in 1899 and in five other states between 1904 and 1913. The first Federal Labor Government was formed in 1904.

3 Jill Roe, *Social Policy in Australia*, Cassell, Sydney, 1976, p. 5.

4 John Pilger, *A Secret Country*, Vintage Books, London, 1990, pp. 187–238.

5 *Business Review Weekly*, June 1986.

6 *Australian Financial Review*, December 5, 1996.

7 Pilger, *A Secret Country*, p. 286.

8 For details of the widening economic gap in Australia, see, among others, the OECD report, cited in *Age*, October 28, 1995; studies by the National Centre for Social and Economic Modelling, cited in the *Australian*, December 6, 1996 and the *Sydney Morning Herald*, October 5, 1997.

9 Australian Bureau of Statistics, *The Health and Welfare of Australia's Aboriginal and Torres Strait Islander Peoples*, Canberra, April 1997.

10 Ibid.

11 World Council of Churches and Amnesty International research papers.

12 *Courier-Mail*, Brisbane, April 19, 1983.

13 *Canberra Times*, May 28, 1997.

14 *Sydney Morning Herald*, April 8, 1997.

15 Ibid., May 8, 1991.

16 Aboriginal and Torres Strait Islander Commission, *Indigenous Deaths in Custody, 1989–96*, Canberra, November, 1996.

17 *Sydney Morning Herald*, October 11, 1986.

18 Ibid., September 23, 1996.

19 Ibid., April 22, 1997.

20 Ibid., April 30, 1997.

21 Ibid.

22 Pilger, *A Secret Country*, p. 132.

23 *Sydney Morning Herald*, May 31, 1997.

24 Jan Roberts, *Massacres to Mining: The Colonisation of Aboriginal Australia*, Dove Communications, Melbourne, 1981, p. 47.

25 Radio Australia, January 3, 1994.

26 Ibid., May 13, 1996.

27 *Age*, December 28, 1996.

28 *Canberra Times*, January 5, 1997.

29 *Age*, June 9, 1997; *Green Left Weekly*, June 4, 1997.

30 *Australian*, June 9, 1997.

31 *Age*, May 10, July 3, 1997.

32 Geoffrey Blainey, *All for Australia*, cited by Jock Collins, *Migrant Hands in a Distant Land*, Pluto Press, Sydney and London, 1988,

pp. 212–22.

33 Russel Ward, *Man Makes History: World History from the Earliest Times to the Renaissance – for Boys and Girls in the First Year of Secondary School Courses*, Shakespeare Head Press, Sydney, 1952, p. 9; cited by Andrée Wright in *Australian Racism: One People, One Prejudice*, research paper for *Island of Dreams*, Channel Seven, Sydney, 1981; cited by Jan Roberts, *Massacres to Mining*, p. 68.

34 Henry Reynolds, *The Other Side of the Frontier*, James Cook University of North Queensland, 1981, p. 163.

35 *Sydney Morning Herald*, October 25, 1996.

36 Human Rights and Equal Opportunity Commission, *Bringing Them Home: National Inquiry into the Separation of Aboriginal and Torres Strait Islander Children from Their Families*, Sydney, April, 1997.

37 The work of historians Rosalind Kidd, Heather Goodall and Peter Read cited by Debra Jopson, 'The Baby Snatchers', *Sydney Morning Herald*, June 30, 1971.

38 *Age*, May 28, 1997. On August 1, 1997, the High Court of Australia ruled that a 1918 ordinance which had facilitated the removal of Aboriginal children from their families was constitutionally valid. The court's decision called into question the Constitution itself, which is about the powers of government not the rights of people. Australians have few constitutional rights, other than those set by precedent with common law.

39 Cited by David Marr, ibid., May 31, 1997.

40 David Day, *Claiming a Continent: A History of Australia*, Angus & Robertson, Sydney, 1996.

41 *Sydney Morning Herald*, February 25, 1987.

42 Kevin Gilbert, *Living Black: Blacks Talk to Kevin Gilbert*, Penguin Books Australia, reprinted 1984.

43 Kevin Gilbert and Eleanor Williams, *Breath of Life: Moments in Transit Towards Aboriginal Sovereignty*, Canberra Contemporary Art Space, 1996.

44 Kevin Gilbert, *Because a White Man'll Never Do It*, HarperCollins, Sydney, reprinted 1994.

ANZAC DAY

1 I am grateful to the late Michele Turner for this detail of

Celestino's death. See her book, *Telling East Timor: Personal Testimonies, 1942–92*, New South Wales University Press, Sydney, 1992, pp. 13–18.

2 *Canberra Times*, April 25, 1997.

3 John Pilger, *A Secret Country*, Vintage Books, London, 1992, p. 168.

4 *Sydney Morning Herald*, November 28, 1996.

5 J. A. C. Mackie, 'Australia's Relations with Indonesia: Principles and Policies', part 2, *Australian Outlook*, 28, 1974.

6 Joint Standing Committee on Foreign Affairs, Defence and Trade, *Australia's Relations with Indonesia*, Australian Government Publishing Service, Canberra, 1993, p. 96.

7 *Age*, September 13, 1974.

8 *Sydney Morning Herald*, September 16, 1974.

9 *National Times*, Sydney, May 30, June 6, 1982. See also 'The Timor Papers' section in Brian Toohey and Marian Wilkinson, *The Book of Leaks*, Angus & Robertson, Sydney, pp. 143–95.

10 Interview with the Australian Broadcasting Corporation, Kuta, Bali, February 9, 1991, cited in *Indonesian News*, vol. 19, no. 2, February 1991.

11 Toohey and Wilkinson, 'The Timor Papers', *The Book of Leaks*.

12 Ibid.

13 James Dunn, *Timor: A People Betrayed*, Jacaranda Press, Australia, 1983, reissued ABC Books, Sydney, 1996, pp. 343–4.

14 Ibid. p. 344.

15 *The Times*, October 12, 1976.

16 John Taylor, *Indonesia's Forgotten War: The Hidden History of East Timor*, Zed Books, London, 1991, p. 139.

17 Ibid., p. 141.

18 *Sinar Harapan*, Indonesia, August 17, 1983.

19 Gareth Evans, *Co-operating for Peace: The Global Agenda for the 1990s and Beyond*, Allen & Unwin, Sydney, 1993. For Evans's admission of Andrew Mack's 'collaborative' authorship, see Australian *Hansard*, June 28, 1995; *Campus Review* (Canberra), August 3–9, 1995.

20 Ibid.

21 See letters' page, *Sydney Morning Herald*, December 1, 1994.

22 *Sydney Morning Herald*, October 20 and December 6, 1990. After the contents of the briefing document were published in the *Herald*, Evans replied in a letter to the paper on December 19, 1990. 'The truth is', he wrote, 'that in a statement circulated [at

Paris] on August 28, 1989, I described, as one of "five stumbling blocks . . . identified in the work of the Committees, and by the Co-presidents" the following: "whether it is appropriate or not to refer specifically to the non-return of genocidal practices of the past". Other "stumbling blocks" I referred to were such matters as "the composition and powers of the transitional administration" and "whether it is appropriate to acknowledge or not the presence of Vietnamese or other settlers in Cambodia". The point is simply that I was making a value-neutral assessment of where we were then at in the negotiating process, identifying controversial words and phrases and issues generally which remained to be addressed . . .'

23 Australian Government, *Informal Meeting on Cambodia, Issues for Negotiations in a Comprehensive Settlement: Working Papers,* February 26–8, 1990. As Ben Kiernan has pointed out, 'The Plan soon degenerated into a refusal to take any action without Khmer Rouge acceptance – not at all a means to exclude them.' See Ben Kiernan, *Cambodia's Missed Chance,* Yale paper, 1990, p. 5.

24 *Indonesia News,* vol. 10, no. 2, February 1991.

25 Mark Aarons and Robert Domm, *East Timor, A Western-made Tragedy,* Left Book Club, Sydney, 1992, p. 66.

26 *Sydney Morning Herald,* December 28, 30, 1991.

27 *Age,* June 6, 8, 1994.

28 *Sydney Morning Herald,* December 28, 30, 1991.

29 *Age,* Melbourne, February 21, 1994.

30 *New Statesman and Society,* July 29, 1994.

31 Amnesty International statement before the UN Special Committee on Decolonisation, July 1992, AI Index: ASA 21/11/92.

32 *New Statesman and Society,* July 29, 1994.

33 Amnesty International, *Power and Impunity: Human Rights Under the New Order,* London, 1994.

34 *Canberra Times,* September 29, 1994; *Australian,* October 11, 1994.

35 *Australian,* December 21, 1994.

36 *New Statesman and Society,* July 15, 1994.

37 *Age,* Melbourne, March 17, 1994.

38 Cited in *New Statesman and Society,* July 14, 1994.

39 *Sydney Morning Herald,* April 18, 1993.

40 Greg Sheridan, *Tigers: Leaders of the New Asia-Pacific,* Allen & Unwin, Sydney, 1997, p. 112.

41 *Sydney Morning Herald,* September 17, 1993.

42 Ibid., October 29, 1993.
43 *Tribune*, January 12, 1966.
44 *Australian Financial Review*, July 30, 1996.
45 *Age*, December 12, 1995.
46 *Australian*, November 15, 1996.
47 Amnesty International, *Power and Impunity*.
48 *Big Issue in Scotland*, no. 121, May 29–June 4, 1997.
49 *Sydney Morning Herald*, November 16, 1994.
50 *Australian*, March 17, 1995.
51 *Herald–Sun*, Melbourne, December 21, 1995.
52 Ibid.
53 *Australian*, December 21, 1995.
54 *Bulletin*, November 21, 1995.
55 *Australian*, December 7, 1995.
56 *Weekend Australian*, August 12–13, 1995.
57 *Australian*, February 18, 19, 1994.
58 As told to the author. See *Age*, May 16, 1995.
59 Communication with the author from ABC executive.
60 *Age*, March 15–16, 1997.
61 *Australian Journal of International Affairs*, vol. 51, no. 2, 1997.
62 *Australian*, March 18, 1994.
63 Ibid., February 14, 1994.
64 *Sydney Morning Herald*, June 14, 1997.
65 *Australian*, March 4, 1997. See also *New Straits Times*, June 10, 1997.
66 Ibid., June 1, 1994.
67 *Courier-Mail*, Brisbane, April 27, 1983. See also *Sydney Morning Herald*, December 5, 1996, for account of an East Timorese witness who told activist Jim Aubrey that three of the five newsmen had been burned alive. José Ramos-Horta said he, too, knew about this witness.
68 *Sydney Morning Herald*, October 20, 1997.
69 See John Pilger, *Distant Voices*, Vintage Books, London 1994, pp. 265–70; James Dunn, *Timor: A People Betrayed*, ABC Books, Sydney 1996 and *East Timor: The Balibo Incident in Perspective*, Australian Centre for Independent Journalism, Sydney, 1995; also 'Timor Murders Planned: Soldiers', *Age*, Melbourne, October 26, 1995.
70 *Weekend Australian*, October 21–2, 1995.
71 *Australian*, October 25, 1995.
72 Dunn, *East Timor*, pp. 32–3.

73 Ibid.
74 *Report on the Deaths of Australian-based Journalists in East Timor in 1975*, Australian Government, June 1996.
75 *Herald-Sun*, January 16, 1997.
76 As told to the author.
77 *Sydney Morning Herald*, June 28, 1996.
78 *Herald-Sun*, January 16, 1997.
79 *Age*, July 16, 1996.
80 *New Statesman and Society*, June 21, 1996.
81 *Age*, August 5, 1996.
82 *Canberra Times*, November 27, 1996.
83 *Age*, June 2, 1997.
84 *AM*, Australian Broadcasting Corporation, May 30, 1997.
85 *Weekend Australian*, June 7–8, 1997.
86 Ibid.
87 As told to the author.
88 *Sydney Morning Herald*, October 18 and November 4, 1996.

WE RESIST TO WIN

XANANA

1 Gabriel Defert, *East Timor: The Forgotten Genocide*, Editions de l'Harmattan, Paris, 1992.

JOSÉ RAMOS-HORTA

1 *War and Peace*, vol. 1, 1995; *Sunday Age*, Melbourne, November 19, 1995.
2 José Ramos-Horta, *Funu: The Unfinished Saga of East Timor*, Red Sea Press, New Jersey, 1987, pp. 38, 39.
3 John G. Taylor, *Indonesia's Forgotten War: The Hidden History of East Timor*, Zed Books, London, 1991, p. 169–70.
4 Daniel Patrick Moynihan, *A Dangerous Place*, Little Brown, New York, 1978, p. 247.
5 Cited by Stephen Zumes in *Christian Science Monitor*, October 17, 1996.
6 Ibid.
7 *War and Peace*; *Age*, October 14, 1996.

BISHOP BELO

1 *Sydney Morning Herald*, April 5, 1997.
2 Note to the author.
3 East Timor Action Network/US, *Network News*, issue no. 12, November 1995.
4 Ibid.
5 *Herald-Sun*, Melbourne, January 18, 1997.
6 First CAFOD Millennium Speech, Westminster Theatre, London, June 7, 1997.

JO, ANDREA, LOTTA AND ANGIE

1 From Andrea Needham's untitled book about the Ploughshares' action, awaiting a publisher.
2 Statement to the author, November 1993.
3 *Independent on Sunday*, July 21, 1996.
4 TAPOL, *Bulletin*, no. 135, June 1996.
5 From Andrea Needham's book.
6 Letter from Joanna Wilson to the author, March 3, 1996.
7 Thanks to Bernadette Meaden, *A Farewell to the Arms Trade*, Wild Goose Publications, The Iona Community, Glasgow, 1997.
8 *Guardian*, July 30, 1996.
9 Evidence of Christopher Foster; cited in *Observer*, July 28, 1996.
10 Meaden, *A Farewell to the Arms Trade*.
11 Ibid.
12 *Manchester Evening News*, July 31, 1996.
13 BBC Radio 4, August 1, 1996.
14 *Guardian*, July 28, 1996.
15 Ibid., August 3, 1996.

THE INVISIBLE REVOLUTION

1 Milan Kundera, *The Book of Laughter and Forgetting*, Penguin, London, 1983, p. 5.
2 Numerous sources for the numbers killed in Suharto's seizure of power include Gabriel Kolko, *Confronting the Third World*, Pantheon, New York, 1988, pp. 180–1.
3 *New Internationalist*, March 1994.
4 US press reports cited by Noam Chomsky in his preface to José Ramos Horta, *Funu: The Unfinished Saga of East Timor*, Red Sea

Press, New Jersey, 1987.

5   *New Statesman*, August 9, 1996; Jeremy Seabrook's *In the Cities of the South* is published by Verso, London, 1996.

6   *Green Left Weekly,* Sydney, August 7, 1996.

7   *Independent*, June 2, 1997.

8   *Green Left Weekly*, June 4, 1997.

9   Andrew Higgins, *Guardian*, June 5, 1997.

10   Tapol, *Bulletin*, no. 129, June 1995.

11   See James Petras, 'A Marxist Critique of Post-Marxists', *Links*, no. 9, November 1997–February 1998.

12   *Green Left Weekly*, November 6, 1996.

13   Ibid., November 19, 1997.

14   *Socialist Review*, May 1997.

15   As told to the author.

THE DOCKERS

1   *Sunday Times*, February 28, 1993.

2   Peter Aughton, *Liverpool: A People's History*, Carnegie Publishing, Preston, 1993.

3   Eric Taplin, *Near to Revolution: The Liverpool General Transport Strike of 1911*, Bluecoat Press, Liverpool, 1994, p. 12.

4   As told to the author, September 1996.

5   *Guardian*, February 12, 1996.

6   Michael Lavalette and Jane Kennedy, *Solidarity on the Waterfront: The Liverpool Lock Out of 1995/6*, Liver Press, Birkenhead, 1996.

7   As told to the author, November 13, 1997.

8   Copy of the contract in possession of the author. Memorandum from Gary Whitby, CPSA BEC rep, to Kevin O'Hagan, CPSA Branch Secretary, 'Health and Safety at Liverpool Docks', March 13, 1997. See also evidence given by Gordon Waddell, Mersey Docks and Harbour Company Managing Director, to the Commons Education and Employment Committee, inquiring into 'The Employment Implications of the Industrial Dispute in the Port of Liverpool', Minutes published by HMSO, July 17, 1996, p. 7.

9   Greg Dropkin, *LabourNet Report*, June 1997.

10   *Liverpool Echo*, September 27, 1996.

11   *Independent on Sunday*, January 21, 1996.

12   Dylan Griffiths, 'Sale of the Century', *PdL* magazine, October 1993.

13   Cited in Merseyside Port Shop Stewards' Press Release, September

1996; also summary of press coverage of the dispute, October 1996.

14 MDHC Annual General Report cited by *Liverpool Echo*, March 21, 1996.

15 House of Commons Employment Committee, minutes, September 1995, p. 30.

16 Ibid.

17 As told to the author, September 1996.

18 Bill Hunter, *They Knew Why They Fought: Unofficial Struggles and Leadership on the Docks, 1945–89*, Index Books, London, 1994, p. 12.

19 Ibid., p. 14.

20 John Pilger, *Heroes*, Pan Books (rev. ed.), 1989, pp. 535–7.

21 Hunter, *They Knew Why They Fought*, p. 113.

22 As told to the author.

23 Ibid.

24 *Lloyd's List*, December 6, 1995.

25 Commons Committee, minutes, p. 19.

26 My letter to Bill Morris, copy on file, October 28, 1996. Morris referred to my 'refusal' to submit questions to him in a letter to E. W. Shannon, Secretary 1/449 Branch, TGWU, December 19, 1996.

27 AEEU Federation of Professional Associations Conference, Liverpool, October 24, 1996.

28 Thanks to Maureen Lee for this reference.

29 Lavalette and Kennedy, *Solidarity on the Waterfront*, p. 112.

30 Jack Heyman, Open Letter to Richard Flint, ITF Communications Director, 'ITF Betrayal of the Liverpool Dockers', October 24, 1996.

31 *Los Angeles Times*, January 21, 1997.

32 Facsimile from Ray Familathe to Bobby Morton, January 20, 1997.

33 *Tribune Business News*, January 21, 1997.

34 Statistics from the Environment Agency, Merseyside Communities Against Toxins, collected by the Merseyside Ships' Stewards' Committee.

35 *Financial Times*, October 1, 1996.

36 On October 25, 1997, at a meeting of the TUC North-West Regional Council, Ian McCartney replied to a question from docker Bobby Morton that the government had received no communication from Bill Morris on behalf of the dockers. In September, Morris had told the TGWU Executive Council member Mike Carden that he had written to the government.

ON THE FAMINE ROAD

THE ROOTS OF WAR

1   Terry Eagleton, *Heathcliff and the Great Hunger: Studies in Irish Culture*, Verso, London, 1995.
2   Thomas Gallagher, *Paddy's Lament, Ireland 1846–1847: Prelude to Hatred*, Poolbeg Press, Dublin, 1988.
3   Cited by Hazel Croft, 'Starved to Death by Market Dogma', *Socialist Worker*, June 14, 1997. See Christine Kinealy, *A Death-Dealing Famine: The Great Hunger in Ireland*, Pluto Press, London, 1994; Liz Curtis, *The Cause of Ireland*, Beyond the Pale Publications, Belfast, 1994, pp. 40–59.
4   Cecil Woodham-Smith, *The Great Hunger*, Hamish Hamilton, London, 1977, p. 86.
5   Ibid., p. 411.
6   Cited in *Independent*, June 3, 1997.
7   Christine Kinealy, *The Great Calamity; The Irish Famine, 1845–52*, Gill & Macmillan, Dublin, 1994.
8   *Irish Times*, May 10, 1995.
9   *New Statesman and Society*, June 9, 1995.
10 Woodham-Smith, *The Great Hunger*, pp. 84, 310–11.
11 *Irish Times*, March 14, 1995.
12 *Independent*, June 3, 1997.

THE RISE AND FALL OF POPULAR JOURNALISM

FORWARD WITH THE PEOPLE

1   *Daily Mirror*, October 14–18, 1963.
2   Letter from Mirror Group, May 17, 1996, in reply to letter from Tony Maughan, General Secretary Pensioners' Parliament, May 7, 1996.
3   Maurice Edelman, *The Mirror: A Political History*, Hamish Hamilton, London, 1966, p. 1.
4   Hugh Cudlipp, *Publish and Be Damned*, Andrew Dakers, London, 1953, pp. 10–11.
5   Matthew Engel, *Tickle the Public: One Hundred Years of the Popular Press*, Victor Gollancz, London, 1996, p. 152.
6   Ibid., p. 156.
7   As told to the author.

8   Charles Wintour, *The Rise and Fall of Fleet Street*, Hutchinson, 1989, p. 135.

9   Cited by Hugh Cudlipp, *British Journalism Review*, vol. 7, no. 4, 1996.

10 Cudlipp, *Publish and Be Damned*, p. 128.

11 Ibid., pp. 128–9.

12 *Daily Mirror*, September 30, 1938.

13 Cudlipp, *Publish and Be Damned*, pp. 142–3.

14 *Daily Mirror*, September 4, 1939.

15 Cudlipp, *Publish and Be Damned*, p. 132.

16 Ibid., p. 133.

17 Ibid., p. 146.

18 Ibid., pp. 147, 148, 150, 169, 196.

19 Engel, *Tickle the Public*, pp. 167–8.

20 Ibid., pp. 219–20.

21 Cudlipp, *British Journalism Review*.

22 *Daily Mirror*, July 5, 1945.

23 Cudlipp, *Publish and Be Damned*, p. 234.

24 Quoted by Anthony Howard in *Age of Austerity*, ed. Michael Sissons and Philip French, Hodder & Stoughton, London, 1963, p. 16; cited by Engel, *Tickle the Public*, p. 173.

25 Cudlipp, *Publish and Be Damned*, p. 240.

26 *Daily Mirror*, February 20, 1951.

27 Charles Moran, *Winston Churchill: The Struggle for Survival 1940–65*, Constable, London, 1966, p. 500; cited by Engel, *Tickle the Public*.

28 *Daily Mirror*, August 14, 1956.

29 Ibid., September 22, 1969.

30 Ibid., August 14, 1970.

31 Ibid., October 14, 1964.

32 *Evening Standard*, January 15, 1985.

33 Cudlipp, *British Journalism Review*.

34 Ibid.

35 *Daily Mirror*, January 16, 1968.

36 Readership was then estimated at four times the circulation.

37 *Daily Mirror*, April 12, 1973.

38 *Guardian*, September 1966, quoted in Phillip Knightley, *The First Casualty: From the Crimea to the Falklands; the War Correspondent as Hero, Propagandist and Myth Maker*, André Deutsch, 1975, p. 390.

39 Tony Benn, *Office Without Power: Political Diaries, 1968–72*,

Hutchinson, London, 1988.

40　Memo from Hugh Cudlipp to Cecil King, cited in *The Times*, April 29, 1987.

41　Wintour, *The Rise and Fall of Fleet Street*, pp. 147–8.

BREAKING THE MIRROR

1　As told to the author.

2　*Sun*, November 15, 1969.

3　Peter Chippendale and Chris Horrie, *Stick It Up Your Punter: The Rise and Fall of the Sun*, Heinemann, London, 1990, p. 49.

4　*Daily Mirror*, June 7, 1974.

5　Ibid., January 20, 1977.

6　Ibid., September 12, 1979.

7　Paul Foot, *Words as Weapons*, Verso, London, 1990, p. 7.

8　Chippendale and Horrie, *Stick It Up Your Punter*, pp. 76, 78.

9　Ibid., p. 118.

10　*Daily Mirror*, May 6, 1982.

11　*Sun*, May 7, 1982.

12　*Daily Mirror*, May 8, 1982.

13　Ibid., November 6, 1991.

14　Reed International press release, October 13, 1983.

15　Granada Television, *What the Papers Say*, July 27, 1954.

16　Audit Bureau of Circulation, cited in *Media Week*, July 19, 1985.

17　*Marketing Week*, January 31, 1986.

18　Mike Maloney, *Flash! Splash! Crash! All at Sea with Cap'n Bob*, Mainstream Press, London, 1996, pp. 10–11.

19　*Daily Mirror*, March 4, 1985.

20　Ibid., August 6, 1985.

21　Ibid., January 19, 1985.

22　Ibid., August 21, 1984.

23　Seamus Milne, *The Enemy Within*, Pan Books, London, 1994, pp. 83–4.

24　Ibid., pp. 138–9.

25　*Daily Mirror*, November 23, 1994.

26　Roy Greenslade, *Maxwell's Fall*, Simon & Schuster, 1992.

27　Milne, *The Enemy Within*, p. 68.

28　Ibid., p. 107.

29　Ibid., p. 430.

30　Ibid., p. 436. The DTI report on Richard Budge was first disclosed on the BBC's *Panorama*, May 1, 1995.

31 *Daily Mirror*, November 6, 1991.
32 Ibid.
33 Ibid., December 4, 1991.
34 Ibid., June 6, July 1, 1997.
35 Ibid., November 26, 27, 1996.
36 *Daily Mirror*, February 6, 1997.
37 Ibid., June 5, 1996.
38 Ibid., April 30, 1996.
39 Roy Greenslade, 'Return of the Prodigal Son', *Guardian*, January 19, 1998.
40 *Independent on Sunday*, February 23, 1997.

THE MEDIA AGE

A Cultural Chernobyl

1 Rt Hon. Lord Justice Taylor, *The Hillsborough Stadium Disaster 15 April 1989: Final Report*, HMSO, 1990.
2 *Sun*, April 19, 1989.
3 Peter Chippendale and Chris Horrie, *Stick It Up Your Punter: The Rise and Fall of the Sun*, Heinemann, London, 1990, pp. 283, 284, 288.
4 *The World This Weekend*, BBC Radio 4, July 30, 1989.
5 *Midweek*, BBC Radio 4, October 16, 1996.
6 *Sun*, September 14, 1994.
7 Ibid., September 9 and 26, 1994.
8 Ibid., September 18, 1996.
9 *The Press and the People*, 35th Annual Report of the Press Council, London, 1988, pp. 150–2.
10 Chippendale and Horrie, *Stick It Up Your Punter*, pp. 166–8.
11 *Sun*, March 1, 1984.
12 Dimity Torbett, 'Rupert Murdoch in his own and others' words', News Unlimited Conference, Sydney, February 1989.
13 Richard Neville, *Hippie Hippie Shake*, Bloomsbury, London, 1995, p. 37.
14 As told to the author.
15 *Breaking the Mirror: The Murdoch Effect*, Carlton UK Television, ITV, February 18, 1997.
16 Thomas Kiernan, *Citizen Murdoch*, Dodd, Mead & Co., New York, 1986.
17 Chippendale and Horrie, *Stick It Up Your Punter*, p. 84.

18 *Literary Review*, December 1995.

19 Richard Belfield, Christopher Hird and Sharon Kelly, *Murdoch: The Great Escape*, Warner Books, London, 1994, p. 87.

20 Ibid., pp. 79–81.

21 Michael Leapman, *Treacherous Estate*, Hodder & Stoughton, London, 1992, p. 73.

22 *Panorama*, BBC Television, 1981, cited by Belfield, Hird and Kelly, *Murdoch*, p. 78.

23 *Guardian*, March 8, 1991.

24 Memo from Rosie Waterhouse to Robin Morgan, May 1988, cited by Roger Bolton, *Death on the Rock and Other Stories*, W. H. Allen, London, 1990, p. 29.

25 *Political Quarterly*, October 1984, p. 385.

26 Ibid., pp. 386–7.

27 *Sunday Times*, February 23 and March 2, 1997.

28 Thanks to Nick Cohen for the reminder: *Observer*, March 30, 1997.

29 Tape of Kelvin MacKenzie addressing *Sun* staff, January 23, 1994.

30 Letter from Tony Isaacs to Tony Britton, January 12, 1986.

31 Letter from G. W. Richards of Farrer & Co. to Bruce Mathews, December 20, 1995.

32 Belfield, Hird and Kelly, *Murdoch*, p. 95.

33 Ibid., p. 100.

34 Interview by Mary Goldring, BBC TV, October 15, 1989.

35 Interviewed by the author.

36 *New Statesman and Society*, July 28, 1995.

37 *Breaking the Mirror: The Murdoch Effect*.

38 Ibid.

39 *Sun*, July 21, 1995.

40 Cited in *Hansard*, April 16, 1996. Lewis Moonie interviewed for *Breaking the Mirror: The Murdoch Effect*.

41 Andrew Neil, *Full Disclosure*. This quotation is from the introduction to the paperback edition, Pan, 1997.

42 The original account of the meeting appeared in the journalists' newspaper, the *Clarion*, December 1986, and has since been substantiated by the author from sources within News Limited. See also Gavin Souter, *Heralds and Angels*, cited by Brian Toohey, *Sun-Herald*, February 24, 1991.

43 David Bowman, *The Captive Press*, Penguin, Sydney, 1988, p. 173.

44 *Sydney Morning Herald*, December 17, 1986.

45 Letter to the author from Ian Macphee, October 31, 1988. See also Australian *Hansard*, December 21, 1989.
46 *Australian Financial Review*, July 1, 1996.
47 *Independent*, November 27, 1995.
48 *Four Corners*, ABC Television, March 13, 1989.
49 *Breaking the Mirror: The Murdoch Effect*.
50 *Sun*, September 11, 1995.
51 *Independent*, November 30, 1995.
52 *Guardian*, February 1, 1997.
53 *Broadcast*, February 18, 1994. The media silence on the Murdoch threat to digital television has been broken by Polly Toynbee in the *Independent*: September 15, 1996; June 25, 1997.
54 Bob Franklin, *Newszak and the News Media*, Arnold, UK, 1997.
55 Norman Abjoresen, 'Turning On, Tuning Out', *Canberra Times*, August 4, 1996.
56 Franklin, *Newszak and the News Media*.
57 *UK Press Gazette*, September 20, 1996.
58 Franklin, *Newszak and the News Media*.
59 *Guardian*, October 23, 1996.
60 *Observer*, February 23, 1997.
61 William Shawcross, *Murdoch*, Pan Books, London, 1993, p. 591.
62 Matthew Engel, *Tickle the Public: One Hundred Years of the Popular Press*, Victor Gollancz, London, 1996, pp. 271–80.
63 Belfield, Hird and Kelly, *Murdoch*, pp. 50–1.
64 *Adelaide Review*, February 1996.
65 Ibid., November 1996.
66 *Sydney Morning Herald*, December 21, 1996.
67 Bowman, *The Captive Press*, pp. 226–7.
68 *British Journalism Review*, vol. 1, no. 2, Winter 1990.

GUARDIANS OF THE FAITH

1 *UK Press Gazette*, April 29, 1985.
2 *Times Literary Supplement*, September 15, 1972; reprinted in Everyman's Library edition of *Animal Farm*.
3 David Bowman, *Adelaide Review*, February 1996.
4 BBC World Service, August 16, 1996.
5 Mark Curtis, *UK-Indonesia 1965 article*, October 15, 1996.
6 Third World and Environment Broadcasting Project, *Watching the World: British Television and Audience Engagement with*

   Developing Countries, 1996.

7   Thanks to Sharon Beder.

8   *Independent*, September 22, 1997.

9   Patrick Renshaw, *The General Strike*, Eyre Methuen, London, 1975, p. 207.

10 Phillip Knightley, *The First Casualty: From the Crimea to the Falklands; the War Correspondent as Hero, Propagandist and Myth Maker*, Pan Books, London, 1989, p. 97. I acknowledge Knightley's work as a consistently valuable source.

11 Ibid., p. 109.

12 Ibid., p. 97.

13 Ibid., p. 354.

14 *Sunday Times*, September 22, 1985.

15 Ibid., August 28, 1983.

16 ITN, June 29, 1983, cited by Greg Philo, *War and Peace News*, Open University Press, Milton Keynes, 1985, p. 138.

17 BBC TV, June 27, 1982.

18 *Daily Express*, May 9, 1984.

19 NCCL, *Civil Liberties and the Miners' Dispute*, cited in *New Statesman and Society*, April 19, 1985.

20 Seamus Milne, *The Enemy Within: MI5, Maxwell and the Scargill Affair*, Verso, London, 1995.

21 Lyn Smith, 'Covert British Propaganda: The Information Research Department, 1974–7', *Millennium: Journal of International Studies*, vol. 9, no. 1 (thanks to Robin Ramsay).

22 *Observer*, August 18, 1985.

23 'The British Embassy Honors the Project in Washington', *British-American Project Newsletter*, June/July 1997.

24 Tom Easton, 'The British-American Project and the Successor Generation', *Lobster*, Summer 1997.

25 *Guardian*, July 5, 1997.

26 *Independent*, March 26, 1992.

27 Sandy Gall, *News from the Front: A Television Reporter's Life*, Heinemann, London, 1994, pp. 122–59.

28 Memorandum to Director of CIA, from Task Force on Greater CIA Openness, November 18, 1991.

29 John Ranelagh, *CIA: A History*, BBC Books, 1992, p. 228.

30 William Blum, *The CIA: A Forgotten History*, Zed Books, London, 1986, p. 334.

31 Independent Television News, July 26, 1994; BBC Short-wave Broadcasts, October 1994.

32   Noam Chomsky, *Year 501: The Conquest Continues*, South End Press, Boston, 1993, pp. 204, 207.

33   Mark Curtis, *The Ambiguities of Power: British Foreign Policy Since 1945*, Zed Books, London, 1995, pp. 166–7, 172.

34   Lawrence Freedman and Efraim Karsh, *The Gulf Conflict, 1990–1: Diplomacy and War in the New World Order*, Faber & Faber, London, 1993. Cited by Curtis, *The Ambiguities of Power*, p. 203. As Professor of War Studies at King's College, London, Freedman ran a summer course (1997) for ten Indonesian military officers, which he described as a 'mind-opening experience' for them. *Observer*, June 15, 1997.

35   Charles William Maynes, editor of *Foreign Policy*, wrote, 'CIA officials privately concede that the US military may have killed between 7,000 and 10,000 Somalis', cited by Noam Chomsky, *Z* magazine, Summer 1995.

36   *Newsnight*, BBC Television, September 7, 1992.

37   Chomsky, *Year 501*, p. 249.

38   *New Statesman and Society*, March 24, 1996.

39   Ibid.

40   *British Social Attitudes*, Report no. 13, Dartmouth Press, UK 1997; *General Household Survey*, cited in *Observer*, January 26, 1997.

41   Sources for the rejoicing in Blairdom: *Guardian*, May 7, 13, 24, 26, 28, 30, June 3, 17, July 26, 28, 1997; *Observer*, May 4, 11, June 1, 1997; *Independent*, May 23, 24, 28, June 3, July 3, 1997; BBC radio news, June 3, 1997; *Newsnight*, BBC TV, May 9, 24, 1997. And thanks to Hugh MacPherson, *Tribune*, May 30, 1997.

42   *Independent*, September 16, 17, 1997.

43   Cited by Hilary Land, *Red Pepper*, October 1997.

44   Karen Gardin, *Bridges from Benefit to Work: A Review*, Joseph Rowntree Foundation, 1997.

45   See note 41.

46   Ibid.

47   Ibid.

48   Ibid. I asked Emma Forrest if her article was a spoof. She said no, but she was trying to be funny.

49   Ibid.

50   *Guardian*, October 1, 1997.

51   *Independent on Sunday*, November 16, 1997.

52   *Guardian*, July 16, 1993.

53   *Observer*, August 11, 1996.

54 Letter from Lord Normanbrook to Sir Burke Trend, September 7, 1965, cited by Michael Tracey in correspondence. See also Michael Tracey, *Decline and Fall of Public Service Broadcasting*, Clarendon Press, Oxford, 1997: *Sanity Broadsheet*, no. 6, 1980; *Guardian*, article and letters, September 1, 3 and 6, 1980.

55 Hugh Greene's speech, 'The Conscience of the Programme Director', delivered to the International Catholic Association for Radio and Television, Rome, February 1965.

56 Peter Watkins, *Cine-Tracts*, vol. 3, no. 1, Winter 1980.

57 Liz Curtis, *Ireland, the Propaganda War: The British Media and the 'Battle for Hearts and Minds'*, Pluto Press, London, 1984, pp. 279–90.

58 David Miller, *Don't Mention the War: Northern Ireland, Propaganda and the Media*, Pluto Press, London, 1994, p. 63.

59 ITN, October 18, 1988.

60 Miller, *Don't Mention the War*, p. 277.

61 *Red Pepper*, January 1997.

62 *Independent*, May 30, 1996; *Guardian*, April 4, 1996; *Morning Star*, June 24, December 12, 1996; *Irish Post*, December 21, 1996.

63 Ibid.

64 Miller, *Don't Mention the War*, p. 64.

65 Frank Kitson, *Low Intensity Operations: Subversion, Insurgency, Peace-keeping*, Faber & Faber, 1971.

66 *Observer*, January 9, 1997.

67 Communication to author from Derry sources.

68 Cited in *New Statesman and Society*, March 1, 1996.

69 *Morning Star*, November 26, 1996.

70 *Observer*, January 12, 1997; *Guardian*, January 4, 1997.

71 *Observer*, January 12, 1997.

72 *Nine O'Clock News*, BBC TV, November 28, 1996.

73 TV 2, French Television poll, November 25, 1996, showed 74 per cent support for the truckers' action and 87 per cent believed their demands justified.

74 *PM*, BBC Radio 4, November 29, 1996.

75 *Guardian*, November 30, 1996.

76 BBC Short-wave Broadcasts, September 1994.

77 *Guardian*, October 19, 1996.

78 *Guardian*, September 20, 1997.

79 Mark Leonard, *Britain TM*, Demos, 1997, p. 46.

80 *Guardian*, September 18, 1997.

81 Ibid., September 3, 1997.

82 Edwin P. Bayley, *Joe McCarthy and the Press*, University of Wisconsin Press, Madison, 1981.

83 George Orwell, letter to Sir Richard Rees, July 28, 1949, *Collections and Essays*, vol. 4, Secker & Warburg, 1968, p. 505.

84 *Guardian*, March 8, 1997.

85 T. D. Allman, 'Eulogy to Wilfred Burchett', read at a New York memorial service, March 31, 1984.

THE LAST VOICE

1 *New Yorker*, November 13, 1995.

2 Cited by Carole Tongue, in her speech 'Gatekeepers of our Society', *Guardian*/Fabian conference, 'Multi-Media Europe: Ownership and Control', London, December 2, 1995.

3 Speech given by Rupert Murdoch to advertisers, London, January 1, 1993, cited *Independent*, January 30, 1997.

4 *New Yorker*, November 14, 1995.

5 Thanks to Stephen Vines and Teresa Poole of the *Independent* for this information.

6 *New Yorker*, November 14, 1995.

7 Author's BBC/News International source.

8 Analysis by *Third World Resurgence*, issue no. 12, 'Manufacturing Truth: The Western Media and the Third World', published by Third World Network, Penang, Malaysia.

9 Ibid.

10 *Guardian*, March 4, 1996.

11 The Television Show, Design Centre, London, March 14, 1997.

12 Thanks to *Red Pepper*, March 1997, for this analysis.

13 *Observer*, December 1, 1996.

14 Bob Franklin, *Newszak and the News Media*, Arnold, UK, 1997.

15 Marshall McLuhan, *Understanding Media: The Extensions of Man*, McGraw-Hill, New York, 1984, cited in *New International*, December 1996. This issue offers one of the few sustained critiques of the new technology.

16 Norbert Wiener, *The Human Use of Human Beings: Cybernetics and Society*, Houghton-Mifflin, Boston, 1950, cited in *New Internationalist*.

17 Vandana Shiva, *Monocultures of the Mind*, Zed Books, London, 1993.

18 *Red Pepper*, March 1997.

19 *Guardian*, December 27, 1996. Julian Petley, of Brunel University

Human Sciences Department, has written widely on the media, including a forthcoming book on journalism.

20 'Real Women of the Real World', *Guardian*, April 19, 1997.

21 Thanks to Mike Phipps in *Labour Left Briefing* for this observation in his review of Timothy Bewes's book, *Cynicism and Post-modernity*, Verso, London, 1997.

22 *Observer*, March 17, 1996.

23 Tommy Sheridan with Joan McAlpine, *A Time to Rage*, Polygon, Edinburgh, 1994.

24 *Third World Resurgence*, issue no. 8, April 1991.

25 Alex Carey, *Taking the Risk Out of Democracy*, University of NSW Press, Sydney 1995, cited by Noam Chomsky, *Covert Action*, Fall 1995.

26 Ibid.

27 Sharon Beder, *Global Spin: The Corporate Assault on Environmentalism*, Green Books, UK, 1997, pp. 20–1.

28 Tom Baistow, *Fourth Rate Estate*, Comedia, London, 1985.

29 *Guardian*, May 13, 1996.

30 Ibid.

31 Beder, *Global Spin*, p. 15.

32 Cited in ibid., p. 16.

33 Thanks to David Bowman for this chronicle.

34 *24 Hours*, Sydney, April 1996.

35 *Manchester Guardian*, August 5, 1919, cited in David Ayerst, *Guardian: Biography of a Newspaper*, Collins, London, 1971, p. 432.

36 Ibid., November 25, 1996.

37 *Reportage*, Sydney, Summer, 1996/7.

RETURN TO VIETNAM

STILL A NOBLE CAUSE

1 Gabriel Kolko, *Anatomy of a War: Vietnam, the United States and the Modern Historical Experience*, New Press, New York, 1994, p. 551.

2 Compared with an estimated 300,000 Vietnamese, there are 2,477 Americans officially listed as MIAs. This is the lowest American figure this century. 78,751 Americans are still 'missing' from the Second World War and 8,177 from the Korean War: Library of Congress, 1985.

3 Phillip Knightley, *The First Casualty: From the Crimea to the Falklands; the War Correspondent as Hero, Propagandist and Myth Maker*, Pan Books, London, 1989, p. 400.

4 *Life, Observer*, April 2, 1995.

5 Alexander Haig, *Caveat*, Weidenfeld & Nicolson, London, 1984, p. 202.

6 Dwight D. Eisenhower, *The White House Years: Mandate for Change, 1953–6*, Doubleday, New York, 1963, p. 372.

7 Philip Taylor, 'The Green Berets', *The Historical Journal of Film, Radio and Television*, March 1995.

8 Ibid.

9 Richard Holmes, *Firing Line*, Jonathan Cape, London, 1985, p. 68.

10 *Guardian*, April 10, 1995.

THE FINAL BATTLE

1 As told to the author.

2 Estimate provided by Dr Duong Quynh Hoa at Saigon's Paediatric Hospital No. 2.

3 Telford Taylor, *Nuremberg and Vietnam*, cited by Alex Carey, *Sun-Herald*, Sydney, June 30, 1985.

4 Linda Mason and Roger Brown, *Rice, Rivalry and Politics: Managing Cambodian Relief*, University of Notre Dame Press, Indiana, 1983, pp. 135, 159.

5 William Shawcross, *The Quality of Mercy: Cambodia, Holocaust and Modern Conscience*, André Deutsch, London, 1984, pp. 289, 345, 395.

6 *Nhan Dan*, the Communist Party's official daily newspaper, March 1, 1996; also *Tap Chi Cong San*, the party's theoretical monthly, March 15, 1996, cited by Gabriel Kolko, *Vietnam: Anatomy of a Peace*, Routledge, London & New York, 1997, p. 102.

7 *Viet Nam News*, Hanoi, May 5, 1997.

8 *IndoChina Digest*, February 17, 1995.

9 Kolko, *Vietnam*, p. 602.

10 Ibid., p. 102.

11 *Third World Resurgence*, no. 47, January 1994.

12 World Bank, East Asia and Pacific Region, *Viet Nam: Transition to the Market*, Washington DC, September 1993.

13 *IndoChina Digest*, February 17, 1995.

14 World Bank, East Asia and Pacific Region, *Viet Nam: Poverty*

Assessment and Strategy, Washington DC, January 1995. Report on Poverty 1995.

15 Cited by Chossudovsky, *Third World Resurgence*.
16 Ibid.
17 Overseas Trade Services, Department of Trade and Industry, *Vietnam, General Information*, London, January 1995.
18 Dr Le Thi Quy, *Some Remarks on the Situation of Women Workers in Foreign-invested Enterprises in Ho Chi Minh City*, 1994; also *Gender: The Relations Between Research and Policy-making in Vietnam*, Asian and Pacific Development Centre (APDC), summer institute, Kuala Lumpur, May–June 1994.
19 Chossudovsky, *Third World Resurgence*.
20 Cited in *National Project Education Sector Review and Human Resources Sector Analysis*, vol. 1, Hanoi, 1992, p. 39.
21 Chossudovsky, *Third World Resurgence*.
22 United Nations Development Programme, *Report on the Economy of Vietnam*, New York, p. 183.
23 World Bank, *Viet Nam*, p. 145.
24 Senator Gaylord Nelson: speech to Congress, August 25, 1970. Source: US Senate Library.
25 *Vietnam Investment Review*, June 16–22, 1997.
26 Kolko, *Anatomy of a War*, p. 590.
27 Interviewed on BBC Television, cited in BBC Summary of World Broadcasts, February 8, 1991.
28 Peter MacDonald, *Giap: The Victor in Vietnam*, Warner Books, London, 1993, p. 42.
29 Associated Press, cited in *Sydney Morning Herald*, March 29, 1997.
30 *Tap Chi Cong San*, cited by Kolko, *Anatomy of a War*, p. 93.
31 Reuters, July 26, 1997.
32 Kolko, *Anatomy of a War*, p. 94; *Saigon Giai Phong* (daily newspaper of the Ho Chi Minh City Communist Party), July 17, 1997.

CHINA BEACH

1 Ralph McGehee and other former CIA officers have since confirmed that the pretext for 'Operation Rolling Thunder', the bombing of the north that reached Dresden proportions, was also fake. This was the 'Gulf of Tonkin Incident', in which North Vietnamese gunboats were said to have attacked a US destroyer,

the *Maddox*, in August 1964. On the basis of 'intelligence reports' that provided the basis for a White Paper, Congress gave President Johnson virtually unlimited powers to wage war without declaring war. The truth was that White House officials had written the Gulf of Tonkin Resolution two months before the alleged attack on the *Maddox*.

2 Martha Gellhorn, *The Face of War*, Virago, London, 1986, p. 254.

EPILOGUE

THE VIEW FROM DIMBAZA

1 Eastern Cape Socio-Economic Consultative Council, *A Statistical Snapshot*, 1997.

2 *Daily Dispatch*, East London, January 16, 1969.

3 Cosmas Desmond, *The Discarded People*, Penguin, Harmondsworth, 1971, p.79.

4 Geoff Berridge, *Economic Power in Anglo-South African Diplomacy: Simonstown, Sharpeville and After*, Macmillan, London, 1981, pp.34–5.

5 William Minter, *King Solomon's Mines Revisited: Western Interests and the Burdened History of South Africa*, Basic Books, New York, 1986, p.279. Thanks to Mark Curtis.

6 Miranda Strydom, 'Black Empowerment: Is There Really More to It Than Equity?', *Cape Times*, October 10, 1997.

7 Hugh Murray, 'The Privatisation of Cyril Ramaphosa', *Leadership*, July 1997.

8 Strydom, 'Black Empowerment'.

9 *Star*, Johannesburg, October 3, 1997.

10 *Observer*, December 21, 1997.

11 *Mail & Guardian*, Johannesburg, May 23, 1997.

12 R. W. Johnson, *London Review of Books*, October 17, 1996.

13 Although statistics are in abundance in South Africa, most are rough estimates. Taking the studies of the Central Statistical Services of the Reserve Bank and Professor Laurence Schlemmer, it is evident that job losses are running at over 100,000 a year in both the official and unofficial sectors.

14 Report by the Central Statistical Service (CSS), cited by *Sunday Independent*, Johannesburg, October 10, 1997.

15 World Bank figures cited by *Green Left Weekly*, December 3, 1997.

16 Ibid.
17 *Mail & Guardian*, July 15–25, 1995.
18 Estimate by Cardinal Basil Hume, *Observer*, December 21, 1997.
19 *Weekend Guardian*, February 15, 1997
20 Speech to Congress of South African Trade Unions (COSATU), September 1993.
21 Cited in the *Independent on Sunday*, December 7, 1997. Thanks to John Cassidy for his piece, 'The Next Big Thinker'.
22 Cited by Colleen Ryan, 'US in Grip of Surging Protectionism', *Australian Financial Review*, November 15–16, 1997.
23 *Independent on Sunday*, December 7, 1997.

Index

ABC *see* Australian
     Broadcasting Corporation
Abdication crisis 382–3, 400
Aborigines, Australian 12,
     230–2, 238–9, 244–8
     genocide 223, 239–44
     Native Title legislation
     234–8, 246
Action from Ireland: Famine
     Walk 361–2, 364, 366
Adams, Gerry 515, 518
Adams, Jack 358
Adelaide *Advertiser* 482
Adie, Kate 50, 51–2, 55,
     57–8, 485
Africa 9, 531
     see Kenya; Nigeria; South
     Africa
Age (Melbourne newspaper)
     265, 483, 542
Agence France Presse 531
'Agent Orange' 56, 581, 587
Ahmed, Moudud 405
Aid for Trade Provisions
     (ATP) 121
Aird, Malcolm 563
Aitken, Jonathan 130–1,
     495
Ajibade, Kunle 15
Alatas, Ali 257, 264, 272
Albright, Madeleine 54
Alexandra, Queen 380

Algeria: death of journalists
     545
Allende, Salvador 63, 64,
     123, 330
Alliance of Independent
     Journalists 137
Allman, T. D. 525
Amin, Idi 124
Amnesty International 120,
     123, 147, 158, 186, 187,
     189, 218, 262–3, 266,
     283, 550
Amoco 217
Amorin, José 313
'Andy Capp' 392
Antrim, HMS 336
Anyawu, Chris 15
APEC *see* Asia Pacific
     Economic Conferences
Aquino, Cory 208
Argentina 27
     see also Falklands War
Aris, Michael 173, 203, 208,
     209, 210, 212, 218
     Freedom from Fear
     (introduction) 200–1
Aristide, Father 66
arms industry/sales:
     British 6, 7, 115–19, 120,
     122–3, 132–4, 135,
     138–9, 144–7, 149–52,
     505, 506–7

to Chile 123–4
to Indonesia 119–20,
122, 136, 137, 139–44,
147–8, 292
to Iraq 125–30
to Malaysia 121, 122
to Oman 122
to Saudi Arabia 130–2
US 7–8, 30, 121, 123,
134–5
to Indonesia 292, 301–2
to Saudi Arabia 56–7
see also nuclear weapons
Armstrong, William 118
ASEAN (Association of South
East Asian Nations) 177,
178, 180, 182, 213
Asia Pacific Economic Conferences (APEC) 76, 324
Asian Development Bank 62,
570, 573
Associated Press 531
Astra (corporation) 170,
127–9
asylum seekers (in Britain) 36,
136
Atlantic Container Line
(ACL) 350–1
Aubrey, Jim 254, 277
Aubuisson, Roberto d' 27
Auletta, Ken 529–30
Aung San 192–3, 197
Aung San Suu Kyi 14, 155,
159, 167, 171–4, 175,
176, 178, 179–80, 193,
199–204, 214–15, 216,
218–20
Freedom from Fear 200–1,
204–5
interview with author
204–12

Australia 76, 77, 227–30, 506
and APEC 76–7
feminism 92
and First World War
249–50
and Indonesia 14, 254–6,
258, 264–9, 270, 272–3,
278–9
media and press 246, 260,
273, 470–4, 481–2, 542,
543–4, *see also* Murdoch,
Rupert
think tanks 541–2
and Vietnam War 254,
265
see also Aborigines; Evans,
Gareth; Hawke Bob;
Howard, John; Keating,
Paul; Sydney
Australian (newspaper) 76,
270, 272, 471–2, 481–2,
542
Australian Broadcasting
Corporation (ABC) 52,
180, 241, 271–2, 450
Australian Financial Review
229
Australian Human Rights and
Equal Opportunity
Commission 223, 232–3,
241
Bringing Them Home
(report) 240
Aye Chan 197, 198

Ba, General Kyaw 187–8
Babcock Thorn 152
Babson, Bradley 575, 577
Bacall, Lauren 509
Bacon, Wendy 273
Baghdad Observer 125

Baird, Vera 321
Baistow, Tom: *Fourth Rate Estate* 540
Baker, James 63
Baldwin, Stanley 491
Bali, Indonesia 168
Balkans: ethnic cleansing 40
Balls, Edward 95
banana trade, Grenada 75–6
Bandler, Faith 246
Banks, David 436, 464
Banks, Dr Ian 80
BAP *see* British–American Project for the Successor Generation
Barber, Lynn 481
Barber, Michael 90–1
Barclays Bank 86, 93
Bartholomew, Harry Guy ('Bart') 381, 382, 383, 402
Batista, Pedro 268
Bayfield, Richard 542
Bayley, Edwin P.: *Joe McCarthy and the Press* 524
BBC (British Broadcasting Corporation) 484–5, 486, 487 and BAP 497
  Martin Bell on 524, 525
  and China 530, 533
  CIA series 499, 502
  and Discovery Channel 533
  journalists refused posts 496–7
  and Kissinger 23
  and 'market' bureaucracy 532
  and Murdoch 533
  Newsnight 111, 322, 501–2, 505, 507, 517, 533
Panorama 456
People's Century series 502, 503
political correspondents 503–4
Radio 4 448
TV news reports 2, 478
  Clinton's attack on Iraq (1996) 19, 57
  Princess Diana's death 522–3
  Falklands War 492, 493
  French truckers 520–1
  Gulf War 45, 47, 50, 51, 52, 501
  Haiti 67, 500
  Liverpool strike 354
  Northern Ireland 516, 517
  poverty in Russia 521–2
  Vietnam War 563
  The War Game (film) 513–14
  World Service 487–8, 496
Beatles, the 376–7
Beaverbrook, Lord 390, 391
Becker, Arnold 479
Beckett, Margaret 94, 147
Bedawi, Zeinab 144
Beder, Sharon: *Global Spin* 68, 540
Beeston, Nicholas 125–6
Belfast Telegraph 517
Belfield, Richard, Hird, Christopher, and Kelly, Sharon: *Murdoch: The Great Escape* 456
Belgrano, sinking of the 419, 420
Bell, Martin 144, 524–5

Bell, Steve 506
Bello, Waldon 78
Belloc, Hilaire: *The Modern Traveller* 118
Belo, Bishop Carlos 143–4, 264, 279, 304, 305–12
Bendana, Alejandro 29
Benetton: Formula One racing company 511
Benn, Anthony Wedgwood 98, 408, 449
Bennett, Ronan 514, 519
Bennis, Phyllis 56
    Calling the Shots 40
Beresford, David 603
Berridge, Geoff 600
Bevan, Aneurin 98
Bevin, Ernest 138, 342
Bevins, Anthony 508
Beyrer, Dr Chris 180
BHP *see* Broken Hill Proprietary Company
Biafra 139, 407
Biffen, John 125, 455
Biko, Steve 5
Bilderberg Group 95
Billiness, Simon 166
Birmingham Barbed Tape company 116–17
Birt, John 487, 516
Biwater Corporation 606
Black, Clementia 394
Black, Conrad 470
Black, Ian 497
Blainey, Geoffrey 238
Blair, Cherie (*née* Booth) 85, 138, 437, 468, 509
Blair, Tony/Blair Government:
    appointments 85–8, 95–8
    and arms industry 95, 133, 135–6, 138, 140–50
    and asylum seekers 36
    belief in 'globalisation' 61
    and Criminal Justice Bill 136
    and death of Princess Diana 523
    and Ecclestone and Formula One 511–12
    economic policies 3, 61, 77–8, 81, 86–7, 88–9, 504–5, 509–10
    and education 11–12, 89–91
    election victory 11, 85, 504
    influenced by Clinton/USA 3, 88, 89, 94–5
    Irish 'apology' 366–7
    and the media 5, 84, 85, 437, 468, 504–6, 507–8, 509, 510–11, 537
    and the *Mirror* 436, 437
    and Rupert Murdoch 81, 85, 436, 468–70
    and 'New Britain' 522
    social and welfare policies 6, 63–4, 78–85, 87–8, 89, 93, 94
    and Margaret Thatcher 80, 82, 133, 469, 509
    and unions 346, 352, 354
Blake, Lord 413
Blake, John 549
Bland, Sir Christopher 485
Blum, Jack 31
Blum, William: *The CIA* 499
Blunkett, David 90, 91
BMARC 170
Bocquet, Kevin 354
Bolivia 27, 31
Bolton, Roger 457

Bond, Alan 229
Bonham-Carter, Helena 185
Booth, Cherie *see* Blair,
    Cherie
Bosnia 34, 40, 116, 302
Bottomley, Virginia 529
Boutros-Ghali, Boutros 310
Bowen, Jeremy 47, 50
Bowman, David 481–2, 483,
    543, 544
    The Captive Press 484
BP *see* British Petroleum
Brabazon of Tara, Lord 136
Bradley, Bernard 346
Bradshaw, Brendan 366
Brazil 63, 74, 330
Brecht, Bertolt: *The Solution*
    8
Bretton Woods conference
    (1944) 62
Brewer, Pat 92
Bridgewater, Carl 418
Briggs, Geraldine 246
British Aerospace 123, 124,
    125, 132
    Hawk aircraft 94, 115,
        119, 120, 121, 135, 137,
        140–1, 142, 144, 148,
        292, 507
    Heckler and Koch
        automatic weapons 119,
        147, 267
    v. 'Ploughshares
        Movement' 313–22
British Airways 158–9, 217
British-American Project for
    the Successor Generation
    (BAP) 96–7, 497
British-American Security
    Information Council 147
British Broadcasting

Corporation *see* BBC
British Digital Broadcasting
    476
British Guiana 25
British Home Stores 217
British Petroleum (BP) 86, 93
*British Social Attitudes
    Survey* 11, 504
Brittan, Samuel 11
Britton, Tony 460–1
Broken Hill Proprietary
    Company (BHP) 233–4,
    258, 272
Brookes, Michael 418
Brown, Cedric 439
Brown, Gordon 81, 88–9, 95,
    103, 438, 475, 504, 505,
    509–10
Brown, Roger *see* Mason,
    Linda
Brown, Tina 480
Brown, William 176–7
Brunei 74
BSkyB (TV) 476, 532
Budge, Richard 433
Budiardjo, Carmel 306, 320
Buerk, Michael 322
Bulger, James 334, 477
Burchett, Wilfred 491
Burger King 69, 86
Burma:
    AIDS 181
    army 156, 157, 159, 193,
        199
    ASEAN membership 178,
        213
    and Australia 178–81, 182,
        206
    British arms deals 170–1
    and British rule 191–2
    Buddhism 155, 157, 162,

191, 193, 196, 206, 212, 214
drugs trade 6, 178, 180–2, 219
ethnic minorities 188, 189, 191–2, 194, 196, 220
foreign trade 156, 160, 166–70, 171–2, 175–6, 177–8, 214, 216–17, 219
gas pipeline 166–7, 170, 177
labour camps 158
Mandalay 159, 160, 183, 186, 191, 196
MI14 174–5
National League for Democracy (NLD) 159, 179, 201, 202, 215, 219
under Ne Win 193–5, 213
oil companies 166–8, 177, 216
Pagan 155–6
railway construction 160–1, 164–6, 168, 172, 187
Rangoon 156–7, 158–9, 190–1, 193, 194, 214, 219
and sanctions 203, 207, 216–17
and Second World War 159–60, 192–3
SLORC 160, 170, 199
Tavoy 160, 162–3
tourism 156, 158, 160, 169, 172, 182–8, 189, 207, 214–15, 217–18, 219
uprising (1988) 190–1, 195–9
women 212
World Bank report 215–16

see also Aung San Suu Kyi
Burns, Nicholas 42
Burton Group 217
Burwell, Dolly 537
Bush, George 6, 7
and Gulf War 20, 32, 44, 49, 51, 55, 501
'humanitarian intervention' in Somalia 43
and invasion of Panama 29, 32
BusinessMap 602
Butler, Billy 447–8
Butler, Eric 463–4
Byrne, Gabriel 364

Caal, Dano 364
Cable News Network (CNN) 476, 529, 532
Cadagat, Edgar 545
Caetano, Marcelo 294
Callaghan Government 140, 402, 417
Callejas, Manuel 27
Calley, Lieutenant William 556
Cambodia:
American bombing 23, 32–3
and China 260–1, 568, 569
Evans's 'UN plan' (1989) 260–1
Hun Sen's 'coup' (1997) 42
Mirror coverage of 417
UN 'peace operation' (1992) 42–3
Western support for Khmer Rouge 33–4, 136
see also Pol Pot
Cameron, James 563
Campaign Against the Arms

Trade 115
Campaign for Nuclear
 Disarmament 458
Campbell, Alistair 468, 509
Campbell, Irene 345
Campbell, Jimmy 338, 342,
 345
Canberra Times 236, 243,
 264
Cantona, Eric 59, 60
Cape Times 603
Capone, Al (quoted) 19
Carden, Mike 343, 349, 350
Carey, Alex: *Taking the Risk
 Out of Democracy* 539
Carey, Peter 267
Cargill Corporation 72
Caribbean Publishing and
 Broadcasting Association
 69
Carlsberg 217
Carlton (television company)
 476, 529
Carrington, Lord 125, 498
Carter, Sergeant Herbert 556
Carter, Jimmy, US President
 302*n*, 305, 568
Carter, William 542
Casey, John 39–40
Casey, William 96
Cassandra (William Connor)
 377, 382, 385, 386, 388,
 403, 404
CAST 351
Castro, Fidel 32
Central Television:
 Charlotte Street
  documentaries unit 526–9
 Cook Report 430, 494
Chalker, Linda 122
Chamberlain, Neville 383,

384, 386, 387
Channel 4 television 479, 493
Channel 5 television 532
Channon, Paul 125
*Chant of Jimmy Blacksmith,
 The* (film) 245
Charles, Prince 119, 392, 450
Chiba, Fumiko 177–8
Child Poverty Action Group
 (CPAG) 105, 110
children:
 Aboriginal 231, 240–4
 in Britain 104, 110–11
 as Burmese slave labour
  164, 187
 as cheap labour for Western
  companies 59–61, 65
 and consumerism 68–9
 in Iraq 2, 53–4, 55
 and poverty 3, 72, 104,
  110–11, 367
 in South Africa 599–600
Chile 23, 25, 62–4, 80, 123,
 124, 330, 419
China:
 and BBC 533
 and Burma 170, 176
 and Cambodia 260–1, 568
 and East Timor 301
 and Hong Kong 72
 invasion of Vietnam 568–9
 and Maxwell 426
 and Murdoch 530–1
 toy factories 60
 on UN Security Council
  123, 134
Chippendale, Peter, and
 Horrie, Chris: *Stick It Up
 Your Punter* 419–20,
 446, 452–3
Chiquita Brands (banana

multinational) 75–6

Chomsky, Noam 11, 37, 72, 539, 541

Chossudovsky, Michel 41, 573, 575

Christiansen, Michael 372–3

Churchill, Winston 384, 385, 386, 387, 389, 390, 391, 392

CIA (Central Intelligence Agency):
  and Afghanistan 498
  BBC series on 499, 502
  in British Guiana 25
  Britons in pay of 496
  and Burma 187
  and Cambodia 33, 34
  in Chile 63
  and Contras 26–7, 31, 499
  and drugs trade 6, 30–1
  in Haiti 66
  and the media 496–7, 499
  and General Noriega 32
  report on East Timor invasion 257
  report on Iraqi sanctions 44–5
  in Vietnam 62, 592

Clairmont, Frederic F.: *The Rise and Fall of Economic Liberalism* 62

Clarendon, Lord 366

Clark, Alan 121, 124, 125, 322

Clark, David 149–50

Clark, Manning 246

Clark, Ramsey 49, 51, 53, 54–5

Clark, Reg 224

Clark Commission 49, 53

Clarke, Kenneth 88, 438, 575

Clarke, Renfrey 330–1

class:
  in Britain 11–12, 80, 82, 91, 399, 403
  in USA 70

Clifford, Max 540

Cline, Dr Ray 34

Clinton, Bill, US President:
  attack on Iraq (1996) 19, 57
  and Burmese regime 176–7
  and Etzioni 83
  and Indonesian dictatorship 265, 272, 278, 302n
  influence on Blair 3, 84, 88, 89, 98
  and invasion of Haiti 66–7
  nuclear arms programme 7–8
  and ruination of Grenada 75–6
  social and economic policies 3, 12–13, 70, 71, 84, 87, 89, 239, 505
  and Vietnam 570
  'war on drugs' 71

Clwyd, Ann 143

CNN *see* Cable News Network

coal strike (1984–5) *see* miners' strike

Coalition for Corporate Withdrawal from Burma 166

Coca-Cola company 69, 72–3, 607

Cockburn, Andrew 56–7

Cockburn, Claude 544

Cockburn, Leslie 56–7

Cockcroft, David 353

Coe, Jonathan: *What a*

Carve Up! 218
Coe, Paul 246
Cohen, Mike 175
Cold War 23, 28–9, 330, 495, 496, 501, 502, 512–13
Cole, Chris 315
Colombia 27, 30, 74, 86, 489
Columbia Journalism Review 46
Connolly, James 367
Connolly, Pat 377
Connolly, Patrick 234
Connor, Bob ('Son of Cassandra') 410
Connor, William *see* Cassandra
Contras, the 26, 31, 499
Cook, Robin: and arms deals 6–7, 94, 138, 140–2, 143–6, 148, 152, 506–7
Cook Report 430, 433, 494
Cooley, Michael 151–2
Corbyn, Jeremy 123
Cornwall, Rupert 506
Correspondent (newspaper) 466
Corrigan, Dr Dominic 363
Costa Lopes, Martinho da 306, 307
Council for Aboriginal Reconciliation 245
County Securities Australia 229
Courtauld's 86–7
Covert Action Quarterly 52
Cowell, Adrian 527
  Decade of Destruction (TV documentary) 528
Cowley, John 381, 383
Cox, David 603

Cox, Sir Geoffrey 485
Crapp, Lorraine 226
Creasey, Richard 527–8
Croatia 116
Cronau, Peter 273
Cu Chi, Vietnam 549–50, 554
Cuckney, Sir John 128
Cudlipp, Hugh 381–5, 388, 393, 399–400, 406, 484
  antagonises Churchill 387
  and Cecil King 382, 400, 409
  on 'Jane' 388
  on post-war election 390, 391
  and Marjorie Proops 393
  and the *Sun* 410–11, 415
Culligan, Michael 588
Cummings, Joe: *Lonely Planet* guide 218
Cummings, Sam 150–1
Cunningham, Gary 274, 275
Curtis, Anthony 254
Curtis, Mark 489, 500
  Ambiguities of Power 22, 55

Daewoo (multinational corporation) 585
Daily Express 44, 390, 391, 433, 491, 493
  cricket XI 372
Daily Herald 411
Daily Mail 84, 391, 440, 467, 519
Daily Mirror see Mirror
Daily Star 44
Daily Telegraph 21, 37, 467, 512

Daily Worker 387
Dale, Derek 373
Daley, William 607
Damazer, Mark 478
Dang Van Quang,
    Lieutenant-General 551
Darling, Alastair 475
Davidson, Basil 405, 437
Davidson, Kenneth 237
Davies, Jimmy 356
Davies, Liz 93
Dawson, Geoffrey 272,
    383–4
Day, David: *Claiming a
    Continent* 245
Day, Sir Robin 485
Deakin, Bishop Hilton 310
Dean, Brenda 460, 461, 462,
    463
*Death of a Nation: The
    Timor Conspiracy* (Pilger
    documentary) 161, 262,
    308, 314, 528
Death on the Rock (TV
    documentary) 456–8, 486
De Faux, Simon 270
Defert, Gabriel: *East Timor*
    284
de la Billière, General Sir
    Peter 487
DeMatteis, Alfonso L. 570–2
democracy and New
    Democracy 67, 80
Demos 83, 522, 541
Deng Xiaoping 426, 530–1,
    568
Depleted Uranium (DU) 56
Desmond, Cosmas: *The
    Discarded People* 599,
    600
Devitt, John 226

Diana, Princess: death 5,
    522–4
Diego Garcia (island) 19–22,
    26
Dili massacre *see* East Timor
Dimbaza, Eastern Cape,
    South Africa 598–601,
    604, 608
Dimbleby, David 45
Discovery Channel 533
Disney (Walt) Company 66,
    69, 529, 532
Dita Sari 326
Dodson, Mick 246
Dodson, Pat 246
Doherty, Faith 180–1
Dollar, David 572, 577
Donaldson, Robert T. 240
Donoghue, Lord 86
Donovan, Jim 348–9, 351
Donovan, Paul 514, 516
Dooley, Pat 338
Dors, Diana 393
dos Anjos, Celestino 251–3
dos Anjos, Virgilio 252–3
Downer, Alexander 180–1,
    278, 279
Dragon Oil 178
drugs trade:
    and Burma 6, 178, 180–2,
    219
    Robin Cook's 'war' on 6
    US 'war' on 30–1, 71
Dubai arms fair 119
Dubbins, Tony 461, 462
Dunblane massacre: and
    handgun ban 146–7
Dunhill tobacco company
    566
Dunn, James 258, 275–6, 277
Dunn, James (pensioner) 377

Duvalier, 'Papa' Doc 65, 66
Dyer, Clare 322

Eagleton, Terry: *Heathcliff and the Great Hunger* 362
East, Roger 274, 275, 277, 285, 289
East Timor:
  Australian betrayal of 251–9, 260, 261–80, 285, 292–3, 364–5
  author's film (*Death of a Nation*) 161, 262, 308, 314, 528
  and use of British arms 7, 94, 119–20, 123, 137, 140–4, 267, 292, 311–12; *see also* British Aerospace v. 'Ploughshares Movement'
  and China 301
  continuing struggle 14, 134, 323, 327–8
  death of TV crews (Balibo, 1975) 273–7, 285, 332–3
  Dili massacre (Santa Cruz cemetery, 1991) 260, 261–4, 267–8, 271, 272, 273, 308, 314, 317
  Fretilin (resistance movement) 253, 258, 259, 275, 286, 297, 300
  Indonesian invasion (1975) 252–3, 255, 257, 283–5, 288–9
  Kraras massacre (1983) 252–3
  and Portugal 252, 279, 286, 288, 294, 299–300, 303
  in Second World War 250–1, 268
  Uatu-Lan massacre 289
  and US arms sales 23, 123, 264–5, 301–2, 302n
  Viqueque massacre 306
  see also Belo, Bishop Carlos; Gusmao, Xanana; Ramos-Horta, José
Ecclestone, Bernie 511
Economist, The 363, 391, 433
Ecuador: British arms sales 122
Edelman, Maurice: *The Mirror* 378
Eden, Sir Anthony 392
education (in Britain) 11–12, 89–91, 93
Edward VII: lying in state 380
Edward VIII: Abdication 382–3, 400
Eisenhower, Dwight D. 71, 73, 560–1
Eisner, Michael 532
El Salvador 27–8, 458
Eliot, T. S. 410
Elkin, A. P. 241
'Emily's List' 92–3
Engel, Matthew: *Tickle the Public* 481
English, Sir David 467
environmentalism 539–40
Eritrea 14
Eslar, Gavin 522–3
Etzioni, Amitai 82–3
Eurofighter, the 149, 507
Europe, media coverage of 520–1
European Monetary Union 520

Evans, Gareth 259–60
  and the Burmese
    dictatorship 178, 189
  and Cambodia 260–1
  supports Indonesian regime
    258, 260, 261–4, 266,
    268–9, 292–3

Fairclough, Alan 437
Falantil 284
Falk, Richard 22, 37
Falklands War 21, 125, 512
  media coverage 47, 418–21,
    449, 453, 481, 488,
    492–3
Falt, Eric 42
Familathe, Ray 353
Far Eastern Economic Review
  194
Farnborough Air Show/arms
  fairs 115–17, 124, 147
Farrar-Hockley, Sir Anthony
  487
Fatchett, Derek 176
Faulkner, Alderman C. C.
  225–6
Feather, Vic 343
feminism/feminists 91–4, 394,
  535–7
Fesl, Eve 246
Field, Frank 63–4, 87–8, 367
Field, Xenia 373
Financial Times 11, 21, 131,
  176, 323, 477, 510, 532
Finnerty, Louise Hoppe 217
Fischer, Tim 179–80, 206,
  278
Fisk, Robert 514, 535
Fitzgerald, Father Arthur 320,
  321
Foley, Gary 246

Follett, Barbara: 'Emily's List'
  92–3
Foot, Michael 459
Foot, Paul 417–19, 423, 424,
  436
Foreign Office, British 23,
  136–7
  and arms to Iraq 125–30
  complaints of US
    imperialism 26
  on East Timor 309
  Information Research
    Department 495–6
  and Malaya 24
  and Mauritius 20
  silence about Balibo
    murders 275
Foreman, Carl 393
Formula One racing: and
  sponsorship 511–12
Forrest, Emma 510
Foster, Christopher 321
Fox, Neil 358
Fox, Sonny 479
Fox TV network, USA 451,
  479, 529
France 123, 331–2
  media laws 467–8
  truckers' strike 520–1
Frankland, Mark 560
Franklin, Bob 480
  Newszak and News Media
    477, 479, 534
Fraser, Dawn 226
Fraser, Malcolm 257, 258,
  481
Freedman, Lawrence 501
  and Karsh, Efraim: *The*
    Gulf Conflict, 1990–1
    501
Freney, Denis 273

Fretilin 253, 258, 259, 275, 286, 297, 300
Freedland, Jonathan 522
Friedman, Milton 64
Fritz Werner (German firm) 177
Fry, Ken and Audrey 303–4
Furedi, Frank: *New Ideology of Imperialism* 35, 38, 39
Furlong, Trevor 341, 350, 357
Futrell, Denis 373
Fyfe, Hamilton 380

Gaddafi, Colonel Muammar al 32
Galeano, Eduardo 14, 323
Gall, Sandy: *News from the Front* 498–9
Gallagher, Thomas: *Paddy's Lament, Ireland 1846–1847* 362
Galtieri, General 27
Garcia, Domingo 28
Gelbard, Robert 182
Gellhorn, Martha 406, 608
The Face of War 593
George, Bruce 322
Germany 468, 520
Gestrin, Phyllis 34
Gibbs, (Sir) Philip 336, 491, 492
Gilbert, Kevin 246–8
Because a White Man'll Never Do It 247
Breath of Life 247
The Cherry Pickers 247–8
Living Black 247
'Memorials' 248
Gilchrist, Sir Andrew 139
Gill, Adrian 459

Glasgow Media Group 493
Glencross, David 485
'globalisation' 4, 61
Godwin, Peter 171–2
Goktepe, Metin 545
'Golden Triangle', the 180
Goldsmith, Sir James 96
Gomes, Amandio Da Costa 280
Gormley, Joe 343
Gott, Richard 494–5
Gowan, Peter 67
Granada Television 354–5, 476, 529
Grand Metropolitan 86
Gray, John 9
Green Berets, The (film) 561–2
Greene, Sir Hugh 514
Greenham Common, Berkshire 513
Greenslade, Roy 431, 432, 452–4
Maxwell's Fall 432
Greenwell, George: photograph of St Paul's 388
Gregory, Martyn 142, 143
Grenada 47, 75, 76
Grigsby, Michael: *Living on the Edge* (TV film) 528
Guardian 6, 43, 45, 83, 110, 115, 358, 382, 476, 480, 544
Aitken libel action against 131
on Blair and New Labour 504, 505, 507, 509, 510, 511
on British Aerospace v. 'Ploughshares' 322

on CIA payment of British
  journalists 496
on death of Princess Diana
  522
on French truckers 521
Martha Gellhorn in 406
and 'Gott affair' 494–5
on Iraq 45, 125
Kissinger in 43
on NATO 497
on Russia 522
on Scargill and miners'
  strike 432, 433, 493
reviews *Some Mother's Son*
  519
Guatemala 27, 63, 120, 330
Guerin, Veronica 545
Gulf War (1991) 2, 20,
  29–30, 32, 40, 44–54, 55,
  56, 58, 185, 488, 501
Gumbley, Christopher 128
Gusmao, Emilia 290, 294
Gusmao, Kay Rala Xanana
  259, 284, 286–95, 303
'Generations' 291–2
Gusmao, Nito 290, 294
Gusmao, Zeni 290

Habibie, B. J. 265
Hackney, London 109–10
Hague, Sir Douglas 83
Haig, Al 19
Hailey, Lord 23
Haines, Joe 423, 435
Haiti 65–7, 500
Halabja: gassing of Kurds
  125–6, 127, 133
Hale, David 610
Halifax, Lord 386
Hall, Edward Smith 543, 544
Hall, Rodney 237

Hamill, Pete 440
Hamilton, Adrian 29
handguns, ban on 146–7
Hani, Chris 608
Hanley, Jeremy 175
Hanoi, Vietnam 553, 564–6,
  569–72, 575, 580, 585,
  587, 593
Hanson (conglomerate)
  131–2
Hanson, Pauline 233, 234,
  235, 239
Harding, Dr Richard 80
Hardy, Jeremy 522
Hare, David: *Pravda* 454
Harman, Harriet 85, 94, 508
Hartree, Michelle 526, 527
Harvey, Brian 438
Hassell, Keith 316
Hattersley, Roy 85
Hawk aircraft *see* British
  Aerospace
Hawke, Bob 92, 179, 206,
  228, 229, 258, 471, 472,
  473
Hayden, Bill 258, 472
Healey, Denis 139
Hearst, David 522
Heath, Edward 413, 492
Heathfield, Peter 428–9, 430
Heffer, Eric 428
Heineken 217
Henderson, Colonel 556–7
Henderson, Gerard 541–2
Herald and Weekly Times
  (group) 471, 472
Herd, Les 398
Heritage Foundation 96, 97,
  541
Hersh, Seymour 559
Heseltine, Michael 522

Hewett, Tony 246
Hewitt, Patricia 93
  About Time 93
Heyman, Jack 352
Hickey, Michael 418
Higson, Mark 126–8, 137, 141, 513
Hillingdon hospital cleaners 89
Hills, Captain Brian 184–5
Hillsborough disaster 334, 445–8
Hird, Christopher: *Breaking the Mirror* 466, 474–5
  see also Belfield, Richard
Hiroshima: atomic bomb 491
Hitler, Adolf 330, 383, 384, 385, 386, 484
Ho Chi Minh 553, 560–1, 564, 586–7
Hogan, John 254
Holbrooke, Richard 33, 568, 569
Holland, Steven 226
Holley, Tim 439
Hollick, Lord 86
Holmes, Richard: *Firing Line* 562
Honduras 75
Hong Kong 72, 328, 437, 530
Hongai, Vietnam 117–18, 567–8
Horrie, Chris *see* Chippendale, Peter
Horta, Francisco 299
Horta, Natalina 296–7, 298, 304
Hounman, Peter 438
Howard, John, Australian Prime Minister:

and the 'American Way' 77
anti-Aborigine policies 232, 234–5, 237–8, 239–40, 242, 245, 246
anti-immigration policy 232–3
and Indonesia 277, 278
and Murdoch 473
Howard, Lee 407, 410, 411
Howard, Michael 135
Howarth, Mary 379–80
Howe, (Lord) Geoffrey 26, 126, 500
Howe, Stephen 365–6
Howitt, Richard 86
Hoyt, Harold 69
Hugenberg, Alfred 483
Hughes, Peter 185
Human Rights Watch 186
Hume, John 517
Hun Sen Government 42
Hunting Engineering company, Bedford 115–16
Huntington, Samuel: *The Clash of Civilisations* 35–6
Hurd, Douglas 23, 40, 44, 119, 121, 125, 136, 148
Hussein, Saddam 2, 32, 36, 44, 45, 50, 51, 54–5, 56
  British arms sales to 32, 125–6, 169
Huxley, Aldous: *Brave New World* 9
Hytton, Thomas 542

Iley, Chrissy 459
Ilois people 20–2
IMF *see* International Monetary Fund

Independent 79, 93, 111, 169–70, 433, 466, 467, 475, 504, 505–6, 507, 508, 509, 510, 517

Independent on Sunday 48, 85, 512

Independent Television (ITV) 86, 414, 456, 457, 458, 476, 479, 529

Independent Television Commission (ITC) 476

Independent Television News (ITN) 46, 57, 477, 479, 492, 493, 500, 515–16, 532

Index Bookshop 527

India 59–60, 120
  Self-Employed Women's Association, Ahmedabad 536

Indonesia (*see also* East Timor) 324–5
  and Australia 254–6, 258, 264–6, 267–9, 272–3, 275, 278–9
  British arms deals 121, 122, 134, 136, 139–40, 146, 147, 148
  GOLKAR 169, 327
  treatment of journalists 137–8
  Kopassus 119–20, 147, 266–7, 271
  media coverage 270, 488, 507
  PDI (Indonesian Democratic Party) 326
  PRD (People's Democratic Party) 327
  uprisings and strikes 323–4, 325–6

  and US policies 278–9, 302n, 503

International Labour Organisation (ILO) 348

International Military Services 127, 128

International Monetary Fund (IMF) 12, 62, 63
  and Burmese regime 168, 207, 216
  and Chile 64
  and the Philippines 3
  and South Korea 13, 329
  praises Gordon Brown 88
  in South Africa 600
  and Vietnam 570, 573

International Publishing Corporation (IPC) 411

International Transport Federation (ITF) 351–2, 353

Internet 68, 532

IRA, media coverage of 514–19
  see also Death on the Rock

Iran 25, 32, 63, 120, 170

Iraq 34, 53–5, 120
  sanctions against 2–3, 54–5, 56, 57
  US attack on (1996) 19, 57
  see also Gulf War; Hussein, Saddam

Ireland:
  Famine Walk 361–2, 364, 366
  Irish Famine ('Great Hunger') 361–7
  see also Northern Ireland

Irian Jaya *see* Papua, West

Irish Times 365, 366, 517

Isaacs, Sir Jeremy 485

Isaacs, Tony 460–1
Islam (Muslims) 32, 34–5, 36, 45, 51, 309
Israel 37–8, 57
ITN *see* Independent Television News
ITV *see* Independent Television

Jackson, Jesse 98
Jackson, Judy: *In Search of the Assassin* (TV documentary) 528
Jacobson, Sydney 410
Jagger, Bianca 509
'Jaipur limbs' 593
James, Gerald 127–8, 170
James, Dr John 104
James, Pat 167–8, 169
James, Roger 528
Jarratt, Sir Alex 422–3
Jay, Peter 433–4
Jefferson, Thomas 67
Jennings, Richard 384–5, 386, 387, 437
John Paul II, Pope 271, 524
John, Elton 448
Johnson, Joel 7
Johnson, Lyndon B. 406, 561
Johnson, Dr Samuel 403
Jones, Cyril 276
journalists 486–7, 535–8, 544–6
   and CIA 496–7, 499
   and IRD 495–6
   'pool' reporting system 47–8
   Third World 76
Jowell, Tessa 511
Juddery, Bruce 273
Juppé, Alain 520

Kachin, the (Burma) 189, 192
Kantor, Mickey 75
Karen, the (Burma) 165, 187, 191, 192, 220
Karlin, Marc: *The Serpent* 4–5
Karsh, Efraim *see* Freedman, Lawrence
Katz, Ian 519
Keane, Fergal 490
Keane, John 538
Keating, Paul:
   and APEC 76
   and Blair 92, 470
   defeat (1996) 232
   effects of social policies 229–30
   Indonesian policies 258, 262, 264–6, 268–9, 278, 279, 292–3, 365
   and Rupert Murdoch 470, 471, 472, 473, 474, 483
   and Native Title legislation 235
   on Second World War 249
Keith, Max 73
Kelly, Paul 272
Kelly, Sharon *see* Belfield, Richard
Kelman, James 354, 355
Kendal, Felicity 480
Keneally, Paddy 250–1, 253
Kennan, George F. 35, 59, 502
Kennedy, Jane *see* Lavalette, Michael
Kennedy, John F. 68, 404, 496, 506, 560
Kennedy, John F., Jr 509
Kennedy, Ludovic 514
Kennedy scholarships 95

Kenya 24–5, 495
Kenyatta, Jomo 25
Kerr, Sir John 481, 497
Kerry, Senator John 31
Kettle, Martin 506
Khin Nyunt, General 169, 179, 203, 213–14
Khin Zaw Win 213
Khin, Yuzana 199
Khmer Rouge 32, 33–4, 42, 136, 176, 260, 261, 553, 568, 569
Khomeini, Ayatollah 125, 126, 524
Khun Sa 180
Kieman, V. G. 25
Kiernan, Thomas 451–2, 455, 479
    Citizen Murdoch 451
Kim Young Sam 328
Kinealy, Christine: The Great Calamity 365
King, Cecil Harmsworth 373, 381, 382, 385, 386, 389, 400, 402, 407–9, 411
King, Tom 130, 427, 428
Kinnock, Neil 82, 93
Kipling, Rudyard: Mandalay 191
Kissinger, Henry 22, 23, 32–3, 36, 43, 62–3, 302n, 459
Kitson, Frank: Low Intensity Operations 517–18
Knight, Chris 352
Ko Htun Oo 197
Kolko, Gabriel: Anatomy of a War 552, 573, 582, 583
    Vietnam: Anatomy of a Peace 573
Konrads, Ilsa 226

Konrads, John 226
Korea 12–13, 72, 75, 141, 328–9, 492
Korten, David 8
Kovic, Ron 590
Kraras massacre, East Timor 252–3
Kronlid, Lotta 313–22
Krupp, Alfred 118
Kulud, Abu 46–7
Kundera, Milan: The Book of Laughter and Forgetting 159, 323
Kurds 23, 45, 50, 51, 52, 54, 57, 120
    Halabja gassing 125–6, 127, 133
Kuwait 32, 54, 55
Kyi Maung, U 215

Labour Government, British see Blair, Tony
Lamb, Larry 413, 415, 416, 419
land-mines 116, 505
Lane, Max 277, 324
Langdon, Julia 426
Lange, David 302, 303
Langford, Stephen 277
Langton, Marcia 246
Lankester, Sir Tim 121
Last Dream, The (TV series) 241, 528
Lavalette, Michael, and Kennedy, Jane: Solidarity on the Waterfront 338
Lawson, Nigel 110
Laxton, Tim 128–9
Le, Nhu T. 10
Leapman, Michael 456
Leatherbarrow, Eric 338,

339, 341, 342, 344
Lebanon, Israeli invasion of 37
Lebow, Victor 68
Lee Kuan Yew 77, 178
Lehrer, Tom 459
Lenin, V. I. 228
Lennock, Jean 53
Le Pen, Jean-Marie 331–2
Levi, Primo 246, 544
Levi-Strauss company 217
Li Ka-Shing 132
'liberal containment' 62, 63, 82
Liddle, Roger see Mandelson, Peter
Liechty, Philip 285
Lightman, Gavin 430
Lilburne, John 542–3
Lindner, Carl 76
Ling Ming-xian 178
Lintner, Bertil: Outrage 191, 194, 196, 198–9
Literary Review 454
L!ve TV 435–6, 439, 477, 533
Liverpool dockers 3, 13, 89, 334–58, 521
Liverpool Echo 340, 345
Lloyd George, David 491
Lloyd's List (newspaper) 341, 346
Lo Hsing-han 178
Loach, Ken: Hidden Agenda 519
   Questions of Leadership (TV documentary series) 343–4, 528
Long, Douglas 425
Los Angeles Times 65, 352
Lowery, Alan (and Pilger):

The Last Dream (TV documentary) 241, 528
Lu Zaw 173
Lucas Aerospace 151
Lucie, Doug: The Shallow End 476–7
Lusane, Clarence 30–1
Lusardi, Linda 426
Luu Van Hoat, Dr 568
Luyken, Reiner 452, 483–4

Maastricht Treaty 331, 520
'Mabo decision' 234–5, 236
Mac Thi Nhan 588
McCain, John 213–14
McCann, Eamonn 514
McCartney, Ian 357
McCoy, Alfred: The Politics of Heroin 30
McDonald, Ian 512
MacDonald, Peter: Giap 584
McDonald, Trevor 57
McDonald's 69
McGehee, Ralph 592
McGuinness, Martin 518
Macintyre, Donald 507
McKay, Ian 420
McKay, Marcia 420
MacKenzie, Kelvin 419–20
   coverage of Falklands War 420, 449, 453, 481
   and Roy Greenslade 452, 453
   reporting of Hillsborough disaster 445–6, 448
   and L!ve TV 436, 477–8
   and Mirror Group 439, 440
   and Murdoch 416, 419, 420, 435, 446, 448, 449
   and Wapping strike 453, 459

Mackie, J. A. C. 255
McKinley, Michael 260
McLachlan, Hugh 237–8
McLaughlin, Greg see Philo, Greg
McLuhan, Marshall 534, 544
MacMichael, David 26
Macmillan, Harold 38
MacNally, Charlie 337, 349
MacNally, Doreen 336–7, 349, 350
McNamara, Robert 82, 563
McNaughton, Andrew 277
Macphee, Ian 472, 473
Macpherson, Hugh 91
McUmiskey, Jimmy 358
Madeley, John: Diego Garcia 20, 21
Madison, James, US President 67
Magginnis, John 342
Mahathir bia Mohamed 78
MAI see Multilateral Agreement on Investment
Major, John 51, 84, 85, 129, 354, 518, 530
Malaya/Malaysia 23–4, 76, 78, 121, 122, 495
    see also Singapore
Malik, Adam 140
Malone, John 529–30, 533
Maloney, Mike 424
    Flash! Splash! Crash! . . . 425
Manchester Guardian 491
Mandalay, Burma 159, 160, 183, 186, 191, 196
Mandela, Nelson 175, 203, 510, 601, 604, 605, 606, 607, 609
Mandelson, Peter 6, 81, 82, 96, 437, 470
    (with Roger Liddle) The Blair Revolution 81
Manhattan Institute for Policy Research 96
Mann, Delbert 562
Manuel, Trevor 607
Maralinga, Australia 234
Marlboro tobacco company 566
Márquez, Gabriel García 30
Marqusee, Mike 5–6
Marr, Andrew 467
Marr, David 246
Marsh, Richard 343
Martin, Graham 551–3
Mason, Linda, and Brown, Roger: Rice, Rivalry and Politics 33, 569
Mason, Roy 141
Mates, Michael 518
Mathews, Bruce 461
Matrix Churchill affair 127, 141
Mau Mau, the 24–5, 495
Maung (Burmese student) 198
Mauritius 19–20
Maxim, Sir Hiram: machine-gun 118
Maxwell, Ghislaine 428
Maxwell, Ian 423
Maxwell, Robert 86, 378, 412, 421, 423–30, 432, 433–5
Mayman, Jan 243, 245
Mbah, George 15
Mbalala, Stanley 598, 599, 600, 601
Mbeki, Thabo 603, 606, 607
Meaden, Bernadette: A

Farewell to the Arms Trade 321
media, the:
  power of 4, 6, 9, 543–4
  and technology 8, 9, 12, 532, 534–5
  see journalists; television
Medical Educational Trust 52–3
Medina, Captain 557
Medway Ports 340–1
Melbourne *Herald-Sun* 277
Mellor, David 125, 127, 438
Menges, Chris: *East 103rd Street* (TV documentary) 528
Menzies, John (company) 546
Menzies, Robert 234, 254
Mercedes-Benz 607
Mersey Docks and Harbour Company 337–42, 345–6, 350, 351, 356, 357, 358
Mexico 3, 39, 330
MI5 430, 431, 433, 494, 496, 516, 517
MI6 127, 495, 498, 499
Michael of Kent, Princess 185
Miles, Tony 403, 410
Miliband, David 95
Miller, Arthur 44
  The Price 5
Miller, David: *Don't Mention the War* 515, 516, 517
Miller, Robert C. 492
Mills, David 511
Milne, Seamus: *The Enemy Within* 431, 432, 433, 494
Mil-Tac (British arms company) 120

Milterton, Lord 23
Minchen, Nick 235
miners, Durham 397–8, 429–30
miners' strike (1984–5) 428–30, 458, 493–4
Minority Rights Group 20, 21
Mirren, Helen 519
Mirror (formerly *Daily Mirror*):
  and author 371–4, 375, 396–9, 401, 403–7, 425, 426, 427
  first 378–9
  history: 1903–45 378–91
    in the 1950s 391–3
    in the 1960s 375–8, 394–5, 399–403, 406–9
    in the 1970s 403, 416–17
    in the 1980s 418–23, *see also* MacKenzie, Kelvin
  'Jane' 388, 392
  under Maxwell 421–35
  on miners' strike and Scargill 428–33
  under David Montgomery and Piers Morgan 435–41, 535
  name change 440
  and *Sun* 395, 396, 412, 413, 414–16, 417, 440
Mitchell, Josephine 277
Mitton, Geraldine: *A Bachelor Girl in Burma* 156–7
Mobutu, Sese 489
Moi, Daniel arap 25
Molloy, Mike 375, 381, 398, 403, 414, 415

Molloy, Patrick 418
Monbiot, George 320
Monde diplomatique, Le 31
Monks, John 95, 347–8, 436
Montgomery, David 435–7, 437, 439, 533
Montserrat 94
Moonie, Dr Lewis 469
Moore, Richard 364
Moore, Suzanne 510
Moran, (Lord) Charles: *Winston Churchill* 392
Moreno, Colonel Anthony 51
Morgan, Alec: *Lousy Little Sixpence* 241
Morgan, Peter 332
Morgan, Piers 378, 435–6, 437, 438–9, 440
Morgan, Robin 457
Morland, Martin 194, 195–6
Morning Star 144
Morris, Bill 89, 346–7, 349, 356–7, 358
Morrison, Bill 258–9
Morrison, Herbert 387
Morton, Bobby 350–1, 353, 355
Moser, Brian: *Before Columbus* (TV documentary series) 528
Moulmein, Burma 196
Mountbatten, Lord 193, 408
Mowlam, Marjorie 96
Moynihan, Daniel Patrick 302*n*
Mulgan, Geoff 83
Connexity 83
Mullan, Don 362
Muller, Robert O. 589–93
Multilateral Agreement on Investment (MAI) 73–5

multinational corporations 65–6, 72–6
and unpaid taxes 84, 88
Munro, David 161–4, 203, 528
see also Death of a Nation
Murdani, General Benni 259, 273
Murdoch, Anna 85, 451–2, 468
Murdoch, Dame Elisabeth 451, 456
Murdoch, Elisabeth 470
Murdoch, Lachlan 470, 482–3
Murdoch, Rupert:
American citizenship 466
and Australian press 76, 229, 237, 270, 450, 470–3, 481–2, 483, 542
background 450–1
at BAP meeting 96
and Blair 81, 85, 468–70
and British media 1, 69, 412, 455, 456, 467, 484, *see also Sun; Sunday Times; Times*
and Chinese Communist Party 530–1
grooming of heir 470, 482–3
'Humanitarian of the Year' 459
Karlin's film 4
and Kelvin MacKenzie 416, 419, 420, 436, 446, 448, 449
private life and persona 451–2, 454, 465
tax evasion 84, 473–5

TV empire 1, 449, 451,
    466, 471, 472, 475–6,
    479, 529–31, 532–3
and 'Wapping revolution'
    434, 459–67, 481
and Harold Wilson 413
Murray, Andrew 347
Murray, Arthur 246
Murray, Charles 87
    The Bell Curve 87
    Losing Ground 96
Murray, Joe 366
Murray, John 464–5
Murray, Leila 246
Murray, Lord Len 343, 429
Murton, County Durham
    397–8, 429–30
Muslims 32, 34–5, 36, 45,
    51, 309
Myanmar see Burma
Myers, Kevin 365

Naing Oo 198
Nam Phann 34
Napoleon Bonaparte 445
Nasser, Gamal Abdel 524
Nation 518
National Dock Labour
    Scheme 339, 344
NATO (North Atlantic
    Treaty Organisation) 7,
    36, 40–1, 95, 96, 487,
    497, 505
Naw Angelene, Dr 182, 188
Nay Min 213
Ne Win 170, 193–5, 199,
    201–2, 213, 214
Neal, General Richard 51
Needham, Andrea 313–22
Needham, Richard 141, 142,
    171

Neely, Bill 500
Neil, Andrew 456, 457, 458,
    464, 469–70
    Full Disclosure 456
Neill, Sir Patrick 511–12
Nelson, Senator Gaylord 581
Neville, Richard 450
New Labour see Blair, Tony
New Light of Myanmar 173,
    174, 213, 214
New Statesman 140, 381,
    432, 503
New York Daily News 440
New Yorker 480, 529
New York Newsday 51, 52
New York Post 452
New York Times 12, 56, 96
New Zealand 14, 245, 302–3
News Corporation 85,
    468–70, 473, 474, 529
News Group Newspapers Ltd
    460–1
News International 460, 461,
    474
News of the World 412, 435,
    460, 468
News on Sunday 466
News Publishers 474
News Times Holdings 474
Newsweek magazine 37, 559
'newszak' 477
Newton, Tony 125, 126
NGOs (non-governmental
    organisations) 144–5
Nguyen Co Thach 568
Nguyen The Khan 565, 583
Nguyen Van Linh 570, 585
NHK International Inc.
    177–8
Nicaragua 26–7, 31, 330,
    499, 500–1

Nicholas, (Sir) David 515–16
Nichols, James Leander (Leo)
    174–5
Niemöller, Pastor 526
Nigeria 15, 120, 139, 546
Nike (shoe company) 69,
    584–5
Nippon Oil 167
Nixon, Richard 32–3, 551,
    559, 566, 568, 570, 590
Nobel Peace Prizes 175, 303,
    304, 306, 310, 459
Nolan, Jimmy 345
non-governmental
    organisations see NGOs
Noriega, General 32
Normanbrook, Lord 513–14
Norodom Ranariddh, Prince
    42
Northcliffe, Lord (Alfred
    Harmsworth) 378, 379,
    380, 391
Northern Ireland 495–6,
    514–19
Norton-Taylor, Richard 496
Nott, John 125
Nsadhu, Basoga 74
nuclear weapons:
    America and Britain 6,
        36–7, 96, 133–5, 149–50,
        496, 497, 507, 512–13
    and Blair 97–8, 133,
        149–50
    and Russia 8, 41, 513
    Third World threat 36
Nyerere, Julius 531

Oakley, Robin 485, 503
Oanh, Nguyen Thi, Dr 586
Oanh, Nguyen Xuan, Dr
    576–7

Obi, Ben Charles 15
Observer 29, 50, 111, 432,
    481, 496, 504, 505, 513,
    518, 538, 559–60
O'Callaghan, Sean 516–17
O'Connor, Kath 277
OECD 73
Ogoni people 120
oil industry:
    and Biafran war 407
    in Burma 166–8, 177, 178,
        216
    in Colombia 86
    and East Timor 256, 257,
        258, 272, 278
    Iranian 25
    and sanctions against Iraq
        2–3, 56
O'Kane, Maggie 535
Olin Foundation, USA 541
Oliver, Nick 142, 143
Olympic Games 69
Oman, Sultanate of 122
One False Move (film) 69
Orbach, Susie 510
Organisation for Economic
    Co-operation and
    Development see OECD
    73
Oriental Express brochure
    158
Oriental Express Group 183
Orwell, George 485, 522,
    525, 537–8
    Animal Farm 486
    Burmese Days 163, 192
    Nineteen Eighty-four xi
Osborne, Milton 269–70
O'Shane, Pat 246
Owen, David 96, 140
Oxfam 29, 567

Pa Pa Lay, U 173
Packer, Frank 373–4
Packer, Kerry 229, 237, 470, 471
Pagan, Burma 155–6, 183
Paine, Thomas 283
Pakistan 74, 120
Pakpahan, Muchtar 325
Palestine 34, 37–8, 597
Pan Ko, U 163
Panama, US invasion of 29, 32, 47, 501
Panjaitan, General Sintog 267–8
Papua, West 329
Papua New Guinea 12, 256
Parenti, Michael: *Inventing Reality* 4, 541
Parer, Damien: *Men of Timor* (film) 250
Paris arms fair 117, 123
Parish, Alf 466–7
Parkinson, Cecil 125
Parrish, John 562
Parry, Robert: *Fooling America* 11
Paxman, Jeremy 322, 507
Pearce, C. 226
Pearce, Edward 432
Pearl, Cyril: *Wild Men of Sydney* 373
Pearson, Noel 234, 235, 246
Peirce, Gareth 319
'Pensioners' parliament' 378
People's Daily: and Murdoch 530–1
Pepsi-Cola company 217, 438
Peres, Shimon 37
Perkins, Charlie 230, 246
Peters, Brian 274, 275
Peterson, Douglas 581

Petley, Julian 535
Petras, James 538–9
Pew, J. Howard 96
Pew Charitable Trusts 96
Pham Van Dong 566
Philippines, the 3, 39, 76, 185–6, 208, 329, 545
Philips electronics company 177–8, 485
Philo, Greg, and McLaughlin, Greg: *British Media and the Gulf War* 45
Pilger, Richard 335
Pinochet, General Augusto 63, 64–5, 123, 124
Pinwill, Bill 273
Plater, Diana 245
Platt, Jack 223
'Ploughshares Movement' 314–15
  action against British Aerospace Hawk 313–22
Podnik, Juris: *Hello, Can You Hear Us?* (TV documentary) 528
Pol Pot 32, 33–4, 42, 158, 169, 213, 261, 284, 515, 553, 568, 569
Polgar, Tom 552
Ponsonby, Arthur 491
Portugal: and East Timor 252, 279, 286, 288, 294, 299–300, 303, 307
poverty: in Britain 79–80, 82, 87–8, 91, 93, 99–111, 507, 508
Powell, Sir Charles 128
Powell, General Colin 55, 501–2
Powell, Jonathan 96, 97
Prabowo, Major-General 147

PRB 128
Premier Oil 167, 178
Prescott, John 437
press, the:
  freedom of 542–3
  see also journalists; and
    specific countries
Preston: Larches Estate 84
Price, Morgan Philips 544
'prison industries', US 70–1
Procurement Services
  International 142–3
Proetta, Carmen 457
Proops, Marjorie 393–6, 410,
  411
Prosser, Sep 224
PR Week 540
public relations 540
Purcell, Peter 572

Qana, Lebanon: massacre
  37
Quy, Dr Le Thi 578
Quy, Professor Vo 587

radio 533–4
  BBC 448, 507
  BBC World Service 487–8,
    496
  commercial/local 480,
    533–4
Ramaphosa, Cyril 602, 603,
  607
Ramos-Horta, José 13–14,
  143, 279, 297–304, 316,
  320
  Funu: The Unfinished Saga
    of East Timor 300
Ramsay, Robin 81
Ranelagh, John: CIA (BBC
  TV series) 499, 502

Rangoon, Burma 156–7,
  158–9, 190–1, 193, 214,
  219
Rantzen, Esther 485
Rather, Dan 52
Raymond, Phil 446, 447
Raymond, Philip 446
Reagan, Nancy 30
Reagan, Ronald/Reagan
  administration 7–8, 34,
  56, 70, 75, 96, 132, 134,
  499, 540, 541
  and BAP 96–7, 497
  and Murdoch 466, 469
  and Vietnam War 549, 554,
    569, 592
Rechem (waste disposal
  company) 356
'Reclaim the Future' 355–6
Reebok 217
Reed International 411–12,
  415, 422
Reid, J. B. 258
Reid, John 149
Reith, Lord 490–1
Renn, Margaret 436
Rennie, Malcolm 273–4,
  275
Renshaw, Patrick: The
  General Strike 491
Reuters 531
Reuters Television 531
Reynolds, Henry 236, 244
  The Other Side of the
    Frontier 239
Richards, Geoffrey 461
Richards, Steve 503, 504
Richardson, Bill 203
Riddell, Mary 433
Rifkind, Malcolm 174–5
Riley, Rob 243–4, 246

Rio Tinto Zinc (RTZ) 86, 329
Rivera y Damas, Archbishop 28
Road to Mandalay (cruise ship) 184–6
Roberts, Paul 49
Roberts, Stephen: *History of Australian Land Settlement* 239
The Squatting Age 239
Robertson, George 96, 97, 148–9, 507
Robinson, Anne 433
Robinson, Geoffrey 81
Robison, Robin 133
Robson, Carol 137
Rodrik, Dano: *Has Globalisation Gone Too Far?* 610
Roe, Jill: *Social Policy in Australia* 228
Rogers, Paul 320
Rolls-Royce 132, 171
Romero, Archbishop Oscar 27–8, 305, 307
Rooney, Bill 358
Roosevelt, Franklin D. 67, 70, 391
Rose, Murray 226
Roth, Stanley 176
Rothermere, Lord 380–1, 383, 389, 391, 509
Rowbotham, Sheila 536–7
Rowntree (Joseph) Foundation: report 508
Royce, Knute 52
Rushdie, Salman 458
Rushing, Byron 217
Rusk, Dean 21
Russell, Lord 366

Russell, William Howard 409, 544
Russia 41, 123, 330–1, 496, 521–2, 545
see also Cold War

Saatchi and Saatchi 68–9
Sackur, Stephen 50
Said, Edward 296
Culture and Imperialism 9
Said, Wafic 131
Saigon, Vietnam 549, 576, 583, 584
American evacuation from 550–3
Caravelle Hotel 585–6
Centre for Scientific Studies of Women 578
Tu Du Hospital 580–2
'Saigon South' 577
Sainsbury, Roy 105
St Louis Post-Dispatch 406
Sampson, Anthony 498
The Arms Bazaar 151
San San Nwe 213
Sandinista Government (Nicaragua) 31, 330, 500–1
Sands of Iwo Jima (film) 562
Sankore, Rotimi 15
SAPs *see* Structural Adjustment Programmes
SAS, British:
in Colombia 86
in Gibraltar 456–7
in Indo-China 25, 34, 136
Saudi Arabia 2–3, 56–7, 147
Al-Yamamah arms deal 130–2
Saw Maung, General 199, 215

Scargill, Arthur 428–9, 430–1, 432–3, 493, 494
Schmidt, Hans 500
Schofield, Hugh 521
Schumpeter, Joseph 609
Schwarz, Michael 558, 562
Schwarzkopf, General Norman 45, 51, 69
Scott, C. P. 382, 491
Scott, Robert Falcon 380
Scott, Ted 544
Scott inquiry 128–30, 145, 170, 513
Scrine, Gil 273
Sea Containers 183, 185
Seabrook, Jeremy: *In the Cities of the South* 325
Sebe, Lennox 598
Sedley, Judge Stephen 315
Sein Lwin 195
Sein Wein, Dr 180
Shackleton, Greg 273–7, 333
Shackleton, Shirley 276, 277, 332–3
Shan, the (Burma) 191–2
Shanks & McEwan 356
Shao Huaze 530
Sharpeville massacre, South Africa 124, 600
Shawcross, William: *Murdoch* 481
Sheldon, Robert 130
Sheridan, Greg 272–3
Sheridan, Jim 519
Sheridan, Tommy 538
Sherman, Tom 277
Sherwood, James B. 183–4, 185–7
Shi'a Muslims 45, 51
Shilowa, Sam 603

Shiva, Vandana: *Monocultures of the Mind* 534
Short, Clare 93–4
Shukman, David 45
Shultz, George 23
Siemens 177, 607
Sierra Leone 489
Silverstein, Josef 212
Simon, Lord 85–6
Simon, William 541
Simpson, John 52
Simpson, Wallis 383
Singapore 77, 78, 139, 169, 170, 178
single mothers 99–104, 105, 475
  Blair Government's attack on 78, 79, 84, 89, 93, 94, 508
Sissons, Peter 47
Sky Television 456
Slabynko, Oleg 545
Slater, Ann Pasternak 204–5, 211
SLORC (Burmese junta) 160, 170, 199, *see* Burma
Smith, Chris 96
Smith, Joan 83
Smith, John 82
Smith, Martin: *Burma* 193
Smith, Sydney 363
Smith, W. H. (company) 546
Snow, Jon 479–80
Snow, Peter 501–2, 505
Soe Moe 205
SOGAT 460
Solarz, Stephen 42, 176
Somalia 30, 34, 43, 501
Some Mother's Son (film) 519

South Africa:
  ANC 597, 601, 602,
    604–5, 606–7, 609
  Bantustans/homelands
    597–600
  black-owned companies
    602–3
  British trade 175, 600, 603
  Dimbaza 598–601, 604,
    608
  economic apartheid 13,
    603–5, 606–9
  foreign companies 600–1,
    602, 606, 607
  health care 605
  Houghton, Johannesburg
    601–2
  house building 604, 606
  land legislation 604–5
  police and prisons 604
  privatisation 606
  sanctions and boycott 203,
    207, 216, 217, 404–5
  water supplies 597, 606
Sparks, Allister: *The Mind of
  South Africa* 13
Spearitt, Adam 445, 446
Spearitt, Eddie 445, 446–7
Spellar, John 143
Spencer, Countess 435–6
sporting goods companies:
    cheap labour 59–61, 65
Spring, Dick 365
Stahl, Max 253, 314
Stahls, Chris 597, 607
Steketee, Mike 279
Stevenson, Robert Louis 544
Stevenson, Steve 251–3, 257
Stewart, Michael 21, 139–40
Stewart, Tony 273, 275
Stohl, Michael: *Current*

*Perspectives on
International Terrorism*
22, 27
Stone, Oliver: *Born on the
  Fourth of July* (film) 590
Stott, Richard 421, 434
Strachan, James 160
Straw, Jack 78, 135–6, 146–7
Structural Adjustment
  Programmes (SAPs) 63,
    66, 74, 135
Stubbs, John 542
Suarez, Bolivian President 27
Subandrio 287
'Successor Generation'
  network *see* British-
  American Project for the
  Successor Generation
Sudradjat, Edi 148
Sugar, Alan 86, 509
Suharto, General Thojib
    25–6, 139, 213, 293,
    324, 327, 488
  and America 278, 302*n*,
    503
  and Australian Government
    255–6, 258, 264–5,
    268–9, 270, 275
  and Bishop Belo 310
  see also East Timor;
    Indonesia
Sujatmiko, Budiman 327
Sukarno, President Achmed
    255, 256, 324
Sukarnoputri, Megawati 326
Sun:
  and Blair 468, 469
  Bouverie Street
    headquarters 460
  Falklands War coverage
    420–1, 449, 481

Gulf War coverage 44, 46
on Hillsborough disaster
   334, 445–6, 447–8, 465
lies and vilification 448–9,
   457, 475
under Kelvin MacKenzie
   419–20, 478, 481
on miners' strike 429, 493
and the *Mirror* 395, 396,
   412, 413, 414–16, 417,
   440
and Murdoch 410–15, 453,
   467
on Trident 134
and Wapping strike 462,
   463, 464
Sun Oil Company 96
Sunday Independent 545
Sunday Pictorial 386–7
Sunday Times 87, 334, 416,
   454, 455, 456–9, 469,
   476–7, 518
Sweden: press 468
Sydney 223, 225, 229–30
Bondi Beach 223, 224–5,
   227
Marrickville memorial 253
North Sydney Olympic
   Pool 225–6
Sydney Institute 541–2
Sydney *Daily Mirror* 450
Sydney *Monitor* 543
Sydney Morning Herald 77,
   232, 240, 244, 245, 255,
   482, 483, 542
Sydney Morning News 265
Sydney *Telegraph* 372, 373–4
Sykes, Roberta 246
Symons, Elizabeth 96

Tanjung, General Feisal 147

Taplin, Eric 334
Tarantino, Quentin 69
Taufik, Ahmad 137–8, 545
Tavoy, Burma 160, 162–4
Tawney, R. H.: *Equality*
   91
Taylor, A. J. P.: *English
   History, 1914–45* 371,
   391
Taylor, Allan 270, 276
Taylor, D. J.: *A Vain Conceit*
   537
Taylor, Jo 354–5
Taylor, John: *Indonesia's
   Forgotten War* 259
Taylor, Lord Justice: inquiry
   445, 447
Taylor, Martin 86–7
Taylor, Peter 514
Taylor, Telford 568
Teicher, Howard 132
television 486
agencies 531–2
digital 475–6
news 476–80, 488–90, 532,
   see also Independent
   Television News
US 1, 479, 529, 539
see also BBC; Central
   Television; Murdoch;
   Thames Television
Tell (Nigerian magazine) 15
Tellman, Ann 78
Tempo (Jakarta weekly) 137,
   269
Teresa, Mother 571
Tewkesbury, John 542
Texaco oil company 167
TGWU *see* Transport and
   General Workers Union
Thailand 6, 60, 76, 216

thalidomide campaign
  416–17
Thames Television: *Death on
  the Rock* 456–8, 486
Thanbyuzayat, Burma:
  Commonwealth War
  Cemetery 159–60
Thanh, Dr Pham Viet 581–2
Thatcher, Margaret:
  anti-trade union laws 461,
    465–6
  arms deals 121, 123–6,
    127, 128–30, 131–3
  on Biwater board 606
  and Blair 77, 80, 82, 133,
    468, 469, 509
  and *Death on the Rock*
    457, 458
  and Falklands War 21, 125,
    419, 420, 492, 493, 511
  and Saddam Hussein 56,
    126
  and miners' strike 428, 494
  and Murdoch 453, 456,
    469
  and Pinochet 64, 124
  social and economic
    policies 95, 105–6, 400,
    414, 603
  Vietnam sanctions 567
Thatcher, Mark 131–2
Thida (Burmese student)
  197–8
Thien Thi Tao 554–5
'think tanks' 83, 540–1
Thomas, Sir Alan 122, 123
Thomas, Anthony: *Thy
  Kingdom Come and Thy
  Will Be Done on Earth*
  (TV documentary) 528
Thomas, Cecil 381

Thomas, Richard 110
Thomson of Monifieth, Lord
  485
Thornton, Clive 422–3, 460
Tiananmen Square massacre
  530
Time magazine 8
Times, The 37, 125–6, 185–6,
  272, 336, 383, 403, 491,
  495, 500
  and Murdoch 435, 450,
    455, 467
Timor *see* East Timor
Timor Gap Treaty 257, 278
Tin, Colonel Bui 583
Tin Oo, General 215
Tinh, Mrs Thai Thi 553–4
Tit-bits 371, 372
Today (newspaper) 435, 466
Todd, Helen 267–8
Toohey, Brian 265
  and Wilkinson, Marian:
    The Timor Papers 273
Torside (company) 337, 338,
  346, 357
Total oil company 166, 167,
  176, 177
Townsend, Peter 79–80
toy factories: child labour
  60–1
Tra, General Tran Van 583
Tracey, Michael 486
Trades Union Congress
  (TUC) 89, 93, 95, 347–8,
  349
Transport and General
  Workers Union (TGWU)
  89, 342, 343, 344, 345,
  346–8, 356–8
Traynor, Christopher 446,
  447

Traynor, Joan 446, 447
Traynor, Kevin 446, 447
Trend, Sir Burke 513
Trevelyan, Lord Charles 361, 363, 367
Tribune 468
Trident submarines 6, 133–4, 149–50, 507
Truong Thi Le, Mrs 557
TUC *see* Trades Union Congress
Tung Chee-hwa 328
Turkey 58, 120, 147, 148, 489, 545, 546
Turner, Michele 273
Turner, Ted 476
Tutu, Archbishop Desmond 207, 604
Twain, Mark: on Australia 227
Tyndale, William 542

Uganda 25, 74
Ugarto, Celestina 26
Un Tin Shwe 202
UNICEF 3, 54, 213
unions, trade 13
    anti-union laws 461, 465–6
    see also Liverpool dockers; miners' strike; Wapping 'revolution'
United Nations:
    Cambodian 'peace operation' (1992) 42–3
    Commission on Human Rights 27, 158, 262, 263–4, 311
    Food and Agriculture Organisation 53
    Human Development Report (1997) 80
    Security Council 27, 40, 54, 123, 134, 257, 300, 301
United States of America 69–72
    and Americanisation 68–9, 77, 88, 94–8, 497
    arms industry 7–8, 30, 36–7, 56–7, 121, 123, 134–5, 292, 301–2, 496, 513
    corporations/corporate propaganda 65–6, 72–3, 539–40
    imperialism 26, 61–3, 502–3
    media and television 1, 451, 479, 529, 538–9
    unions 13
    see also Bush, George; CIA; Clinton, Bill; Reagan, Ronald; Vietnam War
Universal Declaration of Human Rights (1948) 59, 67
Unocal oil company 166, 169, 176

Vang Pao, General 31
Vanunu, Mordechai 14
Vasquez, Juana 364
Venezuela 74
Verwoerd, Dr Hendrik 238, 598
Vickers 118, 119, 150
Vidal, Gore 28
Vietnam 549–50
    American post-war policies 563, 566–8, 570
    'boat people' 569–70, 587–8

Chinese invasion (1979) 568–9
Communist Party 10, 569–70, 582–3
Doi Moi ('renovation') 566, 570
education 572, 573, 578–9
Export Processing Zones (EPZ) 577–8, 584, 585
foreign investment 564–6, 570–3, 575–8, 584–5
health services 572, 573, 574, 579–82, 593
poverty 569–70, 573–5, 583
and World Bank 573–5
see also Vietnam War
Vietnam Veterans of America 591, 592–3
Vietnam War 9–10, 24, 62, 406, 553–6
American bombing and massacres 117–18, 555–9, 563, 580
American chemical warfare 24, 56, 556, 581, 587
American evacuation 550–3
and Australians 254, 265
and British SAS 25
films 561–2, 590
media coverage 118, 406, 492, 559–61, 563, 592
My Lai massacre 556–60, 561
'Operation Phoenix' 62
'Operation Ranch Hand' 581
'Operation Speedy Express' 558–9
veterans 589–93
Villers-Bretonneux 249–50

Vincent, Peter 340–1
Virgin Islands 169
Vo Van Kiet 576–7
Voice of America 488
Volvo car company 607
Vu Trong Huong 581
Vulliamy, Ed 535

Waddell, Gordon 341, 356
Wahid, Abdurrahman 326
Wainwright, Eric 374–5
Waldegrave, William 125, 127, 129
Walden, Brian 84, 399
Walker, Jack 398–9
Wall, John 129
Wall Street Journal 39
Wallace, Colin 516
Wallace, George 233
Walsh, Pat 277
Walters, Barbara 509
Walters, Patrick 270
Wapping 452
'revolution' 434, 453, 459–67, 481
Ward, Colin 14, 607
Ware, John 514
. Warner, Jane 426
Warner Bros 69
Washington, George 67
Washington Post 518
waste disposal, hazardous 74, 356
Waterhouse, Keith 403
Waterhouse, Rosie 457
Waters, John 366
Watkins, Peter 514, 525
The War Game (film) 513–14
Wayne, John 561, 562

Wayne, Michael: *The Green Beret* (film) 561–2
Weale, Sally 509
Welch, Jack 609
welfare-to-work schemes 89, 505, 508
Weston, Simon 449
Whelan, Ann 418
White Deer, Gary 364
Whitehead, Ian 136
Whitlam, Gough/Whitlam Government 228, 255–6, 257, 275, 276, 481
Whittaker, Brian 188–9
Whittaker, Jacqualine 188, 189
Wiener, Norbert: *The Human Use of Human Beings* 534
Wigmore, Barry 434
Wik people, Queensland 236, 242
Wilde, Oscar 99, 546
Wilentz, Amy 500
Wilkinson, Marian *see* Toohey, Brian
Wilkinson, Paul 35
Willetts, David 497
Williams, Eleanor, ed.: *Breath of Life* 247
Williams, Graham 246
Williams, John 437
Wills, Freddie 374
Wilshire, J. R. 226
Wilson, Charles 435, 439
Wilson, Harold/Wilson Government 19, 25, 38, 139, 142, 399, 400, 401, 402, 406, 407–9, 413, 423
Wilson, Jo 313–22

Wilson, Peter 382, 404–5, 410
Wilson, Sir Ronald 223, 241–2
Win Htein 204, 214
Winchester, Simon 514
Windlesham, Lord: *Death on the Rock* inquiry 458
Windsor, Roger 430, 431
Wintour, Charles: *Rise and Fall of Fleet Street* 381
Wiranto, General 147–8
Witcher, Sally 105
Women on the Waterfront (WOW) 349–50
Woodward, Admiral Sir Sandy 487
Woolcott, Richard 256, 257, 261–2, 272, 273, 276, 277
  Pathways to Diplomacy 272
Wooldridge, Michael 231
Woollacott, Martin 521
Woollard, Dr Keith 231
Wootten, Hal 473
Worde, Wynkyn de 542
Worfield, Derek 364
World Bank 12, 62
  and Burmese SLORC 168, 207, 215–16
  in Chile 64
  and East Timor birth control programme 307
  and Haiti 67
  'liberal containment' phase 82
  and the Philippines 3, 208
  and Vietnam 567, 570, 572, 573–5, 579

see also Structural
    Adjustment Programmes
World Development
    Movement 75, 121, 122,
    146, 152
World Food Programme 33,
    569
World Health Organisation
    53, 212, 367, 567, 569
World Television Network
    (WTN) 531–2
World Trade Organisation
    (WTO) 73–4, 216
WOW *see* Women on the
    Waterfront
Wrigley, Alan 269

Xanana *see* Gusmao, Kay
    Rala Xanana
Xang, Professor Nguyen Van
    580

Yeltsin, Boris 522, 582
Yom Kippur War 415
Young, Hugo 458, 506, 509
Youth Training Scheme,
    British 427
Yun Yat 158
Yunupingu, Galarrway 246
Yurtcu, Ocak Isik 545

Z magazine 52
Zaharoff, Sir Basil 119
Zec, Donald 392–3, 403,
    410, 411, 459
Zec, Philip: cartoons 387,
    390
Zeit, Die 452, 483
Zelter, Angie 314
Zia, General 120, 498
Zuckerman, Sir Solly 408
Zuma, Dr Nkosazana 605–6
Zumach, Andreas 41